LOVE AND MYSTERY;

OR,

MARRIED AND SINGLE.

A Romance.

" If love, with all its subtle arts,
Be not a mystery—in earth,
In air, or in the hidden depths
Of ocean, where the diver shrinks aghast,
There are no secrets ; and the world
Is as a book, which he who runs may read."

FARQUHAR.

London :

PUBLISHED BY E. LLOYD, SALISBURY-SQUARE, FLEET-STREET.

MDCCCXLIX.

PREFACE.

In concluding the Romance of "Love and Mystery," the author feels it deeply incumbent upon him to tender his readers his best acknowledgments for the distinguished patronage which the work has met with.

It has been his aim, throughout the accompanying pages, to draw a faithful picture of real life, and never to strain after an effect at the expense of probability; and at the same time he hoped to be able to contrast the simple-minded virtues of some of his characters in a highly advantageous point of view, as compared with the tortuous philosophy and entire want of principle in others.

The unlettered but warm-hearted Tony Thorpe presents the greatest possible moral contrast to the learned, clever, but unprincipled Dr. Wilkins, and it is the opinion of the author—an opinion borne out by the judgment of the public—that there are always abundant materials for the writer of fiction, in the moral contrasts of human nature, without seeking for that morbid adventitious aid in creating interest, which is too frequently considered to be the staple of the romancist.

This romance, likewise, aims at a high moral, for it shows that such men as Lord Battaney fail—miserably—in their search for happiness by means of self-indulgence, and that pure motive, such as Kate Destern's, is, like gold, the brighter and the more beautiful, the more it is tried in the furnace of affliction.

Again, thanking the reading public and the press for the reception this work has received, the author begs to present it to his readers in its complete form at a price which places it within the reach of all.

LOVE AND MYSTERY;

OR,

MARRIED AND SINGLE.

A ROMANCE

BY THE AUTHOR OF THE " STRING OF PEARLS," &c., &c.

" Woman! experience should have told me
All must love thee who behold thee."—BYRON.

CHAPTER I.

THE LOVER'S MEETING NIGHT. — THE
RIVALS.—AN AGITATING SCENE.—THE
CONTEST FOR BEAUTY.

IT is the soft twilight of a summer's
eve—such a twilight as we but rarely
have in England, but which when we do
see it with its calm lustres, beautiful
aspect comes upon the hearts of all who
can appreciate the glory and the magnificence of nature with a holy chastening
influence. Two persons are standing on
the brow of a hill which overlooked
London, and gazing upon the far-spread
mass of human habitations that were

within their gaze, and yet they saw them not. The eyes may look without discerning; and these two persons were by far too much occupied with their own thoughts to attend to the aspect of external nature.

They were both young, and one was beautiful—a girl, in whose face of child-like innocence and feeling, there was such a world of loveable expression, that one had to look and look again to find in what features dwelt the charm of so much beauty. Kate Destern—for that was her name—was but sixteen, and surely Heaven never fashioned a more lovely being.

But hers was the beauty of repose and of innocence—an Arcadian loveliness. There was no dashing, take-you-by-storm sort of charm about Kate. She did not set up to be a wit nor a slaughterer of hearts. Her figure was small and delicate, even to an appearance of fragility. She was all affection—all gentleness—all truth.

He who was by her side—and one arm was wound round her slender waist, while with the other hand he held one of hers in his—was a young man of, to all appearance, not more than nineteen or twenty years of age. His eyes were dark and lustrous—perhaps at that moment intense feeling lent them some fire. He was slight and handsomely formed, and at this time his face had upon it a flush that was far from accurately representing the paleness that usually belonged to it. His name was Harry Dean, and the relation in which he stood to the beautiful and amiable Kate Destern will soon be discovered by their conversation.

The twilight was slowly fading away, as a quick, nimble step sounded near to them, and a child of about seven ran up to where they were, and cried,—

"Sister Kate, sister Kate, why don't you come home now? Here's a handful of wild flowers, Kate,—and you, Harry, you will tell me all their names, and I won't tell anybody that you love Kate."

"Lucy! Lucy!" said Kate.

"Well, then, come soon," said Lucy; and with an arch smile, she again wandered down the hill-side in search of flowers.

"Kate, dear Kate," said Harry, "what that little fairy says is true enough; we must go home soon, But my own dear girl, why are you so sad? Do you not know that I love you—that I shall ever love you—that all things may change and decay but my affection?"

"Yes, Harry, yes, I do know that you love me. But why this mystery about yourself? Why is it that my mother has asked in vain who and what are you? Our acquaintance was an accident—you were thrown from a horse, and sought the repose of an hour at my mother's. Since then you have visited us, and as she says, all she knows of you simply is that you are Mr. Dean."

"Kate, I—I——"

"You pause, Harry."

"Because I am fearful of going on, Kate. Oh! if I could but master courage to tell you all."

"And why not? Courage to tell me—and tell one whom you love! Oh, Henry, Henry, you do not know me yet."

"What, Kate, if I were to tell you that I am poor?"

"I should ask you if riches ever yet purchased happiness or love."

"What if I were to tell you that the very name I go by is not my own, and that I am afraid to call myself by my own name, for fear of consequences? What if I were to say that I am poor, homeless, nearly friendless, and although myself innocent, forced to seek happiness under a disguise?"

"Oh! Harry, Harry, how much need have you for some one to love you!"

He turned, and looked her full in the face, and his eyes glistened through tears, as with deep emotion, he said,—

"And is that your answer? Do you not cast me from your heart? Do you not see the danger of loving me?"

"I see you, Harry, and that is enough for your Kate."

An expression of such exquisite joy came over his face, that it was a charm to look upon it; and at that moment from behind a bank of clouds in the south, the harvest moon peeped out and shed a flood of silvery light far and wide.

"My own Kate," he cried; "my dearest, heart's best, holiest treasure, my darling, how have I deserved of Heaven such a boon as this? Kings—emperors might envy me the possession of such a heart as yours. May Heaven shower its choicest blessings on you. May your life be one unchequered scene of joy."

"Yes, Harry, we may be happy, although poor."

"Poor—poor! No, we ——"

"I'm going home," said little Lucy, as she again approached. "It's all very well, Kate, for you and Mr. Harry to be play-acting here, but I shall go home now."

"So shall we," said Kate.

"We!" repeated Harry; "not me, dear. I must bid you adieu, as usual, by the corner of the lane. But we will meet again to-morrow, and then you shall know all; and if that—that I don't know what to call him—odious Mayston, who lodges at your mother's cottage, dares to give you any annoyance, I ——"

"Hush! Harry, hush! He cannot annoy me. But see, now that we are on the other side of the hill, you can see no more of London. Do not the trees and hedges look beautiful by this harvest moon? Who would now suppose we were near such a city? And there is my mother's cottage; so good night, Harry. We may thank little Lucy, our only confidant, for the joy of these meetings."

"Good night, dear Kate, good night."

"No kissing," said Lucy; "I won't allow it."

Harry Dean laughed, and catching Lucy in his arms, he kissed her affectionately, saying,—

"You will be the sister of—of —— Never mind yet, Lucy. We will all hope for the best. Good night—good night. I go back again to the din and the turmoil of London. But the time may come when we may all live in some sweet sequestered spot in a little world of trees, and flowers, and winding rivulets of our own, and then we will with the poet

> Wonder how the world can be unhappy
> While Heaven has left it hope and love.'"

He looked at the retreating forms of Kate Destern and her little sister Lucy, until he could see they had reached the cottage door; and then, with a deep sigh, he crossed the brow of the hill again, and slowly made his way down its southern declivity, which led across some meadows to the northern suburbs of London.

"She loves me!" he cried; "yes, she loves me! I have awakened in her bosom an interest that will never die. She loves me!—oh, happy thought—she loves me!"

If there be anything in all this world of care, turmoil, and trouble which shall act as a great recompense for all suffering, surely it is the true, the enobling, and the virtuous love of woman. If there be anything yet lingering upon the earth that is near akin to Heaven in the majesty of its beauty, it is surely the affection of a young heart in all its fresh and fragrant purity, unsullied by even a knowledge of evil. Oh, woman! what would all the varied beauties of earth, sea, or sky be if thou wert not present as a rejoicing angel to add the one charm that like the sunlight makes the beauty of all beside!

It is the love of some fair, and kind, and gentle being that has inspired the poet—lent sternness and power to the eye of genius—strength to the conqueror—eloquence to the statesman. Oh, woman! if thou should'st ever depart from this world, let the sun go out, for chaos has come again.

Harry Dean came to a stile which separated the hill from the adjoining meadow. There was rather a precipitous bank, too, covered with wild flowers and weeds, up which he ran, and then he was about to vault over the stile, when his progress was stopped by a man, who suddenly rose up from a crouching posture on the other side.

"Stop! sir," said the stranger; "I must have a word with you before you go any further. I am armed, so you had better hear what I have got to say quietly, sir."

"Your name is Mayston," said Harry, "I know your voice, although you have a half-mask on your face. What do you want with me?"

"To say good night, that's all, and to ask you if ever you saw a prettier girl than Kate Destern. You are a lucky man, Mr. Dean,—a very lucky man. I give you joy, sir. Good night—good night."

He turned, and walked along the side of the hedge, leaving Harry in no small astonishment as to what all this might mean.

It was quite clear that when he first stopped him, Mayston had something to say and a quarrel to pick, but it was quite wonderful how soon he had altered his determination.

Harry Dean remained for a longer period, considering these things at the stile, than he ought to have done, but the idea somehow came home to him that there was danger to Kate, and a strong desire to go back to the cottage came over him.

He ascended the hill again, but when he came within sight of Mrs. Destern's house, and saw that all was quiet, and that it presented the very picture of repose, he began to ask himself why he should go and disturb it, and, moreover, if he should see the mother instead of the daughter, which unquestionably he would, he might be awkwardly situated to know what to say exactly.

He retraced his steps, and descending the hill again, found himself at the stile where he had met with Mayston.

"How vacillating I am to-night!" he said; "but I suppose that feeling is but one of the concomitants of the passion of love. Ah! my Kate, you shall live yet to bless the accident that brought me to your home!"

There was the sharp report of a pistol—a cry burst from the lips of Harry, and he reeled back down the precipitous bank, and fell heavily upon the green sward below. His blood soon dyed the grass around him, and he lay bereft of motion and sense.

A man with bustling eagerness climbed the stile—he half jumped, half rolled down the bank, and stumbling, he put his hands into a pool of blood. With a shriek, he recovered his feet, and then, as if it were necessary to awe himself into silence, he cried,—

"Hush! hush!—not a word—the gibbet else—the gibbet else! 'Tis done—the deed is done! I—I am a murderer. 'Tis done! He is dead—dead! How red and strange the moon looks! What's that? Mercy—mercy! No, no. I—did not do it. Oh, God! Hush! hush! Home—home, and to bed now—home and to bed. I shall have the money! To bed—to bed. How strange the—the grass looks, and the trees—all

red! This is imagination! Strange that I who have ever laughed to scorn such fears should now be their slave! What's that? Who is that following me? No, no,—and yet I thought I heard a step upon the grass. It is night, and I—I am mad—surely mad!"

He crept on, until he reached the cottage of the Desterns. Mrs. Destern was a widow, and eked out a scanty income by letting a portion of her cottage, and evil fortune had brought such a man as Mayston to be a resident beneath her roof.

With a latch-key he admitted himself, and while his teeth chattered, and his knees shook from fright, he slowly made his way up the narrow staircase to his own room.

He cast himself upon the bed, without undressing, for he intended to rise early, and get to London, where he would know as soon as anywhere else any particulars of the finding of the body of Harry Dean, and be likewise out of the way of being at all suspected by any agitation of manner he might otherwise have shewn to the Desterns. Oh! what a night of agony and apprehension he passed in that humble abode of beauty and innocence!

CHAPTER II.

THE MORNING. — BREAKFAST AT A NOBLE LORD'S.—THE JACKALL AND THE LION.

MAYSTON, who slept not at all, had no difficulty in rising by the earliest dawn. He did so, and throwing on his coat, which was the only article of his apparel that during the course of the night he had taken off, he looked at himself in the dressing-glass.

He absolutely started at the change in expression which had come over his countenance in one night, but it was not so much a change of expression as a change of colour. He was of such a death-like paleness that he seemed chiseled from stone.

"This will not do," he muttered; and approaching a cupboard that was in his room, he took out a bottle, from the neck of which, without troubling himself with a glass, he drank deeply. "Better, better," he gasped; "I shall be much better now. This shall be my charm against memory."

It wanted yet an hour to the ordinary time at which the Desterns rose, so that he felt certain of getting out of the cottage without speaking to any one; and he soon crossed the trimly kept little gravelled walk in front, and leaving the little gate to swing open or shut, as it liked, he walked rapidly up the slope of the hill.

When he turned the brow of it, and came within actual sight of the spot on which the murder had been committed, and where he fully expected yet to see the body of his victim lying, he began, as on the previous night, to tremble, but surprise soon got the better of that feeling. The body was gone!

He rapidly descended the hill.

Upon reaching the stile, he saw the marks of blood upon the ground, and he saw where the dead man must have lain, but there he lay no longer, nor was he anywhere at hand whither he might perchance in his agony, before death sealed his eyes, have crawled.

Mayston searched the hedges — he peeped into every leafy spot, but no trace of the dead or of the wounded Harry Dean could be discovered.

"He has been found," he thought, "by some persons early abroad in the fields. He has been found, and no doubt by this time half of London is aware of the fact that a murder has been done. I—I will walk on, and—and shall soon hear some news."

He met a labouring man, sauntering along, and he bade him good morning, enquiring if there was any news, but he answered in the negative.

He reached London, but there was no excitement — the news-mongers knew nothing of it. All was to him a mystery; and finally, faint and weary, he went into a tavern to procure for himself some refreshment.

Let us leave him for awhile. It is necessary that we should introduce our readers to another scene.

* * * *

Those who have walked through the Albany, from Vigo-street to Piccadilly, or the other way, and noticed the very quaint air of respectability there is about that aristocratic region, have but little to guide them to the doings and the life within some of those splendid apartments.

The exterior of some of those houses presents but as faint an exposition of what they are within, as some of the squalid habitations of Constantinople, in the Jew's quarter, do of the magnificence and oriental luxury that grace their interiors.

But there it is a policy to seem poor —here it is policy and custom that combine to make the outside of our dwellings cold and cheerless.

It is with the interior of one of these aristocratic dwellings that we have now to do.

In a room of not very considerable dimensions, but made to seem so by the multitude of mirrors which were disposed upon its walls, sits Lord Battaney at breakfast, for the hour is twelve. He is a man of about forty years of age. His features look swollen, and about his mouth particularly there is an air of sensuality. His hair was elaborately fashioned and glossily got up by a neighbouring perfumer, who brought it every morning. It certainly was Lord Battaney's own, for he paid for it.

He was attired in a cashmere robe, or dressing-gown, of most ample dimensions.

The room was a costly litter; it abounded with everything which could at all contribute to the comfort or convenience of its noble occupier. Superb satin hangings shaded the windows—the carpet was of the softest and richest texture, and the chair on which he sat was so capacious and so crowded up with cushions, that it was quite a pattern of luxury.

Slowly, and with an appearance of languor, his lordship sipped his coffee. At the further end of the room was his valet and personal attendant, polishing a glass, and watching the eye of his master, in case he should want to be helped to anything on the table that might be just out of his easy reach.

"Simpson!" said his lordship.

"My lord!" replied Simpson.

"Has Mayston been yet?"

"No, my lord. Mr. Mayston would hardly think of intruding upon your lordship quite so early. You know, I flatter myself I have taught him better manners. But the old woman has been here again, and wants to see Mr. Smith."

"Ha! ha! ha!" laughed his lordship.

"Ha! ha! ——" began Simpson; but a look from Lord Battaney silenced him.

"Tell her when she comes again," he said, "that she had better name a price that will satisfy her, for that Mr. Smith is going to leave the country; and as for her daughter, she can get her married as quickly as she likes. Oh! I did not see the paper. Debates—debates; nothing but debates, Simpson."

"And scandal, my lord."

"Yes, you are right there,—and scandal. More coffee—and scandal, as you say. Let me see. Ball at the palace—party at Lansdowne-house—regatta—police. How dull the papers are!—Russian finance—hang Russian finance; what is it to me? Some cream, Simpson. The long range—long fiddlestick!—domestic tragedy—tragedy—suicide. Hem! Why, Simpson, what is this? 'Last evening, at sunset, a respectable young female, of great personal attractions, was observed in a state of great agitation on Waterloo-bridge, and before 122 K, who observed her, could reach her, she mounted the parapet, and plunged into the river. The body has not been found, but a letter addressed to a Mr. Norval Smith was picked up on the seat of the bridge from whence she had cast herself into the stream. The following is a copy of its contents.' Put a little more candy into this coffee, Simpson. Let me see, where was I? Oh! 'The following'—yes—'the following is a copy of its contents:

" ' NORVAL,

    " 'May God forgive your unhappy Amelia, as your unhappy Amelia forgives you. Oh! pray for me, Norval, pray for me.

    " ' AMELIA ANGERSTEIN.'

"Eh? Why, Simpson, what do you think of that? Ring for the cutlet I ordered. It's the very girl!"

"Yes—yes, my lord," gasped Simpson.

"Well, who would have thought it? Poor Amelia! More coffee—no chocolate this time. Drowned herself, has she? Well, you can tell her old mother when she calls that it can't be of any use bothering me now, you know. Order my cab at one, Simpson. Where the devil can Mayston be?"

A rap at the door at that moment sounded upon their ears, and in a few moments Simpson came back, looking very pale, and said,—

"She—she won't go away. I—think she's a little mad or so, my lord."

"Hand me the cream. Who?"

"The—the mother of—Amelia, my lord. She—she says she has found out who you are; and—and I can't see a policeman."

"Don't let her in here, Simpson. Of all things in the world I do detest scenes. Keep her out—get rid of her. I don't want her here. Do you understand me?"

"Yes—yes, my lord, yes. I—I—— Oh, here she is!"

A woman, advanced in years, pushed the door of that superb breakfast room open, and slowly advanced towards Lord Battaney, who pushed his chair back as she did so, until the wall stopped him from going further. Even his rubicund countenance became pale as he looked upon her, while Simpson's face was screwed up to a perfect pitch of agony.

But what pen shall describe the look of unutterable woe that was upon the face of that dejected woman? In what language would it be possible to describe the hopeless despair that was manifest in every feature? Her hands shook, and as she clasped them together over her heart, as if in an effort to still its tumultous beating, she said,—

"You are the destroyer of my child!"

"Go—away, woman—go away," he gasped. "Give her some money, Simpson;" and then appearing to be more angry than alarmed, he raised his voice, exclaiming, "How dare you intrude upon me?"

"You are the destroyer of my child!" she said again.

"I don't know you. A mad woman

Simpson,—a mad woman! Curse you, why did you let her in here?"

The bereaved mother—for such indeed she was—the bereaved mother of her who had found at length a place of rest in the still waters, uttered a sudden sharp cry, as if of agonized recollection; and then she spoke in a very different tone to her former one, for there was loud and wild denunciation in each word now that fell from her paralyzed lips.

"Betrayer," she cried, "of innocence! —perjured false-swearer!—wretch, that with a serpent's wiles, stole into the Eden of my child's happiness, and killed her! May the curse of the betrayed and of her who now stands before you weigh horribly upon your head here and hereafter; may your death be one of violence and sudden pangs; and if Heaven has given you a daughter, may you before that death releases you from mortal suffering, know what a pang it is to be told that she has been the victim of such a villain even as thou art!"

"Take her away. Don't let her go on cursing here."

The mother lifted up her hands, and her lips moved slightly, as if she were bidding the recording angel of human vows and curses not to omit that which had just escaped her lips. Then with tottering steps, she turned and walked from the place.

Lord Battaney was more disturbed than Simpson had ever seen him. The fiend-like, fashionable, calm, affected indifference with which he treated as a general thing, all mothers, had nearly gone. At all events, it was rudely shaken, and he wiped from his brow some dew of perspiration with his embroidered handkerchief, ere he spoke.

"Simpson!"

"My lord!"

"Did you hear what that old woman said?"

"The mad woman, my lord?"

"Oh! yes—yes," cried Lord Battancy; "the mad woman, of course, the mad woman—oh! quite mad!"

It was a great relief to his lordship to hear anything like a belief in the madness of the poor mother, whose life now, in losing the only dear tie she had in the world, had lost its chiefest charm. If she spoke but from the impulse of in-

sanity, the curse she had launched on his head, seemed in his imagination to have lost some of its horrors.

Lord Battaney was superstitious—it is strange that the most wicked and the most unprincipled members of society are generally the most superstitious—it is so.

"You—you are sure she was mad, Simpson?"

"Oh! yes, my lord. Anybody could see that in a moment. Mad as a March hare, my lord."

His lordship gave a sigh of relief, and then turned his attention to his breakfast, which had been so singularly interrupted. Something stronger than either the coffee or the chocolate which he had been imbibing was near at hand, and his lordship appealed to that. It was some foreign liquor, and it certainly had the effect of stilling his noble senses a little.

In a few minutes his usual colour returned to him; and Simpson was glad enough when he saw his master, like the crook-backed tyrant, "himself again."

A soft, low rap at the door now announced another visitor, and Simpson with some amount of satisfaction—for he thought that in such society his lordship would recover in some measure his usual indifference—announced,—

"Mr. Mayston, my lord."

"Admit him."

CHAPTER III.

THE PLAN OF OPERATION. — FURTHER VILLANY OF MAYSTON.—THE BRIBE.

THERE was something about the appearance of Mayston when he came into Lord Battaney's breakfast room, that made that noble peer open his eyes a trifle wider than usual, as he said,—

"What's amiss?"

"Amiss, my lord!" replied Mayston, while the colour first rushed to his face and then returned again, as if he feared that Lord Battaney could actually see in his face that he had committed the offence against God and man, of which we know he had been guilty. "The matter did you say, my lord? Oh, there is nothing amiss—nothing, nothing."

"I'm glad to hear it. Sit down, Mayston. I'm dull, cursed sick, and tired of everything—that is, I want a new excitement."

"Well," said Mayston, in soft, oily accents, as he seated himself with his back to the light, so that any occasional agitation of his features should not be seen; "well, I hope your lordship will find in the society of that fair young creature, Kate Destern, one who I hope will soon lighten your lordship's weariness."

"Ah! say you so? Any progress?"

"A little, my lord."

"By Heaven, since I have seen her, I have scarcely been able to get her charming, *naine*, innocent, cherub-looking face out of my head. Mayston, if ever you did me, or wished to do me good service, do so now. That girl must and shall be mine!—she must, I say, and she shall! By Heaven, I will not relax in my pursuit of her while I have life. Well, well,—what news?"

"My lord, your lordship will remember that when last we talked over this matter, it was quite understood that the greatest obstacle was the—the previous attachment to a young man, named Dean—that obstacle I have removed!"

As Mayston uttered these words, he made a strange movement with his face and head, as if he were making a desperate effort to swallow something.

"Why, what on earth is the matter with you?" said Lord Battaney. "I suppose you have frightened the fellow away, and in the process have frightened yourself?"

"Yes, yes, I have frightened him away, my lord; and now, at all events, the coast is clear—quite clear. I don't think, from what I know of the parties, in consequence of taking the lodging the old woman had to let, that any distant proposal from your lordship would be received; indeed, I may say I am sure it would not."

"Then, Mayston, you must just do as you have done before, you know. You must actually marry the girl, and then— ha! ha!—surrender her to me! I suppose you show you have money, and all that sort of thing? There will be no trouble about that—eh?"

"I don't know, my lord. She is a strange girl—a very strange girl, and I have my doubts. I have, however, frightened away the principal obstacle.— You understand me, my lord, that I have done that much, and it is surely good service. You know that, my lord, so that if I do no more in the affair, I— I ——"

"No more! What do you mean? You don't want to make out that you will desert the undertaking? No, no, Mayston. Something has gone amiss with you, I can see that well enough—a man with half an eye could see it; but don't think of leaving any of the work you have to do for me unfinished.—I won't allow you!"

"But my lord ——"

"Hush! I will have no *buts*. I tell you that by fair means or by foul, I will have that girl in my power, and if the worst comes to the worst, and she is obstinate, you know that the house at Fulham is very well adapted to silence opposition."

"Your lordship, then, would carry affairs as far as that?"

"Why, what on earth made you doubt it, sir. Do you think that I pay you for nothing but to amuse yourself with failing in doing by fair means what you must assist me in doing by foul? No. Mayston, you are mere body and soul, and you should always recollect that if you have sold yourself to the devil, you get very well paid."

As his lordship spoke, he took from his pocket a small pocket-book, and from a roll of such pleasant little documents, he took a bank note, which he handed to Mayston, and a glance at which seemed to remove a vast number of his scruples and fears. He made as good a bow as a man could who was sitting, and who had his hat in one hand and a bank note in the other; and in a low voice, he said,—

"I am entirely at your lordship's service."

"Of course you are. And now, as you say you have removed the obstacle of a rival—I care not how, and shall not inquire—you will be so good as to lose no time. I swear it, that that young girl, whom each moment I love more and more devotedly, shall be mine before many days have passed over my head!"

"It shall be so, my lord."

MAYSTON'S INTRUSION RESENTED BY KATE.

Mayston rose, and moved towards the door. He paused a moment, to see if Lord Battaney had anything more to say to him, but the noble individual took up a pamphlet that was on the table, and was, or pretended ·to be, reading it

There was a short, whispered congratulation between Mayston and Simpson before the former parted, and then the villain, whose frightful situation is now transparent to the reader, walked away, with the wages of the most black iniquity in his pocket.

But how haggard he looked! How cold, clammy, and corpse-like! What a mode of life had that man chose—the jackall to such a lion! Can it be possible that human nature produces such creatures?—yes, yes. London—mighty, majestic London, which contains eloquence and virtue enough for kingdoms, likewise contains vice enough to vitiate all human excellence and purity, and to make the—

     " Angels weep,

to think that man, in the very likeness of divinity, should so depart from what ought to be the high and ennobling aspirations of his nature.

CHAPTER IV.

THE DEATH.—A STRANGE REVELATION.

" SISTER, sister Kate! Dear, dear!"

Thus spoke little Lucy to her sister, about a quarter of an hour after Mayston had left the house on the morning after he had done the deed of blood, so close at hand.

" Sister Kate—oh! sister Kate, I thought I heard something!"

The little creature, who slept with her sister, nestled closer to her bosom.

" What, Lucy? Heard what? You have been dreaming, dear."

" Yes, Kate, I think I have. But, Kate, I don't know why I did not tell you. You know, dear, that when we got to the cottage door last night, I found I had forgot my flowers, and I ran back, while you waited for me, to the meadow; and I saw Mr. Mayston. He was stooping down behind a hedge, and he was loading a pistol."

" A pistol, dear! What do you know about pistols?"

" Ah! now, Kate, did not Harry show us two once, with such pretty silver ornaments upon them, and did not he laugh and say that both you and I should know how to load them, and fire them off, Kate?"

" He did—he did."

" So you see I have not forgotten."

" No, dear. And well; so Mr. Mayston was loading a pistol?"

" Oh, yes; and he was tearing up with his teeth a bit of newspaper to cram into one of them, and as the night wind, you know, Kate, had began to blow, it caught up one of the pieces, and it came to me, and I picked it up."

" But what interest could it be to you, dear?"

" I don't know, Kate. It is here."

A light was always burning in the sisters' chamber, and as little Lucy gave Kate a little crumpled piece of paper from under the pillow. The latter rose, and opening it, read upon it the words— " If a murder, a circumstance would serve to prove the old saying, that ' murder will out,' has ——" Then the torn edges of the paper interposed, and no more could be made of it.

" I shall keep it, Kate," said Lucy.

" But why, dear? Why keep at the heart a worthless and uninteresting piece of paper?"

" I don't know, Kate."

Apparently overcome by some feeling which she could not account for, the child threw herself upon her sister's bosom, and wept. Then suddenly starting up, she cried,—

" The noise again!"

This time Kate herself fancied that she heard a low moaning noise; and the cottage being a detached one, she could not attribute it to anything else than something actually within the walls of that humble home.

She at once rose from the bed, and enjoining Lucy to remain where she was, she took the light, and tripped across the little landing that separated her door from her mother's, and softly opening the door, which was unfastened, she said,—

" Mamma, mamma, did you hear anything?"

There was no answer; and then Kate uttered a cry of terror, as she approached the bed, and saw that a most remarkable change had taken place in the aspect of her mother's face—rapidly approaching death was stamped upon it, and it was from her lips that there came the faint moaning sound that had first alarmed little Lucy.

The cry of Kate found its way to the ears of Lucy, and the little thing was at her side in a moment; and when she looked upon her mother, she burst into a passion of grief, and clambering upon the bed, besought her, in every variation of tenderness of tone and language, to speak to her.

Kate was to some extent stunned by the suddenness of the blow, and it was some few minutes before the idea of getting medical aid came across her mind, but then she was leaving the room for that purpose, when, apparently with a great effort, the mother pronounced her name.

She was back again at the bed side in a moment.

"Mother, dear mother, what can we do for you? Oh! speak to us—speak to us!"

Mrs. Destern clasped her hands, and seemed to be silently praying; after which, she spoke in a low voice, while the tears streamed down her cheeks.

"My children,—my own dear children, I am going from you! I have prayed for power to speak to you before I do. Kate, Kate, listen to me!"

"Oh! mamma, mamma—my own mamma!" sobbed Lucy.

"I will run for Doctor Davis," cried Kate, distractedly. "Lucy, stay with mamma, dear."

"No, no, no," said Mrs. Destern; "'tis of no avail. My time has come. Sit down by me, Kate, and listen to what I have to say to you—to my dying words. Oh, God! oh, God! why am I not spared yet awhile, for the sake of these dear ones? Hush! hush! why do I repine? Heaven will be to you, my children, father, mother, and friend; and yet—yet it is hard to leave you."

"Mamma—my mamma," cried Lucy, "take us too—we will all die!"

Kate was sobbing as if her heart would break; and after a pause, Mrs. Destern continued,—

"Kate, my own kind and good girl, there is a secret, which at this moment I dare not keep from you. Bring me the—the book."

She pointed to a book that was upon a shelf in the little room, and when she had it in her hands, Kate thought that she must be distracted, for her great effort was to remove the white page of paper which was on the inside of the cover.

Even as she strove to accomplish this purpose, her voice sunk, and the few words she uttered became gradually incoherent.

"Kate, Lucy, where—where are you both? All dark—my children—my little ones—more light. Hark! what a rushing sound of wings! God! God! God!"

She fell back in the bed, and Kate Destern, overcome by her emotions, dropped in a kind of swoon upon the floor, while Lucy clung to her mother's neck, shrieking aloud, and calling upon her to look up and speak to her again.

Alas! she called upon the dead—the dead, to whom no voice but that of the Eternal shall speak otherwise than in vain.

The book was in her lifeless hands, and the secret to which she seemed so anxious to draw Kate's attention had died upon her lips!

What could it be? What was it that that tender, good, affectionate, blameless, and gentle mother had to tell her child, that weighed so heavily upon her mind at the dread hour of her departure from this world to that—

"Undiscovered country whence no traveller returns."

Kate was aroused from her swoon by a loud knocking at the door of the cottage, and she looked up with something of the aspect of one suddenly awakened by some extenuous and merciful voice from a horrible demon.

Had she had any other sight to fix her eyes upon than the sad one that met her gaze, she might for some time longer have thought it but a dream!

———

CHAPTER V.

THE PROPOSAL OF MAYSTON. — THE WATCH FOR HARRY, AND THE DISAPPOINTMENT.

THE knocking at the outer door increased in violence, as Kate stood tremblingly looking on the wreck that had once been her mother.

As for little Lucy, with that small comprehension of death that children have, she looked terrified at a something that was new and strange to her, and which she could give no name to.

"Kate, Kate," she cried, "oh! speak to mamma!"

Kate could not reply to her for tears, but she lifted her from the bed, and taking her from the room, she closed the door upon the dead.

The knocking continued.

When Kate had hastily thrown on, with trembling hands, some of her apparel, she opened the cottage door, and found that the applicant for admission was a neighbour,—a friendly enough, though ignorant, and often tiresome woman,—but she was very welcome now.

"Why, Miss Destern," she said, "here have I been knockety. knockety, knock at your door, and nobody come. Why, where have you all been? Goodness gracious me, what's the matter? and do you know why I knocked? Only look here, Miss Destern."

She drew Kate's attention to the door as she spoke.

There was upon it the broad full imprint of a hand, that had evidently been sopped in blood. It had a ghastly and horrible appearance, and no wonder that Kate looked upon it with a shudder.

"What does that mean, Mrs. Williams?" she said.

"That's just what I should like to know, Miss Destern. You see, I had just firsted some of my things, and I thought I'd get up early, and go through with 'em again. This is such good drying weather atween the showers; so, says I to myself. as Mrs. Smithson's basket will be here in the day sometime, I'll get the Hocklebrain's things out of the way, and so ——"

"But about this dreadful mark?"

"Well, I'm a-coming to the *pint gradewally*. I says to myself, considering the piece o' soap, you may wear yer hands to the bones, and not get a livin', and we do the Whagglebhurn's things, you know,—I mean, in coarse, the smalls, at a shilling a dozen all round."

Kate burst into tears, and sobbing as if her heart would break, she said,—

"Come in—pray come in. My poor mother ——"

"Lawks a mussy, what a turn you give me, Miss Kate. She ain't *hill*—is she?"

Kate could not bring herself to say the fatal word, "dead," but she brought Mrs. Williams to the bedside, and that experienced personage saw at a glance what had occurred.

"Gracious providentials be good to us! Who'd a' thought o' that? Well,

we is ashes, sure enough—dust I means. Dear heart alive! here we is, as the psalm says, and here we isn't! How did it happen, Miss Kate? Ah! it's a *norrid* blow for you!"

Kate told her as well as she could the whole affair; and Mrs. Williams laid a sheet over the dead, after attempting to take the book away from the cold hands, but they were clasped so closely upon it, that she exclaimed with a superstitious reverence,—

"There will be no end o' bad luck to whoever takes anything away from a *corpus!*"

Mrs. Williams was now anxious to get out of the house, in order to spread the news among the neighbours that Mrs. Destern was dead; and soon the quiet cottage home was beset by half the woman in the parish, who came to commisserate and to satisfy their curiosity.

Oh! what a wretched, wretched day that was for poor! Kate! The small sufferings of her whole previous existence came not in all their accumulation to anything near the endurances of that one day.

Little Lucy sobbed herself to sleep, and the neighbours looked after the domestic affairs of the house, until the soft shrewdness of reason came again, and then Kate began to hope that the only being she could call a friend in all the world would come to her.

Harry Dean. It was to him she now looked to be the gnide and the comfort in her deep affliction.

Alas! how little she suspected that a few short hours had left her all so desolate, and that he, too, in all likelihood, was with the dead!

The twilight deepened into night. There was a hasty footstep on the gravelled path, and Kate's heart beat high with hope.

"'Tis he!" she said; "oh! Lucy, it is Harry. Run, dear, and—and tell him."

"No, Kate," said Lucy; "that is not our Harry—oh, no!"

The child knew the footstep. In another moment Mayston stood before them.

"No light?" he said; "no light?"

Kate lit a candle, and then Mayston closed the door.

"This is a house of mourning," said Kate. "My mother is no more! You—you will find your room ready. The kind neighbours have—have assisted us."

He took the candle from her hand, and placed it on the table.

"Be seated, Miss Destern," he said. "I had heard of your sad bereavement before I reached your door. I met one of the neighbours who told me of it. I am very sorry."

"I thank you, sir," said Kate, coldly, but in such a tone of heart-rending desolation, that Lucy flung her arms round, and turning her face to Mayston, she said,—

"Go away, Kate don't like you, nor do I. Go away, ugly! We don't want to speak to you about our poor dear mamma. Go away!"

A dark scowl came over the face of Mayston, and he gave Lucy such a look of concentrated hatred, that if looks could kill, there would at once have been an end of the earthly career of that young and beautiful child, who looked so like an angel, while he looked so like a villain.

"Hush! Lucy, hush!" said Kate.

"Oh! don't mind what the child says," cried Mayston. "Children's opinions are as wayward as the wind that blows. We shall be good friends some day."

"No, indeed," said Lucy, "we shall not. Go away."

"Miss Destern," added Mayston, waiving his hand, as if defeating any further interference on the part of the child; "Miss Destern, I came home to-day on purpose to say something to you, and I don't know why I should not say it now, although something has happened of a disagreeable nature."

"To-morrow, sir, if you please," said Kate.

"Nay, perhaps it will divert your thoughts a little from what has occurred. I don't know, Miss Destern, if I have, while residing here, made it sufficiently intelligible to you that I love you, but ——"

"I cannot bear this, sir."

"Nay, there is no harm in it. I will make you my wife, and you shall live a life of luxury and great enjoyment. I have ample means; in fact, I only came to live here at all because I had become enchanted with your beauty, and it was a great satisfaction for me to be near you."

"I will not listen to this, Mr. Mayston."

"But consider—only think, now. I make a formal offer of my hand."

"Which I as formally reject!"

"Mind what you say, Kate Destern, and don't stand in your own light. By Heaven, you do not know yet what it is you refuse. Think again, and give me a better answer than that."

"Lucy dear," said Kate, as she rose; "we will go and sit in some other room, since Mr. Mayston turns us from this. Come, dear, come."

"Indeed! So this is the reception of one who brings a note from Harry Dean?"

"Harry! A—a note from him?"

"Yes. As I came near the cottage, a stranger accosted me, and after asking me if I did not live at Mrs. Destern's, gave me this note, with a polite request to deliver it to you. Take it, and you may perhaps be happier with Harry Dean than with me; but he cannot love you better than I do."

Kate did take the note, and hastily opened it. It contained the following words:

"KATE,

"I must throw myself upon your goodness to forgive me. I was libertine enough to think to win you, but you have conquered, by your purity, my evil passions. I cannot marry you, and therefore I bid you adieu for ever.

"Yours,

"HARRY DEAN."

Kate unloosed her hold of the note, and let it fall at the feet of Mayston, as she said,—

"Take back your forgery, sir!"

"Forgery! What, do you think I wrote it? But I can tell you, Kate Destern, that when time passes, and you see nothing of this gay young spark, you will think differently of him, I trust. That will prove whether this is a forgery or not. We shall see."

"Come, Lucy dear, come. We will prefer sitting by all that is left of our dear mamma, than the company of this man."

"Oh! you need not trouble yourself," cried Mayston, as he snatched up his hat; "you need not trouble yourselves at all about it. I'm not going to stay. You and the dead old woman may have the place between you, for all I care. I have made you a fair offer, and you are fool enough to reject it. Well, we shall see what will come of that!"

He dashed the door open, and leaving it swinging upon its hinges, he rushed from the cottage, with bitter curses on his lips.

He was thwarted; and although he, from what he had said to Lord Battaney had shewn that he expected nothing else, yet probably he had not altogether looked forward to the ready conclusion to which Kate had come respecting the forged letter he had shewn her, as purporting to come from one who could not have written such an epistle.

CHAPTER VI.

THE ABDUCTION OF KATE.—THE FATE OF LUCY.

"WELL, my dears," said Mrs. Williams, as she left the orphans—orphans! what a world of pathos is in the word—for the night in the cottage. "Well, my dears, we will to-morrow have a long talk as to what is to be done. Goodness gracious! what troubles there is in the world! I've got to iron the Meadows's to-night before I go to bed; and I always think best while I am ironing, so that perhaps, you know, by the morning I shall have hit upon something —who knows?"

"We are greatly obliged to you," said Kate; "we have nothing but thanks to offer."

"And I'm sure I don't want anything else. I'm sure, as I often say, when people gets into the suds of misfortune everybody ought to try to give them a wring out."

So saying, Mrs. Williams went to her own cottage, which was not a very luxurious one, and which was situated about a couple of hundred yards from that of the Desterns.

A light that gleamed from her lattice window soon shewed that she had commenced operations in the ironing department.

"Lucy dear," said Kate.

"Yes, dear."

"Will you go to bed? You must be tired."

"And you, Kate,—you will come too? I can't sleep without you, you know, Kate dear. Do come."

Kate was silent for a few moments, and then she said,—

"No, dear Lucy. Go to bed and to sleep, this one night, by yourself. I don't know exactly why or how it is, but I have a strong disinclination to go to bed to-night; and I will sit here, and read or work, until the morning's light."

"What all alone, Kate? Oh, you will not like to sit all alone."

"No, dear, I shall hardly think myself alone, for I will keep the curtain of the window drawn as it is, so that I shall be able to see Mrs. Williams at work. Don't you see her shadow on her window blind, Lucy? That will be company to me, together with my own thoughts; and indeed, dear, I would rather you went to bed, for God knows only how much need you may have of rest while you can procure it."

Little Lucy yielded at length; for to tell the truth, the child was drooping much from fatigue; and in a short time Kate was really alone in the little parlour of the cottage, but still, as she had said to Lucy, she did not feel herself quite alone while she could see the cheering light from Mrs. Williams' window. But there was silence if there was not absolute loneliness.

In that silence, the thoughts of the young girl naturally reverted to the painful circumstances by which she was surrounded, and the idea that now both her and her little sister Lucy were destitute rose up like a hideous phantom before her.

She had seen, and many a time relieved poverty, and she knew something of what it looked like. All she knew of her mother's affairs was that once a month, from somewhere or some quarter, a small sum of money was fetched by her, but from what source the supply was procured she had no idea. Perhaps that was the secret which her poor mother would have told her, had she had the power to do so before the hand of death stopped her utterance.

That this monthly pittance—let it come from whom it might, or where it might—was a very small one, was sufficiently evidenced by the fact that even in her humble way of life, Mrs. Destern had been glad to let off one of the rooms of her cottage, and to bear the disagreeable of having a stranger in the house, which certainly could not have been a thing of choice. But still, if she, Kate, did but know from whence came that monthly small sum, it might afford her a clue where to find some friends.

This train of thought then led her further to wonder that she had never recollected seeing any one at their home who claimed affinity with them; and more and more she wished that her poor mother had lived to tell the secret that was hovering upon her lips when she was stricken by the shaft of death.

A distant clock struck twelve.

It was midnight; but still Kate found herself not quite alone, for there was the light still streaming from Mrs. Williams's window; and amid the solemn stillness of the night, Kate could fancy that she heard the dab of the iron with which Mrs. Williams was at work.

Her thoughts wandered back to her own infancy, and she was trying to put together in something like a tangible shape some disjointed recollections of the past, when the light from Mrs. Williams's window was suddenly obscured, and as suddenly came again, while Kate thought that a shadow of something had passed across the casement near to where she was sitting.

Now, as the cottage was in its own garden, and as the rays of light from Mrs. Williams's window fell full upon the parlour casement, it was clear that for the shadow of any one to establish itself for a moment there, it required the substance to be in the garden.

Kate listened, scarcely daring to draw a breath as she did so, and then she felt confident she heard a footstep again; and upon looking intently at the window, she saw, placed close to one of the small panes, a face!

This was not, perhaps, of itself, under any other circumstances, a very alarming idea, for it might be a neighbour, but now we may easily suppose that Kate was rather nervous; and she sat glaring at the face in silence, for she was so terrified that she was unable to speak or to move.

In the course of about a minute it moved away, and then there came a knock at the door—a double knock, but very subdued and quiet, as if from some one who did not wish to disturb the inmates of the house, but yet felt necessitated to knock for admission.

Still Kate did not stir.

The knock, after about half a minute, was repeated, and then she heard a voice say,—

"Miss Destern, you need not hesitate to open the door. It is a friend who speaks to you."

The tones were completely strange to her ears, and she hesitated some few seconds; and then, rather from a fear that any protracted parley or knocking might disturb Lucy, she approached and lifted down a bar, which at night was always laid over the door, and which, when it was removed, left it merely upon a common lift latch.

"Come in," she said, for she did not lift the latch herself; but she soon saw it raised, and a man walked into the cottage.

He advanced towards Kate, who retreated as he did so, until they had actually exchanged places, and her back was to the open door. Probably she would have rushed through it, had it not been for the thought that Lucy was alone; so she confronted the intruder whom she had rather imprudently admitted at such an hour.

"Who are you?" she said, assuming a courage and a presence of mind which at that moment she was really far from feeling, for grief, want of rest, and deep anxiety had worn her spirits.

"I am a fortune-teller, lady," he said, with a hideous grin.

"Leave this place; it is one of mourning. Jests are ill-timed here."

"You will go a journey soon," he added, while the detestable smile upon his sinister-looking countenance grew more apparent; "and you will captivate a great gentleman, who will grant you every wish!"

A strong sense of immediate danger came over Kate, and she was about to turn and fly from the cottage, to get assistance from the neighbours, when she found herself suddenly seized from behind, and a cloth was thrown over her face and eyes, and bound round her so tightly, and with such rapidity, that she had only time to utter one half stifled shriek for aid.

"To the carriage!" cried a voice; "to the carriage. Quick with her! There's not a moment to be lost!"

The cry she had uttered did reach the ears of little Lucy, who had been awakened by the opening of the door, and she gave utterance to a much more practical and effective scream, as rushing down stairs in her night clothes, she reached the parlour at the moment that Kate was being dragged from it.

"Kate, Kate," she cried; "oh, sister Kate, dear Kate!"

She clung to the man who had flung his arm round the light, fragile form of Kate, to lift her to a carriage which was quietly drawn up at some distance from the garden gate; and so pertinacious was the hold of Lucy that she effectually prevented him from attaining his object.

"Here, some of you," he cried, with passion; "knock this brat on the head. She'll spoil all if you don't. Twist her hands off if she won't leave go her hold!"

Another man darted forward, and forcibly tearing Lucy away, he flung her to the further end of the room, heedless of the injury he might do to the young thing, and then they banged the door shut upon her, and bore Kate, half fainting as she was, down the garden path.

But there they met another obstruction, in the person of Mrs. Williams, who had heard Lucy's cry, although she could not hear Kate's, and who had just reached the scene of action, with a large and very hot flat iron in her hand.

Now Mrs. Williams was an admirably practical woman, and the first thing she did was to try the hot iron upon the face of the man who was carrying Kate, and he, with a howl of pain and rage, was forced to let down his burthen. There were too many of them, however, for Mrs. Williams, unaided, to cope with.

She was brutally knocked down, having only succeeded in horribly singeing one of the ruffians; and in another moment Kate was placed in a close carriage, and the door slammed shut upon her, almost dead, as she was, from suffocation.

"Murder! murder!" shouted Mrs. Williams, and she threw the flat iron after the party.

Alas! the deed of violence was done; and the carriage, Kate, and the men who had thus forced her from her melancholy home, were all soon out of sight!

CHAPTER VII.

THE COUNTRY HOUSE AT FULHAM.

THERE was a man in the coach, and when it had proceeded a considerable distance, he spoke to Kate.

"If you will make no disturbance, there is no longer any occasion to keep the bandage over your mouth," he said; but she could not answer him, and that was a fact which seemed then to strike him, for he added, "Oh! well, we shall see."

He then removed the cloth from before her mouth, although he doubled and placed it over her eyes, and she had what was then the real pleasure of breathing freely.

The blood, which was coursing, but sluggishly, for want of that breath of life which vivifies it, though her veins, now again bounded onwards, and with a long drawn sigh, she recovered herself sufficiently to have perception of what had happened.

"Help!—oh, help! mercy!" she cried.

"Ah! I see how it is," said the man. "You want that cloth again on your mouth."

"Oh! no, no. Spare me the agony of such a death. Oh! no, no."

"You will be peaceable—eh?"

"Oh, God! yes, I must be patient. But you will have mercy upon me? You are human, and there must be some touch of compassion in you heart. Have you a child? Oh, think what she would feel!"

"Silence!—will you? I'm not going to sit here for half-an-hour to be talked at in that way."

"But surely it is the poorest privilege of suffering to plead for mercy.

Why am I thus torn from my home? It was my home, sad and sorrowful as it had become."

"I answer no questions. Let it satisfy you that escape is impossible. You are in too good hands for that, I tell you. You talked of patience just now; you had better have as much of that commodity as you can, for perhaps you will want it, for all I know. But when I come to think of that, I know nothing. My work begins at the door of your cottage, and ends at the door of somebody else's house; so it's no use bothering me any more about it."

All this was spoken with an air of careless, brutish indifference that made Kate feel how hopeless and humiliating a thing it was to expect mercy from such a source.

She wept in silence, while she was conscious that the carriage was going along at a very rapid pace indeed, and from the nature of the noise that the wheels made, and the darkness, and the stillness, she was tolerably well assured that it was upon a country road they were travelling.

"When and how will all this end?" she asked herself. "Oh! wretched, wretched that I am! Why am I singled out for this dreadful persecution? Lucy! what will become of you? Harry! Harry! where are you, now to look around me and protect me? Alas! alas! I am desolate!"

"Ah!" remarked the man who was in the coach, "you may cry as much as you like, and perhaps it will do you good. I hope you don't object to a cigar?"

As he spoke he lit one, without waiting for her reply, and she had the additional discomfort of finding the air tainted with the vapour of a filthy and obnoxious weed.

She shrunk as far back in the carriage as she could, and resolved to say nothing more to the man, who was evidently her guard, but at the same time she made up her mind that she would not be terrified into silence, if any opportunity should occur of making her situation known to any one who might interpose for her protection.

An opportunity of the kind did seem to her now to occur, for the carriage was suddenly stopped at a turnpike gate.

"Go on—go on!" shouted some one who was behind in the vehicle. "Go on, I say!"

"Oh! it's all very well to say go on," said the tollman; "but pay me sixpence first, if you please."

"A man on horseback paid you, and told you the carriage was coming."

"Ha! ha!" laughed the pike keeper. "Oh! yes, of course. Jolly green—

aint we? The Duke of Nothink wasn't here with one eye out!"

"Help! help! help!" called Kate.

"D——n you!" cried her companion, and he made a blow at her, which in the dark missed her, and his hand went through the glass window of the coach door.

"What's that?" said the pike-keeper.

"Keep the change," cried a loud voice. "Drive on—drive on! Whip on!"

With a sudden launch, the carriage was dashed forward now at a prodigious rate, and Kate found that the chance of succour had gone by.

"Now you may howl as much as you like," said her companion, as the vehicle turned some corner rather abruptly, and the sound of the wheels was soft and subdued, as if they were going over grass. "You may make just as much squalling as you think fit. I don't care about it, and nobody else will. Confound you, I've cut my hand all through you, and just because you couldn't be quiet. I don't know what anybody sees in such a holy face to make such a fuss about, or to take one half of this trouble with; but there's no disputing about tastes—eh? Oh! you can't say anything now? Very good. I don't want you to do so. Sulkiness I admires on these little occasions. It's the quietest thing that can happen, so you may give us as much of that as you like."

It seemed to Kate that this man now wished to get her into conversation, but she was resolved to disappoint him by holding none with him; so she made not the remotest reply to what he was saying, but turned all her attention to trying to discover where she was.

The carriage still rolled gently over grass, and occasionally the bough of a tree would dash against the windows, so that it would seem as if the vehicle was going through some garden or plantation, but which was completely a mystery to her, as she had no means of knowing, or of making an observation of it.

This mysterious kind of progress continued for about half a mile, and then the wheels grated upon rough gravel, and then stopped entirely.

The bandage across the eyes of Kate had shifted, and she could see that the vehicle was at the entrance of a house, close to which were some tall old trees, the foliage of which made a gentle murmuring noise in the night air. There was a flashing of lights, and the carriage door was opened.

"Come, get out," said the man who was with Kate. "Get out—will you?"

She was half handed, half dragged from the vehicle, and hurried into the house.

She said nothing, lest any remark she might make should lead to the idea that she could see, despite the bandage that was over her eyes; and she felt, in the midst of her terror, all the advantage of being able to make some observations of the place, and the people among whom she was.

There was a woman standing a few paces in the passage, but her countenance was so very far from being prepossessing as to make Kate think that everything in the shape of evil was to be expected from her.

She was tall, and rough-looking, while there were evidences upon her face and about her eyes, of intemperance—bad enough in a man, but in a woman hideously revolting.

Kate shuddered as she crossed the threshold of that house. An unknown terror took possession of her, and as she was hurried on she felt as if death would be a great relief.

"Stairs !" cried a voice, as she reached the foot of a handsome staircase, which she saw, although they thought she did not.

She ascended, perforce, for her arms were tightly held; and so she was led into a suite of rooms, along which she was hurried, until a small one seemed to be the last, and there all was quite dark.

The bandage was taken from her eyes, and she was left alone.

Kate clasped her hands, and sank upon her knees, as she cried, with gasping sobs to interrupt her speech,—

"Is this a dream? Oh! Heaven, is it but a dream?"

Her head sunk upon her breast, and she seemed for a time to be without sense or motion.

There was a faint streak of daylight coming in at a window immediately opposite to where she was crouched up in her posture of despair, that first recovered her, and she looked up.

The window faced the east, and she saw that the morning was coming. She rose and tottered to the casement; it was iron barred, so as to preclude the possibility of an escape by it; and it seemed as if the trees had been cleared away, so as to afford an uninterrupted view of the eastern horizon, which each moment now was acquiring a warmer glow, and spreading the soft tints of the morning far and wide over the whole face of nature.

She heard the birds carolling gaily to each other from bough to bough of the tall trees around, and the melancholy lowing of cattle came upon her ears. She fancied, too, that between the trees, although the foliage was so thick that she could not be certain—she saw water, as if some considerable stream was close at hand; perhaps it was the Thames.

At all events, she knew that she could not be very far from London, considering the time that had been taken to bring her to that place; and she was lost for a time in a maze of anxious thoughts with regard to the locality of the house, to which she had been in so mysterious a manner, and so unjustifiably dragged.

She listened intently, but no sound met her ears, except those of the brute creation—alas ! not half so brutal as man—which we have mentioned; but as the light grew stronger, she became anxious and earnest in her glances round the apartment in which she was a prisoner.

She now found that what she had thought a small room was only so comparatively with much larger ones that she had passed through to reach it, and now that it was not so contrasted in her mind, she thought it large.

A handsome bed was in one corner; but before she could pursue her investigations further, she heard a key thrust into the lock, and her heart beat violently as she felt assured that some one was coming.

CHAPTER VIII.

THE FATE OF LITTLE LUCY.—A CHILD'S DETERMINATION. — THE MOTHER'S GRAVE.

WE left little Lucy Destern, for whom we entertain a very great regard, in a situation which prompts us to return to her at the earliest opportunity.

The ruffianly manner in which her opposition to the abduction of her sister had been set aside, had had the effect of nearly stunning her; so that, at all events, she lay until the carriage had fairly driven off with its prize, incapable of movement. Indeed, it was not until Mrs. Williams, accompanied by some of the neighbours, who had been aroused by the disturbance, went into the cottage.

Then Lucy, trembling and hurt, but still calling upon Kate, was picked up; and a scene of the greatest confusion prevailed in the cottage, for it was nearly filled by sympathizing and wondering neighbours, while some ran for police, and others took a direction which it was supposed the carriage had gone, and half-a-dozen of them at once tried to question little Lucy about the matter.

She could tell them nothing further than the reader is already aware of, as regards the manner in which she had seen a man dragging away Kate, and been herself by main force repulsed; so that all was complete conjecture and dismay.

Mrs. Williams seemed to be the only one having a little common sense about her in the emergency.

She took little Lucy home with her, and shut up the cottage of the Desterns, with its dead.

"You can't think of staying there, my dear," she said. "You would be frightened out of your wits; so come home with me, and you shall go to bed, and in the morning we will think of what's to be done."

"Oh! no, no," sobbed Lucy. "Now, now—think now, Mrs. Williams."

"But, my dear, I don't know what to think. I'm all of a fluster, and can't think at all. As for going on with my ironing, I'm sure I shan't be able; and what to do I no more know than the man in the moon. Oh, the wretches! I marked one of 'em, and if he gets rid of that iron mould as I gived to his countenance in a month, it will surprise me!"

A policeman at this moment, who had been sent by one of the neighbours, reached the spot, and looked about him with a strong determination to take up somebody, if he only did but know who.

The affair was explained to him, and at its conclusion he rubbed his nose with his truncheon, and said that to the very best of his belief, he didn't know exactly what to think of it.

"Then what's the use of you, I wonder!" said Mrs. Williams.

"Come, come, my good woman, don't abuse the force. Come, come, don't obstruct me. I'll report all about it to my inspector in the morning. But don't obstruct me!"

"Me obstruct yer!" exclaimed Mrs. Williams, and she advanced unconsciously with a red hot iron heater for an Italian iron in her hand, which the policeman no sooner saw than he bolted out of the cottage with the utmost precipitation, and took into custody a boy who laughed outside.

"Well I never!" cried Mrs. Williams. "Marry come up! What is the use of the policemen, I wonders. You wait till the morning, my dear, and then we'll go to Mr. Sleek, the churchwarden. I do up their smalls; and we shall hear what he has got to say about them more by token, as through him I gets something riglar from the parish every week. It's only a trifle, but every little helps, you know, as the cat said when she run away with a pork chop."

We may in a very few words indeed pass over the next six days.

An appeal was made to Mr. Sleek, the churchwarden, who advised a statement to a magistrate, and the result of that was that his worship bit the end of a pen, and said he didn't see exactly what to do, further than ordering an officer to see to it, and spare no pains to get at the facts.

As for Lucy, she remained at Mrs. Williams's in an agony of grief.

Mrs. Destern was buried on the Sunday succeeding her death; and when Lucy left the side of the grave, with Mrs. Williams, she felt she was desolate indeed.

"My mamma—Kate—Harry, all, all gone!" she sobbed. "Oh, why is Lucy not dead?"

It was a deeply and strangely affecting thing to hear one so young wishing for death; but as Mrs. Williams wiped her eyes with the corner of her apron, she said,—

"My dear Lucy, don't you say such things. Times will brighten up, you know; and we must all die some day. So don't fret about your mamma; and who knows but your sister Kate may come back safe and sound."

But little Lucy was not to be consoled by any abstractions and philosophical arguments with regard to death; and as for Kate coming home safe and sound, it required the absolute fact of seeing her do so, before any effect of a joyous nature could be produced upon the mind of Lucy.

It is the present that children look to. Hope is a passion, or rather a feeling of education, more than one would suppose it to be, notwithstanding it is one of the inherent and never-to-be-extinguished principles of human nature.

To the great surprise of Mrs. Williams, when she reached her cottage she found a very important personage indeed awaiting her arrival. This was no other than the well-fed clerk of Mr. Sleek, the churchwarden—a fawning, hypocritical-looking scoundrel, with a perpetual faint smile upon his face, as if he had always just heard something that was of a very doubtful character indeed.

"Ah, Mrs. Williams—ahem! How are you?"

"Pretty well, thank you, Mr. Selby. How are you, sir?—and Mr. Sleek, sir?"

"Why—ahem! tolerable. But Mrs. Williams, you know you get two shillings a-week from the parish—ahem! What's to be done with this girl?—destitute I hear—ahem!"

"No, Mr. Selby, not while I've got a crust to give her. No, sir, I'll manage to get on somehow, with the Lord's help, Mr. Selby."

"Yes, oh, yes—ahem! But what I

have called to say is, that there's been a meeting of the board yesterday, and they have made up their minds, on the idea and movement—the Lord willing—of the Reverend Josias Smith, that if you can keep other people's children, you can do without the two shillings a-week; otherwise this pauper girl must come into the house. You needn't get in a passion, Mrs. Williams—ahem! We go upon broad principles of political economy. That's our system, Mrs. Williams."

"Broad \ \..t, you narrow-minded wretch?" cried Mrs. Williams, and she seized an iron, but Mr. Selby got out of the place quickly having delivered his systematic message, so strictly in accordance with the poor laws.

"Never mind—never mind me, Mrs. Williams," said Lucy, who clearly understood the point of contention; "I have been thinking that I must go about and look for Kate or Harry Dean. I shall never find them by staying here, and I should do nothing else but cry all the day. So you see I will go now and ——"

"Stop!" cried Mrs. Williams; "you will do no such thing—no, not if I works my fingers off, and does large and small for ninepence a dozen, and only charges ninepence for *counterpins*. No, no. Besides—leastways, how are you to live?"

"Surely somebody will have compassion upon me."

"No, they won't."

"I shall trust to Heaven, where my dear mamma is."

"No, you shan't. You shall trust to a flat iron; and so long as I can give one a rub, you shall never want for anything."

Adversity is a rapid teacher; and little Lucy had learnt more of the world and its ways in the week that had succeeded her mother's death, and the abduction of her sister Kate, than she had done all her life before.

She perfectly understood the dilemma she had placed Mrs. Williams in, and she saw, likewise, that that good soul would not permit her to leave of her own accord; so she made up her mind to the course she would pursue.

"The world is a large place," she thought; "but I shall find Kate and

Harry, surely. I will wander about, and when I see any one with soft eyes and a kind-looking face, I will tell my story to them, and ask for any news of Kate and Harry; and then I want so little, that some good person will give me that, and it's the dear summer time, too. Mamma—my mamma, why did you leave your Lucy?—my own dear mamma!"

She rose that night, while the soft moonlight was steeping all things in a bath of beauty—she rose, and slipped from the cottage unperceived, and she sought the spot where her poor mother lay in the long sleep of death. She could not think of leaving without once again kneeling to offer up a prayer by the grave of one who had been so unvaryingly kind and good to her.

"My Mamma—my mamma! Oh! where are you now? Will not God let you come back again?"

Tears choked her utterance, and the little creature could only keep at intervals calling upon her dear mamma and her sister Kate to come to her.

Alas! it was sad indeed for such a child to be alone by that grave, and at such an hour too.

How the night wind whistled about among the old tombs, as if sighing at the fate, darkened as it now was, of one so young and beautiful!

At length, exhausted by the violence of her own emotions, and still feeling, as it were, the necessity of getting further and further from the spot where she had already endured so much, she rose, sobbing, to move away, and as she did so, she saw a small bright wild flower growing close to her mother's grave.

She plucked the frail armorial, kissed it, and placed it in her bosom, as she said, gently,—

"I will keep this; it will remind me of my dear mamma and of Kate."

With many a lingering look upon the grave, she walked from the place; and that young, beautiful, and artless creature commenced a pilgrimage which the boldest might well have shrunk from—a pilgrimage, in search of the only two living beings—if they were still living—from whom she knew she should receive protection and love—her sister Kate and Harry Dean.

Poor Lucy! May the blessing of Heaven hover around you like a shield of adamant!

CHAPTER IX.

THE VICTIM IS VISITED BY THE DESTROYER.

KATE held her breath in her deep anxiety to listen, as she thought, or rather she felt certain, that some one was approaching her prison.

A moment or two elapsed, and then she heard plainly the rattle of a key in the lock of the door. The fall of a bar, too, came with its dull, heavy sound upon her ears; and in another moment the woman, whom she had before seen, made her appearance.

She had a large bundle with her, besides a basket upon her arm.

Kate having before made an unsuccesful attempt to induce this woman to speak to her, now, with a natural kind of resentment, would not commence a conversation; but looked at her as coldly and as calmly as she could, while the contents of the basket were spread out, and found to consist of every requisite for a breakfast, only that a light-looking wine was substituted for tea or coffee.

When this was done, the woman's countenance extended into what she intended to be a smile, and she said, in an hypocritical, whining voice,—

"There, you see, we are not going to starve you—oh! dear, no. You will be as happy as a princess here, that you will, my little ladybird!"

Kate turned aside, but made no answer, although her heart was swelling with indignation.

"Come, come," pursued the woman, as she proceeded to untie the bundle she carried; "we must be better friends than this, and no doubt we shall be soon. It's a shame to see such beauty as yours in such mean dresses as that you have on. Look at this."

A magnificent satin dress was produced from the bundle, and the old hag looked from beneath her shaggy brows at Kate, as much as to say, "There, are you not struck with that?"

The look of contempt, however, which was upon the face of Kate convinced her of her resistance, and dashing the bundle of finery on the floor, she cried,—

"I said so—I said so! I was sure of it!" and then she flew out of the room.

She did not forget, however, to fasten the door behind her, and she left Kate rather more puzzled than enlightened by the interview that had just taken place.

An anxious question now arose as to whether or not it would be prudent to partake of the breakfast that was placed before her. But after a time, commending herself to the care of Heaven, while the tears gushed to her eyes at the forlorn and desperate condition she was in, she ate sparingly of some of the bread.

The wine she did not touch, but was better pleased to quench her thirst with some water that was on the toilette table in the apartment.

Feeling now much refreshed by this simple sustenance, the courage of the friendless and unhappy girl—whose only crime was that Heaven had made her beautiful—revived; and she was able by the morning light to take a more accurate survey of the room.

Despite, however, all her dread that there might be something in the shape of a secret door or hiding-place in the room, she found nothing of the sort; and after her vain search, she again resumed her interrupted observation of the prospect from the window.

Through the openings left by the trees, she now saw what at the moment rather startled her, and that was the slender mast of some pleasure boat; but a moment's reflection sufficed to convince her that her former supposition that she was near the river was the fact, and that it was some boat gliding on the Thames, the topmast pinnacle of the mast of which she now saw.

"Oh!" she thought, "if I could but get down to the water's brink—if I could but now escape from this place, and make myself heard, surely some one would be found who would step forward to my rescue. Harry, Harry, where are you now?—oh! where are you now? And you, my poor mother, too! Thank Heaven you have been spared the agony of knowing that your child is so unhappy! Lucy, too,—my dear little fond Lucy—where are you, and what will become of you, now that I am gone from you?"

These were sad recollections, and for a time the spirits of Kate gave way completely under them; and leaning her head upon her hands, she wept bitterly.

But those tears were not to be regretted. It was wonderful how they relieved her over-charged heart, and what a glow of fresh hope, and courage, and serenity crept over her as she wept; and when her tears had subsided to sobs —her sobs to sighs, she felt herself better able to contend against whatever her evil destiny had in store for her.

And so the day passed, until the sun, with a fiery glow, began to dip in the western horizon.

There was a strange crimson haze in the sky, and at times a gust of wind would sweep over the face of it, altering, as if by magic, the shape and complexion of every cloud, and particle of long feathery vapour that floated between earth and heaven. Once Kate thought she heard thunder.

It might, however, have been merely imagination, for now and then a door would slam shut in the house, awakening many reverberating echoes, and going far to convince her that it was only a portion of the mansion that was either furnished or occupied.

No more provisions had been brought to her, but the breakfast which had been laid before her, when the singularly unsuccessful attempt to impose upon her imagination by the love of dress had been made; nevertheless, there was more than sufficient for her, and she made no complaint of her fate on that score.

But as the shadows of evening began to steal on, and the trees without began to lose colour and distinctness, a feeling of great apprehension came over her, and she shuddered to think of what horrors the coming night might usher in.

She had heard nothing, and was not prepared for the sudden opening of the door, so that when it did so open, and a man walked across the threshold, a cry of alarm escaped her lips.

The door was closed again by some one else, and the intruder stood glaring at Kate, but without, for some few moments, advancing.

There was a death-like silence, and Kate held her hands upon her heart, as if by dint of pressure, she should be better able to still its wild, tumultous beating.

Then the stranger, finding that the beautiful person would not break the silence, himself spoke.

"I hope," he said, "you have experienced every attention here; and that you will pardon an affection which so far carried away reflection, as to cause me to have you brought for your own happiness here."

"Command the doors of this prison," said Kate, "to be opened, and let me go. I then pardon you, and I pray that Heaven may do so likewise. I will not ask who or what you are; I will make no complaints; I will not call down upon your head vengeance nor justice; but, oh! if you for one moment think and feel that there is a God above us, let me go free!"

"Oh! you do an injustice to your beauty. You never had your fortune told, I dare say, but I will tell it. You will at once step into a station, the delight of which will exceed anything you can imagine—your own carriage—your servants—an establishment where you please—your box at the opera—dress —jewels ——"

"My mother—my mother," sobbed Kate, convulsively; "my mother, oh! save me!"

Then suddenly drying the tears that had for a moment gushed to her eyes, she spoke.

"Sir, who you are in the world's estimation, I know not. There may be those who call you a gentleman, and perhaps you may be esteemed as a man of courage; but is it not cowardly and base thus to persecute one whom you have deprived of the power of shielding herself by flight from so odious a persecution. There must surely be some slumbering feeling of right even in such a heart as yours. God send my words! —my distress may awake it. Open your doors, and let me free, and I will bless you!"

"And what do you suppose would be your fate? Are you not perfectly destitute?"

"No. It's a great world, and no one is destitute who has courage and innocence enough to put their trust in Heaven!"

He laughed bitterly, but suddenly changing that tone to rather a high one of threat, he cried,—

"Look ye, my girl. You don't know what you say. If you go from here now—if I were to order the doors of this house to open at your bidding—you would go forth, deprived of what you affect so much to value—character! Think yourself well off, and remain contented where you are, or rather say 'yes' to my offers. I am a nobleman!"

"Neither are you noble nor a man. You are undeserving of the one or the other title!" said Kate, gathering courage and indignation. "A man properly so called, is not an oppresser of weakness and innocence, but their best protector; and he is only most noble who is greatest in virtues, and that is nobility, which you can never reach."

"Ah! do you defy me?"

"With all my heart and soul I do."

There was as much of admiration as of anger in the gaze he now cast upon her, as with one of her small hands resting upon the table, she confronted him, with a brightened colour upon her cheek, and her whole attitude one of the most charming, natural grace and simplicity.

He paced the end of the room nearest the door, and to which he had as yet confined himself, with unequal strides, as if some mental contest was going on; and then suddenly pausing, he said, in a voice that seemed to be struggling with emotion,—

"Your destruction be upon your own head! You have converted a preference for a pretty face into a charming passion. Had you, with a mawkish sentimentality, yielded to me, making the shadow of a resistance, you would have been valueless; but now I swear that if earth, hell, and Heaven ——"

He paused and shrunk back, for the promised storm at that moment commenced, and it seemed as if his impious words had called down a warning voice

from the jugment-seat of God. The thunder that rattled and boomed in the air shook the house to its very foundation, and appeared as if it would be ceaseless in its echoes. A dull, purplish-looking glare was in the sky, and shone into the room upon the face of the betrayer, giving clear evidence of the evil passions partially subdued by fear that sat fairly upon it.

He recovered himself by a great effort.

"Fool that I am," he said, "to be appalled by a clap of thunder! Kate Destern, no power shall save you! You shall be mine! I loved you yesterday, but to-day I adore you. You have yourself rivetted the chain that before hung but loosely upon me. You must and shall be mine!"

He made a movement to approach her as he spoke, and then she took from the table the knife that had been brought with the breakfast things; but he laughed at the demonstration of defence, as he cried,—

"Pshaw, girl! I am not to be frightened at a rose because it has a thorn. Do your worst!"

"And my best," she said, as she turned the blade against her own bosom, and placed both her hands upon the handle. "God will forgive me this deed. My hand may deal the blow, but you are the murderer!"

"Hold—hold! What would you do?"

"Rejoin my mother."

There was an air of fervid and holy determination about her that he could not doubt, and the libertine paused. Again came the rolling, rattling peal of thunder. There was a loud crash from a distant part of the mansion, and then some screams.

With an oath upon his lips, Lord Battaney—for it was he—turned and dashed out of the room.

She heard him fasten the door; and then pushing before her the heavy table by which she stood, until it reached the entrance, and feeling that it was some sort of protection, she dropped the knife from her hand; and falling upon her knees on the floor, she wrung her hands and wept, calling upon Heaven to deliver her, or to send its lightnings to save her by destroying her.

CHAPTER X.

THE QUARREL AND ITS RESULTS.—THE RIDING HABIT.

THE cries of distress which had come upon Lord Battaney's ears, and which, in conjunction with the storm, and the heroic conduct of Kate, had driven him from the apartment where she was kept a prisoner, did not decrease; and when he came to the lower part of the house, he met a terrified domestic, of whom he demanded the cause of the uproar.

"Oh! my lord, a stack of chimneys have fallen in. Then the lightning, my lord."

"But if they have, what need there be all this tumult?"

"Why, my lord, Mrs. Green is—is killed!"

"Indeed! Killed?"

"Yes, my lord,—smashed. She was in the room that the roof came in of, and—and she's smashed."

The man was trembling to such an excess as he spoke, that he could hardly give clear utterance to his words; and when Lord Battaney turned from him, he followed, saying,—

"If—if you please, my lord, I'd rather leave."

"Leave what?"

"Your lordship's service."

"Get out of my way!"

Lord Battaney walked into a room upon the ground floor, and slammed the door after him.

There was a handsome chandelier dependant from the roof, one only of the burners of which was lighted; and in an arm-chair nearly under it sat a man, looking as pale as death itself, and evidently holding on by the arms of the seat to endeavour to stop himself from trembling to a noticable excess.

That man was Mayston.

When Lord Battaney entered the room he made an effort to rise, but he sunk back again, muttering something about the storm.

"So," said Lord Battaney, in a bitter, concentrated voice of passion; "so, sir, you have deceived me."

"I—I deceived you, my lord? I—I——"

"Yes; you told me that I should find Kate Destern as compliant as I could wish. You told me that from her habits, her poverty, and from all you knew of her, that I should have no difficulty whatever, although she might shew a little reluctance to embrace her good fortune. Did you not tell me all this?"

"Ye—yes; I—I——"

"And what do I find her?—I say, what do I find her?"

"A very charming girl, I'm sure, my lord," said Mayston, making an effort to recover some portion of his usual effrontery and manner. "Your lordship will go far before you meet her equal."

"I shall; for she will meet death before—before, and well that is the word—before dishonour. You have deceived me concerning her, sir. Had you told me what she was, and how she was likely to behave—and you ought to have known—I should have acted differently. You, however, were too intent, you scoundrel that you are, in grasping at your reward. But you have not got it yet."

"How can I, my lord, answer for the caprices of a girl?"

"You might have told me that before."

"You have her in your power. If fair words won't do, foul ones may; if tenderness and promises don't succeed, force may. You know that, my lord; for if your lordship remembers ——"

"What?" thundered Lord Battaney.

Mayston was mute.

"I know well to what you allude, Richard Mayston."

"My name is Alfred."

"Confound your name, and you too! You have deceived me, and that is sufficient for me. When I employ a scoundrel, I, at all events, expect him not to play me false."

"Birds of a feather, my lord, flock together. Perhaps your lordship will be in better temper to-morrow. I will then call upon you. But I consider that I have done all I bargained for. You have got the girl, and it remains with you to improve upon that circumstance or not, as best you may."

Lord Battaney turned sharply round, and struck Mayston a blow on the face.

"Take that," he said, "for your insolence; and if you dare to come near me any more, you will repent it!"

Mayston half drew a knife from his pocket, but then, although the blood was starting from his lips, he put it back again, saying,—

"No, not that, my lord; we shall meet again. You have made an enemy now who ——. But no matter; we shall see—we shall see. I have the honour of bidding your lordship good evening. My vengeance will keep remarkably well, my lord, and all the better that it will be certain."

Lord Battaney was pacing the room, and paid not the least attention to what Mayston said. When he was alone, however, he no longer concealed the rankling disappointment that was at his heart; and it was in a voice that almost shrieked with rage that he exclaimed,—

"And am I to be crossed in this way? Am I to be thus disappointed and defeated by a girl yet but a child in years? Am I, who have achieved so many triumphs over the greatest difficulties, to be at the very moment of success thus held at the arm's length of defiance? But—but that scoundrel Mayston says what is true, when he bids me remember that she is in my power. Yes, Kate Destern, you are in my power—how the thunder roars and rolls! Ah! what a blinding flash of lightning that was! It is a night of storm, indeed. What shall I do?—shall I now surrender this prize—shall I give up this rare jewel I have had such pains to get at the very moment of possession? She defies me—she in the—the strength of her weakness! Now, if—if I could be virtuous."

He flung himself into a chair—it was the one Mayston had quitted—and he uttered a deep, long-drawn sigh, as the many vicious events of his life rose up before his mental gaze.

"What am I," he said, "and what might I have been? What a life blasted has mine been! I am forty-five —not an old age—and what an awful twenty-five years have the last been. I am known as the *roue*—the libertine—a walking desolation—a blight and a curse to virtue—the destroyer of innocence!"

His head drooped upon his breast, and for a few moments he remained in a quiescent state.

His valet glided with noiseless footsteps into the room, and when he saw his master in that state, he gave his head a slight toss, as much as to say, "Oh! that's it, is it!"

He then went to a cupboard in the room, and poured some brandy from a decanter into a silver goblet, and with that he approached his lordship.

He slightly touched his hand with the rim of the goblet.

Lord Battaney started up.

"What's that—what's that?" he cried.

"It's only me, my lord."

"Oh! Simmons, is it you? Oh, yes. I—I don't know what I was thinking of. I'm glad it's you, Simmons. I—I don't exactly want any one else to see me in—in this state."

Simmons made a half-and-half kind of bow, and still handed to Lord Battaney the silver goblet, and in another moment he quaffed off the contents. He drew a long breath.

"Your lordship is better now?" said Simmons.

"Oh! yes, yes—much better. I am myself again. Any news, Simmons? I hardly expected you here as yet."

"No, my lord, no news. Your lordship's brother, though, and Lady Hastington are beginning to find out that your lordship's pattern of a nephew, the young Marquis of Ribley, is not quite such a wonderful piece of virtue as they thought him."

"Indeed!"

"Why, it appears the young marquis was suspected of an intrigue, and he has now disappeared."

"Ha! ha!—good. Why, Simmons, all the world is alike, only some are greater hypocrites than others. Send for Madame Zadzed from town. There is want of her here. She has tact enough, I think, to do something with this girl, Kate Destern. I—I do not like to use force. If Madame Zadzed cannot persuade her to yield to me, I—I ——. Well, well, we can think of that afterwards. I can say no more about it just now. We shall see—we shall see."

"Your lordship shall be obeyed. Is Mayston here, my lord?"

"I suppose not. I have discharged him."

Simmons rather opened his eyes at this piece of intelligence, but by the manner in which Lord Battaney had given him the information, he saw that any questions would not be very welcome upon the perhaps disagreeable subject, so he made up his mind to wait until accident should reveal to him what had been the cause of the quarrel.

It would have been a vast relief to Kate could she in her desolation of spirits have but known that for that night she was to experience no further annoyance; but that knowledge, welcome as it would have been, she had no means of getting at, and consequently she remained a prey to the most miserable forebodings.

Lord Battaney's repentance came only by fits and starts, and it quickly yielded to the influence of something very strong, which Simmons knew very well how to administer to his master, and then he was as bad and as reckless as ever; and yet the very fact that he was visited at times with such confusion of spirit was sufficient to shew that the germ of something like virtue, although it had been prevented from expanding, yet was not altogether extinguished in his heart.

If, however, it did not predicate at any time a return to a better mode of life, and a deep, sincere repentance for all his follies, it went far to establish the idea that at some time or another the mental sufferings of the lordly libertine would be frightfully acute, and that there would come a time, even if it only but slightly pended his dissolution, when he would suffer pangs of remorse, such as human nature can only garner up for itself, for the mercy of Heaven could never inflict them.

It is the betrayer that is to be pitied by those who look closely at human nature, and not the innocent and the betrayed.

CHAPTER XI.

LITTLE LUCY MEETS WITH SOME ADVENTURES.

WE cannot but feel deeply interested in the fate of little Lucy. Let us follow her in her melancholy wanderings after she left that lonely churchyard, with nothing as a memorial of her mother but a simple wild flower that was in her bosom.

If Lucy had not had a strong and fervent hope of meeting with Harry Dean, she would have turned her face to that country which God made, instead of the town which is the work of man; but with a child-like reliance upon those she loved, she thought that if she could but find Harry all would be well, and that with some magic might he would at once be able to restore her sister Kate to her.

Therefore was it, then, that knowing he ever came from that direction, she turned her steps towards the great and distant town, the turmoil of which she could distinctly hear, even from where she was.

Oh! what a crusade for that young, beautiful, and innocent child to undertake in such a place as London—a search for an unit of its population, amid its thronging, crowding, breathless streets, and a reliance upon goodness and compassion for support, until she should find him whom she sought. Alas! poor Lucy, you know but little of the dangers of the enterprise you were about to start upon. The shield of Heaven should be and perchance is over you. God looks down through the soft eyes of ministering angels upon that young child, and the light of his love and his mercy will light her on her way.

> "Some angel unseen, yet felt,
> Shall lead her by the hand,
> While fluttering in the ether blue
> Float on a Heaven-born band."

The little creature looked up for an instant at the night sky, with her deep, earnest eyes, and then folding over her gentle bosom a thin shawl she wore—it had once been Kate's—she commenced her holy, most holy, pilgrimage.

On, on through the suburb of the mighty city slowly wended the child, and soon having got clear of the fields, the gardens, and the sweet smelling flowers, she came to regular rows of houses and shops, and in her simplicity she thought that she would ask some one for Harry Dean, and she thought, too, that if she asked the best and kindest-looking person she could see, there would be a good chance of getting news of him, for was not Harry kind and good too?

A boy—a lad—perhaps almost a young man he ought to be called—was putting up the shutters of a shop, and there was a something in his face that the child liked. She paused, and looked at him until he had completed the shutting up of the shop, and then she spoke to him.

"Did you ever hear of Mr. Harry Dean?" she said; and she looked earnestly in his face, while the lad looked as earnestly in hers, with his mouth open, as if that would assist him in being of service to her, and answering her inquiry,—

"Mr. who?"

"Harry Dean; he lives somewhere in London."

"Oh!"

The boy looked confused, and then he smiled, as he added,—

"This here's a hadwenture. I say, little girl, did you ever read 'The False Fairy; or, the Goblin Monarch and the Haunted Back Kitchen?'"

"No."

"'Cos you see in that Leila, the good fairy, is just like you, and kums up to the woodman and says, says she, 'Have you seen Prince Flimiskhin?' says she, and then ——. Oh, lor'!"

"I'll teach you to be gossiping," cried a rough-looking man, rushing to the door, and hitting the lad a severe blow on the head with an iron bolt which belonged to the shutters; "I'll teach you when you are put to shut up my shop to do it, and not be talking to every vagrant you meet with at the door, you lazy hound, you."

"Oh! no, no, no," cried Lucy, stepping forward, and laying her little soft hands upon the man's arms. "Don't hit him; he was only talking to me, and I talked to him first. Don't—oh, don't."

"I'll hit you too if you don't be off."

The brutal fellow raised the bolt in his hand. God knows if he meant or meant not to strike the child; but the lad, who seemed to have such a turn for romantic literature—fate be propitious to him—thought that she was in danger. His face became of a glow, and his eyes flashed as he closed at once with the ruffian; and wresting the bolt from his hand, laid him prostrate on his own shop floor, with one hearty blow just between his eyes.

He dropped the bolt when he had done this deed of retribution, and looked for a moment puzzled to know what to do; then turning to the terrified Lucy, he said,—

"Little girl, this ain't by no means no place for me now. The Baron—tut, tut, I mean my master—will kill me for this here, or else put me in one of the dungeons under the castle—I mean the shop; so I'll walk off while the drawbridge—I mean the door—is open. Come along, little girl, I'll walk with you a little way. Come, now, are you a fairy or ain't you? Ah! this puts me in mind of the story of 'The Baron Bumbusticus; or, the Demon of the Haunted Pound.' But if you is a fairy, you know, all I can say is, it's very kind of you to take to a poor fellow in the butchering line."

"The what?" said Lucy, who began to think her companion was a little deranged, and yet there was a simplicity and a kindliness about his tone that had charms for her unsophisticated ears.

"Why, didn't you see that it was a butcher's, little girl, where you spoke to me? I haven't been there long, and I didn't like it; so after all I don't much care, you know, about going away. He was a cruel, hard-hearted baron—butcher I mean. I could put up with a good deal myself, but when he raised his hand agin you, all the blood in my body went bang into the tip of my nose, and then down he went, you see."

"You are very good to me," said Lucy. "What makes you call him a baron?"

"Why, you see, it's my edication. I reads a good deal, you see, though I am in the butchering line, and—and I—I—ha, ha!—I writes a little. But where are you going to?"

"Nowhere," said Lucy, with a sigh. "I'm looking for Harry and my dear sister Kate."

The butcher's boy stopped and looked all round him, as if he expected to see one or other of those personages close at hand; but as there was no one who came up to his idea of Harry or Kate, he said,—

"Where?"

"I don't know. I think Harry Dean is in London, but I don't at all know where poor Kate is."

"But—but where's your father and mother?"

Lucy shook her head, and said,—

"I have none."

"And where do you live?"

"Nowhere."

The butcher's boy took off a fur cap that he had on his head, and gave his hair a vigorous pull, as if to brighten up his intellect a little; and then he looked at Lucy, and then up to the sky, and then all around him; after which, he said, in an inquiring tone,—

"Runned away?"

"Eh?" said Lucy, for she did not understand the question; and that ignorance convinced the boy that she had not, as he called it, "runned away" from anywhere; so having now got some distance from the vicinity of the butcher's shop, he pointed to the step of a door, and said,—

"Let's sit down here, and talk it over. It's quite an adwenture, though I am in the butchering line. Sit down, dear."

Lucy was tired, and gladly enough complied with the invitation, and told him, in a very few words, her simple and unadorned story, which evidently deeply affected him, for he took out a cotton handkerchief, nearly eight inches square, with a striking portrait of the queen and Prince Albert in the centre, and wiped one eye with the queen's face, and the other with the prince's.

"And so you're a-going about, without not nothing," he said, "a-looking for somebody? Lor' bless you, you might as well look for a bottle of hay in a needle, as anybody in London! What a foolish little thing you is, and so is I—so is I. A pfeu! pfeu! I ain't a-crying now, mind. My name's Tony Thorpe, so they says; I ain't not got no father and mother, and never had any. The blessed parish pulled me up, and then they put me out to the butchering line, you see; and the only person as I knows is Mrs. Blinks, you see; and if it hadn't a-been for the books as used to cheer me up of a night, I think I should have gone out of my mind; but when I come for to go, all for to find how Amelia the fascinating was persecuted by the Baron of Bluebhlastometor, and was put into dungeons, and out o' dungeons, and dragged about, and poked through the sliding panels, and all that ere sort o' thing, I said, 'Who is me that I shouldn't have my disagreeables?'

"And then, you know, it all ends happy which teaches of us as we should never despair. Now, there's 'Arabella, the Heiress of Fontenoy; or, the Demon of the Enchanted Ring.' You wouldn't a-thought when she was throwed into the castle vaults, and left to think of nothing but her latter end, that she'd a come at last to be the missus of that ere castle, and married the "Knight of the Heron's Plume, would you now?"

"I never heard of it," said Lucy. "But I must go now and look for Harry and Kate.—Good night, Tony."

"No, no, stop a bit, there is two *orphins*, and you shall go with me now to Mrs. Blinks's, I shall take care of you till to-morrow, and perhaps put you in the way of finding out Mr. Harry Dean, if you can tell her anything about him. Who know's—come along. It's a going to rain too. Just hold that ere little shawl round you.—Lor, what bits o' hands to be sure.—Well I never.— Come along, do.—We is like two knight-errants, that we is, a seeking out lots o' *hadwentures*. I haven't been to Mrs. Blinks's for a long while, but I expects we shall find her out."

There was a slight misty rain falling, and Lucy, who felt that at night she could not very well prosecute her enquiries, was glad of having found a friend, so she tripped on, holding the great hard hand of poor Tony Thorpe. His heart was softer though than any coquette's, vain of her soft taper-fingers, and sweetly dimpled knuckles; and as he looked down upon the confiding, gentle face of the little girl who was by his side, he loved her for her innocence, and her fond confidence in him, and as he involuntarily quickened his pace, he muttered to himself,—

"Yes, he'd have hit her with the bolt, the villain. Oh I am so glad I knocked him down, even in his own castle—his shop I mean. The rascal—he might have hit me as much as he liked, but not her.—Oh, no, not her. Don't hurry, dear. Don't hurry."

CHAPTER XII.

MR. MAYSTON HAS AN INTERVIEW WITH MADAME ZADZED.

IT was twelve o'clock on the day succeeding that on which Kate had felt all the pangs of frightful expectation in her gilded prison, that in a handsome drawing-room of a house situated in Upper Baker-street, there sat a female at breakfast, to whom it is now necessary that we should introduce the reader of this most veritable narrative.

This female, we cannot for the life of us call her lady—was of what is called a certain age which seems always ready to mean a period of life at which the age to all but the person most immediately interested is made to be as uncertain as possible. But she was not young, and she was not handsome, although along with the former she might have been the latter.

Whatever, however, had been her condition in life, and whatever had been the adventures she had gone through, it would appear that she had managed to take care of the main chance, for there she sat in her own drawing-room, at breakfast, surrounded by all sorts of luxuries, and the hour too of partaking of that meal showed that the partaker of it had nothing to do, but that most difficult thing of all, namely, to slaughter time.

She seemed, however, to have all the means and appliances at hand for getting rid of that fiend *ennui*. The morning papers lay upon the table before her, and the most tempting viands that are permissable at a breakfast table were before her.

And this was Madame Zadzed.

The reader may expect a Frenchwoman, we should from the prefix to the name but in the present instance that had only been lent to the female by a Mons. Zadzed, who had long since gone the way of all flesh, while the widow gaily enough jumped out of her weeds but retained the foreign, as some people think, rather distinguished name as a preface to her marital appellation.

After this Madame Zadzel may be anything, but she *was* Irish, and, although she had been long imported from the "gem of the sea," she now and then betrayed her origin by some expression more euphonical than elegant, and there was a smouldering fire of evil passions in her breast too much to be found among the inhabitants of that land of emeralds—*Anglice* potatoes when they *were* good.

The half-hour past twelve sounded from a little time-piece of elegant construction and fanciful design, that was upon the chimney-piece, and then a servant came in and said—

"Madame, there is some one wishes to see you."

"What name, eh?" said the mistress, quickly.

"Mayston, madam, Mr. Mayston."

"Oh—admit him. Has he been here long?"

"Not above ten minutes, madam."

"What can he want," muttered the lady, stretching forth an arm more powerful than beautiful, she hastily dragged down the blind of the window that was nearest to her, so that a shade was cast all over the spot on which she sat, and she would have the advantage in a conversation of observing any play of her visitor's countenance without exposing the emotions of her own, provided she should exhibit any.

In another moment Alfred Mayston entered the room, being ushered in by a servant, who, in obedience to a look from the lady of the house, removed some of the breakfast things, so as to break up the appearance of that meal being still going on.

"Well, Mayston," she said, when they were alone. "What is it now? I think this is only the second time I have had the honour of seeing you in this p'ace since I recommended you to the service of Lord Battaney?"

"By which," said Mayston, "it will be seen that I don't trouble you after I have left Lord Battaney."

"Blur-anouns!—I—I—mean I'm surprised."

She bit her lips with vexation at having let slip this rather genuine bit of Irishism, for it was one highly calculated to awaken the inquiry of where did she learn so much of the colloquial? Mayston, however, took no notice of it, but continued—

"Yes, I have left him. I did him good and faithful service; I was well paid; I put up with ill-humour—contempt—abuse; but I could not put up with a blow!"

"And you come to me for—for——"

"Revenge!"

There was a silence of a few moments duration, and then she said, faintly—

"And what induces you to think that I will help you to revenge?"

"Your general conduct to me. You Lave been the only friend I ever had in all the world. You are the person who rescued me from a miserable condition. You have done all that any one could do for me. I now ask you to do one thing more, and that is to help me to revenge against Lord Battaney."

"Tell me all the circumstances."

Mayston winced a little as he related the affair of the abduction of Kate Destern, and the odious part he had acted in that business, but he kept nothing back. She heard all that he had to tell, and when he had concluded, she spoke, saying—

"I must think of this. Lord Battaney has sent to me to say that he wants me to go to the house at Fulham, before night. You can call upon me here to-morrow at this hour, and if you do not find me, you can call the day after, or the day after that."

"And is this all you can say to me? Is this all the hope and consolation you can give me?"

"It is. Revenge is a good keeping quality. Yours is not of the true mortal if it cannot support itself for a few days. Go away, now, I have other matters to attend to."

Probably he knew by experience that there would be no good in pressing Madam Zadzed to be more explicit, or to take up his cause more energetically, but yet he lingered a little; and when with something like passion, she said to him,—

"By the holy, what does the man stay for?" he approached her, and spoke in a lower voice, saying.—

"Once upon a time you intimated to me that if you had an opportunity you would not be disinclined to revenge yourself upon Lord Battaney. You—you further intimated to me that you had a sense of injury."

"Well?"

"I relied a little upon that."

"Well?"

"Oh! nothing further; I merely called it to your recollection, that's all, with the hope that it might induce you to help me."

She rung the bell, and when a servant appeared, she said,—

"Show Mr. Mayston out."

He bowed, and without another word left the room; but when he got clear of the house, he looked back, and gave

utterance to some frightful maledictions against its mistress, and ground his teeth together with passion.

"I don't know how it is," he said, "but that woman always cows me. Nothing but the present emergence would have induced me to cross her threshold, but I know she has some mysterious power over Lord Battaney, and the hope that she will exercise it, so as to aid me in my revenge, will make me put up with all his overloading inso-lence. But there will come a day when I can, perhaps, afford to repay her scoff for scoff—aye, that's the word—afford. What a number of things I will do when I can afford to do them."

The lady was not without her re flections when she was left alone. She walked to a window that commanded a view of the street, and she saw the rage of Mayston, as once he shook his clenched fist at the house. She trem-bled, as she said, mournfully,—

"Is it so? Well, well, it is perhaps better. We must never know each other very well. He would then—for well I know his disposition—play the tyrant as easily, aye, and easier too, than he now plays the slave. No, no, it is far better as it is."

She rung the bell, and desired that her own waiting maid, "Swam," as she called her, should be sent for at once; and when that individual made her appearance, and they were alone, Madam Zadzed said to her, quite confidentially,—

"Swam, I want you to set out at once, and find out carefully, and without creating any corresponding enquiry, all you can about a family named Destern. But I will write the particulars, while you go and get yourself ready to go. You can have the carriage, but don't shew it."

"I'll be ready in ten minutes," said Swam; and away she went to put herself into out of doors trim.

Swam was not the most engaging-looking creature in the world. Swam had but one eye, but that was as good as anybody else's two, although it gave rather a sinister expression to her not, certainly, very captivating countenance. But there Swam was—but hold, Swam is what she is, and probably if she had had the fashioning herself, she would have done so more according to the generally received notions and ideas of mundane beauty.

In rather less time than she had mentioned she was duly equipped for the expedition her mistress wished to send her on, and having received a written paper with instructions, which she made herself mistress of at a glance, she started in Madame Zadzed's carriage for the northern suburbs of London, where she intended to alight and pursue her inquiries on foot.

Those inquiries were eminently successful, and she came back with the news that is already known to the reader; and the circumstance that a book was so clasped in the hands of the dead Mrs. Destern, that it was only the undertaker could take it away, and that that book, which was not a religious one, was now in the hands of Mrs. Williams, did not escape Swam.

"You must get that book to-morrow, Swam," said Madame Zadzed. "I want the carriage now myself."

"Certainly, madame," said Swam.

CHAPTER XIII.

ANOTHER DAY FOR KATE.—THE AT-TEMPTED ESCAPE.—THE SPECTRE OF A GUILTY CONSCIENCE.

THE evening had fairly and effectually deepened into night before Kate Destern rose from her knees by the door of her chamber, and looked tremblingly around her.

"I am alone," she said; "oh! thank Heaven I am alone. All is darkness, but I am alone! No one comes to mar the solitude of this place. I—I am safe for a time. Thank Heaven for so much mercy!"

She went to the window, and drawing aside the curtains so as to admit as much of the dim and hazy light which preluded the rising of the moon into the apartment as possible, she listened, with a soothed and easier feeling, to the murmurs of the night wind among the branches of the tall trees, some of the straggling foliage of which almost touched the window panes.

Thus half-an-hour passed away, until she was suddenly startled by some gravel being cast against the window from without. The minute stones came with a rattling sound upon the glass, and when, after a few moments, the alarm was repeated, she felt certain that it was intended as a signal for attracting her attention.

Hope sprung up in her heart, and slowly she opened the casement. A rush of cold air came into the apartment, but that was more welcome than otherwise to her, and besides, she was by far too intent upon discovering what was the cause of the attempt to attract her attention, to heed any minor circumstances connected therewith.

She leant out at the window, and strove to penetrate with her eyes the darkness below, but the trees sent about there by far too impenetrable shadows; and she feared to speak, lest she should be betraying some one who was disposed to be friendly towards her.

All was still now, and a feeling of disappointment began to creep over her, when a stone was cast up, and narrowly missing striking her, it bounded into the room.

At the same moment she heard the lock of the door moving. The bar was thrown down, and some one made an attempt to open the door, but was prevented by the table.

"Who is there?" said Kate.

"Oh! you needn't be afraid," said a female voice. "I've only brought you a light and something to eat. Dear me, some people are in a mighty fright about nothing. Perhaps your betters ain't quite so particular; and I don't see, after all, that a table is much good put against a door. There, you see, it's easy enough pushed aside, if any one has a mind to do so."

This address was not one that Kate was very desirous of answering, so she stood with her back to the window, and allowed the intruder to push the table aside for herself.

This was a young woman, whom Kate had not yet seen, and, if that were possible, she looked more atrocious than the old hag who had formerly played the part of jailor to her, and of whose fate she (Kate) knew nothing, although it will be recollected, probably, by the reader that Lord Battaney was informed she had been killed by the fall of the stack of chimneys, during the storm that had taken place at an early hour in the evening.

But still there was to Kate some hope that this woman, who now brought her provisions and a light, might be merciful, and she spoke to her, saying,—

"You are young, and have perhaps a long life before you. Why will you seek to embitter it by the consciousness of injustice?"

"Eh? What do you mean?"

"Sooner or later there will surely come a time when you will repent not having been kind to me. Oh! think of what joy it may be at some hour of sadness and sickness to feel that you have done even one good action in saving me from this place. Heaven will most amply in that way reward you. Have some mercy upon me."

"I don't like preaching, and never did," said the girl, with a brutal sort of laugh.

As she gave utterance to these words, she threw down the provisions, and then turning round, as if she had been insulted by this appeal to her better feelings, she bounced out of the room.

"It is all in vain," said Kate. "There is no one in this dreadful house with feelings of compassion."

Temporarily she had quite forgotten the incident of the stone that had been cast into the room, but now she fully remembered it; and looking upon the floor, she soon found it, and saw, with a flush of anxiety, expectation, and delight, that a piece of paper was wrapped round it.

By the aid of the light she soon removed it, and found that there was written upon the paper these words:

"A friend suggests to Kate Destern that if she wishes to free herself from the presence of Lord Battaney to-night, should he pay her another visit, she should attire herself in a riding habit that she will find in the lowest drawer of the wardrobe."

"What can this mean?" she thought. "How can my attiring myself in a riding habit alarm Lord Battaney, if that be the name and title of the bad man who keeps me a prisoner here?"

Although she had no means of forming the remotest conjecture as to how it was that so trivial a circumstance should save her from the dreaded presence of one concerning whom she could not think without a shudder, she took the light and proceeded towards a wardrobe, which was in one corner of the room, and opening the lowest drawer, she searched for the riding habit mentioned, and there found one which had all the appearance of having been laid by for a considerable time, as a complete rout of moths took place as she took it out from the drawer, and proceeded to unfold it.

It seemed to have been a rich and costly habit, elaborately trimmed with velvet.

"What tale of grief may not be attached to this dress," sighed Kate. "Oh! that I knew who had been the wearer of it. Shall I or shall I not take the advice of the writer of this anonymous note, and attire myself in that garb? It cannot hurt me, if it do not save me!"

By a further search in the drawer, she found a lady's riding hat, and a pair of long, exquisitely soft white gloves; so that if she chose, there was as complete an equestrian costume as she could desire.

But still Kate hesitated. The events of the last twenty-six hours had, for the first time in all her life, taught her the bitter lesson of suspicion.

How could she tell but that contingent upon her wearing that riding habit there was some horrible plot or scheme in contemplation, improbable as such a thing seemed?

And so she hesitated, until she heard a clock from afar off—the faint sound of which was only brought to her ears, in consequence of the stillness of the night, and her having the window open—strike twelve.

A sudden revulsion of feeling seemed to take place in the breast of Kate; and approaching the dressing table, she proceeded hurriedly—she scarcely knew why—to array herself in the riding habit.

It was not the work of more than a few minutes to do this, and then she put on the hat and gloves; after which she began to question the wisdom of the proceeding, and she sat down upon a chair, near to the dressing-table, on which was the light, and it so happened —surely Heaven planned it—that the reflection from the dressing glass fell full upon her face and bosom, giving a white, spectral-like appearance to her, as contrasted with the very dim light, for the candle was untrimmed, that shone over the apartment.

She began now, too, to feel the effects of undue exertion, and to wish much for rest.

"Oh," she said, mournfully; "oh, that I dared lie down and sleep!"

She started, and all her senses became preternaturally mute as she uttered these words, for there came suddenly upon her ears a low grating sort of sound, which was not in the direction of the door. It seemed to her to be issuing from one part of the wall which was immediately by the side of the bed.

She felt her position becoming diffi-cult, and the cold dew of fear stood upon her brow,

The grating noise increased, but she did not stir; and then a voice said, in subdued accents,—

"Hush! Do you sleep?"

She returned no answer, for even in the midst of her fears and her intense nervousness, she thought that the question was but put to ascertain the fact, and not from any friendly feeling towards her; for if she had a friend at all, surely it was he who had thrown to her the mysterious note.

In this view she was confirmed, for in another moment the voice said,—

"All's well! She sleeps!"

She kept her eye intently fixed in the direction from whence the sound proceeded, and to her surprise she saw a portion of the pannelling of the room slowly receding, as if a small door was opening; and when it was completely open, she saw the figure of the man who was named Lord Battaney in the note she had received.

In his hand he held a small night lamp. There was a strange flush of colour upon his face, and it was evident that he was agitated, for the hand in which he held the light shook perceptibly.

He cast his eyes upon the bed, where, doubtless, he expected to find his slumbering victim, but there she was not; and then he shaded the night lamp with one hand, while peering over it he cast his eyes round the room with a look of surprise.

He saw her.

Gradually the hair seemed to stiffen up upon his head, and the shaking of his hands continued, until the lamp dropped from him, and fell upon the bed. Then covering his eyes with both his hands—for he seemed to be rivetted to the spot, and unable to move from it, he shrieked aloud; and then, in a voice of great agony, he spoke in a strange and incoherent strain.

"Oh! no, no, no. Oh! God, no. Anything but that—any shape but that. Have mercy upon me. I did not kill you! The cold waters of the river would never have held your shrinking form had you consented to be happy! Away, away! Why am I cursed with such a vision? Avaunt, frightful, yet beautiful spectre! Help, help! Oh, God, preserve me from madness—madness—madness. Off, off, off—I say—I —I say, off!"

With a strong effort he wrenched himself away from the panel that he had opened, and the terrified Kate—scarcely less terrified than he was—heard him shouting, "Off, off, off!" as he stumbled down a staircase that was behind him.

"Merciful Heaven!" she gasped, "what is the meaning of this?"

For some few moments she was totally unable to move; but then, as she saw the open panel before her, the idea that it might possibly afford her a means of escape, rushed across her mind, and that revived her once again. She sprung to her feet.

"Yes, yes," she cried, "this may, after all, be one of those interpositions of Providence that I ought not to neglect. To Heaven's guidance I commit myself, and may God be merciful to me!"

Seizing her light, and still wearing the riding habit, the sight of which had proved so awfully obnoxious to Lord Battaney, she advanced towards the the bed, and mounting upon it, she looked and listened for a few brief moments at the opening of the yawning, chasm-like flight of stairs that revealed themselves within the open panel; and then mustering all her courage, she commenced what, from the ruinous state of the stairs, was a perilous descent.

CHAPTER XIV.

THE ALARM IN THE MANSION.—THE RE-CAPTURE OF KATE.

THE staircase down which Kate now, with careful and faltering steps, went, was a winding one, and had evidently been constructed so as to occupy as small a portion of the space left between two walls for that secret passage as possible.

By the quantity of dust, too, that was upon each stair, and which could be perceptibly felt beneath the feet, it was quite evident that that secret place had not been visited for a very considerable time. Perhaps there were some associations connected with it which invested the riding habit that Kate now wore with some portion of its horrors.

Immense thick spiders' webs hung from the walls, and Kate shuddered as these homes of the long-legged spinners wafted across her face, sometimes almost blinding her for a moment, before she could, with her disengaged hand, free herself from their troublesome embrace. But she proceeded, and went onward, determined that no trifling difficulty should stand between her and the chances of an escape from that dreaded house.

She had long ceased to hear anything of the footsteps of Lord Battaney, and only once during her descent did any sound now reach her ears, and that consisted of the slamming shut of a door suddenly, but from whence it came she could not, in that extensive mansion, with which she was so little acquainted, take upon herself to say.

It was only for a moment that she paused to listen to the reverberations caused by the sound, and then again mentally commending herself to the care of Heaven, she proceeded on her lonely way.

She began now to think that she must have reached the lower part of the house, and soon she was quite convinced that such was the fact, for she came to the conclusion of the winding staircase, and found herself in a small square place, not much larger than a sentry-box, from which she did not see any means of emerging.

But it was so evident that there must be some outlet, that Kate proceeded, by the aid of the light she carried, to examine the walls, which were of wood, with the greatest minuteness, and finally that examination was rewarded by the discovery of a small steel spring, upon pressing which she had the satisfaction of finding a long narrow door open, and the odour of flowers at once crossed her senses.

At first she thought she was in the open air, but when she passed through the little doorway, she saw at once that she was in a large conservatory, filled with choice plants, the delicate perfume of which quite loaded the air with sweets.

As she held the light high she saw

how sweetly its rays fell upon the multitude of glorious tints of every shade and hue around her, but she soon roused herself from the task of gazing upon these glorious imitations of the rainbow, and felt the necessity of not pausing if she really hoped by flight to escape from her thraldom.

She passed onwards towards a door at the further extremity of the conservatory, but upon opening it, she found that it led into a large and handsomely-furnished room; and fearing that that again would conduct her to other interlinked portions of the house, she retreated, hoping that the other end of the conservatory might lead her into the open gardens, for if once she gained them she had a great expectation of escape.

It was so; a door, beautifully fitted with stained glass, led at once into the open air, and she found herself in a gravelled path, the borders of which were thickly strewn with flowering shrubs.

At once casting down the light, as she considered that now it would be but a guide to any one who might search for her from the house, she darted forward, but found herself arrested before she had gone many paces, by a hand grasping her arm.

Almost fainting from the suddenness of this attack, she was for a moment or two silent, trembling like some young bird in the hands of the fowler; but when she did find power to speak, the imploring accents would have melted any heart but that of him who held her.

"Oh! pity me," she cried, "rather than detain me! Rather—be you whom you may—aid me to escape from this dreadful place, than detain me for one moment longer in it. If ever you knew what affliction or suffering was, have mercy upon me!"

"Hush! You cannot escape," said a voice.

"'Tis Alfred Mayston," gasped Kate.

"True," he replied, "I am Alfred Mayston; and I say again that you cannot escape, Kate Destern, from this place without my connivance. The gates are well guarded, and the walls are of sufficient height to laugh to scorn any efforts to scale them. But I can take you out."

"And—and you will?"

"On one condition."

"Condition?"

"Yes, one simple condition. If you stay here, you stay to a fate of horror to such as you. Only say that you will be mine, and in ten minutes you are free. Say that you will be my wife—that you will marry me when I please, and nothing shall prevent you from leaving this abode of villany and criminality. Call Heaven to witness that you consent to be mine, and I will take your oath, and conduct you to a coach that I have in waiting."

"No, no, I cannot."

"You cannot?"

"Alfred Mayston, I shudder even at your voice. If it be God's will that I should perish, perish I may; but I cannot—cannot be yours! If upon no other than that frightful condition you can save me, leave me to my fate, and to the guidance of that power which yet, perchance, will not let me be wholly lost."

"Girl, you rave! You have but one friend here, and that is myself. It was I that cast the stone into your chamber, containing the note with advice that has scared Lord Battaney half out of his senses. I wished to thwart him, and I have."

"Yes, revenge has been your motive, not repentance."

"Repentance? Pshaw! I leave that to the sick and the weak-minded. Come, Kate Destern, there is not a moment to lose. Fly with me. Surely it is better far to be the wife, even if it be of one who has not yet acquired a hold of your girlish fancy, than to stay here, and be the sport of such a man as Lord Battaney. Can you—dare you hesitate for one moment between two such propositions?"

"I do not hesitate. To consent to your proposal is certain misery. I can save myself from Lord Battaney!"

"You can?"

"As Heaven hears me, I can and will."

"How—how? Why, you are absolutely mad, girl! How can you save yourself from Lord Battaney?"

"By death."

He was silent for a moment or two; and the clanging sound of a bell came from the house.

"'Tis too late," he said. "Your flight is discovered, and those who guard the gates of this place are now upon the guard, and no one will be permitted to leave without further orders. Remain, and perish in your obstinacy; and let whatever fate come to you, you shall have now in addition the horror of knowing that you might, by an honourable alliance, have avoided it."

"Not honourable! Unhand me, ruffian!"

"Ah! has it come to that? What ho! Help, help! This way! What ho! Lights here, lights! Ha, ha, my pretty one, you may struggle, but you shall not be free! What ho! This way—this way. Ha, ha, ha! Do you repent now of your mad-brained obstinacy?"

"Oh, villain, villain!"

"Rail on! That is the most delightful music to me now. They come—they come; and as surely as the sun shall shine to-morrow, you will be the enforced victim of Lord Battaney."

There was a flashing of lights, and a hurried sound of footsteps—voices, too, came upon the night air; and at length, guided by the loud and reiterated calls of Mayston, three servants, bearing torches, reached the spot, and at once laid hold of Kate.

"There," cried Mayston; "there, I caught her, and you may go and tell Lord Battaney who did so. Perhaps he may be sorry then that he has picked a quarrel with Alfred Mayston. Take her away—take her away. What a pretty set of fellows you are! She would have escaped had it not been for me; and when you get to the house, order the bell to be rung again, so that I may be let leave the place, for I have no desire to stay here after the treatment I have experienced."

"Why, what on earth are you raving about, Mayston?" said one of the servants.

"Nothing to you," was the polite rejoinder; and Mayston darted away, and was soon lost to sight among the surrounding trees and shrubs that grew in such great luxuriance all around.

Kate felt that it would be a waste of words to attempt to move the pity of the men who had now re-captured her, and she submitted in silence to a fate she could not control, and walked towards the house, preceded by one of them, and followed by the other two.

When she reached it, the first person she saw was the young, repulsive woman who had brought her the light and the provisions; and this woman, advancing with fury in her looks, seized Kate by the arm with an iron clutch, and shook her furiously, digging her nails into her flesh, exclaiming,—

"So you would get us all into trouble, would you, by running away? Oh, you are a nice, dainty bit of goods, to be sure. I'll shake the life out of you; and if it was not for getting blamed, I'd soon spoil that baby face, by leaving the marks of my nails in it—I would."

For a moment indignation got the better of every other feeling in Kate's mind; and with a power that no one would have at all expected from one so delicate and fragile-looking, she snatched one of the burning links from the man nearest to her, and dashed it in the woman's face.

A howl of rage and pain succeeded, but the men threw themselves between Kate and the woman, saying that their master would make them answerable for any harm coming to the young lady; and so they took her into the house, out of the way of the woman, who looked quite a hideous spectacle, covered with half-burnt tar, and scorched as she was by the link.

CHAPTER XV.

LUCY AND TONY MEET WITH A DISAPPOINTMENT.—THE PLACE OF REFUGE.

CONVERSING together, as if they had been the oldest friends in the world, Tony Thorpe and little Lucy made their way to the not very salubrious part of the town where Mrs. Blinks resided, and where her Tony hoped to find a shelter and a welcome for poor Lucy and himself.

They arrived at a narrow street somewhere about that region that lies between the end of the Hampstead-road and Somers Town, and from that narrow street they turned into a court, and at No. 2, Tony knocked, saying to Lucy as he did so,—

"You see, Mrs. Blinks hasn't got rooms in any of the blessed palaces, but a precious many folks has, I should say, as don't deserve 'em half so much."

"Very likely," said Lucy, as she looked at the dingy-looking houses of the court, and thought that certainly a more unpalace-like-looking place she had scarcely ever seen.

To be sure it was but a poor cottage in the country that she had lived in with her mother and Kate, but then no place in the country can be so utterly squalid as poverty in a great city like London.

"You mustn't judge o' things by how they looks," said Tony. "In this here house you will get a welcome, and a bit of something, and a drop of something."

Now, the latter part of these words of Tony's appeared to be quite prophetic, for scarcely were they out of his mouth when the "drop of something" came, in the shape of a basin of soap-suds, flung out of the second floor window, the party throwing them kindly saying, afterwards,—

"Below there!"

"Thank you for nothing, missus," said Tony, as he looked up. "If we had been a standing ever such a little bit further out from the door, we should have caught rather too much of that."

"Who are you, that's so particular about a drop of soap-suds, I wonders!" cried the lady, in a shrill, alto key, as she slammed shut her window.

"Civil that, ain't it?" said Tony to Lucy; but before she could reply to the ironical remark, the door was opened, and another female appeared, and announced her readiness to hear what the visitors had to say, by the brief permission to speak comprehended in,—

"Now then?"

"We want to see Mrs. Blinks," said Tony.

"What, Mrs. Blinks as used to go out a-*cheering?*"

"Yes, yes."

"Dead!"

Bang went the door in their faces, and Tony staggered back, until he was stopped by the opposite houses, and recalled by a cobbler, who worked in the parlour, to the impropriety of stopping up the light from him, as Tony's back was towards the only square of glass that had not a fracture, and was not half covered by paper.

"I begs yer pardon," said Tony. "They tell me that Mrs. Blinks is dead. Do you know anything about it?"

"Do I know? Why do you ask me, when the state of the country is such, that unless every man has the right to vote according to his conscience, we shall all go to rack and ruin? What do you think of the whigs now? They don't mean to do anything; and I can only say that until every man has a vote, and parliaments are elected once a month, there will be no good done. What do you think?"

"Lor' bless you," said Tony, "I minds my own business when I've got any to mind."

"You are a fool!" said the cobbler, with great indignation; "you are a fool!"

"Ah! very likely," said Tony. "Did you ever read 'The Knight of the Sanguinary Nose; or, the Blue Spectre of Bludendghuts,' old fellow?"

"No."

"Then you're a fool! Come along, Lucy. If poor Mrs. Blinks is dead, bless her, we need not stay here, dear. Come along; we will find, perhaps, some shelter somewhere, and then in the morning we will hold a grand counsel, you know, as to what to do. This way, dear."

"But where can we go, Tony?" said Lucy. "I am so tired."

"Why, Common Garden market, afore the improvements and the new policemen, used to be a nice place, and quite a countrified place to sleep in, too, cos o' the smell o' the vegetables, you see. I don't know how it is now, but as I can't think of anywhere else at present, let's go and try."

"Common Garden," said Lucy, adopting Tony's vernacular; "where's that?"

"Oh! the market—this way. Perhaps we shall be able to stay there long enough to get some rest, if they do

hoist us off soon in the morning. But I say, Lucy dear, ain't you hungary?"

The child burst into tears.

"Stop," cried Tony, "stop. Just you wait here a minute, will you, and don't you move for love or money, that's all."

He darted off, and presently returned with a penny loaf, and something else which was new to Lucy, but he told her it was a saveloy, and with that and the loaf they made a meal which, at all events, allayed the pangs of present hunger.

There was a pump, too, the ladle of which had not yet been stolen, at the corner of the court, and a draught of the pure, cold, sparkling water was wonderfully refreshing; so that Lucy did not feel half so tired as she had been, and holding by the hand of Tony, they set off together towards Covent Garden market, just as the streets were getting rather thin of people.

"Ah! poor Mrs. Blinks," said Tony, "I thinks I sees you now!"

"Where?" said Lucy.

"In my mind's eye, Horatio. So you have gone dead, has you? Well, peace be to your *mane*, says I. A more better old soul there wasn't. You won't go out a-*cheering* no more—you won't do a day's washing now for nobody in this here world! I wishes I had a something as belonged to you to remember you by, if it was but one of your old pattens as used to go chink, chink on the blessed pavement in wet weather. Ah! well, there's no being poor where you're gone to, Mrs. B.; no—oh, no. Your romance, in never so many wolumes, is over, and you're gone to the binder's now, you has."

Much of this monody on the departed Mrs. Blinks was lost upon Lucy, who, as she trotted along by the side of Tony, looked up in wonder at him as he spoke.

And so they went on, until they reached Covent Garden market, which they walked round several times in despair, for there seemed, as Tony said, in consequence of the improvements, no resting-place for them within its precincts.

At length they paused irresolutely opposite to a woman who was sitting on an upturned fruit basket, smoking a short pipe. This lady had on a man's coat over her feminine habiliments, and a man's hat was upon her head. She was a remarkable lady, and her face looked like some old wrinkled, decayed apple.

But there was yet a something about her which looked kindly, and Tony spoke to her.

"If you please," he said, "may this little girl sit down here and rest herself?"

"If I plase!" exclaimed the lady with the pipe. "Why, ye spalpeen, what do you mane by my plasing? It's the good-looking young cratur that she is, any way; and sorra be to them that would wish harm to her. Sit yerself down, darlin'."

Lucy did so, and Tony, finding the old Irish woman so kindly disposed towards them, sat down likewise; and upon a heap of all sorts of odds and ends—baskets, cabbages, porter's knots, and potatoe sacks—both Lucy and he soon fell fast asleep, while the Irish lady smoked her pipe, and crooned out the burthen of some ancient song, in a dialect that if anybody had heard it they would have been none the wiser for.

It was about half past four in the morning that Tony was awakened by a cry from Lucy, and upon starting up, found a sturdy, ragged lad trying to take from her neck a little coral necklace.

At the same moment, too, the nymph from the Erin isle was aroused, and before Tony could collar the offender, she caught up a great flat basket, and gave a blow on the head with it that levelled him.

"Take that, you thief o' the world," she cried; "take that and be aisy!"

"Why, you have killed him," said Tony.

"Sorra' come to him, no. It's a hard head he has! I know his people—the Caseys—the murthering Caseys. Och! the divil a bit is he kilt even."

The scion of the Caseys soon proved this to be a fact, for after lying insensible for a time, he got up and rubbed his head, winked a little, and finally walked away.

"There now," said the maid of Erin, "didn't I be after telling you so?"

"You did indeed," said Tony. "I'm glad you sarved him out, missus; for you see this here little girl ain't got no friends."

"No friends! Oh, murther and turf! Take this, my darlin'."

It was a large orange that she handed to Lucy, and very acceptable it was, for the saveloy was a species of food that the young girl had not exactly been accustomed to. Seeing Tony, too, looking wishfully at the oranges, she picked out a damaged one for him, so that he, too, had what he considered as a very good breakfast, although it was yet too early to get up from the inartificial couch upon which they lay.

"You had better take another sleep, Lucy dear," he said.

"Yes, I will, Tony. That was a dear orange."

"Was it? Well, perhaps she'll give you another in the morning."

"Hilloa!" cried a policeman, coming

up; "what child is this—eh, eh? And who are you, boy? Come, come, this won't do."

"Faith, then," cried the Irishwoman, "and what won't do? Ain't my own friends to sleep on my own stand, you murthering villain?"

"Well, Judy, I didn't know they belonged to you. But you know I must do my duty."

"You're ugly enough for that same, or for anything else, any way. Is that a squint in your left hand eye? What did you stale last? Wasn't your mother *thransported*, you thief o' the world? Who made you a paler the likes of me wishes to know!"

"Oh! a plague take your tongue," said the policeman, hurrying away, for the eloquence of Judy appeared as if when it was once let loose, it would be inexhaustible, and probably the policeman had some former experience of the powers of the lady in that particular. But she celebrated her triumph by lighting a new pipe of tobacco, and exclaiming,—

"Arrah! there goes the puppy, wid his tail between his legs."

CHAPTER XVI.

MADAME ZADZED GIVES CONSOLATION TO MAYSTON, AND RECONCILES HIM TO LORD BATTANEY.

IT is not to be supposed that, indignant as he was, Mayston neglected calling in Upper Baker-street, at the house of Madame Zadzed, according to the commands she had given him.

He did not find her at home, but there was a note left for him, which contained the following brief order:

"MAYSTON,

"Come to me at Fulham forthwith. I have paved the way for you to make your peace with B. Your best road to revenge is through that new and better order of things.

"Z."

"Humph!" said Mayston; "brief and dictatorial as usual. But no matter, so that it answers my purpose. To tell

the truth, I have a great objection to Lord Battaney, but no objection to take my fee for that last affair; and besides, now, probably, I shall get some sort of golden compensation for the blow I have had; so that, madame, I will, because it suits me, obey your commands."

Upon this, then, as the principal, if not the only business now that Mayston had in hand, was connected with the fortunes of poor Kate Destern, he at once hired a boat to take him to Fulham, and in the course of an hour and a half he landed at a private water-gate beneath the shade of some majestic elms, that grew upon part of Lord Battaney's estate.

But that mansion and grounds were by no means known to be in the occupation of Lord Battaney; on the contrary, there was the greatest secresy observed, and some of the neighbours, even, who made the greatest exertion to pry into the affair, could not discover in whose holding the mansion was—so well drilled were the parties who did such good, or rather we may say, bad service to Lord Battaney in that establishment.

It is a sad reflection that money is so omnipotent in London, but in all highly civilized nations it will be so, and the rich will always be able to purchase the reputations of the poor.

Mayston was, as may be well supposed, quite familiar with that house and its grounds, so that he had no difficulty in finding his way to a small lodge entrance, that was carefully closed, and most jealously guarded.

Upon a well-understood signal, however, a man appeared and scrutinized the intruder.

"It's I," said Mayston; "it's all right."

"Oh! is it you? I thought you had gone off in a huff, so some of the fellows said last night."

"They were mistaken."

"Very well; pass on. Of course, it's no business of mine, and I have had no orders to exclude you."

"Is madame here?"

"Now, how the devil should I know who comes in by the other entrance? All I can tell you is that she did not come by water, or else, I suppose, she would have come in this way, which she certainly has not."

"Thank you—thank you."

Mayston passed on through the most beautiful and shady walks, until he reached the house, but he did not go into it by any of its principal entrances, but sneaked round to the domestic offices, and so made his way into the mansion. Perhaps he had a reasonable dread of meeting Lord Battaney before he should be thoroughly assured by his friend, Madame Zadzed, that his peace was made.

He inquired of the first one of the household whom he met for Madame Zadzed, and was told she was in a room that was called the yellow room, in consequence of the prevailing colour of its hangings, and thither he sought her.

Opening the door without much ceremony, he walked in, but he was rather taken aback, and shrunk a little, when he found Lord Battaney likewise in the room.

"Oh! here he is," said his lordship, thereby inferring that the previous conversation had been about him.

"Yes, I sent for him," said Madame Zadzed.

Mayston did not know very well what to say, but Lord Battaney moved towards the door, and somewhat relieved him from his confusion, by saying, as he did so,—

"Very well, then, madame, I shall leave the matter to you; and as for you, Mayston, perhaps you will find it to your advantage to have a short memory."

Without waiting for any reply from Mayston, he left him and madame together; and then the latter spoke.

"Mayston," she said, "you like two things."

"Indeed," he said, with a half smile.

"Nay," she added, hastily, "perhaps I should say but one, and that is yourself."

"Somewhere near the mark, always excepting my devotion for you, madame."

"Which can be put on or taken off, according as it may be convenient or otherwise. Mayston, I know you; and when I said you liked two things, I was going to add, money and revenge."

"Aye, do I."

"Well, here is one," she said, handing him a cheque of Lord Battaney's for fifty pounds; "and as for the other, I can give it you if I like—aye, and such ample revenge that, perhaps, you would shrink from. You look surprised, but I can do what I promise. Lord Battaney has asked me to remain, and bend this stubborn girl to his will. Shall I do it? No, no. You shall marry her, I say, you shall marry her, Mayston. I have said it, and you shall."

"Shall is a word easily uttered; but I believe if she were to be torn to pieces by wild horses for her non-compliance, she would not have me."

"You think so?"

"I am certain of it."

"Well, I will try my best, and then you will have ample revenge upon Lord Battaney."

"But how?"

"By taking care of your wife: that you will find to be fully sufficient. I see you are still in the dark—of course you are; but I cannot explain more to you just at present. The time will come when I can do so, but it would not be prudent just now, Mayston. I know you too well for that. No, no, you must have patience yet awhile before you know more."

"You are always telling me that you know me so well. I wish to Heaven I knew you ever so little."

"That you may yet, before you die."

"Consolatory! But, however, if I don't know you, madame, I have faith in you; so I do leave this affair in your hands. Am I to remain here or stay somewhere else?"

"Here, of course."

"Good. Then here I am, and here I wait."

There was such an air of triumph about Madame Zadzed, that she could not conceal it. Her eyes flashed, she drew her breath hurriedly, and her whole manner betrayed it.

Mayston stepped up to her, and looking her in the face with more familiarity than he usually pretended to towards her, he said,—

"Madame, I can well perceive that while you are serving me in this affair, you are likewise serving yourself; you are helping me to revenge, and yourself to conquest."

"And if I am?" she cried, fiercely.

"By the blazes! I—I mean, if I am, what is that to you?"

"Absolutely nothing, only I am quite happy that such is the case. I shall obey your orders in the minutest particular, as I have always been in the habit of doing; so you may dismiss from your mind the smallest uncertainty as regards my share in the transaction."

"'Tis well. I—I will send for you. By the bye, you know this Harry Dean well?"

"Know him well? Confound him, I know him too well."

"You know his voice—manner? You could, perhaps, imitate his mode of utterance of a few words? Could you do that much, think you?"

"I could; and now I begin to see ——"

"Nothing; for the more you guess, the more likely are you to be at fault. You cannot tell precisely what I mean; for as yet but half formed in my own mind is the plan which may make you or mar you. Oh! you will have most ample revenge—great revenge."

She went hastily from the room, as she uttered these words, leaving Mayston in a great state of bewilderment; for although, at moments, he thought he had some sort of inkling of what she meant, yet again he found himself in a sea of conjecture; and he paced the apartment in a wild, disordered manner, asking himself a variety of questions, not one of which he could answer in a satisfactory manner for the life of him.

"Mysteries thicken around me," he muttered, "but I must e'en swim with the stream; for I feel how very helpless I am to contend with it."

The door opened, and Madame Zadzed again entered the room, hurriedly.

"Mayston," she said.

"Well, madame," he replied, "I am here."

"It has become necessary, from something that has happened, that I should have again from you a most solemn assurance that, however strange and contradictory what I ask you to do may seem, you will do it. Will you give me such a promise?"

"I have already done so."

She paused a moment, and then she added,—

"I must have your solemn oath upon the subject—I cannot trust mere words. Do you believe in anything that can be invoked to make an oath sacred to you? If you do not, I shall dread to go through with the business that I have commenced."

Mayston was much surprised, as well he might be, at all this; but as the agitation of Madame Zadzed seemed to be excessive, he concluded that something of a very important character must have taken place; and he said, accordingly,—

"I feel myself, madame, and have always felt myself, so much devoted to your service, that I cannot, for one moment, hesitate about taking any oath you think fit."

"Will you swear, by all your hopes hereafter—and surely you must have some—that you will obey me in what I shall demand of you?"

"I do so swear, madame."

"I am satisfied."

She accordingly left the room.

CHAPTER XVII.

THE DESTITUTION OF LITTLE LUCY AND TONY THORPE.

WE feel a strong interest—an interest which we hope is shared in by our readers—regarding the fate and prospects of Tony Thorpe, and our friend little Lucy.

We left them in far from an enviable position—houseless, friendless wanderers in London.

Yes, a person may be, without fault of his, even without taint of character, or moral blemish of any kind or description, an outcast in London, among its nearly two millions of inhabitants, and its millions of wealth!

Probably if the whole of the gigantic city had been searched through it could not have produced two more simple-minded, honest, and estimable persons than those two whose faded fortunes we are now about to follow, and for whom we feel so much sympathy.

Of little Lucy it would be impossible to say more in a commendatory strain than that she was a beautiful child, with a mind of an original and acute character, developed beyond her years, and that her heart was a shrine in which every virtue that can adorn humanity had found a home.

Tony Thorpe had seen more of the world, but all the buffetting about that he had got during his enforced acquirement of that information, had failed to knock out of him his good and kindly feelings.

His heroic conduct—for it was heroic —towards little Lucy, is the best proof we can give of what he really was, and the best practical comment we can make upon his character.

But now behold them both wandering in London, and not knowing whither they can go, or what is to become of them.

The bustle of the day has fairly begun; and then why are those two helpless beings insulted, or passed by, by the heartless throngs, intent only upon their own business or pleasure, that hurry through the densely crowded streets of the monarch of capitals—London.

But it is not that human nature is so hard-hearted that it is deaf and blind to misery. The reason why in London so little regard is paid to apparent destitution is that there is so much of it that the feelings become blunted at last to it, like those of a humane man who goes into the army, to the horrors of the battle field.

Those horrors, and the sights he sees around him, at first fill him with grief, and excite his warmest feelings of sympathy; but in time he treads about among the dead and the dying with a callous indifference, the offspring of custom.

And so it is with the people of London. They see so many instances around them of the very depth of human misery, that the sight loses it effect, and crowds of thousands of persons will hurry by a starving family, only noticing them by a passing glance, as if such things belonged of right to the regular order of things, and made up a part of society in the city.

To be sure, neither Lucy nor Tony presented the worst appearances as yet of destitution, but if any one would have taken the trouble to look at them well, the conclusion must have been that they were houseless wanderers; for dejection was upon their countenances.

"Tony," said Lucy, "Tony."

"Yes, here you is," said Tony.

"What can we do? Oh! Tony, if we could but find Harry Dean now!"

"Yes, if ——"

"What crowds of people! Surely some of them ought to know him."

Tony shook his head.

His thoughts were busy about providing some sort of meal for his little companion; and we can truly do the poor fellow the justice to say that it was of her he thought, and that his own wants appeared even to himself of secondary importance.

"I must do something," he said.

Alas! how many persons rise up in London with a similar remark every morning of their lives, and yet they no more know what that something is to be, than they can dive into futurity, and know what is to happen upon that day the next year.

Twelve o'clock came, and nothing was done. The something seemed to be as far off as ever; and they were passing down a tolerably quiet street, when they saw a gentleman, in pulling a handkerchief from his coat pocket, likewise drag out a pocket-book, which fell upon the ground.

Tony picked it up, and ran after him, and touching him upon the arm, he said,—

"Sir, sir, you dropped this."

The gentleman turned round, and at once recognised his pocket-book. He snatched it from Tony, exclaiming as he did so,—

"How did you come by it?"

"You dropped it; I told you so once. You dropped it, and I picked it up."

"Oh! stuff, stuff! Don't tell me. I never drop anything. Don't tell me. You picked my pocket of it, and thought somebody saw you; that's the fact. Go away—go away; and think yourself well off that I don't give you to the police!"

"I'm much obliged to you," said Tony.

"What can he mean by that, Tony?" said Lucy.

"Why, my dear, he don't know very well himself, perhaps; but I dare say he's some great phil—phil—— what do they call 'em? Oh, great philanthropist. That's it, I think. They never give nothing to nobody unless it's printed in the *Times* newspaper, I've heard say."

"How wicked!"

"However, never mind, I did not ask him for anything. It was his pocket-book, but he ought not to have tried to make me out a thief, only because I picked it up. But I suppose a person must be something bad with a hole in the elbow of his jacket."

Poor Lucy could not, for the life of her, understand the last remark of Tony's. The two things did not seem to her to be cause and effect, by any means; and after thinking on the remark for a few moments, she said,—

"But, Tony, the hole in your jacket is because it has worn out, and you have not got money to buy another. You cannot make money, you know."

"That's true, Lucy; but to be poor is the greatest crime you can commit,"

"Is it?"

"Yes, to be sure. Lor' bless you, didn't you know that? A poor person is always considered a dishonest one."

"No, I did not know that, Tony; and it seems to me that if a person is very poor, it's quite a proof they have not got anybody else's money."

"It ought to be. But look here; there's an object!"

The object to which Tony directed the attention of Lucy was a rather corpulent female, carrying an immense market basket, apparently crammed with provisions of all sorts, and which was either rather beyond her strength, or she had already carried it far enough to be heartily tired of it.

"Let me help you, mum," said Tony.

The large lady looked at him for a minute, and then said,—

"Twopence."

"Anything you like," said Tony; "only give me a lift on to my back with it, and I'll manage it. Come along, Lucy, and carry my hat, dear. That will do."

The extensive female hoisted the basket on to Tony's back, and then she gave a sigh of relief, which, like Hamlet's, seemed calculated to

"Shatter all her bulk,"

and commenced vigourously fanning herself with a large red handkerchief.

"Oh, gracious me," she said, "what a *perspiration* I am in! I hadn't an idea it was such a weight, nor near so *fur* as I had to go. How do you feel, young man?"

"All right," said Tony.

"And is this your little sister?"

"No, it's a young friend of mine, mum, that's all; and I'm glad of the twopence you spoke of for her sake."

"Lor', is it possible? Why, you do look hungry. Ah! hem! let me think. Now, I tell you what, do you think you can go as *fur* as Paddington?"

"Oh, yes."

"Well, my daughter Mary is a-going to be married to-day to a very *spectable* young man indeed, and things is so horrid dear our way, I thought I'd go further a-field to market, and I have made some good bargains, I rather think."

"Weighty ones," said Tony.

"You may well say that. I felt as they was. But we have a world o' things to do; and if so be as you and the little girl will stay for an hour or two, and make yourselves useful, I can promise you plenty to eat, as well as the twopence."

"Thank you," said Tony; "there's corn in Egypt! Lor', Lucy, things never is so wery bad but they mends. Come on; and you see, mum, if we don't make ourselves useful above a bit —I believe you."

Having made this arrangement, the good lady would stop and bestow upon Tony half a pint of beer, and upon Lucy a penny bun, in order to inspirit them both on; and these expensive treats had that effect, so that Tony stepped out well, and the party reached Paddington in quite an unprecedented short space of time, considering all things.

The lady turned down a narrow street, and her followers kept close to her. She opened the door of a little house with a key she got from her pocket, and then there was a rush of people from the parlour, and such a gabble of voices, all declaring they ha not expected her for the better part of an hour yet, and asking her success in the marketing line.

CHAPTER XVIII.

THE IRISH WEDDING.—THE FIGHT.— THE STREETS AGAIN.

TONY and Lucy were duly introduced into the kitchen of the mansion, and there they understood from a girl, who was already hard at work in culinary operations, that the name of the lady was Tracey, and that she was a widow of one Mr. Dennis Tracey, an Irishman, and that the marriage was to take place between Miss Bridget Tracey and a Mr. O'Mulligan.

All this was not very interesting to Tony and Lucy, but still they listened attentively to it, and made themselves useful in all sorts of ways.

The wedding was to take place at two o'clock, and great was the gathering of friends on both sides at about half past one, and then the party started.

At about half past two they all came back, the ceremony being over, and Miss Tracey bore the old and euphonious name of Mulligan.

Never did people appear to be in such good humour with each other; and by dint of great exertions on the part of the corpulent lady and her assistants, the dinner was got ready by four o'clock.

She declared she never could have got on without Tony and Lucy.

There was a large roast leg of pork, a round of beef, and an immense pie of all sorts. Then there were whole bushels of potatoes, heaps of greens, and a row of gallon cans of porter, that would have done any one's heart good to see.

Oh! it was a glorious feast that at the O'Mulligans' marriage. A row of black bottles, too, placed under a sideboard, said, as significantly as they could,—

"Here is whiskey."

Now, the servant-girl was a Tracey *fur* off, as Mrs. Tracey said, to intimate that she was not by any means a near connection; so upon the auspicious occasion she was allowed a seat at the table, and the like honour was accorded to Tony and to Lucy.

Nor did this arrangement in the least interfere with the attendance at the feast, for all the tables in the house were joined together, and the whole of the eatables placed before the guests, and therefore there was no further need for anybody to be below.

We recommend this course to those who do not like to be watched by servants at their meals, than which, in our opinion, nothing can be more decidedly unpleasant.

The dinner went off in capital style, and the harmony was perfect. It was wonderful, too, to see how, when the feast in its eating department, was over, the tables were cleared. That operation was then accomplished.

"Ladies and gentlemen," said Mr. O'Mulligan, "there's some of the most illigant whisky that ever tickled the throat of a Tracey or a Mulligan under the sideboard, but the plates and the dishes are in the way, by Jasus!"

"Then what's to hinder each mother's son of us, by the holy," cried another, "from taking down stairs just what happens to be before him?"

Upon this hint they all acted, and the tables were cleared in an exceedingly short space of time.

The porter had been pretty well all drunk, and the whiskey so feelingly alluded to by the O'Mulligan, was produced, and began to circulate tolerably freely.

The bridesman rose to make a speech. He was a Tracey.

"Jontilmen and ladies, I rises to perpose a toast."

"Hear, hear, hear the Tracey. Good luck to your sowl! Silence—order! Stuff a praty into that blackguard's mouth."

"A toast and a sintiment," continued the orator.

"Now for it."

"Will you be after houlding your tongue? I say a sintiment. May we be all dead or alive at the first christening."

This sentiment was received with great applause; and a voice cried,—

"Three cheers for the Traceys."

Three cheers were accordingly given, and then a voice shouted,—

"Four cheers for the O'Mulligans."

"And why," cried another, "should the blackguard Mulligans have four cheers? The things of this world I'd like to be after knowing any how."

This remark produced the rejoinder of a glass of whiskey in the inquiring gentleman's face.

Strong symptoms now of something in the shape of a row became apparent, and Lucy clung to Tony's arm in consternation, whispering.

"Let us go, Tony, oh, let us go."

"It was an easier thing, however, to wish to go than to accomplish the wish, for Tony and Lucy happened to be seated under the window, at the greatest possible distance from the door, so that to get out they would have to get the leave of so many Mulligans and Traceys that it at that moment, when both parties were busy, was a matter out of the question.

At first, the gentleman who had the glass of whiskey thrown in his face seemed too much astonished at the audacity of the act to speak; then he took up a bottle that was close to him, and flung it at his opponent.

The aim was good, and the Tracey, who certainly had committed the first breach of the peace, lay prostrate, with a blow on the forehead that would have smashed any head in the world but a negro's or an Irishman's.

The Mulligan was then, in his turn, felled by a blow from a Tracey; and the row began in earnest, and in a few minutes assumed quite a terrific character.

Lucy screamed, and the combatants swore. Bottles and glasses flew about in all directions; and then, instead of making a vain attempt to get out at the door, through the throng of combatants, Tony thought of another and much more expeditious mode of leaving the house.

"Keep close to me, Lucy," he whispered.

"Oh, yes, yes."

He then made an effort to open the window; it was not fast, and he at once succeeded.

Luckily, they were in the front parlour, and the height from the pavement —for there was no area—was not above four feet. Escape was easy. He lifted Lucy out of the window, and then followed her.

"Good bye to you all, you quarrelsome set," he said; and taking Lucy by the hand, away he walked from the scene of contention, leaving the O'Mulligans and the Traceys to crack each other's skulls, if they chose to do so, until they should get tired of that exciting and peculiarly Irish amusement.

Lucy trembled very much.

"Why, you need not be afraid now," said Tony.

"Oh, no, but I was so terrified."

"And no wonder too. But we had a good dinner, you see, Lucy, and I have got the twopence that Mrs. Tracey promised me besides."

"Have you, Tony?"

"Yes; we are quite rich, Lucy, ain't we?"

"Yes; and I am so glad we have got away. I don't tremble now, you see, Tony. How could they quarrel so? I'm sure they might have been very happy, without knocking each other's heads so dreadfully. Don't you think so, Tony?"

"Yes, dear, you and I think so; but then that's part of their amusement, you know."

"Is it really?"

"Yes, and always will be, I suppose, to the end of the world."

"It's very strange."

They wandered on, conversing, until they got a considerable distance from Paddington, and at length, as Lucy was very weary, Tony proposed that she should sit down upon the steps of a house at the end of a short street leading out of Oxford-street.

There was a large building, with a court-yard before it, opposite to them, and Tony, in answer to Lucy's questions, told her it was the Middlesex Hospital, and the worst, as he had heard, in all London.

The night was creeping on, and as the weather was unusually serene and warm, they rather enjoyed the rest upon the door-step, humble abiding place as that was.

"Well," said Tony, "here we is, like the babes in the wood."

"And who were they?" inquired Lucy.

"What, don't you know? Did you never read the 'History of England?'"

"Oh, it's there, is it?"

"Yes, to be sure, it is. I thought everybody knew that well enough. I'm afraid you ain't what they calls a very literary person, Lucy."

"No," said Lucy, with all the simplicity in the world, "I dare say I am not, Tony. Are you?"

Tony smiled, and looked half shy, as he replied,—

"Lucy, I rather think that when I make a sensation, it will be by something or another in that sort of line myself."

CHAPTER XIX.

TONY GIVES A SPECIMEN OF HIS POWERS IN A MIDDLE-AGE ROMANCE.

LUCY looked at Tony, enquiringly, and perhaps that was just what Tony wanted her to do; for he said, with a knowing sort of nod,—

"Don't you remember?"

"Remember what, Tony?"

"Why, that I promised to read you some of my productions some day."

"Oh, yes, you did, Tony, but you never have."

"Well, but better late than never. You see here's a jolly great gas light here, that throws quite a blaze upon us, and as I write rather large than small, I know I shall be able to see capital; and besides, it ain't long, and I know most of it by heart, in case I can't see very well, and here it is; so if you don't mind hearing some, here goes."

"Oh, I should like to hear it very much."

"Very good."

Tony produced from one of his pockets three or four rather small, and not very clean, pieces of paper, written over, and smoothened them out upon his knee—a process they rather over much required; after which, although his audience was small, and not very likely to be violently critical, Tony gave two or three preparatory hems, and looked a little flurried.

"The title of the work," he said, "is 'The Ghastly Demon; or, the Blue Fiend of the Blood-stained Pool.'"

"Indeed," said Lucy, and her eyes looked preternaturally wide open.

"Yes. I flatter myself that's rather striking, ain't it? That's the thing to take the British public—eh?"

"I should think it would frighten anybody."

"Ah! that's the grand object. Now, listen."

INTRODUCTION.

CAUTION.—This romance is not to be read just before going to bed, as it is warranted to give anybody the worst nightmare they ever had in all their lives.

CHAPTER I.

THE CASTLE. — THE GROAN. — THE SHRIEK. — GOUTS OF GORE. — THE DEMON.—THE BLOODY BARON.—THE SANGUINARY SPECTRE.—THE HEADLESS TRUNK.—THE RUIN AND DEVASTATION OF EVERYBODY. — A DREADFUL BLAST.

IT is night. Bang—crash—smash—whiz—pop, goes the sanguinary drawbridge into the blood-stained moat. The one-eyed ghost appears on the ramparts, with a ponderous portcullis in its right hand; and the Baron of Bhumblepuppi tears his hair out by the roots. Hark! a storm comes on, and the gentle and affectionate Adelinda throws her washhand basin over the ramparts, smash into the court-yard.

"Down below!" she cries, but the gentle warning comes too late; and a man-at-arms, who was intently watching the careering clouds, is smashed.

A demoniac laugh resounds through the castle, and the baron seeks the apartment of the Lady Adelinda.

"Is this possible?" he cries; "are my gallant warriors to be whopped in this way, and sent to the infernal regions by you?"

"Yes, monster! May the most elaborate and vital storm-clad, heaven-born, hell-forged curse that can be conceived, light upon your head, caitiff and thief!" said the gentle and mild Adelinda.

"What!" shrieked the baron, tearing out the last handful of hair he had left upon his head, and casting it at her feet; "Am I to be thus taunted in my own castle?"

"Yes, you *is!*"

"*Is* I? Oh, Heavens!"

"Yes, a thousand time, yes; and may heaped horrors consume you!" said the Lady Adelinda. "You know well, wretch that you are, that I am your prisoner, and, consequently, I dare not say all I would; but I wish you may be condemned to roll on burning rocks, and to swallow boiling oil for countless ages!"

"Then you shall die," said the baron; "or come immediately to the castle chapel, and become the Baroness of Bhumblepuppi."

"Never!" said Adelinda. "I defy you; and not wishing to call any names, I must say you are the most hideous, wolf-looking cannibal I ever saw."

The baron was enraged.

"Ha!" he cried, "you brave my power, I begin to find, and in time you may get abusive. You shall be mine! I swear it; you shall be ———"

The castle clock struck twelve. A thousand hideous and demoniac shrieks all at once sounded in the air. The moat bubbled and boiled—the drawbridge fell down—and through a sliding panel came the one-eyed ghost.

"Beware, monster!" said the spirit; "beware! I am the ghost of your murdered wife. You knocked out my left eye first, and then murdered me by making me try to swallow it, but it stuck in my throat; and you know you had the heartlessness to remark that I could then see what was the matter, at any time, with my digestion. Tremble, tremble, tremble!"

"Oh!" said the baron.

"Rash man!" cried the Lady Adelinda, "you perceive what an awful spirit your villany has invoked."

"Bother you all," said the baron. "I don't care a bit. You shall be mine, or you shall perish!"

The ghost advanced with a howl, and cried,—

———

"Come, get off this step, will you? I won't have anybody on my steps."

These words came from one immediately behind Tony, and upon looking round, he saw that the door of the house was open, and its probable owner standing just within the passage.

"Oh! bother your house," said Tony. "We don't want to stay. Come along, Lucy. I'll finish the story of the baron another time for you. Come along."

Little Lucy, to tell the honest truth, had been rather terrified at the story that Tony had been reading, and she was not sorry that it was interrupted; so she moved away from the steps, without making anything in the shape of a remonstrance against the arbitrary command that had issued from the house to do so.

Tony, however, was highly indignant.

"It's a hard case," he said, "when a stone step on the outside of a door is grudged as a resting-place for those who have no other place to go to."

"Never mind," said Lucy; "we are rested now. But, Tony!"

"Well?"

"Was all that you have been reading to me true?"

"True? Oh, yes, in a manner of speaking. It might have happened, you know, and that's quite enough, at all events, for me. We can call it true. All barons do that sort of thing."

"What sort of thing, Tony?"

"Why, they always get hold of some young lady, and put her into a turret, and there they keep her, and have a regular bully with her every day; and some ghost or another is almost sure to interfere at last, and then there's no end of a disturbance, as you would have seen if I had gone on a little further. But you shan't lose it. Some other time I'll finish it for you."

"Thank you," said Lucy; but somehow she did not seem to be so enthusiastic in the matter as Tony could wish, and he began to think that he was scarcely appreciated by one so young.

And that was a very consolatory thought to Tony; but when will an author think that he may be a little to blame as well as his audience?

They were rested, it is true, those two wanderers, and that was all. They were in the same state as regarded their affairs as before, and the night was now sufficiently advanced to make Tony again most anxious to know what he should do with his young and fragile companion.

He fancied that he saw she was drooping, and that she did not look near so well as she had looked; and the thought was one of great bitterness and anxiety to the poor fellow.

"Lucy, dear," he said, "you must keep up your spirits, you know."

"Oh! yes, I will, Tony—I will."

"Are you quite well?"

"Yes, I think I am."

A sympathetic shiver belied the assertion, and Tony said to himself,—

"Ah! poor young thing, if I didn't think as much. She has caught cold, now, all owing to sleeping in the open air last night. But what could I do?—

and, alas! what am I to do this night likewise? Was ever a poor fellow so tormented? I must and will get her a house somehow or somewhere to-night, come what will of it."

While Tony was trying to consider of some scheme of operations for Lucy's benefit, she felt illness, slowly but certainly, creeping over her

———

CHAPTER XX.

THE STRANGER FROM THE HOSPITAL.— AN UNEXPECTED MEETING.

SHE began to walk slowly, and poor Tony got more and more alarmed each minute, for the idea came across him that now, in the midst of their troubles, she was going to be seriously ill, and in that case, he knew not what on earth to do with her.

"Lucy," he said, "do you think you can get on?"

"Hardly, Tony. Where are we now?"

"Why, close to where we were, Lucy. Don't you see the hospital gate?"

"And what is a hospital, Tony?"

"Why, it's a place where all sorts of people go to when they ain't well, or break their necks, or anything of that sort, Lucy."

"Then—then, Tony, I ought to go there, for I am not well."

She paused as she spoke, and clung to the railings of the hospital, and then she shivered again.

It was quite clear that the child had caught a severe cold, by sleeping in the damp atmosphere of Covent Garden market, and that if neglected, her indisposition would more than likely turn to some much more serious kind of fever.

Poor Tony was nearly at his wits' end.

"I don't like to part with you, Lucy," he said; "but I must do so if you are so ill. I wonder if they would take you into the hospital, and be kind to you."

"What is that?"

"It is a clock striking ten."

It was the hospital clock, and when it had ceased all was still again.

There were not many people in the street. It was a time of the evening in London when the streets are not particularly full. There are particular periods in the metropolis when it may be called high tide, as regards the thronging streets, and between ten and half-past eleven is certainly not one of them.

Lucy sat upon a step close to the hospital gate, and then she rested her sweet face upon her hands, and seemed too much overcome to move.

Now Tony really had not much notion of the hospital, by the gate of which he was; and he thought that if he could get her a home for the night, with some decent, motherly woman, it would be much better, but how could he go seeking for such a thing without money?

That was the greatest difficulty; but as he stood by the side of Lucy, and saw that now and then well-dressed, and apparently well-to-do, people passed him, he began to think that surely some of them could and would give a trifle for the sick child's sake.

"It ain't exactly begging," thought Tony; "and I don't think I could do it for myself at all. But for poor dear little Lucy I can do anything; so I will ask for something just to get her a lodging for the night, and we will see how she is in the morning."

"Sir," said Tony, to rather a pompous-looking, but well-dressed individual, "if you please ——"

There was no occasion to say any more. The outstretched hand of Tony sufficiently proclaimed what he wanted, and the well-dressed individual walked on, full of virtuous indignation to find, as he said, the streets so infested with beggars.

"Well," thought Tony, "that's a bad beginning."

At this moment he saw a lady in black apparel, approaching. She looked, if one might judge from the sombre nature of her garments, as if she had known sorrow; and to her Tony thought surely an appeal on behalf of Lucy would not be made in vain.

"Ma'am," he said; "if you please ma'am."

The lady stopped.

"Oh! I'm so much obliged to you, ma'am, for stopping to hear what I have to say. This little girl is very ill; and what I want is a trifle, in order that I may get her a lodging for to-night, poor thing. She ain't fit to sleep in the open air."

"I suppose you are very poor?" said the lady.

"Rather," said Tony. "I have got twopence, to be sure, and that's all."

"And you regret being poor?"

"Of course I do, ma'am."

"Oh, you wicked wretch!"

"Wicked! — wretch! What for, pray? What have I done to be called such names?"

"Much—much. You say you regret being poor; and it is quite clear that all your thoughts are upon getting money. Oh, mammon, mammon!"

"Who, ma'am?"

"And at a time," continued the lady, "when your eternal welfare ought to be uppermost in your mind. You ask for money, as if you had no soul to think of. Pray, young man, pray that you may be saved from the wrath to come. Oh, what wickedness there is in the world, to be sure! I'm afraid—very much afraid—you are a heathen! Of course! I shall give you something, and that shall be a something much more valuable than you asked for."

"Thank you, ma'am."

"Take this tract, entitled, ' The Sinner's Link through the Fog of Despair.' Keep it clean, and bring it carefully back to No. 2, Tabernacle-walk, close to Ebenezer Chapel, and then you shall have another, entitled, ' The Gospel Flesh-brush; or, the Heathen scrubbed into Eternal Salvation.' "

"I tell you what," said Tony; "you are a humbug."

"A what?"

"A humbug."

"Go on; I like to be abused. Oh! those words are registered in my favour at the last day! Call me something else."

Tony turned away, too indignant to hold any more converse with her; and finding such to be the case, she thought it the best course to move on, exclaiming,—

"A frightful case of heathenism! A horrible case! I never heard of anything so bad as this since the Reverend Ezekiel Droggswill backslided into Romanism."

The lady was shaking her head, and looking upwards, with such an awful squint, that she did not see a very unctuous piece of orange peel on the pavement before her; and in giving emphasis to the last words she uttered, she trod upon it with a dab that sent her sprawling.

"Murder!—murder! Help!" she cried.

"Help yourself," said Tony. "That's backsliding, I think. Never mind about tumbling down, old 'un, but think of eternal glory."

With some difficulty, the lady got up, and Tony was quite certain that he heard her utter a deliberate d—, which was not at all extraordinary in so very religious a person.

"Ah! Lucy, dear," he said, "I'm afraid we shall get no help. How do you feel now?"

"I am better sitting still, Tony."

"Well, I am glad to hear that, dear; and so I won't despair, but I'll ask somebody else, and we may meet with some one, who, for the love of God, will help his creatures."

"Oh! Tony, I am such a trouble to you."

"Now, don't you be saying that, Lucy. You ain't a trouble at all to me, and never will be. If it hadn't been for you, I should be very unhappy; and even now, when we are so very poor, and don't know where to lay our heads to-night for shelter, I still seem to think that happy—very happy days are in store for us. I wonder who this is coming so slowly out of the hospital. A gentleman he looks, and pale too, as if he had been ill."

"A gentleman?" said Lucy.

"Yes; and one who looks as if he had known what suffering was. Only look at him, dear. I shouldn't wonder, now, if he said something kind to you as he passed you. He is coming."

Lucy, sobbingly, told Tony that to her mind all the gentlemen in the world did not come near her dear Harry Dean, and she paid but little heed to the advancing stranger, who was, as Tony had said, so pale and wan-looking, and walked so slowly, as if from weakness, that it seemed as if he had only just emerged from one of the wards of the hospital, in a state, perhaps, of what might be called convalesence, but not strength.

He came slowly—so very slowly—towards the poor wanderers, but as he passed within the glare of a gas lamp, Tony saw, or thought he saw, so much goodness and gentleness of expression on his face, that the idea of addressing him on behalf of Lucy came quickly to his mind.

"She is ill," he thought, "and I must not throw a chance away, however slight it may be, of obtaining kindly sympathy for her. Who knows what and who this gentleman may be."

As the stranger was about to pass out of the gate, Tony raised his voice, saying,—

"Sir—this little girl, sir, is—I don't speak for myself—but she is ill, sir, very ill, and getting worse."

"Poor thing!" said the stranger.

With a scream of joy, Lucy sprung to her feet, and rushed into the stranger's arms.

"Harry! Harry! Oh, it is you, dear Harry Dean!"

CHAPTER XXI.

THE MYSTERY.—HARRY DEAN COMES OUT IN A NEW CHARACTER.

An indifferent spectator could not have failed to have been struck by the remarkable manner in which those last words were pronounced by Lucy, and that they had reference to some foregone conclusion was most evident.

To Tony Thorpe they were a sublime mystery, for he had not the remotest notion why she should be so deeply affected at the appearance of this stranger from the hospital.

The fact was that Tony had not caught the name which Lucy had given him, or from her previous conversation upon the subject, he would have had a tolerable lively idea of whom it was she was addressing.

But although he ought to have identi-fied the individual by name, his perplexity to think how he came there would certainly have not been diminished, for all along, with the information that there was such a person as Harry Dean in the world, Lucy had carefully enough let him know of his total disappearance.

No wonder then, that with open eyes, Tony looked upon them both.

"Oh! Harry, Harry," cried Lucy, "and is it really you? I don't think it is a dream. It must be you, Harry, and none but you."

She was right; it was, indeed, Harry Dean—he whom—we beheld stricken down, and apparently deprived of life by the villain Mayston, but the mysterious disappearance of whose body certainly afforded us a hope that at some juncture he would turn up again as one of the living dramatis personæ of our tale.

And if Tony was astonished to see the manner and hear the tone in which Lucy spoke to him, and if Lucy was delighted and astonished beyond all manner of telling, to the full as delighted and as astonished did Harry Dean appear to be.

At first he stood, as it were, transfixed with astonishment. He passed his hand across his brow, as if he would assure himself of his waking existence, but to a mind like his such a hesitation in the reception of an evident fact was not likely to last long; and flinging his arms around her, he exclaimed,—

"You are Lucy—little Lucy—my old friend? But by what combination of circumstances you are here I cannot conjecture. Ah! what is this? She faints!"

Illness for the last hour or two had been making rapid strides in poor Lucy's frame. It was but a temporary excitement that had enabled her to arouse herself to sufficient energy to speak to him as she had done, but when that temporary excitement was over, and when she found herself really clasped in his arms, a sudden reaction ensued, and she lapsed into utter insensibility.

"Gracious Heavens!" he exclaimed, "what is the meaning of all this? She is ill—she is dying! You, who seem to be her companion, answer me at once upon your peril.'

"She is ill," cried Tony; "but I could not help it. We've no money and no friends. But if you want to blow up anybody, just begin upon me, and go on as long as you like, so that you do something for poor Lucy."

"But—but who are you?"

"Tony Thorpe's my name; only never you mind about that. Look to Lucy, if you can do so, though she told me how poor you were, the more the pity."

"True—true. I will look to her; it is my paramount duty. Poor, said you? She shall want nothing that gold in heaps will purchase—there is no luxury which the highest and the noblest of the land can call their own which shall not be lavished upon her. Follow me, and when she has been well cared for, you shall relate to me by what strange train of circumstances she came to this spot."

"All's right," said Tony. "I'll follow you to the end of the world, and a mile and a half further, if you will but be good to poor Lucy. Bless you, you've no notion what an engaging little thing it is. She's as patient as possible, too, and kept me up by her cheerful ways and pleasant looks, when I do think, by myself I should have sunk down completely; and then when things were never so bad, and there didn't seem to be a hope of getting anything to eat and drink, she didn't complain, but I do believe she thought more of me than of herself; and so you see —— Do you hear, sir?"

"Yes, yes. Go on."

Tony Thorpe might well ask Harry Dean if he heard what was being said to him, for, with the insensible form of Lucy in his arms, he was walking through the streets at a pace which made it a matter of no small difficulty for Tony to keep up with.

Whither he was going was known only to himself, and probably but for the high character that Lucy had given of him, and the almost frantic delight she had exhibited at seeing him, Tony might have been inclined to question the right of having her thus walked away with without any explanation.

Then Tony had heard from Lucy how poor Harry Dean was, and what a struggle it was for him to live and be the gentleman he really, by habits, education, and manners, deserved to show himself.

Where could he thus be going with Luey? What species of home could he be taking her to, and what sort of assistance did he expect to procure for her?

These questions were tolerably soon answered, for, to the utter astonishment of Tony, Harry Dean stopped not until he reached the aristocratic pavement of Bond-street; and then, to the still further astonishment of our humble friend, he entered the door of an hotel, of great pretensions, in the hall of which were several powdered lacquies, who looked completely taken by surprise at the sudden irruption.

"Follow me," cried Harry Dean to Tony, "and fear nothing."

One of the servants stepped forward, as if to challenge the right of such poor-looking people to expect any accommodation in that quarter, and Harry was about to brush past him, when a side door opened, and a pompous-looking man, exhibiting a vast display of white waistcoat, made his appearance.

This was the landlord of the hotel; and one of the footmen made himself very officious, by saying to him immediately,—

"Sir, these persons have just pushed their way in, and don't seem disposed to go."

"Eh?—where?—what persons? Come, come, this is no house for common people, and we never encourage beggars."

He turned sharply, and confronted Harry Dean as he spoke, when the instant change in the owner looked little short of magic.

He took his thumbs from the armholes of his waistcoat, where they had been ostentatiously placed, and bowed most profoundly.

"A thousand pardons. I really—really ——"

"Peace!" cried Harry Dean; "I want no excuses. Let one of your best chambers be got in immediate readiness. Get a qualified nurse, at any expence, and send instantly for a couple of the first physicians that are in town."

"Certainly, certainly. Oh yes, of

course. I can never sufficiently apologize. A best bed-room, instantly! This way, if you please, this way. Be so good as to follow me. Allow me to carry the young lady."

"No; she's a dear friend of mine."

With great haste, the landlord rushed along the hall, and began ascending the principal staircase, closely followed by Harry Dean, who was again as closely followed by Tony.

But after he had got up to the first landing, the landlord was seized with a desire to make another very low bow and turning for that purpose, he saw Tony, whose dress and general appearance certainly but ill-befitted thie gorgeously-appointed staircase, up which he was travelling with mute wonder and admiration.

"You infernal rascal," said the landlord; "how dare you? Here Jenkins —Simmons, turn out this fellow, and see that he's got none of the spoons."

"Pardon me," said Harry Dean, "that is another friend of mine."

"Oh! in that case, I really—I really—certainly—most certainly. Jenkins, you needn't count the spoons, of course. This way, if you please, this way. A private sitting room, I presume?"

"Yes," answered Harry Dean, "certainly."

"Well," thought Tony, "if this ain't a leaf out of the 'Arabian Nights,' I don't know what is. I'm blessed if ever I seed such a house in all my life. It's as good as a romance itself, that it is. I suppose I shall wake up presently, and find myself upon some jolly old door-step, along with poor Lucy, and nothing but a penny buster and the fag end of a poloney atween us."

It was on the first floor that the landlord paused, and casting open the door of an apartment, he bowed Harry Dean and his charge into it, bestowing, likewise, a low salaam upon Tony, who gave him a pat on the head, by way of encouragement, that nearly precipitated him on to his nose.

The best apartment of that hotel was certainly no joke. It was resplendent with everything that could be attractive and beautiful; and when Tony fairly stood in the centre of it, and saw himself in no end of mirrors, and felt his feet sink into the soft, down-like carpet, he rubbed his eyes again, fully expecting that he was being deluded by a dream, uncommonly life-like and real.

Harry Dean surrendered his charge to some of the females of the establishment; and then feeling assured that the directions he had given with regard to the species of attendance that Lucy was to have would be rather improved upon than neglected, he turned to Tony, and said,—

"Now, my boy, give me as brief and complete an explanation as you can of how you came in company, with this young girl."

With the most artless simplicity, Tony recounted the circumstances already well known to the reader; and when he had finished, Harry Dean said, in a voice of emotion,—

"Is this possible!"

CHAPTER XXII.

TONY'S ADVENTURES IN THE GRAND HOTEL.

"POSSIBLE!" exclaimed Tony. "I don't know about that, but it's true."

"Then, in the first instance, you deprived yourself of the means of subsistence, in consequence of your chivalrous interference in her behalf, and afterwards you have been her only friend, her adviser, and companion?"

"Well, that's about it," said Tony; "but I don't see anything extraordinary in that. Who wouldn't, I should like to know, when they saw a young creature, such as she is, with neither house, money, nor friend,—who wouldn't, I say, do as much as they could for her, and stick to her like old bricks?"

Harry Dean paced the room for a few moments in an agitated manner, and then turning to Tony, he said,—

"Remain here till I return to you. Order freely whatever you may take a fancy to. Make yourself quite at home. I shall not be gone long."

With these words he left the apartment, closing the door behind him, and Tony was left alone in that, to him, enchanted region of glory and beauty.

Tony stood for some moments in perfect silence—then he turned slowly round and round several times, until he had thoroughly surveyed the room in all its aspects.

"My eye," he said, "here's a go! I'm to order what I like, am I? Yes, it's all very well to order what he likes, and stick him in a place like this. Of course, they won't bring nothing to eat in here, for fear of spoiling the carpet. Here'll be a pretty adventure! But I know what'll be the end of it—the station-house, of course; that's where we shall get to, as safe as a tenpenny nail. I knowed it from the very first!"

While it lasted, however, Tony thought he might as well have a rest, and as a very tempting easy chair was close at hand, he sat down in it.

The moment he did so he sank so far in a down cushion that he got a little alarmed, and in kicking and struggling to get out, he touched a spring, which made the back of the chair fall back, and away he went, fancying that he had got into some diabolical contrivance, from which escape was out of the question.

A very rich tassel was close to his arm, and Tony seized it, as a means of dragging himself out of the chair, when down came the bell-rope, to which it belonged, and almost immediately the door was flung open, and a footman, in rich livery, with his hair powdered, made his appearance.

"Now for it," thought Tony. "The next thing will be a policeman."

"Did I have the honour to hear you ring, sir?" said the footman.

"I shan't answer no questions," said Tony; "nobody ain't going to criminate themselves."

"Beg pardon, sir, but we thought you rung. Would you like to take any refreshment, sir?"

"I tell you what, old fellow," said Tony, "I should like to get out of this ere blessed machine."

"Machine, sir?"

"Yes, if all ain't a dream. Give us a hand."

"Oh! the reclining chair, sir. Certainly, sir, certainly."

Tony was lifted up, and the chair resumed its original position with a snap.

"Well," said Tony, "of all the rum goes that ever I seed that beats 'em. I've heard of the back of a chair coming off when you didn't want it, but the idea of making one on purpose to slip about in this ere way, and frighten you out of your wits, when you want to sit down, is a odd start."

"Patent reclining chair, sir, very much improved," said the footman. "Self-acting sofa, sir, in the corner."

"No," said Tony, "I've had quite enough of the chair, without the sofa. This looks like a decent thing to sit down upon."

"That, sir? Oh! dear, no, sir; that's a foot ottoman."

"Never mind whether it's a hottentot or not, it does very well for me."

"Well, sir, of course, it's just as you please. Will you take any refreshment, sir?"

"What's it made of?" said Tony. "Is it roast or biled?"

"Why, really, sir, I—I really, sir,—you can have anything you please, of course. We have everything always ready at a moment's notice."

"Well, I don't know why I should not," said Tony. "I was told to make myself comfortable. Bring us a couple of hot saveloys, and don't be sticking a fork in 'em, and letting out all the fat."

"Hot what, sir?"

"Saveloys, stupid. Why, if you haven't got them, a yesterday's faggot, warmed up, will do; and don't be slobbering up all the gravy before you bring it to me."

"I—I really, sir, am very much afraid we haven't any of those delicacies in the house. Perhaps anything else, whether it's in season or not, we shall be very happy to provide it."

"Why, I thought you said you'd got everything. But as you haven't got them, I'll have a sheep's head, and a pint of half-and-half, with the chill off."

"Why, really, sir, I beg your pardon, but I rather think we haven't any of the articles you name, sir. We shall be very happy, sir, to lay lunch for you; and perhaps if you were to leave it to us, we might be able to attract your appetite, sir."

"Well I never!" said Tony. "Here's a pretty place! Talk of having everything. Then I suppose one's to be put off with a bit of cold mutton? Well, be off, and fetch something. I begin to feel quite at home."

Thus commissioned, the waiter disappeared, and presently returned with a tray, on which there was a nice little something under cover, which, to Tony's apprehension,—he not being acquainted with French cookery—looked remarkably like the half digested meal of some dog, who had found it disagree with his stomach.

There was, however, in a sauce-boat some nice-looking gravy, of which Tony took a good draught, but the moment he had done so, he felt as if his mouth and throat had been converted into a mimic hell, so burning hot was the horrible character of something, a minute portion of which had been intended to titillate the palate.

"Murder! murder!" cried Tony; "I'm poisoned!"

"Good God, sir," cried the waiter, "you've taken enough *sauce au diable* to last you your life."

"My life!" cried Tony, "I've lost my life. Give me something cold to drink, and plenty of it."

A tumbler of iced spring water, of a frightful degree of frigidity, was handed to him, and the sudden transition set his teeth chattering, and was productive of the most disagreeable feelings.

Tony, for once in a way, was put out of temper, and the waiter, whom he thought was accessary to playing him all these tricks, received a knock on the head, that enveloped him in a cloud of powder from his own wig.

It was lucky that at this moment Harry Dean arrived, or there is no knowing what confusion might have resulted from Tony's non-appreciation of polite cookery.

"What is the meaning of all this confusion?" cried Harry.

"Really, sir," said the discomfitted waiter, "I don't know, sir, but this gentleman don't seem to be aware of what he wants."

"Yes, I am," said Tony, "but they haven't got it. There's nothing good to eat in the place. They give you something to burn you one minute, and then they freeze you with something else. Of course, Mr. Dean, I didn't wish to ask for anything out of the way."

"And what did you ask for, Tony?"

"A couple of hot saveloys, to be sure."

"Well, well," said Harry Dean, scarcely controlling a smile, although his heart was ill at ease. "I'll set all that to rights. I will order you something plain and substantial that I think will suit you."

This was done most effectually, and in the course of ten minutes, a smoking hot surloin of beef, from which only a cut or two had been taken, was placed before Tony, and that being followed by a silver flagon of porter, thoroughly satisfied him.

To the surprise, however, of Harry Dean and the waiter, he put the first slice of beef that he cut upon a piece of bread, and then clapping another piece on top of that, he said,—

"Come, I shall take this to Lucy. Just show me where she is."

"Content yourself," said Harry Dean, "she is well cared for. I have had the opinion of two of the most eminent physicians in London concerning her, and have the satisfaction of informing you their opinion is that rest, and a little judicious, nourishing diet, will completely recover her. She has been speaking of you, and were she not now sleeping, you should go to her and see her."

"Give us your hand," said Tony. "You're a trump, that you are. I know you'll suffer for it, 'cos you can't afford it. I say there, don't be touching that beef—I ain't begun yet. Lor' bless you, I'll let you see what a fellow with a appetite is. This is a prime cut. Well, I haven't had such a drop of half-and-half for one time. I drink towards you, old fellow,—you with the flour on your nob. Come, take a pull, and let's be friends. I forgive you for serving me as you did."

Harry Dean said something to the waiter in an under tone, which completely satisfied that worthy personage; and Tony was left with the sirloin of beef to do what he pleased with.

Harry Dean had correctly enough reported what had been done with Lucy, in fact, nothing particular was the matter with her, but exhaustion and a low fever, consequent upon insufficient nourishment and exposure to the inclemency of the weather.

Her fainting had rather been a result of her overjoy at suddenly meeting with Harry Dean than of her indisposition.

But now she lay softly cushioned in one of the best beds, in one of the best hotels in London; a noiseless and attentive servant glided about the chamber, while that chamber itself was replete with every comfort and every luxury that the most refined and fastidious taste could congregate within four walls.

She slept the calm sleep of innocence and trustfulness; and oh, what a change had come over her fortunes now!

In lieu of being the desolate and destitute child, dependant upon the chance bounty merely of any compassionate passenger who might meet her in the public streets, no young princess could have fared better than she was now faring, or have been so completely surrounded with what would render life charming.

And who, in the whole world, could deserve better to feel all the delights of mundane existence than that fair and most beautiful girl—beautiful in much more than the mere beauty of form and feature, for she was beautiful in that true beauty of mind which wound around her like a charm.

Sheer fatigue had, for a time, buried in forgetfulness even the remembrance of her sister, whose violent and most unwarrantable abduction from the cottage had given her such a world of uneasiness.

When that bodily fatigue and the exhaustion contingent upon absolute want shall pass away, she will then again awaken to an appreciation of her former grief.

And such is the career of human nature. One care but for a brief time blunts the edge of another; but care there is, and ever will be.

How Harry Dean—who has been represented, as he represented himself, to be poor, and a non-possessor of those worldly advantages which we now see him dispensing with so liberal a hand, came to have the power to do so, and to change so entirely, we shall soon see.

How, too, he escaped the assassin, Alfred Mayston, will be tolerably evident. The story is very brief upon that point.

He was picked up in the fields bleeding, and quite insensible, by some labourers, and as he could answer no questions that were put to him, and seemed to be in a most desperate condition, they adopted the wisest course they could, namely, to borrow a shutter, and convey him to the nearest hospital, which, although it happened to be the worst in London, was still better than none. His good clothing, too, got him attention.

CHAPTER XXIII.

KATE'S ATTEMPT AT ESCAPE. — THE INTERRUPTION.—HER GREAT PERIL.

WE regret to have left Kate Destern for so long a period of time in such very desperate circumstances, but the novelist labours under the disadvantage of not being able to present to those who favour him with their attention two sets of incidents at one and the same time.

Thus if the situation of a hero or a heroine be ever so critical, he or she must wait until those other circumstances are disclosed, which it is essential should be known, previous to a continuation of the main plot of the story.

Although, however, we return to Kate Destern and her more immediate fortunes now, we do not for a moment suppose that little Lucy and Tony Thorpe are so little esteemed by our readers, that anything in which they are largely concerned is a matter of indifference.

To attempt to depict anything like the actual state of mind to which poor Kate Destern was now reduced would be in vain. It was one so closely bordering upon absolute agony, that it was only her naturally strong powers of intellect which really prevented the frightful shadow of insanity from wrapping her up like a shroud.

It will be remembered that there was a sort of pause in the proceedings at the villa, which was in the occupation of the libertine, Lord Battaney; for having experienced so much more resistance from his victim—or rather her whom he meant to make his victim—than he expected, he was rather puzzled to know how to act.

Hence was it that he had sent for his prime agent, Madame Zadzed, for the purpose of seeing what her skill would accomplish in the way of overcoming the resistance of Kate Destern.

That this atrocious woman, Zadzed, had some especial reasons for working his lordship's evil purposes, there can be no doubt; and likewise that there is some very mysterious connection between her and the villain Mayston, is but too apparent.

Those are riddles which will unravel themselves as we proceed with our story.

Let us suppose another day to have passed away at the mansion, which was the prison of Kate Destern; and peeping into the principal room of the house, we shall see Madame Zadzed and Lord Battaney conversing together, while outside the window of that apartment, on a kind of raised terrace, leading to the garden, is hovering Mayston.

"And so, my lord," said Madame Zadzed, "you have set your heart upon this girl, and nothing will turn you from your pursuit of her?"

"Nothing—nothing."

"And yet you want your accustomed boldness. You will not adopt the means you have before, without any sort of scruple, adopted, to make her yours. You have turned faint-hearted."

He paced the room for some time before he made an answer, and then he said,—

"To you I can say anything, and I don't mind owning that I have shrunk from—from violence—fear or treachry with this girl. If she can be won, let me win."

"And if not, you will let her depart in peace, and never look upon her face again. Would that content you?"

"Oh! no, no. I must not—cannot lose her."

"And yet ——"

"I know what you would say. And yet I will not adopt the only course to gain her. But I hesitate."

"I see you do. You have sent for me to aid you. The girl is inexorable. No talking, in the shape either of threat or of promise, will avail with her. You will not, I say, be able to win her. You must let her go at once, or ——"

"No more, no more. I—I will think. She is truly beautiful! Shall I be foiled? Shall I, the hero of a hundred such adventures, after all suffer myself to be defeated by a young girl like this? Shall I own a defeat? No, no. Madame, I consent to your terms. She shall be mine!"

"You are right; always, of course, assuming that you really admire the girl. Ah! my lord, there was a time when to me you used such fine expressions, that if they had been used to her, I almost think she would have fallen. I was what she is."

"Pshaw! You always fancied that I would marry you. Why, I was a boy. The whole affair was between twenty and thirty years ago."

"You took me when I was but a girl from my home. You promised to marry me. You know you took me from a good and a happy home. You protected yourself from the consequences of that abduction by your rank. Italian blood flows in my veins. All my friends are dead; and here am I, a poor lone woman, and you my betrayer!"

"Ha, ha, ha! Upon my life, this is good. Ha, ha, ha! Why, Madame Zadzed,—since that fanciful name was chosen by you—I have not been treated with such a rich bit of comedy as this. I really do admire your acting. Bravo! bravissimo! Ha, ha, ha!"

"Is that your only reply?"

"To be sure it is, and I think a very flattering one too. You have made me laugh—what more would you have? You have pleased your master."

"Master!"

"Yes; you know me, woman. Do not carry this mighty good jest too far. I can see there is a lurking devil in your eye, which would prompt you to do so. Beware, I say! You are my dependent, and you may live to repent goading me too far. Peace, and know what you are."

The flush of rage that for a moment lit up the eyes of Madame Zadzed, and lent a stranger colour to her cheeks than ever she would have thought it prudent to allow revenge to do, was tremendous, and the effort by which she subdued herself must have been a very great one indeed, and said much for the quality of the intellect that had been perverted to the basest purposes.

She laughed loudly—a wild, strange, hysterical kind of laugh.

"A good jest," she cried; "a good jest, after all. Ha, ha, ha! Only a jest! I used to talk of being revenged upon you some day, but it was only jest. You are secure in your position—most secure. A nobleman, with an enormous income! What can a poor, weak woman do but obey you? Ha, ha, ha! That is all—that is all. Ha, ha, ha!"

"Silence! I don't like this mirth of yours, I tell you, it is not of the right sort. Peace, woman, peace!"

"I am your very humble servant, sir."

"That is well. Give the girl some drugged wine—remember; and to-night I will make my good fortune have no comparison with my former defeats. She shall be mine!—I swear it, she shall be mine! I loved her before she was thus obstinate, but now—now I would stake my life upon my passion. She shall be mine!"

"Bravely said! This is like yourself, my lord."

"You will remain here, mind you, and do your duty."

"Of course—of course. All shall be well. Ah! my lord, if your noble relations did but know one half of the life you lead, how they would open their ignorant eyes with wonder."

"They suspect half of it, and treat me with coldness, accordingly. It is a matter of taste; let them be what they call virtuous, if they like it."

"Oh! quite a matter of taste—quite. Ha, ha!"

"Why do you laugh in that strange, sneering manner, as if there was a something that strangely pleased you in your thoughts?"

"Did I laugh?"

"You know you did. But no matter. I have determined upon my course, and that is enough for you. You know what you have to do."

"Right well. I hope, my lord, that notwithstanding what has passed, we are still as good friends?"

"Oh, yes, yes. No more of that."

"'Tis well," said Madame Zadzed, when she was alone. "Nothing moves him. The recollection of my own wrongs seems but to point a jest. Ha, ha, ha! He laughs to scorn the feelings he has trampled on. Be it so. We shall see if there may not arise out of this affair a revenge for me, so absolute and so complete, that he shall be driven to madness, when first its awful truth bursts upon his bewildered senses. Ha, ha, ha!"

She started, for there was a slight tap upon one of the window panes. It was Mayston.

"What now?" she said, approaching the window; "what now?"

"I only wait for orders."

"Ah! yes, I recollect—I recollect. Come to me here in about an hour. I have some letters to write, which you must go to town and deliver, according to the directions."

"No mischief, I hope? I heard you and his lordship at high words."

"Well?"

"So I thought that, perhaps—perhaps you might be imprudent enough to quarrel with him, and—and ——"

"Fool! Idiot! Do as you are bid. Oh! what a sickening thing it is to be compelled to employ tools we despise to work out great purposes. Come to me in an hour; and remember that your very heart and soul are mine, and pledged to my service. Beware how you palter with me! You see you do not know me yet. Come here in an hour."

CHAPTER XXIV.

THE ATROCIOUS ATTEMPT.

NIGHT's sable mantle is spread upon the earth—all around is hushed. Not a sound, save the low note of some accidentally awakened bird, breaks the calm stillness and repose of nature.

It is the hour when the innocent are wrapped in balmy slumbers; the hour when good men are in the land of smiling dreams; the hour when the vicious are enduring, from imagination, some retribution, even in this world, for their crimes, or are prowling about to add new crimes to the already frightfully swollen list of their offences.

It is midnight.

Kate Destern still occupies the chamber where she was first placed upon her arrival at the villa, but sleep is a stranger to her eyes, although tears are not. Amid that solemn stillness of all things she is praying to that God who forsakes not the unfortunate.

She prayed for those who were dear to her—she prayed that the light of a better feeling might dawn in the hearts of those who were now persecuting her, and as the trembling words came from those lips of purity and beauty, a holy gentle calm came over her, and she felt almost happy.

Yes! she, the victim of the lawless violence of those who had torn her from her only fond associations, she had felt that she could be happy even where she was, and had a great confidence that yet Heaven would rescue her from the hands of those who would do her wrong, and hence there was a serenity about her heart, which such a man as Lord Battany, or such a woman as Madam Zadzed might have envied, but could never enjoy.

Her prayer was done, and she looked out from her window upon the silent night. How beautiful it was. The sky was not cloudless, but the vapours that then floated were of a pure and ethereal looking character, and the silver moon beams struggled through each crevice, to make the world look beautiful.

Oh! could any human thing, looking upon such a night as that, think of such black wickedness as that which filled the minds of Lord Battany and Madame Zadzed?

How long she had been gazing at the moonlight, watching the light fleecy clouds as they tempered without destroying the soft light by passing over the disc of the sweet orb, Kate did not know, but she was suddenly roused by hearing the lock of her chamber door touched.

Her heart beat violently, and it was something of a relief to her to see that it was a woman, although an interview with Madame Zadzed, who now appeared, had but ill prepared Kate to endure a a second. The young girl drew herself up with conscious innocence before one who was not so.

"Up so late," said madame.

"I am a prisoner," said Kate; "I have, I perceive, the privilege of sleeping or waking in my prison. I would I could say I likewise had the privilege of escaping unwelcome visits."

"Indeed. You are still bold."

"I ought to be. It is you who are what you ought to be, cowardly."

"Really."

Kate turned aside, wishing to say no more, but after a pause, Madame Zadzed esumed.

"Foolish girl, you know not what you say. Does it not strike you as possible, that you might wish me a friend?"

"No, no, no!"

"You would reject such an offer of friendship and of service, then?"

"Not of service. Open my prison doors and set me free. That would be a service, and entitled to my thanks for it, and my forgiveness, hearty and sincere, for the past."

"Your forgiveness? A great good is that to one such as I am. But enough of this. He who loves you has gone away; he no longer pursues you, and to-morrow morning you will be at liberty to leave here if you please."

"To-morrow—to-morrow?"

"Yes. Make yourself easy now, and to convince you that you may consider your troubles as over, I have brought you what I dared not have brought you were he here—some choice wine. It will help to recruit your strength, after all that you have suffered, and you will pass a good night. Farewell."

"Stop! stop!" said Kate. "As an aggravation to my miseries, I have been kept for the greater part of this day without food and water. Give me some of the latter—I will not drink wine."

"I regret that there is nothing else," said Madame Zadzed, as she placed upon the table a small decanter of wine and a glass. "You will find this both meat and drink, but you need not take it unless you like. It is kindly meant, but you can refuse it if you please."

So saying, Madame Zadzed left the room, for to remain and betray any more anxiety about inducing Kate to drink the wine, would be probably to awaken a suspicion that it was what it was—drugged.

"This is very cruel," murmured Kate, when she was alone. "Do they think to starve me into a submission. And the wine too. It looks so tempting to my parched lips. Shall I—dare I? What is it? What may it be? Oh, no! I must not, and yet my strength is most essential to every hope I have of escaping from this dreadful place."

She poured out a small portion of the wine. She half raised it to her lips—still she hesitated a moment—should she, or should she not. Again she raised the glass—another moment and she would

LORD BATTANEY'S VISIT TO KATE AFTER PUTTING THE DRUGGED WINE WITHIN HER BREACH.

have drank of the contents, when a pane of glass at her window was suddenly broken from without.

"Hold!" cried a voice.

"Mercy—have mercy upon me!" gasped Kate.

"Hush! There is no danger. Don't drink the drugged wine. Beware! I was your enemy, but I have been treated so as to become your friend. Beware, I say, beware!"

"Alfred Mayston!" said Kate, for she recognised the voice. "Alfred Mayston, is it possible?"

Mayston—for it was, indeed, no other —mounted on the topmost steps of a ladder, was about to make some reply, when there was the sharp report of a pistol from the garden below, and he gave a shriek of pain.

He dashed his hands through two of the window panes, to cling to something in his agony, and then with a frightful lurch, he fell backward and disappeared.

Kate stood transfixed with horror.

"Help, help, help!" she cried. "Oh, God, what horror is this?"

Her door was suddenly opened, and Madame Zadzed appeared. At this moment, Kate was so far overcome with fear that she could not speak; and after a glance at the chamber, and seeing that some of the wine was gone—for Kate had dropped the glass she had been raising to her lips—she burst into a fiendish laugh, saying,—

"'Tis done—ha, ha, 'tis done! I wonder much what meddling fool has been attempting to scale the window. But be he whom he may, he has met with his reward—Battany has most surely shot him."

She raised the almost insensible form of Kate in her arms, and flung her upon the bed that was in the apartment; then leaving her there, she darted from it, to inform Lord Battaney of what she considered the success of the horrible scheme for placing his victim at his mercy.

All this had happened with such frightful rapidity, that for a few moments more poor Kate was thoroughly bewildered, and knew not where she was, but as most happily she had not touched the drugged wine, she soon recovered to a sense of her situation.

A glance towards the door of her apartment showed her that Madame Zadzed had, in her exultation and certainty that the poor victim was incapable of taking any advantage of the circumstance, omitted to fasten it, and a hope of escape sprung up in the heart of Kate.

"Now, Heaven aid me," she said, and she rose from the couch.

Her light, for she had had a candle in the room, had now nearly gone out; for want of attention it had got consumed much sooner than it would otherwise have done; and as she advanced somewhat timidly towards the door of her apartment, the flickering flame showed that it was just upon the point of expiring.

"If I had but light," she said, "I might succeed."

She turned to the table on which the candle was, for the purpose of making an effort to re-illumine it, but it was too far gone.

In another moment she was in darkness.

And how was she, in the intricacies of a house of which she knew nothing, to escape in the dark? Might not the very steps she took lead her into the presence of those who might be the most dangerous to her? Most assuredly; and yet could she, with the door open, make up her mind to remain where she was?

"No, oh, no," she said. "There may be danger in attempting my liberation, but yet there is hope. I will trust to the guiding hand of Heaven, and venture it."

Full of this determination, she turned towards the door, but just as she would have crossed the threshold, a faint gleam of light met her eyes, and she heard a slight tread, as if some person was approaching with great caution.

She drew back to listen.

CHAPTER XXV.

THE PERILOUS NIGHT CONTINUED.

KATE trembled excessively. Let who might be coming with the light, whose faint beams came upon her eyes, it was not likely in such a place to be any friend to her.

She held by the balustrade at the head of the stairs, and listened. It was evident that the person with the light was approaching from the lower part of the house, but a hope just flitted across the mind of Kate that after all, her chamber might not be the one sought, and that by going again into it, and closing the door, she might escape a rencontre, which, if she remained where she was, would be quite inevitable.

The moment this idea, which was a rational enough one, and, at all events, could be productive of no harm in its carrying out, found a home in her brain, she retreated to her chamber, and closed the door as gently as she possibly could.

Oh! how her heart beat with ill-repressed dread for the next few minutes, as she heard the light footstep still approaching; and now a gleam of light shoots in a thin pencil of beauty through the key-hole of her chamber door, and she knows that the intruder, be he or she whom they may, has reached the head of the stairs.

The next few fleeting seconds of time must disclose whether her chamber was sought, or some other of the numerous rooms upon that floor of the mansion. Those few seconds were seconds of agony. The mystery was soon solved; the handle of the lock of her door is touched, but very softly—slowly the door itself yields to a gentle pressure from without, and the glare from a light carried by the approaching person lights up the apartment.

At that moment Kate was too much affected to speak, but her sense of being seemed to be preternaturally acute; and she heard a man's voice say,—

"She sleeps soundly. The drugged wine has done its work!"

"Horror! horror!" gasped Kate, but it was but in a whisper, for absolute terror froze up her faculties; she could only utter that word, and clasp her hands, as if her last hour had come.

The door opened wider still—the light shone more and more, and then Lord Battaney, attired in a superb dressing-gown, and with soft slippers on his feet, which had accounted for the very noiseless tread with which he had approached, made his way into the room.

The sight of him roused Kate from the state of torpor into which she had fallen, and she rushed forward, and flung herself upon her knees at his feet.

"Mercy, mercy," she said. "Oh, have mercy upon me. You see me kneel to you—I who never before knelt but to God. I ask you to have mercy upon me."

The light he carried trembled in his grasp, for he was taken completely by surprise to find her not in the state of insensibility the drugged wine would have reduced her to, had she been imprudent enough to have partaken of it. He stood like a man transfixed by some horrible sight.

"Oh! leave me, sir,—be you whom you may, I pray you leave me. If I am to be a prisoner here, at least let me have the poorest privilege of a prisoner —the solitude of my prison. But if you have power here, and can command those who hold me away from all that is dear to me, I pray you to release me."

"Not—not sleeping! The wine—you had the wine?"

"Ah! now I remember you. You are my persecutor. Oh, shame, shame, sir, upon your manhood, that you would thus array the cunning of a fiend against a poor, defenceless girl! Eternal shame upon your name. But you will have mercy—you repent?"

"Mercy—repentance!"

"Ah! yes, you are human yet. You see I weep."

"Beautiful being! You urge me to leave you, and yet by each word and action you rivet the chains that bind me to you. I love—adore ——"

"No, no, no. Peace; no more of this. I am weak, and I ask you to be merciful, for you are strong. I am here in your house; I can but die, but why should you kill me?"

"Kill you—I kill you! Perish the thought. No, I would encircle you in these arms, and were death knocking at your heart, I would warm you to life again by my caresses. You shall be mine! You can now shake off these silly fears, and look with sparkling eyes upon your brilliant destiny. I have fancied that I loved many, but I never yet felt the passion that I feel for you. My fortune is large, and you shall revel in all the delights that wealth can produce. You shall be my sultana—the cherished jewel of my heart. Think again, beautiful girl, and mar not your happier destiny by the folly of scruples, which the world will never give you credit for."

"Oh, Heaven!" cried Kate, in an agony of tears, "must I suffer this?"

"Suffer!"

"Yes, each word is a wound. Monster, respect the innocence that is unknown to your own heart, but which holds a home in mine."

"You really loathe me?"

"I do."

"Then take the consequences. I tell you, foolish girl, that I will not be foiled. I love you. Never before have had such a world of trouble in accomplishing my will. You live, remember, in my house; all here are my creatures—remember that. You may cry, rave, pray, or shriek, as best may suit your fancy, no one will heed you."

"Oh! yes, yes, there is one."

"One—one?"

"The eye of the great God is upon you. The ear of Heaven will be open to me."

"Ha, ha! The age of miracles has passed away. If that is your reliance, you lean, indeed, upon a broken reed, and build the mansion of your hopes upon a foundation of sand. But I tell you, girl, I know you and all your sex too well to be deceived thus; all this passion of yours is nothing in the world but mere rank coquetry. You shall be mine!"

He advanced a step.

"Hold!" cried Kate. "Oh, yet a moment spare me."

"Why should I pause? Beautiful being, I will hold you to my heart, and love you, though you were armed against my life."

"Hush, hush! Do you hear nothing?"

Lord Battany had placed the candle upon the table, and now he paused to listen, and he trembled as he did so, for a strange noise came upon his ears—a most unearthly sort of sound, between a groan and a shriek. It might have been the last attempted cry of some one in the agonies of a horrible and violent death.

"What—what is that?" said Lord Battany.

"Listen," said Kate, "listen. It is for you to tremble, surely, and for me to hail anything that comes to me in the shape of a deliverance. Listen, and let those sounds sink deep into your guilty soul. Who knows but they may be such as you may utter at that dread moment when but a few short respirations of breath separate you from eternity."

He raised his hand, as if he would prevent further speech until he should find out what the strange and horrible sound portended.

And now it was sufficiently evident that it came from without the house, and as it came nearer and nearer, it seemed to be approaching the outside of the window in the room, the panes of glass in which had been so shivered by the recent occurrences that had taken place in it.

A terrible fear came over Lord Battaney. His countenance, which had been flushed with passion, looked dull and white, and he drew his breath short and thickly.

"Are there devils in the world?" he said.

And now between them, as they both gazed earnestly at the window—between them and the night sky, there rose up outside a horrible-looking object. It seemed a human form, but covered so with blood that no feature was recognisable.

Even Kate, much as she considered anything in the shape of an interruption a blessed chance for her, was terrified, and could not repress a cry of alarm at the advent of so frightful an apparition.

Lord Battaney held out both his hands, as if he would so have warded off any impending ill, and kept far from him that terrible object.

But soon a voice came from the horrible bleeding spectre, and that voice at once dispelled all idea that the figure was a supernatural one. It was the voice of Alfred Mayston.

"Revenge! revenge!" he howled. "Blood and revenge!"

The moment his voice was recognised the thing was explained. He had been shot upon the ladder by Lord Battaney, while giving a warning to Kate not to drink the drugged wine; but although seriously wounded, and having had a frightful fall to the garden, he had, after lying for a time to all appearances dead, sufficiently recovered to get up, and in his bleeding, desperate condition, to be seized with a desire for revenge.

Mayston expected to find Lord Battany in the chamber of Kate, or at all events, thought that would be his least observable mode of getting into the house, and had actually clambered up the ladder again, groaning and shrieking with the agony of his wounds as he came.

"Help, help, here!" cried Lord Battaney.

Mayston heard him, and with a yell of

rage at the new prospect of having something like an opportunity for vengeance, he dashed himself through the window into the room.

Lord Battaney made an effort to reach the door, but his foot got entangled in a portion of his costly dressing-gown, and in another moment he was in Mayston's grasp.

They fell together—then struggled and tore at each other like two fiends, and then rolling across the landing, they went headlong down the staircase.

CHAPTER XXVI.

RETURNS TO LUCY AT THE GRAND HOTEL.

THE prognostications of the physician regarding the state of health of little Lucy turned out to be strictly true, for after she had enjoyed a long period of rest—that is to say, a long period counted by hours—she awoke, rather languid certainly, but quite a different creature to what she had been.

The fever, which had been the worst symptom that had before oppressed her, had entirely left her; and though in the superabundance of care which was directed to be taken of her, she was not permitted to leave her room, yet convalescent she was, to all intents and purposes.

And now we may consider that there were two persons, each alike curious to become acquainted with further particulars concerning the adventures of each other, and those two persons were Harry Dean and Lucy Destern.

Burning with impatience as Harry Dean was to learn all the particulars of her story, and likewise the fullest details that she could give him concerning the abduction of Kate from her home, he had still controlled that ardent desire until rest and judicious refreshment had done their beneficent work upon her frame; and she, too, had been compelled to yield to the languor of incipient disease, and instead of relating to Harry Dean all that she had suffered, and receiving from him—which she was sure to do—that tender sympathy which is

the food of the unfortunate, she had been compelled to postpone those revelations until a more fitting opportunity.

Now, however, we will suppose him seated by her bedside, with a feeling that all personal danger was past concerning her health, he felt he might question her closely.

He did so; and with the aptitude of childhood for particulars, she told him all, and perhaps with far greater graphic effect than as if many more years had passed over her head.

All the wounds of his heart were opened afresh, and in a voice of exquisite anguish, he spoke to her.

"Lucy," he said, "while I was lying on a bed of sickness in that hospital, to the door of which surely Providence conducted you, my hourly consolation was that at least Kate was safe and happy."

"Ah!" said Lucy, "we shall never see our dear Kate again."

"Do not despond," cried Harry; "be she hidden where she may, love can find her. She shall be recovered from those who have torn her from our arms. The villain Alfred Mayston must be the man."

"Yes, Harry, yes, it was Mayston—it was Mayston. But, Harry, we thought that you were poor, and yet what a beautiful place this is you live in. Oh, Harry, you are doing too much for me."

"Let not that trouble you, Lucy. All is well as regards my circumstances and ability to do what I am doing. I cannot, and will not attempt to disguise from you, Lucy, that there is a secret connected with me."

"A secret! Ah, Harry, I tell you all my secrets."

"And believe me, Lucy, it is from no want of confidence in you that I do not tell you all mine; but I am sure you will believe me when I tell you that it is better you should not know this secret yet."

"I am quite content, Harry, content, and—and ——"

"What would you say? You ought to know, Lucy, that you can speak freely to me."

"I was only going to say something about poor Tony Thorpe."

"And that something, Lucy, was to urge me to behave kindly to him for your sake?"

"It was."

"Be assured that I require no such urging. In proving himself your friend, he brought with him a letter of recommendation, than which nothing could be more to the purpose. Depend upon it, he is as happy and comfortable as he can be, and the moment you are quite well enough to leave your chamber, you shall yourself be the minister to all his wants."

Tears of surprise and gratitude darted into the eyes of Lucy, and as she hung upon the neck of Harry Dean, whom she loved with all the tenderness of a sister, she told him there was nothing wanting to her happiness now but the presence of Kate.

He was too much affected for a short time to make her any reply, but when he did so, it was to assure her that from that moment he devoted himself entirely heart and soul, to the recovery of her whom he loved, and should ever love while life remained to him.

We are well content now to leave Lucy and Tony Thorpe in such a condition, and to follow Harry Dean, or whoever he may chance to be, in his pilgrimage, in search of the beautiful girl, whose abiding place, as well as the great perils that surround her, are already well known to the reader.

His first and most rational step was to proceed to the country-house, or cottage rather, which had been inhabited by the Desterns, and there from the neighbours attempt to learn all the particulars that he could concerning the abduction of Kate, with the hope that something in addition to what Lucy had related to him would result from his inquiries.

He soon reached the place, and as Lucy had mentioned the benevolent care which had been bestowed upon her by the poor laundress, he made his way to her cottage in the first instance.

There he learnt more fully the particulars concerning the death of Mrs. Destern, and the singular fact that the book to which she had clung so desperately in her last moments had not been taken from her hands, but had literally been buried with her.

This circumstance, however, connected with the book, curious as it was, did not seem to be in any way associated with the fortunes of Kate, and although at some other time it might have greatly excited his curiosity, he did not now think it expedient to follow up such a clue.

The reader is, moreover, aware that this piece of information from the laundress is a defective one.

The book was rescued from the hands of the dead, and had got into the far worse hands of Madame Zadzed, who was using it, probably, for some purposes, or reserving it for some purposes, best known to herself.

What provoked him more than anything else consisted in the fact that the rumour of his own supposed murder—a rumour which had been promulgated by the Desterns—seemed to have taken a far greater hold upon the inhabitants of that little district than the abduction of Kate.

What puzzled him exceedingly was the news that some kind-hearted lady had inquired concerning the Desterns, and although we happen to know that that was Madame Zadzed's messenger, he could form no conjecture.

He returned to town with this scanty information; and as he had left at the hospital some articles belonging to him, he directed the carriage in which he had gone to draw up at the gates, for the purpose of recovering them.

Harry Dean, who now made his appearance at the hospital gate, was a very different looking personage from the Harry Dean who had been brought into that establishment but a short time previously, disfigured by blood, and his clothing in a miserable state from the clay of the fields.

He was dressed in the first style of the English gentleman of wealth and fortune, and the carriage was one of those aristocratic equipages, only to be seen in the streets of so vast a metropolis as London.

There was quite a bustle produced at the door of the hospital, as the equipage dashed into the court-yard, and several of the official personages connected with the establishment came out to do proper honour to the probable arrival of some distinguished donor.

It not a little pleased Harry Dean to find he was not recognised, and he said at once,—

"Was there a poor fellow in the hospital a few days since, who had been wounded by a pistol shot?"

"Oh! yes, sir, there was certainly."

"Well, I am a particular friend of his, and I have called to remunerate most amply those of the hospital attendants who paid him the greatest attention. He has desired me, if it should be proved that the house surgeon treated him even with common decency and civility, that that gentleman should be presented with a fifty pound note for his pains."

This was said to the porter, who, from his station being at the outer doorway, was not so well qualified to recollect Harry Dean as a late patient as any of the nurses would have been.

"Certainly, sir," said the porter, with a stare of astonishment. "Mr. Green, the house surgeon, is at home, of course; but I never heard before of anybody ——"

The porter paused, as if he seemed to think he was going rather too far with a stranger.

"You may speak to me freely," said Harry Dean, with a smile. "Don't you recollect when that same poor fellow left the hospital, you offered him a shilling?"

"Yes, I did, sir, because I thought he wanted it. He looked so pale and woebegone; and while he'd been here, there hadn't been a friend to visit him."

"Well, the shilling has borne interest, and this is the result."

The porter stared at a bank note which Harry Dean placed in his hands, and when he saw that it was in truth an order upon the bank of England to pay Mr. Matthew Marshall twenty pounds, he opened his eyes to that extent that it seemed doubtful if they would ever close again to their natural proportion.

"You're joking with me, sir," he said; "you're joking with me."

"Do you really think so; look at me well."

The porter did look at him, and then his face broke into a smile, as he said,—

"Why, what a fool I am, to be sure. It is you—it is you, sure enough. Well, I am so glad to see you. Give us your hand. Why, you must have come into some property—a whole hundred pounds, perhaps. Come, come, take back your twenty. I'm not going to rob you—not I; and as for Mr. Green, I really wish you would see him."

CHAPTER XXVII.

A HOSPITAL SCENE.—THE MYSTERIOUS NOTE.

IN the few strictures that we have thought proper to pass upon hospital practice, it is by no means our wish to detract from the usefulness of those most eminently serviceable institutions.

Perhaps there never has been anything growing out of the wants of a large miscellaneous population, so thoroughly legitimate, as the public hospital—a home for those upon whom the heavy hand of sickness is laid, and a place of immediate refuge for those who have been snatched away from their daily usefulness and daily avocations, by one of those numerous disasters which will befal individuals in the ceaseless progress of the social machine.

But if we admit that the institution of a public hospital for the sick and the wounded is a something growing most specially out of the wants of society, and a something most specially to be commended, how great and how glaring must be the iniquity of those persons, who, perverting the intentions of munificent donors, make these public hospitals a place of mental agony, if it be one of relaxation from bodily infirmities.

Why is it that in all the relations of life and throughout the whole social system of this country, want of feeling, sensibility, and delicacy of appreciation, should always be considered co-existent with a want of money?

Is it to be endured that because a man seeks the aid of a hospital, to cure him of wounds, perhaps honourably received in the pursuit of some meritorious profession, he is to be treated as if he were a stick or a stone, and to be considered a fit subject for the gibes and shallow wit of some beardless puppy, whose too partial friends have made him a surgeon's apprentice instead of a hairdresser's?

Is a man to be exposed to indignities in his most helpless of all conditions, because he avails himself of a public institution expressly reared for such as him?

Such a man is paying, amply paying, for every kind word that could be uttered to him—every morsel of nourishment that passes his parched lips—every surgical bandage that envelopes his shattered frame.

The large sums subscribed to these institutions belong to the patients, and not to the officials, although the latter evidently take a very different view of the subject, considering the patients but as an uncomfortable and disagreeable drawback to the sweets of office.

In this condemnation of the hospital system, as carried on in London—not of hospitals—we speak advisedly. But let it pass; we will return to our tale again.

After intimating, then, to the porter, his wish still to see the great Mr. Green, the house surgeon of the Middlesex Hospital, he was ushered into a little room upon the ground floor, and an individual, attired in the first style of fashion, with a mincing gait and a supercilious air, made his appearance, and upon seeing that his visitor appeared to be a gentleman of distinction, he executed a most fashionable bow, and requested to know to whom he had the honour of speaking.

"You had," said Harry Dean, "a man here hurt by a pistol shot; his name was Dean."

"Ah! yes, very likely."

"He left the hospital the moment he had strength enough to do so, but much against his will. He left something of importance undone. You behaved to him with an insolence, a heartlessness, and an assumption of puppyish superiority disgraceful to you as a gentleman, and particularly disgraceful to you as a man under the circumstances."

"Sir!"

"Sir, I hope you understand me."

"Ah! I begin to think you are that audacious individual."

"You are perfectly right; and what I omitted to do upon leaving here was this."

Harry Dean explained the rest manually, for he took hold of Mr. Green by the nose, and gave that rather prominent organ so tremendous a grip and a pull, that the house surgeon roared murder, and when he was let go, tried to escape through a doorway behind him—a proceeding which was accelerated by Harry Dean saluting him with a kick behind, which materially increased his progress.

Without, then, taking any further notice of any one on the establishment, or being himself impeded in what he was about, Harry Dean left the place, and was upon the point of stepping into his carriage.

Before he could do so, however, the porter touched him on the arm, saying,—

"I'd quite forgotten, sir, but a few hours after you had left yesterday, a man came with this note addressed to you."

"To me—here?"

"Yes; he said he was aware you were lying here unwell, and seemed much surprised at being told that you had left, nevertheless, as he said his orders were to leave it, he did so, and here it is."

The note was in a handwriting unknown to Harry Dean; and after thanking the porter for delivering it to him, he got into his carriage before he opened it; then, and not till then, he found how deeply interesting its contents were to him.

The note was as follows:

"SIR,

"It would be madness to attempt to persuade you that the hand which dealt the blow upon you, which left you prostrate, and all but dead, was not that of a rival.

"You know who it was that did that deed, and probably you will do all that you can do to bring him to justice; but this letter is for the purpose of supplying you with reasons why you should exercise a forbearance, which, probably, you would not feel otherwise inclined to think of.

"Kate Destern is beautiful—so beautiful that she has attracted more gazers than one, and among those there is one who ranks high in the muster-roll of his country's nobility.

"I was his agent—I did his work—and since then he has struck me; that blow made me your friend; and if, as I expect you will, you recover from the wound which I have inflicted upon you, you may seek Kate Destern at an old house near Fulham, called the turret, and you may seek him who has torn her from your arms likewise there, in all human probability, and you may know him by the name of Lord Battaney.

"Probably this information will induce you to forget that you have been so deeply injured by

"AEFRED MAYSTON."

The letter fell from the hands of Harry Dean. A flush of colour came across his cheeks, and then abruptly vanished, leaving them of a death-like paleness.

"Lord Battaney," he exclaimed; "Battaney! Can this be possible? Is he then really the villain popular rumour has ever painted him? Oh, no, no; there is blood flowing in his veins which should contradict the supposition; and yet this seeming circumstantial piece of information—information, the truth of which is so easily tested—changes my judgment, and upsets all my preconceived ideas. What am I to do? What am I to think?"

The carriage was rolling on towards the hotel, where Lucy was enjoying the sweets of competence, and a very short time would have sufficed to have reached that establishment, but he checked the coachman, and directed that he should drive to Portman-square, which seemed to be a sufficient address to enable the servants to know whither he was bound, for in as short a time as the distance could be traversed, the carriage stopped at the door of a splendid mansion, the hall of which was crowded with liveried dependants.

Harry Dean seemed to be perfectly well known, and he was at once received with abundance of courtesy.

"Is the earl within?" was his question; and upon receiving an answer in the affirmative, he desired that his presence might be announced, and in a few moments he was requested to walk into the Earl of Hartington's study.

The Earl of Hartington was an old man, high in the counsels of his sovereign. He received Harry Dean with a smile, but it speedily vanished when he gazed upon the agitated countenance of the young man.

"Good heavens, Harry," he said, "what is amiss?"

"Do not ask me questions, my lord," cried Harry Dean; "but answer me one if you can. Is Lord Battaney in England?"

"Yes, and has been for some time. Were you not aware of that?"

"My lord, I would give all that I am worth in this world, and the reversion of all that I am likely to be worth, to have been convinced that Lord Battaney was still upon the continent. Pardon me if I say no more, and if for a time I keep to myself the cause of the great embar-rassment you now see me suffering. I need not ask you to be assured that it is from no disrespect that I thus act; but the story is too long a one for immediate recital, and its circumstances are such as to call upon me for immediate action."

"But Harry, Harry, stay a moment."

"Pardon me, my kindest and best friend, I dare not. Think me not unkind or ungrateful towards you that I must now leave you."

Apparently, then, fearful that he should be delayed by further interrogatories, Harry Dean pressed the old man's hand between his own, and then dashed from the apartment.

When he reached the door-step of the earl's house he paused a moment, and appeared to be in deep thought; after which, he said to his servants, who had charge of the carriage,—

"I shall not want your attendance to-day again. You may bestow yourselves where you please."

He then walked away with nervous and rapid strides.

CHAPTER XXVIII.

THE FURTHER PROCEEDINGS AT THE VILLA.

HORRORS were accumulating thickly upon the imagination of the unhappy Kate Destern. Scarcely did it seem that she was upon the point of being relieved from one agonizing woe, when another would rise up of more alarming character than its predecessor.

She stood in her little chamber, after Lord Battaney and the fearfully wounded Alfred Mayston had dashed so precipitously down the staircase, perfectly transfixed with terror.

To be sure, the giant evil that had oppressed her, namely, the terrific presence of Lord Battaney, had been certainly spared her; but in what a way was that accomplished—in how fearful a manner had he been dragged from that chamber, which he had purposed making the scene of so awful an iniquity.

With what a fearful amount of retribution had he been visited, and that, too, by one of the very agents he employed in his vices, and that agent the very one, among all others, whom he thought he had placed far beyond doing him any mischief.

"Oh! heaven," cried Kate, "when will all these horrors end? - Am I to be driven distracted by a succession of events, which come before my mental vision like the hideous phantasma of a dream? Save me, save me!"

She sunk exhausted upon a couch that was in the apartment, but in another moment she became aware of the presence of some one, and upon looking up, she saw the diabolical, distorted features of Madame Zadzed.

This fiend in the form of a woman had come down from one of the upper rooms in the house, full of rage and curiosity, to know what had produced the tremendous uproar below, when she expected all would have been quiet, and that the poor victim, abandoned by consciousness, would have become the prey of the destroyer.

She stood glaring upon Kate with eyes that seemed to flash like flames of fire.

"Speak, minion," she cried. "I heard an uproar as of men struggling. What was it?"

"You are a woman," cried Kate, "and there must be some touch of heavenly compassion lingering at your heart. Save me, oh! save me, I implore you, and take me from this dreadful place."

"How is this?" muttered Madame Zadzed. "Has the sleeping potion taken no effect? Where is he whom you should consider your master?"

There was a violent ringing of bells in the lower portion of the mansion, and Madame Zadzed became too much interested in what that might portend to urge Kate further for a reply.

All she did was to snatch up the light, and muttering some unintelligible words, she hastened to the door, and made her way down the staircase as quickly as possible.

It was an impulse rather than a matter of reflection which induced Kate to follow her; and guided by the light, she made the best of her way down the great staircase to the basement story.

All was bustle and confusion. The sound of many voices proceeded from a particular room, and guided by that Babel noise, Kate opened a door, and found herself in presence of a scene which requires something of a minute description.

It was a large and handsome drawing-room—curtains of rich silks and satins depended from the windows; the floor was laid with exquisite carpetting; and a chandelier, carrying an amazing number of wax lights, lent a soft and chastened brilliancy to the whole.

The floor was strewn with articles of furniture of a most luxurious description, costly pictures adorned the walls, and altogether the apartment presented a perfect picture of excessive refinement and luxury.

We do not mean to say that Kate, in the agitation of that moment, beheld these things, but it is necessary for our purpose that they should be described and known, inasmuch as by such means we may come to a just appreciation of the character of the titled voluptuary who called that place his own.

But there were living pictures more interesting in that apartment than the mute ones upon the walls.

On a couch near the centre of the apartment, and which seemed to have been drawn from the wall, reclined Lord Battaney. Several of the vile domestics of that place—pandars to his vices, were congregated around him, in surprise and terror.

Well might they, as they looked upon the livid and convulsed features of him, who had been for so long their lord and master, fancy that their occupations were passing away, for if any judgment could be come to from his looks, he seemed indeed like a man who was bidding a hasty adieu to the world, and all that appertained to it, but whether in his case that adieu was to herald him to a better, was a very doubtful proposition indeed.

Even Kate could not look upon him, bad as she knew him to be, and suffering as she had done from his persecutions, without something of that heaven-born pity, which forms a part of such natures as her's, and can never be absolutely obliterated from them.

"She is here. She is here!" cried several of the servants as Kate emerged from the shadow of Madame Zadzed into the light.

It would appear from these expressions that Lord Battaney had made some sort of reference to her, or request to see her, before she came into the room.

"Good God!" said Madame Zadzed, "what has happened?"

Lord Battaney opened his ghastly eyes, and glared around him. It did not seem by the character of that look, as if he at all at the moment, knew where he was.

"All is lost! All is over," exclaimed Madame Zadzed. "The effects and the work of half a life-time are lost, I shall even yet be baulked of my revenge."

She cast herself upon a chair, and covering her face with her hands, she rocked herself to and fro, as though she had given herself up to the most abject despair.

Kate shuddered.

"Where is she?" said Lord Battaney, in a faint voice. "Where is she?"

Before any one could reply to this interogatory, which all seemed to know at the moment related to Kate, there arose a bustle outside the door, and a small thin pale man with a slightly Jewish cast of face, made his appearance.

This man's attire was singular enough. It was partly European, and partly oriental, and his sharp sparkling eyes were most intelligent, although there was a something in his countenance, which no prudent man would have trusted, however hard it may be or seem to be, to condemn any one by their looks.

The assembled servants stared at this man as though he had been an apparition, and at the sound of his voice as he spoke a few words of simple inquiry, Madame Zadzed sprung to her feet, and looked for all the world as though she had just seen an apparition.

"This is all a dream," she said.

"It is no dream," said the new-comer, mildly.

"Then the grave refuses to hold two such as you and he."

She pointed to Lord Battaney, as she spoke, and once more she sunk into the chair, from which she had arisen and seemed again to give herself up to despair.

The mysterious stranger slowly approached the prostrate form of Battaney, but as he did, that demon of iniquity managed, hurt and apparently dying as he was, to hold out both his hands and make an endeavour to ward off the approach of the new-comer

"No—no—no!" he cried, with yells of anguish, "not yet—not yet. I am still in life. Not yet can I or ought I to consort with beings of another world. Off horrible spectre, off!"

"Is it so," said the stranger, with a slight smile. ' Do you indeed believe me to be no more. My suspicions are but confirmed."

As he uttered these words he cast a glance of such meaning at Madame Zadzed, that she gasped again for breath, and it was a few moments before she could manage to speak. When she did, her voice was hoarse and thick, and she trembled violently.

"No—no. Do not accuse me.—Do not accuse me!"

"A guilty conscience, madam, needs no accuser. You thought you saw me perish, I know you meant me to perish. But as regards his lordship's share in the transaction, I own I have my doubts."

"He—is—innocent," gasped Madame Zadzed.

"For once, I believe you," said the stranger.

"I swear—I swear that I regretted your supposed death," cried Battaney, "instead of having any hand in it.—I swear that, mind."

"Do not swear it or you will make me doubt it. Let it rest. You seem hurt or ill. Ha! how is this.—He faints.—What has happened?"

"You are a man of skill," said Madame Zadzed. "You are a physician, learned in all the learning of the east. You were once fond of money as a means to an end."

"Which end was power."

"Yes.—You shall name your own reward if you can restore Lord Battaney to health."

"Indeed, do you love him so much?"

"No. There is a passion stronger than love. A passion which wishes often to preserve those who have inspired it, for special purposes."

"Hate!" said the physician.

Madame Zadzed nodded, and nodded silently to the still form of Battaney, which now indeed, did not seem to have within it one spark of vitality.

The physician approached, and tearing open the vest of Battaney, he laid his ear flat over the region of the heart, and listened intently for several seconds. Then he rose up, and turning to the servants, he said:—

"Carry him to a chamber."

"He will not recover," said Madame Zadzed.

"He will," said the stranger.

He was now about to leave the room after the servants, who had lifted Battaney from the ground, but Kate, who, up to this moment had been an astonished and silent spectator of the strange scenes that had been going on, sprang after him, and clutching him by the arm, she said:—

"Save me!—oh, save me! As you are a man, I charge you to save me!"

"From what?"

"From worse than death; from that dreadful woman!"

"Indeed—do you not like my old friend, Madame Zadzed? Well, I may regret it, but I make it a rule never to interfere in what does not concern me. You are here, but how you came here, or who, or what you are, I know not, and care not. Unhand me."

"Oh, no—no. You surely must have some feeling—your heart is not all marble."

"Unhand me, I say!"

With brutal violence he tore himself from her grasp, and then at once hurried from the scene, leaving her transfixed with a horror that for some moments could find no utterance. And yet when she did a little recover from the shock of finding herself so rudely repulsed by one whose pity and protection she had implored, she did not feel disposed by any means wholly to give way to the perils that surrounded her. A determination to make an effort for life and liberty came over her, and she rushed towards the open door through which the physician had passed.

By this time, however, Madame Zadzed had sufficiently recovered to be aware of what was going on, and she said aloud to the servants who remained:—

"Stop her—stop her, as you value your lives. All of you are committed in the guilt that has found a home under this roof, and all of you are interested in keeping the dreadful secrets of this house. If she escape, you are lost."

Thus called upon by one whom they had been as much in the habit of obeying as Lord Battaney himself, the servants threw themselves in the path of Kate, and who found the only chance of escape, if indeed it had been a chance at all, completely cut off. The feeling of despair that took possession of her was truly dreadful. Her feelings prompted her to struggle with her assailants, but what would that have availed her against brutal men whose very touch was contamination? She shrank back into the room almost fainting from grief and apprehension.

"Take her away," said Madame Zadzed. "There is a stronger place in this house than any she has yet seen. Remember that upon the safe keeping of this girl depends all your liberties, and perhaps your lives too."

The servants appeared to be fully aware of the importance of keeping Kate a prisoner, and one man of herculean strength, and ferocious mein, approaching her said,—

"Follow us quietly, and no harm will come to you, but if you don't feel disposed to do that I shall carry you."

Anything was better than the touch of such a monster.

"I will follow," cried Kate. "Oh, yes, I will follow."

"'Tis well. This way.

The fellow snatched up one of the lights and left the room, closely followed by Kate, whose greatest apprehension at this moment was that he would carry his threat of laying violent hands upon her into execution. He led the way through several rooms until they came to one which had all the appearance of well-ordered library. There were compartments of books all round the apartment, and the ceiling which was of a dome shape was beautifully painted.

To the surprise of Kate the man touched a spring at the side of one of the book-shelves, and about the size of an ordinary, door in the shape of a complete compartment of books, swung open disclosing beyond a dark passage.

"Come," he said.

"Oh, no — no. Have you no mercy?"

"Confound you! Will you force me——"

He rushed upon her, and seizing her by the wrist, he dragged her through the opening in the wall, and the spring door closed upon them with a loud snap.

CHAPTER XXIX.

THE PHYSICIAN AND HIS PATIENT.

THE mysterious man who had arrived so opportunely at the villa residence of the infamous and wounded Lord Battaney, followed that personage from the room, after he had behaved in so rude a manner to Kate. The servants conveyed the apparently dead form of their bad master to a handsome chamber, and by direction of the physician they laid him upon a bed.

"Leave the room,' said the mysterious man.

He was obeyed immediately, for there was a certain something about his manner which awed the domestics, and that, combined with the evident control he exercised over the proud and haughty Madame Zadzed, gave them a very high opinion of him. They closed the door behind them, and he was alone with Lord Battaney.

The light which they had left threw a strong glare upon the still features of the insensible man, and for several minutes the physician regarded him in silence. When he did speak it was in such a tone of concentrated bitterness, horrible to hear, and which would have frozen the very life-blood about the heart of Lord Battaney, had he been in a condition to listen to it.

"The cup of revenge is at my lips," he said. "What prevents me from quaffing at one draught the rich contents? Why do I not at once crush the lingering spark of existence that is only hovering around this bad man's heart? Oh! how I have panted for a moment like this, and yet, now that it has come, I pause to debate."

Silently he paced the room for several seconds, and then stopping at the side of the couch, he spoke again.

"There is but one consideration," he muttered, "that stays my hand. I must and will have wealth, and if I slay this man now, my best and most glorious chance of achieving that falls dead with him. No, he must live for a time to enrich me; and he shall do so, or great, indeed, shall be my revenge!"

He took from his pocket a small morocco case, which, when opened, disclosed about half-a-dozen minute phials. One of these he selected, and unscrewing the stopper from it, he approached the dressing-table that was close at hand, and poured a small portion of the contents into a glass, which he afterwards filled up with water. The mixture had then a pale pink colour.

Again approaching Lord Battaney, he partially raised him with his left hand, while with the right he poured some of the mixture into his mouth. The effect was almost instantaneous. Lord Battaney opened his eyes.

"Do you know me?" said the physician.

It was evident from the wandering and distressed look that Battaney cast around the room that his faculties were in anything but a very lively state, notwithstanding that his eyes were open.

"Do you know me?" again said the physician.

"Oh! God, yes. I am with the dead," faintly murmured Battaney. "It is Caroli who speaks."

"Yes, but you are with the living Caroli."

Battaney turned his gaze upon him for a few seconds, and then with a shudder he said,—

"I saw you go down in the surging waters!"

"You did, but my time had not then come. I live for vengeance. Try to move."

"I cannot—my limbs are full of aches and pains. I cannot move."

"What, then, if I now chose to place my hand upon your throat, and at once requite you for all your treacheries towards me? I could do so with the most perfect safety. No one even would suspect the deed. I have but to leave the house, saying to whom I might chance to meet that you were past my skill, and dead."

"Help! help!" shrieked Battaney.

The physician, whom we may now call by his name of Caroli, closed upon Battaney in an instant, and grasped him by the throat.

One more effort he made to shriek for aid, but the tightened grasp that his enemy had of him made it die away in an indistinct and horrible gutteral sound.

Then Caroli relaxed his hold a little, as he said, in a hissing whisper,—

"What price do you put upon your life? You have often times valued the existence of others cheaply enough. What is the price that you put now upon your own?"

"Upon my life?" gasped Lord Battaney.

"Yes, your life. Do you not understand me? I say what price do you put upon your life? Why do you not answer me? Are you deaf or dead already, or do you doubt the certainty of your own danger?"

"Mercy, mercy," said Battaney.

"Ah!" cried Caroli, with a fiend-like laugh, "I now begin to perceive that you are awakening; so once more I propound my question of what price do you put upon your life? Name the amount."

Battaney looked at him with eyes blood-shot and ghastly, and then in a thick, hoarse whisper, he said,—

"Name what you want."

"Ten thousand pounds," said Caroli; "not a fraction less. Will you draw a cheque now for that amount, or will you in preference go to that habitation of the damned you have so certainly fitted yourself for?"

Battaney's eyes wandered to a table, on which lay materials for writing, and Caroli immediately raised him up, and dragged the table towards him. He placed a pen in his hand, and after trembling for some moments, the nearly dead man wrote a cheque upon a well-known banking-house in the Strand for the sum of ten thousand pounds. Caroli eagerly placed it in his pocket, and then from another of the little bottles he had

in the narrow case, he gave Battaney a few drops. The effect was almost instantaneous, and the libertine noble fell back upon the bed in a deep sleep.

CHAPTER XXX.

LUCY'S DANGER AT THE HOTEL.

WE left poor Kate Destern in circumstances of no little peril and difficulty, but Lucy's situation at the hotel still claims so much of our regard, that we feel compelled now to detail an adventure which befell her almost immediately upon the departure of her friend, Harry Dean, upon that mission which terminated in the recognition of Lord Battaney.

The state of mind of the young girl was now, with one exception, of the most serene character, and could she but have been absolutely assured of the safety of Kate, she would have been perfectly happy.

As it was, however, with that confidence which childhood has in the boundless resources of those whom it loves, she considered that now Harry Dean had fairly set about discovering Kate, that her safety was almost guaranteed.

Indeed, the wonders that Harry Dean had already accomplished had been so great, that nothing now seemed to be to him impossible or improbable.

"Yes," murmured Lucy, "yes, all will be well and happy again. Harry will find Kate, and we shall all live together in some place quite full of flowers, and we shall sing all the day."

These were the serene and blissful thoughts that filled up the mind of that pure and spotless being, and in the indulgence of them she slowly dropped into a deep sleep.

What occurred during her repose deserves relation.

Scarcely had Lucy fallen into that innocent slumber, when a dashing carriage drove up to the door of the hotel, and all the servants of the establishment were on the alert to do honour to the apparently distinguished arrival. The door of the vehicle was opened by a footman attired in splendid livery, and a lady alighted.

This personage was dressed in the first style of modern fashion, and she at once asked for the landlord of the house, who obsequiously shewed her into a small reception room, and then stood awaiting her commands.

"We will relieve you of your charge," she said, with a sweet smile, and in a voice which was slightly foreign in its accents.

"Charge—charge—that is, charge, madam?" said the puzzled landlord, who could not make out what she meant.

"Yes, your charge. But I forgot; I ought to repeat to you the words agreed upon—one, two, three, fidelity! You understand?"

"Why, no, madam. I—I really—"

"Dear me, how shocking."

"Shocking, madam?"

"Yes. Did not he whose pleasure it is to be called simply Mr. Dean tell you his aunt was coming?"

"No, madam."

"Then call him, if he be in the house, at once, for it is quite essential that the child should come with me at once. Of course you know that I am Lady Villiers Hope?"

"Oh! yes, madam. I—I ——. Of course, Mr. Dean's aunt is Lady Villiers Hope, of course, madam."

"Precisely," she said, with a light, joyous sort of laugh. "Well, Mr. Dean said he would tell you I was coming, but that for fear of any mistakes, as we know we have unscrupulous persons to deal with, I was to give you a kind of pass-word, which was to consist of 'one, two, three,—fidelity,' but I suppose I must take a seat until he comes in, as I have got here before him."

"Oh! no, madam. Perhaps he is here—I will go and inquire."

This was a ruse of the landlord, who thought he was being very clever and cautious to get out of the room, and the moment he did so, he went to the door and beckoned to the footman of the carriage, and when that personage reached him, he said,—

"Is your lady really the Duchess of Clareton?"

"The what?"

"The Duchess of Clareton? She says she is."

"Then she has forgotten her name, for she was the Lady Villiers Hope."

"Oh, dear me, yes. Ha! ha! What a fool I am. Of course. Ha! ha!"

"Well I think you are a fool," said the footman.

"It's all right," muttered the landlord, as he went into the hotel again. "Oh, it's all right. It was just as well though, to make the enquiry in that underhand sort of way, because if she had been an impostor, of course, that fellow would have thought she had chosen to name herself, the Duchess of Clareton to me, he would have said, 'Oh, yes.' As it is, however, there can be no sort of mistake."

With this conviction he went into the small reception room again, and with more profound bows than before, he said, in terms of great reserve and respect,

"Madam, Mr. Dean is not within."

"How provoking. Not within?"

"No, madam, but any commands that you may favour me with, will, I am sure, be as faithfully executed as though that gentleman were here himself to see to them. If you will favour me with your orders, I shall esteem myself highly honoured."

"Why, the fact is, I was, at the request of my nephew, to take away a little girl who is here, to my house in May Fair. I made him such a positive promise to that effect, that I don't really know what I shall say to him when he dines with me to-day and I cannot show him his young protegee."

"Madam, you can of course, remove the girl."

"Then you are not suspicious?"

This was said with such a fascinating smile, that the landlord was fairly bewildered, and could only bow and mutter something about how honoured and delighted he was, and so on. After this he led the lady to the chamber of Lucy, who being awakened by their entrance into her room, looked up with a something of alarm in her face, and then shrunk farther among the bed clothes.

"My dear," said the lady, "Henry Dean has sent me for you. Are you ready to come to him, or would you rather stay where you are?"

ARRIVAL OF MAYSTON AT THE VILLA AT PUTNEY.

"Oh no—I will go to Harry Dean anywhere. Take me quickly to him."

The landlord in obedience to a hint from the lady left the room, and in the course of ten minutes, little Lucy, although feeling very weak and ill, was dressed and ready to go. She tottered rather in her walk, but the lady supported her, and they together left the hotel. In another moment they were in the carriage, and before the landlord who executed a profusion of bows, could recover the perpendicularity of his back they were off.

"Is it far to Harry Dean's?" said Lucy.

"Hark you!" said her companion, "I think you are old enough and intelligent enough, to understand what I am about to say to you."

The child looked alarmed, and the lady continued—

"I don't supose you know what the meaning of the word hostage is, but it is a hostage that you are to be; I anticipate danger from this friend of yours, Harry Dean, and I want to keep you, until I have made my terms with him. If you attempt to struggle or scream, your own life, perhaps will be taken, but if you keep quiet no harm is intended you, or is likely to befall you in any way. Now I think you thoroughly and completely understand me, and your own position. Why do you not answer me?"

The fact was, that poor Lucy was at the moment too much terrified and bewildered, to make any answer to a speech which had filled her with dismay. In another moment she burst into tears.

"Ah!" said the lady, "you may cry as much as you please."

"Oh, Harry, Harry—Tony, Kate. Where are you all?" sobbed Lucy.

"Peace! you brat, peace I say."

The face of the lady, who was no other than that accomplished actress, Madame Zadzed herself, grew pale with passion, and the expression of that countenance was really so alarming, that Lucy was awed at the moment into silence. She let her head rest upon her hands, as the carriage rolled rapidly on, a feeling of terrible agony and desolation came over the heart of that innocent and loveable child.

Madame Zadzed had no objection in the world to poor Lucy crying as much as she felt disposed. It was anything in the shape of noise or tumult that that lady dreaded, so she allowed the fair young creature to taste for as long a period as she liked that feeling which, with a large amount of poetic licence has been called—

"The luxury of woe."

Alas! it was anything but a luxury to poor Lucy, to be condemned to shed such bitter tears as those were that now came in scalding streams down those sweet cheeks. Illness, too, yet held the frame of the young creature in its enervating clutch, and no wonder that she felt completely prostrated, by the horrors around her.

The carriage stopped at a dingy-looking house. A bell was rung, and Madame Zadzed said to the footman with a patronising air—

"I shall of course inform your master, that I am quite well pleased with the manner in which this affair has been conducted. I shall not want you again to-day."

She tried to rouse Lucy, but what she thought at first was obstinacy, and then sleep, she found out to be a fainting fit, which had come over the young creature. Lucy was carried insensible into the house, and the street door was closed instantly, and well barred and bolted against all comers.

* * * * *

Tony sat at the hotel in perfect ignorance that anything was taking place that he could feel interested in. He had been told sometime before that Lucy was asleep, and with that assurance he felt abundantly satisfied.

After then having satisfied his hunger and thirst, and made a considerable gap in the sirloin of beef, he looked about him for some amusement, and seeing writing materials at hand, the love of literature came over Tony, and he commenced what he called "Swigisbunder the Beautiful, a Tale of the East."

The opening passage will convey some idea of the powers of the writer.

"The Sultan Sticinthemud called for his boots, and as the slave who had the care of them, had forgotten the blacking process, his head was struck off and fixed on the city gates. 'Brother of the moon,' said the grand vizier, slowly advancing, 'we have taken a christian captive.'

"'A what,' cried the Sultan. 'Is it a he, or a she?'

"'A she uncle of the prophet,' added the vizier, 'and her beauty is like that of the full moon, with both its eyes open.'

"The sultan looked around him, upon the sublime apartment in which he was."

At this stage of composition, Tony looked around him, and as he did so he ejaculated. "What a fine house this must be to be sure. If I was to go all over it and have a good look at it, how nobbily I should be able to describe such places, when I comes really to write a romance in seven volumes full of all sorts of rummy goes, and ghosts and barons, and injured innocences, and sliding panels and dungeons, and long passages, and skeletons, and rusty daggers. Oh, won't I have a try at all risks. You can't come it very strong in the way of a description, if you haven't seen the blessed place."

Tony was quite in his innocence ignorant of the fact, that Tourists and Newspaper critics not unfrequently do come it stronge, in a way of a description of what they never saw. But then Tony was purely unsophisticated as King Lear has it.

Full, however, of the idea of finding material for future elaborate description, Tony made up his mind to make a grand tour through the hotel. For this object he considered that it was just as well to take no one into his confidence, so opening the door of the room in which he was, he observed a staircase immediately opposite to him, up which he stole with stealthy steps.

Everything to poor Tony, inartificially brought up as he had been, was a gorgeous novelty. Even the stair carpets appeared by their yielding softness, to be deserving of being particularly noted by him, and when he arrived upon the landing he nearly fell headlong down again with fright, in consequence of suddenly coming face to face with a statue, which he had not observed until he was in such proximity to it.

"Bother it," said Tony, "I thought it was somebody to be sure, but its only an image after all. What a goose I am."

A room door was open, and in Tony went, but of all the mysterious-looking rooms that he ever heard of, this was the most mysterious. It was very small—and in the middle of it was a curious looking affair like a scanty bed with curtains all about it. Tony cautiously opened one of the curtains, and then he heard some one ascending the stairs. Full of dismay at being caught in a place which to him seemed as mysterious as the Blue Chamber of Abomilique, he hastily stepped behind the curtain, and stood at once fairly in the sentry-box. Then close to his face he saw a little tassel, to which he gave a sharp pull, and in an instant he was drenched with a gallon of water. Tony had never been in a shower bath before.

_____

CHAPTER XXXI.

THE FATE OF KATE IN THE RECESSES OF THE VILLA.

WE fear we have left poor Kate for too long a space of time in the power of those desperate persons whose conduct was swayed only by the worst of passions, and who heeded not what suffering they inflicted upon the pure and good. We hasten now to take another glance at the varying fortunes of our heroine.

We left her just as the secret panel in the wall of the library had closed upon her with a loud snap.

All was darkness now, of the most intense character. At this moment she remembered that she had heard casually from one of the servants that the house had been famous at one time during the wars of the Commonwealth as a place of security and secrecy for cavaliers true to the royal cause.

She had not much time for thought, however, as the man hurried her on, the sound of the closing of the panel still ringing in her ears with a fearful sound, for it seemed as if she had been suddenly shut out from all aid.

Kate shuddered, and endeavoured to pause in her hurried advance to she knew not whither. The intention seemed to have been anticipated by the man, whose arm immediately gave an additional impetus to her motions, and when she endeavoured despite this hint, to pause, he said,—

"Come, come, young lady, you needn't stay here, you will have rest enough presently, so come on."

"Have pity on me," said Kate, with a great effort, for she felt the greatest repugnance to the man, and to speak to him.

"Pity, aye, we'll say nothing about that now, but you will have pity upon somebody by-and-by, I'll be sworn. If some of these crop-eared rascals had you now, they'd show you what was pity."

"Man—have you no sister, no mother, if so for their sakes and for Heaven's sake save me from this horrible fate."

"Don't fret," said the man, "and as for my sister or my mother, why do you know I never meddle with family matters —its against rule to mention such things in the regiment, besides, my pedigree and connections can have nothing to do with the case. Make yourself perfectly easy and enjoy the present moment."

Kate shuddered as she heard the fellow speak, and she feared his cool, easy tone was an assurance that no entreaty would prevail with him. She shed tears, and could barely sustain her own weight, though she endeavoured to do so as much as possible, to avoid the contaminating touch of the man.

They passed through several chambers —they were strange, old places, where there were but few signs of recent habitation. Strength and secrecy seemed to be the grand desideratum, which seemed effectually secured.

The fitful light of the lantern added a deeper gloom—almost a horror to the place, for ever and anon it shot forth a glimmering ray, that was lost down a long passage, now on this side, and anon on that, and then it glided along the floor as they proceeded onwards.

At length, after going through many passages and apartments, which she could not have examined well, had she been so desirous, there was one excessively gloomy above all the rest; the man paused at a door which he opened, and then taking her in, he said, as he turned the light of his lantern around the apartment,

"This will be your house for a time, make yourself easy, and don't try to get out, because you can't, and it will only give you trouble for nothing;" so saying, the man quitted the apartment.

Still Kate was not one wholly to despair, if she could see any glimpse of hope in any direction; and such a dread had she of the presence of Madame Zadzed, that to be without the influence of the basilisk-like gaze of that woman, was of itself something resembling an advance to freedom.

The light which the man had carried he had left, so that by placing it in a position to cast its rays as widely around as possible, she had a very good view of the room in which she was imprisoned.

It was an apartment of considerable size, besides being well appointed; and most singular was it, that such a place, with all its rare finishing, should have been suffered to go into decay. There were sufficient chairs, tables, and hangings, of an age gone by, to set up any of the trumpery shops in Wardour-street for twenty years. Some very cogent reasons indeed must have induced the total desertion of such interesting apartments.

By the rays of light from the lanthern, Kate was enabled to make many special observations of the place.

She walked across the floor with that noiseless tread, which the presence of silence and antiquity commonly induces all persons to adopt unconsciously, and as she glanced around her at some of the pictures that adorned the walls, she did not heed where she was treading, until she found that there was something under her feet, which nearly threw her down.

Upon stooping, she found that it was a sword, and close by was a glove. Both were of ancient workmanship, and as Kate looked at the blade, and saw a strange thick rust upon it, she shuddered to think that, probably, the last time it was in human hands, was for the purpose of being used for some deed of blood.

"What a fearful tale, dread instrument of vengeance, might you relate," she said, "could you by some magic process be endowed with the power to speak."

She took the lanthern now, and looked narrowly at the portion of the floor where the sword and glove had lain, and it was quite clear to her that some unusual moisture upon that spot had hastened the decay of the rich carpetting that in the other parts of the room was only covered with the dust of many years' collecting.

This peculiar appearance of dampness, too, she found she could follow distinctly across the room, and she did so with an eager and panting curiosity, to know whither it would lead her.

With slow steps, holding the lanthern close to the floor, so that she should not lose the trail upon which she was, she proceeded entirely along the greatest length of the apartment to a door which was closed.

It required some courage and presence of mind, in such a place, to open a door at all, which might possibly involve some more imminent danger even than that by which she was at present surrounded; but, nevertheless, urged by an insatiable desire to know whither the damp spots upon the carpet would lead her, she laid her hand upon the handle of the door, and essayed to open it.

The latch was stiff from rust and long disuse, but yet she found no great difficulty in turning it, and the door creaked upon its hinges as she flung it open. Probably, not for half a century, or, perchance, a whole one, had these hinges been brought into use.

Before advancing through the doorway, Kate was naturally desirous of seeing as much as she could of what was upon the other side, and for this purpose she held the lanthern up as high as she could, so as to cast its rays as far and wide as possible, and then she looked most earnestly about her.

It was a room of considerable dimensions, longer indeed, she thought, than the one she was in, and it had about the same appearance of costly furniture, and the same appearance of decay. Still there was nothing at all of an alarming character about the place, so with only the natural hesitation, which under such circumstances was likely to mark her progress, Kate crossed the threshold, with the lanthern in her hand.

Before continuing the trail of the damp spots upon the carpet which might or might not be blood, but which a horrible idea floating in her mind, in connexion with the sword, seemed to tell her really were blood, she looked at the appointments of the room.

The only respect in which they differed from those of the apartment she had just left, consisted in the presence of a number of small mirrors on the walls, which no doubt were considered very costly and exquisite when first put up, but which now would scarcely find admittance in that bathos of all that is comfortable, a London lodging house.

To follow the damp spots through the room, was a matter of no difficulty, and she reached a door that was just partially open. All was still, and she pushed it wider, and entered a third room.

The most prominent feature in this room, was a couch, and upon that couch was a bundle of something, which Kate trembled to look at—breathless she approached it—she held the lanthern towards it, and to her horror, she saw that it was the mouldering remains of a human body, richly attired.

Horror almost froze up her faculties for a time, as she looked upon this truly frightful spectacle. She felt fascinated by its very terror, and for fully the space of two minutes, she was unable to move from the spot.

In vain she tried to turn her eyes from the dreadful spectacle. It was only when the light began to fade, and actually had faded away sufficiently to make the spectacle upon the couch, only dimly visible, that she succeeded in turning about, and flying through the middle room into the first apartment.

When there, she sunk into one of the old fashioned unwieldy chairs, and thought for a few moments that her senses were really going from her, amid the horrors and accumulated disasters, by which she was surrounded.

"Oh, Heaven!" she exclaimed, "when will these persecutions cease? Better, far better, that I were in the quiet grave, by the side of my poor mother, than exposed to these terrors, that shake my reason on its throne."

Scarcely had she uttered these words, when she felt she was perpetrating an injustice against that Providence, which had hitherto supported her through the grievous trials, she had been compelled to endure, and as the tears gushed to her eyes, she uttered a short prayer to the divine Being, who is the shield and father of the innocent.

There seemed nothing now but patience, that could in any way benefit her, and as she sat amid the dust, the desolation, and the faded magnificence of that apartment, she made up a fanciful picture of the present and the past, that any painter would have gladly seized, and then as memory went back to the happy days of her childhood she spoke.

"Alas! alas!" sobbed Kate. "What will become of me? Where shall I look for hope? When dream of consolation?. Who would, if told this tale, believe for one moment, there was such oppression in happy England."

Great as had been the misfortunes, and great as was the grief of Kate Destern, she yet knew little of the real weight of human misery, which was to be found in the giant city, with which she was surrounded. Had she but guessed at a tenth part of the agony, that London alone shut up in its vast recesses, she would perhaps have thought more lightly of her own miseries.

But "sufficient for the day is the evil thereof," for such pure spirits as hers.

And yet her situation was one full of pain and dread. Unknown dangers hovered around her, and she knew not a moment when death itself might not be preferable to the danger which might be now at hand. It was the horrible uncertainty of her situation that cast so terrible a gloom over her spirits, and lay like a black pall upon her soul.

"I will not, if Heaven will give me strength to resist," she said, "I will not give way, even to the weight of horrors that now oppress me. It is a duty I owe to others, and to myself, to resist, and I will do so,"

With these feelings she rose from the chair, into which in the agony of her spirit, she had cast herself, and commenced a more careful examination of the room in which she was than she had before made. Indeed, her former glances about it had been more with reference to the peculiarities of it as an old fashioned apartment, than to its capabilities as regarded an escape, but now she turned all her attention to the proposition.

CHAPER XXXII.

THE ATTEMPT TO MURDER MADAME ZADZED.

WE must now return to little Lucy, whom we left with great reluctance in the hands of the ferocious, and most unscrupulous Madame Zadzed.

What was the object of this abduction of so innocent and inoffensive a young creature as Lucy, by such an intriguante, will soon develope itself, but from the pains that had been taken to get possession of Lucy, it was sufficiently evident that that object was considered to be one of great importance indeed.

When the door of the large house was closed upon the insensible form of Lucy, it seemed indeed as if all hope and joy were closed against her, and as though she was taking an eternal farewell of all whom she held dear, That state of insensibility into which she had fallen, was at the time a most happy one, for if she had retained the power to think, her feelings must indeed have been acutely sensitive.

In that house every !one appeared to be completely subservient to Madame Zadzed, and the deference that was paid to her was of that slavish character which at any opportunity, always turns into defiance.

Lucy was carried up stairs to a chamber upon the second floor, and then in an imperious voice, Madame Zadzed demanded to know where Swam was.

The reader will probably recollect that Swam was the euphonious name of Madame Zadzed's maid of all work, who did whatever was required of her—for a consideration.

This lady was not exactly visible, and when she did appear there was a certain amount of confusion in her looks which Madame Zadzed was rather puzzled to account for, and this confusion was the more suspicious, inasmuch as she made the most strenuous efforts to hide it from the observation of her mistress.

"What is amiss?" said the latter.

"Nothing," said Swam, "oh, nothing."

"Well, Swam, I must say that I never saw you so agitated in all my life, but, however, I have business of importance at Fulham, and what I have to say to you now is that our future connexion depends entirely upon the care you take of this young girl in my absence. Her detention here is a matter to me of the very greatest importance."

"Very well, madame."

"You perfectly understand then, that upon the safe keeping of this child depends your future fortunes, so far as they are at all connected with me.—Do you attend to me? You seem to be wandering."

"Oh, yes," said Swam, "I attend madame, and I perfectly understand."

"Very well; now get my diamond necklace, and I will be off."

Swam left the room very hurriedly to obey this order; but, instead of getting the diamond necklace of Madame Zadzed from her dressing-room, where it might naturally be expected to be kept, she rushed to her own apartment, and hastily tearing open a trunk, she took, from amid a variety of miscellaneous articles, the necklace.

Then Swam breathed more freely, and in a faint voice she said—

"What an escape! In another five minutes she would have caught me at the door. Oh, what an escape! But am I, after all my plans to rob her and elope, after all to be deprived of the principal article of value I was to take with me? Am I really to surrender this diamond necklace? Oh, no, no—and yet what can I do. I must think. But she must have it now. Yes, she must have it now, and I must think of what to do."

With this, Swam rushed back to Madame Zadzed, and, with as calm an air as she could assume, presented her with the necklace, although her state of trembling anxiety did not escape the penetration of her imperious mistress.

"I shall return, Swam, some time to-night."

"Yes, madame."

"Until I do, you will keep the house close, and admit no visitors."

"Certainly not, madame; in your absence, I make it a positive rule not to allow any one to get past the passage mat. Shall you be late, madame?"

"I don't know. Mind you look carefully to your charge, and, if I am after midnight, you may go to your rest, for then it will be doubtful when I shall be in."

With these words, Madame Zadzed clasped the necklace around her neck, and left the house to proceed at once to Fulham, where we know such strange and horrible scenes were enacted at the villa of the despicable Lord Battaney.

What occurred there the reader is already acquainted with, so that we need not follow Madame Zadzed to the villa, but on the contrary, leave her to proceed alone upon her wicked enterprise, while we take cognisance of the conduct of Swam, with whose nefarious projects we are already slightly acquainted.

For some short time after Madame Zadzed had left the house, Swam paid no sort of attention to poor Lucy. She was profoundly silent too, and seemed to be in deep cogitation concerning what she should do next.

A single knock came upon the street door, and Swam uttered a scream. At the same moment Lucy chanced to recover from the swoon that had come over her, and stretching out one of her arms she touched Swam upon the shoulder, conveying to the vivid imagination of that lady, an impression that the evil one himself was about claiming her as his due, somewhat earlier than she had anticipated.

"Murder! Oh! murder! fire!" cried Swam.

"It's the doctor, mum," said a servant popping her head in at the half-opened door of the room.

Swam gave a sigh of relief.

"Oh, the doctor," she said. "Mr. Carter, you mean; pray bring him here."

The individual who presented himself as the doctor, deserves some description at our hands, and rogue as he, is he shall have it, for such persons ought to be held up as beacons to the unwary not to approach the treacherous shoals of their companionship.

Imagine a tall gaunt-looking man, with a heavy sand-coloured and chalky complexion—a head of hair like the back of some hog with the mange, and little grey eyes that had about them a look of cunning which made up the sum of the intellect of the animal, and you have a tolerable portrait of the doctor who came to hold a consultation quite extra-professional with Swam.

"Oh, it's you," she said.

"Yes—yes," replied the learned personage, rolling his tongue about in a singular manner, and occasionally gasping and pausing in his conversation like a cod-fish in convulsions. "Yes. Is it not disgusting to be treated as I am. Here I have paid a man £367 2s. 2½d., and he sues me then for £447 11s. 10¾d. I have been all my life as you know, scheming to live upon other people, and raising money by all sorts of manœuvres, and now is it not disgusting, after as I have just said, paying £242 9s. 3¼d."

"You said a different amount just now," said Swam, drily.

"No. I'll explain to you. You know that some people call me a humbug—you know I have been kicked, and you know I have been pumped upon—now I am actually disgusted when anybody wants to be paid. But to come to the point, are you prepared to fly with me. Just look at this writ, is it not positively digusting to be made pay £567."

"Peace!" cried Swam. "Will you never get sufficient control over yourself to avoid lying to me?"

"Lying—I lie?"

"Yes, you know it. Hark you, Mr. Carter, we understand each other. You are as great a scoundrel and as crafty a villain as ever lived; you are a poor adventurer—now, knowing all this of you, I yet choose to fly with you to the continent; but Madame Zadzed has gone out——"

"Well—well——"

"With the diamond necklace upon her neck."

"The devil! It is worth five hundred pounds!"

"It is—it is, and, therefore, the question occurs as to whether we shall go off without it or not."

"Go without it? Certainly not—you must get it."

"But there will be a difficulty. She will not return for some time. Not until midnight, perhaps, and then I have known her to throw herself on the bed without divesting herself of a single article of her apparel, or any one of her ornaments, and as it is absolutely necessary, for I have all the things packed, that we should be off before daybreak, I ask you what can be done?"

The doctor was evidently somewhat puzzled, but after awhile the colour of his face assumed a strange pallor and he said to Swam, who eagerly listened to him.

"Would you have any objection to cut her throat?"

"Good God!"

"Very likely, but I ask again, would you have any objection to cut her throat?"

"I—I don't know. That is I think I should have no sort of objection to having her throat cut, but I should not exactly like to do it myself. Perhaps you would not have the same objection—Ah! Gracious Heavens!"

The cause of this sudden exclamation of Swam's, was the recollection that Lucy was in the room, and the dread that she had overheard the conversation that had just taken place, almost deprived Swam of her breath at the moment. She could do nothing but point to the little sufferer as she lay upon the bed.

The learned doctor's knees smote each other, and fright imparted to his countenance a ghastly hue. He slowly approached the bed, and looked attentively at Lucy.

"It is all safe," he said. It is all safe. Oh what a relief."

"How do you mean by all safe. Is she dead?"

"As good, for she sleeps soundly."

Swam made an observation too, and certainly to all appearance the young creature was in a deep and dreamless sleep.

Surely it was power given her by Heaven itself, at such a time, to imitate repose so well, for in reality, Lucy had heard all that had passed between the two wretches, who talked so calmly and deliberately concerning the perpetration of a murder, and seemed so nearly to have made up their minds to commit it.

"We had much better," said Swam, "remove from this room. The little brat may awaken. By the bye, I must lock her in, for she is to be taken good care of, it appears, for some reason or other."

"It's very disgusting," said the doctor, "when you are talking of your private affairs, to be overheard in this way, and if she had been awake, I should have felt myself under the painful necessity of giving her throat a squeeze. But, as you say, it is at all events prudent to leave the room, and hold council in some other."

"Certainly," said Swam, "come this way; I really think that something of a bold character must be done, and that quickly, too. Suppose now, we were to wait until she came home, and then —"

The door closed upon the half-uttered sentence, and, pale with fright, Lucy opened her eyes and looked around her with an aspect of such terror, that to see it would have excited compassion in the most callous heart that ever beat in human breast.

,‘Oh, what shall I do,” she said, “what shall I do?”

Fearful then that her voice, although she spoke in a faint whisper, might reach some unfriendly ears, she abruptly ceased speaking, and commenced sobbing bitterly. Never had poor Lucy since that awful moment when convinced of the death of her mother, felt so much of the real agony of woe as now.

At length she rose from her seat, and with trembling hands endeavoured to open the door; but the crafty Swam was too experienced in such duties as Madame Zadzed had now charged her with, to have left a prisoner's door unfastened. Poor Lucy soon discovered, to her dismay, that the door was locked, and that there were iron bars stretching across the windows, which effectually prevented egress that way, even if she had been well enough, or strong enough to attempt it. She again sank down on the chair in dismay.

CHAPTER XXXIII.

HARRY DEAN MEETS WITH A DREADFUL ADVENTURE IN LONDON.

HARRY DEAN was returning to the hotel, wrapped in his own thoughts, and but little observant of the events that were passing around him; though they were of no character to interest him, yet they might, even in the most casual observer, have excited an occasional thought.

The day was waning, and the town had become busy, as if every one was anxious to hurry over the remaining portion of the day, and reach that time which each one calls his own; coaches and vehicles of all sorts were hurrying to and fro, people were walking about as if everything depended upon their own individual efforts to carry the world safely through the day, and insure the moon a quiet rising.

In the midst of all this tumult and turmoil Harry Dean picked his way along as if he heard or heeded not the thronging of man or brute, but yet he was not so entirely withdrawn from the scene in which he moved, as might have been imagined, as will be seen from the following incident, which attracted his observation while it escaped the attention of confessedly more observant men.

Just as he had crossed before a hackney-coach, or what he took to be such, and he had to make several hasty strides ere he could get out of some danger that he ran of being run over by it, but he had scarcely done so before a blow was aimed at the glass of the window, and a slight shriek issued from the coach window.

Harry Dean looked up, the coach was going on at a rapid pace, and the driver was exerting himself to urge his cattle onwards with all the speed they could travel.

He thought he had been mistaken, but the coach turned a corner very rapidly, when the light from a lamp shone across it, and he perceived what he believed to be a struggle in the coach, and then a piece more glass fell from the window, and he thought he could distinguish a cry for help as coming from the coach.

"What can it mean?" he muttered to himself, "they are surely bearing some one away who objects to be carried off."

Then came a strong temptation to know more of a matter that seemed so curious, so full of adventure.

"At all events, I will watch where the coach goes to, and I may be better able to ascertain the intents and objects of those inside than if I caused a disturbance now."

This caused him to hasten up the street after the coach, but it went along at a rapid rate until it reached another corner when he lost sight of it.

He now ran up the street as rapidly as he could, and he reached the corner down which the coach had turned, as it was making another turn—but another short run brought him up in the rear of the coach, and then he paused to regain his breath.

To follow the coach at a run, which he must, would be to attract attention, and that he desired not to do, so after a little consideration he came to the conclusion that it would be better to get up behind the coach, and go with it to its destination.

This was easily done. The coach was now traversing some back streets, where there were but few persons, and the lamps shed but a dim and dismal lustre.

Dean ran behind the coach, and then slowly mounted the footboard behind, despite some good-natured spikes placed to prevent intrusion, and secured himself in his position.

The coach continued its route at the same rate, and Harry Dean could hear plainly the voices of some persons in conversation, and more than once, from the nature of the motions of the coach, he believed a struggle was maintained, but eventually subdued.

This was exciting; but what was to be done? he must remain there without exciting suspicion, or his efforts would be nugatory. He did all he could do to get a peep of the actual state of the case, but he could not do so.

An envious little pad was hanging in front of the glass that was placed at the back of the coach, and prevented his looking in; and though he had a great desire to look in at the side windows, he could not; he feared each movement or attempt to lean over might cause the coachman to turn his head and discover him.

Half an hour had been thus spent when the coach came to a sudden stop.

Harry Dean had not paid much attention as to the nature of the locality where he was going to, or even to that through which he was passing, but finding the coach come to a halt, he began then to look about him.

It was a lonely neighbourhood; the streets ill-paved, the houses old, lumbering and frowning.

"Now then," shouted the coachman, from his box, apparently at the house, but he never stirred from his seat.

Harry Dean got down carefully and quietly behind, and then walked up to the side of the carriage next to the road, and looked in at the window, unperceived by the occupants.

From the hasty glance that he got, he believed there were two men and a female, apparently young, and he dared say she was beautiful too—that was a common speculation, and one which he was justified in making under the circumstances, for all adventures have a pretty girl in them, or where is the inducement to action?

He hastily retreated to the back of the coach, and then listened to the results that were about to follow.

The coach door was suddenly opened, and a man jumped out, and then there was a renewal of the struggle.

"Keep her in, Jack," said the fellow, who jumped out, as he ran up to the door of the house.

"Come—come," said a voice inside, "don't be silly—you're safe; but if you kick up a squall and scratch, you'll make it worse for yourself. I shall be obliged to stuff the handkerchief all the further down your throat. I know the young gentleman loves you."

"Mercy!—have pity, and let me go."

"Aye, when he takes you I will; but not till then."

"My friends will amply reward you. For mercy's sake let me go; you don't, can't surely mean to resign me to so horrible a fate?"

"Horrible, indeed! there's a great deal of nonsense in what you say; and all I can say is that you will oblige me to be unkind. I'm going to give you over to the gentleman as loves you, and

I reckon I shall have a pretty tidy amount of conscience money."

"God help me!" exclaimed the young girl, for such she was, "God help me! for man will not."

"You are right, my dear," said the brutal fellow, with a laugh. "Hilloa! none of that if you please."

She shrieked out aloud now for help, and struggled fiercely in the carriage, and Harry Dean would have rushed to her rescue, but for two considerations, one of which was, that if he interfered while she was in the coach it might be driven on; he must wait till she was dragged out; the other reason was, the man after having opened the door, which was left in the charge of a third, now came down the steps, saying,—

"Let her come, Jack, let her come, confound her, what a row she does make, out with her, that will do, now we have her—now we can carry her up without any trouble."

"Villains, let go," said Dean, coming forward, and as he spoke he dealt one a blow that stunned him, while the other stepped back and let go his hold upon the young girl, who no sooner found herself free, than without a further thought she ran away as fast as she was able.

At that moment, a man from the house rushed down and pointed out to them the flying form, and they made an attempt to follow, but Dean prevented them, and a fierce conflict ensued, in which he received a blow that felled him senseless, and when he recovered, he found himself surrounded by three or four strangers, all the others having escaped upon his fall, and the approach of other persons.

CHAPTER XXXIV.

THE DENOUEMENT OF HARRY DEAN'S ADVENTURE.

It was some moments before Harry Dean came to himself sufficiently to recollect what was the matter, and he muttered only half audibly,—

"Where is she—where am I?"

"Oh," said a gruff voice, "you are safe now, but you had an ugly knock on the head, any how, don't be uneasy.

you'll be better presently. Here, give him more room."

"Where is she?"

"Oh, a she, was it? well now, I thought such a smack must have been given by a man."

"I saw three men run away," said another. "I heard a noise, and I ran here, and seeing three men run away, I stopped here."

"And I," added a third, "a few moments before, passed by a young female who was running like mad—and then I heard the noise and came up."

"Which way did she go," enquired Dean, hastily.

"Why, I met her round the corner, and she went straight ahead, but she went very fast."

No more was said, for Harry Dean thought that the young girl might still fall into the hands of those from whom he had as yet, barely rescued her.

He started off at a quick pace, leaving the people who had picked him up, [behind, looking after him with some amazement, and not quite certain that the blow he must have received had not caused some derangement of his intellects.

However, Dean ran on to the end of the street, and then turned the corner, and seeing nothing but dim lamps, still ran on, not much noticing where he was going to.

When he got to the end of the street he was about to run round the corner of the street at the same rate, but was suddenly brought to a dead stand by violently running against some one, and then in a few moments some one tumbled, and Harry Dean fell over them on to the pavement.

Oh," shouted a voice, "oh, you villain —I'll teach you to commit such a horrible, atrocious assault, young feller; let me get my rattle out, and I'll have a posse of brother officers to seize you and bind you, you are some rebelious radical."

At the same moment the springing of a rattle sounded gratingly in Harry Dean's ears. He was so bewildered for the moment, that he did not know what had happened, or what enormity he had unwittingly committed.

"Hilloo," shouted the same voice, "I've got you, and I won't stir, I'll just remain where you knocked me, and let them see the full extent of the assault. Oh, you're a leveller, sure enough, you're a radical!"

"What do you mean?" inquired Harry Dean, "What do you mean by talking in this way."

"What do I mean.—Why, sure, the meaning's quite clear enough.—You've knocked down one of the conservators of the public peace, and you are a violent radical."

"Good God!" said Harry Dean, his patience being quite exhausted, "what do you mean by calling me a radical, and saying I have assaulted you; does no one ever run against a policeman by accident, but a radical?"

"I'm assaulted, and you shall answer it."

"Well, I've no objection, but I did'nt see you, or I should not have picked out a big man like you to run at."

"What's the matter?—A 59, on the stones? Who's done this—you did'nt fall, did you?"

"Yes, I fell, because I was forcibly thrown down by this man, who has committed a violent assault, my clothes destroyed, and my hat thrown into the kennel."

"Ah," said the other policeman—"he must have a night of it."

"What, you do not mean to say, you will take me into custody, for a mere accident?"

"Accident, you may call it, but I call it something else. Yes, that is a pretty piece of business.—I'm to suffer loss and inconvenience," cried the policeman, "merely because you have an accident. Oh dear, no—I knows a gentleman, when I see's one, and though I don't wish to be hard upon anybody, I must do my duty."

"Yes, my duty is to take you into custody," said the other policeman, "we can't be knocked about in the execution of our duty, for nothing, I can assure you, and one of our men ain't likely to be knocked down by accident."

"The magistrates always inflict heavy fines in such cases, and very rightly too, damage to clothes and person."

"Well, my good fellows," said Harry Dean, "I would sooner give you the fine between you, to save any more bother.—I have not done this on purpose—it was purely accidental."

"I'm afraid the magistrate won't think so, sir. At this time of night, sir, I'm afraid its much worse."

"Well, I'm willing to go to the station-house, if it must be so my character is above impeachment, and I have nothing to fear, but if you choose to accept a crown each."

"I'm worse off than my brother officer, who has not been knocked down at all."

"Do you wish me to commit another assault, to bring him to an equality with you?" enquired Dean.

"No sir, but you may raise me to an equality with him, by making my compensation something more than his—say two crowns instead of one."

This was agreed to, and Harry Dean then quitted the two sharking policemen, and went on his way. It was useless to pursue the adventure further —no doubt now remained but the young girl had escaped, and after more than half an hour's walking, he found himself on the steps of an hotel

CHAPTER XXXV.

KATE IN THE VILLA.—THE DREADFUL VISITOR.

IT seemed to Kate Destern, as if the long weary time that she was doomed to spend in the villa at Fulham, would have no end. Hour after hour certainly sped away, but so slowly, that in the silence and solitude of that room in which she was imprisoned, she could not but shudder at the dim thought, that perchance she was forgotten, and might be left to starve.

This was an idea that each moment gained strength, and when she came to consider that Lord Battaney was probably too much injured by the dreadful fall he had had, to interfere himself actively in the affairs of the establishment, she could not but consider that as an additional reason for believing that such might possibly be the case.

If anything more than another was calculated to nerve her to renewed exertion, for the purpose of obtaining her liberty, such thoughts as these certainly might be supposed to have such an effect.

The only weapon she had with which any effort might be made, was the sword, and although it was, she verily believed, encrusted with the blood of the man, whose frightful and decomposed corpse was to be found in the inner room, she grasped it fairly by its hilt.

If ever, for pure and holy purposes, a sword was in the hands of a human being, that one was in the hands of Kate Destern, for objects that the very angels might have blessed, from out the pure depths of their native skies.

"I will strive," she said, "for freedom, and with Heaven's blessing, who shall tell me that failure will come. Oh, Lucy, my poor Lucy, and you too, Harry, whose faith and constancy I will not injure by a doubt, what must you both suffer in ignorance of my sad fate."

These were thoughts suggestive of the greatest amount of grief, and with some difficulty Kate now resisted the temptation to indulge in a violent outburst of grief, but she did resist it, and was soon occupied in making efforts for her release.

The first effort she made was, to see in what situation the windows were, as regarded external objects. This was a matter of considerable difficulty, for there was not yet sufficient light without, although the morning was rapidly advancing, to make objects distinctly visible. It so happened, however, that the lamp which had been left with her, by him who had acted the part of her jailor, suddenly went out, and then being no longer dazzled by that light, she found she could see much better without.

The principal object that met her gaze, consisted of a tree, the trunk of which and some of the branches grew very close to the window, and offered something like a means of escape, but yet it was a fearful thing to her to decide upon adopting such means.

How far she was from the ground too, was to her quite a mystery, for although to reach the rooms in which she was she had certainly descended some stairs, yet she was so confused altogether by the intricacies of the place that she could not take upon herself to say, on what floor of the building, she then really was.

Abandoning, therefore, the thought of an escape from the window, just at that juncture, she adopted another mode of discovering some means of egress from the place. That was, to strike the walls with the hilt of the sword, with the hope of finding by some hollow rever-beration, a secret means of leaving, similar to the panels, by which she had been conducted from the library.

This search was for a time singularly unsuccessful, but at length, there was a sound returned at one particular portion of the panelling, which con-vinced her that behind it there was a hollow space, and the question arose of how was she to open it.

Surely Heaven must have had its eye of omniscence upon her movements, for at that moment a long pencil of light— the first of the early dawn—shot into the room, and fell upon the ornamental cornice, by the side of the panel she had just been trying with the sword hilt.

The cornice was now as light as Kate could have wished it to be, and at the very first glance she gave to it, she saw a small knob of brass which certainly had no sort of connexion with the ornamen-tal matters around it.

To press upon this knob forcibly with the hilt of the sword, was the work of a moment, and at the instant that she did, a tall narrow door in the wall sprung open inwards, and so suddenly and violently too, that she was nearly struck down by it.

What was her horror though, when there stepped through the opening, and into the apartment, a man with a strange smile upon his face. It was the physician, who had so recently extracted so large an amount of money, from the fears of Lord Battaney.

Kate's heart sunk within her, as she staggered to a chair, into which she sunk, with a feeling as if hope itself had fled for ever from her.

The stranger was silent for a few moments, during which he observed her with a scrutiny that was positively pain-ful, shifting his position now and then too, in order too get as much of the light as possible upon her. Had he been about to paint her portrait he could not have been more solicitous to obtain an accurate idea of her form and features.

At length he spoke—

"It is so," he said, "I feel that it is so."

Kate looked at him in silent wonder, mingled with terror.

"What is your name?" he said.

There was a something in his tone, which was more conciliatory and friendly than anything she had heard, since she had been in that house, and she replied to him.

"My name is Kate Destern; oh, save me from this place, if you have the power so to do."

"Destern, Destern!" he repeated to himself, thoughtfully, as if trying if he could fish up from the depths of his memory, some remembrance of the name, but paying no attention to her appeal, to be rescued from the dangers that surrounded her.

"Destern! Destern!" said he, again. "'Tis strange I never heard the name."

"Have you no pity?" said Kate.

"Pity?"

"Yes. Oh search your heart, and if there you find one spark of that heavenly feeling, fan it, I pray you, into a flame for me."

The physician still regarded her with a fixed and earnest look. After a time then he spoke to her, and even his usual cold and callous indifference appeared to be much overcome as he did so.

"Girl," he said. "You know not what you say. You know not to whom you appeal. Tell me, have you any very early recollections."

"Yes—yes."

"What are they?"

"I seem at times as if I remembered strange costumes, and many boats, and much water, while the sun of a warmer clime fell upon my brow."

The physician drew a long breath, and paced the apartment, muttering to him-self,—

"God, it is true."

Then suddenly pausing, he cried, sharply,—

"And so Madame Zadzed told you to say this, which you know to be untrue. Forgive me, that look is sufficient, I am sufficiently skilled in that panorama of passing thoughts, the human face, to read it with tolerable distinctness. You have only spoken as you feel."

"And you have but done me justice," said Kate.

"What are your feelings and opinions regarding Lord Battaney?"

"Dread and abhorrence."

"He is struggling betwixt life and death."

"Heaven have mercy upon him."

"Humph! Heaven will need have abundance of charity and mercy to look with calmness upon the deep iniquities of such a man as Battaney. But that is beside your present purpose. You wish to leave this place, and you may, upon one condition."

"Oh, name it—name it. If it be possible——"

"Possible? nothing is more easy. Look at me. I do not pretend to be an Adonis, but I have that within which passeth show. I am a man before whose intellect the high and mighty have bowed down, I was poor, but a fortune has come into my grasp, and I can, at all events, promise you competence, until you can give me wealth. What say you?"

"I do not understand you."

"Be mine, and there is no power in this place to detain you another moment within its walls."

"Oh, horror—horror."

"You refuse me?"

"Refuse you. Oh, sir, you are but trying the patience of one who here is shut out from all friends, and from all hope. There are those in the great world without this prison, for a prison it truly is, who would with their lives stand between me and all wrong. If gold be your object, I cannot promise it to you, but that which is more golden than gold, the gratitude and the prayers of the innocent you shall have, if you will exercise that power which you say you have, and save me from the horrors of this place."

"I have placed the means within your grasp, and you have refused them. The consequences of your own obstinacy be upon your own head."

He made a movement to leave the place, and Kate again gave herself up to despair. She sank to the ground, and as she did so, her hand touched the hilt of the sword that she had in her sudden terror at the appearance of that callous and cold-hearted man, dropped to the floor of the apartment. A notion at once took possession of her, that she would not perish without one noble effort for freedom, and springing to her feet, rushed forward with the weapon pointing at the breast of the physician.

It was only by suddenly darting aside, that he escaped the point, and Kate then at once passed him through the panel door in the wainscot.

Staggered as he had evidently been at first, by the sudden courage displayed by Kate, the cool, calculating man whom she had to deal with, was not likely for any length of time to remain inactive, and accordingly, in another moment he darted after her through the panel.

The passage was very narrow, and very dark, and it was fortunate for Kate, that she still retained her hold of the sword, as without doubt, it was now her best friend. She heard by the sound of the footsteps of her foe, that he was rapidly gaining upon her. In a loud and imperious voice, he likewise called to her to stop in her swift career.

There was but one resource, and she adopted it. That was to turn abruptly, and present the sword against his further progress.

It was his own act that he ran against the point of the weapon, and received a really serious wound. With a cry of pain, he drew back. Kate still retained her hold of the sword, and thus rushed onwards in the narrow passage, she knew not whither.

All she wished at this moment, was that she might be permitted to escape from the man whose style of conversation had sufficiently shown how callous he was to all gentle impressions, and for several minutes she certainly rushed along the passage in which she found herself, with a want of caution that might have exposed her to much danger.

This hurry and excitement of her feelings was not, however, likely to last long, and after a few more moments had sped by, she paused to breathe.

All around her was darkness of the most profound character, and she had not the remotest notion of where in the villa she was, nor did it seem to her that she was near to any means of outlet from that singular channel of communication within the solid wall of the building.

That it led, however, to some apartment, was sufficiently evidenced by the fact of her having had a visitor by its means, and she therefore determined to pursue its labyrinths with patience and perseverance. She had the sword, too, which had already proved itself to be so servicable, so she did not fear so much as though she had been without such a companion.

How strange that so gentle a being as Kate Destern should be compelled to rely upon a sword as a friend in the hour of her adversity and distress!

A faint glimmer of light at some distance in advance of where she was, came upon her observation, and in a moment the knowledge of its existence fell like a blessed harbinger of hope upon the heart of Kate.

"I shall be free!" she said. "Oh, yes, yes. I shall surely be free at last!"

Hurrying forward to where the light showed itself, she soon came to the spot from whence it proceeded, and which she found to be a number of perforations apparently in a wall. The real fact was, that in the depths of some ornamental panel work on the other side, holes had been cut, so that air and light both were freely admitted to the secret passage.

The means of opening the panel were very perceptible upon the side of it next to the passage, and after listening for a few moments to assure herself that all was still upon the other side, she touched the spring, and a similar door flew open to that by which she had entered the secret passage.

What was her terror to find herself in a superb bed-room, where somebody lay slumbering upon a bed with the curtains partially withdrawn. To discover who the shape was, however, was a matter of the most intense curiosity to her, but she almost fainted upon the spot as she recognised the pale and ghastly features of Lord Battaney.

"Gracious Heaven!" she exclaimed, "how horrible is the chance which has brought me into the presence of my worst enemy. Should he awaken, I am lost indeed."

Scarcely had these words passed her lips, than she heard the sound of footsteps hastily coming from the direction of the staircase without. There was but time to conceal herself behind some of the massive drapery of the bedstead, before the chamber opened and her late visitor with his face more pale than before, and his dress about the region of the breast spotted with blood, entered the room.

There was a slight stagger in his gait, as though he had either recently partaken of some strong stimulant, or was faint from the wound which he had received at the hands of Kate. She did not observe until he actually came close to the bed, that he had in his hand, a sword, not much unlike that which she carried, and still held firmly by the hilt.

"I will have my revenge," he said. "Yes, I will have, by one blow, my revenge uopn both.—I will take the life of him whom I have often wished to dash into the grave, but never yet wrought up my mind fairly to kill, and it shall seem by the nature of the wound, and the circumstance that this girl will be found in the villa armed, that it is her act. Ha! ha! She scorns me, but she knows not how fearful will be my revenge against her. I will swear I saw her do the deed, after telling her of that secret, which when once she knows it, will harrow up her soul, and make her sigh for death as the greatest boon that can be bestowed upon her.

He raised the sword, and then he paused, as if some feeling of uncertainty had suddenly come over him, and he feared to strike, but it was really with no intention of sparing his intended victim, that that pause was made, on the contrary, he only wished to render his diabolical act more sure.

"I must see where to strike," he muttered.

Then displacing some of the bed clothes, he again raised the sword, and another moment would in all human probability have been the last that Lord Battaney would have known in this world, had not Heaven surely sent Kate to his rescue—she at once appeared from behind the curtain, and lifting up her hand, she cried in terrified accents,—

"Hold! murderer! Hold!"

The sword fell from the paralysed

grasp of the would be, murderer, and he Hegered back to the door of the room.

passed out at it without a word, and fell backward down the stone stairs that led from the lower story.

It was an impulse of humanity that had induced Kate to step forward to preserve the life of one who certainly deserved no consideration at her hands. The wild threat that had been uttered by the physician of mixing her up in the murder was at the instant forgotten.

Now that the room was clear she was about to leave it, when the slumbering man spoke incoherently.

"Help, help!" he said. "There—there she goes down the river. No, no, do not say I drove her to the deed, I offered her money. What could I do but offer her money?"

With a deep groan he turned to the other side, and was silent again.

Wretched—wretched man, who would exchange peace and the lowest lot that ever could set upon poor humanity, for all your wealth, and the lip service that is awarded to your station? There can be no doubt, but that in those sleeping hours visions of past offences against God and man rose up in horrible array before his vexed imagination, making night hideous.

He did not speak again, and Kate turned to the landing of the stairs and listened. All was still in the villa, and she slowly descended, aided by the grey light of morning, which was now gradually diffusing itself over all surrounding objects.

At the foot of the stairs lay the insensible form of the physician, who had either been killed, or so stunned by his fall as not to show any signs of vitality.

Kate passed this object with a shudder.

She found she had now reached the hall, and as no one appeared to obstruct her progress, she opened the door that led into the garden, and passed out on to the gravel path, which wound down to the lodge, when she dreaded to think that better watch and ward might be kept than within the house itself, where all caution appeared now to be at an end.

To pause now, however, would have been positive madness, so without casting a more than a mere passing thought upon the probable dangers that awaited her, she ran for the purpose of making a nearer cut to the lodge across a grass lawn, and was soon in the immediate vicinity of the gothic building, which was inhabited by those whose obvious duty it was carefully to guard that approach to a house which was used for such suspicious purposes.

No one appeared, however, to be stirring when Kate entered the lodge, and she had a hope that she should be enabled to open the small wicket gate that was in the large one, and then let herself out without disturbing any one who might interpose an obstacle to her progress.

It was a moment of great anxiety—she saw that a large key was in the lock of the small wicket gate, and that a bar was likewise placed across it, and those two comprehended all the fastenings. There would be no difficulty in undoing them, provided she met with no opposition.

Approaching the door, therefore, she first essayed to remove the bar, and the only obstacle to her succeeding in doing that easily and effectually, consisted in the state of agitation she was in. That, however, was in some measure to be counteracted by proceeding without any hurry.

The bar was fairly removed, and Kate breathed a little more freely in consequence. Nothing now remained but the turning the key in the lock, and she was about to do that, when the door of the lodge opened, and a coarse, masculine looking woman appeared, with a mop in her hands, which she gave two or three twirls to, before her eyes fell upon Kate.

At first she seemed so transfixed with astonishment, that she was incapable of saying one word, but that state of feeling was but momentary, and she then called out lustily,—

"Simon! Simon! Here's somebody getting away. Simon, I say! Come, my dainty madam, this won't do here. You thought you would be off, did you? but it's as much as our place is worth to let you."

"Stand back," said Kate, "as you value your life."

The sight of the sword awed the woman. The moment was advantageous— Kate turned the key and took it out of the lock. The wicket-gate lagged lazily open; to pass through it, and to lock it on the outer side, were the events of a moment. Then she ran until she neared the high road, when the sight of a cluster of cottages at a short distance gave her hopes of immediate succour.

"Free! free! I am indeed free at last!" she exclaimed.

The rapturous feeling that came over her at the thought of soon clasping to her heart those whom she held most dear, almost overcame her.

CHAPTER XXXVI.

THE DREADFUL NIGHT AT MADAME ZADZED'S HOUSE.

LUCY soon partly recovered from the state of terror in which she had been thrown by the awful conversation she had overheard between Swam and the doctor her admirer ; and now she thought she heard a hasty footstep approaching from the outside ; the footstep ceased, and then, while she sat transfixed with terror, she heard the voice of Swam, on the outside, saying,—

"I tell you, I have my suspicions, and I would sacrifice a thousand such brats rather than run any personal risks."

"No doubt you would," replied her male companion, "and so would I, but I tell you as positively that she, was asleep, and that there is no danger. If there were, I would be as forward as you could possibly be, to put her out of the way. Do you think, I am in love with a halter ?"

"No—but——" '

"Pshaw ! You are full of the fidgets to day. Go in, and satisfy yourself."

At this, Lucy, although half dead with fright, managed to have power and presence of mind enough to scramble on to the bed again, when she lay perfectly motionless, with the one exception that her heart beat so rapidly, she feared it would betray her consciousness.

The door was unlocked, and both Swam and her admirer came into the room.

"Now," said the latter, "look at her."

"You are right" said Swam, "she has not stirred. How nervous I am to be sure—and yet——"

"Yet what ?"

"I am confident she did not lie upon that side when we were here before."

"Do you think so ?"

"I am sure. Come this way."

Swam led the way to a window, and then, in a low tone she conversed for some moments with her companion, who suddenly said,—

"Very well, you can try the experiment. Of course it is better to be on the safe side always. I have no objection to that, of course."

"I thought you would not. You know how much we have at stake. Life, liberty, and fortune."

"Ah, to be sure. Try it. Try it then."

"I will."

Lucy was much 'terrified. The uncertainty of what it was they thought of trying, and the fearful doubt of whether it any way concerned her or not, awakened in her breast the liveliest fears—she had not long however to wait, for a solution of the mystery contained in the few brief words that had passed, between Swam and her admirer, the doctor. They both approached the bed.

Swam laid her hand upon Lucy's shoulder, and shook her, exclaiming—

"Come wake up, wake up. You have had quite sleeping enough, now, I'm sure. Wake up, will you ? I want to speak to you."

Lucy had no resource but to arouse herself, and she looked fearfully in the face of Swam, who when she saw that she was attended to, added—

"Since quite by accident you have overheard what we have been saying, about the jewels, I don't want you here in the house any longer, and if you will promise me not to say anything of what you know, you shall go away whenever you please."

The promise of liberation was sweet indeed to Lucy, but she was upon her guard, and the acute perception of the child, was sufficient to cope even with the cunning of such persons, as were opposed to her—she felt perfectly sure that they only wished to ascertain, if they had been overheard.

"If you will let me go," said Lucy, "I will thank you."

"Yes, on account of what you have heard."

"I cannot hear in my sleep."

"Oh, nonsense. About the diamond necklace I mean."

"Diamond what ?"

"There," said the doctor, "I told you so. She knows no more, than that bed-post ; now come away. It is quite as well as it is, and better too."

"I am satisfied," said Swam, but I was not so before, and at any rate it is far better to be quite certain of the ground you are upon in these affairs."

"Oh, of course, nobody disputes that. Come on."

They both left the room, and Lucy was once more alone, and a prisoner, for she heard the door double locked by them, before they left it.

Lucy burst into tears. Never until then, had she been at all familiar with the aspect of evil, in its most hideous form, as it was exhibited by those who had just breathed, as they thought, in her unconscious ear, the project of their villany.

From what she had heard, she could scarcely bring herself to doubt for a moment, that the intention was to murder Madame Zadzed, for the purpose of possessing themselves of that diamond necklace, which was the object of their cupidity.

And yet what was she to do? How was she, completely shut up from all aid, and with her small power to interfere in any effectual way, for the prevention of the frightful crime. It was true that this Madame Zadzed, who was thus threatened with death, was her, Lucy's, worst enemy, but all that was forgotten in the sense of unmitigated horror, with which the young creature regarded the crime that was meditated.

She lay upon the bed sobbing bitterly, as though her heart would break.

The tears of children are, however, of but short duration, and she was not doomed to shed many upon that occasion. Young as she was, the conviction that she ought not to lie there idle, when any one was threatened with so much mischief, came over her, and she soon dried her tears, and asked herself anxiously what she should do.

This was a question, however, much more easily asked than answered, and after Lucy had addressed it to herself a hundred times, she found herself quite as far from a solution of it as ever. But yet it perpetually pressed itself upon her attention, while the hours were rapidly passing away, in which if anything could be effectually done it was absolutely necessary to do it.

But Lucy was really powerless, and hence was it that at the end of her thoughts upon all the possibilities and probabilities of the affair, she found herself as far off as ever from arriving at any satisfactory conclusion.

Escape was out of the question. She rose and tried the door, but it was quite fast, and the window was far from the ground, and likewise at the back of the house, so that it was quite out of all likelihood that any alarm she might attempt to give, would end in any other way than exciting suspicion against herself, and producing, perhaps, her destruction.

"What will become of me. Oh, what will become of me," she exclaimed.

The pangs of hunger, too, now began to be pressing, and she looked in vain to the door, with the hope that it might open and bring her some relief. No one appeared, and poor Lucy approached the dressing table, and poured some water from a decanter that stood upon it.

As she did so, she observed a small drawer partially open, in which were some oranges, and these furnished her with a simple but agreeable repast. She would not have chosen aught else at that moment of anxiety and apprehension.

Much refreshed by what she had taken, Lucy found herself better able to think of what was the probability of her being able to render Madame Zadzed assistance, and she came to the conclusion that although dangerous to herself, her only plan would be at once to tell her when she saw her, what had passed, and that she should see her when she came home, Lucy did not entertain a doubt. What the time was, she had not the remotest idea, although darkness was now rapidly gathering around her.

The night crept on, and at last, Lucy could no longer distinguish the various objects in the room, and she was afraid to leave the bed for fear of making a noise by running against some article of furniture, and so possibly give an alarm to Swam and her companion in iniquity, the professional gentleman.

The hours now really appeared, as far as poor Lucy was concerned, to lengthen themselves into days, and she cried herself to sleep several times, so that her faculties were in anything but a good state, when the flash of a light at the door alarmed her.

She started up from her recumbent position upon the bed, and in another moment she saw Swam enter the room.

"Are you awake, little brat?" was the enquiry.

"Yes," said Lucy, hesitatingly, for she feared that to feign sleep again might be to produce an amount of suspicion she would find it difficult to quell again in the bosom of Swam.

"Oh, very well," replied that lady. "Very well. That will do. Follow me. It is not a very likely thing that you are to be allowed the use of one of the best rooms in the house."

Lucy followed her, and as she did so, she was so full of fears that she could hardly move across the room. The possibility that after all, the suspicions of Swam were sufficiently awakened to induce her to take her, Lucy's life, came across the fancy of the child, in all its horror.

Such, however, was not the intention of the waiting-woman. Even the most hardened wretches have a shuddering deslike to take the life of a child, and so far from there being any positive proof of a knowledge on the part of Lucy dangerous to the interests of Swam, she only sought to remove the young creature more out of her way than she now was.

Lucy was pushed into a room adjoining that in which she had spent so long, and so weary a time, and the door was closed upon her. The moment that it was so done, however, Lucy saw streaming in from a small hole in the wall, whence a knot in the wainscot had been removed, a bright pencil of light.

She found that by kneeling on the bed she could see well enough into the chamber from which she had just been taken. Curiosity chained the child to the spot, and she saw certainly enough to curdle the blood in her young veins.

In the course of a few moments, Madame Zadzed entered the room in full dress. She was evidently much agitated, and she turned to Swam, who followed her closely, and spoke in a harsh voice.

"Where is the young girl?"

"In the next chamber, madame."

"Oh very well, I shall not want you."

"Good night, madame!"

"Good night! There, there go away, do. Did I not say I should not want you. Go away."

Swam left the apartment, and Madame Zadzed then went to a drawer and took out a small bottle and a lump of sugar.

"The friendly opiate," she said, "must be had recourse to to make me sleep. Without it I should taste no repose. Oh what a day of horror this has been."

She saturated the sugar with the laudanum, and then flinging herself upon the bed without undressing, she fell into a deep sleep.

In another minute the door opened, and Swam appeared, followed closely by the doctor, who had in his hand a large knife.

They approached the bed, and then Swam spoke.

"She is fast asleep. Do it—do it at once."

"I—I—yes—yes. Why don't you take the necklace? I—I shake so."

"There, I have taken it. Now do it—stop, I will hold a basin for the blood. Who knows but it might make its way through the floor and alarm the colonel below."

"A good thought; but—but——"

"But what?"

"Is it quite absolutely necessary to do the deed?"

"Necessary? Of course it is. Do it at once, and don't stand trembling there. I thought you had courage enough for anything."

Swam held a washhand basin close to the edge of the bed and the doctor came quite close to the slumbering form of Madame Zadzed. He turned up the cuff of his right hand; he shook like an aspen leaf, and then, with one frightful gash, he dashed the knife into the throat of Madame Zadzed.

There was a groan, a half stifled scream, and a brief struggle; after which nothing was to be heard, but the warm blood gurgling like water into the basin which was held by Swam.

*   *   *   *

Absolute horror froze up the faculties of poor little Lucy. The dreadful scene she had witnessed was enough to make such an impression upon her young imagination, as to drive her to madness. It was a mercy that there was strength of intellect enough in the child to prevent so awful a consummation, but that strength of intellect made her sufferings, at being the spectatress of such a scene, most frightfully acute.

We cannot say that it was a result of anything in the shape of reflection which kept Lucy silent and quiet while the dreadful murder was doing. On the contrary, all sense but that of seeing appeared to have deserted her, and she was so absolutely stunned with horror, that to have moved or spoken, even if her own life had depended upon so doing would have been far beyond her powers.

She felt as if some hideous night-mare were set upon all her faculties, and upon all her senses save that one of sight, which it would have been a thousand mercies at such a time, to have had merged in the general stagnation of mind that had come over her.

But now the deed was done, and the awful perpetrators of it were conversing in whispers in the room, which to them was certain to be a remembrance of such horror, that better had they each gone to death by the most terrific process the human mind is capable of fathoming, than have laid up for themselves such store of human suffering.

"Are—you—sure," gasped Swam.

"Sure of what," said her companion.

"That—that she is quite dead."

"Pho! She has had enough to kill a dozen. She will never draw breath again, but come away now at once, don't stand trembling there. Come away I say. Every moment is of vital importance to us now. What are you staring at?"

"Nothing—nothing."

"Come on then, unless you wish to stay and be hung."

"Oh, no, no. Do you think the girl heard nothing."

"What could she hear if she slept, and if she had awakened she could not have withstood screaming if she had heard what we have heard to-night. Come along, will you."

They left the chamber together.

CHAPTER XXXVII.

THE TALE OF WOE.—THE REFUGE OF KATE.

KATE when she caught sight of the cottages as related in a former chapter, had been misled by her feeling of exultation at her escape, and imagined that those lowly abodes of peace, were much nearer to her then they were in reality. The truth was, that unknown to her a considerable extent of ground, including more than one deep ravine, intervened between her and the roof where she hoped to find shelter.

Under ordinary circumstances the distance would have been but a trifling obstacle to Kate's restoration to perfect liberty, but she had advanced but a short distance into a field which she thought to cross as a nearer path to the cottages, when she heard the shouts of rough voices in the distance, which she justly supposed to proceed from persons in pursuit.

Such was indeed the case, for no sooner had the woman at the lodge recovered from the fright, into which Kate with the sword had thrown her, sufficiently to regain the use of her tongue, than she commenced a series of alarms with that organ, such as "fire—murder—thieves," and so on, which ceased only on the appearance of her husband, and another male domestic, armed with a pitchfork and spade, the only weapons at hand.

To their enquiries what was the matter, she declared that the fine young lady to whom their master had taken such a fancy, but whom she firmly believed to be a highwayman in disguise, had appeared before her with a tremendous long sword, and a pair of pistols, and after terrifying her nearly out of her senses with the most bloodthirsty language, had vanished in some mysterious way, but whether by the wicket or over the wall she was quite unable to say.

Great was the dismay of Simon on learning the disappearance of the prisoner, as he knew that the consequence would probably be his instantaneous discharge from his situation; and his apprehensions appeared to give no less delight to Geoffrey, his companions, who doubtless calculated on stepping into the berth that would be vacant on Simon's dismissal.

Simon, however, roused himself speedily from the stupor that for a moment or two overcame him, and with an oath, and a blow to his wife that sent her sprawling on the ground, he sprang out at the gate, and was followed at a sharp pace by Geoffrey.

On they went, and by a terrified glance that Kate ventured to take, she perceived that they had taken a road which appeared to diverge from the way she had adopted, and she judged that their design was to intercept her by some means before she could reach the cottages.

Hurrying on rapidly she had nearly precipitated herself down an exceedingly high and nearly perpendicular bank, at the brink of which she suddenly found herself. It was covered with bushes and shrubs from top to the bottom, but so lofty was it, that nothing but the most pressing emergency would have led the young girl to attempt the descent. The road lay at the bottom, winding from the distance behind, and on the opposite side progress seemed shut out by a similar acclivity. The road had in fact many years since been cut between the two steep banks, and the ruffians who pursued Kate had taken the more circuitous but easier path, calculating on her being to a certainty stopped by this dangerous ravine.

But Kate beheld the cottages in view, now only divided from her by those hills; liberty and honour were the prizes she had to secure; and first throwing the sword to the bottom, she at once commenced the perilous descent.

Clinging to a shrub here and a branch there, while her tiny feet found sufficient hold on projecting pieces of wood and stone, she safely descended a part of the face of the hill, when a branch which she had clasped, gave way in her hand, and she fell a considerable distance. Her dress, however, catching in first one obstacle then another, helped to break her fall, and when she alighted on the ground, she thanked God fervently, that though scratched and torn, and partly stunned and much shaken by the concussion, she had suffered no very serious injury.

Picking up the sword which lay at her feet, she darted across the road, and finding less difficulty then she expected in ascending the opposite hill, she had time to envelope herself in the foliage that thickly studded it, before her pursuers arrived at the spot.

They evidently expected to find her lifeless or maimed at the foot of the bank; for they stopped near the spot where she had descended, and scratched their heads in rustic amazement.

"Missus said she wur a highwayman," ejaculated Simon, "but dang me if I don't think she be the devil himself. I know I could not get down the bank in double the time."

"Well, down she is, somehow," said Geoffrey, "and if we stand here we shall never overtake her."

They then set off down the road, at the top of their speed, and Kate with again reviving hope made her way to the top of the bank.

She hastened towards the cottages, which were at no great distance ahead of her, hoping that the inmates would have arisen by this time, but after looking about her for some time, she felt that she stood alone, the inmates of the cottage had not yet arisen.

She looked up at the windows, but all the curtains were down, and not a chimney betrayed a sign of smoke—no fire had yet been lighted.

Had there been the least sign of a single person being up, she would have asked admittance, but there was none, and she hardly liked to knock them up. Kate was irresolute, she was divided between fear, and a disinclination to disturb others on her own account.

"I would they were up," she muttered, "I could then remain, and claim their protection, but I will wait or walk on; should I be in any fresh danger, then I can do that which I am not willing to do now."

She turned her footsteps towards London, when she was suddenly arrested by the sound of wheels and bells, and looking back, she saw a waggon coming towards her, and she determined to pause until it came up.

If I can but walk onwards by the side of the driver, it will be a protection; perhaps, he will not deny me permission to rest in his waggon.

She was very tired and exhausted. She tottered, and sunk by the roadside, where she was compelled to sit down, being quite unable to stand.

Her excitement, want of rest, fatigue, and fears, produced a state of feeling, that quite overpowered her, and she could not refrain from sobbing aloud.

This hysterical feeling had hardly subsided, when the waggon came up, and before the unfortunate Kate could rise and speak, the waggoner accosted her.

"Ho, lass," he said, "'tis early yet to be about, you are on the road full early."

"Alas!" said Kate, "it is involuntary. I am wearied and tired."

"Where are you going to lass?" enquired the waggoner.

"To London."

"You are ill-harnessed to travel so far."

"Will you," said Kate, "let me ride in your waggon a part of the way? I have no means of rewarding your kindness. I am flying from those who would persecute me."

"Ah, lass, people do persecute one another, but I don't know how it is, there are few so helpless as not to do a good turn or an evil one."

"You will assist me?" said Kate, looking up, "to get away from this hateful place—to escape those who would persecute me—who would destroy me?"

"Yes, lass, get in; Lord help you, I hope your intellects are not wrong, you certainly look as if you were not used to work for a living; you may have escaped from some place where your best friends may have left you."

"No—no, none but my enemies could wish to utterly destroy me. I have fled from no friend, but from real danger, from men who fear neither God nor man."

"Well, lass, you shall have a lift, and that willingly."

As the worthy waggoner spoke, he stopped the team, and then assisted her into the waggon, where she found several other persons.

After sitting awhile her eye lighted upon a poor, but apparently kind-hearted woman, who had with her a younger woman not apparently much over twenty years of age, but whose unsettled gaze, at once betokened a mind ill at eas.

"You, too, are in affliction," said the kind-looking woman, after she had gazed upon the sad and dejected countenance of Kate.

"I have indeed," answered Kate, "and have but little else than affliction before me."

"Indeed," said the good woman. "You are young."

"Yes, but I have seen more misfortune and danger, than perhaps a great many."

"And so have I too," added the woman, and she pointed towards the younger woman, who bore a strong resemblance to her. "She has seen more, too, than I hope you have."

"Indeed," said Kate; and she related much of what had happened to her, and her present state of destitution.

"Well," said the woman, "I am poor, but if you will accept a refuge at my place of abode, you are heartily welcome."

"I thank you," said Kate, "thank you sincerely, I am quite destitute, and your offer is most welcome; but is that a daughter, or a sister of yours."

"My daughter," replied the woman.

"I thought something of the kind, there is a strong likeness between you."

"Yes, she has been a great sufferer, poor thing.—You would hardly believe it, but she was once a lively, active and sharp girl—she is not so now."

"And what can have produced this change?"

"I will tell you. She loved, and believed she was loved by one above her station."

"Indeed?"

"Yes, she was deeply in love, herself, poor girl—she thought there was no guile in the villain—he was all honour and truth—but she was sorely mistaken, and the mistake has cost her intellects."

"Poor thing."

"Aye," said the woman. The man who pretended to love her, but lured her on to destruction——"

"Did you not know of it."

"I knew she was sought, and I placed every impediment in the way of the villain, but he succeeded in winning my Mary away from me, despite all my care and vigilance—he induced her to quit me to make a run-away match of it."

"But you would have consented to a marriage," suggested Kate.

"I would, but he said his family would not, so he induced her to quit me, and run off with him — but his object was gained, when he got her out of the house. However, a fortnight had not elapsed, ere they parted, for Mary being fully convinced of his treachery, she at once saw his unworthiness, and left him, frantic, perfectly mad, and hastened to destroy herself."

"She did not succeed," said Kate.

"She would have succeeded, had it

THE MURDER OF MADAM ZADZED.

not been that aid was at hand. She flew to the banks of the Thames, and scarcely paused a moment ere she plunged into the dashing stream, and was carried rapidly downwards by the tide, but fortunately she drifted close to a cutter, and the rowers saw her.

"With some difficulty they succeede in getting her into the boat, but thed it was longbefore she recovered consciousness.

"Raging with fever, she reached her home, and many weeks passed away, ere she recovered, and then it was found that her mind was gone."

During this melancholy recital the waggon had progressed and slowly reached London. The woman and her daughter, with Kate, sought their humble abode.

———

CHAPTER XXXVIII.

HARRY DEAN'S ARRIVAL AT THE VILLA.

WHEN Harry Dean had read the mysterious note sent to him by Alfred Mayston, and had ascertained that it was no other than Lord Battaney with whom he had to cope concerning Kate, it will be recollected, that by a visit in a certain high quarter, he ascertained the fact of Lord Battaney's actual arrival in London, and then alone set out for the purpose of seeing and confronting that vicious personage.

It would be most premature of us to fully reveal at the present time, why it was that Harry Dean felt so much emotion at the mere mention of the name of Lord Battaney. There are secrets in all families, and although all connected with the personages of our tale will be revealed, it would destroy the reader's interest to be very explicit too early.

Suffice it to say, that Harry Dean thought it expedient to go quite alone to the house at Fulham.

It was quite evident that as he went he suffered much actual agony, and when he arrived in the immediate vicinity of that abode of libertinism, he could not, for a time, control the agitation that came over him.

He paused for a few moments to make one effort to recover his firmness, and then walked on.

There was no lack of firm resolution about Harry Dean. Many a noble and gallant nature will shrink, somewhat to all appearance, as a consequence of the fineness of the intellect, although in reality, that apparent shrinking has no real character of timidity.

Thus was it that from causes known to himself, the spirit of Harry Dean shook as he approached the villa at Fulham.

The difficulty of obtaining an entrance to the house appeared to be no new idea to Harry. Either he had actually experienced it or he had heard sufficiently of the place and its inmates to be aware, perfectly aware, that such a difficulty did exist, for when he came close to the entrance, he took from his pocket a pistol, the stock of which was richly mounted in silver, and ascertaining that it was in good servicable condition, he walked to one of the garden entrances, and knocked with the butt end of the pistol for admission.

No heed was paid to him, and after some moments thought he went to the principal entrance, and rung the large bell that was suspended over it.

This summons was attended to, but not in a way to be at all pleasing to Harry Dean, for instead of the door being opened, only a very small square hole was revealed, by sliding aside a piece of panelling, and a man's face appeared with a surly look of enquiry upon it.

"Well, what now?"

"Open the door."

"What?"

"Open the door, I say."

"Well, that's cool. Anything else?"

"I will fire upon you, if you do not admit me," said Harry, presenting the pistol at the man.

Bang went the sliding panel as the fellow with a brutal oath, cried,—"Fire away."

This was sufficient to prove to Harry that the dependants of Lord Battaney were not be terrified into submission from the outside of the stronghold, and after a few moments thought, he resolved upon not flinging away a shot through a panel merely, so he at once left that part of the buiding, and walked round to the garden wall, again looking for some convenient place at which by a possibity he might be able to scale it.

The wall of that villa, however, was too well provided with impediments in the shape of iron work and glass bottles for any one to wish to run the serious risk of scaling it, not that being the object he had in view, Harry Dean would have hesitated about the matter had no other means presented themselves.

But in this case, climbing the wall, while it was the most dangerous, was decidedly not the most efficient mode of gaining an entrance to the gardens of the villa. We shall see that Harry Dean, to whom concealment was not an object, made a more bold attempt to gain admittance to that well guarded place.

Harry arrived at the small garden door in the wall, at which he had fruitlessly knocked already, he looked about him until he found a large stone, and raising it in both hands, he struck the door so heavy a blow, that although the lock did not give way, the hinges which were much older and weaker did.

The door flew open with a crash.

No one seemed to be on guard at that spot, probably as it was not at all expected that any such violent and determined means were likely to be resorted to to get into the place, and Harry leaving the door open in its half-shattered state behind him, walked at once into the garden.

It was likely enough that the recent startling events that had taken place in the villa had, in some degree, disturbed the regularity of the watch and ward, that, under ordinary circumstances, was kept up within its precincts, but certain it is, that Harry Dean walked some distance without encountering any one to stay his progress, or attempt to do so.

Suddenly, however, he met a man face to face, who seemed perfectly astonished at the encounter.

It was the physician who had had so strange an interview with Lord Battaney, and who, for some reasons of his own, was still lingering about the garden of the house, instead of repairing to town.

In a moment Harry Dean held him by the throat, as he exclaimed in more passionate accents than any one would have imagined could pass his lips :—

"Villain, if I accomplish nothing by my visit here but your capture, I am well repaid for what trouble it may cost me."

"Good God!" said the physician.

"Peace. Call not upon the sacred name of that being, whose commands you have for the term of your whole life outraged. You know me?"

"Ye—ye—yes, sir."

"And you know you have cause to dread me."

"No—no, upon my honour."

"Your honour?"

"Well—I will swear—I will take any oath you like that I am innocent—most innocent. I did not do the deed."

"Liar!"

"Mercy, you will strangle me."

"As you heartily deserve. But the law shall deal with you. You are by far too base for my personal resentment."

A gleam of satisfaction twinkled in the deep set eyes of the physician, for well he knew the laws were knotty, and that if couraged to it, he might, by dint of money, in England, let him be accused of what he may, accomplish much.

"Unloose me from your grasp, then," he said. "If I am to consider myself your prisoner, you need not hold me so tightly."

"On your peril," said Harry Dean, as he let the throat of the wretch go, "on your peril make any attempt to escape. I swear by Heaven if you do that I will shoot you through the head."

The physician seemed to have a due regard for an oath from Harry Dean's lips. He inclined his head in token of assent, and then, after a slight pause, he said,—

"I could, perhaps, be of service to you, sir, if you would permit me."

"No," said Harry with a look of disgust, "I can accept no service from such polluted hands as yours."

"As you please, Sir."

It was no small puzzle to Harry Dean, now to know how to dispose securely of his prisoner after he had caught him, so he stood considering what he should do, while this wily physician watched him with an accurate enough appreciation of his difficulty.

To leave the villa now with his prisoner, and so abandon for some hours the idea of rescuing Kate, was what he could not for a moment think of; yet after achieving the capture of a man, for whom he had been looking for years, and against whom he had most special causes of complaint, as will shortly appear, was repugnant to him.

In this dilemma he chanced to see through a hedge close at hand, on a small plot of ground adjoining, one of the domestic offices of the house, upon which some clothes were hanging to dry. In a moment Harry made his determination.

"Follow me," he said to his prisoner, at the same time pointing significantly to the pistol he held in his hand.

The physician followed in wonder as to what was next to be done.

To take down one of the clothes lines and to return to the shady spot where he had first met the physician was the work of a minute, and then it was that the latter saw that his only chance consisted in Harry Dean not being very expert in binding him; for bound to a tree he saw he was to be.

A little sound sense, however, will often stand well in lieu of a good deal of practical experience, although there are people who hold to the contrary opinion; and the consequence was that after a few minutes, the physician found himself bound so securely and ingeniously to a tree, that his utmost powers did not suffice to permit him to try any chance of escape.

In fact the more he wriggled about, the more he succeeded in tightening some particular loop of the rope that was round his neck, so that after a few moments he thought it prudent to remain quiet, with the hope that some of the household would pass that way and release him.

In the mean time Henry Dean proceeded towards the house.

When he got clear of the shrubbery, in which he was, he came fully in sight of the building, and rapidly advancing, he was going down some steps which led to an open door, when a man with a gun rushed towards him.

Henry paused.

"Who are you?" said the man.

"I decline telling."

"What do you want here?"

"An interview with Lord Battaney."

"Confound your impudence. Go back directly the way you came, or my orders are to fire upon you. Get back, fool that you are to come here."

"Your gun is unloaded," said Henry calmly.

The man bit his lips, and by his manner at once betrayed the truth of what in reality could only be a guess on the part of Harry.

"If it is" he said, the but end will do to knock you down with."

As he spoke he raised the weapon and made a furious blow at Harry, who, however, with admirable coolness and precision stepped aside, and not only avoided the blow, but by a movement of his foot sent the fellow sprawling to the ground.

Enraged at this defeat he scrambled half up, and made another attempt to strike at Harry with the gun, but the latter caught it in his hands, after hastily thrusting his pistol into his pocket.

A fierce struggle of a few moments' duration now commenced, but it ended in Harry getting possession of the gun, and swinging it over his head, he was about to strike the fellow with it a blow which would have put him quite out of the way of being further mischievous, but holding up his defenceless hands, he cried,—

"Spare me, sir, spare me, I have children, oh, spare me!"

Harry Dean lowered the gun and cast it to the ground.

"I doubt, he said, "if ever upon any plea you would have spared me, but God knows I would rather spare than punish. You shall have no hurt from me, although I suppose now you will try to do me all the harm you can as a requital for the favour."

"No, sir," said the man, as he rose and spoke in a strange half elevating tone, "I am a bad fellow, and have always been a bad fellow; but—but—"

"But what?"

"I don't know, sir, how to express myself. I am very like a child now. You have sent my mind back as if to my old mother's cottage, and—and I shall never be what I was again. You might have killed me, sir, as I should have killed you. God help me!"

The rough man turned aside, and covering his face with his hands, he burst into tears.

Harry Dean was much affected.

Approaching the fellow he took him by the arm, and spoke to him in a kindly voice, saying,

"Come my friend, for a friend I am well assured you will be, reckon this the happiest hour of your life, as I shall reckon it one of the happiest of mine?"

"Do not speak to me, sir?"

"Nay, why not?"

"I don't deserve it. You don't know what a bad fellow I have been."

"Well."

"Can you say well to such as I' am, sir."

"Certainly; one of those tears is sufficient to blot out a crime. Come, you have ample time for amendment. At some other time you shall tell me more at large who and what you are; but now, if you will enter into my service, and sincerely serve me, I have need of you."

"Your service, sir?

"Yes; will you follow me?"

" Yes, sir, to the world's end. Is not my life yours? and might you not have taken it once, but spared it. Only tell me what I am to do, and it shall not remain undone for want of trying."

" Very well. Answer me now some questions."

" Any you like, sir ?"

" Is Lord Battanay in the house ?"

" Stop a little," said the man.

He took off his coat and flung it down, much to the surprise of Harry Dean, who began to think he might be going out of his senses. Then he took from around his hat a silver band, and flung it away. The black cockade shared the same fate, and then a couple of half crowns he had in his pocket were flung upon the grass, after which he said,

" Now, sir, that's all I had that was Lord Battaney's. I found my other things myself, and so I give up his service, and feel myself free to answer you. He is in the house to the best of my belief."

" Tell me this, if a young girl has been brought here lately ?"

" There has been a row, sir, but what it was all about I can hardly tell you. I think there was a young person brought here during the night, but you see, sir, I am seldom inside the house. However, the servants told me that Mr. Mayston was all but dead, and Lord Battaney too."

" Indeed, how was that ?"

" I don't know rightly, sir. But if any body knows at all about it, Madame Zadzed does, I am sure."

" Who is she ?"

" That I can't tell you, sir. But she is in all his lordship's secrets, and is always coming and going there"

" Well, I don't see that you can more efficiently serve me just now than by coming this way."

As he spoke Harry led the way until they could see the tree where the doctor was bound, and pointing to him, he added,

" Keep watch over that man until I come to you. By the bye, what is your name ?"

" Clover, sir. Sam Clover they call me."

" Very well. Don't let him escape, Sam, on any account."

" Depend upon me, sir."

Sam Clover walked on at a leisurely pace towards the physician, while Harry Dean, at a quick pace, took his way towards the house where he determined upon seeing Lord Battaney,

---

CHAPTER XXXIX

LUCY'S CONTINUED PERIL.—HER TRIAL OF FORTITUDE.

RETURN we to Lucy, who at the house of Madame Zadzed was a witness to the horrible crime committed by Swam and her admirer.

The deed was done, and through the small hole in the wainscoat Lucy Destern had seen a sight which if she were to live to the age of one of the oldest of the Patriarchs she could never forget.

It was a sight which might well

" Freeze her young blood
And make her hair to stand on end
Like quills upon the fretted Porcupine."

For a time she had no power to speak —to move—to pray—scarcely indeed to think whether she was dreaming or awake.

Happily, however, after a time, she did just gather strength enough, to throw herself upon the bed, and drawing the clothes over to feign again to sleep, with the expectations that she would be visited by those who had done the murder, in order that they might assure themselves that she knew nothing—had heard nothing of the awful truth.

A pitchy darkness was now around her, for that room at all times was a dark one, and as she lay there alone and friendless, who shall say what direful thoughts crossed her agonised mind, and what fearful sufferings her excited imaginations gave birth to.

Alas that one so young, so guiltless, so innocent, should be made to feel such a night of woe in being the enforced spectatoess of a scene calculated to harrow up her soul, and to make a lasting impression of horror upon her.

She wept, and then she dried her tears lest they being perceived might lead to the supposition that she knew all, and then she listened until listening became a positive pain, to hear it any footsteps approached the chamber.

Some time—how long poor Lucy had

no means of judging, thus passed away, and no one came to break the solitude of the place. At length, after many false alarms, she felt quite certain she heard some one ascending the stairs.

The chamber door opened, and Swam made her appeance.

"Are you here child?" she said.

Lucy thought it best to return no answer.

Swam now approached the bed with a light in her hand, and passed it rapidly to and fro before her eyes, muttering to herself as she did so,—

"I think it is real."

Lucy kept with great constancy her eyes shut.

Swam, however, shook her by the arms, saying,—

"Awake, awake."

Lucy looked up tremblingly.

Swam held the corner of her handkerchief to her eyes, saying,—

"You are young and innocent in the sight of God. Oh, pray for me, pray for me, Lucy Destern. It is all I ask of any one in this world. Pray for me."

"For you?" said Lucy.

"Yes. You know what a criminal I am. Pray that Heaven may pardon me."

"I do?" said Lucy.

"For stealing, I have stolen; for swearing falsely, I have done that too, and oh, most of all, for the crime of to-night, which you heard committed."

Swam, as she uttered these last trying words, shaded the candle with her hand, and looked earnestly at Lucy, who bore the searching wonderfully, and after a moment added,—

"Yes, and the crime of to-night. Ah, you know."

"I—oh, who else should know so well? But, perhaps, you will restore me to my friends, and then God may forgive the crime of taking me from them."

Swam was silent for a moment or two and then muttered,—

"If I was only sure."

"Sure of what?" said Lucy.

"Nothing, nothing. Do you sleep well?"

"Yes. I seem as if I had slept a long while."

"Do you dream?"

"No."

"Well child, you must bear your lot with patience."

With these words she left the room, and when she was gone, Lucy rose upon her knees in the bed, and really prayed to Heaven to grant her strength to struggle through the painful scenes that might be awaiting her.

It was strange how both Swam and the wretch who had assisted her in taking the life of Zadzed, shrunk from imbruing their hands in the blood of that child.

Yet their doubts and suspicions that she might know of the murder were so strong, that with a kind of awful fascination they lingered in the house, making perfect experiments upon her strength and constancy of purpose. One moment satisfying themselves, and the next doubting as before.

Surely Heaven was directly acting in this instance, to detain the murderers upon the spot where lay the body of their victim, whose blood was crying out for vengeance.

"What will happen next?" was all that poor Lucy dared ask herself.

That she was not yet at the end of her troubles and trials, a something seemed to assure her; so she kept as before, upon her guard, and would not allow herself to give way to any sudden gusts of feeling which might have the effect of awaking more suspicion still than was already directed against her.

Lucy had cause to congratulate herself upon her foresight.

After about a quarter of an hour had passed away, she heard something in the shape of a confusion at the door of the room, during which a man's voice cried in rough loud accents—

"It's my duty, and I will do it. I'm an officer, and let any one stop me at their peril,—I shall trouble you, madam, to get out of my way."

It was Swam, who replied—

"Indeed, sir, I don't know what you want here. Tell me what you came about, and then there will be no objection."

"Oh, no matter to you," replied the voice. "I am an officer of police—that is sufficient, and have a warrant to search this house."

Lucy's heart leaped within her bosom for joy. Here was succour come at last!

She half rose from the bed to welcome one to whom she could speak freely of what had happened. The door of the room opened, and a man entered, buttoned up to the chin in a huge greatcoat. His countenance was begrimed and dirty, and his hair was black —but hid beneath a corner of the wig, for a wig it was that he wore, the quick eyes of Lucy saw a small portion of the reddish bristling hair of Swam's friend, admirer, and fellow criminal, Mr Carter, the doctor, or pretended doctor.

Her heart sunk within her again, and she thought that now, surely, her death was at hand.

"Hilloa!" cried the fellow, "is there any one here?"

Lucy, with that wonderful tact and presence of mind which throughout all the trying and extraordinary circumstances in which she had been placed never deserted her, at once replied to him—

"Oh, save me, sir—save me!"

"Certainly I will. Of what do you complain? I am an officer, and have many persons outside ready to take the part of any one I wish. You are quite safe now, and have only to tell me of what you complain?"

"Oh, thank you, thank you. Take me away, and I will tell you all."

"You must tell me here."

"Well then, sir, I have been brought here against my will—I have been taken away by those who do not wish well to me or to mine. Restore me to those who love me. Oh, do protect me, sir, I pray you."

"But has anything happened since you have been here worthy of telling? Have you no complaint to make about anything—no story to tell of any one while you have been here? Have you seen nothing—overheard nothing? Remember that you are perfectly safe now, for everybody in this house is in my power."

"No," said Lucy, shaking her head. "I only want to go home to those who know me, and love me."

"Is that all?"

"Yes, sir. I have nothing more to say."

"The fellow looked malignantly at Lucy for a moment, and then he said,—

"Well, my girl, if that is all your complaint, I am sorry I cannot at all interfere with you. If anything had happened here, of which you could have given me an account, of a serious character, I could have taken you away at once, but as it is, I cannot."

Lucy was not blind to the fearfully insidious character of this speech, and had she not been so fortunate as to have discovered the paramour of Swam beneath his disguise, it must have deceived her. As it was, she only replied to it,—

"No, no, I have nothing to say. But surely, sir, the taking me away from my friends is enough."

"Not quite."

With those words he bounced from the room; foiled, probably, but yet not quite satisfied after all that he was safe. Truly for the last two hours, the pure and innocent life of Lucy Destern had hung upon the merest possible thread.

One incautious word or gesture, must have had the effect of at the moment destroying her; and those wretches, who would have taken her life, doubtless, would have lived to console themselves for the actual horror of such a deed by saying, it was a necessary means of self-defence.

But Lucy was once more alone, and there was some comfort in that state of things, for most frightful was the situation of the young creature while she was compelled to be playing a part in the presence of those who were on the wait but for one slip of the tongue or gesture indicative of a knowlekge of the guilt to take her life.

She waited for a time expecting that some other ingenuous mode of putting her to the torture might be resorted to, but no one came near the room, and as the light of day was close at hand, she rose and crept gently towards the window of the room.

She had hoped that this window would look into the street, but it did not. All she saw from it was the back entrance of some house in another street.

As she looked despairingly at this back window, she saw the shutters of it suddenly unfastened, and then the blind drawn up, and then the window itself was flung open.

At the window, where there was a little dressing table and looking glass, appeared a man just finishing his toilet. He was putting on a waistcoat, which he seemed to admire very much, and over that he placed a coat with light buttons, and all the while he whistled to the still morning air as thuogh his spirit was as light as any bird's.

There was a good humourd look about him that made Lucy think that if by any chance she could attract his attention, he would do what he could for her, but how to make him cognizant of the fact that she required help without likewise disturbing her enemies in the house, was for a time beyond her comprehension.

At last a thought struck her, and going to the table, with the writing materials, she wrote upon a large sheet of paper in as large characters as she could frame the words,—

" Murder !—Caution !"

Coming to the window again, she very slowly and cautiously opened it, and then she held up the placard she had prepared.

The man was now brushing his hat, and whistling away with more vehemence than ever. Lucy was in a perfect agony, lest he should go away, as was probable enough, without once turning his eyes in the direction of the window where she was, but yet even to prevent such a contingency as that she dared not call our or even chance making the slightest sound to attract him.

He had scarcely finished brushing his hat and was giving the crown of it a very scientific kind of circular sweep which left a little knowing looking piece of silk perched up exactly in its centre, when his eyes caught sight of the strange placard, and down went the hat on the floor.

Lucy now trembled so, that she could hardly hold the placard at all steady enough for him to read it.

Suddenly he disappeared, but in a moment he came back with pens, ink, and paper, and after some apparent trouble wrote a placard which he held up, and upon which were the words—

" What's the row ?"

Lucy hastened into the room, and nervously prepared another sheet of paper, upon which was written,—

" Save me !"

Upon this, her new friend exhibited these words—

" If it ain't a sell—what's your number."

Lucy shook her head and clasped her hands. The man nodded, and then she saw that he was carefully counting the houses, so that when he came round to the street in which she was, he might be able to pitch upon the one at the back of which he had seen her.

Having thus satisfied himself upon this point, he gave some very energetic words, and shut the window.

Lucy retired into the room again, and flinging herself upon her knees in the middle of the floor, she sobbed and prayed without intermission for many minutes, but alas, no aid ca me t

" He will not come," said she. " He will not come, and I am lost, indeed J shall yet die in this dreadful place."

Hush! Hush ! she hears something, what noise is that? something is moving in the lower part of the house. There is a slamming of doors, and a sound as if of voices in contention. Hope once more unfurls her radiant banner in the heart of Lucy—she listens with breathless eagerness to the increasing sounds of tumult.

" It must be," she tells herself, " It must be that he whom I have asked to help me has come. Oh yes, he did as much as say that he would come, and he has come. They cannot kill him, I shall be free. Oh, yes, I shall be free."

She flew to the door of the chamber with the faint hope that possibly, after the last visit of Swam's accomplice to her he might have left it open, but such a hope was fallacious. He was too cautious a villian for that. The door was fast.

Crash came some sound from below as though a door was suddenly broken open, and then the angry voices were louder than they had been, but as if by magic in a moment all was still.

Lucy could not divine what was taking place. The silence fell upon her heart with a chilling effect. It seemed to her as if hope was gone again with the sounds of struggling that had awakened it.

Despair now got the better of all prudence, and in loud accents Lucy cried,

THE ABDUCTION.

"Help! help! help!"

No one answered her, and she became almost frantic from deferred expectations. Again she raised her feeble voice. Its soft accents penetrated but a short way. She struck and kicked at the door. All was in vain. There was no answering voice, not one cheering sound from below met her ears.

"Lost—lost—lost!" she exclaimed. "Oh, Harry you have deserted me and I am lost like poor Kate."

No. 15.

CHAPTER XL.

THE FALSE CHARGE.

A very short space will suffice to inform us of the further proceedings of Harry Dean at the villa at Fulham. It is a matter of absolute necessity that we, at such a juncture in the fortune of any one should break off for a time, in order to bring the proceedings of Harry Dean down to the same point, inasmuch as he appears again upon the scene in closer connection with her fate.

When Harry Dean said that his meeting with Sam Clover was an ample recompense for all the trouble and danger he had had in making his way into the villa gardens, he fully meant what he said, although he by no means intended to draw any inference which would prevent him continuing his pursuit of Kate Destern.

Whether or not she was yet in the villa was the grand point he wished to ascertain, and that, as we have seen, Sam could not tell him, so that there remained no other resource than to pursue his original intention of enforcing an interview with Lord Battaney.

While he is ascending the steps leading to the open door in the villa we may as well attend for a moment to what is passing between Sam Clover and the physician.

The moment the latter personage w Sam approaching, he seemed at once to think that rescue was at hand.

"Quick, quick, my good fellow," he cried, "quick."

"Oh, it's all right," said Sam.

"You are one of Lord Battaney's men?"

"I was."

"Well, well, never mind; you shall have a guinea if you cut this cord with which I am bound."

"Cannot you wriggle out of it in any way?"

"No; I have tried in vain. By skill or accident, it is so fastened about me that the more I struggle the worse it is."

"You don't say so."

"Come, come, you shall have a couple of guineas if you are quick."

"Humph! a couple of guineas. Well, I'll think of it, and mention it to my master when he comes this way again."

"Your master—who is he?"

"A young man with dark hair, quietly dressed in black, and eyes that seem to look through you."

"Why that's—that's——"

"Who?"

"The very person who tied me up here."

"Well, now, if I didn't think so," said Sam, with a look of well affected simplicity. "He told me I should find a vagabond tied to a tree, and that I was to keep an eye on him till he came back."

The discomfitted physician gave a groan, for he saw that there was little or no chance of escape for him. Still feeling and knowing the omnipotence of money, under most circumstances, and being perfectly sure that he himself was capable of anything, provided he got his price, he began to have hopes, that for a sufficient bribe, the man before him must set him free.

The physician was one of those, who give the most limited and commonplace signification to the saying, that every man has his price.

"Now, my good fellow," he commenced, "of course, we all in this world do the best we can for ourselves."

"Surely," said Sam.

"You serve your master for wages?"

"No doubt."

"Well, you would have no objection I dare say now to fifty pounds all at once, and no one but you and I need be any the wiser for it."

"Go on," said Sam.

"Is not that enough, fifty pounds, I say."

"Go on."

"Well, I'm sure you understand me. Fifty pounds, you know."

"Go on."

"Well, well, if I must be explicit, all I want you to do is to cut this confounded cord."

"Oh!"

"You consent?"

"Well, I don't mind. Will a little piece off the end do?"

The physician saw that there was nothing to be done with Sam, and that by conversing with him, he was only wasting an amount of diplomacy and cleverness which under other circumstances might have made his name famous throughout Europe, or infamous, which is about the same thing."

Sam laughed quietly to himself, and sitting down within view of the man of drugs, he looked at him as though he had been some natural curiosity.

While this little scene was being enacted in the garden, Harry Dean had [successfully made his way] into the villa.

The first room he found himself in was a small one, and there appeared about some traces of recent habitation. A hat was upon a chair, and upon the table was a riding whip. A door immediately opposite the fire place attracted the attention of Harry, in consequence of its being a few inches open, but upon examination he found that it was not a mode of leaving the room, but only a cupboard.

Whe he had the handle of this door in his hand he heard a hasty footstep behind him, and turning on the moment he saw a woman, whose coarse bloated features at once showed their owner's intimacy with the bottle. She had come into the room, through a doorway that Harry Dean had not noticed, and at the sight of him, she seemed to be transfixed for a few minutes with astonishment.

Setting her arms a-kimbo in the true virago style, and giving her head a slight shake from side to side, she said,—

"And pray, sir, may I ask who you are?"

"Yes," said Harry.

"Well, sir, who are you?"

"I decline answering."

"You do, do you? Very well, sir. And pray, what may you want here?"

"I may want many things, but what I do want I likewise decline enlightening your cunning upon."

"Oh, very well, young man, I'll pretty soon put a spoke in your blessed wheel as you won't like."

As she spoke, she made a move towards the door, by which she had entered, but Harry Dean adroitly interrupted her saying,—

"You would make an alarm."

"Well—well."

"I don't intend to permit you."

"You don't intend. You—you permit."

"It's of no use, madam, urging the point, or putting yourself in passion," added Harry, "I tell you most explicitly, that knowing very well you will be a hindrance to me if you can, I intend to take means to prevent you."

The lady drew in her breath as though she wanted to inhale enough to last her a fortnight at least, and then she looked at Harry Dean, commencing her investigation at the point of his boots, and finishing at the top of his hat. But her eloquence could no longer be restrained, and she burst out with—

"You insignificant thin puppy—you measel—you—"

"Madam," interrupted Harry, "at any other time I should be most happy to listen to your compliments, but really just at present I am too busy. Do you see that cupboard?"

"That cupboard?"

"Yes, that one. I have the honour of requesting that you will step into it."

"I—I—"

"Yes, yes, and if you do not at once comply with my request I shall be under the disagreeable necessity of using force."

The lady absolutely reeled back a pace or two, she was staggered at the terrific assurance of Harry Dean, and he feeling quite sure that by fair means nothing was to be done with her, he thought it was better at once to profit by the temporary confusion into which he had thrown her, so, darting behind her, he got hold of her elbows before she was aware of his intention, and accelerating her movement with his foot likewise, she found herself in the cupboard and had the door locked upon her before she knew where she was, or could either utter one word of the many eloquent ones that thronged to her lips.

Harry Dean did not wait a moment longer in the room, but darting through the doorway by which the lady had entered, he hastily ascended a flight of stairs opposite to him, and after passing through a bed chamber, he entered a second, where, upon a bed, lay some one whose deep groans filled the air with horror.

An idea that it was Lord Battaney possessed Harry, and he hurried forward. The first glance, however, convinced him that he was wrong, and yet he knew that form which was smeared with blood. It was Alfred Mayston.

For a few moments Dean gazed upon this man who had worked him so much evil in silence. At length he spoke to him, saying,

"Mayston, do you not know me?"

The half dead wretch looked up into the countenance of Harry Dean, and then a spasm shook his frame. His injuries had been numerous, but not sufficient to put at once at end to his life. He seemed scarcely conscious who it was that spoke to him.

"Mayston, do you not know me ?" again said Harry Dean.

A dim recollection seemed to cover the intellect of the dying wretch, and he said, faintly,

"Yes ; you are a spirit."

"No, Mayston, I am no spirit."

"Yes, yes, yes. I killed you."

"Recollect yourself. You thought to take my life, but you yourself knew well afterwards that you had failed to do so. Remember the letter that you wrote to me. Speak !"

"It is all a dream."

"You do not mean to deny to me the information that you before gave me. Speak ! I charge you to speak ! Is Kate Destern in this house, and if she be not, you no doubt have a guilty knowledge of where she is."

"God help me !"

"God will help you as you deserve help."

"A dream—a dream."

"No, Mayston. Rouse yourself to the realities of your situation. You will have yet time perhaps to do what will smoothen for you the path to a nobler and a better world than this."

"No—no—no."

"I say yes."

"It may not be. Even you dare not forgive me."

"I do forgive you freely."

"Is this possible ?"

"It is true."

"Raise me up a little, and I will speak to you. I think, nay, I know that I am dying. They laid me here thinking that it was a corpse they laid down upon this couch, but after a time, when they had left me to myself, my fluttering spirit came back again."

"To give you time for repentance."

"It may be so."

"Be assured that it is so, and likewise be assured that repentance in its very essence means atonement."

"Alas what atonement can I make?"

"Much—much."

"Say, what you will have of me."

"You can tell me no doubt how I can rescue the innocent girl who was torn from her home to be brought to this place. You can tell me rather whether she is hidden here ; or if removed from here, you can tell me whither they have removed her."

"No—no—no."

"You can—you must."

"Do not raise a storm at me ; God knows I am willing to say all I can. Raise me up a little."

Henry Dean slid his arms under the body of the dying wretch, and gently raised him up, saying, as he did so—

"If so be that your time is short, it is the more incumbent upon you to speak freely to me. Say on—say on."

"Yes—yes, all I know you shall hear. All I know. Give me a little time."

Henry Dean held him up, and listened intently to him. After the pause of a few moments during which he seemed to be suffering great agony he with an evidently great effort, continued—

"You—know—you know Madame Zadzed."

"I have heard of such a person."

"Well—well you know—she—she—"

"Yes—yes"

"The book it was in the hands of the dead—the dead—the hands of the dead, the book was—was

"Go on—on—on."

"Yes—yes—I—I—faint—faint."

His eyes closed, he fell doubly heavy on the arms of Harry Dean who could not be sure if it were death or a mere fainting that had come over him ; in either case, however, it was quite in vain to think of obtaining any further information from him.

Indeed if Harry Dean had taken all the pains in the world to recover him, it is doubtful if by any means Mayston had power to tell him, he would have been repaid for the trouble.

Letting him repose quietly upon the couch, Harry left the room hastily, in search of Lord Battaney, from whom he was determined to wrest the information he so much wanted.

CHAPTER XL.

HARRY DEAN AND SAM IN LONDON.

AFTER disposing of the lady who had endeavoured to intercept him in the manner we have shewn, Harry Dean did not find any one else who was disposed to interfere with his progress through the villa.

He accordingly found no difficulty, in proceeding from room to room, in search of Lord Battaney.

For a time, however, all that search was fruitless, and in none of the numerous chambers that he entered, could he find any evidence of the presence, either of Battaney or Kate. At length, forcing open a door that at first resisted his efforts, he came into a room which was nearly in complete darkness, from the shutters being closed.

By the dim light, however, of early morning, that did manage to struggle into the apartment through crevices, he saw that it was a bedroom, and that a large space was occupied by a bedstead.

His first care was to unclose the shutters.

When he had done so, and brought more light into the room, he found that the curtains of the bedstead were drawn quite close, but he did not hesitate to dash them aside, and then he beheld a sight, which at the moment, gave him a severe shock.

It was to all appearance the dead body of Lord Battaney.

Yes, there lay that bold bad man, apparently in the cold embrace of death. The features were pale and motionless—the lips slightly parted, and the eyes looked fixed and glassy.

"At last," said Harry. "Gone at last. I would that you had lingered yet a space, that I might have forced you to a confession of where you had bestowed her, who in comparison to you, is as a radiant angel to the darkest fiend of all who dwell in that home that is without joy or hope.

He then continued silently gazing for a time upon the features of the dead. After which, as he closed the curtains he said,—

"May Heaven in its boundless mercy forgive even such as thou wert, Battaney. Death compromises all offences, and now notwithstanding the deep injuries that you have inflicted upon me and mine, I forgive you and can pray for you."

Harry Dean then closed the shutters of the room again, for no one more than he was likely to pay respect to the dead, although the dead he now obeyed the observances of society regarding, was that of the worst enemy a mortal man could have.

Aye, a far worse enemy to Harry Dean, had Ld Battaney been, although he, (Harry) id not then know it, than even Mayston, when he had aimed at his life.

In another moment he had left the room, but not to leave the Villa until he should be better satisfied of the fact that Kate Destern was not there.

Standing, therefore, upon the principal staircase, he called her loudly by name, but no response came to him, and after wandering from room to room, and calling repeatedly, he became convinced that she was not in the place. He was about to leave the Villa, when a young woman made her appearance with something of an aspect of timidity in her face, as she came towards him with a wish to speak.

"Do you belong to the house?" asked Harry.

"Yes, sir," was the reply—"I am waiting here for Madame Zadzed's return, and I think from what I have heard you calling about this place, that you come after the young lady who was here?"

"Yes, yes," said Harry eagerly.

"Then she has escaped."

"Are you certain?"

"I am, sir, she has been away from the place some hours. You may depend upon what I tell you, sir."

"I can believe you," said Harry, "for not only is there an air of truth about you, but my own close search in the villa, corroborates your story, I will go, and I can only say, that I wish you a more respectable service than you are in."

"I am forced to be here by my mother, sir."

"And who is she?"

"Mrs. Green."

"I am none the wiser, is she a tall woman, dressed in green silk?"

"Yes, yes."

"Then when I am gone, but not before, you can let her out of a cupboard in the room where there is a large bookcase and a bronze chandelier."

The girl looked rather astonished, but Harry Dean did not wait to have any further conversation with her, b hurried into the garden, to rejoin his new follower, Sam Clover, whom he had left in charge of the physician, and who we happen to know had well performed his trust.

When he came within sight of the tree, he found the physician still tied to it. Sam sitting comfortably enough upon the gnarled roots of another, opposite, looking at him.

At the approach of Harry, Sam rose and touched his hat.

"You must bring your prisoner along," said Harry.

"Certainly, sir."

"Listen to me," cried the physician. 'I will make such a full confession as will place you in a position that——"

"Peace," said Harry, "I will not treat with you. You may say what you like, and here is a witness to hear it, but I will make no conditions."

"Then wild horses shall not tear from me what I know."

"Wild osses," said Sam, "lord bless you, poor creature, we don't do such things here. Come on now, and don't be obstropelous."

Sam untied the doctor, but kept a loop with a running nooze round his neck, saying,—

"Now then, old fellow, if you want to be hung before your time, just try to run away, while I hold the other end of the cord, that's all."

"You will suffer for this," said the fellow.

"Very likely," said Sam.

"Of what am I accused? I won't stir a step, until I know of what crime or offence I am accused."

"Come up," said Sam.

He gave the rope such a jerk as he spoke, that the physician thought it prudent to say no more, but to run on at the pace which Sam himself chose to adopt, and that was a tolerably fast one, as Henry strode on very quickly through the garden.

To say that Harry Dean had at this moment any very precise object in view would be to say more than he himself knew, for after his latter disappointment at the villa, where certainly he fully expected to find Kate Disten, he was like a ship at sea without rudtderor compass, tossed hither and thither at the mercy of every wind that blew and every wave that roared and lashed in the sounding main.

Still London was his object.

But before he reached the metropolis he wished to get rid of his prisoner. Turning therefore to Sam, he said,

"Do you know of any magistrate in the neighbourhood?"

"Oh yes, sir."

"Near at hand?"

"Certainly, sir; quite close. Sir John Newdam lives hard by, and he is a magistrate."

"Very well, take the nearest way to his house."

"This is absurd," said the prisoner. "You cannot really be so foolish as to take me before a magistrate, and so commit yourself by making a charge against me which you must either substantiate or give up entirely, and in either case you seal my lips."

"Go on, Sam," said Harry.

"Yes, sir."

The physician was dragged on despite his remonstrances, and as the cord was still round his neck, he found the great inconvenience of not adapting himself to the pace of his captors, and being by this time tolerably well convinced that all further solicitation or expostulation was useless, he contented himself by muttering curses upon anybody and everybody.

This style of discourse, however, was as little calculated to have any effect upon his audience as any other which he might adopt, and neither Sam nor his new master paid the slightest attention to the torrent of convictions that came from his lips.

Sam stopped at the lodge, advanced to a handsome stone house, and rung a bell.

A man in livery appeared, and then Harry Dean took him aside and spoke to him for a few moments, after which the man touched his hat with great respect, and motioned towards the house.

"I shall not be many minutes, Sam," said Harry. "Remain where you are with your prisoner."

"Yes, sir," said Sam.

Harry Dean had an interview with the magistrate, the result of which was that a couple of constables were at once ordered to take possession of the physician, and convey him upon a remand to the common gaol.

In vain did he protest against [this unconstitutional infringement of the liberty of the subject; he was dragged off, and Harry and Sam were at liberty to proceed without such an encumbrance.

When they reached London, Harry Dean, for reasons of his own, sought out a private lodging for himself, and his new attendant, and then telling Sam to wait there for him, he was absent for the remainder of the day, organizing a mode of search for Kate, which he considered could not fail of finding her or discovering what fate had befallen her in the course of a few days at the very furthest.

It was night when he reached the lodging, and though thoroughly worn out and fatigued by the exertions he had undergone, he soon fell into a deep sleep.

* * * *

It seemed to Harry as if he had slept no length of time, and yet was shaken by his new attendant, who said in a loud voice to him,

"Sir, sir, I'm sure you will excuse me for awaking you when you know why."

"I dare say I shall, Sam; what is it?"

"I must tell you in regular order, sir, if you please."

"I wish I had not gone to bed, Sam."

"Why, it's morning, sir."

"Morning? Impossible!

"Indeed, sir, it is; there, you see, sir, now that I have opened the shutters, it's quite light."

"It is, indeed. Well, Sam, while I dress you can tell me what it is that has induced you to awaken me."

"Well, sir, you must know I sleep in the back room down stairs, and just as I was brushing my hat, intending to take a little morning walk before you got up, I happened to cast my eyes towards a back window of a house in the next street, and what should I see but a girl."

"Pho, pho, Sam. You will have enough to do in London if you watch the girls at back windows."

"Well, but, sir, hear me."

"Very well; go on, Sam."

"She was quite a young creature, and I saw that she was full of distress and misery by the look of her face, but I was more surprised and afflicted still when she held up a paper on which was written the words—Murder! Caution!"

"Indeed."

"Yes, I wrote a reply, and then she sketched the words 'Save me,' upon which I counted all the houses to know which one it was, and came at once to tell you."

"You did right, Sam. What sort of young girl is she?"

"As well as I could see, sir, a beautiful young creature, with long light brown hair."

"Good heavens, if it should be——"

"Who, sir?"

"Some one, Sam, in whose fate I feel the greatest possible amount of interest, but at all events, if it be a stranger, we are bound to render all the assistance in our power."

"Certainly, sir. When you are ready."

"I am now."

"Then I think I can show you the house, sir."

"Come on then."

Both Sam and Harry Dean sallied out from this lodging in order to render assistance to one who Harry little really thought was Lucy, for although he had been so struck by Sam's description of her, he thought it by far too extravagant a chance that he should thus light upon one he was going to search London for.

And Lucy, too, how far was she from from imagining that the man whom she had seen brushing his hat at a window, and to whom she had applied for assistance was an attendant upon Harry Dean, and that in two minutes time the news would reach his ear. Oh, how her heart would have leaped with joy if she had had any such real idea.

The house was the fifth from the corner," said Sam, when they arrived in the street."

"Are you certain?"

"Quite, sir; I counted them as carefully as possible, and there can't be the least particle of doubt about it, sir."

"Very well. I am armed, and we will insist upon going into the back room at the window of which you saw the girl."

"Yes, sir."

"By the bye, as I have two pistols you had better take one of them, for heaven only knows what sort of a house this may be, and what sort of resistance we may meet with. There are many houses of tolerably fair exterior in London that conceal within them the very worst of characters, who are capable of the worst of crimes."

"If they open the door even but a hair's breadth, sir, they shan't get it shut again against me, you may depend."

"I am fully well assured of that. Go on now."

Sam Clover knocked at the door, but there was no reply. Again he knocked louder than before, but still no attention was paid to him, and it seemed to be a determination on the part of those who were in the house that they would pay no attention whatever to any demands for admission.

Such being the case, Sam and his new master felt that they were rather foiled than otherwise in what they wished to do, but after a brief consultation, Sam said,

"I have been looking down the area, sir, and I am pretty well convinced that the kitchen window is unfastened; moreover, I am sure there is no one there. If you please I will climb over the rails and go down, effecting an entrance that way, and so I shall be able to let you in myself at the door."

"If it can be done, Sam, without too great risk," said Harry Dean, "I should be glad of course."

Without another word then Sam surmounted the iron railings, and soon made his appearance at the street door, which he opened, having encountered no one in his progress through that portion of the house.

CHAPTER XLII.

THEIR RESCUE OF LUCY AND THE RECAPTURE.

HAVING now brought the adventures of Harry Dean down to the same point of time as those of Lucy in the house of Madame Zadzed, we once again invite the attention of our readers to the chamber where little Lucy was awaiting in an agony of expectation the issue of the exertions that were being made for her release.

The sounds she heard below aroused each moment in intensity, and although she had no doubt at all but that they were sounds of hope, yet she was left in the most torturing state of anxiety with regard to the issue of the conflict.

Again she made a more vigorous effort to open her chamber door, but it resisted the, after all, puny efforts she could bring to bear upon it, and in her anxiety she shrieked aloud for aid.

Her cries were unheeded for a time, and then there came a sudden stillness over the house, after which a loud voice cried,

"Police! police. Watch! watch!"

Lucy hoped that that voice was the voice of one who came to her rescue, and indeed she could not with anything like a feeling of probability believe that it was the voice of any of those personages in the house who themselves were most obnoxious to the authorities.

As she continued to listen there came a violent knocking at the street door, and then the trampling of feet upon the stairs was again renewed, after which she heard high voices in the adjoining rooms, and thinking that it was possible there might be some one there who would befriend her she cried in a loud voice that was quite sure at all events to reach so far,

"Help, help, help!"

Lucy was not wrong in her conjecture that she would be heard. The voices suddenly ceased, and in another moment a rough-toned man upon the outside of the room door cried,

"Who is in here?"

"Oh, no one but a child," said another voice.

"Yes ; but she cries help."

"Very likely she is dreaming, I dare say. You need not trouble yourself about her, sir."

This was not a moment at which Lucy should keep quiet, and she accordingly again called out with all her strength of voice,

"Save me! "Save me!"

"Where's the key of this door," said the rough voice.

"Oh—oh—key—the key you want."

"Yes ; and will have it, or else I shall take upon me to break the door pretty quickly."

"That even your power as a constable," replied the other voice in lower

tones, "I believe' does not permit you to do."

"Yes, it does," said the gruff speaker. "If I hear the cry of murder I may break open any door."

This was said aloud, and Lucy was not slow in taking the hint which it conveyed to her. In a moment she shouted, "Murder, murder."

"That will do," said the officer, for an officer he really was. "Now, where is the key? If it be not produced in one moment away goes the door."

"Oh, you are joking," said the other, "and as for the key, I really believe it is now mislaid somewhere or other."

"Very good, here goes then."

The officer had retreated a step or two, and then flinging himself with all the force of a large heavy man against it, the door burst open with a loud report, and Lucy stood trembling in the entrance.

"Now, my good little girl," he said. "What's the matter?"

"Oh, protect me, sir, protect me."

"You are quite safe. Do you belong to these people ?"

"Oh, no, no."

"Who are you, then ?"

"My name is Lucy Destern. They stole me away from my friends, and have carried me up here."

"Ah, I thought as much. Come this way, my dear. We have a prisoner down stairs, or rather two prisoners by this time I should say, upon a very serious charge indeed, but if you will point out those who imprisoned you here I will take them likewise into custody. It seems an odd sort of house altogether."

"But, sir, listen to me."

"Never mind just now. You can tell me all about it afterwards. My friends will, perhaps, be wondering where I am."

The officer then, not having the least idea of the importance of the revelations concerning the murder of Madame Zadzed, which Lucy was intent on making to him, conducted her down the stairs to the dining room, where there was a throng of persons.

"Here, Godfrey," he said, as he entered the room, addressing a brother officer who was with him. "I have found a child here who says she has been kidnapped."

"Then the best thing we can do," replied Godfry, "is to take every one we find in the house into custody."

"If you pursue that course," said a voice, "it will reconcile me in some degree to the unjust violence with which, upon insufficient evidence, I have been treated."

Lucy knew that voice in a moment. The tones thrilled through her very heart. Never was music so enchanting to the most extatic lovers of its mellifluous sounds as those were to Lucy. They were the tones of the voice of Harry Dean.

"Harry, Harry," she cried. "It is I—it is Lucy."

The moment he heard her speak, he made a rush towards her, crying as he did so,

"Is this possible? Oh, Lucy, this indeed repays me for much. I did have a faint thought that it might be you who was imprisoned here, but I rejected it again on the ground of its great improbability. Only tell me that you are well."

"Quite well, Harry, and you ?"

"Oh, well enough Lucy ; only you will see that I am here a prisoner, and cannot hold you to my heart a moment for these manacles upon my wrists."

"You a prisoner, Harry. For what ?"

"You may well ask, miss," said Sam. "They accuse him of murder, and me of being his accomplice."

"Murder !"

"Come along," said one of the officers. "Its lucky we happened to be passing this house at the time police was called. But we have no time to waste here in explanations. All you have to say, one or the other of you, can be best and most properly explained before a magistrate."

"Where's that long fellow who made the charge," said the other officer.

All eyes were directed to the door of the apartment where stood Swam's admirer and accomplice, the doctor. His face was of an ashy paleness, and he seemed to see nobody but Lucy, whom he watched with an intenseness that was absolutely painful.

Lucy was upon the point of declaring all she knew of the murder, and if she had but seen Swam herself in the room, she would have done so at once.

In vain, however, did she look for that personage, and then the thought struck her that if she made a premature disclosure of what she had seen, Swam might escape.

She pointed at the doctor, saying,

"I accuse that man—"

"Of what," he shrieked, "of what ?"

"Of locking me up in a dark room."

The doctor gave a deep sigh of relief, and then slipping into the passage, he cried out in a loud voice,

"Miss Swam, Miss Swam, its all right. Come down. We had nothing to do with the kidnapping the child, and of which the child only accuses us. All that was poor Madame Zadzed's doing."

He laid a stress upon the word only, for the purpose of giving an assurance to Swam that Lucy knew nothing of the murder.

In a few moments Swam made her appearance from some hiding place in which she had deposited herself.

"Your servant, madam," said one of the officers. "We shall feel obliged by your accompanying us."

"Oh, certainly," she said, in rather a

flurried manner. "I can have no sort of objection. Mr. Carter, pray give me your arm. This murder in the house is a very shocking thing."

"Why," said Sam, "I should not like to be so dusty as those who know all about it."

"Dusty! What do you mean, you wretch," cried Swam.

The officers smiled to themselves, for wherever Swam had been hiding, she had certainly brought away a great quantity of dust upon her apparel. Sam, however, made no further remark, and a coach being called, the whole party left the house to proceed at once to the nearest police office.

Lucy insisted upon sitting by Harry Dean, and in a low tone of voice she said.

"Harry, of what do they accuse you?"

"Of murder. I made my way into the house, and after going from room to room, I at last entered one the shutters of which were closed, while I was unfastening them so as to admit light into the place, the door was locked upon me immediately, after which there were loud cries of Police; in the course of a few minutes I was taken into custody, charged with the murder of some dead woman who lay upon a bed in the room."

"And he who is with you?"

"He is a servant of mine, and is likewise on that account implicated in this absurd charge."

"I think," remarked the officer who sat nearest to Harry Dean, "that the less you say the better it will be."

"If I was guilty, certainly," said Harry, your advice would be good, but knowing no more of the murder than you do, I cannot by any human possibility commit myself in any way."

"Very well, please yourself."

"What must be your feelings," said Swam, with an affected shudder; as she looked at Harry Dean.

"Much as usual, Madam," said Harry, "what are yours?"

Sam at this moment whispered something in the ear of one of the officers, who in reply smiled and nodded. Swam changed colour as she noticed this, and said hastily—

"What's the matter?"

"As how?" said the officer.

"What did that man say to you?"

"Oh, nothing particular."

"If it was anything against me, I defy him and all his malice."

"Lor bless you ma'am," said Sam, I was'nt thinking of any one half so dusty as you—you may depend."

"Silence," said the doctor, darting a look at Swam, which he intended should be highly condemnatory of the imprudent manner in wihch she was allowing her tongue to wag. "Silence."

"He is right," said one of the officers. "The least said, madam, is soonest mended."

"Decidedly," said Sam.

Swam was prudent enough to take good advice even it came in an unpalatable shape, so she held her peace forthwith, and the only conversation that ensued was between Lucy and Henry, who, in the consciousness of their own innocence and the purity of their feelings and emotions cared not if all they said was overheard.

"Have you no news of our dear Kate," said Lucy.

"Alas, none."

"Oh, Henry what can have become of her?'

"I know not. It is distracting to think of it, Lucy. But take some comfort, for I have made such preparations for discovering where she is, that I think I cannot fail of success."

"Ah, how pleased I am to hear you say so."

"And I too Lucy"

"And Tony,—is Tony well?"

"Well enough in health, Lucy, when last I saw him, but quite distracted with the thought that you were in danger."

"I shall be glad to see him."

"And he, you."

"Well," said one of the officers, "for a man going before a beak on a charge of murder I think you take things about as coolly as possible."

"Why should I not," said Harry, "knowing my own innocence."

"Your innocence?" commenced Swam.

"Silence!" said the doctor.

"Oh, very well."

"I don't think, Bill," said the officer, to whom Sam had whispered something, to his comrade, "I don't think, Bill, we need incommode our prisoner there —pointing to Harry Dean—by the darbies."

"Very well, as you please, Godfrey."

Godfrey immediately released Harry's hands from the handcuffs which had been roughly put upon him. That he had good reasons for acting thus we shall soon discover when the party appears before one of the metropolitan magistrates.

It was a grateful relief to Harry Dean to be quit of the manacles in which his wrists had been held, not that he attached any sort of disgrace to the fact of being confined in them, for when, with tears in her eyes, Lucy had regarded them, he had said, with a smile—

"If I deserved these, Lucy, I should feel them upon my heart, but as it is, they are as nothing, and the disgrace is to those who have managed to have them placed upon me, knowing my innocence."

There were few, indeed, who would have taken so philosophic a view of the matter as Harry Dean did, but then, not only was he quite conscious of innocence, but he was likewise quite conscious of safety, notwithstanding the cunning manner in which the real perpetrators of the murder had endeavoured to fix it upon an innocent person.

There can be no doubt but that full of all kinds of fear, Swam and her accomplice had lingered in the house, and that the sudden arrival of Harry Dean and Sam, both strangers to them, had at the moment give birth to the idea of implicating them in the murder.

Even a remand for a few days of the falsely accused persons would have given Swam and the doctor ample time to make their escape from England, and so defeat the ends of justice.

CHAPTER XLIII.

KATE'S ILLNESS.—THE PARISH DOCTOR.

It is due to the trials, the constancy, the virtue, and the firmness under severe afflictions, of Kate Destern, that we take now something more than a mere passing glance at her fortunes.

We left her in the care of poor, but honest people, who no doubt would do all for her that lay in their power, but how little that all was likely to be.

Kate, however, after having succeeded in effecting her escape from the villa at Fulham, thought all evils that could befall her slight—but she knew not, as we happen to know, that if she had remained but a few hours longer at the villa, she would have been rescued by Harry Dean himself, whom it was now the great object of her life to discover in London.

Kate knew not the thousand difficulties that lay in the way of finding any one in such a place as London. Chance may throw two people together when they least expect it—perhaps least desire it —in one of its throughfares, but years may elapse ere they meet again.

When Kate reached the little humble home of the poor woman who had offered her an asylum, she was anxious at once to set forth in search of those whom she loved.

Of course the cottage at Hampstead was the first place to which she wended her footsteps, for she expected at all events to find Lucy, knowing nothing of the mass of events which had taken place, and in which poor Lucy had been compelled to play a prominent part, and even her abduction from the cottage.

The poor woman who had told her simple story so unaffectedly, would fain have prevailed upon Kate to rest herself for that day at least, before she proceeded on her journey of enquiry ; but Kate's anxiety to see Lucy overcome all feelings of fatigue, and after partaking of such scanty refreshment as they could afford, she started on foot to Hampstead.

The way seemed long and weary, but at length the beautiful heath met her longing eyes.

With hurried steps she now sought the cottage where her mother had breathed her last ; she pushed open the little gate, but a dog darted from his kennel and opposed her progress.

The ferocious barking of the cur aroused the attention of a woman, who advanced, and in a peremptory tone demanded to know what she, Kate, wanted.

Poor Kate was thoroughly bewildered, she looked around her with the full expectation of finding that she had made some mistake, and come to the wrong cottage, but such was not the case. There was every object that had been for years familiar to her.

"Madam," she said, "was not this Mrs. Destern's cottage?"

"How should I know."

"But—but, it really was."

"Perhaps it was—perhaps it was not. I'm plain as I'm pleasant, and don't want to waste my time ; so be off."

With these words the amiable new occupant of the cottage turned into the building again, and the dog taking his cue from his mistress, again began furiously barking at Kate.

For a few minutes she stood quite distressed, not knowing what to do, but then it occurred to her that surely some of the old neighbours would be there, and accordingly thinking of the kind hearted laundress who had been so good to her and Lucy upon the death of their mother, she hastened to her house which was hard by, and lifted up the latch of the door.

The good woman was engaged in some of the mysteries of starching, and for a few moments she looked at Kate as though she had seen a ghost, and then upsetting a tea-cup full of starch upon the cat, she exclaimed with her eyes wide open—

"Goodness gracious, it's come true."

"What, oh what!" said Kate.

"My dream to be sure. But is it really you, Miss Kate?"

"It is indeed ; is Lucy here?"

"Lucy, Lucy?"

"Yes, my sister Lucy."

"Oh, oh, oh, oh!"

"God of Heaven, she is not dead?"

"No, but nobody knows where she is. Sit down and rest yourself while I grill you some coals on a rasher of bacon. God bless me, what am I saying.

"Oh no, no," said Kate, "I want nothing but news of those whom I love, tell me all you know, I pray you."

The good woman then with many tears related to Kate how the parish officer had threatened her with the loss of her little weekly allowance if she dared to keep Lucy, and how Lucy, therefore, had slipped away without her wish and knowledge, she knew not where.

Kate heard all this with a deep sigh.

"More trouble, more trouble," she said.

She then burst into tears, for the disappointment she experienced in not finding her little kind affectionate sister was severe in the extreme. One of the greatest consolations she had had during all the dreary time she had been left at the villa of Lord Battaney, had been in the idea that Lucy was safe in the care of Harry Destern.

But now that hope was dashed from her she felt desolate indeed. She wished at that moment she was dead.

"Come, come," said the good woman, "we ain't all lost as is in danger, you know.

"What shall I do—oh! what shall I do?" said Kate.

"Stay here to be sure, and we will try what can be done to find Lucy, depend upon it we will think of something between us."

"No, no," cried Kate, "I should go mad here. The only thing that will keep me alive in my senses will be an unceasing search for Lucy. I must find her."

"Gracious goodness! but how?"

"That I know not. But it is to London she would go, I feel assured, to look for me, and there must I go to seek for her."

"Then I must go with you."

"No—no. Believe me I have some friends in London, who will aid me, but should I require the help of one whose heart I know well, I will at once apply to you."

It was in vain that the good-hearted woman urged upon Kate to remain with her, she would not be persuaded, but rising at once, persisted, notwithstanding the fatigue she had already suffered, in making her way again to the metropolis.

She hastened as much as she could, but the way was long, and darkening clouds that all the morning had been gathering in the southern sky, now overspread the whole face of the heavens, and gave evidence of a coming storm of no light character.

But still Kate hurried on, for she

thought she might possibly reach London before the storm clouds burst over head. In this hope she was, however, defeated. Large drops of rain began to fall. A peal of thunder shook the earth, and Kate before she could reach any shelter, was completely drenched with the now rapidly-descending rain.

Under these circumstances, she thought it would be unwise to pause, so went completely through the storm, and at length arrived at the house of the widow drenched with rain—tired beyond all tiredness that she had ever known before, and in a state of mind bordering upon destraction.

She almost fell down as she reached the room, and for some time she could not speak in reply to the kind and compassionate enquiries that were made incessantly by the poor woman.

At length Kate was just able to tell her of her bitter disappointment, in which she was much commiserated. Her wet garments were removed from her, and while an attempt at a little miserable fire was made to dry them, she was glad to lie down on the humble bed of the widow.

While she lay, she tried to revolve in her mind what would be the best means to adopt for the purpose of discovering Lucy in London, but she was alarmed at the strange incoherence of her own thoughts; she felt, too, at times, in a burning heat, and then, with the greatest rapidity of alternation, she would shiver with cold.

The conviction that some serious illness was coming upon her crept each moment more and more surely across her mind.

Oh what an additional pang that was to poor Kate.

"If I had continued well," she thought, "I might have done much, but in sickness, I am indeed worse than helpless."

She spoke half aloud, and the good woman said to her,—

"What do you say, my dear?"

"I am very ill," replied Kate.

At that moment, it seemed to her as if all objects around her suddenly resolved themselves together into one confused mass. Kate fainted, partly from illness, and partly from the dread of it.

* * * *

How long she remained in that state Kate had no means of knowing, but when she recovered, she heard the confused sound of voices, conversing in low accents, in the room.

"What did he say?" said a voice.

"That he wouldn't come without an order."

"But did you tell him she was very bad and might die?"

"Oh, yes, and he said she might please herself about dying, as it was no business of his, one way or the other."

"Gracious! what shall we do?"

"Try the vinegar again."

"I am better," said Kate, "I am better."

Several women who were in the room hearing her now speak, crowded round the little bed on which she lay.

"Are you better," said one.

"Speak again," said another. "Would you like to have anything? You have only to say, and poor as we are, we will manage it somehow among us."

"Good Heavens, where am I?" said Kate.

"You are with me," said the widow woman. "But you are very ill, and must remain quiet my dear."

"No—no. I will rise, I am not ill—I must rise, I have much to do, I have my poor sister to look for in London. Do not tell me I am ill, for I have need now of all the energies that God has given me. Yes, yes, I must rise."

As she spoke, she made an effort to get up, but the moment she lifted her head from the pillow on which it lay, it seemed to her as though all the room was spinning round with her, and the death-like faintness that came over her alarmed her exceedingly.

She was compelled instantly to lie down again.

"You see how ill you are," said one.

"Alas! alas!" sobbed Kate, "what will become of me?"

"Come now," interposed the widow woman, in as cheerful a voice as she could assume. "Come now you must not give way in that manner. You know well enough what is to become of you."

"What, oh what?"

"Why you will get quite well in a few

days, and until you do so, you shall want for nothing here."

Kate could not reply to her for the blinding tears that filled her eyes, and the choaking sobs that rose in her throat, but she stretched out her hand, and grasped that of the friend who had been surely by Heaven raised up for her in her hour of need.

At that moment a heavy footstep sounded upon the stairs, and the attention of all present, was directed towards the door of the little humble apartment.

CHAPTER XLIV.

AN OFFICIAL PERSONAGE.

POOR Kate was but little interested in any one who could bring her no news of those concerning whom she was so anxious to hear, so when the door of the room was only just opened a little way, and a large, round, fat face popped in, of which she had no knowledge, she turned her eyes away, without feeling any interest.

"Hilloa!" said the owner of the voice.

"Oh sir, is that you?" said the widow.

"Is it me. Of course it's me, did you think it was the parish pump, eh?—eh?"

"Oh dear no sir. When I called at your house sir, I only hoped you would come soon."

"Yes, that's always the way. Poor people are out of hand the most troublesome in all the world. If they get ill it's always at somebody's meal time."

"Well sir, I'm very sorry, but the young lady, sir, is only staying with me, and she really seemed so very bad."

"Pho! pho! pho!"

"But sir."

"Don't speak to me, I'm sure what with one and another of you, it's enough to make one's life a burthen. Who would be assistant to a relieving officer, I should like to know?"

"But where are we to go to, sir?"

"Ah, that's always the way. First of all without the means of paying for proper advice, you have the confounded obstinacy to get ill, and then you have the infernal impudence to come to me for a medical order."

"What is all this," said Kate faintly. "Is it on my account?"

"Never you mind, my dear," said the widow. "You require medical advice and you must and shall have it."

"Eh? eh?—What's that you say Mrs. What's-your-name?—Don't aggravate the parish, mum, if you please. Shall have it, indeed, well that's a good idea, a pauper says she shall have it!—I wonder what the world will come to next. Come, come, young woman, no nonsense; now I suppose you are about as much really ill as I am. Lazy, I fancy—That's about what we must bring it in."

Kate would just as soon have thought of making a direct reply to the barking of a dog as to this speech.

"Does she know who I am?" roared the relieving officer's assistant, looking fiercely at the widow, "does she know who I am, that's what I aske of you all?"

"Indeed, sir, she is ill," said the widow.

"Oh, is she? Well I tell you what she must do—Come into the house at once. What do you say to that!"

"Good God!" said Kate, addressing the widow, "who is this man, and what does he want here. He will drive me distracted."

"My dear, you were so bad, that we all thought you ought to have a doctor, and as we could not afford to pay for one, we applied to the parish for a medical order, and this gentleman has come to give one, I suppose, that is all."

"Don't be in such a hurry, ma'am, I have not come to do any such thing. Let her come into the house."

"Oh, no—no," said the widow.

"Very good," said the relieving officer's assistant, giving a grin at his own cleverness. "Very good. Then I refuse an order, that's all. We have made up our minds to offer anybody the house, and if they don't like that, why, we have done our duty, and there's an end to it. I wont stay bothering here all day, so I'm off now, and you may think about it."

"What does he mean?" said Kate, faintly.

"Oh, no doubt you are precious green,

and dont know nothing. You a pauper, too. I never knew a person who was forced in any way to apply to the parish who was'nt up to all the villany in the world."

"How's the young woman?" said a voice at the door, and the coal-begrimed head of a gigantic coal heaver was popped in. "How's the young woman as wasn't well, poor thing, eh? My missus is a making a little weal broth for her."

"What!" cried the relieving officer, "Weal broth for a pau——Good gracious, it's him!"

This curious termination to the speech of the relieving officer, and the appearance of absolute fright with which it was accompanied, quite astonished all the persons assembled in the widow's little apartment.

The coal heaver came a little further within the doorway, and looking seriously at the terrified parish official, he, too, astonished everybody, by saying,—

"Lor! it's him!"

"What do you mean, Mr. Williams?" said the widow.

"I'll tell you, mum. You sees that ere fellow. Well now, he's the relieving officer's fag in this here parish, in a manner o' speaking, and when I was out last winter, when there was never such a frost kiverred up everythink, my little girl Lucy, took ill; poor thing, she's in her grave now, I—I—lor! what a fool I is, I thought I had done crying about that ere."

"Good day," said the relieving officer, as he sidled towards the door with a nervous look of alarm. "Good day—govd day—I—I wish you all good morning."

"Don't go yet," said the coal heaver, as he grasped the official personage by the collar, and gave him a throw into the extreme corner of the room. "Don't go yet, Mr. Vullamy."

"Murder—murder."

"Be quiet, will you?"

"Yes, Mr. Williams. Yes, if you will be so good as not to murder me. Would you all like something to drink. Let's be friends. I'll give the order you want, mum. Ha! ha! ha! It's pleasant now really, aint it, to find we are all such very good friends, all of a sudden. Oh, very, very."

"Will you be quiet?"

"Oh dear yes, Mr. Vullamy—quiet as a lamb. I often think of your little girl, and I says to myself, if ever there was a angel belonging to a coalheaver, she was her, I says."

"You won't be quiet."

"Yes—yes—I—I will—oh dear me, yes."

"Well, as I was a saying," continued the coalheaver, making a great smear down his face as he wiped away a tear, "as I was a saying—I thought I was done crying about Lucy, but I finds as I haven't."

"And very proper," said Vullamy, "very proper——"

"Be quiet, will you?"

The coalheaver accompanied the last remonstrance by a knock on the top of Mr. Vullamy's head with a pint pot he happened to have in his hand, and the sound produced was quite of a startling sort of a character. It had the desired effect, however, for Vullamy only rubbed the top of his head, and said nothing.

"Well, as I was a saying," continued the coalheaver, "you knew my little Lucy, mem?"

"Yes, Mr. Williams."

"Well, mem, you know there never was such a child in this here world. Well, mem, and ladies all on you, when she looked ill, and got never so bad, this here fellow, Vullamy, comes, cos I sent for him, and I says to him, says I, Measter Vullamy, I'm out o' work, cos you see the river is froze, and wont let no coals come, so all I wants is a little help for my child.'"

"Bless me," said Mr. Vullamy, "I forgot, I left somebody at the door; I'll just run down and tell him not to wait, and then be up again in a minute."

"No you wont," said the coalheaver. "You'll just stop where you is, will you?"

The relieving officer's assistant gave a sickly smile, and again rubbed his head, while Mr. Williams continued his story.

"Well, all I asked of him was an order that the doctor might see Lucy; but putting on a sort of a grin, he says, says he, 'You can all come into the house if you can prove your settlement,' says he, 'and not without.' Why, says I, my child may be dead

long before that. 'What's the odds,' says he. 'There's more children than enough in the parish already.'"

"Did he really?" exclaimed the widow.

"No, no, no," said Vullamy.

"Hold your tongue, will you? Well, ladies, I was going at that moment to give him a good shaking, when my little Lucy called out to me, 'Father,' says she, 'I can't see you.' I went to her and held her in my arms a minute, and then she gave a sort of shudder, and her little head dropped upon my breast, and—and she was dead—dead—dead."

"I'm very sorry, I'm sure," gasped Vullamy. "I—I don't mind at all sending for a pot of beer."

"Do you think that an ocean of beer, you humbug, would make me forget my child?"

Mr. Vullamy shrunk back aghast.

"Come along. I suppose, ladies, as you don't want to be troubled with this here fellow any more."

"Certainly not," said everybody.

"Good, come along, Mr. Vullamy, I believe you said once that you wouldn't give a drop of cold water to a pauper to save him from choaking."

"Oh dear, no—no. It was Mr. White, the overseer, who said that—I—I only laughed, you know. I was obliged to laugh when Mr. White said anything funny."

"And you call that funny, do you?"

"Ye—ye—yes—it was meant, you know, to be funny."

"Was it."

"A—a—little. I didn't laugh much."

"Well, Mr. Vullamy, you laughed when a drop of water was grudged to a pauper, I wonder if you will laugh when you have plenty."

"What do you mean, Mr. Williams? You are joking sir. What a funny man you are."

"Am I. Very well. Come along, for the best of the fun is to come yet."

"What do you mean sir ?"

"I suppose you came by the end of the court close at hand, cos if so be as you did, you must have seen the pump that has been put up."

"Yes, yes, Mr. Williams."

"Very good. What are you in such a way about. I'm only going to give you a drop out of it."

"Murder !"

"What?"

"You are going to pump upon me, Mr. Williams. I have been pumped upon before, and kicked too. Oh, don't. I shall catch my death of cold, Mr. Williams."

"Never mind."

"But Mr. Williams. Mr. Williams?"

"Well."

"You really don't mean it."

"Very good."

By this time, the coal-heaver had got Vullamy down the stairs, and fairly out into the street. Now close about the pump, some ladies were washing some fish. They all knew Mr. Vullamy perfectly well, so that when the coal-heaver said, "Allow me," they got out of his way at once, and indeed, one was so civil, that she volunteered her services to pump, while Mr. Williams held Vullamy under the spout.

"Murder, murder, police !" cried the overseer, but who ever heard of a policeman coming when he was wanted ?

The handle of that new pump had not been so well exercised since it had been erected, and when Mr. Williams let Vullamy go, the latter looked more like some drowned cat, than anything even so human as a relieving officer.

CHAPTER XLV.

LORD BATTANEY FINDS OUT THE ESTIMATION HE IS HELD IN BY HIS SERVANTS.

IT is pleasant and refreshing to the mind, even to hear of such small pieces of moral retribution as that which befell Mr Vullamy, the relieving officer's assistant.

It is quite delightful to fancy, what must have been his feelings, while beneath the spout of the pump, but now we must request the attention of the reader to a much darker scene.

We leave Kate Destern in the full faith, that youth will triumph over the sickness that at present oppresses her, and so once again we must step into the chamber of the wicked, frightfully suffering Lord Battaney, at that villa, near Fulham, which had been the scene of so much wickedness.

The physician who surely had played some very conspicuous part in the early career of Lord Battaney, had left him for dead, and Harry Dean ¦too had looked upon that pallid face, and outstretched form, without a doubt of the apparent fact, that death had claimed its victim.

It is no less strange than true, however, that such men as Lord Battaney, cling to life with a most wonderful pertinacity.

The injuries which would send a good and a just man to his grave, and to that judgment which he has no cause to dread, will not have that effect upon one, whose mortal race has been run in the devious paths of wickedness.

We cannot pause to ask why is this, but all who have paid any attention to those curiosities of general experience, which are passing around him, must admit the truth of this remark.

Even ordinary accidents, rarely fall

to the lot of worthless reckless men, it would seem as if the spirit of Sin, which they worshipped, had at least the power of carrying them scathless, while they were employed upon his business.

It was so with Battaney.

Despite the deadful injuries he had received, despite the fearful condition of utter personal helplessness to which he had been reduced, he lived.

Yes ; life still lingered around the heart, and in the brain of that bad man, although he lay such a total wreck, comparatively to what he had been.

And would not even death, let it come with what sharp pang it might, have been a boon, now ?

The vitiated spirit lingered, however, in its earthly tenement, and after a time he recovered sufficiently to open his eyes and look about him.

He had but a dim kind of recollection of all that had befallen him, but he knew that he was in his own chamber, and that the objects he saw around him were familiar to his gaze.

He made an effort to move, but a cry of pain was forced from his lips by that effort, slight as it was. One of his legs was broken, and the displacement of bones, consequent upon even the trifling movement he had made, brought to him the most exquisite agony.

"Gracious Heaven!" he cried, "what is this?"

Alas ! Lord Battaney did not cry gracious Heaven because he thought Heaven was gracious, or because of any awakening feeling that after all his impious doubts and sneers there was a Heaven above him—no, it was with him a mere expletive, meaning to his mind, no more than as if he uttered some common place oath of the character that usually came from his profane lips.

He was silent now, for some time. Pain had almost produced insensibility again, but as the acute agony slowly subsided, he once more looked about him.

"I am in my house," he muttered, "but where are those who have been accustomed to wait upon my every look. Have they all deserted me ?"

If it had not been for rather a powerful ray of sunlight that found its way between two of the shutters of the room, he would not have been able to see about

him at all, and now he began to wonder and to be much alarmed at the stillness about him.

"What is the meaning of it," he said again, in a low moaning voice. "What is the meaning of it? Do they really think I am dead ?"

This to such a man was truly a dreadful thought, inasmuch as it seemed to bring him nearer that eternity which at the bottom of his heart he dreaded more than anything else.

"Oh, no, no, no," he moaned, " anything but that. Why should I die ?"

He lay perfectly motionless for a time, then there came slowly back to him, a recollection of all the various events in their proper order, which had reduced him to his present condition.

Last of all came to his memory the scene he had passed through with the rascally physician, who had extorted from his fears the cheque for so large an amount, and furious passions soon took the place of all other feelings in the heart of Lord Batterey.

At least that, and the sensation of pain devided his mind completely.

"Oh, that I once more was able and capable as I was yesterday," he groaned, "that I might take that man by the throat, and hold him until I saw his dying agonies. I could die myself then without so much regret."

Evil passions and human revenges found a home in the breast of Lord Battany, even at a time when he must have considered it possible that he was near to the shores of eternity.

He found that by lying profoundly still, he, in some measure, got rid of the intense pain which, upon the slightest movement, was almost enough to drive him distracted, and so he lay for nearly an hour, ruminating upon his most desperate state.

At some short distance from him, and really not above twelve inches beyond his reach, was a silken tassel, which communicated with a bell. He thought that if he could but reach that he should at all events succeed in summoning some one to his chamber.

But to reach it in his present state was really a fearful affair, for when he knew that the slightest movement brought on an unceasing pain, beyond all bearing, or at all events beyond his powers of patience, he dreaded to ma an attempt to reach the bell-pull.

The perspiration stood in cold drops upon his brow as he, after much consideration, tried slowly to drag himself along in the bed the required distance.

A shriek burst from his lips: he had got hold of the bell-rope, but it was at the expense of giving himself another pang of a far worse character than the former.

So exhausted and overcome with the pain was he that for some few seconds he could not pull the tassel he now held in his cold clammy grasp. But he did not forego the clutch he had of it, and in the course of a minute he made an effort, and gave it a hasty tug.

Amid the stillness of the villa he heard the tinkling of the bell quite plainly even where he lay.

They will come, he said. Even if they thought me dead they will come now.

If the sound of that bell came plainly enough, and satisfactorily to the ears of Lord Battaney, it came much too plainly and much too unsatisfactorily to the ears of some others.

The few domestics who belonged to the villa, and who had been some in the grounds, and some out of the premises altogether, at the time of Harry Dean's visit, had returned, with some exceptions.

They consisted of two women, one of whom was a most hag-like looking personage, and two men, who officiated in the respective situations of coachman and groom.

Now these persons had been to the chamber of Lord Battancy, and like Harry Dean, had mistaken the state of syncope in which they found him for death.

With some hurry and trepidation they had retired to the lower part of the house, and then held a council of war, for it was a species of war they meditated, as to what they should do.

"He's dead," said the groom.

"Yes; dead as a hind wheel with the tire off," said the coachman.

"What can we do."

"I'll tell you what you are to do," said the old hag of a woman, whose name was Gill. "I'll tell you what to do, if you aint all of you too faint-hearted to do it."

"What is it ? mother Gill," said the groom; "out with it. What is it, eh ?"

"Just this. We are alone in the villa. There is no one to interfere with us, and there is plenty of plate and valuables. Let us all carry off what we can, and get to London with it, where we can sell it and divide the money."

"A very good idea," said the other woman.

"I don't seem much to like it," said the coachman.

"Nor I," said the groom: "but I suppose it would be tolerably prefitable."

"Profitable!" said Mrs. Gill; "of course it would be. Why, I'm quite sure there are watches and jewels enough in Battaney's dressing cases to set us all up in business."

"Do you think so ?"

"I'm sure of it. We have only to take what is at our hands, and fools we should be if we didn't."

"He's dead to be sure," said the groom, "and can't miss what we take from him now."

"There's something in that," said the coachman. "I wonder how much a piece it would bring us all in—a hundred pounds, Mrs. Gill ?"

"More."

"You don't say so."

"There are only four of us, and it will be hard indeed if in this place there aint more than four hundred pounds worth of plate and jewels. Oh, there's double, I'm quite certain."

"How shall we manage it ?"

"Each of us carry what we can, and then lock up the villa, and be off to London as quick as possible. Come to Lord Battaney's room now, at once, and let us see what's in his dressing cases and trunks. Oh, I'll be bound we shall make a good thing of it, and dead men, you know, tell no tales. Ha, ha !"

Tingle, tingle, tingle, went Lord Battaney's bell at this moment.

Each of the party uttered an exclamation of alarm, and they ran against each other in their fright, for nothing could be so completely unexpected as a summons to that chamber, which they fully believed contained nothing but a corpse.

"Let's run away," cried the coachman.

"Where to," shouted Mrs. Gill.

"Perhaps after all we were deceived, and he is not dead."

"Not dead. Then our plan falls to the ground."

"I don't know that. At all events we can go and see what sort of condition he is in. What are you all afraid he will eat you up? He can't do that, dead or alive."

Mrs. Gill took the lead, and being ashamed to express any more fears, the others followed her to the chamber of Lord Battaney, whom they found, as we have shown, alive, but in no condition to be a hindrance to them.

"You vile wretches," he exclaimed; "why am I thus deserted? Go to the town, some of you, directly, and fetch all the medical advice that is to be had."

"Why, as to that, my lord," said Mrs. Gill, "we are rather too busy. Can't your lordship get up?"

"No, no; the slightest movement agonizes me."

"Is it possible," replied Mrs. Gill, as she intentionally gave the bedstead a push, which made Lord Battaney give a yell of pain. "Well, who would have thought it. We are going all of us to retire from your service, my lord."

"What do you mean, you old hag?"

"You had better be civil." [Another kick to the bedstead.]

"Murder, murder," cried Battaney.

"Well, my lord, as I say, we are going to retire from your service, and as we think we ought to do so with something handsome, we intend helping ourselves to what we can. There's the dressing case, coachman, you have got large pockets, just take all you can while we open these boxes."

Lord Battaney heard this speech of Mrs. Gill's with the most intense anger, but he had too good an idea of the powers of mischief and the malignancy of that lady to treat her to any more opprobious epithets, although many came to his tongue.

He saw them deliberately packing up trinkets and other small portable valuables. He saw them tread ruthlessly upon those articles which they did not think to be of sufficient intrinsic importance to take with them.

"Wretches!" he cried. "Malignant wretches! have I deserved back again such treatment at your hands?"

"Every one for himself, old chap," said the groom.

"Ah," added the coachman, "my lord, you will only make yourself ill if you get into a passion."

"To be sure he will," cried one of the women, with a laugh. "Don't he look a beauty, now."

"Oh!" he cried, "that Heaven would but grant me one day to be revenged for this. You wretches—you vampires!"

"Come, come," said the old hag,' "come, come, no bad names, my lord; recollect you don't like to be gagged. He! he!"

"Murder!" cried Lord Battaney, as she gave the bedstead a kick that shook him dreadfully.

"Ah, you can cry out like anybody else you old sinner, can ye? Mind I don't give you a good shake."

"I tell you what it is Mrs. Brown,' said the other woman, "I'm thinking about, suppose, after all, he should recover."

"Ah, you wretches, think of that," cried Lord Battaney catching at the faint hope that such an idea might alarm them into something like complacence to him. "Think of that. What if I recover and am well as ever."

"Yes, that is what I am thinking."

"Is it likely?" said the groom."

"You don't say so," said the coachman.

"Well," replied Mrs. Brown, "what do you propose, Mrs. Gill?"

"You thieves,, you had better make terms with me," said Lord Battaney, "while I may, perhaps, be induced to be merciful to you all. I am sure to recover."

"Well, then," said Mrs. Gill, "if that's the case, I propose—

"Listen, Listen, all of you," interrupted Battaney; "listen and take her advice, for again I assure you all, that I shall recover. I have an iron constitution."

"Well, Mrs. Gill, go on," said the groom, "what do you propose? I'm sure I will consent to anything in reason."

"Well, then," added the hag "as we shall be in an awkward position if Lord Battaney should recover after what has happened, I propose that to prevent that, we now smother him at once before we go away."

CHAPTER XLVI.

THE DIABOLICAL SUGGESTION AND ITS RESULT.

WHEN Lord Battaney heard that his hopes of release from his present situation, resolved themselves into the very dubious and doubtful advantage of being smothered, he gave a groan that quite alarmed the servants, for they thought that indeed his last moment had come, and that fright combined with his wounds, would indeed make him give up the ghost.

They all paused in their work of plunder, and looked at him with a full expectation of seeing the hue of death rapidly overspread his features.

"Smother me!" he groaned, "smother me! Is this to be after all, my end?"

"And serve you right too," said Mrs. Gill.

"And this diabolical suggestion comes from you, woman, who no doubt have grown rich in my service. Is it thus I am requited?"

"Oh, a fiddlestick's end. You can talk very fine now, my lord, but a little while ago we were not good enough to dare to look at you."

"Well, well," said the other woman, "let him be."

"Oh its quite immaterial to me," added the other woman. "What do you say, Thomas?"

"I'm for anything in a quiet way," replied the coachman. "Of course as we have got the things I don't wish to be found out."

"Come away," said Mrs. Gill, after tapping her forehead several times with a thimble she wore upon one of her fingers. "Come away all of you. I have it."

"Have what?" said the groom.

"Never mind. I'll tell you all when we get down stairs. Only take care to bring away with you all you can possibly carry."

There was no fear of any of the party disobeying this injunction. Indeed the pockets of the whole of them were well filled already, so that they were at once quite prepared to depart.

Lord Battaney, however, when he saw them going, got nearly desperate, and called aloud to them,—

"Do not allow me to perish here for want of aid. I will say nothing of the robbery you have committed, of the threat you have used towards me, if you will but send me a surgeon."

"Oh, yes," said Mrs. Gill, in a soothing tone. "Make your mind easy. You shall soon be out of your troubles."

"What do you mean, hag?"

"Hag! Well I'm sure,"

"You wretches! you fiends! you horrible set of thieves, how dare you—"

They had all left the room, and proceeding down the stairs with great quickness, they lost the remainder of Lord Battaney's anathemas against them.

They were all curious to know what scheme it was that Mrs. Gill had in her head, which, to her, seemed so satisfactory and assuring them of safety in the present undertaking.

Mrs. Gill did not keep them long in suspense, but upon reaching the hall, she said,—

"One great object, of course, is now to conceal that a robbery has been committed at all,"

"Yes, but how?"

"This way. You see quite plainly that if his life depended upon it, Battaney could not move off his bed."

"Yes, yes. That is clear enough."

"Well, then, he must be very bad, and likely to die."

"Well."

"Well then—you—you need not, I am sure, any of you, think much of what I am going to say."

"Good God! what is it," cried the groom. "Why don't you say it at once, and not keep us waiting here in such a state of suspense about it."

"Then I'll tell you, only I was afraid you might at first rather start at it, you see, that's all. I propose then that we set the house on fire before we leave it."

"On fire?"

"Yes, I said on fire."

"The devil!"

"Who do you mean, sir?"

"Oh, not you. The devil is a gentleman."

"Very well; this is all the return I get for showing you all first how to fill your pockets, and secondly, how to keep what you have got with safety."

"It's a horrid idea," said the coachman. "But—but yet, I daresay people have done such things."

"No doubt," said the groom.

"I wonder if roasting is quite so bad as one would imagine it to be."

"Roasting."

"Yes, to be sure. He can't get up, and don't Mrs. Gill want to roast him. Of course setting fire to the house means roasting Lord Battaney."

"Not at all," said Mrs. Gill.

"Not at all. How do you make that out?"

"Pho! Nobody is ever roasted in a house on fire. They always get smothered with the smoke long before it comes to roasting. You know that well enough."

"Humph! Smothered with smoke. Pleasant that, I should say. But still as we have got the plate and jewels, and as we do want to get safe off with them, it really won't do to stand upon trifles."

"No," said Mrs. Gill. "A few bundles of straw placed on the staircase, will do the business effectually. Now, Mr. Coachman, you go to the stable at once and get them."

"Well, if I must, I—I—suppose I must."

"Of course you must."

The coachman departed upon his errand, and while he was gone, Lord Battaney's bell rung again furiously, for he had once more managed to reach the bell rope, and although he did not expect any of his rebellious servants to come to him, it was some satisfaction to be able to make even that slight species of alarm.

In the course of a few minutes the coachman entered with a couple of bundles of straw upon his back, which were duly deposited under the principal staircase, in such a position that it would be a wonder indeed if their ignition did not effectually set fire to the house.

"It's done," said the coachman, with a scared look. "It's done now, Mrs. G."

"Not yet; have any of you a lucifer match?"

"We are all lucifer matches now in a manner of speaking," said the groom.

"How do you mean, Bill?" inquired the coachman.

"Why, aint we doing the devil's work among us, Thomas. Aint tha quite clear."

"It is, it is."

"You are cowards," said Mrs. Gill, "although you call yourselves men, I dare say."

"Well, well," said the coachman. "All this is not in my line, so you see it puts me out a little."

"And me too," added the groom. "I only wonder what will be the end of it all."

"That's about as foolish a thing as you can do," said Mrs. Gill; "for in any enterprise of this sort your fears are sure to picture to you the worst results. Who has a match, I say?"

No one had the required implement of incendiarism, and Mrs. Gill herself had to go to the kitchen for one. She brought what was more efficient, a candle ready lighted.

"Now all is right," she cried.

"Hark how he's ringing," said the other woman.

"I hear him."

"He suspects—"

"What? Do you mean to tell me that the great, and haughty, and violent Lord Battaney has the least suspicion that he will burnt to death in his own villa at Fulham? No, no, not he. Whatever he may expect hereafter, he certainly does not look forward to one here."

"Fire hereafter," cried the coachman, "Oh Lor!"

"What's the matter now, idiot?"

"I did not think of that."

"Think of what?"

"Oh, the fire hereafter. Oh Lor! Mrs. Gill, don't it strike you, mum, that if there's a fire hereafter, we all of us for this day's work stand a good chance of a very warm place."

"Superstitious dolt!"

"All that may be all very well, but I—I begin really to think that we had better leave the affair where it is. The robbery we might get off for a swinging for, but the—the murder."

"Murder? Who but you spoke of murder?"

"Aint it something very like it?"

"No."

"No?"

"No, I say, we only want to warm Lord Battaney's bed a little, as he is in bad health, that's all."

"Oh."

"Lor, Mrs. Gill," said Mrs. Brown "what a woman you are to be sure. What a wit you have. Come, Mr. Coachman, it's of no use you making yourself uncomfortable about it. You know needs must when a certain old gentleman drives, so take the candle and set light to the straw."

"I set light to it."

"Yes," said Mrs. Gill. "Why not?"

"I beg your pardon, mum, that aint the question. Why should I, that's all I ask?"

"Why you brought the straw and persuaded us all into it, you know; why, therefore, should you object to setting light to your own straw. Upon my word I shall begin to think, Mr. Thomas, that you are a coward."

"Good gracious, Mrs. Gill, don't put it off upon me, mum. You know it's all your own doings from first to last, and I won't set light to the straw."

"Poor fool," exclaimed Mrs. Gill, with a look of contempt, "you make one in the intention, and yet shrink from the act. I will save you all."

"No, no, no."

"Eh?"

"Don't—don't do it," again cried the coachman. "Don't do it; I repent. Let us all repent. Don't do it."

"Repent?"

"Yes, yes."

"And replace the plate and jewels?"

"No—I—I don't mean that."

'What in the name of all that's cowardly and contemptible do you mean then?'

'I thought of going away with the valuables, but not of smothering or roasting Battaney."

"Did you   Did you!"

"Well, you needn't jump down a fellow's throat because he don't exactly relish setting a house on fire, and burning a fellow creature in it."

'Will you go and put a knife in him then?'

"A knife?"

"Yes."

"No, to be sure not. Hardly. Well, come, that is an improvement upon it with a vengeance. No, Mrs. G., you don't catch me at that sort of fun, and I'm blessed if, from what I have seen of you to-day, I don't think you are a regular she devil."

"Think what you please. The thoughts of such as you are matter of indifference to me."

As she spoke, Mrs. Gill, who had not relinquished the candle, because no one would take it, threw it lighted as it was among the straw, to which it instantly communicated a blaze by the magic of its touch.

"It is done," she said. "Let us all be off now to London as quickly as we possibly can."

"Oh Lor!" said the coachman, "I'm afraid we are all done as well. Come on, come on, I know where we are all a going, post haste, in the long run."

*   *   *   *

Let us take a peep at the chamber of Lord Battaney.

It was something to him in the shape of a reprieve from sudden death when the servants left him, for during their stay he did not know a moment when they might be induced by the eloquence of Mrs. Gill to commence upon him the smothering process.

Little did he imagine how much more diabolical a scheme was in the brain of that politic lady, than the one he had denounced.

It was a something, too, to find that the pain he suffered was just about bearable, provided he lay profoundly still, and then he was conjecturing for the first time in his life, how much he had to hope from some latent principle of pity, that might be in the hearts of his servants.

What pity had he ever shown in all his dealings with human nature? What mercy had he ever exhibited to any one of the many who had been in his power? None—none—whatever. And now he murmured to himself,—

"Surely they will not leave me to perish."

After a time he began to call to mind who it was that had been in his chamber, and when he could count up only four, he thought there was a chance of some other of his dependants hearing him if he rung the bell violently, for he knew that four did not comprise all who received his pay, and who ought to be in or about the villa.

It will be recollected that Harry Dean had taken away the one who possibly might have rendered to Lord Bat-

taney the most efficient assistance. At all events we may set it down for a certainty that Sam Clover would not have joined in the plot against him.

Accordingly Lord Battaney again made the painful, but slight movement, which brought him sufficiently near to the bell to grasp the tassel of the pull, and he commenced the ringing, which was such an annoyance to Mrs. Gill and her companions while the coachman had gone for the straw.

No result followed the ringing except that the more violently he did it, the more he shook himself, and added to his pains which were in other respects momentarily increasing, as fever began to take possession of him.

He left off ringing, and lay still and wretched.

His eyes were open, and as he looked towards the window, one of the shutters of which had been opened by the servants, he fancied that a strange dimness was creeping over it.

At first he looked on with a strange inert feeling of curiosity, but then suddenly an awful idea came across his mind.

He thought the strange vapoury dimness must proceed from a failing of his eye-sight, and be the immediate precursor of death.

"I am dying—I am dying!" he said. "Great God, I am dying! and most horribly, for so far all my faculties are in full vigour. Oh that my mind would go with the bodily decay, but it is truly horrible thus to watch the approach of the destroyer, with no hope—no consolation—not one friendly voice near me."

The window at which he looked grew dimmer and dimmer, and he fancied that huge masses of strange vapour floated before it continually.

Then there came suddenly upon his ears a confused, rushing, roaring noise, as though he were in the immediate neighbourhood of some catract. He listened intently, and there was no mental suggestion of what could be the nature of that noise, which momentarily increased in intensity.

He began to think it must be another mysterious symptom of coming death, and he groaned aloud.

It was now some few moments before he summoned courage to try what he considered was his fading sight, by looking towards the window, but when he did so, the revulsion of his feelings was indeed awful, and with a shrieking voice that might have been heard for miles, he cried,—

"Fire, fire, fire! It is fire!"

CHAPTER XLVII.

TONY HAS AN ADVENTURE IN SEARCH OF LUCY.

THE state of mind of poor Tony when he ascertained by what a juggle Lucy had been removed from the hotel, transcended all possible description.

Despite the reliance which he might feel in the assurances of Harry Dean, that if London held Lucy within its mighty precincts, he would find her,

Tony would not be persuaded from himself engaging in the task.

Now poor Tony, although an inhabitant of the leviathan of cities, was about as ignorant of some of its ways and proceedings, as he was of the made dishes with which it was attempted to tickle his palate at the hotel.

Still perseverance will do wonders, and Tony set off on his wanderings in search of Lucy, with no other guide to the object of his search, than that the carriage she was taken away in had a chocolate coloured body.

"I wonder now," said Tony, "how many carriages there are in all London with chocolate coloured bodies to them?"

This was an interesting enquiry to him, but it was not one which he was very likely to be able to answer well or speedily, nevertheless on he went, looking to the right and to the left, with the hope of finding some vehicle answering the description of that which had so powerfully aided in the abduction of Lucy.

Tony soon reached the neighbourhood of Covent Garden, not because he thought that there he was likely to find the object of his search more than anywhere else, but from that natural sort of feeling which takes a man's footsteps to a locality with which he is familiar.

Wandering on he reached Catherine-street, and as there were unequivocal symptoms of rain coming on, Tony stepped into a spacious doorway, as well to think a little as to shield himself from the approaching shower. As he thus stood, he once glanced behind him to see what sort of a place he was in, but all he could perceive was a long gloomy looking passage, at the further end of which was a swinging door of most fearfully faded green baize.

"An odd place" thought Tony, "but the rain has now come in good earnest, so I must wait a little. Oh, Lucy, Lucy, if I had now but the least idea of where you where."

As Tony uttered these words, he heard the door at the end of the passage close with a bang, and in another moment footsteps slowly approached him.

"Ah!" said a voice, "more rain."

"Confound the weather," said another. "You can't rely upon it for an hour at this time of the year."

" Its constancy you mean ?"

" It is constant, in being constant. But come now in, as we are here alone. Have you made up your mind ?"

" About what ?"

" The little girl, to be sure."

Tony was all ears.

" Oh, I think," replied the man to whom the question had been put, " I think I shall be forced to murder her !"

Tony drew his breath short and thick.

" Won't that be rather revolting," said the other, with as careless an air as though he were talking of one of the most indifferent things in the world, instead of an avowed murder.

" Granted. But what am I to do with her ?"

" Yes, yes ! I know the difficulty."

" If you can think of anything else, of course, I shall be most happy, for I don't like much, I confess, the murdering business, although I have often succeeded i n it."

" True—true !"

" Can you suggest any other mode of escape from the difficulty ?"

" Not I."

" Then settled she must be."

" I suppose so. Do you think this rain will last ?"

" I hope not. It looks quizby though."

" Well," thought Tony, " of all the cool, diabolical wretches that eves I come near, these are the worst. Gracious goodness ! if after all it should be Lucy they are talking about."

This thought had such an effect upon Tony, that he felt for the moment, as though all the world were going round with him. But it was no time for inaction, or anything in the shape of irresolution, so he plucked up a spirit, and creeping a little closer to the speakers, he prepared himself to listen to, and treasure up against them, any words they said.

" Shall you go to dinner ?" said one.

" Well I don't know. I think I will settle the murder first. It will be off my mind then."

" Ah, to be sure ?"

" Off his mind, thought Tony.'

" Perhaps," added he who spoke so unconcernedly of a life. " Perhaps by that time, the rain will have given over, and we shall be able to go comfortably somewhere, and enjoy a walk for an hour or two."

" Very likely. Come on."

" And yet I am perplexed."

" About what ?"

" Why, when you come to think of it, there is a very great prejudice, against the murder of a young girl."

" Well, there is."

" And yet what the deuce else to do with her I don't know, because if she is not murdered, how can she be got out of the way, and out of the way she must be got, you know."

" Oh yes, that is settled."

" Well, well, I will speak to Jones about it. Who knows but he may be able to suggest something, although I think he will vote at once for the murder repugnant as it is."

" There is the great recommendation in that course," said the other " that there is no further trouble about her. If you bring her to such a tragic end, why no questions can be asked."

" True, true."

" I would rather murder her ten times over, than spoil the affair.'

They both walked down the passage again with all the unconcern in the world, and passing the baize it swung shut after them, and Tony was again alone.

For a few moments Tony was much too panic stuck to speak. His first act was to wipe the perspiration that had collected upon his face off it with a very original looking handkerchief which was a painfully vivid representation of the National Flag, and then he gave a serious groan before he trusted himself to speak.

" Here's a situation," he said, " gracious goodness, what ought I to do. Here's a situation. People wouldn't believe this in a novel. If I were to write this now, the people would shake their heads, and say, go along with you."

Tony wiped his face again, and then he gave a great sigh as he heard the door at the end of the passage open.

He did not dare to look round him, but he heard a footstep approaching, and presently a boy with a paper cap upon his head passed him, whistling a lively tune.

"Ah," thought Tony, "you don't know my boy the den of cut-throats you have come out of."

The boy went out into the street, notwithstanding the rain, and in a few moments he returned with a pot of porter in his hand.

"Shall I warn him," thought Tony, "or is he an accomplice? Ought I to speak to him."

Urged by the instinct of the moment, Tony said to the boy,

"Hilloa, old fellow."

"How's your mother," said the boy.

"Come, come," said Tony, "no nonsense."

"Nobody asked you," said the boy.

"Why, you fool, its for your own good I speak to you. You don't know where you are."

"Walker! Have yer sold yer accordian yet."

"I tell you, boy, that there will be a murder here."

"So I have heard. There's a precious many on 'em too, during the season."

"The season?"

"Yes. Oh, aint you jolly green to be sure. Kim up Neddy."

Here they boy executed a striking imitation of the harmony perpetrated by a donkey when he is pleased or displeased, we believe naturalists have not quite clearly decided which.

Tony began to perceive that the boy was obdurate, and he said no more, but suffered him to proceed with the pot of porter, which he did in great triumph, fully convinced that he had quite silenced Tony, and achieved a victory which to him was a matter of great rejoicing.

"Gracious Providence," thought Tony "They think no more of murders here. than they do of pots of porter. I—I can't stand this, I must do something, I—I must find a policeman."

Sauntering past the door, came at that moment one of the force, and Tony called to him.

"Hoi! hoi! hoi!"

"Here you is," said the policeman, "what is it?"

"A murder," gasped Tony.

"I've got you. Do you give yourself up. Don't say anything unless you like, old cock."

The policeman accompanied these words by seizing upon Tony in a very scientific manner by the cuff of his right hand and his collar.

"Don't be a fool, it isn't me," said Tony.

"What did yer say it was, then, for?"

"I didn't."

"What do you want then, stupid?"

"Why, there are some people in here going to murder a girl."

"Ah?"

The policeman pulled out his truncheon, and rubbed his nose with the end of it.

"Do   you hear that, idiot?" said Tony.

"Come, none of that to the force, if ye please, young feller, none of that, or else I shall have to lock you up."

"Lock up who you like, but come with me and stop the murder first, whatever you do."

"Humph!"

"Good God, what are you humphing there for?"

"Wait a bit."

"What for?"

"Don't you think it's better to give em time to do it, and then be down upon 'em. That's the way to do business, you know. What's the use of interfering beforehand."

"Hush!" said Tony.

"Hush!" said the policeman.

The door at the end of the passage opened; the same two persons who had been overheard by Tony discussing the propriety of the murder, made their appearance again, walking very slowly, and talking with great earnestness.

Tony pulled the policeman aside into a dark corner, and they both listened attentively to the conversation of the two men.

The policeman perceptibly trembled, and Tony whispered in his ear ominously, —

"I believe, old brick, that you are a coward."

"Me."

"Yes, you, but hold your noise just now, and listen. There, don't you hear them."

The two men passed close to Tony

and the policeman, and the one said to the other,—

"So that is his opinion is it ?"

"Yes," replied the other. "He thinks that a murder, however atrocious and sanguinary, will not make much sensation at this end of the town."

"Perhaps not."

"So, upon the whole, as there is a little difficulty to know what to do with the girl, and she is decidedly in the way, he recommends that without any fuss being made about it she should be quietly put out of the way."

CHAPTER XLVIII.

TONY AND THE POLICEMAN GET INTO A HORRIBLE ADVENTURE.

THE policeman grasped Tony's arm with vice-like power, as he whispered,—

"Gracious ! there's danger."

"Lots," said Tony.

"You—you, don't mean— mean it ?"

"I do though. Listen to what's going on now. If you are in a fever and don't know what to be at, lend me your truncheon, and cut your stick yourself."

"Take everything, but spare my life."

"Hush ! hush !"

"I tell you how it could be managed," said one of the men.

"How ?" said the other.

"Suppose after murdering his uncle, Martin were to fire a pistol bang at the girl, and smash her through the doorway. There can be a terrible shriek, and that will settle the business, so that afterwards we can go on agreeably enough you know."

"Well, that is not a bad plan."

"Now take 'em up," said Tony.

"Hush !" said the policeman, " I've got a plan in my head."

"Have you, though ?"

"Yes."

"What is it ?"

"I—I shall go and put on private clothes, and then you and I can make our way into this place and make a good thing of it. Don't you see if we were

to take these two fellows now, it would be of no good."

"Wouldn't it ?"

"No. Suppose now the girl they speak of is hid, and accessible to none, but they know where to find her, and suppose they refused to tell, what could you do then ?"

"You are right, lobster," said Tony.

"Come, come, don't call me by any uproarious epitaphs."

"What do you mean, I only said lobster, and you had no need to be crabbed about that, I'm sure. Go and get your clothes while I wait here. Perhaps I shall hear something else before you come back—you know."

"Very well, I've only got to go to the court there by the corner, and get a coat, and be back to you in a jiffy."

"Yes, a coat," said Tony, " when you lobsters talk of disguising yourselves you think the coat does everything, as if a policeman's boots wasn't known all the world over."

"Oh, go along with you. You wait quietly, that's all you have to do, and keep your ears open."

"Oh, be off with you, I don't want quite such long ears as you have got to listen to all as is going on here. Don't be long."

Away flew the policeman to get a change of apparel, and the two men who were in the passage certainly looked a little alarmed to see one of the force rush past them at such a rate, and run over the road like a lamplighter.

"What is the meaning of that ?" said one.

"It looks suspicious," said the other.

"And yet we have nothing to fear. The place has never to my knowledge been interrupted."

"Oh dear, no, it has been in this line for years, and the magistrates of the district know it well,"

"The wretches," thought Tony. " Don't we live and learn in London ; here's a place has been in the murder line for some years, and the magistrates well knowing it, don't think of interfering at all in the matter."

The policeman was stimulated perhaps by vague ideas of a compliment from the learned recorder or the erratic common sergeant, for he certainly showed considerable alacrity in making the change in his costume, and got back to the house of apparent murder long before Tony thought it possible he could have made his arrangements.

The only unfortunate thing was, that by the time he came back, the men had again disappeared behind the mysterious swinging door.

"Where is they?" said the policeman.

"Gone," said Tony; "Lord what a guy you look. But come on, let us go through that door and try our luck."

The policeman shook for a moment, as great conquerers may be supposed sometimes to do, and then he followed Tony, having no doubt raised up his courage absolutely to the sticking place, for he looked not like an inhabitant of the earth, so pale was he, as Tony pushed the swinging door.

The door readily yielded, and they found themselves, as it swung close behind them, in a most singular looking place indeed.

A narrow passage, leading to Heaven only knew where, was dimly lighted by a small oil lamp hanging from the ceiling, dust was upon the walls, and an accumulation of the smoke of gas upon the ceiling. There seemed to be no other outlet from this passage besides the one at which Tony and the police-man had presented themselves, except a dirty looking narrow flight of steps at its farther end, about twelve feet from the swing door.

"What shall we do?" said the policeman.

"Come on," said Tony.

The stairs only got a dim illumination from the oil lamp in the passage, and they creaked amazingly as Tony descended them.

He was followed tolerably closely by the policeman, who now probably began to think that there might be as much danger, if not more, in retreating than there was in advancing.

They descended those murderous looking stairs together, until they reached the last one, and then for a few moments they paused to listen when Tony heard voices some distance on to the right hand.

"Come on," he whispered, "come on."

"We is in for it now," said the policeman, "I don't think rather."

"Never mind."

"Oh, it's all very well to say never mind, but—"

"Hold your bothering,—come on, if you are born to be murdered you will be, so, there's an end of it. Make yourself comfortable."

"Comfortable?"

"Hush! come on."

They proceeded some few steps, and then Tony paused to listen to what was going on, and he heard a voice say—

"Hold! I'll give your body to the vultures, and on the beetling crags shall your quivering limbs hang pendant as though crying to the carrion crows, Ha! ha! come and eat me."

"Villain," said another voice, "why does the grave yawn and give up its dead. I wish for help to crush the serpent in his lair, and the hyena in his den."

The policeman made sure the last speaker would be upon them in a moment, so with the instinct of self preservation and a laudable desire to save the life of Tony as well as his own, he seized him by the arms, and hurried him on until they came to a place more singular than any they had yet seen in that house of murder.

It was a large disorderly looking place enough at one end of which a large curtain hung. The walls were piled up with heaps of what looked like old scaffolding and paper-hangings, and the floor was desperately uneven with knots of all sorts and sizes.

"What will become of us. Where are we now?" said the policeman. "I wish I was well out of this."

"Hush! what's that," said Tony.

A strange knocking sound came from below, and then a voice, evidently in some region beneath the floor, said in smothered accents,

"Knock, when it's to come."

"What? oh, what?" said the policeman.

"I don't care, lend me your truncheon said Tony, "and I'll knock, let come what may."

"Oh, no—no."

"Are you ready," said the voice, "or are you going to keep me here all day."

"There," said Tony, as he snatched away the policeman's staff, "I will knock in spite of the devil himself."

Bang—bang—bang, went the staff upon the ground.

In an instant a square hole opened in the floor, and up came an awful looking figure in a shroud, who said,—

"Repent, wretched Baron, repent. I am the ghost of—Hilloa! Who are you, eh?"

"Murder! Murder!" cried the policeman, "murder, don't, oh don't; I'm only a policeman. Oh, dear—oh, dear."

"Why—why," said Tony, "what the devil is all this?"

Four or five persons suddenly now made their appearance in rather a tumultuous manner, all enquiring together what was the matter.

"I'll be hanged if I know," said Tony. "Where am I?"

"Yes," answered the policeman, "have mercy on us, and tell me where we am."

"Why, you are in the Private Theatre to be sure, where we are getting up a new play, called 'The Spectre Uncle, or, the Demon Lover of the Maiden Worth a Million.'"

Tony looked at the policeman, who winked at Tony."

"Then there ain't never a murder going on here," said the latter, with a dolorous aspect.

"Oh, yes," replied a young man, with a laugh.

"Is there?"

"To-night, a friend of mine, who is a very good fellow in the main, is going to murder Hamlet."

"Where is Mr. Hamlet," cried the policeman, "I'll protect him. Why don't he apply to the station at once."

A roar of laughter followed this speech, and Tony said to the policeman,—

"Lobster, they are queering you."

"What? Making game of me?"

"Yes, to be sure."

"Fire and fury, I'll take everybody up, I will—I'll—I'll have vengeance. Am I to be put to all the trouble of changing my coat, and then to be made game of."

A roar of laughter ensued, and the policeman got very desperate indeed. He glared about him indirectly with an anxious wish of finding somebody whom he could wreak his vengeance on, but one of the company stepped up to him, and said in a conciliatory tone,—

"Come, come, you made a mistake, and we have had our laugh at you, so don't bear malice. There's a deal of dust always flying about here, and the general effect is to make anybody thirsty who comes into the place."

The policeman's features relaxed into a grin.

"Well, gentlemen," he said, "a joke's a joke as you say, and tis an odd thing, but I am thirsty sure enough."

"Ah, I thought so. Here, Bob."

"Yes, sir," said a dirty boy with a paper cap on his head, emerging from behind some cumbrous scenery.

"Go over the way and get a couple of pots of the best old ale, Bob, and say they are for me."

"Well," said the policeman, quite giving up all idea of making himself disagreeable, "it was funny after all—and so this is a playhouse, is it?"

"Yes, certainly."

"And," said Tony, ruefully, "there is no little girl kept a prisoner, and going to be murdered."

"None that we know of."

"Well, good bye to you all"

"Why, you're not going without your share of the ale?"

"Yes; I don't want any. I am looking about for one whom I'm afeard I shan't find in London. You don't happen to have heard of a little girl, named Lucy Destern, have you?"

"No; is she in the profession?"

"What profession?"

"The stage."

"Oh dear, no—oh, no."

"I tell you what, Smith," cried one, "I saw a good melo-dramatic scene yesterday."

"Indeed."

"Yes, and in real life. A coach drove up to the door of a tolerably large house in Soho, and a woman, who upon her countenance had the indescribable air of vice that can never be mistaken by those who have lived long in London, got out and literally dragged out a young child, a girl, I ought hardly to call her a child. The little creature was either dying or fainting, I don't know which."

"When was that?" cried Tony.

" Had she fair hair and blue eyes, with very long lashes?   Where was it?"

"She certainly had fair hair, and plenty of it, rather long than thick though, and worn in what you call a crop."

Tony rushed upon the man, and seized hold of him by both arms, crying—

"Only show me that house and I'll—I'll do anything you like—oh, only show me the house."

"Of course, if you wish it?"

"If I wish it? Oh, don't say that—I shall go mad quite if you don't show me at once."

"But what do you want to know for?"

"Don't ask me—I have no time to tell you, unless, indeed, you will come with me at once, and listen to what I have to say as we go along—will you do so?"

"I will; your emotion is real. I say, King, if we could act like this now, we should do."

"Oh, yes; but that is nature.'

"And 'the art itself is nature,' so we ought to do it."

"Oh, come, come," cried Tony, "come; if you know—if you could only guess my feelings at this moment, full of the hope as I am of finding her I was seeking, you would fly with me. Oh, the sickness of—of—the heart!"

Tony reeled back, and would have fallen, but he was caught by the policeman, who cried—

"Come, come, come. Hilloa—move on—I mean what's the matter with you? ain't you well?"

"Yes, yes; only a little—faint—or so."

"Then," said the actor, who had ordered the ale, "take a drop of that, it will do you a world of good."

Tony drank sparingly.

"Enough, enough," he said. "I'm—I'm all right again. Come on, it was only the thought of seeing Lucy that upset me rather—I—I am as strong as a lion now. All's right—quite—quite right. Oh, do come on."

"Look," said the policeman, as he directed Tony's attention to a young man, who, at the back of the stage, was closely imitating Tony's movement when

he nearly fell. "Look, are you going to stand that? They have no more feeling here than a brick-bat. See if that chap ain't making game of you!"

"No—no " cried the person alluded to.

"I saw you."

"No, you are mistaken; I was only taking a lesson from nature, that's what we ought always to do when we possibly can. Believe me, it was from no disrepect to you or your sorrows. Here's my hand upon the truth of my words."

"I believe you," said Tony. "Don't mention it."

"Now, sir, at your service," said the young man, who without doubt had happened to be passing Madame Zadzed's house at the very moment that individual was handing out poor Lucy Destern from the carriage.

Tony did not want a second asking, but set off at a quick pace, accompanied by the player.

"I am almost sorry," said Tony's companion, "that I mentioned this affair in your presence."

"Sorry?"

"Yes; for your disappointment will be so great if it should not turn out to be the person you imagine it possible it may be."

"And yet there is the chance, so do not say you are sorry. I would go to the furthest corner of the world on such a chance merely, and thank anybody, as I truly thank you, who would give me the chance of so doing."

"Well, you are an odd fellow, and all I can say is, I sincerely hope it may turn out as you wish it."

"I hope so, indeed."

Tony did not like to pester his companion with any questions as to whether they were near or far from the house, but as they went along he would occasionally look anxiously in his face to see if he could gather from its expression that they were close at hand.

The player was sufficiently versed in the human passions and feelings, to know what were Tony's thoughts at the moment they reached the street in which was situated Madame Zadzed's house; he said to him:

"Now we are not many doors from the spot. Come on, and I will shew

[The students carrying the corpse of Kate Destern to the cab.]

you the precise house, for I was sufficiently interested by the circumstance to take particular notice of it. There it is, that house with the balcony, directly facing us."

In another moment Tony stood opposite to that residence where Lucy had suffered so much by being a witness to the horrible events we have detailed in previous chapters, and where now lay the dead and mangled body of Madame Zadzed.

CHAPTER XLIX.

KATE AND THE NEWSPAPER.—THE TRANCE.

With some feeling of affliction at the circumstances of sadness in which poor Kate Destern is placed, we return once again to her bedside at the humble house of the widow.

The scene that had taken place when last with the reader we watched the hectic colour upon that fair cheek, was calculated to produce a most injurious effect upon Kate, considering the weak state she was in.

Superadded to all the pains and penalties of sickness—and Heaven knows they are enough in themselves—she now had the sad and sorrowful reflection that she was bringing evil upon those who had succoured her.

It was scarely to be expected but that the relieving officer's deputy would endeavour to take some vengeance upon the coal-heaver, and all who might be considered to have aided and abetted him in the punishment which he certainly caused to be inflicted upon the hard-hearted official.

Kate knew enough of the jurisdiction and application of the laws of England, to feel what an unequal fight the poor always wage with those in place and power ; no wonder, then, that she dreaded the result of the *fracas* that had taken place.

Hour after hour, however, passed away, and nothing was heard of the discomfited official personage, but after twilight had for some time disappeared, there came the sound of footsteps upon the stairs leading to the widow's room.

Kate had relapsed into an uneasy sleep, but it was that species of sleep that the least unusual noise was sure to break, and as one of the two persons—for there were two who were approaching—had on boots that slightly creaked, the sound awakened her in a moment, and she said in a voice of alarm—

"Who is that—who is that?"

The compassionate widow listened, and before she could say anything the voice of their friend, the coal-heaver, banished all fears, as they heard him say—

"This here's the door, sir. Mind yourself, there's generally an old pitcher put here for people to tumble over. All's right. You can see that mop?"

"Dear me, yes," said a voice. "Really if people would but keep their property in doors, what a—the deuce take it——"

"There now, didn't I tell you of the pitcher?"

"Confound it."

"Aye, you have confounded it, I think.

Lor' bless me ! how stupid some people is—no offence, sir. "

"Oh, none in the least. I never adopt a general remark, if I can possibly help it."

The coal-heaver's man knocked at the widow's door, and when it was opened, he said,—

"Well, I've brought a doctor in spite of 'em. Come in, sir. Here's the young lady. Come in, sir. Don't mind falling over anything, sir. All's right. How do you do, mum, by this time, and how do you do, my dear, eh? You'll soon be better now."

"I thank you," said Kate.

"Is you better?"

"I think not—not much."

"You soon will be."

"I thank you for the kind wish that prompts the prediction."

"Oh, I don't purtend to understand above half of that ; but here's the doctor, my dear. And now, Dr. Grey, I've only got one thing to say to you, do your most bestest."

"You may depend upon that. Will you oblige me by allowing me a few minutes private conversation with my patient?"

"Well, that's only reasonable. Come along, mum, you and me will go down stairs."

"We can step into the next room," said the widow ; "no one is there, as it's to let."

"Wery good. Now, mem. We'll come back soon, doctor, and all I says is, do your most bestest."

In about ten minutes, the medical man called to the coal-heaver and the widow,—

"Come in," he said, "I have said all I need say just now, I think, to my patient."

"Wery good," said the coal heaver, as he produced a small canvass bag from his pocket, "wery good, sir. Now I likes to do things in a business like way, and out of debt, you know, is out of danger. There's the young lady, all you have got to do is to cure her as quick as you possibly can, and tell me at once what you'll do it for, and I'll pay down on the nail."

"Well," said the medical man, with a smile, "This is certainly the oddest offer I ever had."

"Odd! what do you mean? If anybody was to come to me, and say to me, Jem, you see that there barge to unload, what will you take to do it, and here's the blunt, I should say that was the way to do business."

"Well, well, leave the question of what's to pay alone for the present, if you please."

"Well, if you wont say."

"I can't, and, for fear of overcharging you, I will until the young lady is well, which, I hope, will be shortly. I will send some appropriate medicines, and have no doubt but that we shall shortly see an improvement."

"In course."

The medical man took his departure, and when he was gone, the coal-heaver said to the widow,—

"You have heard of the murder, mem?"

"The murder! What murder?"

"Lor' bless you, they is crying it about the street now. Here's one 'o the papers. I'll read it to you."

"Perhaps she's asleep."

"No, no," said Kate, "do not mind me, I am not sleepy at present. You will not disturb me."

"Well," added the coal heaver, "here it is. 'Bow-street,'—Bow-street, you know, mum."

"Yes, yes."

"'We have only time to state, that a shocking murder has been perpetrated in the neighbourhood of Soho.'"

"Go on."

"'A shocking murder has been,' oh, I was past that—'Soho'—yes, 'Soho; the culprit, who, we understand, has been apprehended, and brought before the sitting magistrate, upon the clearest evidence of his guilt, is named—named —named——'"

"Named what?"

"Wait a bit, mum, there's a crease in the paper just here; I'll soon smoothen it out."

"Yes, yes."

"'Is named'—ah! here it is—'is named Henry Dean.'"

A shriek from Kate caused the coal-heaver to let fall the paper, and start to his feet, while the widow herself echoed the scream in her consternation.

"No, no, no," cried Kate, as she rose to a sitting posture in the bed, and stretched out her arms, "no, no, not

Henry Dean; it cannot, it cannot be—it is not—no, no, no! Death—is—this death?"

Slowly she fell back upon her pillow again, her hands dropped listlessly to her sides, and she lay as still as the very image of death itself could possibly be.

"Murder!" cried the coal-heaver.

"Help, help!" cried the widow.

"Stop a bit, I'll run for Mr. Grey," said the coal heaver; "no, I'll get the first doctor I can. Oh dear, oh dear! that this should have happened. D—n that pitcher, I've knocked it all the way down stairs. Don't make a row, and I'll have a doctor here in a minute."

The coal-heaver rushed frantically into the first chemist's shop he came to, and seizing a fair haired stupid looking young man by the collar, he said,—

"Come along, come along."

"Murder! fire!" cried the young man.

"God bless me!" shouted the coal-heaver, "I don't want to do you any harm. I'll pay you. It's a young lady as is ill, that's what it is. Come along."

"Oh, oh! yes, of course I'll come; but you should have considered my nerves a little, and not come into the shop in such a way. How far is it?"

"Come along, will you?"

"Oh yes, yes—my hat—yes—where's my hat. I've got it—I'm coming. Don't be violent. What's the use of being violent? Dear me, you are a most extraordinary man—I'm coming."

The coal-heaver hustled the fair haired young man along the street—he pushed him up the stairs, and brought him to the bed side of Kate, saying,—

"Now tell us what you bring it in."

"Why, why—dear me——"

"What?"

"I—I—oh yes."

"What do you mean?"

"She's—dead."

The coal-heaver staggered back till he came to a chair, upon which he sat with a long drawn sigh.

"Dead, dead!"

"Ye—ye—yes, dead."

"Poor young thing! so mild, and so gentle, and so—so beautiful, as sue was too. What had she to do with dying, I wonder. There aint so many in this here world like her. I—I—well it's no sort of use. What is you a crying about, mum, eh? What's the use o' crying? Don't think I—I, it's only a—a silver moth as has flowed into my eye, and made it water a little—that's—that's—all, mum—that's all."

"Oh dear, oh dear!"

"What's the use of crying? Oh dear!"

"I can't help it."

"Who said you could, eh? Don't be crying there. Of course we must all die some day, and what's the use of making a fuss about it. She might have staid a little longer to make somebody happy with her soft voice, and her dear pretty face. Well, well—what are you staring at, stupid?"

"Eh? Bless me," said the young surgeon, " what a very violent man you are, to be sure."

"And why shouldn't I be?"

"Oh—I—I——"

"Of course; perhaps you think this here affair has cut me up, and got the better o' me, but it hasn't. This here's a moth as is in my eye—that's all—stupid."

"Ahem! well, I'm very sorry."

"No you aint. How dare you be sorry? What was she to you Did you ever hear her speak, so thankfully and sweetly, even if any one said half a kind word to her? No, no, nobody has any right to be sorry but me, and I won't. No, I won't, but she shall lay in some quiet spot where she—she——"

"Oh, dear—oh, dear," moaned the widow.

"Where—she shall have a little railing round her grave, and in summer have a few pots of flowers."

The widow again burst into tears, and wept freely.

"Ah, ah, cry away," said the coal-heaver, " you'll never in this world, mum, find such another to cry about."

"But, sir, sir," said the surgeon.

"What now?"

"Perhaps you won't mind telling me who I am to send in my little account to, if you please."

"Account?"

"Yes, its only five shillings; perhaps you will pay it now."

The coal-heaver rose slowly, and there must have been something in his looks that the young surgeon did not exactly

like, for without waiting another moment for his five shillings, he bolted out of the room and down the stairs with the greatest precipitation.

"Oh, very well, go—go," said the coalheaver, " you ain't wanted here any more. I shall never like now to pass your shop. I say missus, just pick up a bit and tell us what's to be done."

" Alas, alas."

"Come—come, its done now."

" Poor thing."

" Ah, poor young thing, look at us, mum, and look at her. Who's the best off now, eh?" We ought not to cry about her, seeing as how she's as happy as a fly in a sugar tub."

" The parish must bury her, poor thing."

"The what? The parish? Do I look like a sort of fellow as would let the parish bury a cat I'd took a fancy too—no—no mum, no parish has anything to do with her, I can tell you. She shall lay along side of my own little child—I—I did'nt think I should ever bring her such good company."

" You will bury her?"

" I will; if it was the last shilling I had in the world I'd do it; but mum I'll off to Mr. Grey and tell him what has happened. Ah, poor thing, she wants none of his physic now—it's we as has had the physicker. I shant forget this day in a hurry.

CHAPTER L.

THE YOUNG STUDENT'S SUGGESTION, THE CONSEQUENCES.

" DEAD!" exclaimed Mr. Grey in answer to the communication which was made him to that effect by the coal heaver.

" Very dead sighed the latter."

" You—you are jesting, surely?"

" I wish I was."

" But—but how was it, come sit down and tell me all about it. How did it happen."

The coal-heaver sat down after carefully depositing his fantailed beaver under the chair, and then in his way giving an account how it was that Kate had expired suddenly.

During this recital a young man had

sauntered into the room, and would have left it again, but that Dr. Grey invited him to remain, saying,—

"Mr. Musgrave, this is a very remarkable case, that I am now having detailed to me."

When the coal-heaver had concluded, he said,—

"Who did you call in ?"

"The nearest doctor, who said she was dead, and dead enough she is, poor thing, as any one may see. I thought I ought to come and let you know,· so that you might take no more trouble."

"I am truly sorry."

"I knew you would be, sir."

"You did me but justice, my friend ; at all events, of course, since a medical man has declared her dead, poor thing, I can do nothing. I suppose an inquest will be thought necessary ?"

"I have seen the beadle of theparish, and he says not as she was ill in bed beforehand."

"But it would be very satisfactory to know of what she died. I suppose some unsuspected heart complaint, was the real cause, and that excitement at hearing what you read from the paper, was the stimulant that caused it to be immediately fatal ?"

"It don't matter, sir."

"Oh, but it does."

"How can it, she's dead, that's enough, and more than enough, by ever so much for those who cared anything about her poor thing. I suppose her time had come, and there was an end of it. I don't care ; who supposes I care ?"

Dr. Guy shook his head, as he said,—

"You care more than you choose to say you do, my friend."

"No I don't."

The coal-heaver took out his canvass bag, and added,—

"What have I got to pay you, sir ?"

"Pay me ? nothing—nothing at all. Why, you hardly suppose, do you, that I am going to take payment for making one call with you to see her, poor thing. No—no, we are quits—I wish it had been otherwise, but you should recollect that in the midst of life we are in death."

"So it seems, sir. Don't mind me. Lately, ever so many of them small silver moths gets into my eyes when I

least *expectorates* un. Good day, sir—good day."

"Good day, I only hope we shall be more fortunate with the next patient you bring me."

"This has taken me rather by surprise," said Dr. Grey, to the young man who had come into the room. "The patient did not appear to be in any danger whatever. She was merely in that kind of low fever which is incidental to a disarrangement of the ordinary functions of the skin, In common parlance, she had caught a cold."

"And is now dead."

"So it seems."

"It's a bad case, not to know exactly the cause of death."

"Yes. I was in hopes there would have been an inquest, in which case, I would easily have procured an order to open the body. She is quite friendless, poor thing, as I understand, and this coal-heaver who has constituted himself her protector, I fancy with the prejudices of his class against dissection would just as soon allow us to cut him up, as the dead body of the girl."

"No doubt, sir, and yet ——"

"Yet what ?"

"I was thinking."

"Of what ?"

"That surely it might be possible to get the body, sir."

"Humph; I must confess, I don't like that alternative at all. I should, for the sake of science, like to have it, but yet I have no great inclination to make the attempt feloniously to obtain it."

"There can be no occasion for you, sir, to mix yourself up in the matter personally."

"How would you manage, then ?"

"I would get the assistance of a fellow student of mine, who is at Bartholomew's, and upon whom I could depend, and all we would require of you, would be to tell us exactly where the body was, and to give us house room for it when we brought it here."

"Well, really I—I ——"

"Consent."

"I suppose I must. It can do no harm, and may do a great deal of good. It is so seldom that a subject can be got which is not in a considerable state of emaciation from disease, that I must confess I should like to have it."

"Wish us success, then, sir, and go with us and point out to me the place where the body lies. If then you will sit up yourself for us, we will at the small hours of the night, when folks are mostly asleep, make the attempt, and if we fail in any way, of course whatever may be the consequences, we shall not compromise you."

"No—I beg of you not to mention my name, however awkward may be your position. It would never do for me to get a reputation for kidnapping the dead bodies of my own patients. The press would get hold of it, and I should never hear the last of it."

"Depend upon me, sir."

"Very well then. Good luck attend you. When will you try it?"

"To-night. Before any approach of decomposition has marred the subject. I hope to be able to make all proper arrangements with my young friend, and by about two o'clock in the morning, pray expect us with the subject, or if we do not appear, you may be sure some more than usual obstacle has beset us."

"Which I think will not be the case."

"Indeed, sir!"

"No."

"Have you special reasons?"

"I have. In the first place, the house is a low lodging house, every room in which is let out to somebody. In such places, each person has his or her key, so that a footstep upon the stairs at night is nobody's business, and as each person sleeps along with whatever belongs to him, nobody will rise to disturb you."

"Excellent."

"All you have to do, is to get a common latch key, not two large, and with your friend walk in at night, and bring down the body, when you must have a cab or coach ready to receive it, and yourselves."

"You think it will be deserted?"

"Probably locked in the room where she died. I don't think any of the parties belonging to the place will care to sleep with the dead."

"Then sir, it is settled."

Mr. Grey went with the young student, and pointed out the house, after which, he said—

"Now you must manage the whole affair yourself. All I promise to do, is to sit up until you come home, or send some message, until three we will say. After that I shall give you up."

*   *   *   *

The young student whose name was Musgrave, called upon a friend of his, named Ireton, and easily prevailed upon him to say he would accompany him upon the projected expedition at night, to steal the body of poor Kate. They met by appointment at twelve o'clock, and Musgrave could not help, even then perceiving, that there was a most unusual dulness in his friend's manner.

"You look like a mute at a funeral," he said.

"Do I?"

"Indeed you do; but I suppose you are up to some trick or another. Come now confess, is it not so?"

"You never shot wider of the mark, than that Harry."

"Say you so?"

"In truth I do."

"Well, well, you will soon be all right. Come now, tax your wits a little, and try what you can devise, as the best means of carrying out this adventure as we go along."

"Don't rely upon me to-night. What there is to do, that will I do, but I am in the subaltern and not the general vein, I assure you; I must be directed."

"Well, well, here we are."

"A poor-looking place."

"Yes, and yet Dr. Grey tells me that she was evidently educated, and that she was the most beautiful creature he ever clapped his eyes upon in all his life."

"And yet lived here!"

"Yes, she lived here. But come, it is time for action—one o'clock will soon strike."

A policeman with a look of supernatural cunning, was going slowly past the house.

"Ahem!" said Musgrave. "I want to speak to you."

"What is it? Anything suspicious?"

"Come here. Are you long-sighted?"

"What do you mean. Come, come. I'll pretty soon lock up such fellows as you are. Move on."

"Nonsense. We are two medical

men, and there's a dead body in yonder house that we want particularly. Now it will do nobody any harm for us to take it, for she has not a relation in the world, we believe, and has died among strangers. There are our cards, and you may easily ascertain the truth of what we tell you, if you doubt it. We don't mind giving a couple of sovereigns, for you to be looking another way when we come out with the body, You dont look like a fool, so I have spoken candidly to you about the affair."

"All 's right; I'm in the line myself."

"What line?"

"The doctoring."

"Indeed, pray explain yourself."

"Why you see sir, afore I was a policeman, I was a light porter at a wholesale chemist's, so I got a inkling of the profession; rhubarb and jalap; pakem croakem,—saline draughts, and an emetic. What do you think of that, I only say so much o let you see that I know something."

"Something, indeed," said Musgrave. Upon my life you know more than many German physicians."

"You don't mean it?"

"Yes I do."

"Give us your hand, sir; you shall have the body, and I shan't see nothing except those two sovereigns you mentioned."

"Certainly. There they are."

"Sir, you are a gentleman; I always likes to assist a brother professional. How are you going to manage it, eh?—a cab?"

"Just what we were thinking of."

"That's the dodge."

"I suppose there will be no difficuty?"

"Difficulty? Oh dear, no, not when they find I'm in the secret, and here's one a coming. How quiet your friend is."

"He is indeed.— Why, what's the matter with you?"

"I don't know," said the student from Bartholomew's, "but the real fact is, I am uncommonly nervous tonight."

"Oh, that will go off."

"I hope so."

"To be sure it will. Hilloa—cab."

"Here you is."

"I suppose you have no objection to earn a guinea?"

"If it's all right, none. Is Sir Robert in the spree?"

"Sir Robert?—who do you mean?"

"Mr. Peel."

"Oh, the policeman. Yes, it is all right."

"Going to crack a crib?"

"Why, you rascal, you don't take us for thieves—do you?"

"Thieves? Oh dear, no, gemmen. Only when a night cab is all on a sudden axed if he ain't got no sort of dejection to a guinea, one has one's own idees, you see? But howsomdever it's no business of mine. What is the caper?"

"Simply the conveyance of a young lady about a mile, that's all. Only we don't want it spoken about to-morrow."

"Close as wax, and down as fifteen hammers, gemmen, that's your sort. Here you is."

"Very well—wait where you are."

The two students went to the door of the house, and from several latch keys, which one of them brought with him, easily, after a trial or two, selected one that would open the door.

"Come on, Ireton," he said, to his companion. "I think it will be all plain sailing with us now, for the house is full of lodgers, and what's everybody's business is nobody's."

"Yes, yes."

"But how terrifically dull you are to-night. What on earth, or in heaven, or the other place, is the matter with you? I never knew you in this state of mind before."

"Hush—hush!"

"What is it?"

"I thought I heard a voice."

"Pho—pho, it was your imagination surely. You have really been as nervous as possible about this affair."

"I have."

"Well, I suppose it is you first?"

"No, not by any means; but no doubt it is from some cause quite unconnected with the transaction. We all know well enough what a little indigestion will accomplish.'

"To be sure. But come, I think we shall make an easy enough affair of this, after all."

"For God's sake don't make any alarm. I dont understand how it really is, but I seem as if I would not forego this adventure for the world, and yet I am such a novice that, as you see, I can scarcely be said to be master of myself sufficiently to go on with it."

"I wish I had a good glass of brandy to give you."

"I wish you had. Come on, since we are here."

Slowly they ascended the staircase together, making certainly no more noise than could not possibly be avoided, and at that hour if they had made more it is not very likely that they would have roused any one.

This security from interruption was of a twofold character, for in the first place they might not awaken any one, and in the second place, if they did do so, it was not very likely in a house full of lodgers that anybody would have taken the trouble to get up to see who it was.

They reached the door of the room, which had been accurately described to them, as being the one in which the much wanted body was lying, and then after fully satisfying themselves that no one was stirring, they plied their skeleton keys, and soon forced back the common lock with which the door was fastened.

"Now for it. Come on."

"Are you sure she is there?"

"Of course, I can just see the bed on which she lies. I will roll her carefully in the sheet, and carry her down stairs to the cab we have in waiting."

"Do—do."

"I am well aware that you are too nervous to-night, to take an active part in the affair.

"You are right."

"Very well, then, all I ask of you is to stand still here, and listen with all your might, so as to be able to let me know if there should be any alarm in the house, or the street."

"Depend upon me, my hearing seems to-night to be preternaturally acute. There will not, I am sure, a mouse be able to stir in this place without my cognisance."

"That's all right."

The student went into the room. The period of his absence from his alarmed companion was not really above three minutes, but to him it seemed an hour. When he did appear, he staggered on like one carrying a heavy burthen.

"I have it," he said, "I have it. Run, on before and get the cab door open I have it. By heaven she is much heavier than one would have supposed. Be quick—be quick with you."

CHAPTER LI.

AN EXTRAORDINARY SCENE AT DR. GREY'S.

SUDDENLY Ireton appeared to recover all his lost energy. He stepped up to Musgrave, and said with animation,—

"Give her to me, I will carry her if you find yourself fatigued."

"In truth the coming down stairs with my burthen," replied Musgrave, "and the necesity of coming slowly has—has—paid me out. I'm glad you have it. Where's the cab—where's the cab?"

"Here close at hand."

The policeman was anxious to see what was going on, although he did not wish to seem so, and he shrunk into a dark doorway, for the purpose of making his observations in quiet,

"Here you is!" cried the cabman, as he contrived to awaken the poor pitiable creature which drew his wretched vehicle, and to bring it close to the curb.

"Hold the door open, Musgrave," said Ireton. "No. Get in—get in and take it of me."

"It," said the cabman, getting alarmed. "Lor gemmen, you don't mean to tell me its a corpus!"

"A what."

"A dead corpus?"

"We have told you no such thing."

"It is though. I wont take it, I shall dream of it for a whole fortnight. I wont take it. Dont put it into my weicle—don't. Oh, sir, it is a corpus."

"Why, what harm can it do yu?"

"Murder, murder!"

"What's the row now?" said the policeman stepping forward. "Ain't it all right?"

"Oh, dear no. I tells you what it is Mr. Peel. It's a corpses, a dead

THE STUDENTS CONSULT OVER THE BODY OF KATE DESTERN.

corpus, and I don't like any such in my cab."

"I'm very sorry," said the policeman to have to make his here hobservation, but you is a *hass*. If you'd had the advantage of a professional education, you'd a knowed as there was no harm in a post mortem, you *hass*."

The cabman looked aghast, and neither Musgrove nor Ireton could forbear laughter, at this learned reproof from the professional policeman.

"Now," said Musgrove smothering his mirth as well as he could, "I hope you are convinced now, cabman, how wrong you are."

"Excessively wrong," chimed in Ireton.

The cabman looked extremely like the man who is convinced against his will, but who is of the same opinion still. Nevertheless he withdrew his opposition to the cab being used as what he called a *nurse*, meaning doubtless a hearse, and allowed Musgrove and Ireton to get in, both of them, with their melancholy burthen.

"Good-night, gemmen," said the policeman, who was still anxious to make a further impression upon the friends, concerning the amount of his medical knowledge. "Good-night, salts and senna—gum-arabic, and globus hystericus, as we say in the profession."

This was too much for Ireton's gravity, even, and he laughed in spite of himself. The cabman, however, rapidly drove off, for he was now as anxious as possible to get rid of his fare, which had turned out to be by no means the sort of thing he liked, for in common with the Athenians of old, he had given his mind to superstition, and thought that the presence of a dead body in his cab would necesssaily leave behind it something of a supernatural aroma, and possibly entail upon him the horror of a few interviews with a ghost.

"Well Ireton," said Musgrove, as the cab rattled on at a good rate. "I am glad you have recovered your fit of despondency."

"I have," said Ireton, but there is a strange kind of anxiety on my mind, yet, which I cannot by any means satisfactorily account for. If I were superstitious, now, which I hope, believe and trust I am not, I should say that something strange was going to happen to me yet to-night."

"I know that you are not superstitious, Ireton," said Musgrove, "but yet it has happened to me more than once, that these strange presages of coming events have taken firm hold of me, and yet resulted in nothing."

"Perhaps not so. Indeed, I am inclined to be of opinion that they never do so."

"You surprise me, for frequently a feeling of that sort has come over me, and gone off again without anything resulting of the smallest importance to me."

"How do you know that?"

"How do I know it?"

"Yes, May not something of vital importance to you have occurred somewhere else at that time. The occurrences that are of the greatest impor-

tance to us, frequently do not happen to ourselves only."

"True, true, I certainly did not ever view the matter in that light; but we are at Dr. Grey's, and I am very glad of it, indeed."

Musgrove put his head out of the window and stopped the cab at the doctor's door, after which, he alighted and rung a bell, which communicated with Dr. Grey's private study, where he was waiting up for them. The neighbouring church clock struck two at that moment, so that upon the whole, they had been tolerably quick in their enterprise, beset with some delays as it was.

"Is that you, Musgrove?" said Dr. Grey, as he opened the street door and looked out.

"Yes sir, yes."

"Come in then. All is right and clear. Have you succeeded?"

"Wonderfully sir. This is Mr. Ireton—Mr. Ireton, Dr. Grey."

They bowed to each other, and Musgrove carried the body closely enveloped in a sheet, into the doctor's house, and the cabman who had been paid his sovereign, drove off as fast as he could, with a great feeling of relief that the job was over.

"Come right into my study," said Dr. Grey, "Mrs. Grey has taken it into her head that something is going on which she would like to know, and I am afraid to tell her the truth, for she has such a dread of a subject being in the house, that I am certain she would jump up if it was the middle of the night and run off somewhere."

"How have you satisfied her, sir?"

"I'm afraid not at all. But come on. Come on. Here's a bottle of wine ready decanted, and I'm sure a glass or two will not do you any harm. Lay the body on the sofa, Musgrove."

The doctor had carefully closed his street door, and preceding the two young men with a light, he reached his study, where, upon a very capacious sofa, Musgrove laid the body.

"Thank you, sir," said Ireton, as he drank the wine offered to him by Dr. Grey. "This I own, comes to me very seasonably indeed. I am both faint and weary."

"But you had no difficulty?"

"Oh, dear no," replied Musgrove,

"nothing to speak of. We had to fee a policeman, who turned out to be a most original character."

"Indeed !"

"Yes ; you would have laughed as we did at him, sir. But another time will do to tell you all that, doctor. I suppose you would like to operate upon the body at once ?"

"Why yes ; but let us finish this bottle amongst us, first. Pray sit down, you seem cold Mr. Ireton, come, the decanter stands with you, sir."

"Why, the fact is," said Ireton, "I have been foolishly nervous all the evening, and quite unable to shake it off."

"Oh, that will happen sometimes, you know."

"Yes ; but with me it is a positive rarity."

"Then you are luckier than most folks. I suppose we shall find some long-standing heart disease in our subject, and yet none of the symptoms she detailed to me favour the supposition, and I must confess I never for a moment suspected such was the case ; and as it is, probably without the strong and sudden excitement, which it appears she was subjected to, she might have gone on for many years."

"Gracious God !" exclaimed Ireton, suddenly starting to his feet, and dropping the wine-glass that was at his lips.

Dr. Grey and Musgrove were both alarmed at this most unexpected exclamation, and rose anxiously together.

CHAPTER LII.

A DOMESTIC MISUNDERSTANDING.

DR. GREY and Musgrove stared at Ireton in amazement, and, notwithstanding they both eagerly awaited an explanation of his extraordinary behaviour, he certainly seemed to be in no hurry to furnish it.

He continued standing still upon the spot he occupied, glaring across the table with the look of one who has suddenly seen something calculated to topple reason from its throne, and for ever destroy the light of intellect in the brain.

"Gracious Heaven !" he again exclaimed.

"Why, Ireton, are you mad ?" cried Musgrove.

"Mad—mad !" he said, abstractedly.

"Is he accustomed to these abberations ?" whispered Dr. Grey, to Musgrove.

"Not that I am aware of, sir."

"It must have been fancy. All is still again—yes it must have been fancy. The fancy of a diseased brain—I shall really begin to think I am going mad if this continues. I pray you pardon me, Dr. Grey, and you, my friend Musgrove. Perhaps the candles dazzled me, but as I sat here, I thought I saw the—the——"

"What ? what ?" said Musgrove.

"The body move !"

"What ? the body on the sofa ?"

"Yes, yes. It must have been a delusion, I am brain-sick—quite brain-sick, and yet I could if I had what I have not—faith in my own perceptions—I could swear to it."

"Could you indeed ? Well—well, Ireton, take another glass, and get rid of such fancies. With you, I am vexed that this should have occurred upon your first introduction to Dr. Grey, I don't know what he will think of you."

"Oh, be under no apprehension of my doing your friend an injustice, in my thoughts ; I can very easily understand how over-excitement may have produced all the feelings he complains of."

"You are very kind, doctor," said Ireton, faintly, "very kind to make such allusions for what looks like folly but—but it is not."

"Certainly not, my young friend. Come, come, probably a little impaired digestion may very well account for all this and much more. Have you ever heard the story of the lady who went to Abernethy with a serious complaint about the ghost of her grandfather."

"No, no."

"Nor I," said Musgrove.

"Here it is then : an old lady called upon him and said—'Sir I am very much afraid something is very wrong with me, I am going to the clergyman of the parish to speak to him about it, but I thought I would come to you first, as my friends advised me. Last night, do you know, the ghost of my poor old grandfather who has been dead these thirty years, came to my bed side and shook his head.' 'Humph. What did you have for supper?' 'Only a small pork-chop, sir.' 'Oh, where's my fee?' 'Here sir, if you please. What is your opinion, sir, of this extraordinary disease?' 'Why, ma'am just this, that if you go home to night and take a large pork chop you will have a good chance of seeing your grandmother likewise. Now be off, for I have no time to waste over the stomach you have so disordered."

"Good," said Musgrove. "Have you had a pork chop, Ireton?"

"Indeed no, but I am better now—much better. I—I enjoy this glass of wine very much. I assure you, Doctor Grey, I hope you will manage to forget that I allowed my imagination to take so great a hold of me as to fancy—— Merciful Providence. There it is again— She moves she moves—Look, look—Oh God, it is no delusion."

Both Doctor Grey and Musgrove now really thought poor Ireton now going quite distracted, but nevertheless they looked intently at the still form of poor Kate wrapped in the sheet as it lay upon the sofa, and suddenly they saw a slight movement as if one of the hands of the corpse was struggling to get free from the covering.

" 'Tis true, 'tis true, and we are more mad than Ireton if we doubt it,' cried Musgrave. "She does move."

"Then this is but a case of catalepsy," said Doctor Grey. "Run down into the kitchen, Musgrove, there is warm water in the boiler by the side of the grate all night long, for the fire is never allowed to go absolutely out. If indeed animation be only for a brief space of time, in a state of suspension, then this will be indeed a good night's work. Run, Musgrove, run, a minute may be of importance.

Musgrove did not know the way to the kitchen, very well, but he contrived to find the stairs leading to that lower region of the house, and the only thing that astonished him, was, that he felt certain, unless indeed he was the victim of some strange delusion, that

some one in a white dress scampered down before him.

He felt a little staggered at this, considering the hour, and he paused a moment and said.

"Who's there?"

He shaded with his hand the light he had hastily snatched from the table in the doctor's study, and strove to find who it was, but he could see no one, nor was there any reply to his interrogatory.

Feeling the importance of getting the hot water, however, to be much greater than anything else, and not being of a superstitious disposition, he ran to the dresser, and snatching a mug from off a hook, he drew it full of water from the boiler, and ran up again as hard as he could.

"Make a little weak wine and water," cried Doctor Grey, "and hand it to me."

This was done immediately by Musgrove. The doctor was supporting the head of Kate as she lay upon the sofa, and now when he poured a small portion of the warm wine and water down her throat she fairly opened her eyes and looked about her.

"She will do," said Dr. Grey, "such a thing as this has not happened to me in all my practice. I ought to have gone and satisfied myself when the coal heaver called and told me she was dead. You may depend some mere chemist, or young practitioner indeed, has seen her, and without proper examination has taken upon himself to pronounce that she was dead."

"It must be so," said Musgrove, "what will you do with her?"

"I will take her up stairs and put her into bed at once. Mrs. Grey will, I am sure, do all for her that is necessary, poor girl."

"Shall I help you?"

"No, no, we shall only impede each other, I will carry her easily, only light me up the stairs one of you, if you please. Mr. Ireton, you were right after all."

"And this is the explanation of all my nervousness to day," said Ireton.

"God knows, it may be so."

"It must be."

"Oh, God, God, God!" commenced Kate, in a tone of voice that was full of such wonderful melody, that it went to the hearts of those who were there to hear it.

"Cheer up," said Dr. Gray, "cheer up, you will be quite well again soon. Look about you, if you can, my dear, and you will soon see you are not in bad hands."

Kate did try to look around her, but her head dropped, and with a deep sigh she fainted.

"I expected as much, but this is only syncope," said Dr. Grey, "I will put her to bed at once. Come, Musgrove, the light, the light, my lad, if you please."

Musgrove caught up one of the candles, and lighted the doctor as he proceeded up stairs with the now again inanimate, but not dead, young Kate Destern. The distance was only up one flight of stairs, and the doctor desired Musgrove to wait at the door of his bed-room a moment, while he went in and spoke to Mrs. Grey upon the matter.

"My dear," Musgrove heard him begin, "my dear. Hilloa! where is she? The bed deserted."

"That, then, was the apparition of the kitchen," thought Musgrove, "Mrs. Gray has been upon the watch to discover what all the mystery means."

Even as he spoke somebody in white rushed past him into the bed-room, and then a female voice said, in not the tenderest of accents,—

"You wretch, Grey, what is the meaning of all this?"

"Murder," cried Dr. Grey, "Where are you, Musgrove?"

"Here," said Musgrove, popping in his head, his hand and the candle in it.

"You brute," screamed Mrs. Grey, as she sprung into bed, and covered herself up in a moment, "Oh, you brute. Is this proper treatment, Dr. Grey, for me. What is this in the bed?"

"My dear," said Dr. Grey, "be pacified."

"I won't."

"Well, if you won't."

"Do, madam," said Musgrove, I will explain all to your perfect satisfaction, I am quite certain."

Musgrove in a very few words managed to put Mrs. Grey in possession of the whole particulars, upon which the tide of feeling instantly changed, and Musgrove having taken his departure from the room, leaving the candle behind him, groped his way down stairs in the dark to Ireton, who had remained in the parlour below.

"It's all right, Ireton," he said, "it's all right, Mrs. Grey and the doctor between them will, I dare say, soon recover the young girl. What a singular circumstance this has been to be sure."

"It has indeed, Musgrove."

"How do you feel now?"

"Oh, quite well; all my strange terrors are over. You will, I hope, no longer think me to be foolishly superstitious, when I another time expect something to result from such a state of feeling as I have been in all this evening.

"Yes, I shall."

"You shall? After this night's experience?"

"Yes, even after this night's experience, for I am quite prepared to battle with you in the cause of rationality. I deny that the affair connected with this young girl was in any way at all consequential upon your nervousness."

"Ah, but was not my nervousness consequential upon that?"

"As how?"

"If you ask me how I cannot tell you. The thing is a mystery, and will remain one."

"It will indeed. The two states of circumstances happened, accidentally happened at the same time, that is all, Ireton. You were out of spirits, and a young girl was in a trance instead of being dead, but those two states of things had not the smallest connection with each other."

"Well, I do not expect to convince you."

"No, in sooth, you need not."

"I will not attempt it, but still I feel I cannot divest myself of my own opinion that there was some ocult sympathy between my feelings and what was going to happen to us all to night. If I were to try to dissuade myself from such an idea I know well I could not."

"In which case, then, it is no use to try."

"I am not going so to do; but I am very anxious to know how the young creature is. Was she not radiantly beautiful ?"

"She was, indeed, Ireton, and to complete the romance, all you have to do now is to fall accidentally in love with her."

"Perhaps I have already."

"Bravo ! bravo ! Well, I will hope still to dance at what the cabman called the corpus's wedding."

"All's right," said Dr. Grey, making his appearance with a smile upon his face. "All's right. She has recovered from the fainting, and I have given her a composing draught which will soon put her to rights, and now we must have another bottle, and Mrs. Grey will join us as soon as she has made her toilet."

"How pleased I am," said Ireton.

CHAPTER LIII.

THE POLICE OFFICE.

WE left Harry Dean in an apparently critical position.

He, it will be recollected with his new attendant, Sam Clover, and likewise with Lucy, was being conveyed to the Bow-street police office, on a charge of murder. Some most strange and peculiar circumstances had combined to make it appear quite possible that he and Sam were the murderers of Madame Zadzed, and with some degree of tact and real amount of impudence, Swam and her admirer, the doctor, had taken advantage of the accidental state of things to free themselves from the direful consequences of their own acts.

It will be remembered, too, that Swam had as yet no sort of notion that the dreadful murder had actually been seen by Lucy.

Probably had she, or Mr. Carter, thought that the fair young child was really in possession of so important a secret, they would yet have taken some means of preventing her from giving evidence on this side of the grave.

As it was, however, she and the doctor fully determined upon putting the murder upon the shoulders of Harry Dean, if possible.

The coach then that was proceeding to the police office, contained Harry, Sam, Lucy, Swam, the doctor, and the two officers, who had by the bye, their own opinion of the matter.

The distance was by no means great to the office, but when the party arrived, another case was already in progress, so they had all to wait until it was concluded and adjudicated upon.

It was during that brief interval that an over zealous reporter contrived to gather the scanty amount of information which appearing in a second edition of a morning paper, had so alarmed poor Kate, and eventuated in all that train of circumstances we have felt ourselves under the necessity of detailing to the reader in connection with her fate and proceedings.

While waiting, Harry Dean and Sam Clover had the opportunity of seeing some cases disposed of, which made them both wonder if they were in London, where there is supposed to be a law which applies to all classes of offenders alike, or in Turkey, where a handful of piastres to a judge secures a favourable decision to the party who has them to spare.

A man was brought up charged with having first seduced, ther deserted, and finally, cruelly struck, and rendered for a time insensible, an unhappy creature who had been simple enough to fall by his arts. The facts were all clearly proved, and it was likewise brought in, cunningly enough, although to all appearance quite accidentally, that the offender was butler to an M.P.

The magistrate bent his brow, and with a solemn-like aspect spoke,—

"This is a very serious case—a very serious case indeed, young woman, the immorality of your conduct is shocking."

"But your worship," said a person who had attended with her, "that is not precisely the question. No personal immorality can place any individual without the protection of the laws."

"How dare you interrupt me, sir ? Who are you ? Do I sit here to be told by you what my duty is ? I dismiss the charge—there now, sir."

"Dismiss the charge ?"

"Yes. Clear the court, officers. I'll commit you, if you say another word."

"I will not only say another word, but it shall be one that will not please you, for it is to tell you that you dare not commit me."

"What — what — officers — officers! Did anybody hear that? The case is not now before the court—it is dismissed. We don't sit here to encourage any sort of immorality, sir."

"But the immorality has nothing to do with it. It is an assault you have to deal with, and nothing else."

" Clear the court, I say."

The officers hustled all the parties out, excepting the offender, who, as the newspapers have it, bowed to the authorities and then withdrew, accompanied by his solicitor, of the highly respectable firm of Dooem and Backbite.

The next charge introduced to the court an emaciated and wretched looking woman, with a child in her arms looking more wretched if possible than herself.

She, it appeared from the statement of an officer, had been employed as a shirt-maker by one of those Hebrew firms who appear licensed to extort splendid fortunes for themselves out of the very heart's blood of their slaves, by tortures almost as cruel as any inflicted by inquisitors of old, on their own persecuted race. To speak more plainly, she made shirts at twopence-halfpenny each, and when the cost of thread and other matters was deducted, could earn fourpence a day! which was to support herself, a husband out of employment, and several children. The consequence, and a very natural one we conceive, was, that she pawned the materials entrusted to her to obtain bread.

We never pass one of the Jewish " emporiums" of gaudy clothing, without reflecting on the miserable poverty of the wretches who are employed in manufacturing the vulgar and tasteless commodities exposed behind their large plate glass windows, and thinking that the public is chargable with the greater part of the misery which exists among the ill-paid class of workmen and work-women by purchasing with avidity anything which at first-sight appears to be cheap.

Yet a little acquaintance with the subject would be sufficient to deter the most silly from resorting to such shops. The Londoners ought surely by this time to have been cheated enough to make them open their eyes. They have alum and potatoes in cheap bread, diseased cows, and pigs, who have " died a natural death," in cheap sausages, sloe leaves in cheap tea, chicory in cheap coffee, sand in cheap sugar, brown paper in cheap sloes, and " devils' dust," in cheap cloth, and so on through the whole catalogue of the necessaries and luxuries of life.

The case before us was an illustration of this, for it appeared that the shirts made by the poor prisoner were sold by the respectable firm of Shadrach and Son at one shilling each. Now what man with any conscience could expect a shirt worth having at all, for one shilling. Yet no doubt there is a demand for the trumpery articles or they would not be manufactured, and as long as there is such a demand so long will poor wretches be condemned by their necessities to " stitch, stitch, stitch," from morning 'till night, in sickness or in health, with heavy eyes and a fevered brain, for the starving pittance of fourpence a day.

Oh Heaven, that such things should be in a Christian land, where thousands of pounds are collected with ease to build and adorn churches and chapels, to increase the funds of Benevolent Societies, and to send expedition after expedition to convert the savage nations of Africa. So true it is that now, even as it was eighteen hundred years ago, we would rather extract the mote from a brother's eye, than remove the huge beam from our own.

But to return to the police office and the pawner of another's property.

Mr. Pighead, as a matter of course was very indignant; he laid it down as a rule always to be indignant with poor people ; it saved him sometimes a great deal of trouble when he was busy; for, seeing that these poor persons had no one to advocate their cause, and no one to remonstrate at anything that might befal them, it was exceedingly convenient to decide on their cases without hearing anything they might have to say.

Mr. Pighead sat on the bench as the representation of offended justice, and as far as his forbidding countenance would go, he was certainly a " terror to evil doers"—of a certain class. He addressed the trembling culprit thus :

" Why dont you look at me—ah, you may well hang down your head. I've seen you before—don't tell me ; I know it, and I cannot be mistaken. Thomson haven't we had this woman here before ?"

"Why your lordship knows best, in course we have—or somebody wery much like her."

"Of course, I told you so. What have you got to say—there, that'll do, don't say anything—you'll only expose yourself. The property of employers must be protected, the law on the subject is very positive—Eh ? oh, Messers. Shadrach don't wish to be hard on you, they don't wish to be put to the inconvenience of attending at the Old Bailey —it does credit to their feelings—you will go to the House of Correction for a month with hard labour, and take care I never see you here again."

The woman was led fainting from the bar ; and the sapient magistrates ire was again excited by the person in court who had spoken before, and who now made his way to the woman with the purpose of offering her some assistance.

"Officers," roared Mr. Pighead, "put that fellow out of court, he does nothing but interrupt the public business."

The officers who had apparently taken some dislike to the person indicated, now seized the offending individual by both arms, thrust him violently out at the doors, knocked his hat over his eyes in the style known to costermongers as "bonnetting," and then accelerated his progress in such a manner as to cause him to roll down the steps into the gutter, to the intense delight of a gang of pickpockets and ladies of easy virtue, who surrounded the office door. Treatment which will no doubt teach the philanthropic old gentleman to be cautious how he interferes' in future with "the pure stream of justice," in a London police court.

"Lucy," whispered Harry Dean, "whatever happens, don't you allow yourself to be frightened here, and say nothing, unless I say to you, Lucy, speak freely about all you know."

"Well," said the magistrate, as Harry Dean was placed in that part of the court which was devoted to the reception of persons accused. "Well, what is the charge against this person—eh ? Oh, there are two of them, are there. Come, come, young man, don't look at me in that sort of way."

These last words were addressed to Harry Dean, who had bent rather too inquisitive a glance upon his worship to suit his fancy of what was proper on the part of an accused person.

"Murder ! your worship," said one of the officers.

"Murder ! Indeed. Where are the witnesses ?"

"Here, your worship."

Swam made her appearance in the witness-box, and made a low courtesy to that august individual, which, as she guessed, had the effect of at once prepossessing him in her favour.

"Oh—ah ! ahem ! Well, woman, what have you got to say ?"

"Sir. If you please—if your lordship pleases, I only want to ask one question first of you, sir."

"Pho—pho, I am not a lord. What is it, eh woman ?"

"I want to know if I am before the great Pighead."

"A—hem ! a—ahem ! I am Mr. Pighead the magistrate, certainly, but I have no sort of pretensions to be called great, madam; of course I cannot help what opinions people please to entertain of me, but I am nothing but plain Mr. Pighead. Go on, madam."

"It's a pleasure, sir, to hear you. All the world knows that you ought to be Lord Chancellor, but that's neither here nor there, I only hope that your worship will not be offended with me. It was always my fault to say just what I think, and many's the scrape I have got into in consequence of that failing, Mr. Pighead."

"Well, well, madam. Come to the case, if you please."

"I hope, sir, I have not offended you."

"Oh, no, no, no. Go on."

"Well then, sir, I am the confidential friend and companion of a lady whose name is—I ought to say was, for she is dead,—Zadzed, a most respectable person, you worship, I assure you. She often spoke of your worship, saying ' It ever, Swam, I have to go before a magistrate to make a complaint against anybody, I do hope I shall meet with that dear Mr. Pighead, who says such proper things to bad characters."

"Well, well, madam. Pray oblige me by stating your case."

"I will, your worship. It was only

THE DISCOVERY MADE BY TONY AND THE POLICEMAN.

last night that Madam Zadzed bade me good night, in all the health and spirits in the world, but this morning hearing a noise in her room, I went in with a gentleman who happened to be staying in the house, and found her murdered, and those two ill-looking fellows in the room."

"A strong case."

"Oh, very sir. Of course we called the constables and gave them in charge, and there they are both of them. Oh, my heart bleeds to see 'em, but still if they were hanged—as I suppose they must be, they ought to bless their stars that they were brought before you, sir,

in the first instance, for as I often said to Madam Zadzed——"

"Well, well,"

"Madam, says I. Have you that blessed *Times* newspaper with all he dreadful lies in it."

"Well, well."

"Because if you have Madam——"

"Silence! Order! Silence!"

"Oh, certainly, sir. But you know one dont often have the pleasure of seeing you."

"Well, sir," said Harry Dean, "have you and this base woman done talking and complimenting each other."

"What?"

"Because if you have, we will come to the merits of the case if you please, which seem to be quite forgotten."

The magistrate's face turned absolutely purple.

"What!" he exclaimed, "what! do I sit here to be told what is my duty to myself and the public, by you, sir?"

"So it seems," said Harry Dean, calmly, "I consider it a most unfortunate thing that a case of this importance should have come before you, but yet I trust that the facts will be such as even your comprehension cannot fail of comprehending."

"Facts!—facts! I have heard facts enough!"

"Your worship!" whispered the clerk, "had, perhaps, better hear the defence."

"No, I wont, I can adjourn the case."

"Oh, yes, if your worship pleases."

"Then I do please; it strikes me," in a whisper to the clerk, "that the prisoner would not be so independent if he had not some triumphant answer to the charge, eh? Don't you think so?"

"It is more than probable, your worship."

"Well, the only way I can punish him a little is to adjourn the hearing of the case until another magistrate is likewise on the bench."

"Your worship can do that if you please."

"Very good, ahem!—Since the prisoner at the bar has thought proper to throw out some hints derogatory to the dignity of this court, and of a nature to lead me to suppose that he thinks he will not get justice at my hands, I am resolved to gratify him by adjourning the future hearing of this case until to-morrow morning, when my honoured colleague, Mr. Martin, will be upon the bench. Remove the prisoners!"

"Hold!" said Harry Dean, "this will not do. This is a state of things that I most fully and completely protest, against, sir."

CHAPTER LV.

SAM CLOVER PROVES A GREAT FOE TO SWAM AND HER ADMIRER.

THE magistrate when he heard these energetic words from Harry Dean looked perfectly aghast.

"What!" he said, "you protest! you, a prisoner, protest!"

"Most fully and completely I do, I have something to say, and something to prove."

"Which I will not hear," said the magistrate, "I have made my decision, and I mean to keep by it, I will hear no more of this case until to-morrow, when my colleague, Mr. Martin, will likewise be upon the bench."

"I have only one thing to say and to insist upon," added Harry.

"Take him away," roared Mr. Pighead, "take him away, if you don't take that fellow away directly, officers, I will have every one of you removed from any attendance on my court."

The officers made a rush upon Harry Dean, and before he could say one word they hustled him out of the court into a sort of yard where there were several little cells, that looked like cellars more than anything else. An officer opened the door of one of them, and pointing in a significant manner with his thumb into it, he said to Harry Dean,

"Now, my swell, march in."

"Ha! ha! ha!" laughed Swam with hysterical delight; "mind you keep fast, officers, and I'll give you something handsome at the next examination, when I shall be sure to be here."

"Will you let me speak to you a moment or two in private," said Harry to the officer.

"Oh yes, my tulip, anything you likes, only don't criminate yourself, unless you have made up your mind to it, that's all, as when you have done your patter, in I goes to the beak and tells him."

"As you please—as you please. All I want is that during our brief, but highly necessary conversation, you detain these people."

"Detain me!" cried Swam, trembling with rage and apprehension. "Detain me, you murderous wretch. What do you mean?"

"Oh, Harry, Harry," cried Lucy. "You are innocent. You know you are —so very innocent. Oh, Harry, Harry, tell me to speak."

"Hush—hush. Not yet."

"It's all very well," said the officer, "your wanting to say something to me, my rum 'un, but we can't detain the witnesses unless they is bound over to prosecute, and can't find the securities."

Harry Dean began to think there was no real resource but really to tell all to the officers, which was a course he did not wish to adopt if it could be by any means avoided for the present. The conduct of the magistrate had so much provoked him, that he had in his own mind determined to let affairs go a little further, provided he could do so without allowing Swam and the doctor to escape. As regarded the latter personage, the state of dread and frightful terror he was in, had in it something truly hideous, and if he had not been so intently occupied with more important considerations, Harry Dean would have desired no better sport than to watch the guilty terrors of that man.

"Come along, my dear," said the doctor to Swam, for he thought they had better assume the aspect of man and wife. "Come along home, I'm quite sure the melancholy end of poor Madame Zadzed has affected your nerves enough. I beg that you will come home at once now, and compose yourself."

"Sam," said Harry Dean, in a whisper, "can nothing be done to detain these people while I speak to the officer for about five minutes?"

"Yes," said Sam.

"Indeed?"

"Leave it to me, sir."

"But you will be locked up, too."

"Oh, I didn't think of that. Then I must set about it at once, that's all. Here goes for a little delay, at all events."

As he spoke he marched up to the doctor, and seizing that remarkably scientific individual by the throat, he knocked his head against Swam's with a vengeance that produced a sound as if two empty beer barrels had suddenly come into violent contact with each other.

"There," he said. "Take that."

"Come—come," cried an officer. "This sort of thing wont do here. You must come before Mr. Pighead again for this."

"Go to the deuce," said Sam. "It serves 'em right, and they know it."

"Oh, my head—my head," cried Swam, "am I to be killed in this way,

and have no redress at all. Where's the magistrate—where's the magistrate? Oh, you villain."

"Oh, dear," said the doctor, "never mind, my dear, come away. It's much the best to come away; do, you know it is, indeed."

"No," said Swam, "not till I have exterminated this villain."

She made a rush into the magistrate's room again, closely followed by an officer, who had witnessed the assault, and collared Sam Clover for perpetrating it in so sacred a place as the precincts of the office.

"Now listen to me," said Harry Dean to the officer he had before desired to say something to.

"Now for it, young fellow, what is it?"

The officer stepped with him into the cell, and there they remained for the space of about three minutes, when the officer emerged with his face rather red, and calling out,—

"Jackson, Jackson!" he whispered something to another officer, who gave a long whistle, and then something was said to a third, and just at that very juncture in affairs, out came Swam again from the public office.

"And so," she said. "I am to put up with all this treatment, and to have no redress. A pretty thing, indeed. So if a fellow is in custody already, he may do anything, I suppose. A pretty thing, Where's the justice in that, I should know?"

From these words of Swam's the nature of Mr. Pighead's reply to the new complaint against Sam Clover may be gathered.

"Come along,—come along," whispered the doctor.

"Oh you idiot!"

"Good God, call me what you like, but come along, will you?"

"When I please."

"Are you," he whispered, "so far gone in foolish anger as to be deaf to reason. You don't know a moment when by some caprice, we may, be detained. Come along, and in twelve hours we shall be far enough off.—We stand upon a mine."

These words rather frightened Swam, who replied hastily—

"Well, well, come at once. But all

is safe. You had no need to be in such a fright; all is safe, I tell you. Come along."

"You will be here to-morrow?" said one of the officers.

"Oh, most punctual," said Swam.

Arm-in-arm she and the doctor left the office, but they little thought that two of the most active officers from the police office, men who in many serious adventures with notorious criminals had already sufficiently proved that they were afraid of nothing, followed closely upon their footsteps, with a fixed determination not to lose sight of either of them.

"There, you see," whispered Swam. "There is no danger, and we shall quite escape the consequences of our crime."

"I hope so."

"You only hope so."

"Well, that's enough, is it not?"

"No indeed, I do more than hope. I make certain of it; I tell you there is no danger, and we must start for Liverpool to-night, so as to be ready to take advantage of any ship that may be going from there to America in a day or two."

"With all my heart. The further we are off London, you may depend the better I shall be pleased. Did you not fancy that some of the officers looked very oddly at us as we came away from the office?"

"No, certainly not."

"Well, I did then. But I am half dead with hunger, and before we go any further, let us step in somewhere and have something to eat and drink; I never an decide well upon anything while I m hungry."

"I should have no objection to something nice," said Swam.

"Well, we will go into the first quiet, obscure-looking place, in the shape of a tavern we can see.

"Very good."

In London people need not look long for houses of entertainment, and Swam and the doctor soon housed themselves in one of those half public houses and half hotels, with which the giant city abounds, and which really in many cases, are decidedly the most comfortable places that any one can seek refreshment in.

Something substantial, and at the same time sufficiently appetite tickling was ordered by Swam, who always had a great idea of creature comforts; and by the time it was placed upon the table a tall gentlemanly-looking man, came into the room.

He made a slight bow, and seated himself at some distance from Swam and the doctor, but still they could both see that he was in a state of agitation and trepidation.

Neither Swam nor the doctor could help looking at him he was so dreadfully fidgetty and anxious about something. At times he took from his pocket a newspaper, and anxiously consulted some portion of it, and then seeing an almanac upon the wall of the room, he eagerly approached it, and pored over its contents for some minutes, after which he sat down with a sigh, and the waiter brought him in a bottle of porter and a biscuit.

"There's something the matter with him," said Swam, in a whisper to the doctor.

"Yes, there seems so. I'll speak to him. A fine day sir."

The stranger started with an exclamation to his feet—

"No, no, I'll give a hundred pound note if you won't take me—I—I——. Good God. I have betrayed myself. My dear lady, and you sir, have mercy upon me, and don't repeat what I have said just now. I am a man who must rot here in jail, or stand upon the shores of America soon."

"How odd," said Swam.

"Very odd," said the doctor.

"You will not betray me. Oh, say that you will not betray me, or I would rather cut my throat with this table knife. I have made all my preparations for departure from London, and if anything should stay me, I am resolved upon suicide to put an end to the distraction to which I am subject."

Swam looked at the doctor, and the doctor looked at Swam.

"Shall I speak," she said.

"I would."

"It's an odd enough thing sir," said Swam, "but we have no objection to go to America ourselves, and if you have made all your arrangements, perhaps, you can tell us, which will be the most ready mode of proceeding."

"You—you. You go to America Ah, you are deceiving me."

"Indeed, no."

"Oh, if this is some deep-laid scheme for my capture, say so at once. Take me, and put an end to a state of suspense, worse than death itself.

"You are quite wrong," said Swam, "we want to go to America for a change, that's all, and we can have no possible objection to go with you. What arrangements have you made?"

"I have a post chaise ready to start with me in the morning, and to-night I have made up my mind to take a bed here. I shall not sleep, but I will go through the ceremony of going to bed, to lull suspicion."

"Then, perhaps if we pay part of the expense," said Swam, "you will allow us to go with you in the chaise?"

"With pleasure you shall go with me, but I do not want you to pay any of the charges. The additional appearance of an ordinary journey, merely, which your presence will give the affair, will be ample recompense to me. Only say you will come with me, and I will take all the expenses of the journey."

"You are very liberal," replied Swam. "I think we had better, then, Mr. Smith, remain here, at this decent-looking house, likewise."

Swam gave the doctor a nudge in his ribs to make him comprehend that he was to answer to the name of Smith.

"Very well," he said, "very well. I am quite willing, quite willing. You know we have to make a call at the house of a deceased friend, that's all."

"Oh, yes," replied Swam, who at once comprehended that it would be prudent to go to the house of Madame Zadzed and take what they could from it previous to their departure.

"Well, I am happier," said the stranger. "My name is Dun."

"Dun?"

"Yes; Michael Faversham Dun."

"Well," said the doctor, with a faint smile, "I hope you never will be done."

"Thank you, thank you. How dreadfully nervous and weak I am to be sure. I feel a little better since I have met with you, but yet, as you see, I am all of a shake."

"You do tremble."

"Indeed I do, and that makes me think that if I had attempted to go off by myself that I should never have succeeded in fairly getting away. Somebody, seeing me in such a state of confusion, would have suspected something, and detained me, I'm quite certain. But now I do indeed feel a sense of security, and I think we shall all of us land in New York as comfortably as possible."

"I hope so," said Swam.

"Make sure of it, madam, make sure of it. Of course you, who are only going for pleasure, and perhaps for profit, can have no idea of my feelings, but I am certain that I shall hail that house of, of —shall I say the vagabonds of the earth, with rapture. Oh, that I stood upon that soil of freedom now, where the cleverest fellow is he who can best succeed in over-reaching his neighbour, and perpetrating the vilest swindle."

CHAPTER LVI.

TONY FINDS SOMETHING WORTH LOOKING FOR IN MADAME ZADZED'S HOUSE.

"Are you quite sure this is the house," said Tony, with panting eagerness to the player, as they both paused opposite to Madame Zadzed's house, in Soho.

"Quite."

"How shall I thank you?"

"By not saying anything about it, or permitting me to assist you in what you are about. You talk of a young girl being kidnapped by a base, bad woman. Surely that is a state of things which any man would wish to alter who deserved the name of man. What do you purpose doing in the matter?"

"Doing," said Tony. "I'll have the house down brick by brick but I'll find her."

"Bravo!"

Tony was not slow in commencing operations. He hammered away at the knocker at a rate that alarmed the whole street, and brought the officer who had been left in charge of the premises to open it in such a hurry that he nearly fell on his nose on the door step, over Tony, who, not expecting his summons for admission to be so speedily answered, fell upon his hands and knees into the passage the moment the door gave way before him."

"Hilloa !" cried the policeman, "what's the meaning of this ?"

"Where is she ?" cried Tony.

"Who ?"

"The young girl. Give her up to me, blue devil, at once."

"Come, come, none of that, young fellow. What do you mean, you maniac, by coming knocking here in such a way. I'll give you in charge as soon as I see one of our men come by, I can tell you."

"Well," said Tony, "if you wait till you see a policeman when he is wanted, before you give me in charge, I am safe enough."

"Come, come, don't speak in that manner of the force."

"Bother the force," said Tony, "all I want to know is if there's a little girl in this house or not."

"A little girl. How should there be. It ain't very likely is it, after the murder, stupid, as has been done here ?"

Tony staggered back. "The murder ? what murder ? You don't mean to tell me—oh no—that anybody has had the heart to murder her ? Oh, no—no—no."

"Yes, they have, though."

Tony held by the railings for a moment, it seemed as if the whole world on its vast rotundity was slipping from him. Recovering, however, from that sensation of faintness, he grasped the policeman by the arm, and said in a voice of much emotion.

"Does she look as beautiful in death as in life—oh let me see her—let me take at least one last kiss of those ruby lips. Let me look upon those soft blue eyes, with their long lashes. Oh, the wretches to have the heart to take away so much beauty and goodness."

"Ruby lips," said the policeman, blue eyes—my eye you must have been very fond of the old woman."

"Old woman ?—what old woman ?"

"Why what has been murdered, to be sure, in this house."

Tony gave a shriek of relief as he said—

"Oh, what a row, what a row. Its only an old woman after all."

"Is it ?" said an elderly lady, whose toes Tony had trod upon as he reeled off the step of the door. "Drat the boy, does he think folks are to be smashed in this

manners. Take that, and learn better manner. Truly, an old woman indeed, I'll old woman you, you young vagabond."

Three or four hearty blows upon Tony's back with rather a stupendous umbrella, accompanied this remonstrance, and imparted rather a vivid effect to it.

"Oh, bother you," said Tony, "go along."

"I hope you'll remember me," added the old lady, giving him a good poke with the ferule at parting. "Only an old woman, indeed. Well I'm sure, a pretty pass things have come to, but its all along o' these radicals, I know. Only an old woman ! I'll old woman you."

"Now was there ever," cried Tony, "such a cursed bother as this ? I say policeman ?"

"Well, what ?"

"Let me and this gentleman come in with you, I want really to look about the place, for there was a young girl hid here, and if she is found, there is some one who will be pleased enough to let you name your own price."

"Come on then," said the policeman, "I'm not at all disinclined for a little company here. It's precious dull. Come in, only you must n't touch the body, or anything in the room where it is till the inquest, you know."

"All's right," said Tony.

The moment he got with the player into the passage, and the street door was closed, Tony raised his voice to the highest pitch it was capable of assuming, and shouted out—

"Lucy ! Lucy ! Lucy !"

The echo of his own voice was the only reply that came to him ; but Tony, in such a case, was not to be easily discouraged, and again advancing a little nearer to the staircase, he called—

"Lucy ! Lucy ! Lucy !"

All was still when the sounds themselves and their reverberations had died away. Tony gave a long sigh as he said,

"I'm afraid she aint here, after all."

"You need 'nt be afraid," said the policeman, "for I know it.

"How ?"

"I have been all over the house; there's nothing and nobody in it, but the dead woman. Should you like to see her ?"

"Not I," said the player:

"Nor I," said Tony, "I don't want to see such sights."

"Very well, just as you like, have it your own way, you know. But some people would come ever so far to see any one as was murdered. It's all as folks take these things, I takes 'em you know in the way of business, and don't care much about 'em, that's the fact. Eh?"

"What?"

"Didn't you hear something at the door of this room?"

"Yes, to be sure," he added, "an odd sort of noise."

The policeman turned rather pale, and drew his truncheon from his coat pocket, as he said—

"Gentlemen, stand by me, and keep the peace. There it is again, what can it be?—it's an uncommonly odd noise. What in all the world can it be?"

"The only way," said the player, "satisfactorily to settle the question is to go and see; I'll soon tell you if it be anything."

"You are a trump," said Tony, "and I'll go with you."

"Very well," said the policeman, "somebody ought to stay behind here, you know, so I'll keep an eye on what happens, and protect you if needs be. Go on, and don't be afraid, now I am here."

"Why, you humbug!" said Tony.

"Never mind him," said the actor, and he flung the door open and disclosed to view a large black cat, who had been scratching at the lowest part for admittance.

"Oh!" said Tony, "it's you, is it?"

"I thought as much," said the actor.

"Confound you," said the policeman, "this is the third time you have frightened me, you black wretch, since I have been in this house, and now I'll settle you."

"No, no, let her be," said Tony.

The policeman made a rush at the cat with his truncheon, but puss seeing that mischief was intended, after some preliminary spitting and swearing, deliberately clambered up one of the window curtains and secured a safe position upon a gilt cornice, the top of which was just like a shelf, at least six inches from the ceiling of the room.

"Now she's safe," said the player.

"And she's flinging things at him," said Tony, as a small book fell to the floor from the top of the cornice.

"That's an odd place for a book," said the policeman. "Let's see if there ain't any bank-notes in it."

He shook the volume well, but nothing resulted but dirt, upon which he flung it on a table, and Tony without much curiosity took it up. It was a volume of religious exercises, but what attracted Tony was some writing upon the fly leaf next the cover, at the beginning of the book.

The moment Tony cast his eye upon this writing, he gave a cry of surprise, and without a word of explanation, he rushed from the room and out of the house like a madman, carrying the book with him.

Whether or not he was pursued by the actor or the policeman he did not know. If such was the case, he distanced them, and he never stopped until he reached the hotel whence Lucy had been stolen by Madame Zadzed.

Rushing in, Tony laid violent hands upon a waiter, and said to him,—

"Is Mr. Dean here? Is Mr. Dean here?"

"Mr. Dean, sir? Oh dear no, sir. Beg your pardon. You be the gentleman as eat the *sauce au diable*, I think, sir; Mr. Dean's friend?"

"Yes—yes."

"Then, sir, sorry he ain't here, sir. Hasn't been here for some hours. Would you like to take anything mild, sir, if you please sir?"

"No—no. How very unlucky to be sure, that he should not be here. Oh, if I could but find him. I'll come back again soon."

"Yes, sir, if you please, sir, Certainly, sir."

Tony knew the volume he held in his hands as he walked rapidly from the hotel without any fixed purpose, was an important one, but he did not know all its importance. He was not aware that that was the very volume which old Mrs. Destern had clasped so tightly in her dying hand when in the last few minutes of her existence speech was denied to her. He did not know that that was the volume which Madame Zadzed had made a point of possessing, and from which she had gathered materials, as she thought, for revenge upon Lord Battaney, who had wounded her pride so deeply.

Such, however, was the volume which now, by so singular a train of circumstances, had at last found its way into the possession of our brave, conscientious, and honest friend, Tony.

He had no precise object now in traversing the streets. All he felt was that he could not be still, and that if he could now find Lucy and Harry Dean, he might really feel that the happiest hour of his existence had come.

He had not the smallest notion upon earth that Harry Dean was accused of the murder of Madame Zadzed.—Probably, if he had remained a little longer with the policeman, and asked a few questions of him, the name might have been mentioned.

He had left, however, too precipitately for that.

"What shall I do?" said Tony, when he was fairly in the street. "What shall I do now, I wonder? Here's a pretty affair. What can I do? I must be at something, that's quite certain. A lawyer! Ah! shall I go to a lawyer? No. They are such out-and-out rogues, that's the fact. Where shall I go, though? Back to the hotel and wait for Harry Dean? Perhaps I might. Perhaps I mightn't."

"Here you have," said a boy, who came bawling up the street, "Here you have the full and interesting particulars of the murder in Soho, with the confession of Henry Dean and Samuel Clover, the two sanguinary murderers. Here you have it for the small charge of one halfpenny, the full and true particulars of—"

"Stop," cried Tony.

"Here you is, master."

"Did you say Henry Dean?"

"Yes, to be sure I did."

"Do you mean to say it again?"

"Yes, Henry Dean."

"Take that then."

Tony dealt the boy a very scientific blow in the region of the stomach, which sent him sprawling into the kennel and all the impressions of the full, true, and particular account flying in all directions.

"A likely thing," said Tony, "as he walked on, "that I'm going to be told my old friend has done a murder, when I know he'd go a hundred miles out of his way to do a good turn to a poor cat. I'm sure he would."

But still, notwithstanding the vigorous manner in which Tony had thought proper to defend the reputation of the absent Harry Dean, it did occur to him as he went along, that just possibly he, Harry, might be the victim of some false accusation, and this was a thought that gave him a serious pang.

"I must do something I suppose, I shall really have to go to a lawyer after all.—Oh dear, oh dear, here's a catastrophe. Lucy lost, I don't know where, and Harry Dean who wouldn't hurt a fly, accused of murdering an old woman."

An old gentleman was coming down the street, and just as he passed Tony, and reached an entry which led into some stables, Tony heard him cry—

"Help! help! They are murdering me!"

"Hold hard," said Tony, "and I'll be in at the death."

Turning in the direction whence the sound proceeded from, Tony saw two fellows striking at the old gentleman, and trying to force his watch from him.

"All right," said Tony, as he knocked one of them down, by a well-planted blow in the face. "All right, never say die, sir. Go it again."

The other ruffian seeing that some assistance had come, ran away, and before Tony could do anything, the fallen one rose and fled.

CHAPTER LVII.

TONY MEETS WITH A NEW FRIEND.

"WHAT do you bring it in now?" said Tony, to the old gentleman, when by the flight of the thieves he was at leisure sufficiently to speak to him.

"Oh dear, oh dear. Young man, I think you have really saved my life. Let me lean upon your arm for a moment."

"They didn't hit you?"

"No—no. But one blow of that bludgeon you saved me from, would have killed me, I am sure. I—I am better now. Who are you young man Who are you?"

"A poor devil enough."

"Poor—poor. Well something can be done to cure that perhaps. It's not the worst complaint in all the world."

"It's a very obstinate one, sir."

"Sometimes—sometimes. But if you will complete the obligations under which I am to you by lending me your arm homewards, I shall be greatly your debtor."

"Oh don't mention it," said Tony.

"I'll see you all right. Those fellows may be lurking about now."

"Oh yes, yes. If I could but see a policeman now."

"A what?"

"A policeman."

"Don't think of such a thing," said Tony. "Have n't you lived long enough in London to know that you never see a policeman when he's particularly wanted. Don't you give up your mind to seeing a policeman again, when anything happens."

"Well, I have certainly heard that before, but thought it was only a joke. Is it really a fact in London '''

"It is indeed. You have found it out to night. Where is the policeman to take care of you, I should like to know ; just look all about you, and if you can so much as see a blue bottle now, it will be a wonder."

"A blue-bottle?"

"Yes, Mr. Peel."

"Mr. who, young man ?"

"Oh, that's what I calls a policeman, but never mind my nonsense. How do you feel now, your'e getting all right."

"You are very kind ; I am, now. Pray go on talking, you much amuse me, young man."

"Do I—I only wish I could amuse myself. But I don't think I shall ever be amused again while I live. Do you want to go very far, and yet it don't much matter. One direction is as good as another to me, but still, perhaps, you can o me some good."

"I will with pleasure, if I can."

"Do you happen to know of a honest lawyer ?"

"An honest lawyer ! Well, I certainly have heard that there is some sort of difficulty in meeting with such a character, but I hope and trust that I do know one at all events. Yes, young man, I think I can answer your question by saying that I know one."

"You do ?"

"I certainly do."

"Where does he live, then, for I have got a job for him that now lies like a lump of lead at my heart."

These words were spoken with such true and genuine pathos, that the old gentleman turned and tried to take a better look at Tony than he had yet taken, as he replied to him.

"If what lies so heavy at your heart, is a something that a lawyer can remove, you may depend upon having it removed if you will come to my house and tell me all about it. I shall be better able to recommend you to an honest lawyer, for to tell the truth, I was in the law once myself."

"Was you, indeed ?"

"Aye that I was ; I believe I was condered both by friends and foes toler-ably honest as the world goes. Come, what say you ; will you make a confidence with me, and take my advice ? It may be of service to you."

"I will."

"Rightly and freely decided. This way if you please, we shall soon be at home."

The old gentleman led Tony to a part of the town with which he was not very familiar, and approached a large handsome house, from which Tony rather shrunk, saying as he did so,—

"I say, do you really live here ?"

"Yes, yes."

"Then you are somebody ?"

"Well I hope I am, I don't imagine that I have lost my individuality."

This was not quite comprehensible to Tony, but when the old gentleman knocked at the door, and it was immediately opened by a footman in splendid livery, who at sight of the old gentleman flung it quite wide and made a low bow, Tony's wonder was much more excited than before.

"Hilloa !" he said, "I have been talking away to somebody or another who is quite a great man without my knowing it at all. I think I won't trouble you any more sir, if you please."

"Not trouble me any further. What do you mean ? Come—come. How foolish you were to fancy that I shall not be able to serve you because I keep a large house. Robert, let lights be brought to the library."

"Yes, your lordship," said one of the footmen.

Tony whistled, and would have made off, but the old gentleman caught him by the arm, and said,—

"Nonsense, you must not go yet. Come this way. Have I not promised to find an honest lawyer for you ?"

"Yes, but ——"

"But what ? Come along, and tell me your story as composedly and quietly as though you were in your own house".

"Well," said Tony, "I will, and who knows but this is the very thing after all, that is to do the most good to all those that I feel for, though Harry Dean is quite rich enough, that's quite clear, yet if I can make a friend for Lucy —ah, that will be the thing."

Tony followed the old gentleman to

a library, which almost struck him dumb with amazement. The footman placed the lights upon the table, and when they were alone, the old gentleman sat down in a large arm-chair, and motioning Tony to take another, he half shut his eyes, and said—

"Now, tell me for what you want an honest lawyer."

Tony thus encouraged, told him the whole story connected with Harry Dean and Lucy, and so far as he knew, about Kate, too, concluding by the finding of the book at Madame Zadzed's, on the fly leaf of which was some important information, which the old gentleman read quietly enough, and of which the reader will soon be fully aware, when other events are a little more ripe.

The old gentleman laid down the book, and continued with his eyes shut for some time. At length he said—

"You tell me you heard a boy in the street saying that this Harry Dean was in custody on a charge of murder, and had confessed."

"Yes. But that was only in a newspaper."

"A good enough argument for doubting its truth," said the old gentleman, with a nod. "The arrest, I dare say, has taken place, but the confession is a doubtful proposition enough. I must confess, young man, I do not see my way clearly through all these circumstances that you have related to me, but I will get you a better, and a more active assistant than I should be."

He wrote something, and placed it in an envelope, after which he rung for a servant, and said, in his usual quiet way—

"Let a messenger go with that at once, and bring some refreshments to this gentleman."

The servant bowed himself out.

"Now," said the old gentleman, rising, "if you will wait here, a gentleman will come to you, to whom I wish you to tell all that you have told me. He is a lawyer, and will undertake the case for you, and follow it out in all its ramifications and bearings. Give him the book you have shown to me. It will be safer in his keeping than in yours, and now you will excuse me, as I am forced to go out on business."

"Oh, certainly," said Tony. "I'm very much obliged to you."

The old gentleman smiled and left the room. In about a minute afterwards, Tony heard a carriage dash up to the door, and then there seemed something of a bustle, and away it dashed again.

"Well," said Tony, as he looked about him. "This is a rum go, at any rate, an uncommonly rum go. I'll just ask the first person I see, who he is, I didn't like to pop the question to himself."

Tony was not long without an opportunity, for a servant brought in a tray upon which were several silver covers, while another carried something that held several wine bottles.

Tony looked on in silence while the tray was placed before him, and then when one of the footmen removed the covers very adroitly, he saw that there was something with a very savory odour before him.

"I hope," he said, "there's nothing to burn one's throat here?"

"Sir."

"No sauce of the devil, or that sort of fun?"

"No sir, oh, dear no, sir! The devil, sir, did you say?"

"Yes I did. But come, who is the old buffer?"

"The what, sir?"

"The jolly old buck, your master. Who is he now?"

"Yes, sir, certainly. What wine would you please to take," said the footman, evidently evading the questions of Tony.

"Oh you won't tell," said Tony; "only say at once like a Briton that you aint to tell, and I won't ask you any more. As for wine I don't want any, but a pint of half-and-half wouldn't be objectionable."

"Certainly sir, we have orders to get you anything you require.

"Have you, though?"

"Yes sir, certainly we have."

Tony's eyes glistened, as he said instantly,

"Do you you know of a good place about here for boiled sheeps heads?"

The footmen looked aghast at each other, and one of them replied.

"No sir, there's not a shop for those delicacies in all this neighbourhood, sir."

"Very well," said Tony who did not much like the manner in which a veal cutlet which was upon one of the dishes, was bewildered by its mode of preparation, "get me the half-and-half, and I don't want this affair any longer."

The tray was quickly cleared, but before the half-and-half made its appearance another footman came into the room and presented Tony with a card upon an elegantly embossed silver salver.

"Eh," said Tony, as he took the card, "Mr. Anderson, who's he? I don't know him; it's a mistake, my trump. Stop, yet I don't know, an honest lawyer was to come, and perhaps this is him. Bring him here, bring him here."

A gentlemanly-looking, plainly attired man was introduced to Tony, at whom he looked with some surprise, and then bowing, he said—

"I was requested to communicate with you, sir, immediately."

"That's right then," said Tony, "perhaps you have no objection to tell me who requested you."

A lawyer always has a great objection to answer a plain question in a straight forward manner. Mr. Anderson, although one of the most eminent counsel at the bar, could not get rid of the prejudice.

"If," he said, "that personage has not himself informed you, I doubt if I ought to do so."

"Well, if ever I came near such a set of people. Have it your own way, don't tell if you don't like."

"I should prefer the answer to that question coming from the personage himself, but I was informed that you had a case of much apparent complexity to detail to me, and I am here to listen to any statement you may be pleased to make, and to act upon it according to the very best of my judgment."

"Oh, then, you are the honest lawyer?"

"The what, sir?"

"The honest lawyer."

"Well—I—I—really I hardly know what to say, excepting that I try to be so, sir. It is not the easiest thing in the world to find out what is right to do in this world, but when you do, it is not much easier to follow that exact course of rectitude. As the friend of the personage that resides here, you may depend upon the advice and assistance I render to you, being the very best that I can possibly command for you."

"Very well, then you shall know all I have to tell."

Mr. Anderson listened attentively to Tony, as he detailed the circumstances which had rather puzzled the old gentleman, and ended by handing to him the book, at which the barrister looked attentively.

"I must confess," he said, "that the affair is complex. But I have no doubt that something will occur to clear it up. I happen to have heard of this murder in Soho, and of the arrest of a Mr. Dean for it, together with a man named Clover, and all that can be done at present is for me to go and have an interview with him."

"Can you find him?"

"Oh, yes, easily, if he remains in custody."

"I'll go, too."

"You will not be permitted to see him. It is only in my capacity, as his professional adviser, that I can demand admittance to him, sir, but if you will meet me in the morning at the police-office, I shall, I hope, be able to put the affair into a better shape than it at present seems to wear."

"I will," said Tony.

CHAPTER LVIII.

KATE'S NEW POSITION AT DR. GREY'S.

THE situation of Kate Destern was now so materially altered, that she might well, as she did, look around her in amazement, when she opened her eyes, in consequence of the sunlight of early morning making its way into the doctor's bed-room.

Strange to say, the cataleptic state into which she had fallen, had had the effect of entirely ridding her of all the feverish symptoms which had previously possessed her, and when she opened her eyes, it seemed to her that not only was her present state a dream, but all her illness likewise.

And yet objects around her were by far too vivid for such a delusion to continue long, and when she found that she was really awake, and in an apartment where every comfort was to be found in profusion, terror took possession of her, and the idea of having again fallen into the hands of Lord Battaney, was uppermost in her thoughts.

That such a notion should bring with it a world of terrors, one can most easily imagine.

Half rising in the bed, she clasped her hands, and looked around the apartment with a vague expectation of something terrible meeting her gaze.

"Oh, God!" she exclaimed. "Am I doomed yet to suffer pangs such as I thought I had left behind. Oh! give me poverty—give me want—sickness—anything but the horrors of association with that dreadful man."

As she uttered these words, the room door opened, and when she fully expected to find some myrmidon of Battaney's enter, she was agreeably surprised at a smart enough servant girl making her appearance.

"Oh, Miss," she said, "are you awake?"

"I am," said Kate. "For the love of Heaven tell me where I am. You look kind and compassionate. Oh, have some mercy upon me?"

"Mercy, miss? Lord bless you!"

"Where am I?"

"At Dr. Grey's to be sure. They won't tell me, but I know as you was going to be made a atomy of."

"A what?"

"What they calls here a subject, only you comed to life again, when they least expected it, and so you see they——"

"Silence, Ann, silence," said Mrs. Grey, entering the room. "Now did I not tell you most particularly to say nothing, but to let me know when this young lady should awake?"

"Yes, mum," said Ann, with a look of injured innocence.

"And yet here you are talking."

"I talking, mum! Well I never, I only just opened my mouth, and said I'd say nothing, and I havn't. Well I'm sure, mum. When I is wrong I don't mind something being said, but when I isn't, it's quite another thing.—Well I never—I only——"

"There, there. Go away, go away."

"Well," added Ann, "of all the—upon my life—talking indeed, as if I

ever talked. Yes, mum, I'll shut the door.—Talking indeed, I as never says half a word hardly to nobody.—After that indeed.—Well—I never did!"

"My dear, how are you now?" said Mrs. Grey.

The tones in which these words were uttered, was a kind one, and it quite overcome Kate. In vain she tried to speak. A choaking sensation came in her throat, and she burst into tears.

"Never mind," said Mrs. Grey. "Never mind—cry on, tears such as those will do you good, my dear. Don't mind me, only recollect that you are with friends, who will do all they can for you."

After this, Mrs. Grey did the very best thing she could, which was to bring some needlework that she had to do, and sit down quietly by the bedside of Kate until she was sufficiently recovered to continue the conversation again herself.

Kate looked at her, hesitatingly, saying,—

"May I know what has happened?"

"Yes, my dear."

"All?"

"Yes, certainly — certainly. You shall know all. There is nothing, my dear, to keep secret, but there is much that may surprise. Are you prepared to listen to all I have to tell you."

"Quite, madam, quite."

"Then my dear, you were very ill, it appears, at the house of a most kind and compassionate widow woman, who not being able to procure for you the attention of those whose duty it is to attend upon any one who is sick and friendless, was compelled to rely upon a friend to do something for you."

"Ah, the coal-heaver!"

Mrs. Grey smiled.

"I see," she said, "that you recollect now something of your position. It was a coalheaver who first came to Dr. Grey, and asked him to call and see you at the widow's."

"Yes. Yes, I remember Dr. Grey coming, but somehow after that all seems vague and dim to me; I must have fallen into some most strange sleep."

"A strange sleep indeed!"

"Was it so very strange?"

"It was indeed. It was the sleep, to all appearances, of death. Pending the time when Dr. Grey was to send you some medicine, it seems that you fell into a trance, which an ignorant practitioner mistook for death, or else if he had the knowledge to know differently, he did not give himself the trouble to apply it."

"So I was supposed dead !"

"Yes, until Dr. Grey got a friend to remove you here, and then you moved. I must refer you to him for any further particulars."

"But how could I have fallen into such a state as to be mistaken for one among the dead."

"Some violent shock to the system. I think they told me something about some newspaper."

"Newspaper ? newspaper ?" said Kate, musingly, as she passed her hand across her brow, striving to recollect to what it alluded. Suddenly then as the paragraph which the coal-heaver had read to the maiden, came fully upon her recollection—she gave a scream.

"Oh, Heaven—yes—yes—yes."

"You recollect ?"

"Too well—too well. They said that he had done murder ! He whose heart is a well spring of the holiest emotions —no—no- no. He could not—he did not do it. Oh, God, no !"

"Calm yourself."

"I recollect now. It drove me then into seeming death, and it will soon drive me into actual madness."

"Do not give way to such feelings, my good girl, I pray you. Reflect with more calmness upon what you have heard? Remember, that you may be mistaken. How would you feel, after you had perhaps done some act under the impulse of a sudden despair, at tidings which afterwards turned out to be false ?"

"You give me a hope," said Kate, sadly. "It may be false. The fact of course I know to be false—the allegation I mean, but it is the accusation which is perhaps true."

"Well, and if it be. Is this gentleman in whose fate you are evidently so deeply, and probably so justly interested, the only innocent person who has ever been accused of murder ?"

"No—no."

"Nor will he be the last by a great many."

"No—no ; something must be one

to show his innocence to the world. Something must be done to clear him even from the shadow of suspicion of such a crime."

"Ah !" said Mrs. Grey with a smile, "now, my dear, you are rational, and we shall hear no more from you of dying or going mad from despair."

"I take shame to myself, madam."

"Nay, that you need not. Come, I will go and fetch Dr. Grey, and what you have to tell, you shall tell both of us together, so that you shall be spared the pain of a double recital of many things that may affect you much. Compose yourself so far as you are able, by the time I return, which will not be for ten minutes yet."

These ten minutes were a good hour to Kate, and she could not but admire the kindly consideration manifested by Mrs. Grey, in leaving her alone for that space of time. It enabled her to collect her scattered thoughts, and to better prepare herself for the interview with the doctor, which was promised her.

Before, too, that ten minutes expired, Kate found time to offer up a devout prayer to the Great Ruler of heaven and earth, that he would be pleased to shower his blessings upon those who were dear to her, and to unite her to her sister Lucy and Harry Dean.

She fancied that if she could hold the hand of Harry Dean with one of her own, and that of Lucy with the other, she should scarcely have a wish ungratified upon this side of the grave. "We should never more part," she said. As she uttered this word Doctor Grey and Mrs. Grey entered the room.

They were, as they well deserved to be, received by Kate with a smile of welcome, and as she held out her hand to the doctor, she said—

"To you, sir, it seems that I owe my life."

"My dear," he replied, "say no more about that."

"No more, sir. It is a theme upon which surely I cannot say too much; I owe it to you that I now am able to say so, and yet to hope for many happy days to come."

"Well," said the doctor, "I don't like to be defrauded of any credit that is fairly my due, and by the sam reasoning, I don't like, to arrogate to myself anything that I don't deserve."

Kate looked amazed and curious.

"First and last," added the doctor, "you must know it, and the real truth is, that two young medical friends of mine kidnapped your body."

Kate looked astonished.

"Ah, I see you don't understand me. Being told you were dead, we took it for granted, and had you surreptitiously brought here for dissection, where you recovered, and now you know the truth."

Kate shuddered, but Mrs. Grey soon overcame by her mild and judicious reasoning, the shock that this disclosure gave to the young girl, and persuaded her to relate to her and the doctor, the particulars of her fortunes.

This Kate did, and in so artless a manner, as won from them their sympathy and esteem. When she had concluded, the doctor said—

"You find the coal-heaver has shown himself a friend indeed."

"Oh, how very kind in his simple, unlettered, and honest way, was that coal-heaver to me. There was nothing that kindness and generous consideration could suggest that he did not say or do to put spirits into me, and make me forget the unhappiness of my condition."

"Well, I owe it to our mutual friend the coal-heaver, to go to him with a full explanation of what has occurred."

"Oh, do, sir—do, sir. And tell him how truly grateful I am to him for all his kindness. Alas! I shall have so much to be grateful for, and so many to be grateful to, that a life time of devotion will not suffice to do more than prove my feelings."

"Say no more upon that head. When I have seen the coal-heaver I will get you all the information that can be got of this Mr. Harry Dean, who seems rather a mysterious personage, if I may be allowed to make the remark."

"Mysterious," said Kate with surprise.

"Yes, is he not by your own account of him, poor at one time and rich at another. Is he not to all appearance penniless and incapable of protecting you one day, and the next one to whom all who encounter him bow down with deference. Surely he is mysterious enough."

Kate blushed, and hung down her head.

"But mark me," added Dr. Grey, "I do not see anything in this mystery which surrounds him any symptoms of evil, it rather seems to me the sort of mystery that an eccentric honest man would wrap his actions and himself in for some good motive."

"I thank you sir, from my heart for your good opinion of him who is so dear to me."

"And I am much pleased with the ingenuous manner in which you say that he is dear to you."

Kate was hardly aware of what the doctor complimented her upon, the ingenuousness that had made so complete an exposition of her feelings towards Harry Dean ; for the fact was she had so accustomed herself to think of him as one so intimately bound up with all her thoughts and actions, that she quite unwittingly applied to him when speaking of him, epithets of tenderness.

Now, however, she was roused to a consciousness of the fact, and she covered her fair face with her hands to conceal the traces of emotion that immediately became visible upon it.

Dr. Grey took the opportunity of quitting the apartment, and in a few moments he left the house, resolved before he returned to have ascertained something more particularly concerning Harry Dean.

CHAPTER LIX.

SHOWS HOW LUCY AGAIN BECAME A FUGITIVE IN LONDON.

IT will be recollected, that Lucy had accompanied the party in the coach, that went from Madam Zadzed's house to the police office, and which coach contained Harry Dean, Sam Clover, Swam and the doctor, besides the two officers who had taken charge of Harry Dean and Sam.

The arbitrary and ungentlemanly conduct of the magistrate could hardly be said to enter into the calculations of Harry Dean, on his route to the police office, and of course he did not imagine there would be any difficulty with regard to his extending his protection to Lucy.

The only circumstance that had at all surprised him was that on the road in the coach, the doctor had taken from his pocket some lozenges, and offered one to Lucy. Harry Dean thought she had not taken it, but partly from fear, and partly from that want of self command in knowing what is best to be done at a moment, she took it and eat it.

The consequences of this lozenge where rather fearful to Lucy.

It was while the examination of Harry Dean was going on, and in the midst of the altercation which unfortunately took place between him and the magistrate, that Lucy began to feel a strange sort of giddiness, and to fancy that she was far from well.

A woman who was in the court observed her change colour, and said to her with a tone of kindness—

"My dear, you are unwell."

"I am, I fear," said Lucy.

"Can I do anything for you."

"Oh! if I could have a draught of that water."

Lucy pointed to a decanter of pure sparkling spring water, which was before the magistrate, but the woman said—

"My dear, the pump where it was got from, is outside, and free to all; I will go with you, as well as seeing you back here again. Have you got any friends here, or do you come only out of curiosity to the court?"

"There is my dear friend," said Lucy, pointing to Harry Dean.

"Oh, well, you will be back again in a moment. Come along!"

Lucy really felt so ill that to leave the court for a draught of that pure cool looking spring water, seemed to her sufficient almost to save her life. She took the hand of the woman, and accompanied her into the street.

There she felt no better, nor did the water, although grateful to the palate, at all dissipate the strange sort of confusion which was in her brain.

The doctor's infernal medicated lozenge which he would not even name or mention to Swam, was doing its work.

Now, the woman was really compassionate, and tender-hearted, and no doubt would have taken all care of Lucy, but an officer ran suddenly out of court, and cried in a loud voice—

"Here's Joliffe's case come on!"

"That's my husband!" cried the woman, " that's my husband!" and she rushed back into the court, leaving the confused Lucy in the street.

Lucy would not have, even with her small experience, found any great difficulty in rejoining Harry Dean, provided she had not anything like a proper or efficient use of her faculties, but that she really had not.

The confusion of her intellect increased each moment, and she wandered across the road, and up a court with a very narrow entrance, she really knew not how.

A feeling of distress and dread came over her. She felt as though she were walking through a mist, and only feeling her way, when she would fain have seen it plainly. A more painful sensation could scarcely have been well imagined.

She saw faintly a house with some steps leading up to it. The lowest of these steps came invitingly in her way, and she sat down upon it with a feeling that it would be quite impossible for her to get half a yard further up the court.

Alas! poor Lucy! Those steps were not attached to exactly the sort of house in which innocence ought to find refuge.

There then he sat and, her eyes closed—her head drooped—and she felt the strange sensation as if all the world was slowly gliding away from her, and leaving her shelved as it were upon some vapour in the vast realms of space.

After this, she knew nothing for awhile.

The door of the house opened suddenly, and a man looked out, and scrutinized the appearance of Lucy.

"Who the deuce is this?" he said, "I say Bill, come here."

"What is it now, stupid?" said a voice, from further down the passage of the house.

"Come on!"

"Well, ain't I coming. Have you found a horse's nest, eh? and are you wanting the eggs? You are always

(Tony exite the anger of the " old woman,")

making up some sort of fine conjurations you are."

"Don't be a goose, now, will you, but come this way, and look at the strange kid. I tell you it's no joke."

"Well, who said it was?"

"Don't be a fool."

After this little bit of dialogue, another man came forward, looked at poor Lucy intently, after which he said,—

"Who is she?"

"Don't know"

"She don't belong to the family, I should say, by the looks of her. What do you say?"

"The same; but, Bill, haven't you often heard of things being, what do they call it—prowidential—ah, that's it?"

"Well, what if I have?"

"Why, this here's one on 'em, that's all. Wasn't we a wondering how we could get hold of anything small enough to get atween them iron bars in the back window of the crib we means to crack to night?"

"To be sure."

"And won't this one do?"

"Humph! I don't know that. What's the matter with her now, eh?"

"Why, somebody has hocussed her, that's quite clear enough, and if we take her in and get her all right again, I should say there won't be much difficulty in frightening her into what we want."

"Well, you can try it."

"Come on, then, my little rum 'un. This is the way."

The man lifted the light, fragile form of Lucy with ease from the door-step, and at once proceeded into the house with her. The experience of the thieves and housebreakers who made that place their home, enabled them at once to pronounce upon what had happened to Lucy. And they were right, for the lozenge which Swam's admirer gave her, had in it some narcotic, which for a time would effectually seal up the senses of even an adult.

No wonder, then, that the effect was great upon Lucy Destern.

There were some women in the house, to whom the thieves, with more humanity and consideration than could have been expected from them, surrendered the care of Lucy, and they being well acquainted with the mode of producing such a condition as Lucy was in, were likewise cognisant of the proper remedies to be applied for her recovery.

The consequence was, that in the course of an hour, the effect of the narcotic was so much diminished, that Lucy could look about her.

The intense surprise with which she did so, was most amusing to those who were watching her.

"Oh, what has happened?" she said. "What has happened, and where am I?"

"Nothing particular," said a woman of immense proportions, who had superintended the recovery of Lucy.

"But where am I?"

"Oh, all's right."

Lucy burst into tears, and with difficulty sobbed aloud,—

"Where is Harry?"

"Come—come," said the woman, "no crying here."

"But, where is Harry?"

"Gone to blazes!"

Poor Lucy could make nothing of this off handed sort of information. A gleaming and indistinct idea that she had been ill, and had left the police-office, came across her mind, and then as memory resumed its functions, she began to recollect everything up to the moment of sitting upon the door-step.

"Let me go," she said, "to my friends. I dare say you have been kind to me, and I thank you; but let me go now?"

"Why, where else would you be but here?"

"With my friends who love me!"

"Oh, we are your friends, and if you make yourself useful to us, we will love you, if that's all you want."

"But—but you do not mean that you will not let me go? Oh! what now have I done that you should not let me go?"

"Don't bother."

Lucy felt as though she could have dropped to the floor, and there died, her mental agony at finding herself a prisoner was so great she could not divest herself of the idea that her cognisance of the murder of Madam Zadzed was known, and that by some most artful means she had been again entrapped by Miss Swam.

In such a case, what could she have to look forward to but death.

The state of her feelings began to be agonising in the extreme, enough almost to drive her mad,

"Mercy, mercy!" she said.

"Why what are you frightened at, eh?"

"You will not let her kill me. Oh tell me that you will not let her kill me."

"Who?"

"Miss Swam. I know that she is here. I expect each moment that the door will open, and shew her to me, all I ask is that you will save me from her."

"Why you little fool, we don't know," ——began the woman, but before she could say any more, another who was present, cried,

"Stop. I want to speak to you, Bess."

They walked aside, and she who had interrupted the other said—

"Don't you see the little wretch is frightened half out of her life at somebody. If we say we will protect her we shall be able to get her to do anything we like."

"Do you think so?"

"To be sure I do."

"Very well, manage her your own way."

The woman who took so politic a view of the affair, and who wished to make use of Lucy's fears, now approached her.

"Hark yer," she said, "I can and will protect you from Swam if you will in return obey me in what I require of you?"

"Oh, yes—yes—yes."

"Very well; but mind me now, the moment you refuse or turn at all disagreeable I will send for Swam, who don't know we have caught you, and then you know what will happen to you pretty quickly."

"She would be sure to murder me."

"Of course she would."

"And you will protect me from her. You really will?"

"Haven't I said so. Of course I will. You have nothing to fear if you will do as you are bid to do. That is all."

"Anything—anything so as you do not give me up to her. I know so well that she would take my life, for she has found out now that I saw all."

Lucy shuddered as she spoke, and the woman would fain have asked her for further particulars, but she feared that by so doing she might loose the hold she had upon Lucy's imagination by letting her know or suspect how little she knew already.

Under the circumstance, therefore, she thought it prudent to say no more, but to leave Lucy to say as much or as little as she pleased of her affairs.

"Wait here," she said, "and don't stir, if you do you don't know who you may run against and then somebody may send for Swam."

"I will not move, madam."

The woman proceeded to the lower part of the house, where the men were, and in a voice of exultation she cried—

"Come now. I think if the swag is good to night I ought to have something extra?"

"What for?"

"Why the young girl would never have made herself useful if I had not managed her."

She then proceeded to relate by which means she had contrived to make Lucy so tractable, a piece of information which was agreeable enough to the housebreakers.

"Well that's all right, Poll," said one. "You are an out-and-out schemer, you are, and we shall soon make something of the little 'un up stairs. It puts an end to a great difficulty it does."

"Of course it does," said another, "what do you say is the rum name she is so afraid of, I shall be forgetting that, I'm sure I shall."

"More fool you then—Its Swam, I'm sure that's easy enough remembered—Swam—Now do you know it."

"In course I does; Swam, what an odd name for a christian to be sure. I won't forget it in a hurry—Swam, Well I'll be hanged if I should like to be called Swam."

"But are you sure she may be depended upon, after all?" said another.

"How can anybody be sure. I think she may, and that is all we can do. I only wish the job was well over, and the swag in the melting pot, Bill."

"So do I, old girl."

"Ah," said the other, "some work will have to be done before that time comes. We all know that sooner or later there must be an end to the game. The grabs must have us all in the natural order of things, and the only question is, how long can we hold out. Aint that about the state of the case, Poll?"

"Yes, Joe, it is; but we don't mean to give in for all that."

"Give in? No, hang it, not I. I'll hold on like grim death, and if some of these days I am nabbed, why I'll face out the beak as best I can, and make the most of a bad business."

"All's right, all's right. Let's have a drain of something to drink on the strength of to-night's work."

"Beware!" said the woman.

"Beware of what?"

"Of the drink. You know well that you came home empty handed the last time you went to crack a crib, besides narrowly escaping the grabs, and all through the something to drink you took before starting."

"It's true, Bill.

"Oh, stuff. Poll is always at me about some nonsense or another, but she knows it aint often that I take the extra drop, and when I do, it aint when such business as this is on hand."

"Well," said Poll, "you are not the worst fellow in the world, but have the something to drink when you come back, and not when you go."

Bill did not seem much to like this arrangement, but a kind of habitual deference to Poll stopped any complaints.

CHAPTER LX.

THE THIEVES' HAUNT.—A RECOGNITION.

THE mental uneasiness of Lucy increased as her bodily indisposition passed away, and by the dusk of evening, which, in consequence of a cloudy state of the air seemed to fall upon London much earlier than usual, she was certainly in no very enviable frame of mind.

She had so many separate and distinct sources of uneasiness that each was enough to produce a state bordering upon distraction. It was truly sad, and at the same time truly wonderful that one so young should be so much tried in the furnace of affliction.

She was kept in the room where she had first awakened to a consciousness that she was in a strange place, and she was not even permitted to go near the windows, lest, it is presumed, she should give some alarm of her condition to some passer-by who might feel disposed to interfere for her rescue.

She felt that there could be no good in a state of things that required so much concealment and caution.

Once, and once more only, did she make an attempt to move the compassion of the woman who had taken charge of her.

"You would let me go," she said, "I am sure you would let me go, if you had the least idea of how much I had suffered."

"Hold your peace," said the woman.

"Nay, but it has been for the good of others that I have suffered. Do not fancy it has been for any wickedness."

"Don't talk to me of wickedness," cried the woman. "Do you mean me, you little brute, eh?"

"Oh, no, no, no."

"Then mind what you are saying, that's all."

The fear of offending this woman, whom Lucy still believed could not but be in league with Swam, now kept her quiet, and she felt that she had no resource but to wait quietly the progress and the course of events.

She hoped, but only hoped for the best.

Soon the darkness that had overspread London became very intense, and those whose prisoner she was began to think that their nefarious designs might well we carried out.

Lucy found that there were whispered consultations going on in the room, while now and then an uneasy glance was cast upon her, as though she were the subject oft he rather uncomfortable consulta ions.

If anything more than another could tend to give her a large amount of uneasiness, this would, and she trembled as the woman suddenly approached her, drew a chair and sat down in very close proximity indeed to her.

"Now attend me," she said.

"Yes," faltered Lucy, "oh, yes, I will indeed. Do not do me any harm."

"All that depends upon yourself; remember that if I send to Swam to say that we have you here, she will lose no time in coming to you."

"Oh yes, yes."

"Well attend to me now, and I will tell you what you ought to do, and indeed what you must do for the purpose of keeping yourself safe."

Poor Lucy listened as though the woman were an oracle.

"Do you know what cracking a crib is ?"

"No."

"Do you know what a beak is ?"

"Oh yes. The beak of a bird."

"Don't bother her," said one of the men. "You see she is not fly."

"You mind your own business."

"Well—well."

"Interfere with me again and I will give the girl up. You can try what your stupid brains can do with her, which I'll warrant would come to nothing at all,"

"Oh bother you, when once you begin to talk there's no such thing, I know, as a fellow calling his head his own."

"Now, you little wretch," pursued the woman, again addressing herself to Lucy, "attend to me if you please, and don't forget a word I say; you must go with these two gentleman to-night to a house where they will show you a little window, you will have to drop through for them and open a door, that's all; now do you thoroughly understand?"

Lucy shuddered, the conviction that it was a robbery she was required to assist in, came forcibly to her mind.

"What's the matter with you now?" said the woman.

"Nothing, nothing."

"Yes, but there is though."

"Do not, oh, do not ask me to do any thing that is wrong. It is true that I dread Swam, and I think that she would kill me, but if you save me from her, do not ask me to be grateful by wrong doing. Oh, do not, I pray you."

"There that's gratitude."

"I am indeed grateful, but—"

"Oh yes, there's always a but. Bill, pop on your hat and run for Miss Swam."

"Oh, no—no—no," cried Lucy,

"Will you consent then?"

"I—I must. I suppose I must."

"All's right," said the woman,

She then rose and held another consultation with the men, after which she heard them say that they must go at twelve, for that would be the safest time. They then told her to lie down and rest herself, for they did not want her to be half asleep when her services were required, and as this advice was almost enforced by the woman, Lucy feeling herself anything but a free agent in the matter, laid herself upon a couch and closing her eyes she gave herself up to thought, but not as she supposed, to sleep.

Sleep will, however, come as often unbidden as it will stay away even when earnestly solicited. In the course of a few minutes Lucy's eyes were closed and she was shaking off the fatigue and exhaustion she had gone through in a deep and dreamless slumber, such a slumber as could only visit the innocent.

How long she had slept she had no manner of means of knowing, but she was somewhat suddenly awakened by the woman shaking her by the arm, and crying.

"Will you awake? Or do you want to sleep on all night, and all day too, you little brute? Come, rouse yourself."

Lucy started wide awake in a moment.

"Come, are you ready?"

"Oh yes, yes. What is it—what is it? Oh, I know now."

"Oh, you do, do you? Then perhaps as you know, you will be so good as to get up, and set about what you have to do."

Lucy rose. The harsh manner in which the old woman spoke completely chilled her, and she waited in breathless agitation for what should be next said to her by her captors.

The door of the room was opened, and one of the men, attired in a rough great coat, made his appearance. He called in an impatient tone,—

"Come, have you got her ready yet?"

"Yes, here she is."

"Come on then, will you."

The woman put upon Lucy's head an old, miserable, small bonnet, and tied a blue handkerchief over it and her head. Thus, taking her by the hand, she led her to the man, who at once hurried her rapidly down the stairs.

In the hall of the house, a lantern stood upon a chair. It was lighted, and emitted some feeble rays. The man paused with Lucy, and pointing to the street door, he said,—

"Do you see that?"

"Yes," she replied, timidly, wondering much what such a question would lead to.

"Well, go and open it.

The street door was secured by an iron bar and sundry bolts, all of which Lucy, after a few moments exertion, contrived to undo. The man watched her keenly, and when she had finished he grumbled out,—

"It's better than I expected. Come on."

Again roughly he seized her by the hand, and a companion joining him at the threshold of the house, they walked rapidly through the streets, dragging the terrified Lucy with them.

———

CHAPTER LXI.

TONY IN THE KITCHEN.—A LITTLE SURPRISE.

For a brief space we return to Tony. It will be remembered, that we left him in very good quarters, in the house of one, who, for the service he had rendered to him, felt a warm interest in Tony, and all his hopes and wishes.

There was really something, to the imagination of Tony, quite enchanting in the amount of mystery which everybody kept up concerning the name of the master of the house. He scarcely wished to know it, inasmuch as the not knowing it gave him such material for conjecture, as quite withdrew his mind from more painful topics.

He moreover considered, now, that he was in a better condition, as regarded Harry Dean, for the promises that had been made by his present patron, were of a nature to make him quite hopeful of a pleasing result to the proceedings at the police-office in the morning, for which he earnestly longed.

Tony had had an idea of still traversing London in search of Lucy, but he was persuaded to remain where he was until the morning, and the time began to grow rather heavy upon his hands, as he sat in the magnificent library, where he was told he might amuse himself.

"Oh," said Tony, "it's all very well to say, amuse yourself, but bother all these books, I can't make anything of them. They ain't my kind at all. What the deuce amusement can anybody find in them is a regular poser to me ?"

After for some time sitting in a very solitary state, Tony went to the door and opened it, just in time to hear a peal of laughter from the lower regions of the mansion.

A door then banged shut, and all was still.

"Well," said Tony, "there are some enjoying themselves here, at any rate I don't suppose it's high treason to try and find out who it is so merry in the place."

With this intent, Tony walked cautiously towards the head of the stairs, which most incontestibly led into the kitchen.

When there, he stopped and listened for some few moments, with the hope of a repetition of the joyous sounds that had so felicitously before broken in upon his sense of solitude.

He was not doomed to be disappointed.

In a few moments the door below again opened, and another roar of laughter came upon his ears.

This was too much for Tony's nature, if not for human nature generally, so he at once, without a thought of the consequences, crept softly down the kitchen stairs.

When he arrived at the foot of the stairs, he found that there was a swinging door, covered with green baize, placed no doubt there with the express intention of preventing any sounds, either of strife or rivalry, from that quarter, from finding their way above.

To open this door a little way, so that there was but a small crevice for him to look through, was the work of a moment to Tony, and then he could hear pretty distinctly what was going on in a very capacious kitchen,

"It's true," said a female voice, as if enforcing the vivacity of some narrative of the wild and wonderful. "It's true, as I'm a sinner, and you may believe it or not, as you like."

"Well, but how did it end ?" said a man's voice.

"I'm a going to tell you."

"Go on—go on ?"

"Well, you must know that after hearing the screaming noise in the cupboard, she sat looking at it, and looking at it, and looking at it, just as I might at that baize door."

"Well—well ?"

"Well, she was so frightened she couldn't move an inch, and so for about ten minutes she did nothing but stare at the cupboard till she thought the door began to move. Then she said, 'Oh, dear, oh !—oh !—oh dear me !'"

"How well she tells it, don't she ?" said the cook, who had been listening with breathless attention to the narrative from the lips of the housemaid.

"Yes, she does."

The housemaid, however, to the surprise of every one, could go on saying nothing but, "Oh, dear—oh, dear !"

Now this looked like over acting her part, but the fact was that it was perfectly real, for she did actually see the door move, for the best of all possible reasons, that Tony was upon the other side of it, inducing such movement.

As, however, he became quite still, after finding that he had in such a way prematurely attracted her attention, she began to think, that after all, it was but a trick of the fancy, and she continued her story.

"Well, you must know, then, after she had looked some time longer, the door just far enough for somebody's head to be popped in and a voice said,—

"'Remember your latter end!'"

At this moment, Tony put on as horible a contortion of countenance as he could, and putting in his head through the opening of the door, which he first opened sufficiently to allow him to do so, he said,—

"Bow! wow! Blood! blood!"

The effect was instantaneous. Of the three female servants and the two male that were in the kitchen, none could stand such a terrifying circumstance. The cook got under the table. The two housemaids rushed into a little cupboard. The footman hid behind the washing stand, and the groom, after a fruitless attempt to get into the oven by the side of the grate, made his way into an adjoining pantry, and effectually hid himself among some casks and bottles.

"Hilloa!" said Tony, as, resuming his natural aspect, he walked into the kitchen. "What are you all afraid of? It's only me. Why, where have you all got to?"

No one answered him, but the disappearance of them all had been so rapid that Tony really for the moment did not know where to find anybody.

The spirit of fun was, however, aroused in him, and seeing in one corner of the kitchen one of those brooms with amazing long handles called Turk's heads, he poked it carefully up the chimney, leaving the handle resting in a dark corner of one of the hobs.

"Ever such a little touch now to that," said Tony to himself, "will bring a dollop of soot, and no mistake."

Having then duly provided himself with such a means of having further frolic, he called aloud, saying,

"It was only a bit of fun. It's nobody of any harm. Where are you all, eh?"

The footman looked out, and said,

"Are you, then, the gent as was up stairs?"

"No," said Tony. "Don't call me that. I'd sooner be called an individual than a gent."

"Oh, dear, what a fright you did give us, sir. Here, cook—Mary—Susan—Bob. It's all right."

One by one they made their appearance, and finding that Tony looked anything but murderous, they breathed more freely, and more freely still when he said,

"Now don't mind me, and call me sir. I heard some fun going on down here, and come to join in it. Now, let us all be good friends, and don't think anything of my frightening you all."

At this assuring speech they quite recovered, and as Tony now set the example of laughing, everybody followed it, and they were all as merry as possible.

"Did you finish your story," said Tony to the housemaid.

"Oh, yes; she fainted away, and didn't come to herself again for five weeks, that's the end of it."

"Five weeks?"

"Yes, exactly."

"Very good. Now, there's nothing I like so much as good stories. Will anybody tell one?"

"I don't mind," said the footman, "telling you all why I left my last place."

"Ah, do, do."

"Well, I don't know how it is, but I never can stay in a place long where there are young ladies in the family."

As he said this the footman arranged his hair and felt for his shirt collar to discover if it was exactly in its right place, so that his audience might fairly infer that the reason why he could not stay in any place where there were young ladies had something to do very particularly with his personal attractions.

"Well," said the cook.

"I'm proceeding, mum," said the footman. "There was three daughters in my last place. Jane was a lovely girl!"

"Really."

"Yes; a lovely gal. Of course I has eyes in my head. Well, it's perhaps not right to say such things, but I know in course it wont go any further, but the fact is from the first day I went to the place I saw Jane had a eye on me."

"You don't say so?" remarked Tony.

"Yes sir, I does."

"Very good—go on. What happened next?"

"Well, I wondered with myself, and I said, Grummet, this has happened to you before, meaning myself, you comprehend. Will you tear from her friends and her family, a lovely gal? Will you be a seducing villain, and be talked of in all the newspapers, or will you be a man of honour, and shew her that you discouage her affections!"

"You asked yourself all that?'" said Tony.

"I did sir."

"And what did yourself answer?"

The footman did not much like the tone of grave irony in which Tony spoke to him, but nevertheless he continued—

"Well, things went on, till one day, Jane took a cold, they said; I thought different, and that her heart was infected, but no matter—they said she had a cold, and a cold I am bound to believe it were."

"Bless me!" said Tony, you'll never get through your story.

"Yes I shall sir. Where was I, oh! at Jane's cold—well, Miss Kittscoffiner said to me—

"Miss who?"

"Kittscoffiner—the lady's maid in the family."

"What a deuce of a name!"

"Well, sir, she said to me — 'John,' said she, 'Miss Jones will want two quarts of hot water placed at her room door at eight precisely. She is no better and is going to put her feet in it.' Excuse me, ladies, for naming feet in your presence, but upon my honour I don't mean any harm."

"Bother your honour. Go on," said Tony.

"Well, at eight I took up the water in a can, and something came over me as I went up the stairs."

"Why didn't you carry it evener, then?" said Tony.

"Sir?"

"Why didn't you carry it evener? You say some of the hot water came over you as you went up the stairs."

"No, sir; it was my feelings came over me. 'Grummet,' I said to myself, 'this is a crisis in your destiny;' but, howsomedever, as I went I determined to do the right sort of thing."

"And what was hat?"

"You shall hear, sir, you shall hear. Well, when I got to the door of Jane's room, I felt unutterable things, as the poet says; but I controlled myself till I found the door was only ajar. 'I knew it,' I said to myself, and just by accident putting my eyes to the opening, I saw Jane looking towards the door so pale and unhappy that my feelings was overcome."

"You don't say so!" cried the cook.

"Well, well what did you do?" said the housemaid.

"What could I do? I flung the door open and rushed in. 'Jane,' I said 'Jane, I know all. Behold me at your feet!'"

"Gracious!" said the cook.

"I'm all hot and cold," said the housemaid.

"Well," continued Mr. Grummet, "can you believe it?—she gave a sort of scream, and Kittscoffiner coming at the moment, took up the can of hot water, and emptied it over me. That cooled me down."

"The devil it did!" said Tony.

"I rushed from the room, feeling that the happiness of Jane was gone for ever."

"And so you left?"

"Why, yes; there was some trumped up story told to one of the family, and he had the vulgarity to kick me into the street; I told him I scorned such an action, but from hat day to this I have not seen Jane. Heaven only knows what her feelings was, and is; I heard her laugh when the hot water went over me."

"If you heard her laugh," said Tony, you knew her feelings pretty well, I should say."

"No, sir, it was a historical laugh."

"A historical laugh! What do you mean by that?"

"Why, sir, the fair sex often laugh historically."

"Do you mean highstirickel?" said the housemaid.

"It's the same thing, Miss Susan

quite the same thing. Only, in very high life, we call it historical."

"Well," said Tony, "that's a very good story of yours, Mr. G., but, I think, I know one which will astonish you all."

"Oh do tell us," said the cook.

"Do, do," said the two housemaids.

The footman smiled benignly, as one who should say, I am quite charitable enough to hear what this person is about to say, although, of course, it is far beneath my notice.

"You won't scream?" said Tony.

"Scream!"

"Yes; it's rather horrid. It will make your flesh creep."

"Is it possible?"

"Well," said the housemaid, "my flesh hasn't crept for a long time, and I shan't mind it."

"Very well."

The party gathered a little closer round the fire, but Tony took good care to get a place where he could readily reach the handle of the long broom he had poked up the chimney.

So intent was everybody upon what he was going to say, that this little bit of manœuvring was quite unnoticed, so that he had all the opportunity in the world of producing an effect at any period of hisstory, when he thought it most applicable, and most sure of being effectual.

CHAPTER LXII.

TONY'S STORY OF A CHIMNEY.

"You must know," said Tony, "that what I am going to tell you is strictly true."

"Oh yes, yes, of course."

"It happened then, that about two years ago, in the house where I lodged, a very strange man came and took an attic. He was very old, and had immense moustacheos and whiskers. He was a foreigner, coming from somewhere in Germany. He seldom spoke to anybody, but the people in the next attic said they often heard him talking in the night to somebody.

"Now who it was nobody could tell, for this night-talking used to go on when everybody was in bed, and the whole house locked up, so that nobody could get in.

"Well, things went on in this way for some time, till at last, in the middle of the night, there was an alarm in the house that the German was dying, and had called for help in his room.

"Of course, the whole room was in an uproar, and among others, in I went. I found the old German sitting up in his bed, and looking rather wild.

"Some one it appears had thought of sending for a doctor, but he said,—

"'No, no; not all the doctors there are, were, or will be, would suffice to do me any good. All is over now. I am dying.'

"'But,' said the landlady, 'its very unhandsome of you to die here in my house, and besides you owe two weeks.'"

"'Unfeeling woman,' said the old German.

"'Hoity, toity!' cried the landlady, 'its all very well to call folks unfeeling, when they only ask for their own.'"

"'Can you speak thus?' he said, 'to one going such a journey as I am?'"

"'A journey. Oh, if it was only a journey, one might expect to see you again, but not now.'"

"'It is a journey,' he said, 'to eternity. Yet madam, you shall see me again, since you so much desire it.'"

"'As he said these words he gave such a peculiar look at the landlady, that I saw her turn pale.

"'I don't want to see you again,' she said.

"The old German, however, paid no attention to this, but suddenly, in a tone of agony, he cried aloud,

"'Oh God! it is true, then, and you have made a third appearance to me. I come, I come. Oh, don't look so frowningly upon me. I know I am doomed—doomed. Oh, yes, yes, doomed.'"

"He spoke these words in a tone of such harrowing horror that all were terrified, and most of all the landlady. She almost fainted away, but we didn't pay much attention to her, for we saw the old German fall back upon his pillow, and we all thought he was dead.

"The landlady, when she heard us say that, all of a sudden jumped up, crying and wringing her hands, as she said,

"'He will haunt me! His ghost will haunt me now. He said so, and I shall never have another moment's peace.'"

"'Stop a bit,' said I, 'he is not quite dead yet.'"

"I had been looking at the old man, and saw that his lips moved slightly, so I thought he might say something if he were pressed to do so, to comfort the landlady.

"She came close to him trembling, and said,

"'Oh, sir, say you won't trouble me after you are gone, and I will freely forgive the two weeks rent, and all the bother of your funeral.'"

"He opened his eyes, and spoke very slowly.

"'I shall not cross your threshold again, except once' in life or in death.'"

"Those were the last words he spoke, and the landlady tumbled on the floor with a groan.

"'He says he'll come to me once,' she cried, 'and I'm as good as a dead woman.'"

"'Why, what a fool you are,' said I. 'Don't you understand him? He says he will never cross your threshold, dead or alive, but once, and unless you bury him in the attic, or throw him out of window, he must be carried out in his coffin, and that will be the once.'"

"Well, this pacified the landlady, and as the old German was really dead now, she could make nothing more of it. In about a week he was duly buried, and everybody thought there was an end of the matter. But there was not."

The circle of attentive auditors drew a little closer to the fire as Tony said these words, and all eyes were fixed upon him with intense curiosity to hear the conclusion of the story.

"Would you like the end?" said Tony.

"Oh, dear, yes," said everybody.

"Well, its rather disagreeable, and don't blame me whatever may happen, mind that."

"Oh, yes, yes; only go on."

"Very good."

"Are you going on?"

"Yes. Well, on the day he was buried the landlady evidently felt rather fidgetty, and her eyes looked red as though she had not had too much sleep the last night, but nobody liked to say anything to her except a great grey cat that she had, and every time that cat passed the door of the room where the German had died, it stopped and gave a sort of spit, as much as to say,

"'It aint all right yet.'"

"This conduct of the cat, whose name was Gargantualamartenspike, rather astonished—"

"But do you mean to say the cat had such a deuce of a name as that, sir," said the footman.

"Certainly, I do. Why might not the cat in my story have a deuce of a name as well as the waiting maid in yours?"

"Oh, I have no *dejection* whatever?"

"Well, that's kind of you. But as I was saying, this conduct of the cat only made the landlady worse, and towards night, though she had fifteen cups of strong tea to compose her nerves, and nine glasses of gin, she was more flurried than ever."

"Nine glasses?"

"Yes, exactly nine. Well, as I was saying she did not feel a bit the better, but like our friend Grummet here, felt that there was a crisis in her destiny coming on in some way or another."

The footman looked rather indignant, for he began to find out that Tony was laughing at him occasionally, but still he felt his interest in the story Tony was telling sufficiently great to chain him to the kitchen, otherwise he would have shown his indignation by returning to the hall.

"Well," added Tony, "the night came as night usually does, and everybody saw the landlady was not exactly the thing. Twice she fell down the kitchen stairs and the cat growled and spat in all directions, and at anybody, until at last the landlady could keep about no longer."

"I should think not, sir," said Grummet."

"Very likely the tea upset her, poor thing," said the cook, "I've known one cup of tea upset me."

"Yes, after a quartern of rum," said the groom.

"A what?"

"A quartern of rum."

"You wretch, if ever I took so much as one half glass of rum in all my life may I be shot, except as a medicine."

"Oh—!"

"Oh! oh!"

"You must be ill every day then, after dinner has been served up," said the groom, "I should think."

The cook felt so aggrieved at this unmanly attack upon her, that after trying to speak again she wept bitterly, and betrayed some symptoms of going into what Mr. Grummet called historical fits.

"Come, come," said Tony, "I shall never get through my story if I'm to be interrupted in this way."

"That's just what I was going to say," remarked the housemaid, "and I really wouldn't go to bed without hearing the remainder of that story on any account."

"Nor me," cried the cook.

"Well, ladies," laughed Tony "after the second fall down the kitchen stairs and making her nose bleed, the landlady got better."

"It relieved her poor head," said the cook.

"Yes," added Tony. "Well down she sat, and the cat sat down directly opposite to her on a low stool. The kitchen clock struck twelve you must know."

"Good gracious!"

"Yes, the kitchen clock struck twelve, a coffin flew out of the fire on to the cat's back, and she didn't know it till a hole was burnt in her fur the size of half a crown.

"But that's not much—a winding sheet came in the candle, and a stranger appeared on the top bar of the grate."

"Enough to alarm her," said the cook.

"Quite enough, and it did; but now really I—I,—"

"You what, sir?"

"I almost dread to go on."

"Oh, dear, why?"

"Because it is so—so very horrid that I am afraid it will quite overcome you all, indeed I am."

"Don't be alarmed sir," said Grummet as he again rectified his shirt collar, "we can stand a great deal. We ain't sugar nor salt to melt away at nothing at all, so go on sir, and be as horrid and as frightful as you like."

"Are you listening then," said Tony.

"Oh dear yes," said the cook, "I'm sure we are all amused and amazed, are we not, Susan."

"Dreadfully," said Susan.

"Well then," added Tony. "There sat the landlady all of a tremble, turning the matter over in her mind. Every-now and then she looked at the great black cat opposite to her, and the cat ——"

"Looked at her," said the footman.

"No," said Tony, the cat looked up the chimney, and at that moment—at that very moment mind you, and not before—but at that moment——"

"Good God, yes. Go on."

"Well I am. Draw a little closer up. Well at that moment it occured to the landlady, that although the German had in a manner promised not again to cross her threshold, there was nothing very particular to prevent his coming——"

"Where? Where? How?

"Down the chimney."

"Good gracious, yes."

As this moment, Tony quite unperceived by his audience, contrived to give the bundle of the Turks head a twist and a pull, when down came a good bushel of soot with an avalanche-like force, that sent it into everybody's lap but his own.

The confusion that now ensued, may, as the newspapers say, be much better imagined than described.

Nobody entertained the shadow of a doubt, but that the catastrophe of Tony's story was coming about there and then, and that the deceased German was actually making his his way down the kitchen chimney of that house.

Screams, oaths, exclamations, shouts for help, and every description of cry which fear could indulge itself in, filled the air, during which Tony managed to blow out the light, and then to make his way up stairs, not a little amused at the mischief he had done.

——————

CHAPTER LXIII.

LUCY FINDS THAT OUT OF EVIL SPRINGETH GOOD.

WE return to Lucy.

The situation in which she was, certainly presented no parallel in her limited experience. It was painful in the extreme.

With her notions and feelings, to be compelled to take part, or to seem to take part in anything wearing the shape of criminality, was to plunge her into a state both of grief and terror.

But yet she did not lose that self command which had hitherto favoured her under the most serious and calamitous circumstances of difficulty, and of danger, both to herself and others.

Over and over again she told herself, that after having gone through so much, she would not flinch now.

She made up her mind not to any precise course of action, but to be guided by circumstances as they should occur, for well she knew from her experience that settled plans are at the mercy of a thousand accidents, any one of which may have the effect of thoroughly deranging them.

She felt a sort of confidence in the open air which she did not feel in the thieves' house, and when the party started to make the attempt to rob the house they had pitched upon, as the source of their depredations, a hope of rescue gradually developed itself in her mind.

The woman had attired her in a loose jacket and trousers, so that she looked much less than in her own apparel, and certainly was more conveniently attired, to assist the housebreakers, if she had as much of the intention to do so, as she had the power.

The most ruffian-looking of the two men held her by the hand, and spoke to her sternly, saying—

"Hark ye, my little lass, I think you know more than you will pretend to know, so I shall just conclude that you will understand every word I am now saying to you."

He paused as though he wished, and expected a reply, but as Lucy was still silent, he went on speaking, but his tone was a little more angry than it had before sounded.

"Very well," he said, "nobody wants you to speak if you had rather not. The least said, perhaps is the soonest mended, so you can listen to me without speaking just as well as though you said yes and indeed at every other word. Do you hear?"

These last words were accompanied by a shake that apprised Lucy of the necessity of making some reply. She said timidly.

"Yes, I hear."

"Why could you not say so before, then?"

"I did not think it necessary; I was attending."

"Very well, go on attending then. We are going on a service of danger. It's every one for himself with us. You may, if you like, have the satisfaction of betraying us, but so soon as you do—look here."

He took a large clasp knife from his pocket and adroitly with his teeth opened a large sharp-looking blade.

"Look here, I'll cut your throat if all the world cried out to me not to do it, so sure as I see you waver for one instant. I'm a man of my word; but mark me, do as we require you in this instance and you shall go free in the morning, we shan't want to have anything more to do with you."

"Very well," said Lucy.

"Come on now, we understand each other."

The fellows strode on at a rapid pace, dragging poor Lucy along with them. They took the most unfrequented route they could, and their accurate knowledge of London enabled them to do that very effectually, so that Lucy knowing how populous the great city was, was rather astonished at the few solitary passengers that crossed the path.

At length they stopped opposite to a large handsome house.

"Bill," said one of the men to the other, in a low tone, which, however, did not escape the ears of Lucy, if they intended that it should. "Bill do you think Hopkins has done his part of the work."

"He was to do it."

"Oh yes, but you know he ain't to be depended on."

"Well, he told me he'd be here about this time, dressed like a first-rate swell, and pretend to be so drunk that the policeman would be sure to go off his beat to take him to the station."

"Well, perhaps he's gone."

"Hilloa, what's that?"

Some confusion at the further end of the street came upon their ears, and the men ensconced themselves in a dark doorway, drawing Lucy after them, threatening her with instant death if she gave any alarm.

The noise approached, and it was soon perceived that it arose from the remonstrances of a drunken man who who was in charge of a policeman.

"Its Hopkins," whispered one of the men to the other. "How well he does it."

"Ah, don't he?"

"He always was a swell."

"Hush!"

The person whom the policeman had in charge, or was rather assisting along, was attired in the first style of fashion, and he certainly played very well the part of a gent, if he utterly failed in that of a gentleman.

"What do you mean, fellow?" he said. "Tell me eh! where's the duke, eh?'

"Why, sir," said the policeman, I really don't know, but you had better come to the station, or you may be robbed."

"Where's the odds? Are you the marquis."

" No, sir."

" Well old fellow, do you know who I am?"

" No sir. But you see you really can't stand without assistance, and it is my duty to take care of you."

" I am the Earl—humph, I need not tell you. No, I feel I am a little tipsy, and it may get into those infernal Sunday papers. Mind, Mr. Policeman, mind, an earl."

" Oh dear no, my lord," said the policeman. " Oh dear me, your lordship may depend upon my discretion."

" My name's Hopkins."

" Oh dear, yes. Ha, ha! Excuse me, my lord, Hopkins. It shall be Hopkins if your lordship pleases. This way, my lord, if you please—this way. Pray lean on me, your lordship has only had a small drop too much."

" You are a fool."

" Yes, my lord."

The policeman and Mr. Hopkins, passed on, while the two housebreakers could hardly refrain from laughing at the truly admirable manner in which their associate and confederate managed to withdraw the policeman from his beat, while they should attempt to perpetrate the robbery, which it was their object to succeed in upon that night, by the enforced assistance of poor Lucy, who was rather bewildered at what had just happened.

" Now for it," said one of the men.

" Hush! The gas?"

" What, do you think that light down there is in our way much?"

" A little. It throws, don't you see, a kind of standindicular sort of ray bang again the fanlight."

" Well, that's soon settled. Give us a leg up."

One of them then assisted the other to climb the lamp-post, and in another minute the gas at that particular lamp was turned off.

The lamp did not seem to have given much light, but it was astonishing what a gloom spread over the street where it was out. The change was by far greater than any one might have expected.

" Now for it, Bill."

" Come on."

" Now you little brat, remember its life or death with you. The knife or,

liberty in the morning to go to your friends. Remember that."

" Yes," said Lucy. " Yes."

The party crossed the street, and plunged into the deep doorway of a house with a portico, immediately opposite to where they had been hiding themselves from the observation of the deceived policeman.

The certainty and the accuracy of the movements of the housebreakers, was now to the preceptions of Lucy, quite wonderful, she watched them closely, and with deep interest as they proceeded.

In quite an incredibly short period of time, one of them had mounted to the fanlight at the top of the street-door, and cut away almost noiselessly so much of the coloured glass and its frame as would be sufficient to leave an aperture that would admit of the passage of the small and tender form of Lucy Destern.

He then rapidly descended.

" All's right," he said.

" Up with the kinchin," said the other.

" Now little un, remember the lesson you had in bolts and bars before you came here, and don't let us have any nonsense. Have you got the rope, Bill?"

" Here you is."

Lucy could not for the life of her, imagine what was wanted with a rope, but she was soon painfully and most alarmingly enlightened upon that score.

A thin but very strongly made cord was produced by one of the thieves. At one end of it was a slip noose, and to the horror of Lucy this was put over her head, and drawn as close as it could be borne without strangulation round her neck.

" You will not murder me," she said.

" That depends upon circumstances."

" What do you mean?"

" Why, just this. You could hardly think we were such flats as to poke you through the fanlight, and trust you to let us in, while you had a thick door between you and us, with good bolts upon it.

" But—but——"

" Pshaw! We dont do business in that way. We shall give you time enough, but we hold the other end of this cord remember, and if you come any of your nonsense we shall have to cut, but before we do that we have it in our power to hang you just by a good pull up, and by fastening one end of the cord to the door handle here."

Lucy shuddered.

"Oh, you understand that."

"I see how I may be put to a cruel death."

"That will do, now go on?"

This was indeed a most unexpected piece of diabolical ingenuity on the part of the housebreaker to provide against Lucy doing what she had fully intended to do, namely, give an alarm the moment she got safely on the inside of the door, but now she felt rather confused, for Lucy could not see how to avoid obeying the behests of the thieves, except by a culpable and deliberate sacrifice of her own life.

To do that would have been for such an object the most extravagant and romantic folly, so she did not of course contemplate it for a moment, but resigning herself to the force of events which she could in no way control, she could only be waiting for some opportunity to occur of confounding the robbers without incurring the fearful risk consequent just then upon doing so.

"Push her up, can't you," said Bill.

"Well so I is," said the other.

Lucy was on the instant lifted up as though she had been no heavier than a kitten to the opening in the fan light.

"I shall fall," she said.

"Not a bit of it, climb in."

"Oh spare me."

"D——n! another word, and you shan't live to baulk us any longer, climb in I say. Remember, the rope and the knife."

"Oh that I had a knife," said Lucy.

She felt herself compelled to clamber into the house by the narrow opening made in the fan light, and certainly in doing so, and in descending to the passage on the other side she found the rope of the greatest assistance to her.

"Be quick," said one of the thieves, putting his lips down to the key-hole so that Lucy started, for it seemed to her that the voice was close to her ears.

"Yes—yes."

"Remember the rope."

"Oh, yes—yes."

"Quick! quick!"

"I am, I am. Oh Heavens! what will become of me," said Lucy, as for a moment before making any attempts to undo the street door, she clasped her hands and felt that a sensation of despair was creeping over her. She could not tell what might be the consequence of once admitting the thieves into the house, and yet not to admit them seemed now impossible.

A sudden thought seized her.

"Hush! Hush!" she said through the keyhole.

"What is it?" said one of the thieves from without.

"Some one is stirring in the house."

"Never mind, open the door."

There was no help for it. She found that there were two bolts and a chain only opposing the entrance of the robbers. To remove such obstructions let her do so ever so slowly could not occupy much time, and in about half a minute the door yielded, and the two robbers made their way into the passage of the house.

One of them immediately produced a small lanthorn with a slide in it, by which it could be darkened at pleasure.

"All's right, he whispered. All's right. It is a small cabinet in the library that we want. This way, this way."

"Mercy!" said Lucy, throwing herself upon her knees at their feet.

"The devil! what do you want now?"

"Oh, do not commit this robbery."

"A good joke, indeed. Give us the knife, Bill, I'll soon settle this little affair—I don't know my lass that you are of much use to us now, but you may be of much injury to us, and you will be so if you can, I take it."

"You will not murder me?"

"No, no—only silence you; murder is an ugly word. We never murder."

Emboldened by the desperation of the moment, Lucy made a sudden rush, and so unexpected was it, that she twitched out of Bill's hands the end of the rope, the noose of which was round her neck, and she darted through a door-way into a large room upon the ground-floor of the house.

It was only a glance by the light of the lantern the housebreakers had, that she got at this room, but it sufficed to show her it was large and handsomely furnished. Her first impulse was to try and hide herself, and she darted under a table, rapidly drawing the rope after her and concealing it, so that it should not betray her.

"There now, you have overdone it," cried one of the men.

"What do you mean?"

"Why, you threatened her, till you made her desperate."

"But she has run into the very room."

"Come on then, come on. She is half dead with fright; let us get what we come for, and then leave her where she is."

"Very well."

The two thieves made their way into the room, but they were both panic-stricken, by seeing some one asleep in a large chair.

By the light of the lantern, they saw that it was but a mere lad; and yet why he should be sleeping there, was beyond their imagination to discover. His dress and appearance, too, were not such as to warrant his being an inmate of such a house as that.

"What's to be done?" whispered one.

"Knock him over the head," said the other.

"It may be the best. Where's the girl?"

"I'll be hanged if I know, what! Quick, Bill, we must not daudle now about what we have to do. Quick, give me the hammer, and I'll soon settle this fellow, and make him sleep sound enough."

CHAPTER LXIV.

A MOST UNEXPECTED RECOGNITION.

THE sleeper in the large chair, was quite unconscious of his danger. One of the housebreakers produced a short hammer from his pocket, and was approaching the lad, who if he had been struck with it, would in all human probability have slept a long sleep indeed, when a voice cried—

"Forbear!"

There was something so strangely sepulchral and wailing, and anguish-stricken about the voice, that the robbers involuntarily started with dismay.

"Hark!" said one. "Did you speak?"

"No!" said the other.

"What was it?"

"I don't know; I thought I heard something, but I suppose it was nothing but some accidental noise, after all. Let's kill this fellow, whoever he may be, for if he should happen to wake up suddenly, and make an outcry, we are lost. Kill him, I say, kill him at once, and make no more bother about it."

"Very well!"

"Thank you," said he who was sleeping, or affecting only to sleep, upon the chair. "Thank you, gentlemen, but if it's all the same to you, I'd rather, be excused."

As he uttered these words, he stepped nimbly from his chair, and got behind it, so that it being very large, and high, he was tolerably well protected.

The two robbers were so completely taken by surprise, that they almost fell over each other.

One, however, drew a pistol from his pocket, and with a terrible imprecation fired at the lad.

"Not yet," he said, as he rose up, after dexterously avoiding the shot. "I can't accommodate you with a bullet, but this leaden inkstand may answer some purpose for you."

As he spoke, he flung a heavy leaden inkstand at the fellow's head, with a precision of aim that was sufficient to bring it, and all its contents with such a smack on his face, that it staggered him, and he was compelled, in a very inglorious sort of way, to sit down upon the floor, and try to get the ink out of his eyes.

"Help! Help! Thieves! Thieves!" cried the lad.

The door of the library, for that was the room in which this scene had taken place, was flung open quite wide, and half a dozen policemen made their appearance, headed by a sergeant of the force.

"All's up," cried Bill, as he made one desperate attempt to dash past the police, by using his head as a battering ram. He certainly did upset one of the

THE ATTEMPTED ROBBERY AT THE LORD CHANCELLOR'S PREVENTED.

force by that means, but the one was not six, and he was collared and hand-cuffed on the instant by the others.

"That's the way," said the sergeant. "All's right. Here we are. Nab the 'tother! All's right. Humph, anybody else. Oh there's another; nab him, pop on the darbies, any one else? oh, all's right!"

"What do you mean," said the lad, who had been sleeping in the chair, "My name is Tony, and I aint one of em."

Yes it was, indeed, our old friend Tony, and the very house which the housebreakers had made the attempt upon, was that of the old gentleman to whom he, Tony, had done so important a service, and who in return had pro-mised his interference in behalf of Harry Dean.

After the fright that Tony had given the servants in the kitchen, he had come up to the library again, and there sat down, and sleep overcoming him he had fairly yielded to its influence.

It was the rush of Lucy into the room, which had awakened him, although he little dreamt that it was she.

He had had the presence of mind to remain quiet, so that he had actually overheard what had passed between the burglars, and had managed, as we have seen, to start up, at the critical moment necessary to save his life, which else would most certainly have been sacrificed.

"Do any of you know him," said the sergeant of police.

One of the policemen who was looking ou for promotion, came up to Tony, and afer a pretended careful examination of his face, said, in a broad Irish accent,—

"Oh bedad, yes, its myself that know's him! Haven't I had him in custody twice already, any way."

"Indeed!"

"Wasnt he picking pockets, convanient to Regent Street last week!"

"No," said Tony, "he wasn't."

"Come, come," said the sergeant, "all's right."

"Oh yes," said one of the defeated housebreakers. "He's a pal of ours, and no mistake. He was to help us after we got into the house. There's a girl too, with us, and she's one of us, too ; you will find her somewhere, we told her to hide."

"I am here," said Lucy.

As she spoke, she emerged from beneath the table.

"I am here, but do not, oh, do not think that I have anything to do with these men, except so far as I was enforced ; I fled from them at the very first opportunity."

Her back was to Tony as she spoke, but he knew her voice, although the state of excitement she had been in, and the position close to the place she had occupied, had prevented her from recognising him.

"Lucy! Lucy!" he cried, "don't you know Tony?"

With a scream of delight, she turned round, and flung herself into his arms.

"All's right," said the police sergeant, " go it, they are all of a gang, nab the girl, does anybody know her?"

"Oh by the holy, yes," said the Irish policeman, "Didn't I have her in

charge myself, last Saturday, for stealing a shoulder of mutton."

"Oh yes, she's one of us, and has been for some time," said the burglar, who had already made the atrocious attempt to implicate Lucy from, nothing in the world but pure motives of revengeful aggravation.

"All's right," cried the sergeant, "anybody else."

"Yes," said a mild gentlemanly voice, "perhaps some one will implicate me as an associate." ·

A door had opened in the further wall of the room, and the old gentleman who was master of the house entered.

"Oh, yes—yes," cried the Irish policeman, eagerly, " I had you in custody for stealing a gammon of bacon, and —"

"There, Cassidy," said one, " I'm glad of that. Now you have done it, and the sooner all such vagabonds as you are out of the force, the better."

"Stop a bit," said the old gentleman. "Stop a bit. Come proceed, you, Cassidy, if that is your name. You say you had me in charge for stealing bacon?"

"Oh, you rascal. It aint all right," said the sergeant.

"Let him speak," said the old gentleman, mildly, " I want to know where I stole the bacon."

Mr. Cassidy began to see that he was in the wrong box, and he tried to swagger out of it with a little Irish impudence.

"Did I say bacon?"

"Yes."

"Oh, bedad, that's only a way of mine."

"Then you withdraw your charge against me of stealing bacon, and of being an associate of housebreakers in my own house too."

"Your own house. Oh, the blazes! I mistook you, you are the masther, thin perhaps you will be after standing something to dhrink. Its mighty dry work taking thieves and bad characters, yer honor."

"Oh, you fool," whispered one of Mr. Cassidy's comrades.

"Be aisy, I'll talk him over."

"Indeed!" said the old gentleman, who had overheard the few words spoken, "you wont talk me over. I am too much used, Mr. Cassidy, to be tried to be talked over, not to be tolerably well proof against it now."

"Hold your tongue!" said the sergeant to Cassidy. "I shall report you to the inspector, for saying what you have to the Lord Chancellor."

"The Lord Chancellor!" said Tony.

"The Lord Chancellor!" said Lucy.

"The devil!" said Cassidy.

"Yes; I have the honour to fill the office of chancellor," said the old gentleman; "and since Mr. Cassidy withdraws his charge against me of stealing bacon, I wish to know if he persists or not in his charges against this lad and this little girl."

"Oh, yes, yes, yer honor. Oh, bedad, yes."

"Then I must contradict him. During the course of the past day I received an anonymous letter, telling me that my house would be robbed to-night. Of course I took measures of precaution, and got you and your five men, Mr. Sergeant, to hide yourselves in a large cupboard, or closet, in the hall. From this you could neither see nor hear what passed very well, but from a station I took up, I could both see and hear all."

"Then I am saved," said Tony.

"You are without reproach, and how this policeman and how this burglar pretended to know you I can't say, since the latter tried to shoot you, and the former is so determined a liar."

"What? Is it the honour of an Irish jontleman you impeach?"

"Yes; and his honesty likewise. I shall take good care that you are not only dismissed from the police, but punished besides."

"Oh, murder!"

"Then," said the serjeant, "we are only to take the two men and the girl, your lordship?"

"And why the girl?"

"Oh, bedad," said Cassidy. "I'll swear to the girl."

"And so will I," said the chancellor, "for I saw her kneel to the two ruffians, and I heard her appeal to them to spare her from the sin of even seeming to assist them. It was only by threats of murder that they forced her to do them some service."

"And she's the very Lucy too," said Tony, "I spoke to you about."

"As I suspected."

"Then I am saved," said Lucy, as she burst into tears.

"Confound it, if I live for a hundred years," said one of the burglars, "I'll never try to rob a lawyer again."

"You will not live for one year," said the sergeant, "in this country. All's right. You'll go to what they call a penal settlement."

"Curse you all."

"Take them away," said the chancellor. "These two young persons are friends of mine, and they stay with me. Give my compliments to your inspector, Mr. Sergeant, and tell him I want to speak to him, concerning a prosecution of this man Cassidy."

"Oh have mercy upon me, your honour."

"Mercy? Contemptible villain. How dare you appeal for mercy. I have no mercy, I never will have mercy, and I hope mankind never will have mercy, upon a false witness!"

Mr. Cassidy tried to get up a blubber, but he could do nothing but sneak away, begging everybody to be considerate to him. The two burglars felt that they were thoroughly discomfitted, and it is a great satisfaction to know that they were well aware how much injury they had done themselves, by their atrocious attempt to implicate innocent persons in their offences. Well they knew that all that had taken place, would be duly reported to the judge, who should try them after their conviction, and that the consequence would be all the difference, and no inconsiderable one it is—between ordinary transportation and a voyage to a penal settlement. The police had adroitly enough put handcuffs upon both of the scoundrels, or there is very little doubt but that they would even now have tried to do something of a desperate character, not that they could have any idea of its doing them any good, but from merely a desire of vengeance. As it was, however, they felt how helpless they were, and only muttering to themselves indistinct curses, they were dragged off by the police. Truly now Lucy had found, that out of what seemed to be one of the most calamitous and evil circumstances of her life, sprang good. Was she not once again in the society of Tony, to whom she felt bound by so many ties of gratitude, and had she not the joy of hearing from his lips how well the safety of Harry Dean would be cared for. Her own evidence, too, upon the morrow, could not be otherwise than quite conclusive of the innocence of Harry Dean, and of the guilt of Swam and her villanous paramour, the doctor.

CHAPTER LXV.

THE CHANCELLOR'S PRECISE HOUSE-KEEPER.

YES, once again Lucy was happy—not happy that she was surrounded by so much luxury and refinement—not happy because she was as it were in an atmosphere of elegant repose, but because she could look into the honest face of Tony, and tell herself that there was hope for Harry Dean. And Tony, too, whose affection for Lucy was of that self sacrificing, enduring character, which only in a mind full of peace and noble impulses such as his own could take root, thought, that the end of his troubles had come, and that he might now at least safely lie down, and know that those in whose fate he felt so great an interest, were on the sunny side of fortune's highway.

"It's all right," he said, "it's all right."

"Yes, it is all right," said the chancellor, "we will have a long talk tomorrow ; but now, quite satisfied with each other, we will take some rest."

As he spoke, he rung a bell, and said to the man who answered the summons,—

"You will rouse the housekeeper, and if she is not up, tell her that a young lady, a friend of mine, has unexpectedly arrived, and she must get a bed-room ready for her directly."

"Yes, my lord," said the servant. I —I—yes—my lord."

"What is the meaning of this hesitation."

"My lord—I—that is Mrs. Armstrong the housekeeper, my lord, is rather hasty tempered."

"Very well."

"And so, my lord, perhaps she won't like being disturbed, you see, my lord, at this hour."

"Indeed ?"

"Yes, my lord, she is a very particular woman, indeed, is Mrs. Armstrong.'

"Nevertheless, John, go and wake her up, and deliver my message," said the chancellor, mildly, "tell her I am waiting here in the library for her, as I wish to speak to her myself."

"Yes, my lord,"

The man who had such an abundant fear of Mrs. Armstrong, the chancellor's housekeeper, could make no further resistance now, although he knew the temper of the lady he had to do with so much better than his master did, that he trembled at the prospect of what shape the ebullition of wrath in Mr. Armstrong might take.

"And it is'nt," snivelled John to himself, as he walked up stairs, " as though it was a real young lady as had arrived, only a little girl as comed in quite promiscous. Won't there be a row."

"I see, sir," said Lucy, "that I am disturbing your household, if the housekeeper be unwilling to be roused, I can sleep upon one of these large chairs."

"Hush," said the chancellor, "hush ; this Mrs. Armstrong who occupies a confidential situation here as my housekeeper, was quite destitute when she came here, so that she cannot be so forgetful of what is due to both herself and to me. She is a very religious person, too."

"Ahem," said Tony.

"What do you mean to express by ahem, my young friend."

"Only this," said Tony, "that your very religious people take so much trouble, and snivel, and cringe so much about the next world, that they don't like anybody in this, and go off always like a bottle of ginger beer if they are put out of the way in the least ; did you ever, sir, know a religious person with any temper ?"

"Well—I—really—oh, here she is."

The door opened, and a woman with a severe cast of countenance made her appearance, in an immense morning wrapper, while her head was surmounted by some complicated arrangement, that was half cap and half turban. It was quite evident, as the newspapers say, to the meanest capacity, that Mrs. Armstrong was in anything but a smiling mood. The curtsey she made to the chancellor was low, savagely low. Then she looked right over Lucy's head at the wall beyond her, and with a slightly vibratory movement of the whole person, awaited what was to ensue.

"Now or never," thought Mrs. Armstrong. "The chancellor is of a mild, quiet nature and knows no more of housekeeping then of kite-flying. Now is my time to assume over him the same amount of authority that I have already got over the household."

"Mrs. Armstrong," said the chancellor, here is a young friend of mine, for whom I wish a bed provided immediately."

"A young friend?"

"Yes, Mrs. Armstrong, I said a young friend."

"And may I ask how long you have known this—young—friend, my lord?"

"To-morrow, Mrs. Armstrong, to-morrow there can be no objection to your knowing what has happened to night, but at present, all I wish of you is, to see to the immediate comfort and repose of this young lady."

"Now for it," thought Mrs. Armstrong, who considered herself so useful to the chancellor, that he would not have the courage to fight up against her. "Now for it, I shall make myself more thoroughly than ever, mistress of the house. I am quite glad of this opportunity."

"My lord," she said, "there is no spare bed in the house ready for any one, and as for this person, she can easily get a lodging somewhere in the neighbourhood. It's my duty to keep this house respectable, and to attend to it; I cannot provide beds in the middle of the night for anybody. I have made myself a perfect slave to this house and to your comforts for two years, and I have only to say that I really cannot suffer such things to go on as this; if the young person is respectable, and all that sort of thing, a lodging can be got for her by the footman somewhere, but I am not going to make my beds common to anybody. With my religious feelings, which are the only comfort I have, I could not do it, and I must say it was very inconsiderate of you, my lord, to have me awakened in the middle of the night on any account."

"Will you reconsider," said the Chancellor.

"No my lord, my mind is made up. I have the care of this establishment, and I now mean to take care of it."

"You refuse then to obey my orders?"

"Oh dear, no. Only order what is reasonable, and of course if convenient at all, it shall be done, my lord; nobody can say I neglected your comforts, I have been a slave to this house, and to you."

"And you want me to return the compliment? said the chancelor.

"My lord?"

"I say you want me to return the compliment, by being a slave to you now. Mrs. Armstrong, I have noticed of late that what you have to do here is too much for your strength of mind, and distracts you too much from your religious duty; I know you are a woman of singular and most unpredecented sincerity."

"I always say what I think, my lord."

"Very well, it is quite clear then that we must part, Mrs. Armstrong. You will leave my service instantly,"

If a bomb shell had fallen into Mrs. Armstrong's lap, while she was taking her tea quietly some afternoon, with the little drop of something rather stronger than tea in it, Mrs. Armstrong could not have been more astonished than she was at this most appalling announcement.

"Leave your service my lord, I—I—didn't mean—"

"That;" said the chancellor. "I have no doubt you did not, but I do. John! John!"

"Yes my lord!" cried John, making his appearance with a quickness that proved he was not very far off when the little scene was going on with the housekeeper.

"I suppose, John, there are some female servants in the house?"

"Certainly, my lord. There's poor Mary, the under housemaid, who was to go this morning for giving her poor old mother the tea leaves, and refusing Mrs. Armstrong her regulars my lord and then there's.——"

"Stop, stop—what regulars?"

"You villain!" cried Mrs. Armstrong, forgetting at the moment that she was out of office. "You villain, I give you warning from this moment, and you will get no character."

"Stop a bit," said the chancellor, "I

want to know what Mrs. Armstrong's regulars are?"

"A pound a quarter from every servant's wages in the house," said John; "and if they grumble at it they get notice directly."

"John," said the chancellor. "Go and send Mary here. Mrs. Armstrong, I command you to leave my house this instant."

"I wont go."

"John, fetch a policeman."

"Yes my lord," roared John, and he cut such an extravagant caper of delight that if a look could have annihilated his soul and body, Mrs. Armstrong would have given John but a poor chance in this world or the next. "Yes my lord. Yes; won't I?"

Mrs. Armstrong sat down in a great arm chair, and burst into tears. They were partly drops of vexation, and partly hypocrisy.

"And this is my reward," she said. "Oh dear, and this is my reward."

"Reward!" said the chancellor. "What an unreasonable woman you are; two years ago you were destitute—I made you my housekeeper, and you live in luxury, robbing my servants, and making yourself detestable to all around you, and then you want a reward."

The door opened, and John fairly pushed into the room a neatly dressed servant girl, who was trembling violently.

"Mary, my lord," said John.

"Oh, very well," said the chancellor. "Mary, this young lady wants rest, and refreshment, and kindness."

The smile with which Mary at once, without questions of who or what she was, held out her hand to little Lucy, had all the magic of honest-hearted good nature in it; Lucy flew to her in a moment.

"I'm afraid, however, Mary," added the chancellor, "that this young lady will give you trouble, and that you have been very much put out of your way by being awakened thus in the middle of the night."

"Oh no, my lord, not at all; bless her heart, somebody must get up to attend to her, I can be kind to her while I am here, my lord."

"While you are here, what do you mean by that Mary."

"I am going in the morning, my lord, for I have, I suppose, offended Mrs. Armstrong."

"Well, but you can take care of this young creature, and attend during the remainder of the night to anything required of you, for all that."

"Oh yes, my lord."

"And you can go when you are no longer wanted. Bye the bye where is your home?"

"I have no home, my lord. I—I—am nearly destitute, but if your lordship will ask Mrs. Armstrong to give me a character, I would try to do the best I could."

"And so, my poor girl, notwithstanding you are going tomorrow from here, and are without a home, and doubtful even of a character, through no fault of your own, you are willing to do your duty to-night, even to the loss of your rest."

"I—I ought my lord."

"Oh you vile hussey," cried Mrs. Armstrong. "Oh you brazen-faced wretch, to speak in that way before my face."

"Gently, gently, Mrs. Armstrong," said the chancellor, "because you are pious, is poor Mary not even to be good. I believe Mrs. Armstrong that when you were installed in your position as housekeeper here, I gave you certain keys; you will now hand them to this young girl, Mary, if you please."

"What! hand her the keys! Her! her! Perhaps you had better make her your housekeeper."

"Exactly, I mean to do so. Mary will you accept the situation?"

"I ought not, my lord."

"Indeed—why?"

"Because I am afraid I am not capable; I might not please you by the way in which I should do my duty."

"But you would try to do so, and how much better will it be to put up with your cheerful and happy incompetency, even if you are incompetent, than with the gloomy and most piously uncomfortable talents of that robber."

"Robber! cried Mrs. Armstrong. "You call me a robber. Curse you all, I won't stay another moment in the house—Yes I will though, just to vex you, I won't budge an inch, I won't. I'll stay as long as I like, you are out of your senses my lord, and don't know when you are well off."

"B. 222," cried John, and the policeman, whose symbolical existence was so typified, made his appearance at the threshold of the room.

"Turn that woman out of my house," said the chancellor, pointing to Mrs. Armstrong, "and you, John, get her boxes, and whatever belongs to her, ready, and toss them into the street."

"Now mum," said B 222. "Now mum, if you please."

"Take that," said Mrs. Armstrong, inflicting five scratches down the nose of B 222.

"All's right, all in the way of trade, mum," said B 222, as he unstrapped from his cuff the mysterious looking little bit of striped bandage he wore on duty. "All's right mum. Here you is."

With considerable dexterity, B caught the hands of Mrs. Armstrong, and in the course of a minute had them fairly secured behind her back, with the aforesaid strap.

"Now mum, are you a coming?"

"No, you vile wretch. Murder! murder. Help! murder, murder! I'll soon raise the whole neighbourhood. Murder! murder! murder! I won't be taken quietly by a hundred lobsters. Fire! fire!"

"Oh," said B 222. "That's the caper is it. Now mum, if you please."

That B 222 was an enterprising man, and knew what he was about. Getting behind Mrs. Armstrong, with his back towards her, he very dexterously hoisted her up, like some sack of rubbish, and crying, Open the door, he walked off with her as comfortably as possible. Mrs. Armstrong was really now as much alarmed as she was helpless.

"Oh good gracious," she cried. "Is this the way a religious woman's to be taken through the street, murder! oh, murder, let me down, Mr. Peel—Mr. Blue dev—— I mean Mr. Policeman. I'll walk, I'll walk. What you won't. Then curse everybody, curse——

The maledictions of the tall housekeeper died away in the distance, until silenced in the station-house, where B 222 took her upon the charge of scratch-

ing his official nose, an offence which was far more serious than refusing when ordered to leave the chancellor's house.

"Now," said the chancellor, "this is a night of congratulations truly. I have found a friend," turning to Lucy, "and I have got rid of an enemy, for surely if ever a man can have an enemy in his house, it must be a woman such as this Mrs. Armstrong."

"I never was more pleased in my life," said Lucy, "it's quite as good as a play, that it is."

"Well," added the chancellor, "it is high time we should all endeavour to take some rest, for I have business to transact to-morrow, and so have you all. Remember you must both be at the police-office at on early hour in the morning, when all will be done that can be done for your mysterious friend, Mr. Dean,"

"I can save him," said Lucy, "and will. Oh, sir, you do not know the important evidence that I can give upon the charge that is so falsely brought against that most innocent and truly noble person."

"Evidence? Have you any evidence to give upon the matter in question? What is it?"

"Listen to me," said Lucy, in considerable excitement, and then she related to the chancellor, at length, all that is already known to the reader, regarding the murder by Swam of Madam Zadzed, to which the chancellor listened with the most marked and fixed attention, it was possible to give to anything in the world. When she had fully concluded by bringing her simple, pathetic, and unadorned narrative down to the precise moment when he first looked upon her in his house, the chancellor said with much emotion,

"This is indeed one of the most singular of affairs, but, thank Heaven it is so far elucidated as it is, and now justice will be done to the innocent, if not to the guilty, and even they I hope will not totally escape the law. But now to rest. Leave all these matters entirely with me."

———

CHAPTER LXVI.

A PEEP AT THE VILLA OF LORD BAT-
TANEY AT FULHAM.

THE great disadvantage that the novelist labours under, consists in the fact that while he is relating to his readers, and rendering clear, one combination of circumstances connected with the personage whose career forms the staple of his history, certain other combinations of events get the start of his pen, and he is perforce, in a manner of speaking, compelled to take his readers by the hand and make a retrospective march. Our readers have not forgotten that there is such a person as Lord Battaney, and such a place as his villa at Fulham, close to the banks of the river Thames. Lord Battaney was not dead when last we looked upon his miserable drooping form. The destroyer was hovering around him, and making strange familiarity with the man whose hours—nay whose minutes we may say, might now be easily counted, but not actually had the breath of life sighed itself away from the lips of that bold bad man, who had seemed to think the whole world was little more than a place created for him to display his passions in. But there is one penalty which the iniquitous will always pay for their misdeeds. There is one circumstance which will always happen, to tell them of that which they have done that is ungracious in the sight of earth and of heaven; sooner or later the wicked will be deserted. We do not mean to say that it shall always happen that the hirelings, who for gold have been gathered about the state of some one far less respectable than they themselves, desert the piece of gilt corruption they have tended and flattered, but a far more bitter and felt desertion takes place. All who from affection, respect, or old association, would under ordinary circumstances have remained, drop off one by one, and such even as Lord Battaney find themselves alone in the truest sense of the word, for they can name no one near or distant who loves them, or who can feel any higher aspiration than pity for them, let their fate be what it may. But Lord Battaney's special case was worse, far worse than the common run of such cases. All those who from family ties would have loved and respected him, had long since cast him from them as a blight and a destroyer; a disgrace to them, to virtue, and to every feeling of excellence and shame. Not only was he deserted by all those, but as it turned out, the hirelings who had crowded around him not for love, but for plunder, were to the last true to their motives, for they left him for plunder, and as the reader will recollect, he was alone in his splendid and luxurious abode. He was worse than alone! Harry Dean had thought him dead, but life still lingered about him. Happy would it indeed have been for him, had the destroyer already claimed him. The ordeal, however, that he had yet to go through was far more horrible than any ordinary death could be with all its bitterness. How long he lay in a kind of death-like trance he could not say, but at length he did awaken, and in a few minutes the faculties of his mind returned with amazing perspicuity. He felt that it was quite impossible to move, the injuries he had received were by far to serious for that. A kind of paralysis had laid hold of him, and there he lay, with, if we may be allowed the expression, nothing but his head alive. Yes there he lay with such a vivid perception of the past and the present, as was quite painful to him in its distinctness. The dreadful silence of the house, however, in a few minutes began to weigh upon his spirits, and to awaken all his attention to an effort at hearing some sound which should convey to him an idea that he was in the proximity of human beings. No such sound came upon his longing senses. All was stillness and desolation. The silence of the very grave seemed to be in and about that most luxurious house. Where are they all," he thought, "I recollect they robbed me, I recollect they threatened me, but they cannot be all quite gone; what strange odour is this—what singular floating blue looking clouds are these that come about the room. Hush! what is that? Hush! hush!" A low strange crackling noise came upon his ears. He could not for the life of him divine what it was, and yet he listened to it with a species of fascination, and he felt a conviction that it was something terrible, as well as something closely

connected with him and his future prospects. Not long, however, was this state of doubt and incertitude to last with that unhappy man. The cracking noise increased; the strange vapoury state of the atmosphere in his room became more and more decided—the odour that he had remarked was more forcibly presented to his senses, and after a few moments more, during which he tried in vain to doubt the accumulated evidence of all his senses, he with a voice of the most despairing anguish suddenly cried —"It is fire!"

How little, under ordinary circumstances, would that conviction have affected him, what a small amount of anxiety would it have given him. to behold that his villa, with all its associations, and all its appointments was in flames, provided he had had the use of those physical energies, which while they were his he had always made so bad, and so wanton an use of. But now, what a world of horrors did not that one short word "fire !" suggest to his terror-stricken soul, as he lay there a living head, but a body upon which the fell blight of a gloomy and horrible paralysis had fallen. It is fire ! Oh, horror, horror, unutterable ! Where was now the haughty aristocrat—the man who had made a plaything of human feelings—the man who had laughed at human woe, and made a jest of tears—where was he now —half dead, yet singularly vital in so far as he was enabled to know his condition. Full of life to comprehend his frightful state—full of death after he had made the smallest effort to release himself from its terrors, present and prospective. It is fire ! A shriek burst from the lips of Lord Battaney. Pain he would have braved—mangled and broken limbs he might, with a horrible and groaning perseverance, have dragged from the room, but that was not what he had to contend against. He did not lie so still because it was an exquisite agony to move, but because it was impossible to move. For one bewildering moment he thought he was going mad. It was only for one moment.—So much happiness as the oblivion of sense was denied to him. It was necessary to the mortal retribution that came upon that man, that insanity should not shroud him in its dreamy embrace, nor still the exquisite sensibility of those nerves which remained still intact to suffer. No, no, he did not go mad.

"Help, help, help !" he cried.

How fearfully—how yellingly did that cry resound through the villa. How strangely was it sent back to him with a dull dreamy echo. There was no hope.

"Fire ! fire !" he screamed—" Oh for one drop of water to cast upon my burning throat ! Help ! help ! Tis I—Lord Battaney who calls, I can enrich the hand that snatches me from this horrible fate. Fire ! fire ! Help ! help ! Mercy ! —Fire ! Help ! help !"

His voice grew hoarse. He dashed his head from side to side, and yelled, and shrieked like any madman, but yet he was not mad. He made superhuman efforts to rise, but there he lay inert as a log, nothing of him full of life and energy but that head and that shrieking, yelling, blaspheming voice, for now he began to arraign Heavens justice ; he who had

never used the name of Heaven but to point some sarcasm, or add a sting to some hideous scoff at all that was great and holy. Yes he called upon Heaven at first with shrieks of entreaty, and then when no miracle was done in his behalf, he commenced a course of the worst imprecations that could come from the lips of mortal man. But all this while the blue mist increased about him—the cracking noise was so loud, accompanied by so strange a hissing, that it seemed to him as though the house was full of fiends, who were thus heralding his soul to the infernal regions. An intense heat began to make itself felt too in the thick and heavily laden atmosphere. Suddenly now there was a sharp rattling noise and casting his blood-shot and glaring eyes in the direction whence it came, Lord Battaney saw the flames coming up through the floor of the room. Long dancing tongues of many coloured flames, hissing, roaring, dashing up thousands of red hot sparks, which now began to fall upon him and his bed, in abundance. Now the heat became insupportable. He began to feel a frightful difficulty in breathing, and his eyes ached from the contact with the smoke so greatly, that he was compelled to close them in despair. Piercing shrieks came from his lips. The red hot sparks had set the curtains of the bed in a blaze, although the actual flames from the burning house had not reached him. For the space of about two inches, he lived in an atmosphere of flames, and then as the curtains were all consumed the ashes fell about him, and he lay blistered and scorched, a horrible spectacle. This was a state of things that could not last. The floor was rapidly giving way. One corner of the bedstead was giving way—Lower, lower, still it went, until it was quite clear that if the flames made much further progress in the floor beneath, all must fall together, in one frightful crash. Lord Battaney felt that his fate was close at hand. He knew now that nothing could save him, and the most frightful visions began to chase each other past his disordered brain.

" Away spectres !" he cried, "away— Oh horrible, though I know you not, why do you haunt me ! Off, off, I say. No—no, no nearer. Why do you press upon me with those glaring eyes, untouched by even the spirit of fire: Off, off! Oh, God! no, no, no spectral embraces—They come—hideous throng. Can you laugh? Ha, ha, ha! Avaunt! I, too, can laugh. What chasm is that? Give it no name — a mockery — a mockery! There's no such thing, I say there's no such thing. Help! help! Murder—fire!"

With a roar like the discharge of several pieces of heavy ordnance, the staircase fell. The floor vibrated for a moment, and the flames ambled like living things round the richly carved wood-work of the bedstead. The bed-clothing began here and there to show small flickering blue lights. Lord Battaney was wrought up to the highest pitch of mortal agony. His voice had changed completely. It was like nothing human, and no comparison could be found to it in any sound ever before heard upon the earth, the sea, or in the heavens.

"I burn—I burn! Water, water, water. May the bitterest curse of—

Down went floor, bedstead, and Lord Battany, into the roasting flames beneath. In a few moments the flames were smothered by the descending mass, and then out they burst again with tenfold fury, roaring and leaping up to the roof of the doomed villa.

"Yes," said one of the servants of Lord Battaney, to the crowd that began to collect about the house, near which he had lingered. "Yes there's a fire certainly, but nobody is in the villa. Work away at the engines. There's no life to save."

CHAPTER LXVII.

BOW STREET.

It will be recollected that the beautiful and accomplished Miss Swam, whose beauty and accomplishments were at all events fully on a par with her innocence, considered herself peculiarly a favourite of fortune in the steps that she took for the purpose of effecting her departure to the new world with her admirer, the doctor. No doubt our readers will remember that at the obscure tavern where they repaired for the purpose of getting some refreshment, they met with a gentleman who promised to be exceedingly useful to them, inasmuch as various prudential reasons induced him, likewise, to fancy that the air of the United States of America would agree better with his moral constitution, than that of England. A good understanding then had been come to between these high contracting parties, to the effect that they were to meet in the morning and proceed upon the first stage of their journey. There can be no doubt in the world but that both the doctor and Swam had a similar idea at this juncture, which was that it would be most desirable to go alone. That is to say, the doctor would have had no objection to feel sure that Swam was at the bottom of the Thames, while Swam devoutly wished the doctor at Jericho, or anywhere indeed, that was sufficiently distant and inaccessible, so that she got rid of him. It is to those who have taken the trouble to look into such matters, a well understood and settled fact in the moral obliquity of criminals, that to none have they so bitter and abounding an aversion as to their accomplices. A compact of dishonesty or villany of any description which commences with such an exceeding amount of confidence, and the greatest seeming trustfulness, is certain to end in mutual detestation, if not in mutual treachery; and as regards the two persons under consideration, they would without the least regret have seen each other hanged. The difficulty, however, was to get rid of each other, and although both resolved it in their minds, they could neither of them come to any satisfactory conclusion, and so the time wore on, until the hour for meeting the gentleman who was to accompany them in their flight, was close at hand, and there was no time to do anything but to go with him. He was punctual, and in a whisper to Swam, he said,

"I have got a hackney coach which will take us a part of the way, and then we will have a post chaise for the remainder. I have calculated everything, and am certain we shall get to Liverpool without any trouble."

"Do you really think so?"

"I am sure of it. You see how cool and calm I am."

He was indeed cool and calm, and in these respects he certainly presented a great contrast to both Swam and the doctor, for they really shook in every limb; it seemed as if the last few hours had completely destroyed their nervous system, and rendered them incapable of fighting up against the terrors of their imaginations. It was in vain that feeling how desperately impolitic the betrayal of such a state of mind was, they made the most desperate attempts to shake it off, but the nerves and the circulation will not listen to reason, so that both Swam and the doctor looked pale and shaken, as their friend preceded them to the coach.

"Come, come," he said, "be more active and alive. I have, I dare say, quite as much reason as you to feel unhappy, and out of spirits, and yet look at me how well I keep up,

"Oh yes," said the doctor, "you do indeed. The fact is we leave some very dear friends behind us, who will grieve very much for our departure, and then you know to a sympathetic mind, the very idea of going to America must be something not very agreeable, so that we—we feel—that's just you see what we feel."

"Yes," said Swam.

"My own view of the case exactly," said their new friend. "The white cliffs of Albion, as the song says, and all that sort of thing, is quite sticking in a manner of speaking, in my throat at this very moment, but there is no occasion you know to say anything of this sort before the coachman. Let us be cheerful."

"Oh certainly. Ha! ha!" said the doctor. We cannot say laughed the doctor; the hideous sound he made was as great a libel upon laughter, as Mr. Turner's pictures are upon art.

"Don't do that again my friend, or you will really frighten everybody."

"It's given me a chill," said Swam, "already. One would really think that —that—you—had something on your mind."

"Oh, that is too ridiculous,'" said the doctor.

The coach had started, but Swam whose eyes were here, there, and everywhere, saw a strange man mount upon the box, along with the driver, and she was a little alarmed as she said,—

"Who is that. There's a man upon the box who has no business there.''

"Oh don't be too sure of that," said the new friend. "I dare say he is only a buck."

"Only a what?"

"Bless your ignorance, don't you know really what a buck is? I dare say you do, sir?"

"Not I," said the doctor. "He don't look much of a buck, if it means a dandy, as once it did, I think."

"No. It certainly don't mean a dandy. You must know that there are many men, who have hackney-carriages of their own, but who from some misconduct, have no licenses to drive, so that they would be liable to to a fine if they were to ply in the regular way, and take passengers, but then again there are men who have licences, but no carriage, and these lounge about the stands, until some man without a licence gets a customer, upon which, the licensed man mounts the box with him, and is paid a something out of the fare, for taking the responsibility upon himself, and he is then called a buck, you understand."

"Yes," said the doctor, "I understand that, but another buck has got up behind."

"Indeed."

"Yes, a great fellow as big as the coach almost, has scrambled up behind, and quite sways the vehicle down upon its springs. It's a very odd thing; I wonder the coachman don't take notice of it."

"You don't say so."

"Yes I do though. Only look out for yourself."

"Oh well, after all it don't matter to us you know, who get's up behind or before. All we care about is to reach our destination, and if we do that safely our desires are quite accomplished."

"Yes, but——"

"Come, come, what are you making yourself uneasy about? Are we not going on at a very good pace, considering all things, and is not the morning quite brilliant, I'm sure we ought to be as happy as butterflies."

"Where are we," gasped Swam. "Where are we?"

"It—It looks amazingly like Covent Garden Market," said the doctor, as he glared from the window of the coach, which commanded a view of that emporium o' fruits and flowers — smashed oranges and insolence.

"I rather think," said the obliging man, who had taken so much trouble for them, and who knew everything. "I rather think that it is Covent Garden Market ; I dare say it is some near cut, now."

"Stop," said the doctor, suddenly tapping his forehead. "A lucky thought."

"What ?" said Swam.

"There's Watkin's in York-street, close at hand here, who will take in all letters that come for us when we are gone. Stop the coach, I shan't be two minutes running to his house and telling him. I shall be back in a jiffy."

Swam licked her lips again and again, as though there was something very nice upon them, which she would not lose on any account whatever, come what may.

"Hilloa," said the doctor, "stop ! stop !"

"Why really my good friend," said the stranger, with the most obliging air in the world, "really you need not, I am sure give yourself the trouble to call upon Watkins."

"Why not ?"

"Because a note from Liverpool, when we get there, will answer the purpose just as well, and if you go, you will most likely be detained, for you know it will look very odd to rush into your friend's house, just to say, Watkins, take in letters for me, and then rush out again."

"Oh, not at all, I am so very intimate with Watkins that he will think nothing of it. We both know Watkins."

"Yes," said Swam, "but anything in the shape of hurry or unaccountable behaviour always is less thought of in a woman than in a man. I'll go and say a few words to Watkins, while you wait here ; I shall be five minutes I dare say but not longer you may depend."

"No—no," cried the doctor, "allow me."

"No," said Swam, "I—"

"Really now," said the new friend, you had better both of you leave Watkins alone. "Come, come, make yourselves easy, we are past York-street now, and you know how very unlucky it is in any enterprise to turn back, I wonder how you could think of such a thing.

Here we are in Russel-street, don't you see."

The doctor turned ghastly pale. He took a little pill-box from his pocket, and opening it, he produced a nice looking small rose-coloured lozenge, and handed it to the obliging personage saying,—

"You are right. Will you take a rose lozenge."

"Thank you."

Swam gave a deep groan as the obliging personage put the lozenge into his mouth, and said in a moment,—

"It has slipped down my throat it was so small."

"Which—is—all—the—better," said the doctor, "as he flung himself back in the coach ; I have at all events had my r evenge."

The coach dashed round a corner and Swam with a shriek cried,—

"Why this is Bow-street."

"I know it," said the d ctor.

"You are my prisoners," said the obliging personage, producing one of those ugly looking squat pistols, which the police prefer to all others, heaven only knows why. "You are my prisoners. Make any attempt to escape, and I shall blow your brains out."

"I am not going," said the doctor, "to make any attempt to escape.'

"Lost, lost," said Swam.

"Found, you mean ma'am," said the officer, as the coach drew up at the door of the police-office. "You might have been lost if it had not been for me, but you are found now."

It was a sorry joke, but the officer chuckled at it amazingly.

"Revenge," muttered the doctor, "revenge! I have had my revenge, yes I have had my revenge."

"What do you mean by that," said the officer.

The doctor smiled merely. He thought that all was safe as regarded the officer. The lozenge that he had given him contained an active poison. Swam was so completely subdued and horrified by her arrest that she could neither move nor speak. In vain she tried to collect her scattered thoughts and to ask herself if effrontery might not yet stand her in some stead, but she was perfectly bewildered, and when the officer handed her from the coach, she, to use a popular expression, did not know whether she was on her head or her heels.   But soon she began to see light amid the gloom.

"I know what I will do," she said. "Upon the first flush of] any danger I will turn evidence against the doctor, and I will not only tell all that he has done, but will add to it plenty that he has not ; I will represent how I was led away by him to connive at the commission of crime, his looks wil hang him, for after all what an ugly wretch it is."

After coming to this determinatiod, Swam put quite a bold countenance upon the affair and turning to the officers, she said, in an impressive voice, "And pray of what am I accused?"

"Why, at all events your evidence is wanted about the murder," was the reply.

What a long breath the doctor drew. After all this, it might only be that they were wanted as evidence, and the officers in the natural anxiety to make up a case, had played such a trick to get him and Swam to the police-office again. In that case if they could by any amount of perjury, fix the murder upon Harry Dean, they might yet escape. It was a hope. Oh, what would not the doctor have given, for a quarter of an hour's private confabulation with Swam, so that they might agree to be both in a story. He looked at her, as he said—"Oh, yes, we are both evidence against the young man charged with the murder. We caught him, and we heard him say, ' Well, the old wretch was not so well worth killing as I thought.' That was what he said, I think Miss Swam, and what we can both swear to."

"Yes," said Swam.

"Clever," said one of the officers, putting his tongue in his cheek, and winking at a companion. "Clever, aint it?"

"Oh, very—very," said the other.

Then they both laughed. "What are they laughing at?" asked the doctor of himself. "It was a very disagreeable sort of laugh that; I wonder now if it would be good policy at once to give up Swam, and tell all I know of the affair. It might save my neck, although it would of course transport me. I must think, I must think."

Swam shook, too, a little when the officer laughed. "I must be guided by circumstances," she thought, "but the

moment I see things going queer, I peach upon the doctor."

"This way, this way," said the officer, "the magistrates have taken their seats. Clear the way, there—clear the way for the night charges."

———

CHAPTER LXVIII.

KING'S EVIDENCE.

IT is necessary at this juncture that we take a very brief review of the situation of those personages in whom we are interested, inasmuch as a great crisis is certainly about to take place in the position of each and all of them.   It will be remembered, then, that Kate Destern, after being, in a manner which those who are fond of superstition would not hesitate to call miraculous, preserved from death, had found a refuge with the benevolent physician, who with his young assistants, were quite as willing that she should be ornamental in life as useful in death, which latter had been their first idea concerning her. The shock which the constitution of Kate Destern had received, was undoubtedly a most severe one, and the subsequent circumstances had almost been sufficient to quench the flame of her pure existence completely.   And yet it is astonishing what youth will battle through, and how that sometimes frail and little possession, life, will stand out against a thousand adverse circumstances, preserving its hold in some apparently fragile form, while the seeming strong, who, to look at them, one would say, might almost bid defiance to the King of Terrors, will, at a touch, drop into the grave, and "lie in cold obstruction." From first to last no actual disease had laid hold of Kate.   Fatigue and mental anxiety had only deranged the machine of life, and then the sudden shock she had experienced when she read of the apprehension of Harry Dean, had completed the derangement, and thrown her into that cataleptic state, which, to the young practitioner, who had been suddenly called to her aid, had seemed not only like death but actually to be death itself.   But although bodily indisposition will for a time quench the aspirations of the mind, the latter will soon resume their away, when the mechanism of vitality again rights itself. Hence was it that as she became each hour more convalescent. the deep anxiety of Kate Destern concerning the fate of Harry Dean became more painful and all absorbing. The physician had, however, promised to bring her tidings concerning him, and to betray the impatience that she felt she thought would be almost to insult those kind friends who were doing so much for her. We leave her, then, waiting with no small amount of anxiety, the news which the physician had promised to bring her, and at the same time making the best return she could for the kindness heaped upon her by the wife of the medical man. Little Lucy, that fair young specimen of the truthfulness of youth, that courageous and beautiful creature, who, though in the very spring-tide of her existence, had seen more of life, and gone through more of its most trying scenes than many hundreds of thousands who fancy they have led quite a wonderful career, was as the reader will remember, comfortably enough housed at the Lord Chancellor's. The new young housekeeper of that illustrious person, for he was illustrious, despite his rank, made Lucy as happy and comfortable as a princess. This chancellor of whom we speak, only held the great seal for about four months, during one of those political storms which had for a brief period set to the route the cold, crafty holders of office, but who soon resumed their sway. We make this statement, lest our readers might unwittingly think we were attributing anything in the shape of virtue or goodness to any of those well-known political Jesuits, who, from time to time have in the name of party filled the judicial chair in the court of chancery. Our friend Tony, too, he was there sleeping for the remainder of that night which had been so singularly disturbed, that calm sleep which King Henry alluded to when contrasting his own; kingly anxieties with the security of obscure serenity ;

—————"Happy low lie down,
Uneasy lies the head that wears a crown."

It was their own consciousness of integrity, and confidence in the innocence of Harry Dean, and in that innocence being made apparent, that gave them so much serenity. And now let us turn to Harry Dean himself. The chivalrous spirit which we know had so strong a hold of his heart, affected his conduct very much during his examination before the magistrate. That circumstance which would have ended very differently, if the magistrate had exercised the commonest discernment, or fair play in the matter. But when Harry Dean saw the sort of personage before whom he was brought, and the kind of conduct to which he was to be subjected, he said to himself,

"What now if I were really poor and friendless? What would be the result of all this? Why simply that this man, who is a disgrace to the office he fills, would make me a victim to his bad nature, and I should have no redress whatever ; for when, unless it shall happen to answer some political purpose, when is the cry of the oppressed poor ever listened to in London?"

It was this feeling and this consideration, then, that induced Harry Dean to keep back on that day the proofs of his innocence of the crime with which he was charged, much to the surprise of Sam Clover. He was determined that as the magistrate had began to be unjust, that he should have an opportunity of committing himself to such an extent, that his dismissal from the bench must be the inevitable consequence. Sam Clover did venture to remonstrate a little with his master when they were temporarily locked up together in a kind of cellar in the rear of the court.

"If you please, sir," said Sam "don't you think it might have been made all right?"

"As how, Sam?"

"Why, that stupid magistrate might have been forced to let you go, sir."

"Oh, very likely, but I don't want to go, Sam."

Sam whistled a tune.

"You must know, as well as I, that we have nothing to do with this affair, at least as principals, and that I have the means of proving so much."

"Yes, sir."

"But that magistrate is such a fool that for all practical purposes, you see, Sam, he might as well be a rogue."

"Perhaps he is, sir."

" Well, Sam, it is more charitable if you can, to consider a person a fool than a rogue. But yet, if it be only ill-temper and folly that leads him, he is quite unfit for his office."

" No doubt of that, sir.'

" Then you see, Sam, he must be removed from his office, or this same behaviour may be practised on some one not so able to resist it as I am, but in order that there should be an unanswerable case for his removal, you see, Sam' in order that all should approve of his dismissal——."

" Ah, Sir," interrupted Sam, " I understand. You must give him rope enough."

" Exactly, Sam, as you say he must have rope enough. That is precisely the light in which I view the matter. I am quite willing to put up with a little inconvenience, for the purpose of accomplishing such an object."

" So am I, sir."

" I knew you would, Sam."

After this little conversation, Harry Dean, handed a sovereign to a kind of messenger who made his appearance upon Harry calling for some one, and said,—" Bring here the young girl you saw me with in the office."

" Well sir, I——"

" You what ?"

" I don't know if I ought to let you see anybody."

" Then I do. Prisoners who are not committed, may see any one. That is a rule. You ought to know it, surely."

The messenger looked astonished to find that the accused had such an accurate knowledge of the forms of the court, but he did not hesitate any longer.

" I'll bring her," he said, and away he went.

" I wish her to go to an hotel," said Harry Dean, " where they know me well, and will pay her every attention, until the morning, when she will be wanted here again."

Harry Dean had not the least idea of what had occurred to poor Lucy, during the long period that she was out of his sight, and he fully expected her to be brought to him. What was his consternation when the messenger came back, and said,—

" The girl has left, and no one knows where she is."

" This was a blow, in deed, and his dead was naturally enough, that she had fallen into the hands of Swam, and the doctor ; but when he came to consider that he had said sufficient to one of the principal officers of the court, to have those two personages kept in sight, he got a little easier upon that score ; but still his equanimity was much disturbed at the uncertainty regarding what had become of Lucy. More than once, he thought, of breaking up the present combination of circumstances, and sending for those who would at once have released him from his present position, but Sam, who saw his embarrassment, said to him,—

" Its very likely sir, that seeing how things went, she has gone on purpose to keep out of the way of Miss Swam, and hidden herself somewhere. You will be sure to see her in the morning, and any hunt for her to night might only terrify her.'

There was something in this, and after a few moments more consideration, Harry Dean made up his mind to let things take their course until the follo ing morning.

" Now my tulips," said a rough voice, as the door of the cellar-looking place in which Harry Dean, and Sam Clover had been placed for security, was flung open. " Now my tulips. The wan is ready if you is. Only don't hurry yourselves of course. Oh no, not at all."

Harry walked out, followed by Sam, whose face flushed crimson at the idea of being placed in the police van.

" Never mind," whispered Harry Dean, to him. " Better be innocent and in the van, than guilty and out of it."

" A great deal, sir," replied Sam.

" Tumble in, tumble in," said a policeman. " Now my rum un's all's right, see how you is looked after, riding in your carriage, just like the Duke of Wellington. All's right."

Harry Dean found himself in the police van, with some dozen or so of others, whom the dim light that came from the top of the vehicle scarcely enabled him to see. There was a silence of some few minutes duration, and then a face was placed very close to Harry's, and a voice said,—

" Yours is a scragging job, ain't it, my family cove."

" A what ?" said Harry.

"Oh, yes," said the pickpocket, for such he was, "oh yes, keep the pot a *biling* !"

"I really don't understand you."

"Green as grass, in course. Well, perhaps you knows best. I expects a couple of months at the grinder, cos you sees, my family pal, the grabs can't snoozle on to the vipe."

"Really," said Harry, "you must speak English if you expect me to comprehend you. I suppose that is what is called 'slang' (in which you have been making those remarks ?"

"Oh, how fine we are to be sure! Well, old fellow, if you are in the same ward with me to-night, look to it, that's all. I like a fellow to be sociable ; but I suppose cos you have *dashed* an old feminie's *gobble*, you think you are above talking to a swell prig—eh ?"

"Don't be a fool," said Sam Clover. "Keep your d——d nonsense to yourself, will you—I understand it, but this gentleman, my master, don't—and he don't want."

"Do you really know what he said, Sam ?" said Harry.

"Oh, yes, sir ; he said he supposed you would be hanged ; but that he would only have two months at the treadmill, because although he was apprehended for stealing a handkerchief, the officers could not find it."

"But his last speech, Sam."

"Oh, he said he supposed you were above speaking to him because you had cut an old woman's throat."

"A distinction, certainly," said Harry Dean.

A gabble of conversation now ensued, in the midst of which the officer who was riding in the mysterious looking little box that is fastened behind the police van, cried out—

"You shall be reported for the refractory if you don't be quiet."

This threat had the desired effect. The refractory ward of the prison to which the cargo was bound, was well known to most of them, and they had no wish to feed their imaginations upon its romantic delights. The van rapidly proceeded, and in about five minutes more it rolled under the gloomy gateway of the new prison of Clerkenwell, as it was then called.

"Well, Sam," said Harry Dean, with a smile, "this will be something for us to talk about in time to come. There is nothing like seeing life in all shapes and places in London."

CHAPTER LXIX.

A NIGHT IN A PRISON WARD.

It is rather questionable whether Sam Clover felt quite so comfortable and philosophical as his master, when they were both of them thus unceremoniously consigned to durance vile for nothing at all. But still as Harry Dean put a good face upon the matter, he, Sam, could not very well do anything else but imitate his example. When Harry Dean alighted from the van, he found himself in a kind of vestibule, where several persons officially connected with the prison were waiting, not one of whom, as Sam in telling the story afterwards, remarked, run

the smallest risk of being hung for his beauty, for a more ill favoured set of men could scarcely have been found. The first ceremony Harry Dean and Sam had to go through, was being cursorily searched again, notwithstanding that irksome process had been previously gone through.

"You are sure you have got no 'baccy ?" said the official personage, who was performing the searching process upon Sam.

"No what ?" said Sam.

"Come, come, you know well enough what I mean. Have you got any of the prohibited ? If you have you may as well out with it at once, and save trouble."

"If you mean tobacco," said Sam, "I certainly always carry about a pound of it with me, but as I don't feel at all interested in saving your trouble, I shall leave the discovery of it entirely to your genius."

"You will, will you. Oh, you are a regular hand. We have often had you here before."

"Which is a lie," said Sam

"Hilloa, Jones," cried the man, "just look at these two. Haven't we had 'em here often enough. Look at 'em both, the swell one, and him in the servant's togs. Don't you know 'em ?"

"Of course I does," said Jones, " and indeed it was a matter of course, for the police of London are in in such a fever at the idea of forgetting anybody, that they take care never to fall into such an error by adopting the plan of perfectly remembering anybody. There never was yet the most innocent man in the world taken to a police-office, who would not be at once recognised by the police as an old offender, especially if his worship thought he had seen the face before.

"Very well," said Harry Dean, " you recognise me you say, as having been often here, and I say a more abominable falsehood could not be uttered, but I shall be here once more after this time."

"Take them to number nine," cried Mr. Jones, "that's the ward for such fellows as them."

"Sam was about to say something, but Harry Dean stopped him by a look which said tolerably plainly, rely upon me and fear nothing ; so that they were both led in silence to a long vaulted sort of hall, with ranged round it a number of little sleeping places, something similar to the berths in rather a dirty and ill-fitted ship.

"Number seventeen, and number nineteen," called out the man who acted as guide to the two new prisoners, and then the door was made fast again behind them, without any further ceremony.

"Vich is they," said a gruff voice, "family vuns or milky coves."

"Scrag, lag, or the grinder," cried a man with a brutal expression of countenance, coming close up to Harry Dean and looking him inquiringly in the face; "come no nonsense, which is it?"

"I don't understand you," said Harry.

"New born babbies, I should'nt wonder," said the other, "wot a thing it is to be locked up only on suspicion."

"Five bob," said the ill-looking gentleman who had made the incomprehensible speech, the real meaning of which was a wish to know if Harry Dean's offence that brought him there was a hanging, transporting, or imprisoning charge. "Five bob; if you have comed a horseback, pay it, if you hasn't you had better send to some pal outside the jug for it."

"If you want money of me," said Harry Dean, "you won't get it; is not probable that I am going to pay for being imprisoned here upon a charge concerning which I am wholly innocent."

"Perhaps you don't know me, my swell pal, I's the warder of this ere ward, and if you won't pay your footing I shall take it out of your bones, that's all."

"If," said Harry, "you mean that as a threat of personal violence, I shall certainly upon the commencement of anything of the sort knock you down. You are now fairly warned; I would advise you to look to your own safety."

So audacious a speech to one who was the bully of the place, and who had been elected ward-man because no one dared to oppose him, excited at once the greatest interest and astonishment in the prisoners present. The contrast between Harry Dean's slight agile figure and the brutal looking bulk of the thief was most striking, as they stood at about arm's length, confronting each other for a few moments now in silence. In truth the wardsman was too much astounded to speak or to do anything for some few moments. When he did recover himself sufficiently to say anything, his eyes flashed with passion, and his face turned deadly pale, as he said,—

"So you will have it, will you?"

Harry Dean made no answer.

"I say you will have it, will you?" added the bully. "Take it then."

He must have had some sort of faint suspicion that the man who could say what Harry Dean had said, must be conscious of power of some sort, either of skill or of strength, for in the blow that he aimed at Harry, he put forth all his strength, and likewise all his skill. Slightly shifting his position, Harry avoided the blow easily, and then he made a feint of striking the fellow in the chest, which threw him off his guard a little, and then with the quickness of lightning, Harry struck him such a straightforward stunning blow in the face that the bully reeled again. Without a perceptible interval, Harry followed up his attack with the other hand, hitting the fellow precisely in the same spot, and this blow was decisive. Down he fell as though he had been shot.

"Bravo," cried a voice.

"Hurrah!" cried a dozen in chorus.

"Go it my tulip," said the gentleman who was not particular about his pronunciation of the English language. "Go it my rummy tulip, you have peppered him, down as a hammer. My eye what a go. How does yer feel, Bill, eh?"

The discomfitted wardsman was propped up upon the knee of one of the thieves, while the last speaker spoke to him, saying,—

"Is yer a coming up to the blessed scratch agin, or is it a case of enough and to spare, my rum un."

"I—I haven't been very well to day," growled the fellow. "Curse you all."

"Go it my blue bell, go it. That's sure to take away the swelling on yer nose, my tulip. Well you have met your match at last, my fancy card, that you have."

"Ah, uh! Bother."

"Well, that's what I calls an incommonly sensible remark, I does. Let him down gently, Peter. He aint a coming up to the scratch any more, doesn't you hear?"

The gentleman who had the wardsman on his knee was so disgusted at his declining to come up to the scratch, that he abruptly withdrew that friendly support from him, and let him drop heavily to the ground without any warning, a proceeding which produced a roar of laughter at the expense of the defeated bully, whom nobody seemed to fear now. Truly he had

"fallen, fallen from his high estate,"

and in losing the prestige of success he had lost all his terrors. There was not one there present who did not long to give him a kick in satisfaction of some foregone domineering or insult.

"Will you be wardsman?" asked one of Harry.

"Certainly not."

"Oh, very well. Only as you have whacked him, you may if you like. The turnkeys always let the cove be wardsman as thumps everybody else in the ward. That's the rule here."

"And an atrocious one it is," said Harry Dean. "All I desire is that I and my companion here may be left to ourselves, and in no way interfered with. We shall esteem such indifference as a favour."

"Humph! As you please, master, and as for interfering with you, I don't think now anyone here will be over fond of doing that."

If the night had not soon come on, both Harry Dean and his faithful attendant would naturally enough have wearied much, of this anything but desirable situation, but as the evening came, and a dull, miserable lamp was lighted at one end of the ward, Harry Dean found abundant food for speculation, in listening to the singular dialogues that were going on around him. What most surprised him was the absolute freedom from anything in the shape of shame or indifference with which the various persons there confined confessed their guilt to each other. Such a state of mind he could only attribute to the fact that in such a place innocence was in so fearful a minority, that guilt became in the depressed imaginations of the unfortunates there confined, stripped of all its shame by being stripped of all its singularity. The thieves spoke of their

crimes just as they would, had they been lawyers or money lenders, have spoken of their professional pursuits, with all its prospects and all its risks. Harry Dean watched these things with the eye of one who felt more than curiosity in noticing the failings of his fellows. He was of those who always look upon the failings and short-comings of human nature with compassionate eyes, and he passed some hours in asking himself if indeed education could make honest and virtuous those whom nature seemed to have taken pains to make widely different. There were some, too, in that prison home, upon whose faces was stamped an expression of villany that could not be mistaken. When night came a dim lamp was trimmed at the end of the room, and then, at a sound from the prison bell, the prisoners were ordered to cease all conversation, and to go to rest. Neither Harry Dean nor Sam Clover made any opposition to the mandate, but they both retired to the little shelves, upon which rough horse clothes were spread for their accommodation. In the course of a few minutes now, all was still, for those who were accustomed to that place knew that the penalty for infringing the rule of silence at night was being not very ceremoniously dragged off to a refractory cell. It was not likely that Harry Dean should sleep over well in such a place. Indeed his intention was to remain awake the whole of the night, in that close thought which those only dare indulge in whose consciences will permit them unflinchingly to look back upon the past. There were few who could do this as Harry Dean could do it.

Harry was conscious of his innocence, and he was well aware that his detention would not continue for many hours longer, and he was therefore but little affected by the temporary loss of liberty; but although he was void of all anxiety for his own fate, or that of his follower, his mind was distracted by his uncertainty of what had become of the mistress of his affections, the innocent and lovely Kate Destern. With the recollections which his memory brought before him of the happy moments he had spent with her, were associated all the chain of singular adventures which had lately happened to him; and full of these ideas, he at length fell into a slumber, which soon became peopled with the figures of his waking thoughts.

* * * * *

He thought that he was walking near the sea-shore. At a little distance rose abruptly a vast rock, and on this rock stood a tower against the walls of which the spray from the troubled ocean dashed continually. He took a path-way leading inland towards the rock, when a marvellous spectacle suddenly arrested his footsteps, and he stood for awhile motionless. On a heap of ruinous rubbish near one of the walks sat Kate, his Kate—in the habit in which he had last seen her. As she sat between Harry and the glowing sunset, it appeared that she was surrounded with a golden glory, and the boughs of a shrub suspended from the wall waved in the evening breeze over her head, as if about to kiss it.

"And yet it surely must be an illusion!" said Harry Dean within himself, as he approached the object of his admiration. Nor was he long in doubt. The figure arose. It was indeed clothed as to the upper portion of the body in the well-remembered attire of Kate Destern, but below, in the tattered garments of a beggar. It was bare-footed: and starting at the unexpected presence of a stranger, fled to the rear of the ruins. Harry followed the fugitive, and suddenly found himself in close proximity to a family of gipsies, who were indolently reposing themselves on the ground, and had all their worldly goods spread out before them in the shape of old garments and fragments of all descriptions. A flat-nosed patriarch was comfortably stretched out on the ground, and was luxuriously indulging himself with copious demands upon the soup-pot hanging within his reach. Not far from his side sat an ill-favoured woman nursing an infant: and at some little distance was a half-clad young girl bathing her legs in the spray of the sea. At the moment of his approach, the object which had attracted his notice was in the act of announcing his presence. The old gipsey arose and received the approaching traveller with a respectful salutation. Harry immediately began to enquire respecting the attire of the girl before him, and the

eplies were so unsatisfactory that he was compelled to come to the conclusion that the unfortunate Kate had been robbed and probably murdered. He recognized in particular a silk kerchief, with the corners embroidered by the hand of Kate herself, as well as other articles, and this conviction drove him to madness.

"You have murdered her—you have stripped her," he thought he shouted, "you have murdered her who was my soul's idol; without whom all the world will be to me a blank."

The nursing woman laid aside her infant in affright: the bathing girl hastened in her undress from the water: the old gipsey cast himself at the feet of the angry young man, who was brandishing a stout walking stick in every gesture of menace. But the young girl who wore the questionable raiment shook her head in artless innocence, and implored the forbearance of the threatening assailant: "Handsome young gentleman!" she said, "do not strike my poor father! he has done nothing to give you offence. I it was who found the bundle—for I am always the fortunate child of the family."

"Speak—where—how—when did you find it? Speak—ye thieves, or I'll grind to dust your thievish carcasses!" And as the excited young man screamed these words of fearful menace in their ears, he seemed about to put his deadly design in immediate execution. But the young heroine ran rapidly forwards towards Harry, seized his uplifted arm with both her hands and exclaimed, "Strike not the old man, for the love of mercy, strike him not, but hear me! It is true that in these garments I recognise the dress of that pretty lady whom I have seen you walking with far away from here, and oh! kind sir, I have grieved and wept bitterly in the woods for her since the hour I found these things under a bush."

Harry furiously dashed the poor girl from his side, and she fell heavily on the earth, and writhed in pain—

"Ye vagabonds and murderers," he again screamed, as the flame of resentment and vengeance flashed from his eye; "what has become of the sweet girl? Lead me to the spot where ye did the foul deed of robbery and murder!"

The old gipsy partially raised himself from the ground, and timidly said—

"Have we slain her? have we plundered her? Willingly will I aid in the discovery of the murderers, if she be slain. This woman has the gift of prophecy, and knows all villains, whether they live in hovels or in palaces."

"Prepare yourselves!" sternly ejaculated Harry: "you must all accompany me to a magistrate. Be prepared immediately!"

The gypsies slyly winked at each other with their little eyes, and as if by a preconcerted signal they all dispersed at the same moment, but in different directions into the woods beyond the ruins. They left all their possessions behind them caring only for their personal safety. Harry Dean pursued them as rapidly as possible through the wood; but strange to say, he neither saw nor heard anything more of them, as if they had never had existence, or never fled in the direction, which he had seen them take. He doubted the evidence of his own senses—or as an alternative was inclined to believe the fugitives were in possession of the art of making themselves invisible. Astonished at the mystery before him, he paused and listened for awhile, but hearing and seeing nothing he returned with a heavy heart to the garments. His eyes filled with tears; he contemplated the sad memorials of his lost love. He lifted each article in succession as if to question it concerning the fate of its former wearer. At last he took the silk kerchief, as sacred to the memory of the unfortunate girl, and hastening along the seashore, oppressed with melancholy thoughts, when he was suddenly startled by a loud noise which seemed close to his elbow, and—he awoke!

*   *   *   *

Harry sat for a moment or two in a sort of stupor; he was sensible that he had been dreaming, but he felt likewise certain that the noise that had aroused him had actually arisen close to his actual waking position. "Some one," he thought, "of the prisoners has thrown something down accidentally, and that has fortunately awakened me from a very unpleasant dream."

He did not move, but he fixed his eyes upon the figure of one of the prisoners, whom he felt certain he should easily recollect again, and who was with a stealthy movement creeping about the ward. This man slowly approached the light, and then, after looking about him with an anxious glance to see if he were observed, he suddenly and rapidly extinguished it. All was still now for the space of about three minutes, during which Harry Dean could see the figure of the man who had put out the lamp, creeping along close to the floor among the beds. Curiosity to know what he was about to do, kept the eyes of Harry Dean fixed upon his thin shadowy frame. He leant over one couch, and then the silence of the place was frightfully broken.

"Help, help," shrieked a voice. "Oh, help—murder. He is killing me."

In a moment the place was in a commotion. Harry Dean heard a scuffling of feet. Then there were loud cries for a light, and imprecations upon the head of whoever had put it out, in the midst of which a policeman made his appearance armed with a cutlass.

"What's all this row about," he cried, "Can't you be quiet till you are hung, all of you, as I suppose you will be some day. Who has put out the light?"

Amid a general enquiry and repudiation of the deed of putting out the light, the policeman reillumined it by the aid of his lantern, and then a deep groan came upon all their ears, and upon looking in the direction from whence it came, one of the prisoners was found stabbed to the heart with a clasped knife, which was lying upon the bed of the next man to him. The policeman, upon this rather serious discovery, left the ward and rung a bell, which was only touched by the constable on duty at night, if anything very serious occurred. This bell ringing, soon produced an inspector and then a surgeon, who at once pronounced the man who had been stabbed to be quite dead. The governor of the prison was by this time roused, and a pair of handcuffs were put upon the shaking wrists of a miserable looking old man, upon the coverlet of whose rude couch the blood-smeared knife had been found.

"Is that the man who did it?" said the governor.

"Why, sir, the knife was found upon him, and he was in the next crib," replied the policeman. "It's suspicious."

"Very. Remove the body, and we will see which it is in the morning. It's an abominable thing that if they must do these odd jobs, they can't do them in the day time. Put the murderer in a cell."

"But I am no murderer," cried the old man, recovering himself, and speaking with horror in his very tone, "I am no murderer. Good God, I did not do it. I am here for dishonesty, but I did not take this man's life."

"Ah, you must prove that, my man, before a magistrate to-morrow," said the governor.

"No!" said Harry Dean.

"Hilloa! Confound your impudence. Who are you that say no, I should like to know? I have a great mind to put you in a cell."

"You dare not," said Harry; "I said no to you, because you said that this poor old man must prove his innocence before a magistrate in the morning, when you ought to know he has no such thing to do, for if you charge him with this murder, it is you who have to prove his guilt, and not he to prove his innocence, and I say to you boldly that he did not do this dreadful and bloody deed before us."

CHAPTER LXX.

BOW STREET AGAIN.

THERE was a something about the manner of Harry Dean which commanded respect, and yet the situation in whic heh was, so much militated against any exhibition of such a feeling towards him, on the part of the prison authorities, that the governor, after a few moments silence, during which he felt abashed in spite of himself, said,

"Remove that man, No. 18, I think he is, to the refractory ward."

"For what?" said Harry.

"Oh, no matter for what. We don't ask or answer questions here, my fine fellow. All we care about is to keep discipline, and you will soon find out that we are quite strong enough to do that, without arguing the point with you."

It was quite clear from the chuckle that the governor gave that he thought he had given a most triumphant answer to Harry Dean, whom a couple of officers laid hold of.

"Well," said Harry, "I of course admit, for that is quite certain, that if you choose to exercise it, you have the power of perpetrating, for the time, any injustice within these walls. What may be the ulterior consequence is another affair, but at present it is my duty to discover the man who committed this murder. I know him."

The villain who had actually done the deed, and whose best policy certainly under the circumstances, would have consisted in silence, at this could not contain himself.

"Ha—ha! A good joke," he cried. "He knows who did it, does he?"

"Yes," said Harry Dean, "and it is not I only who have that information."

The fellow sat bolt upright in his bed, and as the perspiration rolled down his face, he said,

"Who—who else knows?"

"You do."

"I—I? Perhaps you would not mind saying that I did it. That would be your best plan. Why don't you accuse me of it. I shall be surprised if you don't."

"I do accuse you," said Harry Dean, "certainly; I saw you do it!"

At these words the fellow absolutely reeled again, and had to clutch by the side of the crib from which he had come, or else he would have certainly fallen, so affected was he at the accusation. But he soon found an unexpected ally.

"Oh, stuff," cried the governor, "I don't believe a word of all this. Who knows but that this fellow who talks so fine," alluding to Henry Dean, "did it himself."

"Well," said one of the occupants of one of the shelf-like sleeping places, "I suppose as I shall be put in the 'fractory ward for saying anything, but the fact is, I seed him as No. 18 says did it, get up out of his crib, and douse the glim."

The governor bit his lips. Here was corroborative testimony at once, so he was compelled to take some notice of it. After a few moments of irresolution, he said in a sulky tone of voice,—

"I shall do nothing in this affair, until the morning. I can't knock up a magistrate at this hour, so turnkeys just shut up the ward again, and let it all be till the daylight. I shall say no more about it."

The police and the turnkeys were not sorry to get to rest again, for there had been something in the shape of a general disturbance among them, in consequence of the ringing of the alarm bell. The door of the ward was duly closed upon both the murdered, and the murderer, and the echoes of the footsteps of the prison officials died away along the vaulted passages. This state of things appeared to Harry Dean to be so monstrous, that he at once took the lead in attempting to effect an alteration in them, and for that object he addressed his fellow prisoners, saying,—

"A murder has been done here, and there stands the murderer. Are we to lie down again to repose, while such a man is at liberty among us?"

"No—no—no."

"Well, then since the proper authorities will not take him into custody, let us do so."

"Who dare lay a hand upon me?" cried the fellow.

"I dare," said Sam Clover, as he sprung upon him, "and if any more testimony is wanted to háng you, I beg to say that I can give it, for I saw you do the deed likewise."

Some dozen handkerchiefs were immediately produced by the thieves, and with right good will they bound the murderer hand and foot, despite his cries and remonstrances, which, b y no means became less, as one said,—

"It would be saving a good deal of trouble to come, wouldn't it, if we were to hang him out of hand, as there's no sort of doubt in the world, but he did it."

"No, no," said Harry Dean, who was rather terrified at the general disposition there evidently was to carry out this suggestion. "No, no. Let him be dealt with according to law. He cannot escape the consequences of his crime. There is more than sufficient testimony against him to convict him of this most atrocious and to all appearance objectless deed."

"Not so objectless," said one.

"Indeed, can you give a reason for the act?"

"I can, this man and he who is murdered were comrades. They are both accused of forgery, and this one who is now dead, was strongly suspected by the other of an intention to turn king's evidence. That was the reason of his death, which that scoundrel would gladly enough have laid at some one else's door."

This explanation was evidently considered quite satisfactory by the thieves, and the accused man only struggled with his bonds, and no longer attempting to deny his hideous crime, gave utterance to the most horrible imprecations. After this it was not very likely that any one in the ward would enjoy much repose, and the ringing of the prison bell, which announced that it was morning, was a welcome sound to all. A very rough breakfast was given to Harry Dean and Sam Clover, after which there was a sort of inspection of the whole of the prisoners in the yard of the prison, and then the van arrived, which was to convey Harry and Sam to the police office once more. How the affair connected with the murder in the prison was being managed, nobody knew but the officials, for the ward in which lay the dead body was locked, and the prisoners who were not to go before the magistrates that morning were removed to another part of the building. Harry Dean only asked one brief question upon the subject, in reply to which he was roughly told to mind his own business, as that might be quite enough for him. To this he did not think it worth while to make any reply, and being hustled into the prison van, along with some real unfortunates, he was soon set down at the door of the police office, in Bow-street, in the midst of a very motley assemblage of persons. Almost every one who alighted from the prison van, with the exception of Harry Dean and Sam Clover, had some friend to greet them; the staple of those greetings being to "never mind;" a recommendation which, if it could have been carried out fully, would certainly have had the effect of disarming cruel fortune of

much of its terrors. To these affectionate admonitions, they who were addressed, usually responded that all was right, a form of expression in vulgar English, which is much oftener used when in reality all is wrong. However, the remark and its rejoinder, appeared to be perfectly satisfactory to the parties concerned, and to be looked for as things of course, by the officers who had charge of the party of prisoners. Harry Dean and Sam, were placed in the same strong-hold, at the back of the office, where on the previous day they were temporarily lodged, but they had not been many minutes there, when one of the officers of the court—one of those old race of Bow-street runners, now quite extinct—came to them, and stepping aside with Harry Dean engaged in earnest conversation with him for some minutes. What rather astonished Sam Clover, was the air of deference put on by the officer, as he spoke to Harry Dean, and which was most strikingly different to the behaviour they had both met with in the prison. Sam Clover was puzzling himself upon this head when the short interview concluded, and Harry Dean returned to him with a look of such satisfaction upon his face, that it seemed to be quite beaming. Of course, Sam asked no questions in words, but he looked a whole volume, upon which Harry said with a smile to him,—

"There is no time just now, to tell you all that I would be quite willing to tell you, but you must be content to feel assured that all will be well."

"That I have all along been quite sure of," said Sam.

"You are right."

In about a quarter of an hour more, the night charges having been disposed of, Harry Dean and Sam Clover were conducted into the office, and placed at the bar, upon the serious charge of murder. There was quite a rush of spectators, and the reporters looked even more pale than usual, and more anxious, as they prepared to take copious notes of the whole proceedings. A couple of magistrates were upon the bench, one of whom was the rather intemperate gentleman with whom Harry on the day preceding had not been at all able to agree, and when he saw the prisoner again, with whom he had had such a rencontre, he tried to look so amazingly dignified, that he really appeared quite contemptible.

"Oh, ah! so these are the prisoners accused of murder," said he.—"Come, come, young man, don't look at me in that kind of way, if you please. Is the evidence ready in this case?"

"Yes, your worship," said an officer.

At this moment Swam and her admirer were ushered into the office. These two worthy personages were still in a state of the greatest doubt as to their precise position. Whether they were merely detained as witnesses, or because their real share in the transaction was suspected, or more than suspected, neither of them could very well tell; and they looked about as thoroughly wretched as any two people in such an awkward situation could very well look. The words of the officer who had brought them to Bow-Street,—"You are my prisoners," rang in their ears, but yet the translation of those words was not quite

clear to them. No wonder then that they both looked with trembling anxiety around them, striving to gather from every face they saw some food for speculation. They both, however, maintained their fixed determination to turn evidence against each other, in the event of the affair thickening and things becoming rather serious in the way of their implication. Swam was placed in the witness-box, and she made a great effort to look composed, as she glanced at the crowd of faces in the court, and then at the two magistrates.

"I hope your worships are quite well," she said faintly.

Then she cast a glance at the doctor, as though she would read his very soul, while he stood like a greyhound in the slips ready to say, "I turn evidence for the crown," the moment he should see that things were taking for him a dangerous course. Swam was duly sworn, and then the magistrate said to her in what he intended to be a very impressive and dignified manner indeed, and one which, he thought, would have quite an effect upon the spectators,—

"Now, witness, mind what you say, for we keep books here. A-hem! Mind what you say."

Swam shook a little, but she was not so easily intimidated as most folks; moreover, she had a very fertile imagination, and when once she fairly started upon the little romance she had got up about the death of Madame Zadzed, she went on with a facility that would have delighted a French novelist.

"Your worship and gentlemen," she said; "you will easily, I am sure, imagine what a painful state my feelings must be in upon this most melancholy occasion. The fact is, I know very little about it, except that my best friend is now no more, and that these two monsters in human form," glancing at Harry Dean and Sam, "did the deed."

"Which yet remains to be proved, I believe," said a voice in the court.

"Who dares interrupt the proceedings of the court?" cried the magistrate; "officers, take that man into custody, and bring him before me directly. We don't sit here to submit to these unmanly interruptions."

"Here I am, officers," said the person who had so spoken; "to be brought before the bench, is the very thing I have been wishing for some time. Pray assist me, for the crowd is so dense I cannot get forward."

By the exertions of the officers, a plainly dressed, gentlemanly-looking man was brought up to the magistrate's seat, and that angry personage, casting upon him a look of great defiance, said,— "Who are you, sir ?"

"My name is Willoughby, and I appear for the prisoners."

At this name, which was that of a member of the House of Commons, and one of the most eminent men at the bar, there was a general commotion, and the magistrate said, in a very odd sort of tone indeed,—"Are you Mr. Willoughby, the member, sir ?"

"Yes."

"Oh ! Ah ! Very well. Of course. Pray step here, sir, and take a seat upon the bench, if you please. A-hem ! A cool day, rather, Mr. Willoughby."

"Very ; but I can do very well where I am, your worship."

"There must be some mistake, here," said Harry Dean ; "I don't know Mr. Willoughby."

'Oh ! there's no mistake, my dear sir. I was instructed by the Lord Chancellor last night, rather late, and fully comprehend the case."

CHAPTER LXXI.

SWAM IN A LITTLE DIFFICULTY.

SWAM really did not seem very well to comprehend what was going on in the court now. She looked from one to the other of the persons, between whom the last little conversation had taken place, with rather a bewildered air. All she seemed to suspect was, that something had gone amiss with her evidence, but, then, what a consolation it was to her to feel that she could get out of her difficulty, by turning evidence against the doctor, and throwing herself upon the mercy of the crown! At least, by such means, she thought she could, at any time, save her neck. Swam thought her neck worth the preserving, although she was certainly singular in that opinion.

"Now," said the magistrate, who took an active part in the proceedings, while his colleague for the present merely looked on,—"now, witness, pray proceed with your deposition, and be as clear and explicit as you can, stating only facts, and not what you think, if you please."

"I don't want to state anything but facts," said Swam.

"Very well. Go on."

"And I rather, upon the whole, decline thinking upon the subject."

Swam wanted a little time in which to collect her rather disordered faculties, and she was determined to have it somehow. The magistrate began to frown, but Mr. Willoughby said, with a quiet smile, that was daggers to Swam,—"Let her take her own time, perhaps she thinks that some slight alteration in her story will make it look a little better. Give her plenty of time, your worship. This is rather an important investigation.— Plenty of time."

These words, "plenty of time" sounded to Swam, singularly, like "plenty of rope," and she winced at them accordingly ; but there was no help for it. There she was, chained, as it were, to the stake, and she must take the consequences of the situation.

"Well," she said, "I have a plain story to tell."

"Tell it, then," cried the magistrate. "We cannot sit here all day, to humour the caprices of a witness."

"A-hem !" coughed Swam, and then she glanced round the court, until her eyes fell upon the face of the doctor. His very lips were white with fear, as he looked, not upon her, but upon Mr. Willoughby, upon whose face he saw, or thought he saw, a look of strange and, to him, the doctor, dreadful intelligence. What could it mean ? He was roused, however, by the voice of Swam, as she began her rather cleverly concocted narrative. The reader, who knows the real particulars quite as well as Swam does, will give her credit for the great ingenuity she displayed upon this particular occasion.

"I was companion to Madame Zadzed."

"Who was ?" interrupted Mr. Willoughby, with provoking interrogation in his look and tone—"who was ?"

"What ?" said Swam.

"That's just what I want to know,"

added Mr. Willoughby; " I want you to tell the court, since you were her companion, who this Madame Zadzed really was. Come, now, you are upon your oath here, recollect."

"She was a lady of independent means."

"And did you know nothing disreputable in her character, or mode of life?"

"No; and it's a shocking thing for a female to be asked such questions. Do you think that I would have been her companion if there had been anything wrong in her conduct? No, sir, hardly. I defy you and all your petty arts."

Swam was getting energetic, but Mr. Willoughby had said all that he had to say at that juncture, and so he took no more notice of her just then than as if she had been a portion of the woodwork of the witness-box in which she stood.

"I was companion to Madame Zadzed," she continued, "and had been for some years. All I know of the murder is, that I was awakened at a very early hour by hearing a half-smothered scream. At first I made sure that it was only my imagination, for I had passed (I don't know why) rather a disturbed night, and I sat up in bed and listened attentively for some few moments. The scream was not repeated, but yet it pressed upon my mind that something must surely be the matter, and, after trying to shake it off and get to sleep again, I at last got up."

"At what time?" asked Mr. Willoughby.

"Don't know," said Swam, rather tartly, who thought it was just as well not to be particular to an hour or so.

"Very well. Go on."

"I mean to do so, however disagreeable it may be to some people."

There was a slight laugh in court, and Swam, who, upon the whole, thought she was getting on very well, proceeded.

"Not feeling, as I have said, satisfied in my own mind about the scream that I had heard, I got up and went to the door of Mr. Carter's room to awaken him."

"You took a deal of useless trouble," said Mr. Willoughby.

"Useless trouble, sir! Pray, what do you mean?'

"Why, that Mr. Carter, if he was asleep, might easily have been awakened by a nudge of the elbow."

This produced a laugh at Swam's expense, but she disdained to reply to it, although she trembled to feel that the counsel had a very just appreciation of her character, and likewise seemed to have an almost superhuman knowledge of her actions.

"I awoke Mr. Carter," she proceeded to say, in rather a hurried tone. "He is a medical man, and I thought if anything was amiss he might be useful. Besides, he was the only man in the house."

"Oh, nonsense!" cried Mr. Willoughby, "to call up a medical man after the extent of injury that Madame Zadzed had received. Why, you know, Miss Swam, that that must have been useless."

"I don't know that."

"Yes, but really, now."

"Oh, I dare say you are very clever," said Swam, losing her temper, which was just what Mr. Willoughby above all things wished—"oh, I dare say you are very clever, and know much more than other folks; but as I had often heard of people whose throats had been cut having them sewed up again by doctors, I called the one who happened to be in the house. Now I hope you are answered, sir, and satisfied."

"Pretty well; but there is a slight difficulty that wants explaining."

Swam looked uncommonly vicious, but she did not yet know where she had committed herself exactly. She was soon, however, doomed to be duly informed upon that head.

"As I say," continued Mr. Willoughby, "there is one slight difficulty that wants explaining in the matter. Pray, Miss Swam, how did you know that the throat of Madame Zadzed was cut at the time, for, if you recollect, you had only just been awakened by a slight kind of scream, which you had almost attributed to imagination. Can you satisfactorily answer me that, Miss Swam? Come now, don't be considering. The truth, you know, can always be spoken at once. Will you answer me, woman? Upon your oath, I ask you, how did you know at that juncture that the throat of Madame Zadzed, the lady of independent means, was cut?"

"I never said it was."

"You did."

"Oh, nonsense, it was you. You don't know what you are saying, and confuse yourself. It was you who said her throat was cut, not I. I only wish somebody would make you sit down, and not interrupt me in this way while I am giving my evidence to his worship as well as I can. I wonder at you, sir."

Nothing in all the world could transcend the cool impudence of this speech. It rather astonished Mr. Willoughby, who, with a smile, sat down, saying as he did so,—

"Go on, Miss Swam. If you are satisfied with the state of affairs, I am quite sure that I am. Go on—go on."

Miss Swam did go on, although she was, in reality, anything but satisfied with the state of affairs, and her voice was evidently shaken as she proceeded with her narrative.

"I awakened the doctor," she said, "and we both proceeded to Madame Zadzed's room, to ascertain if anything was the matter with that lady. The shutters seemed to be closed, and we heard a whispering of voices, which I need not say alarmed me very much. I wanted to rush out into the street, but Dr. Carter would not allow me, as it might, after all, be a false alarm, and so we, after calling Madame Zadzed, and getting no answer, opened the door. Excuse my agitation, gentlemen, but what followed was enough to affect any one's nerves."

"Compose yourself," said Mr. Willoughby.

Swam darted a glance of defiance at him, and proceeded. She knew well what his sympathies amounted to, so far as she was concerned.

"Two men," she continued, "tried to make their escape from the room, but we struggled with them, and an alarm took place. I hardly know how it was that fortunately the officers came, for I was very much agitated when my eyes, upon being directed to the bed, saw Madame Zadzed dead."

"Can you," said the magistrate, "identify those two men whom you saw in Madame Zadzed's bed-room?"

"I can."

"Look at the prisoners at the bar. Are they the men."

Swam made an affectation of looking fixedly at Harry Dean and Sam Clover, and then she said,—

"These are the men."

"Have you any doubt upon the subject," added the magistrate, "or are you quite sure about it?"

"I have no doubt whatever. I am quite sure about it. I could swear to them anywhere. They are the men."

"Which is not denied for one moment," said Mr. Willoughby. "They are the men who were seen in the bedroom of the murdered Madame Zadzed. So far this excellent witness, Miss Swam, is perfectly in the right. As she says, they are the men, but—and in all things of this complexion, there will be some awkward qualifications—they did not do the murder, for all that."

"You must admit, Mr. Willoughby," said the magistrate, "that things look very suspicious against your clients. It is for you to say whether you will protract this examination or not. Probably, as you may perceive that I have sufficient grounds for the committal, you will think proper to reserve a defence for the trial."

"If these men were guilty, I should say yes to your worship's recommendation," said Mr. Willoughby; "but, as they are innocent, I cannot see any evil in protracting the investigation. Every fact that comes out must, of course, under such circumstances, be to their advantage."

"Very well, sir."

"Perhaps your worship will now allow me to cross examine this most veracious witness a little."

"Oh certainly, you can do so if you like, Mr. Willoughby."

"Very well. Now, Miss Swam, if you please. Is this Dr. Carter you speak of your acquaintance, or was he the acquaintance of the late Madame Zadzed?"

"He was an old friend of Madame Zadzed's, although, by coming to the house frequently, I got acquainted with him. I don't see anything very wonderful in that, I'm sure."

"Nor I, Miss Swam, nor I. Now jog your memory a little, and tell me who else was in the house on the night of the murder, if you please. I mean besides yourself and the doctor?"

"The servant—we kept but one—was out."

"Well."

"There was a little girl, too, who was, I think, some relation of Madame Zadzed's, but I don't know no more of her than that she was staying in the house at the time, and had been for a day or so."

"Pray, Miss Swam, what was the name of this little girl?"

"I don't know."

"Perhaps you don't know, either, where she is now?"

"I have not the remotest idea, and I don't want to know, either. I heard Madame Zadzed say that she was a very vicious, lying little thing, and was not to be depended upon for one moment in anything. When I heard that much from one who, of course, I knew too well, I made up my mind that the less I had to say to her it would be all the better. Besides, I saw her character in her looks."

"Well, it's a thousand pities you don't care to know where this little girl is, for then you would be gratified to learn that she was in a private room of this building, and had some most singular evidence to give respecting this case."

"She evidence?"

"Yes; and, as I take it, evidence of the most striking character. She evidently, from the slight conversation I have had with her, labours under an impression that Madame Zadzed's throat was cut some hours before the persons at the bar made their way into the house in which that deed was committed."

Swam changed colour, and grasped the rail in front of the witness box. "Shall I turn evidence against the doctor at once," she asked herself, "or shall I wait to hear what the child says? Yes, yes, I will wait—I will wait. Time enough yet."

"Call Lucy Destern," said Mr. Willoughby, and there was a slight bustle consequent upon the entrance of little Lucy to the court. Her beauty, as well it might, attracted the eyes of all present

---

CHAPTER LXXII.

KATE IN A NEW SITUATION.

It is the misfortune of truthful narrative compositions like the present, that whereas two or more actions necessarily connected with the story are proceeding at one and the same time, it is impossible to place before the reader more than one, and hence, much to the aggravation of all parties, heroes and heroines have to be left in all sorts of extraordinary straits and situations, in order to bring up to the same epoch of action the other characters of the story. Thus, for a brief time, are we compelled to leave our old acquaintance, Harry Dean, and our somewhat nearer acquaintance, Sam Clover, in the court of the police office, at Bow-street, while we take a glance at other proceedings, in which Kate Destern became just at that juncture particularly engaged. We will close the door, then, of the police office, leaving Swam in the witness box, Harry Dean and Sam Clover at the bar, and little Lucy just coming through the crowd like some ministering angel bound upon an errand of rare and exalted charity. There let them all wait, until we can come to them again. We shall not keep them long dull and lifeless in that strange antagonistic position in which they are all placed. The reader who has followed us thus far will recollect a certain personage who came to the bedside of Lord Battaney, and extracted from his purse a large sum of money. This person was named Wilkins, and by profession a physician. It will likewise, no doubt, live in the memories of our readers, that this personage, before he could get so snugly off as he expected with his booty, encountered Harry Dean, who put a stop to his peregrinations by taking him into custody, and lodging him, with the assistance of Sam Clover, in the watch-house at Fulham, there to abide until he should be sent for. Much more important considerations for the time being called Harry Dean to London. He was in pursuit of Kate, but still he was anxious that this man, Wilkins, the physician, should not escape the punishment due to some crime which it was quite clear Harry Dean considered he had good grounds to charge him with. What that crime was, we shall no doubt hear in good time. At present, what we have to do with are the proceedings of Wilkins, who, if tact and talent could make a man respectable, was entitled to that name, for he possessed both in an eminent degree, although there was not one particle of honour or honesty in his entire disposition. Such characters are by no means so rare as they might be imagined to be. Wilkins appeared to give himself up to his destiny, and entered the watch-house at Fulham like a lamb, complaining of indisposition, and was allowed to sit by a fire in the outer room, as he looked so very inoffensive, and such a poor, weak, harmless creature. He then got colder still, and at length, with a sigh, he said,—

"I don't feel very well, I think a glass of hot brandy and water will be beneficial."

This was a proposition which did not present itself in very hideous colours to the constable who had charge of the watch-house, and when Wilkins produced the requisite amount of money, and glancing at the constable and his associate, said blandly,—

"I think, as there are three of us, we ought to have three glasses," the thing became quite fascinating.

"Well, ahem! I'm rather afraid that it's contrary to rule."

"Which will make us careful," said Wilkins, "to say nothing about it. Tell them to make it good."

This conduct of the prisoner's was really quite irresistible, and the brandy and water was duly procured, steaming hot, and with its brilliant mahogany tint, casting bright reflections, like a snake's eyes, upon those whom it intended to betray, for, if ever the foul fiend, the agent of all wickedness, lurks secretly at hand, grinning and smirking at his dupes, it is through the soft dreamy vapour of alcohol.

"What's that?" said Wilkins, suddenly.

"What's which?"

"A scratching at that door, yonder. Ah! there it is again."

Imagination, and the cool impudence with which Wilkins accompanied it made both believe that they did hear a something, and, springing towards the door, they flung it open. All was still, and not a soul was to be seen.

"It was fancy," said the constable.

"Or an accidental gust of wind," said the other.

"Oh, bother!" said Wilkins, "well, gentlemen, the brandy and water, you see, is prepared, and only waits for you to drink it up. Here's a toast, 'May we often have such pleasant cups as this.'"

The brandy had indeed been prepared, for while the two unsuspecting guardians of the peace were looking at the door and the passage beyond it, Wilkins had dropped into each of their tumblers a little something no larger than a pea, which in the hot liquor was immediately dissolved. The toast was drank, another followed, and in three minutes the constables fell to the floor in complete insensibility.

"Fools!" said Wilkins, as he shrugged his shoulders, and stepping over the prostrate bodies left the place—"fools! as long as I have only human machines to deal with, I can thus tolerably carry my wishes into effect."

He soon overtook a public conveyance, and was set down in busy, bustling, heartless London. He remained for some moments musing, and looking at the pump in Oxford-street, near the "Green Man" coach-office, and then as he walked away he muttered,—

"It is not often one thinks of a place which gives safety and revenge at one clutch. Look to it, you who thought you had made a prisoner so neatly—look to it, I will wound you through your heart, and that wound shall never heal, unless I have assurance of safety."

How and when this man then succeeded in procuring the most accurate information concerning the situation and proceedings of Harry Dean and of Kate Destern, it matters little. Suffice it to say that that information was both correct and conclusive, and that he shaped accordingly a course which will soon show itself in all its terrors.

*   *   *   *

It was on the morning of the second examination of Harry Dean at Bow-street, and just as Lucy was, as we are aware, called into court, that a handsome plain carriage stopped at the door of the physician's house where Kate had found so kind a welcome, and where she lay but yet half only recovered from the effects of the terrible and singular circumstances that had brought her there. A gentle, but by no means humble rat-tat at the street-door, from a scrupulously-attired footman in mourning, summoned Dr. Bell's servant, to whom a note was handed, which had upon it the name of "Dr. Wilkins," and no address whatever.

"Is Mrs. Bell at home?" said Dr. Wilkins' footman.

Now Dr. Bell's footman was rather surprised at his mistress being asked for instead of his master, but, as the latter was out and the former was within, he replied in the affirmative. A communication was then made to some one in the carriage, and the door was opened, the steps were let down, and a well-dressed, gentlemanly-looking individual alighted, and walking into the hall of Dr. Bell's house said, in mild accents,—

"Please to announce me to your mistress."

Dr. Wilkins was shown into a reception room, and his card was taken to the lady of the house, who was at the very time conversing with Kate Destern, and telling her that Dr. Bell would be sure to bring her some good news concerning Harry Dean, of whom she so much wished to hear. When the card was put into Mrs. Bell's hands, she turned it over and over, as people will do a strange card sometimes, and said, with an air of much surprise,—

"Dr. Wilkins—Dr. Wilkins! I'm sure I never heard of Dr. Wilkins before. It must be some mistake. He can't want to see me. I don't know any Dr. Wilkins. What kind of man is he, John?"

"Quite a gentleman, mam," said John.

"And where is he?"

"In the dining-room, mam."

"Well, I suppose, then, I must go to him. Say I will be down directly, John. Now, Kate, as I was saying to you, make yourself easy. You are quite safe from all the world here, and you may fairly consider your adventures to be at an end. I will return to you as soon as this unknown visitor has gone."

Kate could only thank Mrs. Bell with her eyes, and in a few moments that lady was bowing to Doctor Wilkins.

"Madam," he said, "my friend, Bell, told me I should have the happiness of finding you at home. We were old fellow-students, and have not met for years before to-day. He wants me to take great care of Miss Distin—no, Destern, I think it is—yes, and bring her to him directly, at Long's Hotel, where he is waiting with a Mr. Dean—yes—I am bad at names, but I think it is Dean, who is taken for somebody else, and wants the young lady to identify him. Bell says the little ride in my carriage, out of which she need not get, will do her good. I can't judge myself, as I have not seen the case, but I'd take Bell's word against the world."

All this was spoken without any hurry or confusion and in the most gentlemanly manner, with a soft rich voice, that was particularly convincing.

"I—I am rather surprised, sir," said Mrs. Bell.

"Ah, Bell said you would be."

Mrs. Bell took a glance through the window at the carriage, and then she said,—

"Well, sir, of course if the young lady decides herself to go—she shall. I will trespass upon your kindness to wait for a few minutes, as Miss Destern keeps her room."

"Oh certainly, madam."

Kate was duly informed of all that had passed. She did not hesitate a moment. An accession of strength seemed to come to her, the moment Harry Dean's name was mentioned, and she was quite impatient until she was ready to go. To be sure she tottered a little from weakness, as she came down stairs, but her spirits supported her as she told herself it was for Harry. The carriage door was gently closed upon Kate and the physician, who with much politeness surrendered to her the seat at the back, saying as he did so, with that kind, cordial sort of voice, which had so won upon the doctor's wife, and disarmed her natural powers of penetration,—

"You know you are an invalid, so the best place is yours, by right."

"Ah, ah, you are too kind to me."

"Not at all; I am quite sure that is not an opinion you will persevere in when you know me better."

The carriage went on at a dashing rate. The sudden transition from the extreme quiet and repose of her chamber

at the benevolent physician's, to the bustle of a carriage, and the being whirled through the open air at so rapid a rate, had a sensible effect upon the nervous system of Kate Destern. More than once she felt as though the next moment she should faint. She spoke in a low tone—

"Have we far to go, sir? I confess that, in leaving the house, I have rather overrated my strength—I am faint."

"The distance is nothing," was the reply of Doctor Wilkins, as he fixed his keen eyes upon her. There was a something in his tone not quite so bland as it had been before, and Kate looked at him with a slight shudder, after which he took from his pocket a small phial, and handing it to her, with the stopper uncovered, he said, not unkindly,—

"If you can but manage to take a few drops of this, it will quickly restore you. I do not say it will cure you, but it will give you a temporary strength to go through what you have to do for Harry Dean."

The mere sound of the name of Harry Dean was a talisman to Kate Destern. She did not hesitate a moment, but placing the phial to her lips, she took a few drops of the potion it contained. The taste was not unpleasant. It was sweet and grateful to the palate, but the effect was anything but what she had anticipated, for, in lieu of feeling any accession of strength, as a consequence of partaking of it, she, on the contrary, felt what little power she had remaining rapidly flying from her. Alarm took possession of her, and she tried to cry for help, but the sound she would have uttered died away upon her lips, and with a feeling of terror, that, had she possessed the power of speech, she would have wanted words to describe, she sunk back in a state of perfect insensibility upon the soft, luxurious cushions of Dr. Wilkins's carriage.

"Very good," said Wilkins; " I could not have had a fairer opportunity of giving her the opiate. She is quite safe now, for twelve hours, at least."

The carriage in a few minutes stopped in a fashionable street, which, however, was not free from lodging-houses, and the doctor alighted. He was met in the hall by the landlady, to whom he said,—

"Madam, I have brought my sick sister home with me, and shall give her to your care. As I before informed you, she must not be contradicted in anything, but agreed with in everything, like a young child. Her madness is of that form, that opposition renders desperate."

CHAPTER LXXIII.

A PALACE AND A PRISON.

"WELL," said Mrs. Bell, as the doctor came home in about an hour, "how about Wilkins?"

The doctor stared, but, being something of a humorist, and thinking his wife was perpetrating some joke at his expense, he replied,—

"Ah, how? As you say, my dear, how about Wilkins?"

"How provoking you are! I mean Dr. Wilkins, your old fellow-student. Come,

now, don't be troublesome and enigmatical."

"Oh, certainly not. Go on. Have you anybody else to inquire about, my dear? How is Kate ?"

"Kate ?"

"Yes, Kate.

"But Wilkins ?"

"Well, Wilkins."

"Do you want, Dr. Bell,"—Mrs Bell always called him doctor when she was in a passion—"do you want, Dr. Bell, to drive me out of my senses? How can you play with any one's feelings in such a way? I ask you now explicitly, if she arrived safe with Wilkins, and if it answered the purpose. Come, now, that's clear enough, I think."

"Remarkably, my dear. Ha! ha! How is Wilkins? Ha! ha!"

"Well, how, and who is Wilkins ?"

"That's right, vary the fun a little. I'm sure if Wilkins is any friend of yours, I shall be delighted to know him."

"Dr. Bell, do you really do all this to try my temper? You know I feel an interest in Kate Destern, and am anxious to know if going out so suddenly, even in a carriage, was not trying her strength rather too much, notwithstanding your friend, Wilkins, was with her to take care of her. What are you staring at, Dr. Bell ?"

"At you, my dear, if it be not high treason to do so."

"And why at me ?"

"Do you feel quite right in your head? any pain across the temples? You look, I think, much as usual, and yet, really ——"

"Really what? you will make one think you are a little out of your wits, if you go on in this way."

"Very good indeed! Well, my dear, I shall just pop up stairs to see how Kate is, and then—"

"Stop! stop !"

"What for, pray? Is there really any mystery? If there be, pray explain it to me at once. What is it ?"

"Dr. Bell, sit down."

Mrs. Bell's voice faltered as she spoke, it was quite clear she was beginning to be deeply affected; she continued,—

"Did not your old friend and fellow-student, Dr Wilkins, call in his carriage from you to fetch Kate Destern to Long's

Hotel, when Harry Dean was to be liberated from arrest upon her identifying him?"

The doctor sat down and uttered a deep groan. Mrs. Bell, who began to have a horrible suspicion of the truth, came up to him, and shook him by the shoulder, as she exclaimed—

"Speak! speak! for the love of Heaven speak! Do you know Dr. Wilkins?"

"Never heard of such a person in all my life."

"Then you—you know nothing of the message from Long's hotel—nor the carriage—nor—nor anything else ; you did not send for Kate Destern at all ?"

"Certainly not."

Mrs. Bell tottered back until she came to a seat, upon which she sunk, saying, in a voice of exquisite anguish,

"Then she is lost to us, for I have given her up, poor girl, to perhaps her worst foes."

"Good God!" said Dr. Bell; "you don't really mean to tell me that Kate Destern, upon any pretext whatever, has been stolen or waylaid from this house? Surely that is impossible."

"It is true. I am to blame. I let her go, and I shall never again know a moment's peace. 'Tis true, 'tis true."

For some few moments poor Dr. Bell seemed so completely cut up, that he could not speak. Much as he wished to know the whole particulars of this affair, he found that it was impossible for him to gather courage to ask them ; but his wife, who saw the state of mind he was in, relieved him by telling him, in a tearful manner, exactly what had occurred, repeating word for word the spurious speech of Dr. Wilkins, which had so completely imposed upon her, and induced her to let Kate go, without a shadow of a suspicion that anything was amiss.

"Now, my dear," said Dr. Bell, "in the first place do not distress yourself further than for the fact that Kate Destern has been taken away from us by a trick."

"But it was my fault, my credulity."

"No, it was neither a fault nor a piece of credulity ; ninety-nine persons out of a hundred would have done precisely as you have done, so comfort yourself, and let us consider the matter calmly."

"Calmly?"

"Yes, calmly and rationally. I have ascertained that Harry Dean is charged, along with another person, with the commission of a murder ; but from what I heard among the officers at Bow-street, there is no doubt at all of his innocence of the charge, and that he will be set at liberty. All we can do, therefore, is to have an interview with him at once, and let him know exactly what has occurred."

"Yes, yes. Alas, poor Kate !"

"Alas, indeed. It is quite evident that some strange mystery envelops her. What it is, time alone can dissolve ; but I do not think we ought, upon a consideration of all the circumstances, to have any notion that she is in real danger. A prisoner she may be kept for some purpose or another, but her life is, I dare say, safe enough.

"I can only hope so.

"It is well to hope the best. This pretended Dr. Wilkins is probably the agent of some one who has special reasons for securing this young girl. That she is not what she seems to be I think we may fairly conclude ; and at the same time I think she is in complete ignorance herself of who she really is."

"I am sure she is. If she had known anything concerning herself more than she told us, we should have heard it. There was no such thing as mistaking her—she was truth and candour itself. There are no such things as truth and sincerity in the world, if she possessed them not."

"I perfectly agree with you, and should be sorry indeed if human nature was not redeemed by some such examples as Kate Destern."

"Then we are both agreed upon that point ; so all we have to do is, to find out where she has been thus, in so abominable a manner, spirited away to. Can you think of any plan?"

Before any reply could be made to this, the servant of Dr. Bell brought into the room a note addressed to him. The doctor received so many notes during the day, that he did not pay any particular attention to this one. He merely said—

"Does any one wait an answer ?"

"No, sir," was the reply. "It was in the letter-box, merely."

"Very well, that will do."

The servant left the room, and Dr. Bell rather listlessly opened the note. He naturally glanced first at the signature, to see from whom it came, and he was not a little startled to see "George Wilkins" signed to it. Mrs. Bell saw that the note was something out of the common way, by the expression of the doctor's face, and she said hastily—

"Any new calamity?"

"No, my dear; but it is from your Dr. Wilkins."

"For God's sake read it. but don't call him *my* Dr. Wilkins. What have I to do with the wretch? Read it, read it."

The note ran as follows :—

"To Dr. Bell.

"SIR,—The abduction from your house of the young girl named Kate Destern, is not without a meaning, and I am well aware that there is one who, from his rank and means, will soon find means to communicate with you upon this subject. What I wish you to tell him is, that the young lady is in the hands of Wilkins, the physician; and that he, Wilkins and the young lady, shall go to the grave together, unless a complete amnesty for the past is insured to him, Wilkins.

"If an advertisement be inserted in the 'Herald' newspaper, to the following effect, it will tend to the restoration of the young girl to him who sighs to see her.

"Dr. W. will find a letter containing a complete pardon for the past, from H. D. at Dr. 'B.'s. W. will no longer be molested by H. D. if K. D. be restored in safety to Dr. B.

"I am, sir, with great respect for your wife's judgment, which was so signally manifested in the interview I had the honour of having with her,

"GEORGE WILKINS."

"The impudent scoundrel!" said Mrs. Bell.

"A cool piece of assurance, certainly," said the doctor; "I am more puzzled now than I was before. What does he mean by a person of rank and means? Is it this Harry Dean?"

"So it would seem."

"Well, there is a great mystery in the whole affair, which, I suppose, some day, will be kind enough to unravel itself; and in the meantime, it seems to be my most obvious course to show this letter, and tell the whole story to this Harry Dean, who is so intimately mixed up with the whole affair."

"Of course you must; so now be off at once, and see if you cannot get an interview with him, for every hour may be of consequence, before that advertisement is inserted, which, I suppose, he will not hesitate about."

"I will go. It is quite a mercy Wilkins did not name the 'Times' instead of the 'Herald,' for the bad character of the 'Times' makes even an advertisement in its columns doubtful in its honesty."

It was rather inconvenient for the doctor, considering his professional avocations, to go in search of Harry Dean; but he was so deeply interested in the fate of poor Kate, that he did not hesitate to make any sacrifice to spare her pain, and he could easily imagine what she must be suffering, when she found out, as no doubt by now she had, how cruelly she had been deceived by the man who called himself Dr. Wilkins, than whom, probably, there was not in all London a greater rogue, which is saying a great deal. To the police-office. then, the good doctor hurried, and arrived while the proceedings were still pending—those proceedings which we were compelled abruptly to break off, in order to follow the course of Wilkins, and to detail to the reader the cruel fate of poor Kate Destern. We shall again look in upon the court at Bow-street, when we have given a passing glance at the condition of Kate, now in the hands of one of the boldest, worst, and most unscrupulous of men that society could produce. Alas! her dangers and deep anxieties were not yet over. What a chequered life was hers! How many storms disturbed the ocean of her pure existence!

CHAPTER LXXIV.

THE GILDED CAGE.

"DEAR me, sir! Bless us and save us, the poor thing! Well, sir, you must not despair; who knows but she may come quite round ? Is she asleep, sir, if you please ?"

These words came from the landlady of the house to which Dr. Wilkins conducted poor Kate Destern, while she was in the state of insensibility produced by the few drops of the powerful opiate he had induced her, upon the false pretence that it would give her strength, to swallow in the coach. Wilkins lifted her out of the vehicle, and carried her into the house with an affectation of great tenderness, at which the landlady, who saw a long and undisputed bill against such lodger in the dim prospective of time to come, thought it incumbent upon her to shed tears of sympathy, and to make sundry remarks, to the effect that it was quite a thing to see a brother and sister so united, and that it was not always the case, as she knew instances where they quite tore each other's eyes out for the smallest possible provocation. During the utterance of all these sympathetic speeches, Kate was carried up stairs to a truly handsome bed-room, with a neat little apartment, half sitting room and half dressing room, attached; for the house was of its kind a first-rate one, and the furniture and fittings were such as would have graced any nobleman's mansion. The landlady had set up the business of lodging-letting with a competent capital, and she "took in" and "did for" no one who made any scruple about the charges. Dr. Wilkins just suited her, for he had never even asked the price of the accommodation he had demanded, which as Mrs. Tig, for such was the euphonious name of the landlady, said, showed at once that he was quite the gentleman, for common people always asked what there was to pay, and he did not. The fact is, the doctor had plenty of money ; and, as he guessed that his stay at Mrs. Tig's would not be very long, he thought that, to bind that lady to his interests, ten or twelve pounds over and above what he ought to have paid would not by any means be ill treatment. Therefore was it that, with his eyes open to the fact, he consented to be robbed.

"Now, madam," he said, "I shall leave you to get my poor sister Kate to bed. She will sleep for some hours, so you may leave her with perfect safety; and now, madam, if anybody should inquire for such a person as Dr. Wilkins,

mind, I don't live here, and you never heard of me.'"

"Lor, sir."

"You understand me. I do not want my uncle the duke,—pooh—what am I saying ?—I mean, I do not want anybody to know where I am just now, for I differ in opinion with the bishop—I mean I differ in opinion with one of my relatives—about the propriety of putting my sister in a private lunatic asylum, as I want to try and effect her cure at home, without their knowing anything about it."

"Certainly, sir, oh yes, sir. What a thing affection is ! "

"By-the-bye, Mrs. Tig, I ought not to trespass upon your purse for any little disbursements that you may have to make for us. There is a twenty-pound note, and you can let me know when it is gone."

All this happened at the door of the drawing-room ; and when Mrs. Tig had grappled the note, Dr. Wilkins bowed to her, and entered his own apartments, closing the door upon her. Mrs. Tig went to her own parlour quite in a flutter, but, before she could soliloquise her feelings, a visitor was announced, who was a Mrs. Frew, a lady in the same line as herself in the street. Here was an opportunity of quite a providential character, to sound the praises of her lodger.

"Oh, Mrs. Frew, Mrs. Frew, you see that my nerves are rather affected."

"My dear, what is the matter ? You have let your first, I think, haven't you, to a carriage and pair ?"

"Yes, yes."

"Well, you are lucky. You know I am quite empty, with the exception of a brougham in my front parlours. All very respectable and so on, but rather mean about extras. If there's any sort of people I hate in all the world, it's those as is mean and despicable about extras."

"So do I—so do I—I can't abide them, Mrs. Frew."

"My dear, I know your principles."

"Yes, as poor dear Tig, who is dead and gone, used to say, my interest is my principle, and my principle is my interest; and I have always kept to the maxim in this life, whatever I may do in another."

"Quite right, Mrs. Tig, quite right ; but what sort of people are they in the first ?"

"Oh, nunsuches—nunsuches!"

"You don't say so ?"

There was a slight tone of acerbity in Mrs. Frew's speech, which a nice ear like Mrs. Tig's detected instantly. The fact is, Mrs. Frew and Mrs. Tig were great friends, and hated each other mortally, being, as Mrs. Tig's cook said, as jealous as " pison" of each other's lodgers. Now, it was the custom between these two ladies to keep up an interchange of visits, and be just as provoking as they could possibly be to each other. It was a strange taste, rather, but if Mrs. Tig did not hear all that Mrs. Frew had to say, she was quite unhappy ; and if Mrs. Frew was not acquainted with all that the fertile imagination of Mrs. Tig could suggest, concerning her and her affairs, there was a decided vaccuum in her happiness. The knowledge that Mrs. Tig had let her first-floor, had, of course, been the provocation to Mrs. Frew's visit.

"Yes, my dear," said Mrs. Tig, continuing the conversation, " I think I have got a fit now."

" Objects to nothing ?"

" Asks nothing. Got an uncle a duke. I wonder if it's the poor, old, obstinate duke they call the F. M. And a relation a bishop, with whom there's a difference of opinion ; only think of a difference of opinion with a bishop !"

Mrs. Frew shook her head.

" Ah, my dear Mrs. Tig, I don't like all that."

" A-hem ! I did not think you would, my dear, exactly."

" My dear, you don't quite understand me. What I meant to say was, that I always mistrusted lodgers, who spoke about great relations, and never asked the prices of anything."

" A-hem !"

" But of course, my dear, you know your own lodgers best. I only say just what comes uppermost, that's all, my dear."

" Oh, don't mention it. By-the-bye, can you lay your hand on change for a £20 note ?"

" Of course I can, and I should think it would not trouble you to do so either, Mrs. Tig."

" But, my dear, I have just paid in all the loose cash I had to my banker's, and as my first-floor has handed me a £20

note for extras, and told me just to say so when it was gone and have another, I wanted change."

The countenance of Mrs. Frew underwent a change, if the note did not.

" Are you sure it's good ?" she gasped.

Mrs. Tig turned nearly blue at the horrible idea that it might be bad ; and then, with an hysterical cough, she produced it for Mrs. Frew's examination, who saw in a moment that it was the real thing ; so that the faint hope that Mrs. Tig had a swindler in her first, vanished like some

————" unsubstantial pageant."

",Well, I'm very glad you are so fortunate," said Mrs. Frew, rising. " A gentleman only, I think ?"

" Why, you may say so, and you may not. There's a little secret."

" A secret ?"

" Yes—a little secret."

" Mrs. Tig !"

" Mrs. F. !"

" I hope, ma'am, you are not going to bring discredit upon this street, Mrs. T. If there"s a secret, it strikes me there's some female at the bottom of it, Mrs. T."

" There is, certainly, a lady connected with the affair, Mrs. F. ; but if your beastly imagination suggests anything that is improper in my house, I leave you to wallow in the mire of your own thoughts."

" Me wallow ?"

" Yes ; I said wallow in the mire, and I don't regret it in the least.'"

" Mrs. T., you are a beast—a hog—an old maid."

" You abominable wretch, you backbiting scum of the earth ! Get out of my house directly. Never show your ugly old face here again. It's only fit for a street-door knocker, and then it would frighten away all visitors from the house."

" You old cat, take that," cried Mrs. Frew, " and at the moment she seized a half-open work-box from the table, and cast the same at the head of Mrs. Tig, who immediately rejoined by casting at Mrs. Frew a blue vase containing about a quart of water, and some half decomposed flowers.

Mrs. Frew thought it prudent now, as she was in her enemy's camp, to beat a retreat, and she rushed to the street-door and opened it so quickly that a baker's man, who was just arriving with some pies, fell with a grand splash into the passage. Now Mrs. Frew was leaving the house with an air, and so of course she fell sprawling over the baker with her face upon the door-step and her legs in the passage. The baker swore, and Mrs. Frew screamed until she was raised by Mrs. Tig's servant, when with a flood of tears and the fragments of the pies sticking to her feet, she made a wild rush into the parlour again, and tore from Mrs. Tig's head a lace cap, and—oh, horror—the whole of that lady's head of hair. Mrs. Tig now fainted, and Mrs. Frew walked off in triumph, like an Indian warrior, with the scalp of her enemy. While this skirmish, of which he was the provoking cause, was going on, Dr. Wilkins paced the drawing-room in deep thought, after which he sat down and wrote the note which Dr. Bell read after the explanation with his wife concerning the disappearance of Kate Destern during his absence from home. One thing was quite clear in the whole of the conduct of Wilkins, and that was his anxious desire to treat with Harry Dean for the restoration of Kate Destern, and therefore was it that he made his name so much connected with the matter, in order that Harry Dean should fall into no mistake as to whose hands she, Kate, had really fallen into. This Wilkins must indeed have been an artful villain. Well he knew, that if there was any way more sure than another of reaching the heart of such a man as Harry Dean, it was through his best affections. He calculated that the desire for vengeance or the strong impulses of justice would give way before the conviction that she whom he loved was in danger. Affection would overcome even the stern dictates of duty.

"Yes," muttered Wilkins to himself, "he thought that he had me in his power, and that, spirit broken, I must of course submit to him; but he will now find that he has more of a giant than a pigmy to deal with, and that he must make terms with me, or place for life a thorn in his own breast."

But faint sounds of the tumult below had reached the ears of Wilkins. The house was large, and the doors in the passage or hall as it is more grandiloquently called, fitted well. Mrs. Tig sent for her hair-dresser and her lawyer. The former to bring her a fresh peruke, and the latter to take instructions for commencing an action against Mrs. Frew, for she was on thoughts of vengeance intent, and was ready to cry with the man in the play—"I have sent for my lawyer; and hang the consequences." Mrs. Tig was determined to pay every possible attention to the sister of her distinguished lodger, and accordingly, when she had got her ruffled plumes somewhat in order, she ascended to the bed-room, where poor Kate lay like some blighted flower. The deep and unnatural sleep of Kate rather alarmed Mrs. Tig, and the more she looked at her the more she trembled to think that something serious was the matter with her.

"I don't want her to die here," muttered Mrs. Tig to herself, "no, not if the F. M. and the bishop were both to come to the funeral. I'll just go and speak to Dr. Wilkins, as he calls himself, about her."

"With this intent, Mrs. Tig appeared at the drawing-room door."

"Come in," cried Wilkins.

"Oh, if you please sir, ten thousand pardons," ejaculated Mrs. Tig, "but the young lady, your lordship's sister—this was a bold stroke of Mrs. Tig's—is asleep yet."

"No doubt, madam."

"But if you please, my lord, it isn't a sleep that I exactly like."

"But perhaps she does, madam."

"Well, if it's all right, sir, of course it's all right, and I am very sorry to have troubled you, my lord; but I thought the sleep did not seem, somehow or another, quite natural-like, my lord."

"The observation does honour to your penetration, madam. The sleep of my poor sister is not at all natural—it is the result of a powerful narcotic, the effects of which will not pass off, until about ten o'clock to night. Then she will awaken, and, as usual, poor thing, I dare say she will say some very odd things."

"Indeed, my lord!" said Mrs. Tig.

"Of which it is no use to take any notice."

"Certainly not, my lord. When folks are mad, they of course are—are not in possession of their senses, as one may say."

"Spoken like an oracle, madam."

"Then, perhaps, I need not trouble bout the young lady just at present, my lord."

"You need not, madam. All you are required to do, as regards her, is to keep the room rather dark, and the door closed."

Very well, my lord."

"Don't call me, 'My lord.'"

"But I suppose, sir, you are a—a lord?"

"That's my affair, madam. Don't call me a lord, that is all I have to say upon the subject. Whether I am less or greater than a lord, can be of no consequence here, whatever it might be at the court of St. James's. And now, madam, I shall leave my dinner entirely to you. Let it be composed of four dishes, and be particular about the cooking."

"Certainly my L—I mean sir; I beg your pardon, but your dinner shall be correct, and— and— regardless of expense?"

"Quite so, madam, and ready at five."

"Here's a prince of a lodger," thought Mrs. Tig, as she walked down the drawing-room, with the quiet tread of a cat—"orders a dinner, regardless of expense, and leaves it to me! Well, such lodgers, I must confess, do almost reconcile one to human nature; really I think I could forgive that Irish captain, who did nothing but tell lies, and get into my debt, and then run away—the wretch—"

"Mr. Fungus, the lawyer, mum, is in the parlour," announced a servant.

"Is he? very good. Now, Mrs. Frew, we will soon see if there's any law in the land can serve you out; and I dare say, one way or another, I shall be able to get all my expenses out of my new lodger. Ah! he is a pearl—quite a pearl."

CHAPTER LXXV.

A PAINFUL INTERVIEW.

WITH the sort of amazement with which a person might be supposed to awaken in a new world after death had spread the filmy mantle of obscurity upon this, did Kate Destern open her eyes, and look around her, after the effects of the powerful narcotic administered to her by Wilkins had passed away. The chamber in which she found herself might well arrest her wondering attention, for it was one such as she had not looked upon since she was a prisoner in the villa of the infamous Lord Battaney at Fulham. It was, in truth, quite a show room. We have before taken occasion to state that Mrs. Tig had done justice to her house in its fittings and appointments, and this bed-room was such as any lordly drone, with his pockets full of plunder from the people, might have laid down in with satisfaction, and a feeling that his accommodations were indeed of a very different order from those of the people who paid for his luxuries, and those of his race. We do not accuse Mrs. Tig, or Miss Tig as she delighted to call herself, of taste —God forbid that we should so libel that lady's character; but the fact was, that at the time she was getting her house in order, and wishing to fit up a show drawing-room and a show bed-room, she had an opportunity of purchasing cheaply the whole fittings and appointments of two such apartments in the adornment of which the most refined taste, combined with the most lavish expenditure, had presided. Thus it was, then, that Kate Destern found herself surrounded by costliness, pale green salle hangings, and many little luxuries of furnishing, in that bed-room. The drug that had been given to her by the doctor was no coarse narcotic, that left the intellect confused and muddled, but its more immediate effects had passed away, so that Kate now felt as well as before she had taken it, at all events, and it will be remembered that that was not very well.

She sat up in the costly bed, and drawing aside the enclosing curtains looked about her for full five minutes in the silence of utter amazement. The idea then that she must be sleeping still, and that all she saw was but some vivid picture presented to her in a dream, came across her, and she pressed her hands upon her eyes to shut out the scene with something of an expectation that when she should look again it would be gone. But no—there it was. There were the pale green silk hangings, the Louis Quatorze chairs, the elegant fatuils,

all as plainly and as distinctly visible as they had been before.

"It is no dream," she exclaimed, "it is no dream."

She then began to closely recollect what had occurred previously to the blank in her existence which the narcotic had occasioned. She had a clear remembrance of the message to repair to Harry Dean—of the obsequious physician—of the luxurious carriage—of taking something from a small phial, but there memory failed her. There was a hiatus until she found herself where she now was, but imagination could easily now account for that hiatus, and Kate said at once,

"That was a sleeping draught, and heaven and my persecutors, for persecutors they must be, know only where I now am, and what my fate may be. Oh Harry, Harry, where are you, indeed, to save me now? What will become of me? Has not cruel fate yet wearied of making me unhappy?t

For a short ime she remained in the

bed in an agony of woe, but then she began to think more calmly upon her situation, and to reason with herself.

"No one is lost," she said, "who does not give himself up."

She had read that sentiment somewhere, and it came strangely new to her mind, but it gave her courage, and courage is strength and hope.

"I will not despair," she said, "no —no. Such ills as it is the will of heaven to visit me with I will endure with such patience as I may call to my aid, and I will fight up against oppression; I have enemies, I know not why or wherefore, but I will not yield to them, they shall not subdue me yet."

It appeared to her she was apparently quite alone in that splendid room. She listened for some few minutes and could not detect the slightest sound of any voice or movement. All was soft repose. She could only guess that the large city was around her by the confused hum of life that came upon the air mingled with the distant rattle of the wheels of many vehicles.

"I may possibly escape," she cried, "at least I will assure myself that such is impossible before I give up the idea of so doing."

As she uttered these words she was about to leave the bed, but was instantly deterred by hearing a voice in the tones of which there was certainly no disrespect say,

"Lady, do not alarm yourself needlessly."

The voice was that of a man, and while the burning blush of outraged delicacy spread itself over the fair face of Kate Destern, the physician Wilkins glided from behind some hangings, and confronted her.

"Kate Destern," he said, "I have for an hour or so awaited your awakening to give you a little explanation of your present position. Will you attend to me ?"

Kate was too much confounded to speak, and after a pause of a few moments, Wilkins added,

"You are naturally alarmed, but compose yourself, for you are perfectly safe, if matters turn out as I fully expect. Indeed I think I shall be able to convince you that your life and liberty are both in your own hands."

"My life and liberty ?"

"Yes, both."

"Leave me, sir, your appearance here is an outrage."

"That is all imagination, Kate Destern. Besides, I am a physician, and so a sort of priviledged person, and no one can wish to treat you with more respect than I. It would not answer my purpose to do otherwise, I assure you, I never defeat my own objects foolishly. You are charming, but I have other objects than in feasting upon your beauty. Throw off your terrors, no word or action from any one here will offend you."

There was a sort of calm truthfulness about these words, which impressed itself strongly upon the mind of Kate, and she looked with wonder at the man who talked in such a strain, and was lost in a complete sea of conjectures, to know why he had made her his prisoner, and thus found it his interest to behave respectfully.

"This is some mistake," she said, "you fancy me other than what I really am, perhaps !"

"No !"

"I am a poor girl, my name is Kate Destern."

"And Harry Dean loves you ?"

"Ah, yes. Harry."

"You see there is no mistake whatever. That is the only fact of importance, that Harry Dean loves you. After that I care not who or what you are. It is upon that fact that I have based this whole proceeding. It will not fail me.'

"You talked to me of explanation," said Kate. "Will you give it to me ?"

"Yes, vulgar villains delight in mystery, but I do not. You shall know precisely how you are situated, and then you can decide upon your own course of action, without being disturbed by any conjectures, which might otherwise obtrude upon you, and much disturb your faculties. You see how candid I am."

"You profess candour, but I have heard nothing yet," said Kate.

"That is well. I am not sorry to find you have an intellect which enables you at once to draw such a distinction ; my name is Wilkins—I am a physician, I have committed a crime which Harry Dean alone can pardon. I have taken possession of you whom he loves with the hope of extorting by such means that pardon ; I wish to offer you as the price of it.

What is your opinion upon that important point?"

The cool effrontery of this man, perfectly astounded Kate. His words wrung in her ears, but it was two or three minutes before she could feel quite sure that she had really heard them a right. Yet they were plain enough.

"Do you completely understand me," he added, upon finding that she still continued silent.

"I comprehend your words."

"That is enough. You will be well cared for here during your stay, which I hope will be very short, indeed, for I am quite as anxious to get rid of you as you can be to go. But all that must depend upon Harry Dean. Do you know where to communicate with him?"

"Indeed I do not."

"Well, that do I. You must write to him, stating how you are situated, and that if he refuses to give me a perfect guarantee of safety, your life is in the most imminent peril."

"My life?"

"Yes your life."

"Oh, what have I done to you? How injured you, that you should take my life?"

"In no way, but if I have an enemy, and I meet his dog, I kick it, so, as you are dear to Harry Dean, if he will have his revenge upon me, I, by sacrificing you, will make him pay probably what in the end he will think a rather dear price for the gratification. Now there is nothing more for you to know, but, that you will be attended upon here by a woman who is in my pay, and consequently in my interest, and who will not believe one word you say, because she is prepossessed with an idea that you are mad. I shall return in about an hour, when you can write under my direction the letter I speak of. Until then, farewell."

Wilkins did not seem at all to care about any reply from Kate. He was one of those stern ruffians who make their own resolutions, and then conclude that all is settled. Besides, what could Kate say? She might ask him questions which he was not disposed to answer, or she might protest against the arbitrary nature of his conduct, but that would be all, and that he did not care to hear, so before she could open her mouth to speak he was gone. Truly that bold, bad man

had adopted a mode of bending the stern spirit of Harry Dean to his purposes which did promise success, for was it likely that, let Wilkins have done what he might, Harry Dean would sacrifice Kate to a wild desire for revenge, so romantic a principle of justice. Ah, no, what would life be to him, Harry, but a dreary blank,

"Flat, stale, and unprofitable!"

without her, who was the one bright and beautiful earthly flower, for which he lived, and hoped, and suffered. Wilkins at once proceeded to his splendid drawing-room, and summoned Mrs. Tig, to whom he said,—"Madam, my poor sister is awake. Will you, yourself, attend to her, as I do not wish this family affliction to meet the gaze of servants. For any extra trouble this may give you, pray put a corresponding item in your bill."

"Oh, dear, yes, sir—a-hem!—my lord—I beg your pardon, F. M. Certainly."

Mrs. Tig was rather confused at the rank of her guest, but if he had desired her to slide down from the first-floor to the hall on the balustrade, and put it in the bill, there is no doubt but she would have at once acceded to the proposition, and done the gymnastic feat. She at once, now, repaired to the splendid bed-room. There was nothing very attractive or hopeful about the cold, calculating face of Mrs. Tig, but still she was a woman; and when Kate saw her, she cried at once, while tears gushed from her eyes,—"Oh! save me—save me.—I am a prisoner here, and I am not mad. I am poor—nay destitute, so do think how dear liberty must be to me, since it is my only possession. You surely have some human feelings. Oh! let me leave this house, or give me the means of communicating with those who love me, and who will come and rescue me."

"Hush!—Hush!" said Mrs. Tig.—"How is your head?"

"My head?"

"Yes. Be quiet, now. Sit down.—Only think what affliction you bring upon your poor dear brother, who is quite the gentleman, and the dear bishop, and the old F. M., too."

Kate looked confounded. She could not, for the life of her, understand what the woman meant by such jargon, and she looked at Mrs. Tig, with a suspicion that she was really mad.

"Come—come," added Mrs. Tig, as though she were addressing some pet-dog. "Lie down.—Lie down. I'll soon bring you a something to eat; but you must be quiet you know."

"Alas! poor Kate! she had little, indeed, to hope for, after she had once let Mrs. Tig know, that, if what she said was really true, she was poor, and had no means in the world of making up the loss of a lodger, who gave a £20 note for contingencies only.

CHAPTER LXXVI.

MORE EVIDENCE AT BOW-STREET.

WE again find ourselves in the public office at Bow-street. Lucy has been called to give her evidence, and, to the joy of Harry Dean, he sees her making her way, by the assistance of an officer, through the crowd. That sweet, delicate little face has upon it the flush of a natural excitement, and in a few moments, panting and beautiful, she is in the witness-box. She is sworn. Swam has a dread of what Lucy is about to say, and makes an effort to stop her.

"That child knows nothing of the value of an oath," she said. "It is absurd to swear her."

"We will see to that," said Mr. Willoughby. "Lucy Destern, do you understand what you have sworn?"

"I do, sir."

"What is it?"

"To do what I always do, tell the truth."

"Very well; now proceed, if you please."

"I was in happiness and safety," said Lucy, "when she, who is now no more, Madame Zadzed—as I find her name is—took me by fraud first, and force afterwards, to her home. I was lodged in the room adjoining that in which the murder was committed."

"Did you hear anything in the course of the night?" said the magistrate.

"Yes, much, and saw more."

"Saw!" exclaimed Swam. "Now that shows your worship the vice—the—the original sin, as I may call it, that is

in children. It shows what a little lying slut this really is. It shows——"

"You are wrong," said Lucy. "It only shows that I found a hole in the wall, through which I looked and saw the murder done, that is what it shows, and I am ready now to tell all that I so saw, for I can never forget the events of that dreadful night."

Lucy shuddered as she uttered these words, and the deep truthfulness of them was quite evident to all in that crowded and interested court. Swam gasped again, and the doctor looked to the door. It was very odd, he thought, that so many officers just at that time completely blocked it up.

"Go on," said the magistrate.

"You cannot believe," said Swam, what this child says."

"Is your worship," said Mr. Willoughby, "enamoured of the interruptions of this woman, that you put up with them so easily. In the name of justice, and of common sense, I protest against them."

"Woman," said the magistrate to Swam, "if you interrupt the business of the court, I shall have you turned out."

How devoutly Swam wished they would turn her out, and pay no sort of attention to her when she was out, but no, she had no such hope, no; she saw that the game was very nearly up, but still she waited to hear what shape Lucy would really put the accusation into. She kept an eye upon the doctor too.

"Two people," said Lucy, "came into the room where I was, to see if I were awake."

"And who were they?"

"That woman was one," pointing to Swam.

"No, no, no—it's false."

"And that man," pointing to the doctor, "was the other."

"I deny it, I deny it," said the doctor, "I did not do it—I am innocent of the murder, quite innocent."

"And so am I. I never murdered any one."

"I have not accused either of you of the murder," said Lucy, "I only say that you both came into my room to see if I slept, and that you satisfied yourselves that I did sleep, although, in truth, I was far from sleeping. It was after that that the murder was done, I stood upon the bed and saw it. Oh it was dreadful; I saw the deed actually done; I saw the blood—the blood!"

"Let me out," said Swam, making a movement to the door of the court, "let me out, I am very far from quite well—I will come back again as soon as my slight faintness goes off—depend upon me, gentlemen, for coming back, I shall only interrupt the proceedings by remaining. Let me go, let me go."

"Stop that woman," said the doctor, in a hoarse gutteral voice, "stop that woman!"

"What," screamed Swam, "is that you—is that you? Seize him! Seize him! Hang him! He did it!"

"Murderess!" said the doctor, "I will keep your culpable secret no longer. You know you did the deed, you have confessed it to me; you know your own guilt! Look at her countenance, look at her! is not her guilt manifest in her face? Oh I was wrong, very wrong, not to tell all I knew before, and let justice take its course; but I will now, I will confess all. She murdered Madame Zadzed for her jewels—she cannot deny it."

"I am king's evidence," said Swam, making a rush at the witness box. "Now, Mr. Magistrate, ask me what you like, I'll tell all about it—now, now. That man did it."

The magistrate looked utterly confounded, and the whole court was in an uproar. Probably the only person who preserved the greatest coolness there was Harry Dean, for he had tolerably well surmised that some such scene would shortly take place. The facts that had come to his knowledge had well enough prepared him for it.

"The officers," said Mr. Willoughby, "will no doubt see the propriety of taking both those persons into custody at once."

Swam was on the moment accommodated with an officer on each side of her, and a pair of handcuffs were about being put upon the doctor, when, with a yell of rage, she made a rush at him, exclaiming—

"It is you who have brought me to this!"

Then, before she could be torn away from him, she had frightfully disfigured his face with her nails. Her yells were perfectly demoniac, and the magistrate, in a voice of terror, cried—

"Officers, why don't you handcuff that woman?"

Swam, if she had been quiet, would not have been subjected to this infliction, but the officers, naturally enough, prized their eyes, and did not know who she might next fly at, they soon accommodated her with a pair of iron bracelets, such as in the height of her criminality and arrogance she had certainly never thought of being reduced to the necessity of wearing.

"This is very dreadful, Mr. Willoughby," said the magistrate, turning rather pale.

"It was to be expected, your worship."

"Expected?"

"Yes; I was quite aware of the guilt of those parties; but was willing to allow it to come out in the regular way."

"You were? Why they might have murdered some of us in their rage and desperation."

"True; but it is your worship who would have been the natural victim; and I do not for a moment doubt but you would willingly have died a martyr to your position in that seat."

"Oh, thank you. Dear me, I feel quite uncomfortable. Officers, place those persons at the bar—and—and I think that the prisoners already there, may be discharged on their own recognisances to come up if called upon."

"Sir," said Harry Dean, "your conduct yesterday to me was so bad that I give you due notice now that I am about leaving the court, that I will speak to the Secretary of State concerning you."

"What?"

Harry Dean did not repeat what he had said, but Sam Clover added,

"And you may depend he will, if he says it. If he were to say Covent Garden Market was to be carried into Lincoln's Inn Fields, I should fully expect to see it there. You have put your foot in it, Mr. Magistrate."

"Hush, Sam, hush," said Harry Dean.

"All right, sir."

"Oh, Harry, stay for me," cried Lucy.

"Do you think I would go without

you," he said, as he leant over the witness box and kissed her affectionately. On Lucy, we part no more after this day you may depend. You and I together will commence a pilgrimage in search of Kate, and something seems to whisper to me that we shall find her Lucy, and all of us be happy yet."

"Oh, Harry, your voice is as joy to me. Kiss me again."

"'Hip! hip! hip! Hurrah!" shouted Tony Thorp, from the middle of the crowd in the body of the court.

Now the magistrate's nerves had been rather unstrung by the whole affair, and when he heard this sudden sound he at once jumped up from his chair and scrambling past his colleague, he tried to make his escape from the court, and would have done so, if he had not entangled his coat in the chair, the arm of which had slipped into one of his pockets, so that he was held quite fast, and had time to see that there was no danger, upon which his wrath became very great, and, reseating himself with as much dignity as he could assume, and it was not much, he said,

"Officers, bring the person who made that noise before me?"

Tony was at once pounced upon, and handed up to the front of the bench, when his worship said,

"What, fellow, induced you to make that disturbance?"

"Because it was all right," said Tony.

"All right, you rascal, and are you to make this court into a bear garden because you happen to think it is all right?"

"Oh, there's no thinking about it," said Tony, "I know it is."

"You know it is?"

"Yes, to be sure, aint Harry Dean acquitted, as was the wrongful murderer, and a'nt the lady and gentleman with the bad looking faces as are the rightful murderers booked. Aint little Lucy a hanging round the neck of Harry Dean, and aint I here. I should say it was the most natural thing in the world for me to make a shout after all that."

"Who are you?"

"Oh, nobody particular."

"Then I shall commit you for a week as a rogue and a vagabond.

"Commit me?"

"Yes, I'm glad I have caught some-body. Officer's remove this fellow. Hard labour for a week;" understand, a rogue and a vagabond who brawls in the court and can give no accoutn of himself."

"Will your worship permit me to say a word," remarked an elderly gentleman, stepping forward to the bench with an air and manner of the most respectful kind.

"No, sir, I will not," cried the magistrate.

"But it is concerning this lad, he is a friend of mine—much as I disapprove of the demonstration that he was foolish enough to make in court, I——"

"Hold your tongue, sir."

"Sir, you must hear me. It is a part of your function to hear any one who proffers information concerning a matter before you. You commit that lad to gaol for a week as a rogue and a vagabond, and I came forward to see if the fact of his being a friend of mine will not clear him from that charge. With regard to the brawling in the court, I think you ought to punish for that to the extent of your powers."

"Oh, you do, do you?"

"Indeed sir, I do. I know the act was not done with an intention to disturb, but still these things cannot be passed over. Demonstrations of opinion on the part of spectators in a court of justice cannot be tolerated."

"And pray sir, who may you be that think the fact of your acquaintance with the boy will rescue him from being a rogue and a vagabond, I think I have seen your face before. You had better be careful."

An Irish policeman at once considered this as a hint from the bench.

"I know him," he cried. "He was charged before your worship for stealing lead from a gutter."

"Lead from a gutter," said the old gentleman with all the coolness in the world. "Pray when was that?"

"Oh never you mind when."

"Yes, but I have I think a pardonable curiosity on the subject."

"Hold your tongue, or I will commit you."

"Very well. If you think proper, do commit me. But to make rather an execrable point confess you would be at the same time committing yourself rather seriously."

" Then I will do it, and you and your friend may enjoy a week at the treadmill together, and meditate upon your position. That efficient policeman recognises you, come sir, what's your name, I suppose you will be puzzled to give a good account of yourself. You are sure you know him, policeman."

" Quite sure, your honour."

"My name," said the old gentleman, " is Marsden, I am commonly called Lord Marsden, and I am the Lord High Chancellor of Great Britain. At least, I was when I left home this morning, and I don't think any change has taken place since then in the administration. Now sir, you can believe me or this policeman at your own discretion."

CHAPTER LXVIII.

A CHANGE.

It would be difficult—nay probably impossible to find words in which to pourtray the effect produced in the police office by the last thunder-clap of a statement made by the Lord Chancellor. The policeman's face turned almost as blue as his coat, and the magistrate who never made so sorry an exhibition of himself, sat upon the chair, he disgraced, looking like a man absolutely petrified. How gladly would he have listened to any one who would have said to him. It is only a dream. Harry Dean too was surprised, and there was not a person in all the court now, who did not make a struggle and a rush to obtain a good view of the chancellor. There was only one faint hope remaining to the magistrate, and to that he clung as a despairing mariner clings to a plank that, but hardly floats upon the surface of the billows. It might be a hoax he thought to himself, and not the Lord High Chancellor at all. Yes, there was hope—faint hope in the supposition, and he looked around him for some confirmation of it. The eyes of the counsel, leaned in the law, who had defended Harry Dean met him, and the lips of the magistrate moved to the question of, is it really the Lord Chancellor. The counsel nodded ; alas ! that hope was gone, and the magistrate felt as if his seat were treacherously gliding from under him.

" Policeman," he said faintly.

" Ye—ye—yes, yer wosheep," said the policeman who had so clearly identified the chancellor as an old acquaintance.

" You are a scoundrel. I shall report you."

"Me, yer wosheep ?"

" Silence, sir. How dare you speak. My lord I—I really—will your lordship take a seat upon the bench, really I can assure your lordship that this policeman shall be reported and duly punished."

" I will take care of that," said the chancellor. " I came here merely as a spectator of the proceedings here ; and am sorry that circumstances have compelled me to become an actor in them."

" If I had only known, my lord—I —I—."

" Sir, I beg that you remember that the office you hold is entitled to respect, and that you will not for one moment think of compromising it by any humiliation of yourself, in public ; I pray you to go on with your duties towards the prisoners."

" Let them be remanded until tomorrow ;" gasped the magistrate, " I— I am not very well, and will leave the court.—Will your lordship oblige me by a few minutes conversation in my private room ?"

" I beg to decline the honour ;" said the chancellor.

The magistrate groaned, for he saw that there was no such thing as explaining away the impression which his mode of administrating justice had made upon the chancellor's mind. He knew not that a few minutes' talk with the Secretary of State, would supersede him in his functions. He felt that he was lost, and rising, he abruptly left the court, by the private door leading to his room.

Doctor Carter and Swam were immediately removed, and made secure in separate cells at the back of the court, and Harry Dean and Sam Clover found themselves completely at liberty. To Harry, however, much that had happened, was quite inexplicable, and to Lucy he turned for an explanation. The chancellor, however, sought him out, and said—

"I hope you will do me the favour of calling upon me this evening. I certainly should like to have some conversation with you, about the extraordinary transactions in which you have been engaged, and if I can be of any service to you, I beg that you will let me know in what way."

"I thank your lordship," said Harry Dean, "and shall do myself the pleasure of calling upon you."

"I suppose my new friend," added the chancellor, glancing at Lucy, "will remain with you."

"You have indeed been good and kind to me, sir," said Lucy, "but this is my oldest friend."

"And you are quite right," added the chancellor, with a smile, "to prefer him to new ones. Nevertheless, I hope in time to become an old friend."

The chancellor then walked away arm-in-arm with the eminent counsel, whom he had engaged for Harry Dean's service, and in a few minutes afterwards Harry, Lucy, Tony, and Sam Clover, left the court. Of course, as they proceeded to an hotel, the conversation turned upon Kate; and Harry had just asked Lucy if she could give him any news of her, when some one touched his arm, and upon turning, he saw a gentlemanly personage, who said—

"I beg your pardon, but I am Doctor Bell."

Harry bowed, and tried to recollect the name; but the doctor continued—

"You are Mr. Dean, I believe. I arrived just now at the court, and they told me the direction you had taken. It is of Kate Destern I wish to speak."

"Destern!" cried Harry—of Kate?"

"Yes, yes."

"Oh tell me, tell me," cried Lucy, "have you found our dear Kate, for we have lost her?"

"My dear," said the doctor, with much emotion, "that is precisely my condition—I have both found and lost her. Pray listen to me, and you will soon find, in a few minutes, how distressed I must feel."

It certainly needed no stronger invocation than the name of Kate to enchain all Harry's attention, and, as the kind-hearted physician related what had occured at his house, he was listened to with an interest that was positively pain-

ful, by Harry and Lucy. Harry gave a sigh when the name of Wilkins was pronounced.

"Ah!" he cried, "that bad man, whom I thought I had placed beyond the power of doing further ill, is at the bottom of this affair. I know him but too well."

"Indeed it seems that he is one who, if you once have anything to do with him, is not very easily forgotten. Who and what is he, Mr. Dean?"

"A physician."

"Really? Then the rascal, after all, did not misrepresent himself."

"Not at all, sir, except in so far as he represented himself as an honest man, which he is far from bearing the smallest resemblance to, as night is from day."

"You know him well, then? If anything, sir, could give me hopes of a speedy release of Miss Destern from the power of that scoundrel, it certainly lies in the fact that you know something of him, and of his haunts; but what do you purpose doing?"

"I must succumb to any terms he chooses to make with me. I can see, as plainly as possible, what are his motives in this transaction. He wishes to live in peace, and free from the constant apprehension that he is now under, of my delivering him up to justice for the crimes that he has committed. He thinks that if he can make a good bargain with me, that he will be safe, and able to enjoy his ill-gotten wealth, for I have no doubt that he is wealthy."

Dr. Bell now hesitated for a few moments, and seemed to be rather uneasy, as though there was a something upon his mind which he wished to say, and yet hesitated to give utterance to. His eyes were all the while fixed upon Harry Dean, who, observing his confusion, said to him kindly, and in the most friendly and cheering voice in the world—

"I pray you, sir, have no disguises with me. I can well perceive you have something to say which you doubt if I like—is it not so?"

"It is indeed."

"Then say it fully; and believe me that it is of intention I judge, and not of words. Now, as I know your intention is all goodness to those in whom I am interested, I shall not readily take

offence at anything you may say to me."

"Well, my young friend, if you will step aside with me for a moment, I will say quite freely to you what is upon my mind at this present moment, hoping a favourable reception for it."

Harry Dean walked on a few paces in advance with Dr. Bell, who said,

"I heard quite sufficient of you from Kate Destern, to be quite easy about your character; so without the smallest doubt, or after-thought, I offer you my friendship; and as you may possibly be in want of friends to prosecute your inquiries concerning Kate, what I have to say to you is, just that I hope you will apply to me under such circumstances, and it will give me real pleasure to assist you."

"And was it so generous and rare an offer as this," said Harry Dean, "that you were afraid would be offensive?"

"Well, I don't know—some people view things in the wrong light."

"But not I, sir."

"Well, I am very much delighted; and I am to understand that you accept my offer?"

"By no means."

"Indeed?"

"Hear me, sir. I accept half of your offer, and that the most valuable half—the friendship you are kind enough to promise me; but the money I do not want, for it so happens that I have more —much more than can ever be absorbed by any legitimate wants of mine."

"I rejoice to hear it."

"Alas, sir, if I am as fortunate in my possession of her whom I love as I am in worldly circumstances, I should indeed be happy; but yet I will hope for the best, and I shall not readily forget that, when you supposed I really wanted it, you made me a generous offer."

"Oh don't say a word about that. Make use of my services in any way you can. There is my address; and remember there can be no more welcome visitor at my house than yourself."

"I shall assuredly come," said Harry Dean, "and report progress to you. I must answer that scandal in the 'Morning Herald' as he suggests, I suppose. Indeed, when Kate Destern is the stake I cannot and dare not falter for a moment. Her happiness and safety is paramount. You shall see me to-morrow, Dr. Bell, when I hope to be able to bring you some news."

And thus, then, upon that most eventful day Dr. Bell and Harry Dean separated, the former to attend to his professional duties, and the other with anguish in his looks to think deeply over the distressing news he had received concerning her who was his heart's idol, and without whom he could know no sort of happiness in this world, let the advantages of his position be what they might. Little Lucy walked by his side in silence, until they reached an hotel, when Harry Dean ordered private apartments, and then she flung herself upon his neck as, bursting into tears, she said,

"Our dear Kate is lost for ever."

"No, no, no."

"Oh, yes, Harry, yes; even you look sad and no way hopeful. She is lost, lost, lost!"

"Just now, my dear Lucy, she is but far from being lost to us for ever. I have, from what I have heard, every reason in the world to believe that she is perfectly safe, and that I can take measures which will rapidly have the effect of restoring her to us."

"Ah, Harry! and yet you are so sad?"

"And yet, as you say, I am so sad."

Lucy looked at him inquiringly, and, after a moment's pause, he said—

"It is true that I see the way by which Kate may be restored to us; but it is at a most fearful price, Lucy, that it can only be quickly done."

"Ah, what money can compare with our Kate? But I see, Harry—you mean that you have not got enough to pay for her?"

"No, Lucy, that is not it; and it is not money of which the price consists. It is stern and immutable justice that must be compromised and tampered with to rescue Kate. I will tell you just how the matter stands, my Lucy, and then you can judge for yourself."

"Do, Harry, do. But how distressed you look!"

"I am distressed, dear, but that will pass away. I am going to speak to you of something which has not passed my lips to any one for a long, long time. I am going to tell you a portion—and the most important portion, too—of a secret that is in my hands, and the hands of some of the principal police authorities of this country only.

Lucy began to look a little alarmed, and as Harry Dean proceeded, her whole soul became wrapped up in the words that came from his lips.

"Once upon a time," he said, with a faint smile, "as the old story books have it, I had a good father, who loved me as—as—in fact, as truly as I loved him, and as you would have loved him, had you known him, Lucy."

"I am sure I should, if he was like you, Harry."

"Well, Lucy, he took ill—seriously ill; so much so, that fancying he was near to death, he was anxious to see his brother, from whom he had been long estranged in consequence of the bad conduct of that brother. My father, however, now wished to see him, and to forgive him, as well as to give him some kind and good advice, which at such a time he hoped would have more than common effect upon him."

" And the brother! was he too wicked to come?"

" No. My uncle, that is, the brother, came, and made a pretence of being much affected, and a sort of reconciliation took place between them, but the danger of my father passed away, and the crisis of his disorder being over, he began rapidly to recover. A skilful physician had done much for him, and we were all rejoicing."

" Oh, how much gratitude you owed to that skilful physician!"

" It was Wilkins."

" Wilkins! The man who has taken away our Kate?"

" The same."

Lucy was quite astonished at this statement, and remained gazing at Harry with speechless amazement.

" Yes, Lucy," he continued, " that skilful physician, whom we loaded with rewards, and to whom we thought we owed so much, was Wilkins. But hear the sequel."

" Yes, Harry—yes."

" Suddenly my father died. In the midst of his family, and when we all thought him convalescent, he breathed his last in my arms. Wilkins was hurriedly sent for, and pronounced that he had expired of disease of the heart, which he had suspected existed, but hoped was not in a sufficiently diseased state to be at all alarming for years to come. Now, it so happened that upon the day after the death of my father, there arrived in London a young man named Adamson, to whom my whole family had been very kind, and who had been studying medicine upon the continent, with means afforded to him by us; and it was quite a thunderclap to him to hear of my father's death."

" Ah, he loved him."

" Yes, Lucy, all loved him who knew him."

" Go on, Harry—go on. You do not know how deeply I am interested in what you say. Go on—go on."

" Well, Lucy, this young Adamson and I sat up late at night, and had a long talk about my father's illness, and the

various symptoms that had preceded his disease, when he suddenly said to me, after rather a long silence,—

" ' Do you know, I think Dr. Wilkins quite mistaken.'

" ' In what?' said I.

" ' Why,' said he, ' none of the symptoms were those of the heart disease. It is a very serious case; and now I am going to say something that may shock you, perhaps, but yet it might not. Will you, unknown to any one, permit me to-night to ascertain really and truly what your father died of?'

" ' By dissection?' said I.

" ' Yes,' he replied.

" ' I consented at once. I gave him the key of the room where the corpse lay, and I sat up waiting for him while he went upon his mission. He was gone about an hour, when he came back to me, looking rather pale and excited, and sat down without saying a word.

" ' Well,' I said, ' have you satisfied yourself?'

" ' Yes.'

" ' And the result?'

" ' Is, that your father has been deliberately poisoned!'

" Gracious Heaven!" cried Lucy, " What did you do, Harry?"

" I sprung to my feet, and I recollect that for about two minutes the room seemed whirling round with me. Then I recovered, and seizing Adamson by the arm I said—

" Upon your salvation, Adamson, are you sure of what you say?"

" I am," he replied; " I have made the subject my particular study, and have not the shadow of a doubt about it in my own mind."

" What, what shall I do?"

" I would recommend you to send for a magistrate—or what do you say to going to Dr. Wilkins first and hearing what he has to say about it?"

" Agreed. Come on—come on."

" It was very late, and the rain was coming down in torrents; but off we both set to the house of Dr. Wilkins, which was only a few streets off from my father's.

" And he? Oh, I now begin to suspect," cried Lucy.

" You shall hear. When we reached his door of course it was no fit hour at which to make an usual appeal to the knocker, and I looked for the night bell, which would let him know that he was wanted professionally. I rang it sharply. In about half a minute he looked from an upper window, and I called to him, saying, —

"Dr. Wilkins, we have made an awful discovery regarding my father's death. Will you come to our house directly, if you please ?"

There was a tap at the door at this moment, and Tony putting in his head said, —

"Oh. Never mind. It's only me."

"Come in," said Harry Dean, "come in, Tony. We have no secrets from you. Come in, and sit yourself down."

CHAPTER LXXVIII.

WILKINS'S VILLANY.

"OH, go on," said Lucy, "and tell me all."

"I will," said Harry Dean. "Tony, you have lost the first part of this story, but I will tell it to you in full at some other opportunity."

"Never mind me," said Tony. "You go on and let Lucy know all about it, whatever it is ; go on. From what I hear now, perhaps I shall be able to guess the rest."

"I doubt if you will be able to do that," said Harry Dean, "but I will not keep you in suspense, Lucy, but proceed with my rapid narration which recalls such painful scenes to my mind at once."

"Wilkins replied to me from the window saying, —

"Good God! what have you discovered ? Is your father not really dead ?"

"Oh yes," I said.

"What has alarmed you then ?"

"He has died from poison !'

"Gracious Heavens, you don't say so. I will dress and come after you directly. I dare say I shall be at your house as soon as you will yourself."

"Down went the window, and Adamson and I walked slowly home again in deep discourse about the sad discovery he had made—a discovery which, since from the distress it has involved me in, I have often wished had never been made; and yet Adamson of course could

not for one moment have felt or been justified in concealing from me the discovery of the mode by which my father's sudden death was accomplished.

"Up to this period I can safely say that I really had not a shadow of suspicion against Wilkins, and I as firmly expected him to follow me home as I expected myself to live to reach there ; but when a whole hour had elapsed and he did not come, my mind began to waver a little, and I looked anxiously at Adamson as I said, —

"Adamson, what can keep Wilkins ?" He shook his head.

"I know nothing of him," he said, "you do."

"What do you mean ?"

"I mean that you know his character."

"Indeed I do not," I replied. "All I know of him is, that he was warmly recommended by my uncle as a man who had performed some astonishing cures. Further than that his whole conversation and manner denote a man of singular ability and discursive education, I know nothing of him.

"Adamson was silent. I saw that he was unwilling to say anything about people of whom ne knew nothing ; but when the whole night had passed away and Wilkins did not come near the house, some of the most horrible suspicions concerning him began to take possession of my thoughts. I leant my head upon my hands, and strove to collect my scattered fancies, and to put them into some form and consistency. They just came to this : 1. My uncle's whole course of conduct for many years had been such as might well make any one think him capable of any villany. 2. This physician Wilkins was recommended to my uncle, at a time, too, when he, my uncle, would benefit largely in more respects than one by my father's death, and might make it amply worth the while of an unscrupulous physician to aid him in any act, which might rid him of my father. 3. Wilkins did not come when his presence was so obviously expected, and was so obviously necessary. At least up to this he had not come. I turned to Adamson, and said, —

"What shall you think if Wilkins don't come ?"

"That it is possible he has some

sonnd excuse, for his absence," replied Adamson.

"It is possible," said I. "Let us go to his house."

"We both started off again; and as it was morning now, although early, we knocked at the door. It was answered by a servant, of whom we asked if his master was at home, naming Wilkins.

"Doctor Wilkins is not my master, sir," she said, "he only lodged here, and he is gone now."

"Gone?"

"Yes, sir, he went in the middle of the night, and left a note upon his dressing table, to the effect that he would not come back. He is quite the gentleman, though."

"How do you mean?"

"Why, sir, he left more than enough money in the note to pay all that he owed, and said I might keep the £2 10s., as I'm a sinner."

"Now, Lucy, you will be surprised how I am able to tell you all this so circumstantially, but I was so deeply interested in it, that not one word escaped me that any of the actors in that fearful drama uttered, or was ever afterwards forgotten. I turned from the door, and leaning upon the arm of my friend, I said in a voice of agony,—

"Oh, Adamson, Wilkins has murdered my father!"

"Hush, hush!" he said.

"Why should I be hushed?" I cried. "Good God! am I to feel that so dreadful a crime has been committed, and to take no notice of it?"

"By no means," he replied. "I wish you now to come to the chief magistrate, and detail all the circumstances. I have no wish for you to lose one moment, but do not as yet directly accuse any one. Only speak of the facts you really know as facts, and leave it to others to draw inferences. Come with me at once to the proper authority."

"We went to the chief magistrate, who after hearing all the circumstances said,—

"I will issue a warrant for the apprehension of this Doctor Wilkins, if you please; but really, however you and I may presume that he is guilty from the circumstances, yet the evidence is not sufficient to convict him. It must be more direct, and all I can advise you is to be as quiet about it as possible at present. Of course the police shall be set to work in every possible way to find out this Doctor Wilkins, but when he is apprehended, which no doubt he will be, you should prepare yourself for the possibility of his criminating some one else."

"You mean my uncle," said I.

"I do. It is a sad case. Let me advise you to consider it, and above all things do not allow your excited feelings to allow you to say anything about the affair until we have more evidence than at present."

"'I will be prudent,' I said, 'find Wilkins at any risk, and confront me with him, that is all I ask at present. Fear nothing from any indiscretion upon my part.' With this meagre consolation, Adamson and I left the house of the magistrate."

"And did you find Wilkins?" asked Lucy.

"It's quite romantic," said Tony.

"You shall know all," continued Harry Dean. "I went home, and, by the aid of Adamson, instituted a rigid inquiry into the whole affair, by which it came to be considered, both by him and by myself, as a fact that could not be controverted, that Wilkins had taken advantage of his position, to administer the poison that was the death of my father."

"And your uncle?" said Lucy.

"Alas! there was every reason to believe that he was the employer of Wilkins."

"Horrible! horrible! Oh Harry, what did you do?"

"I relied much upon the promise of the police to soon apprehend Wilkins, when I intended to have the whole affair thoroughly investigated, regardless of any family considerations; but when the magistrate had talked so confidently about finding Wilkins, he little knew the man he had to deal with. All the exertions of the police were absolutely fruitless, and thus time wore on, and I could do nothing. My poor father was consigned to the grave, and the suspicion against my uncle was much too vague and undecided for me to take any steps against him consequent upon it."

"Did he say nothing?"

"We never met. He went abroad in

his yacht, and more than once I was assured that Wilkins had been seen with him. Mere accident, at last, some few days ago, threw Wilkins in my way, and I immediately arrested him, and lodged him in a watchhouse, from which he has, as it appears, contrived to effect his escape; and no doubt, knowing how dear Kate Destern is to me, he has adopted the diabolical plan of seizing her as a kind of hostage for my clemency as regards the charge he knows well I would otherwise vigorously bring against him."

"Ah yes," sighed Lucy. "My poor Kate, to be in the hands of such a monster!"

"A monster indeed! But fear nothing."

"Oh, if I only knew in what baron's castle," said Tony, "he had placed her, wouldn't I go and do something that would astonish their weak minds, rather?"

"But still there is a mystery," said Lucy.

"What mystery?" said Harry.

"You have not told me who and what your father was, nor who this bad —bad uncle is."

"Will you still permit me, Lucy," said Harry Dean, "for reasons which I assure you are sufficient, to keep that mystery still unsolved, and yet trust me?"

"Trust you! Oh, Harry, you know how really and truly I do trust you. If you were surrounded by all the mysteries in the world, you would still be the same dear, good, kind Harry Dean to me."

"This, Lucy, is real trustfulness, and for a wonder, as regards trustfulness in this world, it will not be discovered. Believe me, Lucy, that we shall all be happy yet."

"To be sure we shall," cried Tony,

" 'Romance for me, romance for me,
    And a nice little bit of mys-te-ry.'

come, come, no crying allowed on the premises. Oh, what a rogue that Wilkins is! I shall never trust a man of the name of Wilkins as long as I live."

"Ah," said Lucy, "I can no longer wonder at your having a dread of such a man as this Wilkins, and that you can shrink to save him from the conse-

quences of his crimes, although to do so, will restore to us our Kate."

"Shrink! Ah, no, I do not shrink!" said Harry Dean. "What is all the world compared to Kate? Oh, no. Any sacrifice must be made for her. All the justice in all the world is as nothing compared to Kate."

Lucy, with a gush of tears, flung herself into the arms of Harry Dean, and lay for some five minutes sobbing convulsively upon his breast, before she could say:

"You do indeed, Harry, love Kate, and she shall be yours, and you will be so happy, as in truth you do so well deserve to be."

"That's true," said Tony, "and you'll have all sorts of sunshine continually shining in your path; and your castle— your house, I mean—will resound with mirth and revelry."

"Ah, there will be something dearer than mirth and revelry in Kate's and Harry's house," said Lucy, as she dried her tears.

"I know that," said Tony, "you mean a family.

' The girls with all their mother's wit,
    The boys with all their father's beauty.'

No, hang it, that ain't right. The boys with all,—no, the girls. You know what I mean. The short and the long of it is, that the children are to be nonsuches, that's what I mean, and of course they will be. That's fully well settled."

"I see," said Harry Dean, with a smile, "that at all events I shall not break down in my happiness for want of good wishes and the kind solace of good friends. But now, Tony, mind, I leave Lucy to your care while I go and take some steps absolutely necessary to the restoration of Kate to us, and her rescue from the bad hands she is in."

CHAPTER LXXIX.

KATE'S NEW DANGER.

WE do not like to leave Kate for long by herself in the power of such a man as Wilkins, so once more we return to the lodging-house where she was placed by that designing and most unscrupulous scoundrel. Kate resolved to make one effort to save herself by working upon the cupidity of the landlady, if she found that her humanity was in no way to be aroused; but in so doing, Kate laboured under the disadvantage of not knowing precisely the situation in which she was, and whether or not she was entirely surrounded by the creatures of Wilkins. Of course she had no means of accurately ascertaining whether it was his house or not that she was in, and anything that might even be said to her in the way of seeming information, she had no means of learning the truth of, and might fairly enough doubt considerably. Still, she did not feel disposed to lose anything by neglect, and when the landlady, who, in obedience to the wishes of her lodger, waited upon Kate herself, came into her room, our heroine addressed her:

"You are a woman," she said, "and cannot be wholly devoid of feeling." Alas! Kate forgot at that moment that she had already, in her brief career, met with some women who were devoid of all feeling.

"Oh! yes, miss, we have quite feeling enough," replied the landlady.

"Then you cannot quietly allow me to be so cruelly treated."

"Cruelly treated! Cruelly treated!"

"Oh, yes! most cruelly."

"What? Can you tell me to my face that you are cruelly treated, when you are in the best bed room, with lace and fringe on the furniture that never, originally, cost less than 7s. 6d. a yard, if a penny piece? Cruelly treated, indeed!"

"Alas! may there be no such thing as splendid misery in this world of woe."

The landlady looked puzzled. Splendid misery was, to her, a contradiction in terms. She had no comprehension of it, and she looked at Kate in vacant wonder, making no reply at all to her.

"You do not, or will not understand me," said Kate. "What pleasure can I, as a prisoner, take in this place, were it ten times what it is?"

"A prisoner?"

"Yes. If I am not, open your doors, and permit me to go free."

"Oh, dear—oh, dear, have you no consideration for the F. M.?"

"The what?"

"He ain't a what. He's a F. M."

It was now Kate's turn to look puzzled. "Ah, poor thing!" muttered the landlady to herself, "it's quite clear that her wits are gone wool-gathering. She don't seem to have the least recollection of the F. M.; and that he's her uncle, or something of that sort, I wouldn't mind betting my hall chandelier to a rushlight."

Kate, however, still clung to the hope of interesting this woman in her favour, and she said to her in a voice of much emotion—

"You may be duped as to who and what I am. Believe me, I am but a poor girl—my name is Kate Destern, and I have been torn from my friends by a villain."

"Now, my dear," said the landlady, "you will never get well, if you go on in that way. You really must give up your delusions. Only consider how unhappy you make your brother by them! Think of that."

"My brother?"

"Yes; his lordship."

"I have no brother."

"Ah! poor thing," sighed the landlady, with a sympathetic look, "it's just as he said. Her poor wits are all in a tangle, I declare, and it don't seem as if they would easy come all straight again. Come, now, my dear, all you have to do is, to make yourself as comfortable as you can. I'm sure I'd be mad myself to have the F. M. for an uncle, and all sorts of dukes and duchesses and bishops quarrelling as to who shall take the most care of me— that I would."

"Mad?" said Kate.

"Oh, dear me, what have I said? I don't mean mad—oh, no."

"Stop, tell me truly. Have you really been so grossly imposed upon as to fancy that I am a deranged person? It may ultimately even answer your interest to speak to me fairly upon this subject, and even to aid me."

"Aid you?"

"Oh, yes, I am indeed much oppressed, but I have friends who will not suffer those who are kind to me, to suffer any loss by such aid, I implore you to save me!"

The door opened, and Wilkins stood upon the threshold of the room. There was a look of awful vindictiveness upon his face, and the veins upon his forehead were swelled with passion, as in a voice that, by a great effort was not furious, he said to the landlady—

"I thought, madam, that I had informed you this style of conversation would be highly calculated to increase the infirmity of my sister."

"'Tis false," cried Kate, with energy, "I am not your sister. The lie is even now imprinted upon your face in the flush of shame that yet lingers upon it. You know you have uttered that which is not true."

If a thunderbolt had fallen at his feet certainly Wilkins could not have been more astonished than he was at this most unexpected boldness of the young girl, who, from her feminine and gentle appearance, he had thought, would be too much overcome by her fears to do anything but pray to him for merciful consideration. For a few moments he looked at her as though he had seen her for the first time, and was now intent upon reading her character in her face. As for the landlady, she glanced from one to the other of them in amazement, quite unable to come to anything in the shape of a definite conclusion concerning them. At one moment he thought that if Kate was mad, there was a kind of

"Method in her madness,"

such as she had never before heard of; then, when she looked at Wilkins and remembered the £20 note for contingencies, which was to be replaced by another when that was gone, how could she relate one word which such a personage had said to her, or should say? No; Kate must be mad, since such a lodger said so. There could be no mistake about it. £20 for contingencies! Pho! How could a man be otherwise than quite correct who did such munificent things as that?

"Sir," she said, "if you will believe me, it was the young lady who began talking to me; but, as regards what she said, I assure you that it goes into one ear and out at the other, like the idle wind that blows. You may believe me, sir, that such is the fact."

"Sister," said Wilkins to Kate, feeling that there was an urgent necessity for him to play his part somewhat better than he had been doing—"sister, let me beg of you to be composed."

"Villain!" said Kate, "restore me to my friends."

"Madam, you had better leave her awhile with me," said Wilkins, "I know how to soothe her when she is rather excited, as at present."

"Certainly, sir."

"Oh, no, no," cried Kate. "You may have little feeling, and you may be weak enough to be easily, as it seems, deceived by this man, but I beg of you not to leave me with him. You are a woman, and in your presence I shall still feel some sense of security."

"Ah, poor thing!" said the landlady, as she moved towards the door.

"You see she is very bad to-day," said Wilkins.

"Very," said the landlady; and she left the room.

Wilkins's first movement was to lock the door, after which he advanced towards Kate until he was only a few paces from her, and in a suppressed voice, between his clenched teeth, he spoke—

"Kate Destern, for certain purposes of my own, it became necessary that I should have you in my power. These purposes will be best answered by trusting you will, and in every possible way respecting your condition and sex; but—and now you, for your own sake, should pay particular attention to my words—but I am a man of violent and headlong passions, and if, by your foolish and utterly unavailing abuse and opposition to your quiet and respectable sojourn here for a few days, you drive me out of patience, the consequences of that folly will be all your own, and too late you will bitterly repent it."

Kate shuddered.

"It is time we came to an understanding with each other," added Wilkins. "Is it to be war or peace between you and I?"

"Heaven help me!"

"You may pray as much as you please; but I swear to you, by that Heaven you appeal to, that if you endeavour to tamper with those who are about you, or engage in conversations full of revilings against me, and mad declarations of who you really are, I will adopt a means of quieting you that you now probably little dream of. You are in my power now, and you cannot escape, but while you are here it

(Wilkins awakening from his horrible Dream.)

entirely depends upon yourself to make your position bearable or unbearable."

There was too much real sound reasoning in this for it not to have some consideration and effect upon the mind of Kate, and that it had such effect she sufficiently testified by her silence; but Wilkins was not going to be satisfied by silence. He wanted something like an assurance against a repetition of the scene that had just taken place, and he said—

"It is necessary that I should have your answer."

"What answer can I give?" said Kate. "How can I know that if I submitted to my present condition without a murmur to any one, that I should be treated with the respect you say?"

"By experience."

"Experience?"

"Yes. You have suffered no indignity since you have been here. The privacy of your apartment, so far as you yourself made it practicable, has been respected. Will you promise silence and acquiescence?"

"No, no."

"You will not?"

"I cannot and will not tamper with wrong in such a way. I may suffer, but I will not barter my own sense of what is right on account of any threats that may be used towards me."

"Very well," said Wilkins, as he moved towards the door, "it is war then; and we shall soon see who will first tire of the contest, you or I. You have made a most unhappy determination for yourself. Kate Destern, I would have respected you, for you are nothing to me except as a mere instrument in my views regarding another, and so long as you would have been a passive instrument I pitied you, but now you have roused a personal feeling towards you which is partly hatred—"

He had the door in his hand and paused a moment, ere he added,—

"And partly admiration of your beauty."

In another moment he was gone. Kate heard the door double-locked upon the outer side, and the key removed from the lock. She was a prisoner once more. And now that she was alone she buried her face in her hands, and as the tears trickled between her fingers she began to doubt if it would not have been much wiser after all, if not by any means so heroic, to have bent a little to circumstances and not breathed so stern a defiance to the man who certainly seemed to have power to treat her with a severity very different from what she had as yet experienced. She thought of Harry Dean and of Lucy, and she blamed herself for not being politic as well as brave in her difficulties. She recalled all that Wilkins had said, and the more she thought on his words the more she felt convinced that what he had said was really true.

"Yes," she exclaimed, "it is as a kind of hostage for the conduct of another that I am made a prisoner by this man; and who can that other be but Harry Dean?"

Full of this thought, and dreading that she might be bringing much misery upon him whom she loved so tenderly, by her defiance of Wilkins she moved forwards, saying as she did so,—

"I must tell him that, for the sake of others, I will succumb to circumstances. I must tell him that the hour of my pride and of my defiance has passed away."

She reached the door, and laid her hand upon the handle of it intending to shake it, and to call to Wilkins, who might not be far off; but even then her feelings revolted against the concession she was about to make to such a man, and with a shudder she shrank back.

"Oh," she said, "if I did but feel sure of what was right to do——"

She flung herself into a seat, and remained for a long time in anxious thought, the result of which was, that at all events she would wait until Wilkins or some one from him should think proper to visit her again, before she signified any change in her feelings towards him; and she did not doubt but that her gilded prison would soon be visited by some one.

"Yes, I will so far submit," she said, "as I shall be able to ascertain that such submission is for the happiness of Harry Dean, but no further. I will demand of this man Wilkins an explanation of his enigmatical speeches, and if he will give it to me I will act reasonably and not passionately."

About an hour now passed, during which no one came to the chamber, although more than once Kate heard footsteps hurry past it. The fact was, that the landlady had impressed upon the minds of the servants, that Kate was rather a dangerous lunatic, and they hurried past the door of her room, whenever their duties over the house forced them to pass that way, with all the fright in the world, as though they expected that at some unexpected moment she would bounce out and attack them. Thus was it that every footstep that came near the door went at a railway speed, until the key was placed in the lock again, and she found some one was coming. Her first impression was that it must be Wilkins, as he had taken the key away with him, after double-locking the door; but when the visitor appeared, Kate saw that it was the landlady with a small tray, upon which were some provisions. When she was fairly in the room, Kate spoke to her, saying—

"If you can give me any information

concerning those whose happiness is dearer to me than my own, that will prove to me that I ought for their sakes to remain here without a murmur, I will cheerfully do so."

Kate waited the reply of the landlady, but she waited in vain. That individual was profoundly silent, holding her lips quite close, and breathing in a distressing and laborious manner, through her nose, as though that was the only way to prevent herself from saying a word to Kate. The fact was, that the landlady had promised her lodger that she would not exchange one word with the fair lunatic, and she was determined to keep her word; so, after depositing the tray upon the table, she left the room again, puffing and blowing like a grampus, and carefully locked the door after her.

CHAPTER LXXX.

A NIGHT OF TERROR.

DR. WILKINS was not the happiest man in the whole world under these circumstances, although he was to a certain extent, having things very much his own way. We will take a glance at him in his solitary magnificence.

It has been before stated in this narrative, that the accommodations of Doctor Wilkins in the house where he had taken up his abode with Kate Destern were of the most *recherche* character, and the contrast which the man presented to the room in which he was became soon sufficiently striking to be worthy of comment. The room had the advantage —no evil passions distorted its gorgeous drapery—no ill-repressed aspirations or fears dimmed the lustre of its gilding. In quiet, calm magnificence, it held that human soul which was nigh bursting with contending emotions. The fact was, that wicked, steeped in guilt as he was, this man Wilkins, being educated, and having abilities of no common order, could not always stifle the pangs of conscience.

Kate, in all the doubt and uncertainty of what might be her fate, did not in her gay prison chamber suffer one-half the pangs that Wilkins, who was free to go or come as he pleased, and who was to all intents and purposes succeeding in

what he was about, suffered. Hers were the terrors of what persecution she might have wrongfully to endure. His were the pangs of a guilty conscience, which felt that nothing he could suffer would sufficiently atone for the wickedness of the past. With all his hardened philosophy, he could not at all times persuade himself that in some other world he might not be doomed to suffer infinite agony for the crimes he had committed in this, forgetting that even in this world and among men merely punishments are not pretended to be inflicted in revenge, and that it was not likely a divinity would stoop to be the slave of such a passion.

But he did suffer, and that acutely, for he, at those moments when his intellects were clouded by his conscientious pangs, doubted but that after all the fables of churchmen might be true. If they were, in what sort of condition was he? If even a pit of brimstone was ignited to grill a sinner in, surely Dr. Wilkins required one all to himself, for his iniquities had indeed been of a fearful evil. When these fits of depression came over him, such as after his last interview with Kate, and began to assail his soul, he always tried what he could to shake it off. His general plan was to march to and fro in the room, wherever he might be, if he were alone, and picture to himself the triumphant life he meant to lead in time to come, when he should have shaken off all torments connected with the threatened prosecution upon the part of Hary Dean. At times, when the still small voice had not been very alarming, he nearly had succeeded in shaking it off, but sometimes it clung to him until, bathed in perspiration, he was compelled to have recourse to much more violent measures to still the enemy conscience, that bosom foe, which, despite all exertion,

" Makes cowards of us all."

Upon this occasion he tried in vain to bring his mind back to its ordinary state of composure. After pacing the brilliant apartment for a considerable period with agitated steps, he at length flung himself upon a couch, and with a deep groan, ejaculated,—

"It is in vain. This is one of my days of torture. Shall I never wholly succeed in steeling my feelings against those spectres of the past? Courage, courage! Why, what an arrant fool am I to conjure up images that are more than sufficient to chase the life-blood from my heart!"

He covered his face with his hands, as though, by so doing, he could effectually shut out the thick-coming fancies that his brain teemed with, but it was in vain. In the darkness so produced he saw forms with glassy eyes, and long corpse-like fingers pointing at him, while the skinny death-like lips moved to the words,—

"Thou art a murderer!"

With a shriek he sprang to his feet.

"Off! off!" he cried, "avaunt, ye spectral host! avaunt, I say. I defy ye. Show yourselves to me now in your worst guise, and I defy you. Come to me now—now—now!"

He sunk back again, groaning. His courage was but the rage of a moment, and in a moment it was gone again— evaporating into thin air. He was once more the poor, weak, trembling, con-science-stricken wretch, terrified at his own shadow, and cowering from every sound.

Alas! who would now, let him be sunk in the most wretched mire of poverty, envy that man all that he had gained?

The evening was creeping on, and he began to see the various objects in that gorgeous room with indistinctness. At first, in his nervous and terrified condition, he was afraid it was some failure in his own vision which had produced such an effect. He staggered to the window and looked out. The lamps in the street were being lighted.

"I am the fool of my own senses," he gasped, as he sat down again. "How weak I am!"

After a short time, as the darkness grew upon him, he began to dread sitting in it, and he hastily rang the bell. Before it was answered, he strove to compose himself so as not to exhibit to the servant any traces of emotion. For that purpose, he took up a book and affected to read.

"Did you ring, sir?"

"Yes. Lights."

He did manage to utter these two words with some degree of composure, and that was all. It was a great effort, however, for so small a result. Two tall wax candles were brought to him. They did things right royally in that house, when they had twenty pounds at a time for contingencies, and no questions asked regarding the mode of its expenditure. But Dr. Wilkins was in not much of a humour to appreciate any of the luxuries by which he was surrounded—to tell the truth, he had already almost outlived his taste for these things, which he had completely bartered his peace of mind to obtain. How common a case! He had hoped, that, after dispelling the darkness, or rather the semi-darkness, which was much more suggestive of powerful emotions than as though it had been total, he would soon have recovered some degree of mental serenity, but such was far, very far indeed from being the case. The stings of conscience were not going to yield to two wax candles, although they were placed in silver candlesticks.

"And has it come to this?" he said, after a long pause of silence, during which his countenance underwent many mutations and changes—"and has it come to this, that all my life I have been striving after a phantom;—that I have been sedulously neglecting a substance, to grasp at one of the coldest and most evanescent of shadows?"

This was just what he had been doing all his life. Instead of making for himself agreeable reflections, and garnering up holy thoughts to light him peacefully and happily from the world, when all its shows and beauties should have become dim to him, he had thought of nothing but the acquisition of money, caring not one straw for the mode by which he acquired it, so that he did acquire it in some way, and hoard it up. He must have had a vague idea of, at some time or other, making some very great and glittering display with his ill-gotten wealth. But now, thus he was like Macbeth,

"In the sere and yellow leaf,"

with almost as few friends as the Scottish tyrant could boast of in that dismal autumn of his days, when all had flown from him but his indomitable courage. Alas! for the wretched Wilkins, he had not even that left him. He was not a man to die

"With honours on his back."

Suddenly he sprung to his feet, for he thought of a means which for a time might cheat conscience of its power to wring his soul with such mental agony.

"Yes," he exclaimed, "yes, it is my last resource. It shall not grow into a habit, but I will take it now. I never yet suffered so much as I have this night suffered."

He unpacked a small portmanteau that he had brought from the adjoining room, which was his bedroom, and from the portmanteau he took a little mahogany box, which he opened with a key that was attached to his watch chain. This box contained a number of small articles of value, besides some medicines. From one receptacle in it he found the drug he wanted—opium, that deceitful and wretched solace of such men as Doctor Wilkins.

"'Tis here! 'tis here!" he said.

He held up the small dose of the deleterious extract to the light for a moment, and as he looked at it, he exclaimed solemnly,—

"What a world of strange thoughts and feelings lie within the compass of this small circumference! Who shall tell what my dreams may be, when I have in the stomach's crucible dissolved this enchanter? but, come what may, I will risk it. Anything is better than my present agony—ay! if it give me a glimpse of the infernal house of the damned, I will yet chance it."

He swallowed the opium. After this, fearful that the drug would take probably a more rapid effect than he expected, he put out one of the tall wax candles which had been brought to him, and leaving the other burning he went into the adjoining room, and, only disencumbering himself of his coat, he flung himself upon the bed.

"Sleep—sleep!" he cried, "come, sleep."

It was some minutes, however, yet before the potent spirit that was locked up in that strange drug began to exert its sway upon the mind of Wilkins. He tossed to and fro restlessly for a time, and uttered deep groans, but after a time they subsided and then all was still, save his hard and regular breathing, as he lay in the stillness of repose upon his bed. The opium was commencing its eccentric labours. The drug was doing its work,

but the work that it does is not exactly always what would be dictated to it by those who like it, and rely upon its powers to drown hideous reflection. At times, this good minister and consoler will betray those who trust to it. In this instance it betrayed Wilkins. Instead of soothing, it drove him nearly to madness. Instead of finding himself in some of those delightful regions to which, in imagination, he had at times been transported by the opium, he fancied he was in a large, damp, mouldy vault, which smelt of the dead. He thought that he stood a living man the centre of a mile of spectres, and as he looked from the face of one to the face of the other he recognised familiar features of those whom he had known upon earth, and by poison sent to their long account. Among that ghastly company was the father of Harry Dean. They each raised their hands, from which the decaying flesh hung in putrid masses, and pointed at him while in hideous yelling chorus they chanted—

"Thou shalt do no murder!"

A green sickly light, he thought, irradiated each of the eyes of the ghastly crew, and by the aid of that supernatural glare he saw a staircase winding up—up from the vault into the world above—that world which was still in the hands of the living, and where he at least would not be terrified by such companionship. He fancied that he made one violent effort, and breaking through the horrible throng, he reached the foot of the staircase. A glance upward showed him that it wound upwards in a spiral to a prodigious height. But it was his only resource. Was he to stay there and go mad? Oh, no—no—no; air, and light, and human faces might be above. With desperate speed he rushed up the staircase. He heard a noise; he turned his head and saw the ghastly company pursuing him—how he flew! But hold, suddenly as struck by the wand of a magician he can only creep along at a snail's pace—they near him—they shriek in his wake—they clutch him, and shout their horrible triumph.

"Help! help!" he cried, as suddenly he sprung from the bed.

All was darkness about him. He rushed into the front room. The wax candle still burnt there, but it was nearly consumed. The wick was quite in the socket of the candle-stick, and flickering and spluttering in the last few moments of its existence. A French clock upon the chimney-piece struck in soft silvery tones the hour of three.

"So—so late !" he gasped. "God, what a dream ! Oh, horror ! horror ! horror ! Such another vision, and I am mad—mad—mad ! Yes, quite mad. What shall I do ? What dare I do ? Does ever the devil's drug fail me ? Am I so utterly lost that all it can do is to conjure up in my brain more hideous images than I fly to it to banish ?"

With trembling hands, and after several bungling attempts and failures, he at length succeeded in lighting the wax candle he had, before lying down, extinguished. Scarcely had he done so, when the light from the other died away.

"I am not in darkness," he gasped, "no, no, I am not in darkness, now, although in another moment I should have been, and that is too horrible to think of. I feel as if I were quite sure they were only hiding—only hiding."

The impression upon his mind was—and a truly horrible one, too—that various of the fiends and terrible spectres of his dreams were still hiding in different parts of the room, only being temporarily scared away from him by the light, which was inimical to their existence. With this impression, he looked at every object in the place with a shudder of terror, not knowing what it might conceal. His eyes seemed to be starting from their sockets, and his hair was in wild confusion, and almost inclined to stand on end,

"Like quills upon the fretted porcupine."

After enduring this state for some time, he sank upon a couch, and sat tremblingly alive to the least sound that came upon his ears, and then suddenly he rose, saying in a voice in which mental agitation was struggling with the first conceptions of a firm resolve,—

"I cannot bear this ! I will fly. Such another night as this would drive me distracted. I cannot chance it. I will have my revenge, and then I will once more make an effort to seek in another land, the peace that I have for ever lost in this, and the safety, too, as well as the peace. Ay, the safety, safety ! Yes, that is everything in my eyes, now. I shall sleep o' nights."

CHAPTER LXXXI.
THE ATTEMPTED MURDER.

THE expression of the countenance of Wilkins, as he uttered these words, was so horrible that it could scarcely be called human, notwithstanding it was but the elaboration of a human passion. He was, after all, only carrying out what people who stand brightly in the world's eye do in a smaller way, every day—namely, intense selfishness. But still there was something to be considered before he committed the deed, the first dawn of which was, in the shape of a frightful suggestion, creeping over his soul. That frightful deed was the murder of Kate Destern ! To bring himself up to the mark, which would enable him to do such a deed, he reasoned thus with himself :—

"Already I have done murder, and such a murder, too, that he who pursues me for it, cannot look over it. He is, consequenly, my most implacable enemy ; and upon him I should gloat upon having revenge. There is no revenge in killing one's enemy, none whatever—all must die, and, when the pang is past, where is the revenge ? Who shall say that a few short years might not have developed some disease in the victim—the mental and bodily agony of which would have transcended by a thousandfold the brief pang of parting with existence by the agency of the dagger, the pistol, or the most agonising poison that ever made war against man's vital functions ? No, no. It is a poor, uncalculating, and weak revenge to kill your enemy !"

The light was burning but dimly and the physician trimmed it—his hand shaking so as he did it, that any one would have fancied him in an ague. He then continued his horribly true course of reasoning—

"No, no, I would not kill this Harry Dean, as he chooses to call himself, for the mere purpose of revenge, if by raising my hand he should be dead. I could not stab him, were he here before me unarmed, and with a dagger in my grasp, that is to say, I would not stab him corporeally, because I can stab him mentally! Why should I stab the body, when I can plant a dagger in the soul?"

A ghastly and horrible smile played for a moment, like a light in a sepulchre, upon the face of Wilkins, as he added in a deep hoarse whisper—

"By killing this girl, I take away, at one blow, all the glitter and joy of the world from Harry Dean. Death would be a relief to him, instead then of a revenge to me. I will do it, for I cannot, I will not, live thus, and I should go mad before that which I have commenced in the hope of negotiation could be settled, while, after all, some cross accident might mar the whole scheme, and give me up to his vengeance without a hostage. Yes, she shall die! She shall surely die!"

Alas, little did Kate dream of her danger.

"I am a prisoner," she had said to herself, "and in the hands of an unscrupulous, bad man, but it is sufficiently clear that his interest lies in treating me well."

And so it did; but the night of horror that Wilkins had partially passed, had changed that now; and we have heard from his own lips what new and dreadful ideas it had given birth to. Having thus, then, settled in his own mind that he would take the life of Kate Destern, Wilkins began to think of all the minor accessions to his plan, as to how he was to do the deed with the least chance of alarm, and how he was to escape from the house when it was done. He was not a man to have anything to chance, if he could possibly help it. In order to counteract the remaining effect of the opium he had made so free with, he took from his medicine chest some nitric acid, in crystals, and having dissolved it in water, he took a liberal dose. Then he began to arrange for a hasty departure. He thought first it would be prudent to extinguish the wax light, and he did so, substituting in its place a small spirit lamp, which enabled him to see sufficiently without its beams reaching far enough to alarm any one. With this spirit lamp in his hand, he crept down stairs to see how the street door was fastened, as for aught he knew he might have to undo it in the dark. There were only

a couple of bolts and a chain. He took down the latter carefully, and then felt certain that in any hurry or emergency he could undo the bolts. Being satisfied, then, that his escape was easy, he cautiously made his way to his room again, and began to place in his pockets such things as he intended to take with him, for, after doing the deed, he wished to walk directly from the chamber of death and to leave the house.

"I will leave nothing to do but to escape," he said, "after it is done. A moment's delay might sacrifice me."

And so, with all this horrible ability and calculation, Wilkins prepared himself for a deed that was one of the most cold-blooded and horrible that the mind of man can conceive—the murder of a beautiful and unoffending young girl—in order to be revenged upon somebody who loved her. In the course of a quarter of an hour more he was ready. The clock upon the chimney-piece struck four. Wilkins startled at the sound.

"The time hurries on," he muttered. "What must be done, must be done now quickly. This night has been, and is to be, one of horror to me, and it shall be one of horror to others, and most of all shall it be a night of horror to him whom I hate—this work for Harry Dean, who, with his show of humility, strives to make poverty look what it is not—graceful."

Once more he looked around him. He had forgotten nothing. No, all was right. The spirit lamp cast its strange gleams upon the costly hangings and the rich gilding of the room, and Wilkins smiled bitterly as, after a search in the breast of his apparel, he produced a small fine poniard, not above six inches in length, and of exquisite workmanship. The handle was of ivory, richly carved.

This weapon he had picked up abroad, and for a long time had always kept it about him in case of any sudden emergency, for that man walked about like Ishmael, with all men's hands against him, and his hand against all men's. In every honest face he saw an enemy. Horrible condition! and yet it was one that for years had grappled with him. There are many such men as Wilkins in the great world, although some may, by superficial observers, escape detection, especially when circumstances do not occur to bring into activity their latent powers of mischief.

"Four!" he gasped, "four o'clock. I must hasten. How this night has sped on! I must lose no more time. Each moment of it may now be precious to me."

With the spirit lamp in his hand, and the poniard concealed partially up the sleeve of his coat, Wilkins slowly crept from his room, and made his way up the softly-carpeted staircase to the apartment occupied by Kate Destern. Oh, how he shook and started at his own shadow upon the walls as he went! How fearfully was his countenance distorted, and how strangely he breathed as he went step by step to the perpetration of this unhallowed deed! One would scarcely have thought such a man as Wilkins would have suffered so much anterior to the commission of any iniquity, save a murder; but there were circumstances that made this projected murder most peculiar. In the first place, although he had taken life before, it had been from motives of a personal character towards the victim. There were no such direct motives in this case. Then again, he had always attained his end by some covert means, such as poison. This was the first time he had actually contemplated the vulgar use of a weapon in the perpetration of a murder, and he had no time for any other mode. No wonder, then, that Doctor Wilkins felt a little nervously disposed, under such a, to him, novel combination of events and conditions; but, nervous as he felt, it was not yet quite sufficient to induce him to forego his intention. He still, with the stealthy step of the cur, crept up the staircase. Once or twice, a thought of the wondrous beauty of Kate Destern came across him, and he whispered to himself—

"Oh, if I could but have got such a creature to fly with me to another land, and gild my retirement with her more than mental charms, I might yet have tasted of happiness; but there is no hope of that. I know she loathes me."

"Right, Wilkins—right. She does loathe you."

Now he fancied he heard a slight noise; and with all his senses concentrated to the aid of that one, he stopped to listen. All was still. It was only one of those strange, unaccountable noises, which, amid the stillness of the night, will occur in all houses—noises which have many a time got folks out of their beds to look for the cause of, and yet always ended in a fruitless search. After a few moments, he got convinced that it was nothing and he proceeded with more courage than before. The slight noise, whatever it was, had broken the frightful chain of thought which had laid hold of his faculties for the preceding few moments. Now he reached the landing. Upon that landing there were only two doors, opening respectively to two bed-rooms. It was in one of these—the most costly —that Kate reposed. The other was to let, as the landlady had informed him, Wilkins, so that he had the whole of that floor of the house to himself, for those two bed-rooms, being very spacious, fully occupied it. No interruption, therefore, was likely to ensue, and as he stood by Kate's door, he felt that he held her fate in his hands, and that he could not possibly have any sort of difficulty in carrying out his dreadful plan. The only sounds that met his ears were the roll and rumble of some night carriages in the streets of the great city, and these came to him subdued by distance into but a faint murmur, after all, and then he was with life and death in his hands. The spirit lamp shed its sickly rays about it, and fell upon the ghastly face of that man, who looked more like some fiend than anything human. But he did not repent him yet of the evil that he meant to do. But now he asked himself some anxious questions.

"Will she scream?" he whispered, "will she scream?"

The idea that he might not, by the first blow he should strike, effectually deprive her of life, haunted him, and he asked himself, what would be the result of her shrieks alarming the whole house, nay, the whole neighbourhood? That would be to him terrible! How should he escape then, with the blood of his victim, perchance, upon him? No, no, she must not be permitted to scream. He must take good care that she had no time for that. But then he would like to do the deed in the dark, or in such partial darkness that he should not see her face. Even he was afraid that a glance at the sweet, almost childish beauty, of that

[HARRY DEAN AND DR. BELL LEAVING THE RAFFLE.]

countenance, would disarm him, and deprive him of the power to strike. 'No, no,' he said, 'I must not—I dare not, look at her. I could not do it if I looked at her; and yet, how can I, in dusk or in darkness, be sure of my blow. Oh, what a horrible position is this! And yet shall I not be revenged upon him who would take my life—who would place me upon a scaffold to be the gibe and jest, and the spectacle to a multitude? Yes, I will have my revenge. This poniard will make a worse cut in his heart than in the heart of this young girl whom he loves. She is doomed for his sake!'"

Now the grand thing was to ascertain if Kate was sleeping or waking. If the latter, he had not determined how to proceed, but if the former, he would despatch the dreadful business at once, for he began to feel with Macbeth, that

" 'Twere well done, if 'twere done quickly."

He listened, with his ear as close to the door as though it had been nailed to it, and he heard, or fancied that he heard, the deep and regular breathing of one in a sound and dreamless slumber. No other sound reached him.

"Yes, she sleeps—she sleeps! Her last sleep! She will not awaken from that sleep in this world. This world? What do I say? There is no other world. I will not believe for a moment that there is, or what would become of me?"

He shuddered as he spoke. It would not do for that guilty man to dream for one moment even of a future. If he had he must have gone mad. He now placed his hand upon the lock of the door, and endeavoured to stir it so gently that the lightest sleeper could not have been awakened by it. This he fully succeeded in, and the door opened noiselessly upon its well-constructed hinges. The moment he projected that hideous visage of his within the doorway he heard more plainly still the deep breathing of the sleeper, and he drew himself a long breath of relief as he said—

"Yes, all is well—she sleeps!"

He was afraid to bring the spirit-lamp into the room, for although the light that it gave was of the faintest character, yet he thought some wandering ray from it might by a possibility fall upon the sleeper's eyes and awaken her. He, therefore, to guard against even this remote contingency of evil, to his purpose, left the lamp upon the landing. The door, however, was a little way open, so that the spirit-lamp sent into the room a dim and dubious sort of twilight. This was all Wilkins wanted —he only wished to see sufficiently to prevent himself from stumbling over anything in the room. He did not wish any light to shine upon the blood—the pure and innocent blood he was about to spill. He dreaded to be for the future haunted by some look from his victim, which might remain in his remembrance while he lived. He had already had some experience in impressions of that kind. Now he removed from his coat sleeve the poniard with which he was to do the fatal deed, and step by step he approached the bed. Oh, Heaven! Had that man's better angel for ever deserted him, leaving the field of his heart in sole possession of the fiend? It would seem so, for he

paused not now in his path towards his victim, whose regular breathing he could still hear. There can be no doubt whatever now, but that Wilkins was in that state of mind which sets all reflection at defiance. The intense excitement of the last few hours had fevered his brain sufficiently to render him quite incapable of any rational power of thought, and for the time being he became a sort of monomaniac—a man without one idea, except the murder of Kate Destern, to be avenged upon Harry Dean. Nothing but violence— nothing but some strong hand striking him down dead upon the spot, would have stopped him in his progress as he wound his way stealthily towards the bed. The room was a large one, so it took some time to reach the bed, at the rate he was going. Oh, if the poor sleeper could but have awakened during that time! Surely it would have been better to have had a struggle for life, than there to be butchered in sleep. To exchange so suddenly and so awfully the sleep of calm repose for that of death! And now he reached the bed. His eyes had got sufficiently accustomed to the dim light to enable him to see the outline of the form and face that there lay. How sound she slept. Alas! poor —poor victim! Awake! awake! Is there no spirit to whisper in your ears "murder?" With his left hand Wilkins felt for the breast of his doomed one. He could not be mistaken. His hand touched the warm bosom—his left hand, and then he raised the right. For one brief instant the dim rays from the lamp fell upon the keen and glittering blade, and then, like a flash of lightning, down it came with a sickening crush! Up—up to the hilt! Up to the hilt in the warm quivering flesh—splash, splash, bubble came the hot blood. The murderer's hand shook, and with a snap the handle broke from the blade of the poniard. There was one faint cry—a choking—a bristling scream, as if from one drowning in blood, and then all was still.

"It is done," said Wilkins. "It—is —done. I—I—am revenged. Hush, hush! It is all over now. Oh, God— oh, God! no—no, there is no God for me. No—no—no—no. Mercy!"

CHAPTER LXXXII.

A CLUE TO THE LOST ONE.

"AND so, Harry, you really think our dear Kate will be restored to us," said Lucy, as, with Harry Dean's hand clasped in her own, she looked occasionally in his face.

"I do, Lucy."

"Oh, happy thought."

"We will do our utmost. Go and tell our friend Tony to get ready to accompany us. We will now, that I have taken the step dictated by the scoundrel Wilkins, with regard to the advertisement promising him an indemnity for the past, go at once to Doctor Bell, and get a more accurate description, if we can, of the carriage in which Wilkins conveyed away our dear Kate."

"Oh yes," said Lucy, "if we did but know exactly what sort of carriage it was, we might meet it in the streets and follow it. Oh, what joy it would be in such a way to find our Kate."

"It would, but you must recollect what London is, Lucy, and how rare i is to find what you search for within its streets. Two of the dearest friends in the world, with all the wish to meet each other, might wander about for years in London without encountering."

"And yet people do meet each other?"

"Yes. By accident. I have sometimes twice in one day met an acquaintance, and then, although we are both of us in London, we have not met again for a year, that is, presuming we are not visiting acquaintance. But," added Harry, perceiving that Lucy looked disappointed, "that shall not obstruct or prevent us from doing all we can."

"No! no! it ought not."

"Come, then, we will go to the doctor's house and talk with him about the whole affair. I should like to criminate the villain if it be possible o to do, with at the same time no sompromise for the safety of Kate, but ce will think over all that at Doctor Bell's."

Lucy and Tony were both soon ready to accompany Harry Dean to the benevolent physician's house—that physician who was so great a contrast to his brother Esculapius Wilkins. In answer to the enquiry, they were gratified to find that the good doctor was within, an they were ushered into the very same waiting room which Wilkins had occupied while expecting Mrs. Bell to make her appearance upon the occasion of his getting possession of Kate. They had not to wait long before Dr. Bell appeared, and holding out his hand to Harry Dean, he said,—

"Ah, my young friend, do you bring me news?"

"Of the lost one?"

"Yes. Yes."

"No. Alas! no. Things remain precisely as they were, and yet, apart from the natural disquietude I cannot but feel at the situation ot Miss Destern, I have no fears for her ultimate safety. The whole affair is one of calculation, and as I shall readily yield—and indeed have already done so—to the result of Wilkins's speculation, all will be well, so far as Kate is concerned."

"But, my dear sir, it is a shocking thing that such a rascal should go unpunished."

"It is a shocking thing."

"Can nothing be done?"

"If nothing, it shall not be for want of trying. The safety of Miss Destern compels me at once to adopt the course dictated by the scoundrel Wilkins, and to negotiate with him upon his own terms for her restoration, but if, finding that by negotiation I cannot by any means discover his retreat, I will soon let him see that his career is at an end."

"Well," said Dr. Bell, "I have no doubt you adopt the only wise course. Can I in any possible way aid in circumventing the rascal. If I can, I need not say what pleasure it will give me to do so. You have but to point out to me a path, and I will take it."

"I do not know that you can do anything more than just give as accurate a description as you can of the carriage in which this Wilkins came to your house."

"For that, you must ask Mrs. Bell. I was not at home, you know—she is in the drawing-room, I think, so we will go to her at once, if you will have the goodness to follow me."

A few moments found the whole party in the said drawing-room, where Mrs. Bell gave to Harry Dean and Lucy, not forgetting Tony, a lady-like welcome, and in reply to the question put to her she said,—

"Really, I hardly looked at the chariot, but—appealing to her husband—I dare say, my dear, that our footman Sam looked at it—servants usually do take notice of such things. Suppose we call him up, and hear what he has to say ?"

"Humph !" said Dr. Bell.

Harry Dean looked rather surprised, but Mrs. Bell explained what the doctor's "Humph !" meant, by saying,—

"The fact is, our footman having a great deal of indulgence from us with regard to the use of his spare time, has joined the—the—what is it, my dear ?"

"Oh, I don't know."

"Well, it's some society for the diffusion of everything; and he has become so scientific that, at times, we, who like things by ther proper plain names, don't know really what he means."

"Yes," said the doctor, "like your societies and institutions for making philosophers of the million. Sam has substituted for a plain language, that he did understand, a perplexing one that he don't, but however we must have him up, and hear what he has to say for himself. He may, or may not have taken notice of the carriage. If he has done so, you may depend upon it he will explain to us in the most scientific manner what he has seen."

The doctor rang the bell, and by good luck Sam answered it.

"Come in, Sam," said Dr. Bell, "I wanted to see you. Shut the door, and come in at once ; you must answer this gentleman some questions."

"Beg pardon, sir," said Sam, "but I have got outside the door a vehicle containing some *fossiliferous cryptomania*."

"Some what ?"

"Vulgarly called coals," added Sam. "I will *expectorate* them into a corner, or some one may *gravitate electrically* over them like a *campanology*."

"Good God ! you are worse than ever to-day," said Dr. Bell. "Do you fancy that all those words you have stuffed your stupid head with may be used just at random ?"

"*Stenographically*, sir."

"Grant me patience ! Mr. Dean, you will be so good as to ask your own questions. You see Sam is like the

learned pig. He picks up a word that he knows about as much of as of the manners and customs of a dinner party in the moon."

"*Dentoulogically*," said Sam, looking as wise as an owl in a fit.

"Now, my good fellow," said Harry Dean, "do speak plain English if you please. Do you recollect the exact colour of the carriage which took the young lady away who was staying here, or did you take accurate notice of the livery of the footman, or if there was a crest upon the carriage, and if so, what ?"

"Not being a *campanologist*," said Sam, "I really cannot *scarify vertically*. But if you will put your questions *crustaceously* I will endeavour to be *efflorescent*."

"You see," said Dr. Bell, "your labour in questioning Sam will be thrown away."

"So it seems," said Harry Dean.

"Perhaps you are not a *numismatical chonchologist* ?" said Sam. "I am."

"Now, Sam," said Dr. Bell, who had been writing a few words upon a small slip of paper which was upon the ta'le, "take this—I think you will find it plain English. You can study it at your leisure. Go away now."

Sam took the paper and read, "I hereby give you, Samuel Gwibbins, one month's notice from this day to quit my service.—GEORGE BELL."

"Oh, sir ! you don't mean that ?" said Sam.

"Pertinaciously yes."

"Oh ! oh ! I can't go. Oh, sir ! I won't be *skientific*, I won't—I'm plain Sam Gwibbins; a month's notice, I didn't expect that. Oh, dear ! gentlemen, I seed the chariot, yellow and black with a cat's head on the panel. The footman in white coat and green plush beg-your-pardonables and one eye—should know the whole affair again any where—two hours afterwards was at the bar of the 'Hedgehog and Water Lily'—saw the same footman having a go of something short."

"Oh, you can speak plainly at last."

"Oh, dear ! yes, master. Do take back this little bit of paper, sir, I won't not never be *skientific* again no how, I assure you, sir."

"Very well, Sam. Now mind, if I hear you call anything again out of its name you shall have this bit of paper again freshly dated."

"And you say you saw the footman at a public house?" remarked Harry Dean, much irritated.

"Oh, yes, sir."

"Did you speak to him?"

"No, sir."

"Then you have no idea where to find him, I suppose. Alas! alas! it is but a faint clue indeed."

"Oh, yes, sir, I know where to find him at eight o'clock to-night."

"Is that possible?"

"Yes, sir; only listen. After he had paid for his go the landlord said to him, 'I think you are one in the raffle ain't you?' 'Yes,' says he, 'when does it come off?' 'Why, to-morrow night,' says he, 'at eight. Will you be here, or shall anybody throw for you?' 'Oh, I'll come,' said the footman; 'I wouldn't be away on any account. You may expect me punctual to the minute,' says he, and then away he went, and you may depend upon it, sir, that will be the place to find him."

"I think so too," said Dr. Bell.

"This is a mercy," said Harry Dean. It is a clue indeed, if there be no mistake in it."

"No mistake whatever, I assure you, sir, if you please," said Sam. That man once seen is known, sir."

"We will talk this over, sir, if you please," said Harry Dean to Dr. Bell, who understanding him, told Sam he might leave the room, and when they were all alone again, Harry Dean added,

"Do you think that what your footman has said can be depended upon? You know him of course better than I, and probably have an opinion as to his character of truth telling."

"He's a goose," said the doctor, "but he has been with us two years, and we never detected him in a falsehood, or in a dishonest or tricky action. My fair impression is, that what he has just now told you is possibly the truth."

"I am rejoiced to hear you say so."

"Ah, so am I," said Lucy, "for now we shall find our dear Kate.

"Do not be too sanguine," said Harry. "We will do our best, and that is all we can do, Lucy."

"What will you do?" said Dr. Bell.

"I will go," replied Harry, "to the raffle for the accordian at the public-house, and if you will permit me, I will take Sam with me to identify the man—then, by threats and promises, I will endeavour to shake his fidelity to Wilkins, if he really have any."

"I will go with you," said Dr. Bell.

"A thousand thanks."

"We cannot be too strong a party, and now, as it is to be this evening, let me beg you and your friends to be my guests for the remainder of this day, and then this young lady can remain with Mrs. Bell while we go to see if we cannot get some news of her sister for her. Who knows but we may be eminently successful."

"With pleasure, sir," said Harry Dean, "do I accept your kind hospitality."

Tears of joy stood in the eyes of Lucy now at the hopeful aspect of affairs, and she could only look from the face of Harry to that of Dr. Bell to gather food for hope from each as far as it was possible to do so.

"It will be desirable," said Harry, "for our friend Sam to disguise himself."

"I will manage that," said Dr. Bell. "Of course if he went in his ordinary apparel, as it is so close at hand, there is very little doubt he would be known for my footman, and then the fellow upon whose fears you wish to operate might be put sufficiently upon his guard to elude you. I should advise, before you speak to the fellow at all, you dog him to his home."

"It shall be done."

"You see in that case, Mr. Dean, you will have some clue to him, whereas otherwise, if he fairly run away from you in the street, perchance you would be no wiser than you are now, and I think you will agree with me, that what is to be done had better be done by arts and by persuasion than by force."

"I do, indeed."

"Very well then, now we will go to dinner, and after it arrange all the little essentials of the plan, which I really begin to think promises as fairly as any thing very well can."

"Oh, yes," said Lucy, "I almost feel as if Kate were aleady restored to us."

"I hope," said Harry, "that we

shall soon be able to tell ourselves that she is so in reality—until then hope, Lucy, hope."

Tony was quite delighted at all these proceedings, they smacked so much of genuine romance that they ensured his full approbation ; disguises—plots—such matters were completely in his line, he put on such a look of mystery that any one who had not known this little peculiarity of Tony, would entirely have thought him just a little out of his senses, and have avoided him accordingly. The day wore on, and it became necessary for Sam to assume his disguise, in doing which he was cordially assisted by Tony, who, however, would have liked him much better to dress as some mysterious bandit. Indeed, Tony went so far as to suggest various modifications of the plans of Harry Dean, but as those modifications smacked much more of romance than usefulness, they were only received by a smile of incredulity.

"Tony," said Lucy, "this will be quite a romance for you to write."

"Yes," he replied; "but I'm afraid I shall never get quite through 'The Murderer's Bride ; or, The Fiend of the Marrowfat Caverns ;' but when I have finished that I shall certainly begin upon another, you may depend."

By the hour of seven the disguise for Harry Dean, which was found to disguise him a little, so as not to appear so much of a gentleman, was complete, and the party, consisting of Dr. Bell, Harry Dean, and Sam Gwibbins, who had not been in the least scientific since the notice to quit, departed for the public-house with the euphonious sign. The distance was very short, but on the route they had time to appoint Sam Gwibbins as spokesman. His instructions were to ask if any chances in the raffle still remained open, and if so to take them for himself and friends.

"You may depend, gentlemen," said Sam, "that there will be plenty of chances left. These raffles are got up for the landlord, and he, after they have hung about for a long while, is, in a manner of speaking, forced to bring the matter to a wind-up, by taking the remaining chances himself, and he will be only too glad to get rid of some of them to us, if we ask him."

By this time they had fairly reached the threshold of the public-house, and e neighbouring church clock struck at th same time the hour of eight.

———

CHAPTER LXXXIII.

THE RAFFLE AT THE PUBLIC-HOUSE.

SAM GWIBBINS was right. The landlord of the public-house had just three shares in the raffle for the "finest accordian as never was," which he could let the gents have, and they had them accordingly. Our friends placed fictitious names upon the list; Sam wrote, in legible characters, "Blue Beard !" as his assumed cognomen, which rather astonished the landlord, who did not really know whether he ought to laugh at the gent or not. Harry Dean luxuriated in the ancient English name of Smith, and the learned doctor thought Jones would be about as anti-suggestive a name as he could very well hit upon.

"Up stairs, if you please, gents, into the coffee-room," said the landlord.

They ascended into this room called a coffe-room ; probably, however, a cup of that beverage had never once been within its walls, in much the same way that a bishop is called holy when his whole soul is intent upon lucre. This room was a large rumbling apartment, with a palpable division in the room to show that it had been composed of two apartments originally, and an awkward step of about six inches high, all along the centre of the floor, down which everybody always fell twice or thrice before they could get into the habit of recollecting that one half of the coffee-room was upon a different level to the other half. Glazy-looking mahogany tables—walnut wood chairs; with excruciatingly hard seats—a pile of hideous-looking receptacles for the expectoration of those who stultified themselves, and became a walking nuisance to others by the use of tobacco, and a number of prints—plain and coloured—upon the walls, completed the apartments of the coffee-room These prints, of course, consisted of a view of Barclay's brewery, the Licensed Victuallers' Asylum, and a long flourishing list of odds and ends, announcing that the landlord was an "Odd Fellow " and belonged to some lodge, and was a past M.W.F.F., or a present F.O.O.L., and a worthy of trotting horse, pugilistic, and by-gone Derby notoriety. Such was the "Coffee Room" of the public house where Harry Dean hoped to meet the man without an eye, or, rather with only one eye, from whom, by fair means or foul, he hoped to extract some information concerning Wilkins. The room began rapidly to fill, and Harry Dean was somewhat startled by a sudden hideous sound, something between a scream and a groan, close to his elbow; when, starting round with the exclamation of "Good God, what's that?" a gentleman with a white hat that had seen better days, said,—

"It's only me a trying of the accordian."

"Is it possible?" said Harry.

"Yes; a good tone, hasn't it?—Difficult to play it."

Harry Dean said nothing, but he thought that if the difficulty should happen to reach the impossible, it would be quite a mercy. He looked everywhere for the man with the defective optics, but in vain, until Sam gave him a nudge of the elbow, and said,—

"There he is."

"Where?—where?"

"Only just come in, and speaking to the landlord, there. Don't you see him, sir? What a bad-looking fellow he is to be sure. There, now he's a looking this way, sir."

"Ah, yes."

"You see him?"

"I do,—I do. Will this raffle business soon be over, think you, Sam Gwibbins?"

"Oh, yes; they are writing down the names now, and then they will put 'em all in a hat, and the one as draws out first will have the first throw with the dice also, as you know."

Harry Dean was not very much enlightened, but he kept his eyes fixed upon the man with one eye, resolved that if he left the room, he, Harry Dean, would be after him at once; but the man had no suspicions, and betrayed no sort of intention to get out of the way; on the contrary, he began to make himself quite conspicuous, and to play off the great man. He became the bustling director of the proceedings, so that there was no sort of difficulty in keeping him in sight. And now the drawing of names

began; a boy—as though in a boy there must be truth and innocence, when all the world knows that boys—but no matter;—a boy was brought in to draw the names, and, as they were drawn and delivered, the dice were rattled, and the numbers of each throw duly scored. The excitement was quite terrific, as the various numbers gained by the competitors were shouted out; but when, with a stentorian voice, the landlord said,—

"Blue Beard, twelve," there was the most intense excitement. A few minutes more, and the raffle was over, the accordian finding its way into the hands of Sam Gwibbins.

"I tell you what it is, Sam," whispered Dr. Bell, "if that infernal groaning and screaming machine comes into my house, a certain notice to quit shall be again produced."

Sam, like the admiral in the song,

"Shook,—'twas for an instant,"

then, with a groan, he said,—

"What shall I do with it, master? I have won it, worse luck, and here it is."

"You may do what you like, but it don't come home."

"I say, young fellow," cried the landlord, to Sam, "would you like to have the accordian in the box, and raffle it again? What do you say to that, eh?"

"Oh, yes," said Sam, eagerly. "Oh, yes, that will be the very thing. I don't want it."

"Then what the deuce did you come here for, and win it, from people as did want it?" said the gentleman with the one eye only.

"Oh, bless you!" said Sam, "what a nice looking creature you are. Any one might eat off you."

This sarcastic allusion to the anything but prepossessing looks of the fellow, produced a roar of laughter at his expense, and glancing savagely at Sam with his one eye, he said,—

"We shall meet again."

"I hope not," said Sam. "It's given me a pain in my inside to look at you this once."

The fellow would have made a rush at Sam, but the company prevented him; and Harry Dean whispered to Dr. Bell,—

"Let us leave now, and meet the rascals coming out in the street."

"Yes, yes."

In a few moments after Sam had left the sum he had to pay for drink, being the winner at the bar, they were all three in the street, waiting rather anxiously for the appearance of their friend, whom they had heard named in the room as Joe Pugsey. In the course of a quarter of an hour he made his appearance at the door of the public-house, and they heard him say to some one—

"I won't be above half an hour; but if the old fool comes home he is sure to walk round to the stable, and if I ain't there, there will be a row to-morrow."

The fellow then set off at a rambling quick pace, without once looking behind him, so that our friends had no trouble at all in following him to a mews in the neighbourhood, down which he suddenly dived. This place was rather dark, and they were afraid of losing sight of him, so they hurried after him with some precipitation, even at the risk of him seeing them, until they watched him pause at a stable-door, and lifting the latch, enter and close it behind him. Above this stable there were two or three dwelling rooms, from the windows of one of which beamed a light; and as Harry Dean watched those windows closely, he saw upon the blind of one of them, a shadow, of which he had every reason to believe was that of Mr. Pugsey. Upon this, our friends called a sort of council of war.

"How are we to proceed, now?" said Dr. Bell.

"I propose," said Harry Dean, "that we go up to the room where he is sitting at once, and force the informa-tion from him that we require."

"But if he refuses, sir?"

"Then I shall take him into custody, most assuredly; and give him over to the police. Perhaps the threat of doing that may open the gentleman's faculties to the propriety of being quite explicit with us upon the subject matter of our nquiries.

"Possibly."

"Well, I will lift the latch as care-fully as I can, and we will, as noiselessly as possible, creep into the stable; come on, come on, as I don't think we ought to lose any time."

"Don't you, young fellow," said a voice, and Harry Dean found himself suddenly seized by the collar, and the light from a policeman's lantern shone in his face. "Don't you?—I rather think you are nabbed now. It's rather lucky, as our superintendent keeps his *oss* in the *oppersite* stable, or else I should not have been here, rather. Sir—sir! I've nabbed some cracksmen.'

"What is the matter?" said a stout man, crossing the dirty roadway of the mews, from a stable upon the opposite side. "What is the matter, now?"

"Nobbled some chaps," said the policeman, "as I overheard just now planning a robbery."

"Indeed?"

"Sir," said Harry Dean, "are you a superintendent of police?"

"Well, what then?"

"I wish to speak to you a few words in private, immediately. I will follow you to the stable you have just come from, if you please."

There was something in the tone and manner of Harry Dean that induced the superintendent to grant the request, although he did not do so with a very good grace it must be confessed, but that undefinable something which proclaims the gentleman stuck to Harry Dean, and the few words he uttered sounded so like a command from one who was accustomed to be obeyed, that almost in a state of unconsciousness that he had an option in the matter, the superinten-dent to the stable preceded him across the way.

"I will return directly," said Harry to Dr. Bell.

A glance from the supreintendent to the policeman let him know that he was to keep charge of the two others, and then he and Harry Dean disap-peared in the opposite stable, where a dim light was burning produced by a candle stuck against the wall.

"Now, sir," said the superintendent, trying to recover some portion of his ordinary importance.

Harry Dean carefully closed the door, and Dr. Bell and Sam Gwibbins entirely lost sight of him and the superin-tendant for the space of about five minutes. When the door was opened again, the superintendent was executing a low bow with his hat in his hand; Harry Dean preceded him for a few

[THE ABDUCTION OF KATE DESTERN.]

feet, and then turning, he said to him in a voice of calmness,—

"Will you be good enough to speak to the policeman?"

"104," cried the superintendent.

"Here!" said the policeman.

"Do you see this gentleman?"

"What the—the—cracksman?"

"No, y u ignorant beast. This gentleman, who has convinced me he is no cracksman; now understand, you are under the orders of this gentleman, and you will do whatever he directs you to do. You fully comprehend that, now?"

"Y—ye—yes," stammered the astonished policeman.

"That will do," said Harry Dean; "I am much obliged."

"Why, what is the meaning of all this?" said Dr. Bell.

"My dear sir," said Harry Dean, "I hope the time will very soon come—nay, I am quite sure it will—when anything that seems a little mysterious in my conduct just at present will be, to your perfect satisfaction, cleared up."

"Of that I entertain no manner of doubt," said Dr. Bell; only I'm much afraid that I am acting with some one to whom I am paying scarcely sufficient respect."

"It is I who ought to pay you respect," said Henry Dean, "considering the great obligations I feel myself under to you, so say no more upon that head. Come, follow me."

"What am I to do, your worship?" said the policeman, who now imagined that Harry Dean must be some magistrate in disguise, and so gave him the common title of one.

"Just remain here within call."

"Yes, your worship."

Harry Dean lifted the latch of the stable door so gently that it gave no sort of alarm to Mr. Joe Pugsey, and the three entered the precincts of not the most salubrious stable in the world.

"Hush," said Harry, "hush; do not speak a word any of you. I should rather like, upon this occasion, to take Mr. Pugsey completely by surprise."

"God bless me!" said Dr. Bell, "what's that? I think I have tumbled over a horse, or some animal as big as one."

Sam coughed, and a horse gave a short sort of half-cough, half-neigh, as though he did not know exactly whether to be pleased or not by the doctor's intrusion into his stall so very unceremoniously.

"Hush, hush," again said Harry; "I have found the staircase. Come on."

"All's right."

"Lay hold of my skirt, and I will guide you."

The doctor laid hold of Harry Dean's skirt, and Sam laid hold of the doctor's, so they got on, up a narrow and rather steep staircase, without any further difficulties impeding their progress than were incidental to some loose articles, such as a pail with a mop in it, and such like, being in the way. Harry reached at length a small landing, and by the gleam of light that came through a parted opening of the door of the room in which Mr. Pugsey was sitting, he could see that gentleman very well, as well as hear the observations he made to Mrs. Pugsey about things in general and his own affairs in particular. Mrs. Pusey was a dark-visaged, cunning-looking, stout-made woman, with an eye that had in it a world of trickery.

"Bother the accordian," she said.

"What!" said Joe, "and arter I had,

in a vay of speaking, made up my mind to have it, for a cove as nobody knowed to come in and vin it, and then treat me to some cheek besides. Oh, if I only catch him some day in a dark place, when there's nobody looking, that's all! Give us the bottle."

"Well, Joe, you oughtn't to complain," said Mrs. Pugsey, "you have done a very good stroke of business lately; but the mare is falling off."

"Is she?"

"Ah, isn't she? and old Arrowdale will soon begin to notice it."

"Well, in that case the mare must have a good feed now and then. We mustn't sell quite so many of the oats to the man that keeps the furniture van, that's all, though it is a good seven shillings a week gained."

"Yes, but things may be over done."

"So they may, old woman."

"That five pounds from the doctor came in rather sweet, Joe."

"Rather."

"And all for nothing but holding your tongue about the job. I suppose Bill as drove got the same?"

"Purcisely."

"Well, it's an ill wind as blows nobody any good. I suppose that young woman has got used to being with the doctor now, for from what you says she was about as much mad as I am."

"Mad! Lord bless you, she worn't mad."

"No, I thought not."

"I tell you what she was, though, that was worse for her a good deal."

"What, Joe?"

"Pretty?"

"Ah, so you have said. What like was she, Joe?"

"I can't tell you, but she was a real out-and-outer—such a pair of lips—such little mites of child's hands, and such teeth. I could not twig her eyes, cos yer sees they were shut up, but I seed enough on her, to know as she was a out-and-outer, and no sort of mistake whatsomedever."

"I wonder, Joe, if anything will ever come of it?"

"Eh? What's that?"

Joe sprung to his feet, as Doctor Bell dislodged a hair broom that was upon the landing, which was clattering down he stairs into the stable, making as much noise as half a dozen hair brooms ought to make.

CHAPTER LXXXIV.

THE VISIT TO THE LODGING-HOUSE.

HARRY DEAN felt that from that moment further concealment was out of the question, and advancing boldly, he flung open the door of the room, leaving his companions upon the staircase, and said in a bold, confident, familiar voice,—

"Well Joe, how do you find yourself to-night? Confound you, why do you leave things in people's way, as they come up stairs. Eh?"

Joe shaded his eyes with his hand from the glare of the light which chanced to intercept his view of Harry Dean's face, and then he said—

"Who the devil are you?"

"Ah, you have hit it."

"Hit what?"

"My name."

"Why you don't mean to tell me that you are the—the real old personage himself. Eh?"

"Anything you like, Joe. But, at all events, I have come to have some talk with you, so be quiet. We have some little affairs to settle together. Don't disturb yourself, madam."

"I tell you what, my fine fellow," said Joe, "I dare say you think yourself mighty clever, but it won't do. I don't know you, and there's the door."

"I see the door perfectly well, but before I pass out at it, just tell me, Joe, how much now you think you have made from first to last by purloining Mr. rrowdale's corn?"

Joe's face turned of an ashy paleness,

"I—I don't purloin—his blessed oats! I—l—don't."

"Pho! Pho! I mean what you sell to the van-keeper in the next street, you know."

"It's all up," gasped Joe.

"Murder!" exclaimed Mrs. Pugsey faintly.

"I'm done up, old un," added Joe, "yet—no—prove it, old fellow. Prove it, I say, if you can. I say prove it."

"Nonsense," said Harry Dean, "I don't care about proving it. You and I know it, and that is quite enough any day or night, Joe. If any one else knew it though, it would cost you more than the five pounds you got from Doctor Wilkins, for keeping snug where he took the young girl to get out of the scrape. Indeed, without my help you wouldn't get out of it at all."

Joe's teeth began to chatter.

"W—w—won't you tell us who you is?" gasped Mrs. Pugsey. "Do you come from down below, sir, if you please?"

Harry Dean nodded, and Joe dropped upon his knees, and commenced an extemporaneous prayer, that had about it a very strange jumble of divinity indeed. At any other time Harry Dean could not have failed to have been much amused at the peculiar turn the fears of Joe had taken. As it was, however, he was by far too deeply interested in discovering where Kate had been conveyed to give any place in his mind to mirth.

"What can you imagine," said Harry Dean, "ought to be your fate?"

"Oh, I shall grill."

"Perhaps not. Even I am merciful. Make a full confession of your iniquities, and I will go away at once, and remove likewise those whom I have brought with me."

"Some of your devils, I suppose, sir?"

"Yes; now begin."

"Oh, dear! yes. I stole Sir Arrowdale's cow,—I sold it to Richards, the van man; I was employed by Dobbs, the stable keeper and jobber, to be a footman for one day to Dr. Wilkins, while Bill Jackson drove him."

"Go on; that is all right so far."

"He picked up a young lady at a Dr. Bell's, and drove her to No. 2, York-place, Portman-square, and then Dr. Wilkins gave me a five-pound note, saying, 'Mind you never tell any human being where you drove me to to-day, and if you keep the secret for a month only, you will have another note, which I shall make it my business to forward to you.'"

"True," said Harry Dean, rising. "Now, Joe, you have told me the truth, so I shall not visit you again for some time; but mark me, Joe!"

"Yes."

"Give the mare a good feed, for she is falling off."

Mrs. Pugsey at these words fainted away; for she had said or thought, she hardly knew which, the very same thing only that day. After this, could she doubt that it was the veritable old Nick himself who was in the sitting-room over the stable? By passing his hand rapidly before the candle, Henry Dean now created a current of air which instantly put it out, and taking advantage of the darkness, he left the room, saying to his two friends upon the staircase, "Come away quickly; I have got all the information I wanted. Come at once; for I have produced an effect upon the mind of Mr. Joe Pugsey which I do not wish should evaporate for some time to come."

Dr. Bell and Sam hastily followed him into the mews, where the policeman made his appearance, saying, with a touch to the rim of his hat, "Want me, your worship?"

"No," said Henry; "there is something for your trouble."

He handed him a sovereign, and walked away, leaving the policeman in a state of wild amazement at such an instance of prodigality, which, however, neither Dr. Bell nor Sam were aware of. They saw something given to the policeman, but probably thought it a shilling.

"What are we to do now?" said Dr. Bell to Harry Dean, as they walked on a few paces in advance of Sam, who had never forgotten the respect he owed to his master, although he was in masquerade.

"We must go at once to No. 2, York-place, Portman-square."

"Is she there?"

"She is. What is the time now?"

"Just eleven by my watch. Have you arranged any precise plan?"

"No; but we can talk about all that as we go along. I know that Wilkins is capable of anything; and if driven to desperation, by seeing that he had lost his game as regarded Kate and me, there is no knowing exactly to what length he might go."

"Would he commit murder, think you?" said the doctor with a shudder.

"God forbid! but he has committed murder, and who shall say he would not again?"

"Who, indeed! You must use stratagem, Mr. Dean. Come on, I know the way to your place very well, and No. 2 will be easily found. I dread now the result even of our own information, for from what you have told me of this Wilkins, he is more a fiend than a man."

"He is, indeed," sighed Harry Dean.

After this, poor Harry Dean seemed to fall into a kind of abstraction, which was very different from the sort of exultation one would have supposed him to feel at the discovery of the hiding-place of Wilkins. But that discovery had now given birth to a variety of thoughts and feelings of the most painful and distressing character. If he had consulted his own feelings and emotions in the matter, he would have moved to the door of the house where the idol of his heart was concealed, and never ceased his efforts until he had forced it open and reached her; but there was too much manifest danger in such a course. He dared not adopt it. It was this consideration, then, that made him still dull and dejected,—that even now that he had found out where Kate was, he was compelled to temporise in some measure with her abductor, by not making a direct attack upon him,

"You are full of sad thoughts," said Dr. Bell.

"I am, indeed."

"May I share them?"

"Alas! they lie upon the surface. I think, if I were to show to this man, Wilkins, that I knew where she was, he would rather take the life of Kate Destern than let me rescue her from his hands."

"Let us pause, then, and think the matter over. Here is the deep doorway of an empty house; we can stand here and consider what had better be done in such an emergency as this."

CHAPTER LXXXV.

THE ELOQUENT MRS. DAWES.

THE house in the deep doorway of which they were now ensconced, commanded a view of York-place, so that after they had taken up their places for a few moments, Dr. Bell pointed to a mansion with green outside jalousies, and said,— "That is no 2."

Harry Dean started, and made a movement to rush to the house, but Dr. Bell restrained him, saying, as he did so,—

"For the love of Heaven, be cautious, for the reason you have advanced to me."

"Oh, yes, yes," said Harry, "but is it not maddening to stand here looking upon the very house that contains Kate, and feel that there is any consideration in the world that ought to hold one back from flying to her rescue—is not this, I say, most maddening?"

"It is—it is; but yet most necessary. It is the life and liberty of Kate Destern that we look at as things of importance much more than the punishment of Wilkins."

"True,—oh, most true! Do with me what you will. Is that a woman pausing at the door of the very house you have pointed out to me? Truly she pauses there."

"She does, indeed."

By the glow of a gas-light that was close to the door of No. 2, this woman could be seen with tolerable distinctness. She had all the appearance of a London char-woman. A large shawl, that looked like a dyed blanket, was around her shoulders; a black polka bonnet concealed her head and face. In fact, the effect of the bonnet to her must have been something akin to living at one end of a tube of some sort, and only looking at something through the orifice at the other end. The lady carried in her hand a pair of formidable pattens, and under her arm was an umbrella, of about the proportions usually used for those London abominations called one-horse chaises. She was evidently pausing before No. 2, York-place. Harry Dean regarded her with the closest attention, and for a few moments not a word was spoken between him and Dr. Bell, as they both watched this woman. In a few moments she rang rather timidly at the area-bell—just such a ring as servants, unless they have an assignation at that house with some friend of their own, never dream of paying the least attention to, so the old woman had, after waiting awhile, to ring again.

"What think you," whispered Harry Dean to Doctor Bell, "is it worth while trying to get any information from that woman? Perhaps she may be able to satisfy the small amount that yet remains about the accuracy of our information. Shall we call her?"

"Hush! Let us send Sam for her."

The doctor whispered to Sam for a few moments, after which, while the faded-looking woman was still in vain wishing for a reply to her ring at the area-gate, Sam walked over to her and spoke to her. In about half a minute she accompanied him to where our friends were hiding. There was a tact about this woman which enabled her to know a gentleman when she saw one, and she dropped her profoundest curtsey to Harry Dean as she said, —

"The young man is goods enoughs to says as yer wanteds to speaks, sir, if yer pleases."

This woman had an odd way of making everything into plurals.

"Yes," said Harry Dean, "I did want to speak to you. I wished to know if you could give me any information concerning the inmates of No. 2?"

"And likewise," added Sam, who understood the best argument to use to the woman, "if a sovereign would be of any use to you to-night?"

"Graciouses Providences!"

"Yes, certainly," said Harry Dean; "you shall be amply rewarded for any information procured through your means, and you may likewise rest assured that the object we have in view is a good one."

The poor woman looked confused.

"It is No. 2, then," she said. "I'm a lone woman, if you pleases; don't be puttings any of your funs at a poors, lones widows, gentlemens—don'ts."

"We are serious, I assure you," said Harry Dean. We want information regarding the inmates of the house at which you were ringing, and we will pay you liberally for the information, as well as for keeping secret that you have been asked for it."

"Nods is as goods as winkses at blind osses!"

"Madam!"

"Why yer sees, sir, my sights is not so goods as they wonct was, and I hardlys knowed as it was number two or number three, but numbers two it is, and I'm sure anythings in an unlawful ways I'm always willing to do."

"What sort of a house is it?"

"Why sir, the cooks says, says she, Mrs. Lupins, we are going to have our monthly, and your had better comes over nights and lights yer places, and so that accounts for that in a ways o' speakings though it's neithers heres, as my poor husbands used to says, as is dead and gones."

Harry Dean shook his head.

"Allow me," said Doctor Bell, as he gave the woman a sovereign, "to ask, who and what are you?"

"I *chairs* sir, Mary Lupins, and I says as perhaps shouldn't—"

"Hush! Who keeps that house? I mean number two."

"I thinks as her name is Mrs. Tug as never was, and I says to myself, says—"

"Hush! Is there any one else in the house do you know, besides this Mrs. Tug and the servants?"

"In course lodgers, when she get ems, for as I oftens remarkses, I—

"Hush! What lodgers are there now?"

Mrs. Lupin was getting so thoroughly bewildered by this reiterated "Hush!" an interruption upon the part of the doctor, that, to use her own expressive and graphic phraseology, she hardly knew whether she was upon her "head or her heels," but still she had taken the sovereign, and she wished to earn it by being as explicit as possible.

"Say it again without the Hushes, sir, if you pleases."

"Are there any lodgers at No. 2?"

"Lodgerses?"

"Pray answer me categorically."

"I knows nothing about the cats."

"Good God, cannot you tell me if there are any lodgers or not at No. 2, York-place, woman?"

"I thinks, as cook said, as there was a Dr. Williams's, and something about a F. M."

"A what?"

"I'm quite sures it was a F. M. She said as she hads overheards her missus say, as she should nots at alls wonders at a F. M. comings to the houses himselfs."

"Are you sure the name was not Wilkins, instead of Williams."

"Now you mentions it, I think it was Wilkins.—What a memorys you musts have, sir, I'm sure now it was Wilkins's or Jones's and there's nobody else—"

"Now is not this enough to drive anybody crazy?" said Doctor Bell.

"But," continued Mrs. Lupin, "the mad young lady as nobody waits on, they say, but Mrs. Tugses herself. Oh, no—she's as mads, cooks says, as a marchs hares she is, poor things."

"I think that will do," whispered Doctor Bell to Harry Dean.

"Yes."

"Very well, Mrs. Lupin, if you say nothing to any one about this matter for three days, and then call upon me at the address you will find upon this card, you will get another sovereign for your trouble."

"*Suttenly.*"

Away went Mrs. Lupin, and Doctor Bell turning to Harry Dean, said,—

"Now, Mr. Dean, as we are quite sure there can be no mistake, let us go somewhere and quietly sit down and think of some clear and distinct mode of action. You yourself are of opinion that, although Kate is a prisoner, she is quite safe, since the game that Wilkins is playing renders it necessary he should treat her with every respect. Calm your feelings, therefore, and let us bring cool judgment to our aid."

"You are right, sir. I will follow you. My mind is much more at ease than it was."

Doctor Bell led Harry Dean to a quiet respectable hotel in the immediate neighbourhood. Having found a private room, they sat down to consult upon the posture of affairs, but while they are doing so it is far more essential that we should follow Mrs. Lupin, than listen to what our two friends are saying. Now with Mrs. Lupin shillings were scarce visitors, and sovereigns never knocked at her door at all. The one she had received from Dr. Bell, was, as she herself said, as she looked at it by the beams of a gas-lamp, "quites a sights for sores eyeses." Now, human nature is not perfect, and Mrs. Lupin had one fault. Shall we confess in full? That one fault was, a predilection for a liquid called Old Tom! It would be a curious

I

inquiry to ascertain why or wherefore Old Tom had such charms for Mrs. Lupin, but we have neither space nor inclination to enter into it. Suffice it to say, she liked — loved — adored — doated on Old Thomas.

"It isn't oftens," said Mrs. Lupin, apostrophizing, the sovereign, "as I sees one of yous. I've onlys hads ones drops to-days, and I'm a sinner's if I don'ts have anothers nows. It's onlys naturals as ones should like comforts as ones is goings downs the hills of lifes into the watersses of it.—I will have a drops if I die for it! There's noberys at number two. I'm afores my times, so here goeses."

Now, in London, if anybody has an Old Tomish inclination and a sovereign in his or her hand, they need not be long without an opportunity of gratifying it to any extent they please, so Mrs. Lupin was soon at the bar of a gin palace, inhaling the perfume of the place which, in itself, she thought was worth a something. The very air was teeming with gin. Mrs. Lupin immediately ordered one glass of the enticing beverage, but that one was naturally enough so suggestive of another, that she had the other as a thing of course, and if one was suggestive of two, how much more likely were two to be suggestive of three! The gold was changed —transmuted into gin. Oh, bathos! Alas, Mrs. Lupin! No less than eight glasses of the liquid fiend! The curse of indiscretion bubbled down the throat of the char-woman, and then having placed her change deep in the recesses of a pocket that seemed bottomless, she left the gin palace.

"Hilloa! what is this? It must be the air—the—blue night air. The street is turning round and round somehow. It can't be the gin?"

Mrs. Lupin paused and smiled; she shook her head sagely. Oh, no, she was not to be taken in; it was not the Old Tom. It was the street that was trying to play her some tricks by presenting to her observation first one end and then another, but she was a woman who had seen a little of life, and was not to be made a victim of, exactly, by bricks and mortar. Not she. She walked on in rather a devious, uncertain sort of way. And now for No. 2:

"success," said Mrs. Lupin. I—goe to Nos. 2: I chairs, and *I—I—likes Old Toms's. Eh! And outs of the ways fellows. Oh! it's only a postesses. I' goes to Nos. 2; I—I—steadys is the words; steadys as rock-sesses: all's rights rings the hairy bellseses!"

CHAPTER LXXXV.

THE SPARE BED AT NO. 2.

TINGLE! tingle! tingle! went the area bell of No. 2. It was really a great relief to Mrs. Lupin to hold on by the area rails until the cook, who could not very well be off testing this appeal to the bell, looked up from the door of communication between the kitchen and the area.

"Is that you, Mrs. Lupin?"

"How—is you," said the charwoman.

"Oh, it is you?"

"Rathers."

"The gate is open, you can come down, Mrs. Lupin; just push it close, and it will fasten of itself. You are rather late, I think, Mrs. Lupin?"

"Go to blazeses!"

"What did you say, Mrs. Lupin?"

Mrs. Lupin made no reply to her interrogatory. She was much too busy in keeping herself steady as she opened the area gate and descended the steps, to reply to any nonsense of the cook's. The only remark she made as she half walked half tumbled down the steps, was,—

"As I'm a females I does believes as the cooks is drunks."

The kitchen was, however, with some difficulty gained. Mrs. Lupin fairly staggered and sank upon a seat. The cook looked at her with dismay, for she could not but perceive that Mrs. Lupin was in a curious condition, and, in fact, that she had felt the enemy in her mouth to steal away her brains. The more the smile came upon the countenance of the char-woman, the more proclamatory was it of the fact.

"Goodness gracious!" said the cook.

"How is you?" said Mrs. Lupin; "keep the coppers a boiling—steadys—steadys."

The cook lifted up her hands in dismay, for the cook was no tlike cooks in general, really temperate and wise in her potations. The sight of a drunken woman, although she was an old char-woman, gave the cook what she her-self graphically called a "turn."

"Why, Mrs. Lupin," she said, "is this really you? I always thought you a sober, honest, industrious woman, and I declare, I am quite shocked to see you now in such a condition. Oh! Mrs. Lupin, you should think of your latter end,—indeed you should."

"Eh? 'never says dies. Keep the flues a bilings."

"This is dreadful! Oh! Mrs. Lupin, if any of your children were to see you in this state!"

Mrs. Lupin was either getting lachry-mose without any provocation at all, as is the wont of some persons in their cups, or this allusion to her family touched a tender chord in her bosom, already softened by gin; but certain it is that Mrs. Lupin began to sob, and shed abundance of tears, notwithstanding that she believed she was the most unhappy woman in the world, and had not a friend.

"Mrs. Lupin, do you know what the time is?" said the cook.

"No—no—times is times."

"Can you look at the kitchen clock?"

"Oh! my poors heart—rally—rally I'm a infortunate woman!"

"Well, Mrs. Lupin, it only wants a quarter to one, and I'm loth to turn you out into the street at such an hour in your condition—I'm going to bed. The fire is nearly out, but in the pantry is Stagghorne's mattress, the last boy we had. You had better lie down on that till the morning, when I shall speak to you, and you may depend it won't be about. coming here any more, Mrs. Lupin. Oh, you abominable woman!"

The cook was for a few minutes puzzled how to leave Mrs. Lupin a light, without risking having the house burnt down by some drunken vagary of that lady; but at last she hit upon the plan of putting about an inch of candle in a flat candlestick and mounting it upon a tall shelf, which she felt certain Mrs. Lupin must be much steadier on the feet than she now was to have any chance of reaching. This candle so high shed a very dismal and spectral sort of ight over the kitchen.

"Now good night, Mrs. Lupin," said the cook, "and reformation to you. Don't touch the clock—I shall be down at six."

Mrs. Lupin was alone. For a few minutes she sat quiet, and then a dim remembrance that she was to sleep somewhere came over her, but she quite forgot that she had been directed to Stagghorne's pantry, where the mattress was to be found.

"I—I should like to lays downs," muttered Mrs. Lupin, "if it's only to keeps the kitchens from going rounds and rounds in this sorts of ways. It's very odds indeeds that's it is—wells I never—oh! my poores heads—my poores heads! It can't be the gins—oh! no—it can't be the gins, I'm quite sure of that."

Mrs. Lupin had risen, and she now tottered across the kitchen, and without paying the least regard to the directions of the cook to sleep in the pantry, she began, holding by the balustrade by the way, slowly and with no small amount of difficulty, to ascend the kitchen stairs. She reached the hall, and then com-menced the first floor flight; and now in that progress we must not dally with her, but merely remark that, much ex-hausted and confused by her exertions, she reached the second floor landing, and pushing open a door which was op-posite to her, she staggered into a room. After some groping about she found a bed, into which she got, and was in two minutes more in a deep drunken sleep. The door of the chamber swung quite close again, and all was still save the deep breathing of Mrs. Lupin, whose animal functions were rather disturbed by Old Tom.

* *

Return we to Kate Destern early in that evening upon which the doctor, when it darkened more into night, had com-mitted the awful crime of murder. Kate, despite all her wish to keep her mind free from dejection, which she knew would have the effect of clouding her faculties and rendering her incapable of reflection, or of taking advantage of any accidental circumstance that might oc-cur to favour her escape, could not help trembling to think what might yet be her fate in the hands of that desperate and vicious man in whose power she

was. She could not possibly avoid being deeply impressed with an idea that Wilkins was daring enough for anything, and that he likewise had a large amount of villanous ingenuity to aid him in his iniquitous exploits; in fact, that he was a man in every way to be feared, as well as hated and despised, she felt sure. But what could she do? That was the question. Must she calmly await what might occur, resigning herself to be the sport of evil fortune, at the same time that she was in a condition to anticipate the worst, or was she to make some effort, however futile, to save herself? To her mind there was a something pleasing, and distracting from the painful thoughts that laid hold upon her, in any species of exertion that in the remotest degree tended towards foiling the wishes and the intentions of those who held her prisoner.

"No!" she exclaimed, "I cannot—dare not, sit brooding over my condition. It would drive me mad to do so. I must do something."

What that something was to be, though, was the difficulty, and Kate sat thinking over it, until thought was so far advanced that she felt she should not have many more visits. Alas! she little suspected the dreadful visit that was yet to be made to that chamber by Wilkins, in the madness of his mental agony. Hearing all in the house profoundly still, Kate rose and tried the door. It was locked, of course, and it was no disappointment for her to find it so. The chance would have been the other way entirely; but the idea occurred to her, that the lock of a room door could not be so very strong, so she might possibly succeed in opening it. As soon as this notion found a place in her mind, she began to look around her most anxiously for some means of carrying it out, but every precaution seemed to have been taken to remove out of her way any weapons of offence or defence. The very fire-place was destitute of its usual "irons." Kate's eyes now wandered round the room, until they fell upon a cupboard-door in one corner. Now this cupboard she knew was open, for she had looked into it, and found it full of clothing and other matters of no moment, but now, she thought she would institute a closer search, as among its miscellaneous contents there might, after all, possibly be something that would assist her. Without any ceremony, then, she threw out the various things from the shelves. There were faded bonnets—worn-out dresses—some spare bed-linen, but for a while, nothing of a sterner character, and Kate was just upon the point of giving up the search, when she saw a brown-paper parcel at the back of one of the shelves. It did not look very promising, but she took it out. Its weight proclaimed it metal, and, upon opening it, she found it to be a dozen new knives and forks carefully greased and laid by, most probably for any emergency when they might be required; and as for this being left in that cupboard, it was one of those oversights so very natural, that it hardly deserved speculating upon. Now, knives and forks are not very available weapons to make an escape with, but still they were something better than old bonnets and artificial flowers. A knife, too, was an ugly weapon if used as a defence, but it was the door of her chamber which Kate was most anxious to get open in the first instance. Snap went the blade of the first knife she tried to make a lever of, to force the lock of the door, and she saw, what she might well have supposed before, how perfectly inadequate so small and flimsy a weapon was to the task assigned to it. She then thought of placing several blades together, so as to give this a combined power; but upon looking over the knives again she found a steel for sharpening them, and as this was much stronger than half a dozen of the knives, she determined upon first trying what she could effect by its aid against the lock particularly. She was now much more fortunate, for by attacking the lock instead of the door, she found she had less resistance. One vigorous wrench broke the steel and forced the door open. The lock was not sent back, but the hasp into which it ran was so twisted on one side that it no longer held it. The door would close and appear locked, although a touch would open it by removing the mere tendency of the hinges to keep it shut.

"One step to freedom," said Kate, as she stood upon the threshold of the chamber and looked out upon the dark landing.

She had a light in her room; it was a small oil night-lamp, convenient to carry, and she now took it in her hand, and advanced to the head of the stairs to listen if all was still in the house. Oh, what a rapturous thought it was that she might possibly descend, succeed in opening the street-door, and in five minutes be free. But was it likely she was left so easily guarded? Was it possible that such a man as Wilkins should be so incautious as to leave her such an opportunity of absconding from him after he had taken such pains to make her a prisoner? This was a sickening reflection, and Kate trembled as it came across her; and yet how still the house was! not a soul appeared to be moving. Sleep seemed to have fallen upon all but her, and yet she knew that twelve o'clock was not far gone into the dim waste of time past. Kate remained for about five minutes listening, and then, although she trembled at the idea of meeting with Wilkins, perchance, she would not forego the hope of escape because it might possibly be foiled. Of course, there was danger—there always was in such matters, and she could not expect that the circumstances in which she was placed would be any exception to the general rule.

"Heaven help me! I will try," she said.

As she spoke she slowly and noiselessly commenced the descent of the stairs. They were too well carpeted to creak, and her footstep was perfectly noiseless. She passed the drawing-room door, but not without a shudder, for might not her enemy be there ready at any stray moment to come out and seize her? Oh, what a temptation it was, the moment she got fairly past that door, to abandon all caution and fly like the wind. She resisted it, and slowly as before, only that she trembled more, she proceeded onwards to the hall. A sound, as if some one was talking in the kitchen, came upon Kate's ears, and she paused to listen. She was not mistaken. The cook and Mrs. Lupin were holding together that brief conversation which we have already detailed to the reader, and the sound came tolerably distinct as voices to the hall, although Kate could not catch above a stray word now and then as regarded the subject matter of the discourse; she remained profoundly ignorant. But now she was only half a dozen paces from the street door, and upon the other side of this barrier of wood and iron was liberty. She hurried forward. Her heart sunk within her. The chain, which at ordinary doors is easily removable, was secured in its place by a padlock. This was a cunning provision of the landlady to make sure that nobody left the house after she had retired to bed. Kate felt her hopes evaporate. At that moment she heard a footstep upon the kitchen stairs, and a voice said, "I shall be down at six."

To be caught making a fruitless attempt at escape might make her situation worse, but could not make it better, and Kate at once flew up the staircase considerably in advance of the speaker, who, as the reader will see, was the cook. Kate stopped not until she reached her room again, and then, panting and completely exhausted, she sat down in the first chair she came to, and burst into tears. She felt that she had calculated too much upon her chances of escape, without considering the many dangers she had to pass through first, and the many difficulties she would have to encounter. She dreaded the arrival of some one in her room, and she opened the door to listen. She advanced to the top of the stairs, and then, as she saw by a flash of light that some one was near at hand, she retreated in her fright, and opened not the door of her own room, but the door of another bed-chamber upon the same floor. Kate discovered her mistake immediately, for the colour of the drapery of the room was essentially different. Her first impulse was to make another effort to reach what she called her own room, but she paused, and said to herself—

"No—no. Who knows, but after all, I may be much safer in this room than in any other?"

CHAPTER LXXXVII.
THE CAPTURE OF WILKINS.

IT will be recollected that Harry Dean and Doctor Bell were left consulting in a private room at a hotel, while Sam solaced himself below. Little did Harry Dean guess Kate's danger, while he was thus deliberating upon the best means of rescuing her without danger to himself. Oh, what agony would have been his, if he could but for one moment have supposed that she owed her life to the trivial circumstance we have related, for we have no wish to keep up a needless mystery to the reader. Kate did escape the murderous designs of the doctor, and the charwoman, who in her drunken insanity had reeled into Kate's bedroom and taken possession of her bed, fell his victim. But Harry Dean was mercifully—most mercifully spared the knowledge for the present of these things. The thought that there had been so much danger, and he not there, would have gone near to kill him. It would have been too horrible."

"Now, Dr. Bell," he said, "all our reasoning must resolve itself to one point, and that, how we shall most easily and most quickly save Kate."

" And most safely," said the doctor.

" Yes, and most safely."

" You have told me, my dear sir, your opinion of this Wilkins fully, and intimated that you really think him capable of taking the life of Kate; so now, what I advise you to do is, to wait about the house until you actually see him."

" Wilkins ?"

" Yes, it is most improbable that he will, although he makes a prisoner of Kate Destern, make a prisoner of himself. You know him doubtless well enough personally to enable you to detect him in any disguise ?"

" Oh, yes."

" Well, there cannot be many hours until the morning ; and by dint of keeping a good watch upon the house, you must see him come out some time."

" You are right, you are right."

" You think well of the scheme, even with all its disagreeables ?"

" I do. What are disagreeables to me, when the happiness and safety of Kate Destern is at stake ? I will wait cheerfully in the street, let the weather be what it may : I shall feel nothing, know nothing, but that I am working for her release."

" Well said. And yet——"

" You hesitate. Speak freely, my good friend."

" I was thinking that you might be spared the fatigue, as well as the risk of discovery of waiting in the open street. What say you to boldly asking leave of the occupiers of the opposite house to watch from the windows ?"

" Do you know the people ?"

" Certainly not."

" Then I fear you will find, that, in England, anything that is at all unusual will meet with but a sorry reception. I shall not mind waiting in the street."

" Probably not : but the damage to our cause by so doing is very great. First of all, you must either get so close to the house, for fear of missing your man, that you will run the greatest risk of being seen by him ; or you must, to avoid that risk, go so far off that you may miss him altogether."

" Alas ! alas ! it is so."

" Well, both of these objections are obviated, if you can get into the opposite house."

" But the hour ?"

" Is rather an awkward one, I grant, at which to call upon a stranger ; yet desperate cases require desperate remedies, you know, so I am for making the attempt."

" Be it so, then."

Delighted in having brought Henry Dean to his view of the case, Dr. Bell told Sam Gwibbins to remain where he was ; and he and Henry then sallied out to make the attempt upon the feelings and sympathies of the opposite neighbour to number 2. First of all they looked up at the house ; and they were glad to see there was a light in the drawing-room, as that carried with it an assurance that, by soliciting admission, they should not be disturbing any one. Dr. Bell knocked a quick, gentleman-like knock, and in a very short time a servant came to the door.

" I'm afraid the hour is late," began the doctor, "but——"

" Hush !" said the servant ; " is it you, gentlemen ?"

Dr. Bell looked at Henry Dean, and Henry Dean looked at Dr. Bell, but the servant, with a mysterious nod, said—

" You must not mind me ; I know all about it ; missus told me. Hush ! Come in, come in ! Don't stand at the door whatever you do ! Hist ! Come in !"

" There must be some mistake," said Henry Dean.

" Oh no, no !" said the girl. " Missus has seen it twice. She's waiting for you in the drawing-room now. That's right. I don't think anybody from opposite saw you come in, did they ? There's no knowing the mystery of some people."

" What shall we do ?" whispered Harry Dean to the doctor ; " we are evidently mistaken for some other persons. What shall we do ?"

" Come in," said the doctor, as he pushed Harry before him into the passage ; " I dare say it will turn out all right. We can easily explain."

" Why didn't you come sooner ?" said the servant ; " missus is so nervous. Will you take anything before you go up stairs ?"

" No, thank you."

" Oh, very well. What's your number ?"

" My what ?" said Harry Dean.

" Your number — you know ; but,

howsomdever, it don't matter, if you'd rather not tell. Come this way. Perhaps you ain't one o' the common ones."

"Is this a mad-house?" whispered Harry Dean to the doctor.

"I don't know; but come up stairs, at all events, and we will see the nervous missus, you know. At all events, she will be quite in my line."

"Very well. I only know that if I am not actually in some dream, this is the most odd circumstance that has happened to me yet."

The servant preceded them up the staircase, which was well furnished, and then throwing open a door which conducted into a handsome drawing-room, she said—

"Here they are, ma'am."

"Oh, thank heaven!" cried an elderly lady, rising from a seat at the window; "I am so glad. You can now watch yourselves, and I sincerely hope it will not be to no purpose."

"Madam," said Harry Dean, "I much fear there is some mistake."

"Mistake?"

"Yes, madam. I and my friend here have ventured to come here to—"

"To watch the house opposite, No. 2, of course," said the lady.

Harry Dean never felt so confounded in all his life.

"Good God!" he said, "am I awake? Is this sorcery, or what is it? Truly the determination to come here, madam, and obtain your leave to watch No. 2, has only been made within half an hour, and yet you seem quite prepared for it."

"Well," said the lady; "I must confess I don't see anything at all surprising in that. Do you, sir?"

"Pardon me, madam, if I do. It appears to me to be one of the most thoroughly inexplicable things I ever heard of in all my life. Could you oblige me by saying how you came to know our intention in so really seemingly magical a manner?"

"I inferred as much, of course, after my letter."

"Your letter?" said Harry Dean.

"Your letter?" said Dr. Bell. "What letter?"

"Gracious goodness, gentlemen, ain't you the two inspectors of police who were to come?"

"Inspectors of fiddlesticks, madam," said Dr. Bell. "We are perfect strangers, and came as such to throw ourselves entirely upon your courtesy for leave to watch No. 2, where a friend of ours, we have reason to believe, is being badly treated."

"A young lady?"

"Yes — yes!" said Harry Dean, eagerly.

"Why bless me, gentlemen, I saw her at the window of a room on the second floor, making such despairing attitudes, and in such dreadful grief, that I made some inquiries, and ascertaining there was a mystery, I wrote to the police about it, and received an answer that two inspectors would come and watch the house from my windows, and talk to me about it."

"Well, madam," said Doctor Bell, "this is most extraordinary. There is my card, madam, and I only hope you will allow us to watch from the windows for that young lady whom you have seen is confined in that house——"

"Confined?" said the lady. "Dear me, I hope it is nothing improper, Doctor a—a—oh, Bell—I beg your pardon, but if the young lady has just been confined, I would rather not interfere."

"My dear madam, you misapprehend me. I do not mean confined in the sense you take it, I only mean that she is kept prisoner."

"Oh, I really beg your pardon. Of course, my house is at your service, and —dear me, who's that?"

A rat-tat came to the street-door, and in a few moments the servant rushed upstairs and cried out with some alarm—

"Oh, ma'am, here's two more of 'em, and they say they are inspectors."

"Ah," said Doctor Bell, "these, no doubt, are the real Simon Pures.— Gentlemen, you are welcome. — Mr. Dean, keep your eye upon No. 2, and I will soon explain to you the state of affairs."

The two police inspectors entered the room, and were soon put, by Doctor Bell, in possession of the whole circumstances, upon which one of them said—

"We are the more anxious regarding this affair, as our commissioners have received a message from the Secretary of State to use every means of discovering a young lady named Kate Destern ; in whose fortune a noble lord——"

"That will suffice, gentlemen," said Harry Dean. "It is of this young lady we speak. She is no doubt in that house opposite. But now listen to me patiently, and do nothing precipitately."

Harry Dean then succinctly explained to the officers the apprehensions he was under, regarding Wilkins's disposition to commit any violence, if he found himself foiled ; but one of the inspectors shook his head as he said—

"I'm afraid it will be our duty, despite all such considerations, to go over to the house at once."

"I forbid you," said Harry Dean.

"You, sir ?"

"Yes. Step this way a moment."

He took the inspector into the recess of another window, and conversed with him a moment, after which Doctor Bell saw the inspector make a low bow, and heard him say—

"We are most entirely at your service, and will act under your instructions solely in this business."

CHAPTER LXXXVIII.

THE MURDERER'S CAPTURE.

DR. BELL was not a little surprised at this sudden and unaccountable deference that was shown to Harry Dean. It seemed as though he, Harry, was some magician, who had but to pronounce some cabalistic word in the ear of any one, when lo ! they became at once his most abject slaves. He looked all the surprise that he felt.

"My dear sir," said Harry Dean, in that winning way which none knew better than he how to assume when it pleased him ; "my dear sir, there are secrets in all families, and I think that in mine there is rather above the average number, but the time will, I hope, soon come, when to a friend like yourself there need be no mysteries."

"If, sir," said Dr. Bell, "you intend any apology to me for your not being more confidential, believe me, it is quite uncalled for, for I am quite content to work with you in the cause of Kate Destern, without knowing more of you than I do."

"You are very good."

"Not at all. But we wont waste time in complimenting each other, but proceed to business at once ; is there anything else that can be done besides watching No 2 opposite ?"

"None at present, I think."

"Well, gentlemen," said one of the inspectors, "as the watch may take some time, suppose we take it hour and hour about, and then we shall none of us get negligent by getting weary about the matter. You, however, sir, know the party who is to be apprehended."

"Yes," said Harry, "immediately apprehended after he has got some short distance from the house, so that he cannot, by any energy of movement, return to it upon taking an alarm. I wish particularly to provide against such a contingency as that."

"Is it probable, sir ?"

"Highly so ; as in that case, a murder might be the result, and a life might be sacrificed which I would freely give my own to preserve."

"You shall, then, give the order for his capture yourself, sir," said the inspector. "Some of our men in plain clothes are below, and if you will take this small silver whistle, and open the window, when you sound it, any one who has come out of No 2 will be seized upon the moment."

"I thank you," said Harry Dean, "it will be a satisfaction to me to do this myself, feeling, as I do, so deeply interested in the result of it."

The inspector handed the little whistle to Harry Dean, who then at once stationed himself at the window, feeling quite assured that he should not tire of keeping watch, let it extend as long as it might into the night hours. He kept his eyes most intently fixed upon the house. It was in vain that Dr. Bell begged him to lie down upon a sofa for an hour, while he took his place, promising to arouse him upon the slightest movement of the street-door opposite.

"No—no. I thank you much," said Harry, "but this is to me a matter of life and death, so you see I am less mentally agitated while looking myself, than if I waited nervously the report of another's watching."

And so he continued at the window. Little did Harry Dean suspect that

Wilkins was at that time dreaming that dreadful dream that fitted him for the awful crime which he committed upon that most eventful night. Truly, Harry Dean's heart would have been frozen with terror if he could but have imagined for a moment such a state of things. Dr. Bell conversed in a low tone with the lady of the house, and thus an hour or two passed away.

"Nothing yet," said one of the inspectors.

"Hush!" said Harry Dean—"hush! Something—I know not what—but some mysterious feeling creeps over me, with the assurance that something will soon happen now.

"Oh, you are getting nervous," said Dr. Bell.

"No, no."

"But, my young friend, it is highly natural that you should do so. I could have foretold you as much."

"For the love of heaven," said Harry Dean, "do not distract me. Hush, hush —all I ask of you is to say nothing to me!"

Dr. Bell was silent. The two police inspectors, who took the whole affair in a very cool, professional sort of way, seemed annoyed at the violence of the emotion that was exhibited by Harry. How little could they understand the feelings that were tugging at his heart. Indeed, one of them, in his ignorance of what Harry Dean was suffering and feeling, poured out a glass of wine, and approaching him, said—

"I am sure, sir, it will do you good, after your long watch, just to take a glass of port. It is good."

Harry Dean, in the agony of his spirit, was about to do what he seldom, indeed, ever did—namely, return an impertinent and angry answer; but he succeeded in checking himself in time, and said—

"No, I thank you. When my watch is quite concluded, I will do myself the pleasure."

"He is a fidget," muttered the inspector to himself; "but, for all that, he is quite a gentleman. Any one can see that."

Truly, any one who was in the smallest degree a judge of what a gentleman really ought to be, would not hesitate to bestow the title upon Harry Dean. Another hour passed away, and Dr. Bell was upon the point of saying something, when he saw Harry Dean suddenly spring to his feet.

"Is he there, sir?" said one of the inspectors.

Harry held back his hand deprecatingly. Dr. Bell flew to the window, and upon the door-step of No. 2 he saw a pale, haggard, ghostly-looking man standing for a moment or two looking about him, as though he were not in his right senses, or as one might suppose some prisoner, who had been immured in a dungeon for many long years, would look upon the world if suddenly and unexpectedly, without house or friends, let loose upon it.

"Is that——"

"Wilkins!" said Harry Dean. "Hush! hush! Leave all to me."

"But——"

"By heaven, I will not be questioned! Leave all to me, now. Hush—there— there he goes, How now? one—two— three — four — five — six raps. Ah, he quickens his pace. They shall have him, now—yes, they shall have him now!"

Harry Dean dashed his hand through a large pane of glass, and projecting the whistle through the aperture into the open air, he blew a shrill blast upon it that might have been heard at that silent time for half a mile.

"That's it, sir!" cried the inspector.

"Yes, that will have him," said the other.

The gaze of Harry Dean was still riveted upon the villain who had caused him so much unhappiness; and we may as well now step into the street, and see more particularly how it fared with the murderer. Wilkins, having made good his retreat to the door-step, leaving the street-door idly swinging upon its hinges, considered that he had as good as completed his escape. Even his fertile fancy could not for a moment picture to itself any danger. Truly the circumstances which had placed Harry Dean and the police in such close approximation to him, Wilkins, were so strange and unprecedented, that Wilkins might well be excused from thinking that by any possibility he was in the way of detection. Hence his strange scared look when he issued from the house was only attributable to the fever of his general spirits, and not to any special dread of detection.

Oh, what a world of horrors filled that man's brain at that time. He thought he had done a deed which would embitter the existence of Harry Dean; but he had, as we know, signally failed in that. His poniard had pierced the heart of the char-woman, while Kate had fallen into a serene slumber in the other chamber, into which she had gone by mistake. And there stood Wilkins upon the door step, and Harry Dean had grasped the inspector's signal whistle. We know he sounded it, but we follow Wilkins, and the events that to him happened. We have before described the state of mind in which Wilkins was when he left that fatal door step; but amid all the apprehensions and all the evil passions that were tugging at his heart, he certainly had not the remotest idea of being taken a prisoner by Harry Dean, or anybody acting for him. He looked more like a ghost than a living man, as he went several steps from the door with a strange swaggering gait down the street. It was then that Harry Dean's whistle sounded in his ears as though it were the last trumpet which was to summon him before an Incorruptible Judge, there to be sentenced according to those things which he had done in life. A man well dressed, but with anything but the air of a gentleman, although he had the clothing of one, slipped from out a doorway and confronted Wilkins.

"A rough night, sir," said the man.

Wilkins cowered back, and thrust his hand into the bosom of his apparel.

"Fool!" he said; "have you set your life upon this cast?"

"What cast, sir?"

"This," said Wilkins, and drawing his knife from his bosom, he was about to make a rush upon the man, when he was caught from behind in the arms of another, who said, in something of the voice of an amiable bear,—

"Gently, gently, sir. 'Don't give way to your bad passions,' as the copy books say. You are my prisoner."

"Prisoner!" gasped Wilkins.

"Yes," said Harry Dean from the balcony of the first floor, in which he had been watching for Wilkins, "you are my prisoner."

———

CHAPTER LXXXIX.

KATE IN THE CHAMBER.

WE left Kate in the chamber where she had, without the smallest previous intimation of doing so, gone for refuge against some one, she knew not whom, coming up the staircase of the house in which she had passed so many dreary hours. Little did she imagine what a frightful tragedy was about to be enacted upon that night of horrors. Little did she imagine that she was so near to such a scene of bloodshed and criminality as she really was. It will be remembered that, after finding that she was not in her own room, she had come to the hasty determination of remaining where she was. That chamber could not possibly present itself to her in a worse aspect than the last she occupied, and she considered that for a brief space she might positively benefit by the change; and as this chamber was not her prison, no precautions had been taken concerning its locks and other fastenings. A key was in the lock of the door, and she had the satisfaction of being able to lock herself in. Listening thus intently, she heard the sound of various footsteps, but at length all subsided into peace. Kate uttered a short and simple prayer, and then casting herself upon the bed, she fell into a deep, dreamless sleep, the first of the kind she had enjoyed since leaving the hospitable mansion of Dr. Bell. With the frightful events that occurred during that night the reader is sufficiently familiar. The murder that was done by Wilkins, within a few feet of where his supposed victim was calmly reposing, was executed with so much quietness that she, Kate, had heard nothing of it, and the soft and beautiful morning dawned into her room, finding no blood there, but such as coursed its way through her veins, and wandered about the truest, gentlest heart that ever beat in human bosom. But before that morning much was done. Kate is sleeping—Harry Dean is upon the balcony of the opposite house, proclaiming, in the terrified hearing of Wilkins, that he is his, Harry's, prisoner.—Two stout men have a firm grasp of the trembling wretch, and his wrists are clasped by the felon's irons.—His face is of ashy paleness.—It something resembled discoloured white wash

in parts.—His lips were unclosed, showing his fury-like teeth, and he shook in every limb. Those words of Harry Dean's—"You are my prisoner!" were more dreadful to him, than would have been any fiat of the Almighty. How could he now escape the consequences of his hideous criminality? What could he now say to move the pity of the man whose heart he fully believed he had rendered desolate?—and in the midst of all, he asked himself, How was it that at such a juncture he should fall into the hands of the man whom he had most cause to dread in all the world? He was stunned. He shook his head, to try to satisfy himself that he was not awake. He closed his eyes for a few moments, with the hope that he should open them upon another scene, and so convince himself that this sudden revulsion of his fortunes was not real. But no. There were the houses.—There were the officers of justice.—There was, above all, Harry Dean on the balcony with his arm extended, and those awful words upon his lips,—"You are my prisoner!" Wilkins lost the hope that he was yet in some dream, occasioned by the opinions he had conjured up in the fond hope that it would be an antidote to his cares. There can be no doubt but that if he had not been so completely stunned, as it were, by the suddenness of his arrest, he would have made some attempt to escape, of a violent nature. As it was, now apparently forgetting that his hands were not free, he commenced a furious struggle with the two officers who held him in their custody. It was a struggle without hope.

"Come, come," said one. "It's of no use your coming it in this way. You're booked, though I don't know for what. The gentleman is coming, and then you can say what you like; but as to getting away from us, you might as well try to move the house; so just be quiet."

"And here are some inspectors," said the other. "It's all right. A long watch we have had of it; but I suppose we shall get something handsome for our pains after all."

Wilkins caught at this expression. It implied that the officers would do anything for money. He thought they had apprehended him because they were paid for it, and why should not they let him go upon the same grounds, particularly if they were paid a hundred fold better?

"Listen to me," he said. "Take off these handcuffs, and let me run away, and you shall have £1000 between you. You shall, as I am a living man. I swear it by all that's sacred."

"Yes," said one of the officers, executing a feat called taking a sight, in vulgar English. "Yes, my rum 'un, at the end of a hook, I supposes."

"No doubt on it," added the other; "such as butchers hangs their meat on."

Another moment, and that last hope, dim and imperfect as it was, had fled. Harry Dean himself confronted Wilkins, and the two inspectors likewise joined the party.

"Wilkins," said Harry Dean, "your career of wickedness is at last over."

Wilkins glared at him for a few moments in silence, and then he lifted his eyes towards the face of Harry Dean, and spoke. He seemed as if,

having recovered from the first shock of his capture, all the violent and evil passions of his nature rose up again in opposition to the depression that for a time had bound him so completely down.

"Yes," he said, "I am your prisoner." It was those words which had implanted themselves in his brain, as though engraven there. "Yes, I am your prisoner, but my revenge is now complete — most complete; and come what may, I am satisfied; and you may, in that which you have yet to suffer, wring pity even from me. You will, proud, and haughty, and revengeful as you look, you will, I say, envy me."

"Wretched man! What new device is now hatching in your brain?"

"Nothing new."

"I defy now all the resources of that brain, teeming with wickedness and malice. Wilkins, you have for once been out-generaled; and you shall now suffer for your crimes as surely as there is a God in heaven, who now looks down upon us both."

"We shall both suffer," said Wilkins; "but you the most. Yes, yes, much the most; Harry Dean, as you choose to call yourself, far, by far the most. Oh, but you will envy me!"

A terrible misgiving came over the mind of Harry Dean; but yet what could he have to dread? Kate must be safe. Wilkins's obvious policy had been to keep her safe, and even to treat her well, and it was impossible that he could have had any notion that he was so closely watched. Besides, if he had such a notion, and was only apprehended in an attempt to escape, what would it have availed him to have done any injury to Kate?

"Oh, no, no, no, she is safe," said Harry to himself. "She, without whom life would indeed be a dreary waste, is safe."

He drew a long breath of relief, as he replied to Wilkins, saying—

"You hint obscurely at some mischief yet in your power to perpetrate, but I defy your power."

There was only one thing that kept Wilkins's tongue tied regarding the real facts of the case—real, as he believed them to be—and that was the faint hope that, amid all the juggles and uncertainties, and the chichaneries of the law, he might, although put upon his trial, find out some mode of escape. It was this consideration alone that prevented him from saying, in a voice of thunder, to Harry Dean—"Go into that house, and look upon the bleeding, lifeless corpse of her whose image sits so near your heart. Look upon the corpse of your beloved!" But he restrained himself. Wilkins was slowly recovering his accustomed caution, and was calculating his chances of escape from the consequences of the frightful crime he had committed. We have before stated that he left the door of the lodging-house open when he walked from it. What cared he, in the plenitude of his ferocity, and the fulness of his fancied security, what happened to the house? He was going to leave it, therefore it might be robbed, or its inmates all murdered, for he cared not a straw. Harry Dean saw in a moment that the house was so left; but he was not likely, even under the circumstances, to take advantage of such a defenceless state of the household. It was true, he thought, that Kate was in some room of that house, but still it was not for him to go from room to room, alarming and disturbing every one, in search of her, for, from what he had heard from the charwoman, he was induced to think the landlady of the house was more of a dupe than an accomplice with Wilkins, in the detention of poor Kate. To knock loudly then, so as to summon the mistress of the house and the servants, was the course Harry Dean thought he ought to adopt. Dr. Bell was by his side.

"Will you ring while I knock?" said Harry Dean.

"Certainly. They can but think the house is on fire; but frightening folks in this way, is better than bouncing into their bed-rooms."

The knocking and ringing had continued for about half a minute, when a faint scream was heard; and when Harry Dean advanced in the passage, and called out in a loud voice, "Who is that?" a flat chamber candlestick fell from a great height, the staircase being a well one, at his feet.

"Murder! Fire! Police" cried a voice; and the landlady, who had dropped the candle and candlestick over the banisters in her anxiety to see who was below, and what was the matter, now came rushing down in her night dress, and fell into the arms of Dr. Bell.

"Oh! is it fire or thieves?" she said.

"Neither, madam," said Dr. Bell; but pray oblige us by telling us if you are the mistress of this house, if you please?"

"Gracious Providence! Of course I am. Oh! what has happened? Tell me, is it fire or thieves?"

"Neither, madam. But had you a lodger named Wilkins?"

"Wilkins, and the F.M., and all that sort of thing? To be sure, I had a house, and means to keep it—a very nice gentleman—don't mind extras a bit, and that's what you can say for few lodgers now-a-days. They kicks at extras like mad. But what is the matter? I am quite astonished. Pray, sir, why are you looking at my feet in such a way?"

These last words were addressed to Henry Dean. Dr. Bell looked at him, and then at the landlady's feet, and then along the passage up the staircase, and by the light of one of the policemen's lanterns, he saw that there were marks of footsteps in blood all the way she had come. The landlady made the same discovery at the same moment, and she gave a shriek of dismay as she did so; and on glancing at her foot she found it stiffened and bedabbled with the same ensanguined hue. Something horrible must have taken place.

"Good God!" said Dr. Bell, "what does it mean?"

"Answer me, woman! and for your life answer me truly,—have you a young lady in your house named Kate Destern?"

"F.M.," gasped the landlady.

"What on earth does she mean by F.M?" said Henry Dean. "Answer me, woman, or you may find the consequences far from pleasant to you."

"The only young lady is Mr. Wilkins's niece—she as is out of her mind. The bishop thinks a private asylum best, but the doctor keeps his niece; and the F.M. you must know——"

"Silence!" said Henry, who had lighted, by the aid of the lantern, the candle that the landlady had let fall over the balustrade. "Silence! Conduct me at once to this young lady. If you have been deceived by this villain Wilkins, you are free from blame; if you are, however, his accomplice, the only way by which you may hope for mercy being shown to you is, by at once disclosing all you know, and conducting me to the young lady."

"What, sir! Mr. W. a villain?"

"Yes; and such a villain as, for the credit of human nature, we will hope is rarely produced. Now, madam, I will follow you."

"Well, I never!" muttered the landlady. "The idea of anybody being a villain who gives twenty pounds for extras, and don't ask how it goes. Oh dear me! There must be some mistake. Dr. Wilkins will soon put this all to rights 'tis sure."

There was, however, no such thing as avoiding the command of Henry Dean to show him to the chamber of Kate; accordingly she said, "well, sir, if you will follow me—I hope you are one of the family—I will take you up stairs to the young lady's room. It's quite a pleasure to me to find that it's neither fire nor thieves."

"Lead on, lead on."

Henry Dean strode after the landlady, and as he went he kept glancing at the staircase. He shuddered as he saw the bloody footsteps repeated all the way up. They passed the first floor, and they were still, for a good reason too, as will be seen. A faint feeling came over him. He began again to recollect the obscure hints of Wilkins that he had had his revenge; yet it was too maddening to reconcile those words with what his heated imagination now suggested as possible. And yet what Harry Dean tried to reject as too much to palm off upon human nature as at all probable, namely, the murder of Kate Wilkins, he actually believed he had done in cool blood, and in the horrible manner we have described.

"Stop!" said Harry Dean.

The landlady stopped and shook, for she too saw the blood prints upon the white damask that covered the rich stair carpets of the house. They were now half way up both of the stairs of the sacred place upon which, it will be recollected, was Kate's chamber.

"Can you tell me the meaning of these prints of blood? Can you, before we proceed one more step, give me any satisfactory solution of this? For the love of Heaven. speak if you can!"

"I cannot, I feel as if I was in a dream."

"Go on—go on—God leave me my reason, let my eyes be blasted with what sight they may! Go on—go on—I will follow you."

Hamlet, when he followed his father's spirit in "arms," could not have done so with more nervous brooding in his soul than now beset Harry Dean, as he followed the footsteps of the landlady up the stairs leading to the sleeping chambers of that house. Suddenly the landlady uttered a shriek and fell huddled up on the stairs, without sense or motion. She had fainted. It was fortunate that Harry Dean himself carried the light, instead of entrusting it to her. He strode over her prostrate form, and then holding up the light, he saw what it was that had so frozen up her faculties with horror. Creeping down the stairs in a thick straining stream, from step to step, came warm clotted blood. He saw it reach the head of the stairs and come gliding down, while the red scent of it filled the air with that peculiar odour which, once known, can never be forgotten.

CHAPTER XC.

THE DISCOVERY.

TRANSFIXED with horror—motionless with dread, or rather immoveable—a certainty of what he was to undergo, poor Harry Dean — poor indeed! thus stood about five steps down the staircase watching the blood as it came over in a mimic, but terrible cataract, to meet him where he stood. At that moment, with a feeling upon his mind approaching closely to certainty of the murder of Kate, he would freely have dropped dead upon the spot, could the choice to do so, or to live even in wretchedness, have been his. But even at that moment of dread and despair, he did not verify the words of Wilkins, that he should envy him. The truth was, that Harry Dean, at that time, did not think of him at all. The frightful calamity which had boomed upon his soul, was of sufficient magnitude to leave all his mind to itself. He quite forgot Wilkins.

"Dead — dead — murdered!" he gasped. "Oh no, no, no; God has angels enough yet!"

"What is it?" cried Dr. Bell from below; "what is it?"

"Murder!"

"Good God! no. You do not surely, Mr. Dean, mean that the villain has done such a deed—you terrify me. You will surely drive my reason from me."

"Come up."

Dr. Bell immediately ascended the staircase and stood by the side of Harry Dean, who silently pointed to the terrible spectacle before him, and then looking in the face of the doctor, he said, in a strange, deep, husky voice,—what is that?"

"Blood!"

"Kate's blood. Oh, God—oh, God —why am I alive to see this hour? Is there no friendly lightning to find my heart, and let my spirit loose?"

The light shook in his hand so much, that Dr. Bell took it from him as he said—

"Be calmer, I implore you. Wait here. Mr. Dean, while I follow this blood track, and ascertain from whence it comes. Do not advance another step, I will faithfully report to you."

"No—no—no——"

"Nay, permit me ——"

"I dare not—I cannot—no—no."

"Let me implore you. The sudden sight of anything dreadful might be too much for you; while, full of grief as I shall be, I am yet more used to scenes of woe than you. I pray you permit me to go and see what has happened."

"The suspense would kill me," said Harry Dean. "The light—the light! give me the light. I must and will see what there is to see, even if it drive me mad."

By a sudden movement, he wrested the light from the hands of Dr. Bell, and dashed up the few remaining steps of the staircase. Dr. Bell followed him, but he followed him slowly. He suspected all that Harry Dean expected, and he dreaded the effect it might have upon his sensitive frame. It was not difficult for Harry Dean to follow the track of the blood. He coasted it, if

we may be allowed the expression, along the corridor, whence it had flowed in a narrow stream, adapting itself to the inequalities of the floor. On, on he went, until he reached a door. It was from under that door that the blood came in a thick and fetid stream, and then he paused for a moment.

"Come down!" cried Dr. Bell. "Come down, for God's sake, Mr. Dean, and leave me to follow up this matter. You are much better below here."

Harry waved his hand, and then he tried the lock of the door. It yielded to his touch, and he shook like one in an ague fit. A voice sounded from the top of the stairs. It was that of the landlady, who having recovered from her swoon, was coming after him.

"Oh, sir," she said, "tell me—do tell me what has happened."

"Peace!" cried Harry Dean.

She paused panic-stricken; and then pointing to the door, and speaking with a great effort—the words, like Macbeth's amen, seeming to stick in his throat— Harry Dean said—

"Woman, is this the room?"

"Yes, yes. The young lady's room, Dr. Wilkins's niece, you know, and the niece of the bishop and the F. M., you know. Oh dear—oh dear, my house will be ruined after this, quite ruined, and I'm ruined too, or shall be."

Harry Dean opened the door, and shading the light with his hand, he looked in. One glance towards the bed showed him the bleeding corpse; all was still. He gave one gasping sob, and then closing the door again, he turned to the landlady. The calmness with which he now spoke was truly frightful, as he said—

"She is murdered!"

"Murdered?"

"Yes. By Wilkins she is murdered, and I am desolate!"

Oh, what a world of anguish was comprised in that one word, desolate, uttered in the tone, too, that it was by poor Harry Dean—we call him poor now, for his sufferings at that time, although all without real cause, made him poor indeed.

We might parody for him the lines of the poet of poets, and say—

He who steals my purse steals trash;
But he who filches from me my soul's idol,

Takes that which not enriches him,
But makes me poor, indeed !

To Harry Dean's comprehension and feelings his soul's idol was gone, and henceforth the world to him was to be "stale, flat, and unprofitable"—an "unweeded garden." Well might he say—"I am desolate !" The strange, unnatural calmness that had crept over him, however, was the very worst of all the features that his agony of mind could have assumed. It was that calmness which the most inexperienced in the phenomenon of the human heart might have safely pronounced was but the prelude to some storm of the passions, which might be most fearful in its character. There was no trembling now, and, but for his ghastly face, no one would have thought that anything particularly agitating had happened to Harry Dean, as he stepped across the corridor and met Dr. Bell, who stood by the head of the staircase.

"Well ?—well ?" said the physician.

"She is murdered !" said Harry Dean, "and lies there cold and weltering in blood !"

Dr. Bell thought he was prepared for this information, but now that it really came with all its stunning force upon him, he was compelled to hold by the rails of the balustrade to keep himself from falling, as he repeated the word "murdered !" as though it was some new idea, and not one that had been familiar to his apprehension for the last quarter of of an hour.

"Yes, she is foully murdered by Wilkins, and that is the end of all !"

"But—but—Mr. Dean——"

"Well, sir ?"

"This horrid calmness ! — this unchanging tone !—this stolidity of face ! Good God ! Mr. Dean, believe me, I would rather see you in an agony of grief. This is unnatural !"

"It is. Don't you think it the commencement of the end ?"

"What end ?"

"Madness ! What a mercy that would be ! Aye, there is hope there—I may go quite mad ! and with a vacant interest find amusement in a show !— ha ! ha ! This comes of walking gently through the world, and trusting to Providence ! But, my friend, will you not go and see my poor dead girl ?—you are used to strange sights."

"I have a worse here," said Dr. Bell, as he took Harry Dean by the arm and led him down stairs. "My good young friend, let me implore you to rouse yourself. Remember that you are young, and that you probably have duties and obligations in this world yet. Do not— oh, do not allow this unmanly sorrow to consume you. Come, sit down in this room, I see it is vacant. Sit down and talk to me."

The door of the magnificent drawing-room, so recently occupied by Wilkins, was open, and Dr. Bell led Harry Dean into it. One of the inspectors of police came in at the moment, and said—

"Need we keep our prisoner longer here ?"

Dr. Bell rose, and taking him to a window, briefly told him what had happened, upon which the inspector looked amazed.

"This is truly serious," he said.

"It is indeed. I think you had better remove your prisoner at once, and oblige me by sending one of your men to Dr. Grant, who resides at No. 9, in Belgrave-street, with my compliments and a hope that he will come to me upon the instant. Will you do that ?"

"Certainly, sir. Oh, of course. Dear me ! What a noise the murder will make to be sure."

"It will, indeed."

At this moment Harry Dean rose and walked rapidly from the room, and down the stairs, before Doctor Bell could stop him. As it was, the doctor and the inspector both ran after him, but Harry stopped not until he reached the step upon which was Wilkins guarded by the two policemen. Advancing then towards him, and holding him by the lappets of his coat with both hands, Harry Dean said to him—

"Devil ! Devil ! What tempted you to do this deed ?"

"Ha ! ha !" laughed Wilkins. "You know it now."

"Fiend !"

"Ha ! ha ! ha !"

"Tell me, what had I done to you that you should set yourself up as the curse and the blight of my young life. Speak to me, and tell me if that you are human ?"

"Ha! ha! ha!"

Harry shook for a moment, and then he fell insensible at the feet of Wilkins, who again burst into a brutal laugh, as he cried—

"I said I would be revenged, and of a surety I am. Do with me what you like now. Take me where you please, I have blighted that man. Yes, blighted is the word; I might once secretly have poisoned his body, and so taken life from him, but I have had a real, subtle vengeance—I have poisoned his spirit, and he shall know peace no more. Ha! ha! ha!"

Dr. Bell spoke not a word to Wilkins, but by the assistance of the inspector he lifted up Harry Dean, and between them they carried him to the drawing-room again, and laid him on a couch. And all this time Kate slept as soundly as one whom innocence and sweet holy feelings blessed,—that sleep, one bliss-ful hour of which is worth an age of restless power and wild ambition.

CHAPTER XCI.

THE DREAM.

Dr. Bell considered Harry Dean's situation to be extremely critical, and he not only sent off immediately for another medical friend, but desired the inspector at once to make a report of the whole affair to a magistrate, and if possible get his attendance at the house, as the whole matter was of more than ordinary gravity.

"There will be an inquest, sir," said the inspector.

"Yes, yes, and I feel that I ought to go and look at the dead up stairs, but really I have not the heart to do so. I loved her living in a different way to what this gentleman loved her, and for the first time I shrink from the dead."

"It's natural, sir."

"It is, I suppose. I would have given all I am worth in the world, to have prevented this horrible tragedy."

"Shall I go, sir?"

"Yes, if you like, just for formality's sake go, and then close and lock the door; of course, you know that nothing must be touched."

"All's right, sir. I have seen one or two queer sights in my life."

The inspector went up stairs, and soon came back with the key of the room in his hand, saying—

"She is stone dead, sir, but——"

"No more—no more. For God's sake, make no remarks to me about her appearance."

The medical friend who had been sent for by Dr. Bell, soon came, for he resided in the immediate vicinity. It was now just the dawn of morning, and Dr. Bell had really not succeeded in restoring Harry Dean to a state of perfect consciousness, although now and then some nervous twitchings of the facial muscles encouraged him to think that he should soon do so.

"How welcome, Grant!" cried Dr. Bell. "This is a sad affair."

"I guessed there was something very unusual, Bell, by your sending for me by a policeman, and in such an urgent manner as you did—what is it?"

A sad case, indeed, just look at this young gentleman, and tell me what you think of him.

"Humph! Syncope, I suppose—not cataleptic, I hope."

"I hope not, but fear it is so. A great mental shock has produced the case. This unfortunate gentleman fell into such a condition as you now see, upon suddenly hearing of the murder of one whom he dearly loved. In fact, I believe he saw the body weltering in blood —a strange, unnatural calmness came over him, and then he dropped off into this state."

Dr. Grant shook his head.

"God help him," he said, "it may be worse when he recovers. You have often heard of the brain being perma-nently affected by such matters?"

"I have indeed, and seen instances too. What do you advise?"

"Let us see if we can rouse him."

They got Harry Dean into a sitting posture, and tried various means of restoring him to a state of consciousness. It was no small gratification to them both to find that it was but an ordinary fainting, aggravated by the deep mental distress which the young man suffered. The vigour of a youthful constitution saved him from any of those worse con-sequences which might have been produced by the serious mental shock he had experienced.

"He will do," said Grant.

"Thank heaven, yes," responded Dr. Bell. "He will do. Temperate living, you see, and a naturally clear head piece, has saved him."

"Yes, such a shock upon a diseased or enervated frame would have been fatal. What is his name, Bell?"

"Mr. Dean, he calls himself; but I have reason to believe he is somebody else of rather more importance than that name would lead you to suppose. He answers, however, as they say of dogs, to the name of Dean, so you can use it in addressing him."

"That will do."

Dr. Grant now raised his voice and said—

"Mr. Dean, allow me, as a friend, as well as a medical man, to advise you to make some strong mental effort to recover yourself from the apathetic condition in which you are. I shall feel much pleased if you will answer me."

Harry Dean looked up in the physician's face, and said faintly—

"She is dead !"

"Well, Mr. Dean, we must all die some day. The world is full of pitfalls, and each day of our brief and petty existence, we escape death a hundred times and know it not. You should consider, sir, that death, instead of being an evil, and a grief, and a pain, is the end of all evil, all grief, and all pain."

"And more especially," added Dr. Bell, "to such as she who has gone from you, in whose life there has not been one action that angels might not record as full of gentleness and heavenly goodness. Do you hear me?"

Harry Dean nodded, and then said faintly,—

"Leave me to myself awhile. I shall recover from this shock. I thank you for what you have done for me. The worst is past. I pray you leave me to myself."

"Freely, said Dr. Bell. "Come, Grant, we may now, I am sure, trust our young friend entirely to his own thoughts. They will guide him free of any perils, I am sure. Will you be good enough, Mr. Dean, to ring when you wish for anything, and I will come to you."

Harry Dean pressed the hand of the worthy physician, and then they left him to himself. He walked to the windows and closed the blinds, so as to shut out even the faint morning light that was struggling in. Then, having darkened the room effectually, he lay down upon a couch, and closed his eyes to think. He was resolved before he rose again to restore himself, if possible, completely to his ordinary frame of mind.

"My heart," he said, is desolate ; "but I have still duties to perform to save the sister of poor Kate, and to others likewise. I shall go through life now a lost and melancholy man ; but in the depths of my own heart I will strive to hide my feelings and my despair."

We will leave Henry Dean in this strange state of mind, while we follow the two medical men from the room into the apartment below, where the landlady, one of the inspectors of police, and an official from the nearest police office were assembled. Wilkns had been taken away and safely lodged in prison, until the time for a preliminary examination, before an investigation should come.

"We have sent to the coroner," said the official personage ; "can any one tell me the name of the deceased person?"

"Yes," said Dr. Bell. "I am sorry to say I can. Her name is Kate Destern—poor girl !"

"Thank you, sir. I suppose you medical gentlemen have seen the lady?"

Dr. Bell shook his head as he said, "you will be surprised at me, a medical man, shrinking from such a sight; but I loved that poor girl as dearly as though she was a child of my own, and it would be a severe shock to me to see her in her present situation. My friend here, Dr. Grant, however, I think, will have no objection to view the body. The policeman has already, I think, seen it."

"I have," said the inspector ; "but I will go up stairs with Dr. Grant, if you please, gentlemen, as I have in my possession the key of the room, which I do not feel myself justified, under the circumstances, in parting with until the coroner arrives."

"You are quite right," said Dr. Grant, "come with me, and as a matter of fancy I will look at the body, so as to be able say that I have done so to the coroner, when he arrives. Come, Bill, be more yourself. Remember that—

"The sleeping and the dead are but as pictures."

"I cannot—I cannot."

"Well, well, don't force yourself. I know how important it is to keep off the mind a distressing reminiscence, so perhaps you are right in reflecting. Now, Mr. Inspector, if you please to produce your key, I am ready to accompany you up stairs at once, sir."

"Certainly, sir, I will follow you."

Dr. Bell looked after them with a

KATE DESTERN RECOVERING FROM HER SWOON.

shudder as they ascended the staircase, but he was raised from the state of stupor which was creeping over him, by the clerk from the police-office saying to him—

"You have important evidence, I suppose, sir, to give regarding this sad affair?"

"Yes, yes, I think I have, but Mr. Dean knows the most about it. There can be no doubt, however, regarding the guilt of the man Wilkins."

"You think not."

"I feel morally certain. It was in fear of him doing such a deed, that I and my friends were upon the spot, but we were too late, as it has appeared. Oh, if we could but have foreseen what was going to happen, how we would have flown to the rescue of so much innocence and beauty. It is horrifying and soul-harrowing, to think that while we were watching the house that dreadful deed was being done, which we would all give anything we possess to have undone."

"A sad thing, sir."

"Most sad, indeed. Oh, here is Dr. Grant returned. Quite dead, Grant, of course?"

"I should say death must have been instantaneous."

"The—the—throat—cut, I suppose?" faltered Bell.

"No, stabbed to the heart."

Dr. Bell shuddered, as he said—

"Oh, when will the sun again shine upon so much excellence and purity, and beauty? The more I think upon this affair, the more it cuts me to the soul. Oh! Grant, you should have known her as I knew her."

"Long ago, I suppose," said Dr. Grant, much surprised at the raptures of his friend, considering that the corpse he had seen was that of an old dowdy-looking woman, not over clean, and smelling, even in death, strongly of "cream of the valley." Dr. Bell took his friend Grant aside into the recess of one of the windows, and looking at him, with quivering lips and a tearful expression, he said—

"She is beautiful, I suppose, even in death?"

"Not very."

"Oh, yes, yes. She could not, even in the repose of death, lose all her charms. I have seen fair faces, still with so much of earthly beauty upon them, although life had fled, that one—

"Still might doubt the tyrant's power;"

and my poor Kate, I can fancy, was one of those. Alas! alas!"

"It's a matter of taste," said Dr. Grant. "Every man to his liking, as the proverb says."

"But she is still beautiful?"

"Humph! not to my eyes—but, as I say, we won't fall out about beauty. I have in my time encountered some of the most strange and absurd tastes that ever a man could be invested with."

"You have no conscience in your disposition."

"Certainly not so much as you have, my dear friend, when you fall into raptures about the personage up stairs. But, come, think of something more cheerful, my friend. You are quite upset about the matter."

"I am, indeed. You have no notion what a shock this has been to me; I must have a lock of her hair, poor thing, as a remembrance of her charms."

"A what?"

"A lock of her hair."

"Well, upon my word, Bell, I did think you a man of some sense, but I do believe you are out of your senses. You are enough to aggravate a saint. A lock of her hair! Ho! ho! ho! Excuse me, but I must laugh, if my life depended upon it, and notwithstanding murder is most foul at the very best, and let who will be the victim. Come, come, Bell, shake off this nightmare of the spirits that oppress you, for I can really call it nothing else."

"You astonish and afflict me, Grant."

"Do I?—damn it, you have fully returned the compliment, and made me swear into the bargain; I must confess I cannot be so plaguily sympathetic. You should not have asked me to see your model of perfection. It has knocked all the nuisance of the matter upon the head. Here, Mr. Inspector. Did you feel struck by the angelic beauty of the corpse up stairs?"

"God bless me, no, sir."

"Stop," said Dr. Bell. "Madam, you are the landlady of this house. Was the young lady who is up stairs beautiful or not. Answer me truly?"

"Quite a pure angel!"

"Did she drink?" said Grant.

"Drink!" shouted Dr. Bell. "You beast!"

"Well," said Dr. Grant, "upon my word, Bell, I think the sooner you retire to a private asylum, the better it will be for yourself, and for society at large. I must for the present, until you are better or worse, decline any conversation with you."

"A good riddance," said Dr. Bell; "I shall go home and come back when the inquest takes place. When will it be, Mr. Inspector, do you think?"

"About three o'clock, the coroner's

clerk has sent word. I shall remain in the house until then, but you had better, sir, attend at the police-office, for Wilkins will be brought up, and just enough evidence taken to remand him until the inquest is over, and then he will be committed to Newgate to take his trial. His fate is fixed, I suppose. What a madman he must have been, to be sure; but I suppose it will all come out upon the trial."

"No doubt, no doubt," said Dr. Bell. "Say to Mr. Dean, if he should ask for me, that I will be back here at three o'olock precisely, and beg him to wait for me."

"Depend upon me, sir. I will not forget your instructions. You will find me here, sir."

Dr. Bell left the house, and as he walked hastily homewards, he muttered to himself—"What a thoroughly insensible pig to anything in the shape of beauty, that Grant must have become lately! The idea of his speaking so disparagingly of poor Kate, who I am sure must have looked beautiful even in death."

Now if Dr. Bell had been a man of rather stronger nerves than he was, or if he had cared less for Kate Destern than he did, how great an amount of suffering would have been spared to Harry Dean and to himself. He would, had he but possessed courage enough to go into the chamber of death, at once have seen that it was not the beautiful Kate Destern who lay there in grim and ghastly repose, but Mrs. Lupin, the charwoman, with whom he and Harry Dean had so recently made a bargain offensive and defensive. In fact; just to think now how curiously things happen in this word—the sovereign that had been given to Mrs. Lupin had, in a manner of speaking, bribed her to die for Kate. As thus— into "Old Thomas," regularly called gin, she had liquidated a portion of the gold, and that had made her *non compus* to the eyes of the cook at No. 2 who in her indignation, went to bed, leaving her, Mrs. Lupin, in the kitchen, who again, in *her* indignation, walked up stairs into Kate's bed-room. One who knew a thing or two has said,—

" There is a special providence in the fall of a sparrow !"

And who shall say there was not a special providence in the fall of Mrs. Lupin ? We will not be so profane as to say a special constable would have been more to the purpose at the moment, but certain it is—Mrs. Lupin had died for Kate Destern, however little of the old spirit of matyrdom there might really have been in that good lady's anti-chivalrous composition.

CHAPTER XCII.

JOY.

IN the meantime Harry Dean had fallen asleep upon the couch in the splendid drawing-room, and had a dream. Exhaustion had hold upon his frame. After a flood of tears, which seemed to wash away the bitterest feeling that had oppressed him, a holy calm spread itself around his heart, and, as if fanned by the breath of angels, he sunk into sleep. It was not a dreamless sleep though, for it was full of strange images. He fancied himself wandering in a country full of all the delights of Asiatic scenery, without any of its enervating influences. Clustering grapes hung pendant from bough to bough of the wild acacia, and the blushing pomegranate wooed his touch. The songs of innumerable birds made the air vocal with primitive melody, and he thought he told himself that this must surely be the lost Eden of our first parents. In the midst of this region of enchantments flowed a silvery stream, upon the margin of which he walked, crushing at every footstep innumerable sweet flowers. The stream was but a step across, and upon the other bank walked Kate. She was smiling, and happy-looking. She held out her hand to him, saying as she did so—" My Harry, you will not come to me. Ah, why will you think me lost to you ?"

But still he lingered upon what might be called his own side of the stream, and although he had all the wish in the world to cross, some unknown power of magic or fascination kept him where he was. He could not make the step, much as he longed to do so, which would place him by the side of his much-loved

Kate. It was strange in what an even course this dream continued, as for miles he seemed to walk side by side with Kate, only separated from her by that little silvery rill. Oh! what efforts he made to reach Kate. At length, he thought that her face wore a melancholy expression, instead of the intensely happy one which had before characterised it, and she spoke to him, saying—

"Harry, we have but one more trial now. It is a strange one. We have both been tried by adversity. We shall both now be tried by joy, and then when that is past, we shall be very, very happy indeed."

"Ah, Kate," he said. "Why are we not happy now?—Why may I not come to you, dear one?"

It was strange, that throughout all that dream, which betrayed a certain activity of mind, he completely forgot all about the supposed murder of Kate. It was a circumstance that appeared completely to have slipped his memory. In reply to his last words, he thought she said—

"Very soon, Harry;" and then she began to fade away from him; but still the last word she had uttered, being his own name, seemed to reverberate in his ears, and he thought he heard, "Harry! —Harry!—Harry!" repeated in a half-frenzied modulation.

    *   *   *   *

At this point, with the reader's permission, we will proceed up stairs, and introduce him or her, as the case may be, into Kate's chamber. We have said that Kate, after fastening the door of the new bed-room, into which she had so accidentally made her way, threw herself upon the bed, and for the first time, in that house, tasted of the luxury of real repose. Had she been asked, she could not have told why a feeling of perfect security crept over her mind, and induced that calmness which enabled her to close her eyes in sleep after that brief prayer to the Author of all good, which she had prefaced her repose with. There she lay, in all her beauty,

"As still as some marble saint upon a marble
    tomb!"

and nothing knew she of what was passing around her, upon that which was decidedly the most dangerous and most eventful evening and night of her existence Now, with your permission,

reader, we will just consider what amount of alarm there was during that night to awaken Kate. First of all, there was the murder itself, which was all done after she slept. But then Wilkins, for his own safety's sake, made as little noise as possible, creeping with Tarquin-like strides to and from the accomplishment of the dreadful deed, which, in every aspect, was the greatest mistake he ever made in his life. He did not make noise enough to awaken Kate, who was the only person sleeping upon that floor ; and Mrs. Lupin herself made no sign. One gasping sigh or sob was all that heralded her into eternity. Peace be to her manes! She did not awaken poor Kate from her sweet slumber. Nothing alarming, then, occurred until Harry Dean knocked at the door, and Dr. Bell rung the bell. She heard neither. The noise of the knocking was much dissipated in that well-furnished house before it reached her, and the bell (not the doctor) was in the kitchen. Then Harry Dean ascended the stairs, and so did the landlady partially, and so did the doctor ; but from the first moment that they had all of them seen the blood upon the stairs, a kind of awe crept over them, and they spoke in whispers and moved like ghosts. From that time there was no noise in the house. The presence of death had had its usual influence, and a dreary stillness crept over the spirit of every one in that place. They seemed to be afraid of disturbing the sanctity of that repose which was the only one that nothing could disturb. But that was nature. And so Kate Destern slept on with despair, and woe, and bitterness, and grief, and horror, all around her—she slept on, the sleep of the young and good, and great—for Kate was truly great—great in her goodness, and in her virtue, and in her beauty. Wilkins was taken away, Harry Dean had fallen asleep in the drawing-room—the police had possession of the house ; and the clear blue eyed morning came, and no one thought it worth while to look into that empty room, where it was thought no person had slept for some time, but where there was such a living precious treasure. It was not broad-daylight, but light enough to see surrounding objects, when Kate quietly and gently awoke, and looked around her.

"What a sweet calm sleep I have h d," was Kate's first remark. "Ah, if I could but escape from this house and that dreadful man Wilkins, as he calls himself, I might always have such happy slumbers.—Oh, Harry, how have you rested this past night, I wonder. Shall I ever have the joy of looking upon your face again?"

Sh[ ]   from the bed and leant her face upon her hands

"In maiden meditation;"

and then with a sigh she arose and approached the toilette to arrange the disordered tresses of that fair hair which Dr. Bell wanted a lock of, and which Dr. Grant thought constituted a piece of insanity in Dr. Bell, that qualified him for a lunatic asylum. Kate began now to think what might be the possible consequences of the step she had taken, of going into another bed-room than the one allotted to her; and the more she thought over the sport of the affair, the more surprised she was that no one had disturbed her.

"They must have missed me by this time," she said, "early though it is, and one would think they would hardly omit looking here for me."

She went to the window and peered out through the glass. It was certainly very early, and the servants might not have yet risen—Wilkins might not yet have sent the landlady up to her room to as sure herself of her, Kate's, safe keeping Along with all this a blissful thought arose, which was, that she might possibly make her escape, now that she was not confined to one particular room. The same use that over night i   d her to abandon all attempts on the street door could hardly now operate, for the house seemed quiet, and that she had not been visited, appeared to her tolerably good presumptive evidence that the household had not risen.

"I will try," she said, "it is daylight, and I am wonderfully refreshed by slumber; if I could get any weapon now, I would strive to break that padlock that foiled me last night. Oh, if I could but once gain the street, I should soon find somebody who would befriend me, and by dint of diligent inquiry, I should find my way to Harry Dean."

The chance of such a consummation as this was so full of hopefulness and joy that Kate could not abandon it without a struggle. She looked round the room with the hope of finding something that would assist her—but, alas! there was nothing. She had a knife, and that was all; but still she would not abandon the hope of freedom, and an idea struck her that she thought better than trying to break open the street door, in which she might be foiled by the noise it would make.

"If I can get into any of the front rooms near the street," she said, "the parlour, for instance, I can surely attract the attention of the police, or of some one who will assist me; I can send some one, on promise of a reward, to Dr. Bell, and if he ever knows where I am I shall soon be rescued."

This was a good feasible sort of plan, and one which Kate was not a little anxious to carry out as quickly as possible. She opened the chamber door and stepped on the landing. What was her horror, to find she had at the first step placed her feet in a pool of blood. She recoiled with a half scream. And yet, horrible and mysterious as was that circumstance, was she upon its account to give up the plan of escape? Oh, no—no—a hundred times no. She recovered herself with courage, and passed on to the head of the stairs. Then she paused and listened intently. It had so happened that while Kate listened no one spoke below sufficiently loud for her to hear, and to her apprehension, therefore, all was profoundly still. In point of fact, that feeling to which we have already adverted, and which is so often produced by a consciousness of death being in a house, and which induces a timid and gentle footstep, had its effect even upon the voices of those who conversed below—whispers were the order of the day. Trembling, and yet with more courage than she had started with, notwithstanding the sight of the blood upon the landing, Kate commenced the descent of the stairs.

"Oh, Harry Dean," she murmured, —" Harry Dean, how you would fly to aid me if you knew where I really was, and with what dangers and miseries I am environed."

How little did the beautiful Kate Destern suspect that she was really now only separated from that very Harry Dean, whom she so apostrophised, by a very few paces, nay, even that her voice, if excited beyond its ordinary pitch, would reach his ears. But so it is—when we are apparently sunk deepest in hopelessness—when the storms of fate most appear to lower around us, some gleam of joyful sunshine may be near at hand to cheer and to compensate us for all that has passed, and wrap the soul in extacy. Step by step went poor Kate, until she reached the landing of the drawing-room floor, and then either she was so much nearer to those who were talking below, that she heard their subdued voices, or they suddenly spoke louder, but certain it is she was horrified by the hum of conversation, most unmistakeably coming from somewhere on the ground floor.

───

CHAPTER XCIII.

AN APPARITION.

KATE felt at that moment as though all her hopes of escape from the splendid prison had vanished like a dream. She clasped her hands despairingly as she said—

"Oh, shall I never again feel what it is to be free?"

How little she guessed that the pure light of that freedom she so sighed for was in effect now around and about her, and that she had not an enemy now in that house, upon the staircase of which she stood so pale and so trembling, alive to the slightest noise, and listening with dread to the murmured tone of the voices which came upon her ears from the room below. But Kate was courageous even in circumstances of the greatest danger—we have more than once seen that she was so ; and under even dilemmas where less exalted souls would have shrunk aghast, and given up all further struggle, she has nobly persevered towards the accomplishment of the objects she had in view. Thus, then, upon the present occasion, confounded as she was for a few moments, and con-

tinuously shocked at the idea that escape by the street door was barred by the persons who were evidently in the lower part of the house, she soon recovered herself sufficiently to say—

"What can next be done for the best?"

This was an anxious question ; yet to her apprehension time was most precious, therefore it was one that required something like an immediate answer, and that answer consisted in a determination to go into the first room that presented itself, open the window she could most conveniently reach, and call upon the passers-by, among whom might be the police, for help. If such a plan failed for the moment, it might lead to ultimate inquiry, and, for aught she knew to the contrary, it might at the moment succeed, beyond or fully up to her most sanguine expectations. She approached the drawing-room—that drawing-room, in which no less a personage than Harry Dean is lying asleep on a couch. He had darkened the apartment, by closing all the shutters, in the hour of his calamity. The light of Heaven was distasteful to him. While Kate's hand lies trembling on the door handle, we will take the liberty of peeping in and glancing at Harry Dean. He had lain for a considerable time in a kind of torpor ; but what would have had a bad effect upon the spirits and feelings of many, tended much to his recovery— namely, semi-darkness and solitude. The shutters of all the windows were closed, save one flap of one of them, and through that opening there came one of those shining, misty-looking rays of sunshine, in which millions upon millions of atoms seem to be dancing and whirling in mad jollity. This ray of light, which was about eight feet only in width, reached from the open shutter to the door. And now, after a time, the slumber which exhausted nature had claimed the right of having, dropped from the senses of Harry Dean, and partially sitting up on the sofa, he leant his head upon his hand, and began to think. Oh! who shall tell what direful thoughts pass through the brain of man, when he feels that the hope of an existence is blighted, the mainstay of a happy life shivered, and he left desolae. Friends may be false, gold may "make unto itself wings and fleed the expectations of ambition may blighted, the budding hopes of chil hood cankered, but there can be no feelings comparable to crushed affections. It is taking the odour from the violet, light from the day, and hope and beauty from all things. "She is gone! she is gone! and I am desolate!"

These were the words which, softly as they were uttered by poor Harry Dean, comprised the reality of his present position. Strange position; for there was Kate holding her hand upon her heart, to still its wild, tumultuous beating, while she gently tried the yielding lock of the door, which alone separated her from the immediate presence of him who mourned for her, and thought her numbered with the bright things that had gone by. Another moment, and she quietly turned the latch. There was no noise; and Kate thought, surely that room was unoccupied. "Yes," she thought, "I will to the window and cry for help. They shall not tear me from it until some one has heard how much I am oppressed."

Unfortunately, or perhaps fortunately, it is hard to say which, the door opened so as to shroud Harry Dean from Kate's eyes until she should be some paces from him, and then she stepped at once into that ray of light, so full of dazzling atoms that she could see nothing. Now Harry Dean's head was turned another way; he had been looking at the dancing atoms, but he looked at them no longer, and he had fallen into a train of thought which comprehended an immediate and long, perhaps an eternal pilgrimage, from the land of his birth. If ever he was to recover the semblance of an outward serenity, he thought it would be by foreign travel, through wild and unknown lands, where even if he left his bones to bleach amid the wilderness, or to rot in pathless forests, it mattered little to that sorrow-stricken man. But a something attracts his attention—a something like a long-drawn breath—it might be the faint sigh of some being of another world, but certainly Harry Dean comes to the conclusion that he is not alone. A strange feeling of superstitious dread and hope commingled, comes across his mind. He feels the blood pause in his veins for an instant, and then rush tingling on with that strange shuddery feeling that great excitement will at times produce.

"What is it?" he mutually exclaims; "is the dead near me?"

He turned his eyes towards the beams of light—that glorious visitant from Heaven, with its millions of inhabitants; for who shall say that the greater portion of those atoms are not living things? Following the ray with his eyes, he then saw that it rested upon a form, and a face that was the very index of his dream. It was the form of Kate!—it was the face of Kate! That this was anything but an apparition, never for one moment crossed the mind of Harry Dean; for one moment it seemed to him that the opinions and the principles of his existence respecting the material and immaterial world were blown to the clouds. There she was, plainly and distinctly before him;—the apparition of the murdered Kate Destern! He could not move; a deep sigh escaped him, and then, much as he wished to speak, he felt the power to do so utterly at fault, but, by a violent effort, he forced himself to rise from the couch, and then, but not till then, Kate Destern saw that there was some one in that room which she had considered unoccupied. She saw the face, too; and pale and ghastly as that face was, she knew it as the face of Harry Dean. No wonder that, under the circumstances in which she saw her lover, it struck her as having a wonderfully different expression to what she had ever seen upon it. We cannot feel surprised at its strangeness, when we come to consider, firstly, what Harry Dean had suffered for the last few hours, and, secondly, that he was then and there under the impression that he was looking upon a being who was not an inhabitant of this world. No wonder, then, that if he thought Kate in the ray of sunlight to be unreal, she thought so strange a resemblance of her lover to that in her imagination a most unlikely place to find him anything but real. That her excited fancy had conjured up a spirit in her mind's eye was Kate's impression, and she felt a degree of nervous horror that quite obliterated the remembrance of what she had come to that room to do. She only felt the wish and the capacity to fly. Turning then, with great rapidity, she rushed from the room; and now, quite heedless whither she went, she made her way down to the ground floor, and opening the first door she came to, which was that of a small room at the back of the dining room, she rushed in, and fell in a swoon upon the floor. Now the police, who were in the dining-room, heard some one come down the staircase with amazing speed, and they looked at each other inquiringly, to know who it could be; but before any one could speak, they heard a noise above, as though some one had fallen heavily to the floor.

"What's all that?" said one.

"Something amiss," said another. "The gentleman is up-stairs. Let's go and see; he don't seem as if he'd get over this affair in a hurry."

"Indeed he don't, poor fellow. Come on."

The officers, in their anxiety concerning Harry Dean, whom they did know, quite forgot to make any further inquiry about the sudden rush of footsteps down the stairs, from some one whom they did not know, or if they did give another passing thought to that subject, it was probably to account for it under the supposition that it was one of the servants, who, having been up stairs upon some errand, was actually anxious to get away from such a scene of horror and bloodshed as was above. The officers had no superstitious fears—their minds were in no chaotic state that would induce them t

"Weave strange fancies;"

and consequently, despite of the sunbeam and the partially darkened room, and the "clots of blood" that they knew were to be seen upon the stairs, but a few paces above them, they walked into the drawing-room, and there lay Harry Dean upon the carpet in a state of insensibility.

"Swounded away," said a policeman.

They lifted him to the sofa, and then one went down stairs again for some water, while the other flung open the window shutters, and again let the light of day shine gloriously upon all the magnificence of that room so lately occupied by the arch villain, Dr. Wilkins. The sparkling sunbeam, with its millions of atoms, was swallowed up in the general floods of light, and the romance of semi-darkness was no more. It was fortunate that at that moment Dr. Bell, who had got through some of his professional business upon that morning quicker than he expected, just then arrived at the house, and when he was admitted he was at once told of the sad state of Harry Dean, and, of course, proceeded at once to the drawing-room. The doctor soon found that it was something more than intense grief that had produced Harry's condition, and after having, by the aid of powerful restoatives, brought him again to a state of consciousness, he desired that he should be left alone with him, and then, closing the door, he spoke to him with the kindness and the firmness of one who knows he is upon the footing of a friend, saying—

"My dear sir, you grieve more than enough those who wish you well by this immoderate giving way to the very extacy of woe. Have you resolved to make no effort to fight up against the agony of your affliction."

"Hush! No more—Do not blame me, Dr. Bell I have seen her!"

"Her!—whom?"

"Kate Destern—I can give but one explanation to the appearance of the vision, and that is, that we shall not be long apart, a joyful interpretation."

"Well, Mr. Dean, I can give another explanation, and I think any dispassionate person will, and that is, that your imagination being over excited, naturally enough, has played you this trick, at which I very much grieve."

"No doubt that is, naturally, as a medical man, and as one who has not seen what I have seen, your inevitable conclusion. If you had not said so, I should have thought you were really playing with my nerves, under the impression that my mind was diseased, which I am glad to find you do not think is at all the case."

"Certainly, my dear sir. The mind may be perfectly sane, and yet the imagination, acting upon the visual organs, may produce such an effect as that you describe to me. If the supposed apparition had been a complete stranger to you, the case would have been much more extraordinary; but as it is, it only chimes in with medical experience."

"I understand you."

"And in time you will have to think with me."

"I doubt that, much, said Harry Dean, shaking his head; "but still, for my own peace sake, I will try to think so; and yet the vision—if vision it was—was so palpable."

"And with all the addenda of it's murder?"

"No, no. Kate was as I have always seen her, save that she was pale and agitated rather, and that a sunbeam that came into the apartment from an only partially opened shutter, seemed to give a

HARRY DEAN AND THE NEW EARL.

sort of spiritual appearance to her face, such as I have not seen it wear. No horrors accompanied the appearance."

"But you had been sleeping?"

"True, I had been sleeping; but, to the best of my belief and perceptions, I had been awake for some time; and then, hearing a slight noise, I turned and saw the figure—a face I knew so well; but upon my rising it immediately disappeared."

"Yes, exactly; upon your changing your position, no doubt. Ah, Mr. Dean, you must get rid of these nervous fancies, or they will lay too strong a hold of you. Dear me, what are they calling me below for, I wonder? I will be with you again in a few moments, Mr. Dean. It's some nonsense, I dare say."

CHAPTER XCIV.

THE HAPPY MEETING.

DR. BELL carefully closed the door of the drawing-room, and when he got down stairs the first person he met was the landllady of the house, sitting upon the passage mat, and looking as though her last hour was come. The next person Dr. Bell saw was a policeman, who looked at the landlady with all the amazement in the world, and was quite oblivious regarding the causes of that lady's trepidation.

"What is the matter?" said the doctor.

"Oh! oh! oh!" cried the landlady. "This house to let on lease on reasonable terms; no fair offer objected to. Oh! oh! oh! It's all over now."

"What does she mean?"

"I don't know, sir," said the policeman; "but finding she was in such a state in the passage, and knowing you were a doctor, I thought I'd better call you down, you see, sir, and stay with the old lady until you came."

"What do you mean, you lobster-looking ruffian?" said the landlady, "by calling me old? How dare you, you wretch? But I shall have to leave the house, for who will move into it now? Oh, dear!—oh, dear! I am a ruined woman, I am a ruined female!"

"Very well," said Dr. Bell, "if you have called me down stairs, madam, merely to hear you rave, and to see you sitting upon a mat, I may as well go again; so I shall have the pleasure of bidding you a very good day, madam, as I am somewhat anxious to attend to my young friend up stairs, who is far from well."

"Stop!—oh stop!" said the landlady, "I beg of you; you ain't a parson, so not quite the right sort of person to *exercise* a ghost."

"Exorcise, you mean, I suppose," said Dr. Bell. "But pray, what ghost, madam, have you seen?—I have had quite enough of that up stairs."

"Hush!" said the landlady, as she rose up from the mat by catching hold of the policeman's skirts, and then gave him a box on the ears for the accommodation; "hush! she's in that room as sure as I am a sinner, and I shall have to let the house, for who will live here now, I should like to know?"

"What do you mean, madam?"

"Why, that I saw in that room, where I went all of a hurry to get a couple of clean wine-glasses, no more nor less than the ghost of the young lady that you all tell me has been murdered up stairs by Dr. Wilkins."

Dr. Bell was staggered at this circumstance. It bore so remarkable an affinity to what Harry Dean had said, that he might well stare, as he did, in amazement, and ask himself if fear was driving any one mad but himself. He looked at the landlady for a few moments in silence, and then pointing to the room, he said—

"There, do you mean?"

"Yes, yes."

"Then I will soon put an end to this seemingly appalling mystery. I much suspect that there is some trick going on, and, in truth, I would much rather find that Mr. Dean has been made the victim of a trick, than incline in the belief which, otherwise, I wish that his own imagination has played him false."

"You won't venture, sir?"

"Will I not; you will soon see if I will or not: I have had too many intimate dealings with both the living and the dead, to fear what, according to current report, is a something betwixt the two—no, no. I will not shrink from a solution of this mystery. You can remain where you are, policeman, I can easily call you if the ghost should prove one too many for me, which I do not expect."

"Very well, sir," said the policeman; I hasn't no objection to nothing — a cracksman, or any of that family, but as to a ghost, sich as this old lady says as she seed, I confesses it's rather out of my line; howsomdever if you calls, sir, in I comes."

Leaving, then, the landlady and the policeman to settle together the new dispute about the old lady, that was now got up between them, Dr. Bell opened the door and walked in. Certainly a female form was lying upon the floor, but the face was not visible, and Dr. Bell, without the smallest idea of discovering any one whom he knew, raised up the head, and then beheld the familiar features of Kate Destern. If Doctor Bell had been asked to say what he felt, he would have found it, quite independently of the sudden surprise, difficult to reply, for his feelings were of so large and multifarious a character, that they jostled each other, and quite defied anything in the shape of classification or arrangement. There he was, a man quite confuted and quite confounded, and probably the popular saying, of a man not knowing if he were upon his head or his heels, might carry the best idea of the doctor's state, after all. Kate continued in her swoon, and the doctor continued gazing at her for the space of about a minute, as though they both had, by the spell of some enchanter, been turned to stone, and never more to breathe—to move—or to speak. At length he recovered sufficiently to exclaim—

"Great God! there is some awful and instinctive mystery in all this, which far, very far, transcends my comprehension. This is Kate Destern, and Kate Destern living, and in the flesh, too; but how she came here, or why she is not above stairs a corpse, I know not, or else I am mad; and from first to last this whole affair is one of the dreams of a lunatic, from which I am only now awakening to comprehend the real from the unreal in this world!"

As he spoke he raised Kate from the floor, and placed her upon a large couch or settee that was in the apartment, and then staggering, rather than walking, to the door, he looked out, and seeing the landlady, he said—

"Come in, madam, for God's sake; there is no ghost here, and nothing whatever to fear, but your womanly assistance may be wanted to a sick person. Come in—come in! I am bewildered."

"Shall I come?" said the policeman.
"No, no."

The landlady slowly crept into the room, but when she saw Kate again, she stopped and commenced trembling like an aspen leaf, exclaiming—

"Oh, there she is! There she is!"

Kate at this moment opened her eyes and looked confusedly around her, sitting up on the settee, and the landlady appeared to feel a sudden conviction that she was real flesh and blood, for she went up to her, while Dr. Bell, as he looked Kate in the face, anxiously exclaimed—

"For the love of Heaven, tell me if this is the young lady who came here with Dr. Wilkins, madam, or not?"

"Oh, yes; the very same! He said she was his mad niece, and spoke of the F.M. and the Bishop. She's the same mad young lady, sure enough, sir."

"Then I am mad, that's all."

"Mad, sir?"

"Yes; stark, staring mad! As mad as a March hare. Take care, madam, that I don't bite you, for I have long had an opinion, founded upon medical practice, that the bite of a mad man is as fatal as the bite of a mad dog."

"Help! murder! He's mad, indeed."

"Oh, Dr. Bell! is that really and truly you," said Kate Destern, clasping her hands and looking doubtingly at him, or am I in a dream; and, after all, still more than ever in the power of the villain Wilkins. If you are really Dr. Bell, oh, speak to me as your niece, as you used to speak to me at your own house, where, saving my concern for Harry Dean, I was indeed happy."

"What shall I say? Kate—Kate Destern, are you a being of this world, or are you some beautiful airy phenomenon come for a brief space upon earth to be the blessing and the bane alternately of those who know you?"

"Alas! sir, I am but what I am."

"And what is that?"

Poor unhappy persecuted Kate. Oh, Heaven, do those whom I have thought to be different from all the world beside, and my real friends, at last deny me, or is this but another freak of a disordered fancy? Speak to me kindly, Dr. Bell—oh, speak to me kindly, or tell me why I have forfeited your esteem."

"My dear, you have not forfeited it at all; but just explain to me why you, who were murdered last night, are here now alive, and beginning, notwithstanding a rather paler face than usual, and something of a more frightened look, to show some of your accustomed aspect? Tell me that, in all sincerity, Kate."

"Murdered ?"

"Aye, murdered; and by about three o'clock to-day the coroner for the district is going to hold an inquest upon you, and Dr. Wilkins is now in custody for your murder, and glories in the commission of the dreadful crime."

"You confuse me," said Kate, passing her hand across her eyes; "you much confuse me."

"Do I ? Then I tell you, Kate, that you not only confuse, but you utterly confound me."

"But—but, how came you here ?"

"Naturally enough—to look for you; but how came you here ?"

"Wilkins brought me."

"Nay, but you are lying up stairs murdered, and the marks of your blood are all the way along the landing, and partially come down the stairs. Pray, Miss Kate, what right have you to be sitting in a back dining-room, staring at me, when you know you are murdered, and a man will in all probability be hanged for it ?"

Kate burst into tears.

"Come, come," said Dr. Bell, "there's some mystery in all this, which, although it is far beyond my present capacity to unravel, must and will be explained shortly. My dear, this is the happiest moment of my life, now that I hold you in my arms, with an assurance that you are alive and well ; I may venture to say so much, now that Mrs. Bell is not within hearing."

"Then I am free from Wilkins," said Kate, "and it is no dream ?"

"Not at all. Now tell me; did Wilkins make any attempt upon your life last night ?"

"Certainly not. The fact is, I made an attempt to escape, and failing in that, I retired to rest, but in another room, which I happened to find open, and not in the one I usually slept, or rather, I may say, since I have been here, watched in."

"Go on, go on ; the mist is clearing. And who occupied your own room ?"

"No one to my knowledge. But you terrify me by this talk about my lying dead up stairs. Have you seen me ?"

"To be sure not. Oh, what a fool I have been, to be sure. If I had but, as I ought to have done, slipped up stairs and seen who it really was who lay there murdered, what hours of pain I might have saved myself and Harry Dean. Oh ! the mist is all clearing away fast now. Why, my dear Kate, Wilkins rose in the night, it appears, and murdered some one in your bed, whom he thought to be you."

"Gracious Heaven !"

"Yes, and I and Harry Dean have been at our wit's end."

"Ah, poor Harry ! How full my mind must have been of him when, in a room above this—and that, by the bye, accounts for my fainting—I fancied I saw his spirit."

"What ?"

"Yes, Dr. Bell, I opened a room door, and there, in a half-darkened apartment, I thought I saw Harry Dean. The sight almost froze the blood in my veins, and in the frantic terror of the moment I rushed down here, and I believe fell upon the floor in a swoon; but I know it was all fancy."

"Hurrah ! Go on !" cried Dr. Bell, in a very excited sort of way. "The mist is nearly all gone. Bravo ! Why, Kate Harry Dean is up stairs, and nearly frightened out of his wits at the idea that he has seen your ghost pop its head into the room where he was sitting upon a sofa, and look at him, so pale and woe-begone, that he will never forget the vision while he lives, and only hopes soon to be a ghost himself, that he and you may go about frightening honest people together."

"Oh—no—no."

"But I say, oh, yes—yes. Nay, Kate, do not tremble so. All will be well, but you must not rush up stairs to Harry Dean just yet. Now stay where you are ; and you, madam, if you please, just attend to this young lady while I go up stairs upon a voyage of discovery, for I shall not believe it is quite all real until I see who it is that Dr. Wilkins really did murder last night, for that he did commit such a crime, there can be no possible mistake."

At this moment there came a tap at the room door, and as the doctor was anxious just until he had prepared Harry Dean for the joyful surprise that awaited him, he himself went to it, and found it was merely one of the police to tell him that Wilkins would not be examined by the magistrate until the morning.

"Very well," said the doctor. "It's all the better. Don't disturb the ladies who are in that room."

"Certainly not, sir."

"Is the room door open where the body lies? You know I am a physician, and know all about the affair, so there can be no objection, I suppose, to my going up to view it?"

"Oh dear, no, sir; as many doctors as like we let go in reason, cos you see, sir, there's all the more evidence about it afore the coroner and his worship. You'll find the key in the door, sir. We leave it there, for there's no fear of anybody in the house going and interfering with such a hobject.'

"I should say not," replied the doctor, as he went up stairs, and then he added to himself, "God bless us! how different I feel to what I did only half an hour ago. Well, I have two things to do. To ascertain who is murdered, and to prepare Harry Dean for one of the strangest and most exciting of surprises."

CHAPTER XCV.

A LITTLE SUBTERFUGE.

THE doctor did not pause at the drawing-room, but went direct on up the second floor staircase to the chamber of death. His great anxiety now—and oh! after all, what a minor anxiety it was to that which had possessed him—was to ascertain who had fallen a victim to the villany and murderous intentions of Wilkins; so, with a feeling that was pitiful enough, but as different as any one thing could be from another from that with which he had formerly looked upon so melancholy a sight, he passed the blood upon the stairs and the landing, and made his way to the room which had well nigh been so fatal to poor Kate. As the policeman had told him, the key was in the lock, so that he had no difficulty in at once opening the door. His first act, then, was to go to the window and open the shutters, so as to let in as much light as possible, and then, turning to the bed, he drew aside the curtains and looked upon the dead. There lay poor Mrs. Lupin, the

charwoman, in the embrace of death, presenting certainly about as horrible a spectacle as could be conceived. There was a something about the face, even in death, which Dr. Bell thought was familiar to him; but as he had quite dismissed from his mind all the now unimportant episode with the charwoman, he did not connect the feeble reminiscence of those features with any of the proceedings of the former night.

"Well," he said, after a pause, "truly my friend Grant must have thought me mad indeed when I talked of the charms of this poor corpse, and of the beauty that death, indeed, could not quench. Faugh! I only wonder he did not have me taken off at once to a lunatic asylum, for to him I must have appeared thoroughly deranged.

The doctor continued gazing at the corpse for some little time longer, and then, unable to come to any sort of conclusion concerning it, he closed the curtains, and left the room, saying as he did so—

"Well, the mystery so far as regards the manner in which Kate has been saved from the villany of Wilkins, is sufficiently solved by her own account of changing her room; but whom this is that Wilkins murdered, in the dark doubtless, is still to me as great a mystery as ever."

The doctor felt now the propriety of informing the police of the quietly attained circumstances of the case, but as the coroner was not to come for some time yet, he, Dr. Bell, considered that he would be doing no harm by keeping this important secret a short time longer, until he had, by a revelation of the extraordinary circumstances that had preserved Kate, in some measure restored happiness to Harry Dean. In Harry Dean's present state of mind, however, this was a delicate task. Joy, sudden—excessive—and quite unlooked-for, is frequently more difficult to bear with anything approaching to composure, than the most terrible of misfortunes, and in the present strangely excited and unusual condition of the mind of Harry Dean, any very sudden shock might be productive of the most disastrous circumstances and results. Moreover, Dr. Bell knew, too, that he was in a state of physical exhaustion, from want of proper food, so that, taking into consideration the whole of the affair, and its attendant circumstance, Dr. Bell told himself that he could not be too cautious in letting Harry Dean know what an amount of happiness was in store for him. It was with these feelings the kind-hearted physician arrived at the door of the drawing-room once again. Having briefly thus made up his mind not to leave that apartment without letting Harry Dean know all that had occurred, Dr. Bell could only determine to be guided by circumstances in his mode of making the all important communication to him. He found the young man sitting upon the couch, with his face hidden in his hands, and apparently in a deep reverie. Who could doubt of the painful and better nature of the thoughts which were chasing each other through his overwrought brain?

"Come," said Dr. Bell, "I understood you to promise me that you would rouse yourself a little, and shake off this overwhelming grief. Be more a man, Mr. Dean. What is done, you know, in this case, melancholy as it is, cannot be undone."

"Say no more," rejoined Harry, looking up, and almost frightening the doctor by the strange and ghastly look of his face. "Say no more, I have but one hope now left."

"And what is that?"

"Soon to be as Kate is—an immaterial spirit. She and I will range the universe, making at times some bright particular star our home."

"Well, I am sorry to hear you talk in this way, as I think, considering you are quite a young man, there may be many ways found by which you might shake off the gloom that is upon your spirits, and live for years in comfort and happiness."

"Indeed."

"Yes, to be sure I do. Why, man, do you think that you are the only person in all the world who has felt the keen pang of such suffering as you now endure, and yet smiled again? Aye, and to laugh as heartily as the best of us. Pho! pho! I tell you this deep-seated grief will have an end. It must be extirpated by some skilful physician."

"He would need to be a skilful physicica indeed, to do that," said Harry Dean, "but you spoke even now of modes and means of conquering affliction, are they earthly or of another world, doctor; for I know not of such.

"Oh, they are quite earthly. First, now, there is music."

"No, no. The softest strains now will become hateful to me; for if they melted my soul at all, they would but serve to remind me of her whom I have lost for ever—my beatiful Kate, whose lightest tone was the very witchery of music's holiest spell: no, no, not music."

"Well, then, the drama; what say you to that?"

"Nothing; but that the most skilled painting of the human bust upon the stage of animate life could present to me nothing so fair as Kate, or so full of joy as the joy of my heart when I should call her mine, nor so grief-like and desolate as my bosom is, now that she is lost to me for ever. No, no, doctor, I want no weak reflex of woe or of joy, such as the stage could give me. I feel too keenly what has been and what is. No drama for me."

"You are hard to please. Would the pages of romance have no charms for you?"

"Romance!"

"Aye. You look surprised at my question; but many an aching heart has been soothed by the pages of fiction, and many a slumbering intellect awakened to the glories of nature and of goodness. Do not despise Providence, my friend; for if God had not given his creatures an imagination, many an hour now spent in harmless serenity might have been much worse employed. The realities of existence are so stern, that we may well recline in the arms of fiction for a time."

"I agree with what you say; but no romance can come near to my horrible reality."

"Ah, there you are wrong."

"Indeed, am I? Can you name any human woe that is equal to mine? any amount of human suffering brought about so strangely as mine has been? Oh, no, no! There is nothing in the page of romance that can come near my own melancholy history."

"You think so, Mr. Dean. Now I will soon convince you to the contrary; for in my own limited experience a circumstance took place which far transcends all that you can possibly say of your affairs; and as I can vouch for the truth of the matter, I will tell it to you."

"Then it is no romance."

"Why—a—hem! not exactly; but it is romantic enough surely, and I tell it to you to convince you that there have happened within the limited experience of one individual, much more extraordinary circumstances than those, from the consequences of which you are now so keenly and so deeply suffering."

"Can you do so?"

"In truth can I. Now listen to me, Mr. Dean; as a personal favour I now ask you to lend me your most serious attention to what I am going to say."

"Very well," said Harry, dejectedly, "I will, of course, listen to you, Dr. Bell; and since you put the matter in that light, I pray you proceed at once, for I am sick at heart."

"About a year ago," said Dr. Bell, "I was rung up one night by one of the most hurried and violent appeals to my night-bell that ever I heard. I sprung from my bed, and huddling on some of my clothes, rushed down stairs, and there found a gentleman, who, in tones almost convulsed with grief, told me a murder had been committed at his house, and that he implored me as a favour to accompany him directly. Now I did not see the utility of my accompanying him, since the murder had been done. Moreover, I was a physician, and the affair lay within the province of a surgeon, but knowing that in their fright people knock or ring up the first medical man they come to, without drawing any very nice distinction, I made no further scruple than just saying—"It is not probable I can be of any use, but, if it be particularly wished, I will go with you, sir, to your house."

He thanked me, and off we went. Are you attending, Mr. Dean?"

"Oh, yes—yes."

"Well, when we reached the house, I, of course, found it all in disorder—no one would venture up stairs where the body lay; and a couple of policemen were there, who had the man who had done the murder in custody. Now the murderer was a disappointed suitor of the young lady who had been murdered, and he said, when I went into the house, I

have taken Kate's life, and I am satisfied."

"Kate's? Was her name Kate?"

"Oh, yes, that's what makes it so singular, and indeed it was the similarity of names that brought the affair into my head. The gentleman who had come to my house, told me in which room above stairs I should find the corpse, saying as he did so—' You will then see, sir, of what a world of beauty death has robbed this unhappy family."

"And she was like Kate whom I mourn—beautiful?" said Harry Dean.

"She was indeed, so they said. But judge of my surprise, when I found in the room where they had told me the body lay, the corpse of an old wrinkled woman, certainly murdered, but possessing, as certainly none of the charms which they had attributed to the young lady they called Kate."

"It was strange."

"It was indeed. But how do you think, Mr. Dean, this mystery was solved?"

"Alas, I cannot guess."

"Then I will tell you. It appeared afterwards, when the affair came out, and was made as clear as day, that the murderer who had secreted himself in the house in the dusk of the evening, knew perfectly well which was the chamber of the young lady named Kate; and, bad as he was, he was afraid that if he took but one look at his beautiful victim, the sight of her charms and her innocence would disarm him of his fatal purpose, so, in the profound darkness of the night, while rain was descending too, so that any slight noise he might make would not be heard, he sought the chamber of his victim."

"Yes—yes. Go on."

"With a poniard that he took with him he stabbed her to the heart, having, with trembling hands, as she slept, felt for her heart."

"The villain!"

"Aye, the villain; and yet he did not do the deed he meant to do, for it happened, by quite a rare accident, that upon that night the young lady had changed her bed-room."

"Oh, rare chance!"

"Rare, indeed. It saved her, and an old woman, who for that night slept in Kate's accustomed bed, fell beneath the

k

snife of the murderer   You under-
tand ?"

"Oh, 'tis very plain."

"Very well, now you see the lover
whom the young lady named Kate really
did love Harry——

"Harry ?"

"Yes, by an odd coincidence between
your case and this I am telling you the
fond and accepted lover's name was Harry.

Harry Dean looked fixedly at Dr.
Bell, and then in a low and mournful
tone, he said—

"This is indeed very—very cruel, Dr.
Bell.'"

"Cruel, do you say ? Upon my word
Mr. Dean, I do not see anything cruel
in it."

"You do not, sir ? Is it fair, or just,
or generous, to make me and my miseries
the subject of an idle tale ? If you think
that I cnm aeea bused and moved from
my grief by any such means, you know
me not, sir ; I now see that it is myself
and poor Kate Destern that you make
the hero and heroine of your pretended
story. Say no more, sir—say no more."

"Oh, nonsense, you will hear it out ?"

"No, no, no."

"But I say, yes, yes, yes. The most
interesting part is yet to come. I was
going to tell you how this lover, who, by
the odd coincidence, was named Harry,
somehow was sitting in the drawing-
room of the house as you might be sitting
here, and how Kate, who had not been
murdered at all, rose up in the morning
and came down stairs, quite unconscious
that anything was amiss——"

"Peace, sir, peace——"

"And looked in at the door, where
there was a ray of sunlight, on account
of the shutters being nearly all closed."

"Good God !" exclaimed Harry
Dean, as he sprang upon Dr. Bell, and
grappled him by the breast of his apparel,
"are you devil or angel? Do you
come to drive me to distraction, by the
most horrible mockery a bleeding heart
was ever subjected to ; or, under the
guise of a fiction, do you seek to prepare
me for such a joy—a—joy——"

He sank to the ground, but Dr. Bell
raised him up, crying with a triumphant
voice—

"I think you can stand it now, Mr.
Dean. Kate Destern lives, and is per-
ectly well—she lives, I say, and the villain Wilkins has murdered some one
else—Kate lives, and is as well as I
am !"

————

CHAPTER XCVI.

HARRY DEAN'S MYSTERIOUS CONDUCT.

DR. BELL was right enough in seeking to prepare, by a round about means,
Harry Dean for the communication he
had to make to him, for even now, with
all that careful preparation, he seemed
quite overwhelmed for some minutes.
Suddenly, then, a plentiful flood of
tears came to his relief.

"All's right !" cried Dr. Bell, "I
like to see that. You will do now, Mr.
Dean. All danger is past, and I'll go
and fetch Kate at once. Now don't
call me cruel again, will you, for I have
really taken all the pains I could to be
kind?"

"Most kind ! Most kind !" cried
Harry.

"Well, well, now sit down and make
yourself comfortable. I suppose you
have no thoughts now of becoming a
ghost, and skimming about the milky
way to find out some bright particular
star to lodge in, eh?"

"Kate ! Kate ! I will go——"

"No, you won't. Come, come, stay
where you are. I restore Kate to you,
and you ought to let me do so in my
own way. You shall see her in a few
moments ; and if you had but had your
wits about you, you ought to have
caught her to your heart when she
peeped in at the door."

"But I thought it was an apparition,
and she fled.—Oh, how happy—happy
I am, Dr. Bell. Kill me now, if this be
not real."

"Kill you, if it be not ! No, no,
Harry Dean, I do not carry jests or
romances quite so far as that. But I
will no longer delay fetching the ghost
again to you, for I see you are quite
sufficiently recovered to smile instead of
to weep."

"I am, I am, indeed ; and let what
sorrow now of the ordinary sorrows of
humanity come over me, I shall contrast
them with what I have gone through
for these last few hours, and think them
nothing."

Dr. Bell left the room and repaired to

the apartment below, in which Kate was, now quite recovered from her swoon, and fully apprised by the landlady of what had happened during the night in the house.

"I am sure, miss, if you ain't mad; and if the doctor, Wilkins, ain't your uncle; and if the F. M. ain't one of your relations, and a bishop another, I ought to beg your pardon for all that has happened; but you see, miss, when a gentleman, as looks like a gentleman, comes and gives you a £20 note for extras, and says there's another when

that's gone, it's quite enough to take in and do for the angel Gabriel himself, to say nothing of a lady, and housekeeper, as has a honest living to get in this world of troubles."

"Say no more about it," said Kate, "I am willing to think that you were deceived by Wilkins, although you should have enquired more closely into his statements."

Dr. Bell came into the room at this moment.

"Come, my dear," he said, "I want to introduce you to the ghost in the drawing-room, who has now no objection in the world to see the ghost of the sunbeam in the darkened room. He is quite prepared now, and knows all."

Dr. Bell led Kate to the drawing-room door, and there he left her, saying—

"I will now go and inform the police that you won't require a coroner's inquest to be held upon you just yet."

We will not intrude upon the scene that ensued between Kate and Harry Dean, for not only are they entitled to a little private chat of their own, but we feel how totally inadequate any language would be to give expression to the feelings that actuated them both during that most happy interview. The doctor proceeded to the parlour. There the police were waiting the arrival of the coroner, and the moment Dr. Bell got into the room, he said—

"Gentlemen, I have to inform you of an extraordinary discovery that has taken place in this house. The young lady, who was supposed to be murdered, is alive and well."

A look of black dismay came over the faces of the police.

"It can't be," said one. "What a pity!"

"Is it possible!" cried another. "And all this trouble then has been for nothing. Well, this is rather too bad, after it promised to be the best case out of all those that we have had this year. I'm quite shocked."

"Are you, indeed?" said Dr. Bell. "It will perhaps then console you to know that a person is murdered, although not the young lady."

"Oh, that's quite another thing, sir. We were only afraid the supposed murdered person had come to life again; but, so as somebody is murdered, of course it can't matter to us a bit who it is, you know. I think that is quite understood; but after all the trouble, it would really be too bad if nobody was murdered at all. That was what we meant."

"Exactly; I understand you perfectly. What letter is that?"

"It has been left here, sir, for a Mr. Dean."

"Ah, indeed. Then it is for my friend up stairs. I shall not interrupt him just now with it, as he is far better engaged, and I shall stay here until the inquest takes place, for, as yet, I don't really

know who is murdered, since it certainly is not, to my great joy, the young lady whom we all thought at first had met with that calamitous fate."

*   *   *

In about half an hour, Dr. Bell thought he might with great propriety tap at the drawing-room door.

"Come in!" cried Harry Dean, in such a cheerful voice, that it was quite a pleasure to hear him; and Dr. Bell entered with the letter that had been left for Harry in his hand.

"Excuse me interrupting you, but here is a note for you, Mr. Dean."

"Many thanks, Dr. Bell."

Harry Dean went to the window to read the note, and while he was so employed, the doctor looked smilingly at Kate, saying—

"I do firmly believe now that these many and grievous trials are all over, and that nothing but happiness is in store for you."

Before Kate could reply, Harry Dean turned from the window, saying—

"Will you spare me, Kate, for half an hour, I have a call to make some two or three streets only distant from here, which is of some importance."

"You will return soon?"

"Indeed I will, and in the meantime I shall leave Dr. Bell, who has my full permission to make violent love to you until my return."

"Have I, in good faith?" said the Doctor. "Then I shall take advantage of the permission, you may depend, in the fullest possible manner. Be off with you at once."

Harry Dean left the room, and shortly the house; and as his visit, a few streets off, and what he did there, are rather mystesious matters, we will follow him on his errand, promising that shortly an ample and satisfactory explanation will be given of all that seems strange in his conduct. He walked rapidly until he came to a large handsome house, at the door of which he knocked, and when the door was opened by a footman, he said—

"Is Mr. Braybrook within? If so, tell him Mr. Dean is here."

"Yes, sir. He is in the library, and I have orders to show you in."

"Very well."

Harry Dean was shown into a handsome room, where sat a man about his own age or thereabouts, who flushed with colour at first sight of him, Harry Dean, and he turned very pale.

"Well, Francis," said Harry Dean, "why have you now sent for me?"

"To tell you," said the other, "that now Battaney is no more, I will no longer delay taking proceedings to prove who and what I am."

"It is already proved."

"How mean you?"

"That you are a bastard. Now, Francis, if your own conduct had not been very, very bad indeed, no one should have said this much to you. But as I have the means of preventing you from making a bad use of large powers, I will do so freely, and therefore all your exertions will be of no avail. You have a large income, and that ought to suffice you."

"Indeed. But I, in addition to that, have a fancy to be pointed at as the new earl."

"Which fancy," said Harry Dean, "if you attempt to gratify, will end in your being pointed at as the old impostor. Let me once again, Francis, advise you, as I once before advised you, to court an honourable obscurity, if you can."

"That is still your opinion?"

"It is, and I can only wonder that you should send for me to hear me repeat it again."

"I did not do so."

"Is not this note in your hand-writing? Although, how you came to find out where I was, to send it to me, I own surpasses my comprehension."

"Then I will tell you that a spy of mine has been always close upon your back, and go where you would, or do what you would, information has been always brought to me within a few hours of the event."

"Is that what you have sent for me to tell me, Francis? Because, if so, I am ready and anxious to leave your house, which I entered most unwillingly."

"Not entirely. Do you see this paper?" As he spoke he produced a legal-looking document from a large desk that was immediately before him.

"Well?"

"This document, then, contains a formal recognition of my legitimacy, which I now expect you to sign."

"Are you mad?"

"No, but you will be if you refuse; for I have made up my mind, if you do, that you shall not leave this room alive. Now, take your choice, Harry Dean, as from some freak of fancy you choose to call yourself; write your name to this properly drawn-up legal declaration, or take the consequences of my fancy; for I tell you, now, that I am a desperate man, and, as there is a Heaven above us I will execute the threat I now hold out against you."

"Indeed?"

"Aye, indeed; nothing can or shall save you."

"Are you legitimate? Are you entitled to an earldom? Anything, and truly anything but a mere shallow adventurer? Deny these allegations, and prove to me that your claim is correct, and not a mere piece of most audacious braggadocia, and I will sign a paper to that effect."

"You refuse, then, to affix your name to this document?"

"Most decidedly I do."

There was upon the table, at which this man, whom Harry Dean called Francis, sat, a large cover of thick brocade; and now that he had received the final answer of Harry Dean, he suddenly put his hand under the cover and drew out from beneath it an unsheathed sword, saying, as he did so—

"Your last hour has come."

The words were scarcely out of his mouth when Harry Dean rushed upon him, and with a force as though the strength of ten men was in his single arm, he wrenched the weapon from the grasp of the would-be assassin. To break it across the edge of the table, and to throw the fragments upon the floor, where the legal paper, which he was asked to sign, had fallen, was the work of another moment to Harry Dean, who then, pointing to the paper and the sword, said—

"Before you threaten, you should carefully estimate your powers of performance. It so happens that at present I am busy about other matters, or the strong arm of the law should curb your insolence; as it is, I leave you, Francis, with contempt, but beware of testing my patience and forbearance."

So saying, Harry Dean left the house

and went instantly back to Kate and Dr. Bell at the lodging-house. With what different sensations did he now make his way across the threshold of the house to those which had sat, like fell despair, brooding at his heart, upon the former occasions, when he fully believed that the dearest object to him in all the world lay there a corpse, slain by the worthless hand of a ruffian, who, in his composition, had scarcely one speck of that God-like feeling of pure humanity which prompts noble and generous actions. Now, there was joy in the path of Harry Dean, and the sincerity of his heart cast the soft and the beautiful sunshine of its own happiness upon all things. Then, there had been nothing but despair, and the beauty of the daylight seemed to be gone for ever. The little incident we have just recorded had for the moment ruffled his temper, but the very recollection of it appeared to pass away as he looked in the face of his own Kate, and beautiful, and fresh as a rose in June, did she now look! She had suffered no hardships in that house of sin, except the fact of being deprived of her liberty, and she had rather improved in health and strength than otherwise; so that now she did, indeed, look something like her former self.

"My own Kate," said Harry Dean, "you must not remain here."

"Ah, Harry, I have but one wish more."

"And that——"

"Is to see Lucy, and feel once again that child's kiss upon my cheek."

"You shall."

"Here's the coroner," said one of the policemen; "here's the coroner, gentlemen, coming."

CHAPTER XCVII..

THE DISAPPOINTMENT OF WILKINS.

HARRY DEAN regretted that he had not left the house before the arrival of this functionary, but he now felt himself bound in courtesy to speak to him, and he made some ordinary civil remarks, to which, with a volubility that would have astonished the most talkative person in the world, he replied—

"Yes, yes—here, and there, and every-where, we are to be seen knocking up horses and breaking down postilions. Half a dozen inquests in a day, and every medical witness an ass, of course. Well, it can't be helped — just finished off a case and come in piping hot. Where is the jury? Beadle made some mistake: of course, all beadles do. Well, well, can't be helped. Now, gentlemen, we will soon settle all. Here I am. Can't be, like a peacock, in two places at once, you know. All's right—a—hem! Get through the week and keep moving—that's the way to do it. Where's the body?"

"Upstairs, sir," said the policeman; "it seems a bad murder, sir."

"Bad murder—Pho! pho! Don't talk of bad murders. Only last week, held an inquest on three bodies. Disappointed man, because his boots pinched him—broke into a house at dead of night—lit a candle — murdered a man; wife knelt by dead body for mercy—murdered wife—hung himself with cord of a bedstead, then finished it all off in twenty minutes. Think I see him now standing with candle in his hand, after murdering man. Clever young friend of mine—all my young friends clever—made a sketch of it. Royal Academicians a set of most infernal humbugs, and, I dare say, would refuse it. Man standing with candle in one hand and dagger in the other, over dead body of victim—woman kneeling for mercy: highly affecting. Now for it though: can't waste time with anything not to the purpose. Everybody is an ass most commonly. Where's the beadle? Beadles are all fools. Now for it. Another inquest at six."

"But sir, if you——"

"That's it, all right. Oh, here's some of the jury."

"But sir, if——"

"Go on. I'm listening.—Capital listener.—Never say anything myself, but—Yes and indeed.—Go on, my good sir.—What were you remarking? —Oh, are you on the jury, sir? Yes. Well, then you are a great deal too fast."

"But, sir——"

"Upon my life, young man, do you want to have all the talk to yourself?—Won't let any one get in a word edgeways.—Oh you are the beadle, are you? a fool, of course."

"But——"

"Well, I have you, I have you.—Wit as thick as Tewkesbury mustard.—Ha! ha! You should see my son.—A fine fellow.—Quite a man at fourteen.—Precocious.—Sure to be.—Brought him into the world on purpose.—Now, gentlemen, can't waste precious time here you know —Let's begin.—Now Mr. beadle, upon my life you are a most uncommon fool, but all beadles are, I suppose."

"Well," said Harry Dean to Dr. Bell, "I shall certainly give up the attempt to say anything to this coroner as perfectly hopeless. "Does he always go on in this most extraordinary manner, Dr. Bell?"

"Most commonly, I believe; and yet, with all his faults, he is a good coroner, and, in his vulgar blundering way, has done some good in his time."

"I am glad to hear it. Now, come, Kate, you and I and Dr. Bell will leave him, for the details of the dreadful crime will not be such as you will care to hear."

"I beg your pardon, sir," said an inspector of police at this moment. "We cannot possibly now do without the young lady's evidence in this case."

"Indeed!"

"No, sir. You see, as I understand it is the young lady herself who was supposed to have been murdered, and so you see, sir, she must give what account she can of the transaction."

"Well," said Harry Dean, "the young lady, of course, would rather not remain, but if it be necessary for the furtherance of the ends of justice that she should, she will, of course, have no objection."

A policeman now came up to the inspector, and said—

"If you please, sir, the cook in the family here has just been u s ta to look at the body, and after saying she knew it, fainted away."

"Indeed!"

"Yes, sir, so perhaps as this gentleman," approaching to Dr. Bell, " is a medical man, perhaps he won't mind stepping up stairs and seeing if he can revive the poor woman."

"Oh, certainly," said Dr. Bell. " I'll go, of course, and the more readily as I see the worthy and exemplary coroner is beginning to talk again, and I know

from that circumstance that I shall have plenty of time, and shall not be wanted down stairs for some time."

With this cut at the coroner, Dr. Bell, after in vain inviting Harry Dean to go with him, went up stairs to exert his professional skill for the cook, who, as the reader has of course surmised, at once recognized the murdered woman as Mrs. Lupin, the char-woman, whose predilection for Old Tom, and such like incitements to inebriety, had most certainly been the cause of her death. We shall leave the doctor to recover the cook, while we proceed with the inquest, during which, who and what the murdered person was must now necessarily come out in full, to the great interest of all whom it might concern. The final examination of several witnesses took place, and then the jury viewed the body, which certainly presented a most hideous spectacle, and after descending again to the dining-room, the coroner said—

"Now, gentlemen, if we can settle the question of identity as regards this old lady—a hem! who lies up-stairs, it will be desirable to do so at once, before we go any further. Is there any witness competent to do that for us?"

"Yes, sir," said the inspector, "I have a witness here."

"Very well, Mr. Inspector, pray don't smuggle him or her up, but let us hear all we can. Oh, it's a female is it? Good God! Well, we must cut her as short as we can, but some people are such talkers."

"They are, indeed," said the beadle of the parish, who was present, and who had impanelled the jury. "They are, indeed; I never in all my life heard anything truer than that."

"Oh, you didn't, didn't you, Mr. Beadle? Pray what's your name?"

"Hoggins."

"Really you don't say so! Couldn't you make it Hog without the 'gins,' eh? It would sound more euphonious, you know, and much more to the purpose; particularly when there's a corporation dinner, eh, Mr. Hog?"

Everybody laughed at the unfortunate beadle, who had dared to measure opinions in a wordy war with the coroner, to whom, in that respect, he was not fit to hold a candle. Very wisely Mr. Hoggins shrank back amongst the spectators, and tacitly owned himself completely defeated. The cook, looking rather pale and agitated, was brought forward by the inspector, and being sworn, and having duly answered to the name of Mary White, was ready to give her testimony.

"Well, Mrs. White," said the coroner, "have you seen the old lady up stairs ?"

"Yes, your worship."

"Pho ! Pho ! don't call me that ; I am the coroner, here, there, and everywhere. Now, Mrs. White, can you be so good as to tell us what was the name of the deceased, and who she was ?"

"Miss White, if you please, Mr. Crowner."

"Bless me, woman, what matters it ? and, for God's sake, dont't call me any more odd names, but tell us at once, upon your oath, who was the presumed to be murdered person ?"

"Old Tom——"

"What ?"

'Was the cause of all, I'm sure and sartin, as I'm a living cook this day as never was."

"Old who ? Mr. Inspector, look out, I hope you will get the person she names into your custody as soon as possible. He ought to be present here now. I have always said prisoners ought to be before me ; and, please the pigs, I'll have 'em as often as I can. Go on, madam."

"Cream of the Valley——"

"Who ?—what ?"

"Old Tom, or Cream of the Valley. I won't, as I'm a living female, take upon me to say, what was the overcoming of poor Mrs. Lupin ; and that's all I know about it, my Lord Judge."

"How remarkably intelligible. Pray, Mrs. White——"

"Miss White, if you pleases. I ain't Mrs. White yet. Miss White, your grace."

"Good God, what next will this woman call me! Do you mean to swear that the name of the murdered woman was Old Tom or Cream of the Valley ?"

"No, Lupin as never was. Mrs. Lupin, leastways her christian name was Sarah, as was making afore providence. Sarah Lupin, and if it hadn't a' been for Old Tom——"

"Stop ! For the love of all that's clear and intelligible, tell us the sirname of Old Tom."

"Gin !"

A roar of laughter burst from nearly all present. Even the sad, solemn character of the inquiry could no longer make successful head against the comedy of the cook's examination ; and now that it had reached such a climax, no one but Harry Dean and Kate could escape the general infection of laughter, in which the coroner himself—for he loved a joke, did that coroner—joined most heartily. When the mirth had subsided, he said—

"Well, Miss White, I think we all understand you now; your evidence goes to state that the name of the deceased was Sarah Lupin, and that gin had something to do in her decease, but as gin could not stab her to the heart, although God knows it has stabbed many families to the very soul, we should like to hear what more you can tell us about this affair."

"Certainly, sir," said Mrs. White, "I will tell all I know, and more too."

"No, no, no !"

"Very well, sir. All I have got to say is, that Mrs. Lupin was to come as it was in a way of speaking overnight was yesterday, and light the copper ; then you see down the area she comes, and I said to myself at once, 'Old Tom,' says I, and sure enough when she got into the kitchen, and sat herself down upon a rush bottom, it was enough the odour of it to knock you flat, so I up and says, 'Mrs. Lupin, it's a disgrace,' says I, 'for a woman as goes a charing to cross——"

"What's that about Charing Cross ?"

"Nothing about Charing Cross, but I says it's a horrid thing for a woman as goes out a charing to cross her own connexion in such a way ; that Old Tom goes as strong as pitch all over the house in half a minute."

"You certainly, Miss White, get the better of me," said the coroner.

"Well, as I was a saying, 'with that I saw as she wasn't at all fit to be trusted with her own lights, so I took my candle and says I, 'Mrs. Lupin,' says I, 'perhaps by the morning you may be a different woman,' says I, 'there's a shake down in the pantry, and go and sleep yourself sober.'"

"From all which, we are to infer, that last night the deceased came to the kitchen of this house in a state of intoxication?"

"Horrid."

"At what hour was this, Miss White?"

"As near twelve as anything."

"Dear me, what hour can that be? Pray be more explicit."

"Just on the stroke of twelve. How stupid some people are—they won't understand plain English; and since I have told you all I know about it, up I goes to bed, and I leaves her to do the best she could, and off I goes and never nothing more did I see, or clap eyes upon Mrs. Lupin, till the blessed day when I saw her upstairs in a gore."

"In a what?"

"A complete weler, as one may say, and all of a bleeding. Poor old soul, I felt as if my latter end was coming at once, and down I went flop till I don't know what brought me to myself. It was all in the bringing about by pepper, I supposes—such lots of sneezing! However, here I am, and that's all I know about it."

"Really, gentlemen," said the coroner, "I am of opinion that we shall get nothing more satisfactory from this witness than we have already. She states the deceased to be a char-woman, named Sarah Lupin, and that she left her in the kitchen of this house last night, about twelve o'clock."

"Yes," said the cook; "you ain't half the fool that you look."

This terminated the examination of the cook, who, in her odd roundabout way, had thrown all the light she could upon the question at issue. Kate then gave her testimony, and Harry Dean and Dr. Bell theirs; for now that they knew who the murdered person really was, they felt bound to relate the interview that they had had with the unfortunate char-woman, which was, without a doubt, the indirect cause of her death, or, if they had not given her the gold, she would not have visited the emporium of the Cream of the Valley, and been so seduced by its sweets. And so the whole affair began gradually to reveal itself to all who listened to the details, and Harry Dean found that, after all—although an innocent person had been the sufferer—he and Dr. Bell had saved the life of Kate Destern by givign the sovereign to Mrs. Lupin. There could not, in Harry Dean's mind, be the shadow of a doubt of the guilt of Wilkins, and had not Mrs. Lupin been in Kate's bed, to receive the death he intended for her, Kate, he would doubtless have searched for her, and sacrificed her, as he still believed he had done.

"I can make but one exhihition of what I feel upon this matter," whispered Harry Dean to Kate, "and that will be by providing for all who were in any way dependent upon Mrs. Lupin for support, so that they shall not suffer from what has saved me from despair."

The coroner now summed up the evidence, remarking upon its clearness, and the jury, after a very few minutes' conversation together, agreed upon their verdict, which they returned as one of Wilful Murder against Henry Wilkins; and the coroner made out a warrant of committal, notwithstanding the villain was already in custody of the police.

CHAPTER XCVIII.

TONY THORPE SMITTEN.

It may be in the recollection of our readers that Tony was left at the hotel to guard it, while Harry Dean and Dr. Bell went upon the expedition for the rescue of Kate, the results of which we have already detailed at some length. Now, there are some sour and crabbed philosophers, who will have it that no one can consent with a good grace to any proposition which does not chime in with some agreeable plan or hope in the mind of the person proposed to; and we must confess that Tony stayed behind with some degree of pleasure upon account of his own private feelings. In the hotel was a little, spare, tidy, black-eyed, red-cheeked, ringletted damsel, who was a sort of "odd man," we were going to say; but she filled the nondescript office—the duties of which were comprehended in the pleasure of making herself generally useful upon all and every occasion. She wore not a "wreath of roses," but a little apron, with two of the most provoking and impracticable little pockets you ever saw, and what with the aprons and the pockets, and the black eyes, and the ringlets, and the red cheeks, Tony fell—as you, reader, would have probably fallen—plump in love. Yes, he did! He looked at her as she went up stairs, and he looked at her as she went down stairs—he listened for her footsteps, her voice, her cough, and he was continually in all sorts of places in the house where he had no business, just to catch a glimpse of this little piece of fascination, who had hooked his heart with the adamantine hooks of love—those hooks that go in and out and around and about such susceptible hearts as Tony's, until, if you were to attempt to tear them away, Heaven only knows what might happen as the natural and inevitable consequence. Now black eyes and ringlets had looked at Tony, perhaps, not quite to such an extent as Tony had looked at her, but still sufficiently to see that Tony was a good-humoured, well-dressed young man—for Tony was well dressed then. The age of rags had passed away; but the young man—for troubles had not let him escape entirely—looked somewhat older than he was. However, as it was evident Tony was well to do, and as it was as clear as the clearest thing in the world—and that, Tony thought, was the eye of the wearer of the tantalizing pockets that he looked so longingly at, she asked herself if she should kill him with a frown, or quite the reverse. The reverse carried the day, and when Tony suddenly trotted out of a room upon hearing her footstep upon the stairs, she only said—

"Oh, sir, how you did frighten me."

"Me?" said Tony. "Did I frighten you. Oh, you duck!"

"Sir?"

"I tell you what it is, miss—I don't know your name, but——"

"Mary Ann."

"Miss Mary Ann, then, you are a dangerous character, and ought not to be allowed to go about a house in the way you do, making people in love with you, and as miserable one minute, and as comfortable the next, as nothing; I suppose, if you were to see in a newspaper that you were the prettiest girl in all England!—ah, and in all the world, too—you would say that's no news, wouldn't you now?"

"Well, I'm sure."

"Oh, Mary Ann, tell me true. Will you have me if I love you? Have you, or have you not a beau? For if you havn't, pray tell me so. Your lips like cherries seem to me, which make my heart no longer free. And with those eyes as black as sloes, away my poor heart quickly goes—against my ribs, thump, thump, thump, thump. And so I make this offer plump.'

"Offer, sir?"

"Yes, to be sure; I ain't the knight who 'loves and then rides away,' not I. Only say, Mary Ann, with beauty bright—by this softly shining light—that you'll be mine by day and night; and through the world you'll find we'll fight, and, perhaps, rise high, like any kite. For, dear one, it is only right that you and I——"

"Get along with you."

"Do you mean then, cruel fair—so to doom me to despair? Oh, no."

"I don't like you at all."

"Very good; there's nothing like beginning with a little aversion, although in this case it's a sort of perversion. So, sweet Mary Ann, pray take this fond kiss. Oh! certainly, I oughtn't to have gone for to cause you to have expected such a box on the ear as this."

"Serves you right."

"Does it? Oh, no. If I was, now, some baron bold, in a castle strong and old—with long-lived ivy on the turrets high—choosing the bright blue of a summer sky—even then, if like an unnatural old mule, I caught such beauty without law or rule——"

"You'd be what you are now——"

"What?"

"A precious fool!"

With this climax, away tripped black eyes and ringlets, making, as folks always should do, a prudent retreat after a good hit.

"Lor!" said Tony, "she's gone. Well, faint heart never won fair lady; so I'll try it on again, for I see it's the fashion with all girls to show off a little at first—I know; but in time all comes right; and when she dotes upon the ground I walk on (modest thing, Tony) then I'll pretend to treat her quite queer.

'Flee love, and love will follow thee,
　　Follow love, and—won't love flee?'

Yes, I believe you—I'll give my head a sort of toss, and I'll say to her——"

"Get out of the way, stupid," interposed no other than Mary Ann herself as she came up stairs again upon some trivial errand.   "Well, of all the young men that ever I saw in all my life, you are the ugliest.   Don't come down to the bar at half-past six to-night, while

I am all alone, and missus is having her tea."

Tony laughed and nodded, at which Mary Ann affected great indignation, and walked away again, with a toss of her head, that made all the ringlets dance again.   Ah, Tony! those ringlets were

THE SECRET INTERMENT OF ONE OF WILKINS'S VICTIMS.

dancing in your heart.   In due course Harry Dean and Kate Destern came to the hotel.   Harry desired Kate to wait in an adjoining room, while he went to prepare Lucy, in some measure, for her reception, as he feared that the acute feelings of the little creature would be too powerfully acted upon if at once he unexpectedly introduced Kate to her.

"Well, Lucy," said Harry Dean, "I have great hopes that we shall soon see Kate."

Lucy looked in his face a moment and then she said, with an arch smile—

"Ah, Harry, have you indeed good hopes?—you have more than hopes now. You cannot look at me without smiling, and say you have not actually seen Kate."

"Why, Lucy, you are a little necromancer."

"Ha! you have really seen her?"

"I have, Lucy, and you shall soon see her; for, to tell the truth, I was afraid to do so suddenly, for fear your joy should be so great as quite to overcome you; and joy is sometimes, I think, quite as hard to bear with patience as grief. Do you not think so, Lucy?"

Lucy burst into tears, and then rapidly drying her eyes and smiling, she added—

"Now you see it is over, Harry; I knew I should cry when I should first hear that Kate was safe and well, and, although you have not distinctly said that she is, your face is like an open book, in which I can read all that, and much more. Oh, where is she?"

"Really, Lucy, you read my face in such an artful manner, I shall have to wear a mask. Sit still, and Kate will come to you."

In a few moments the sisters were in each other's arms, and there, with the instinctive delicacy that was a part of the disposition and nature of Harry Dean, he left them together. Their interview lasted six hours, during which all the hopes and fears that had for so long agitated them were upon each side detailed, and a more delightful reunion than that was could not have been conceived. To be sure, Kate gently chid Lucy, when, clinging to her sister's breast, she said—

"Ah! Kate, we are and ought to be dear to each other, for we are alone now in the world."

"No, Lucy, no; such is not the case. Do not let me hear you say that again, for never were orphans so amply provided with a friend as we are."

"Yes—yes, Kate, I did forget Harry."

"I know you did, Lucy. But now for one moment—in joy or in sorrow—health or sickness—ought we to forget the constancy and generous devotedness of that friend to us?"

"We never will, Kate, and you must pardon me for saying what I did. It came from my lips, but not from my heart, you know; and I will tell Harry that I said it, and ask him to forgive me too—I will, indeed, Kate."

"Nay, there is no need of that, you know, Lucy. I think we shall be very, very happy now; and remember, Lucy, you are to stay with Harry and me.

"Yes, Kate—yes, when you are married."

A slight blush spread across the face of Kate, but she was far above the mawkish sentimentality of boarding-school misses, and, moving her composure in a moment, she said—

"Yes, Lucy, when I am married to Harry Dean, which will be very shortly now, I think, I hope he will go to the country, and in some quiet little happy home, in the midst of birds, and trees, and flowers, seek for that serenity and calmness which is the most enviable lot that human nature can enjoy in this world."

"Kate, Kate, what a picture of joy you draw for us. Ah, we shall be happy indeed; and Tony, you know, who was so kind to me, must come and see us all, very, very often."

"As often as he will, Lucy; we shall always consider him as a very dear friend indeed; but, no doubt, Harry Dean will see to his advancement in life, for, although I know them not, much of Harry Dean's behaviour is to me a profound mystery; I feel confident that he has, from some means or another, ample resources."

"Yes, there is a mystery."

"There is, Lucy; but yet I have that strong faith in Harry, that I am in my own mind assured that he has good and sufficient reasons for such mystery, and that when it shall please him to explain it, that my explanation will contain ample justification."

"No doubt, Kate."

"There cannot be a doubt, my dear Lucy; and if the strange adventures you and I have gone through were to be ever written, the faith, the overweening faith, I have always had in the honour of Harry Dean, ought to be made a point of, notwithstanding all the mystery that envelopes his conduct."

"Then the story," said Lucy, with a bright and beaming smile, "ought to be called Love and Mystery."

"It might, fairly enough," said Kate, "and it would end in the love without the mystery, for Harry Dean will scatter the mystery to the winds, while the love will still remain a constant inhabitant of both our bosoms."

Tony was soon introduced to Kate, and was delighted to shake hands, whispering to Lucy that she was handsome enough, quite, for a Queen; an opinion in which Lucy fully coincided, for there was no amount of praise of Kate which Lucy would not believe, and be ready to declare was perfectly authentic. Tony, however, took Harry Dean aside as soon as he could, and in a very mysterious manner he said to him—

"Mr. Dean, I want to ask you something very particular indeed."

"Very well, Tony, what is it?"

"I want you to give me your advice about something very important, because two heads, you know, are always better than one in any matter."

"Yes, usually. Go on, Tony."

"Well, then, if you were a little bit in love with a nice little creature, with such eyes and ringlets, and were to go down-stairs and find her alone—suppose we say, now, in the bar of this house—while the landlady was at tea; what would you say?"

"Upon my word, Tony, I don't know."

"Oh, yes, Mr. Dean, I believe now that you know very well, because it is rather important—it is indeed—so do tell me. Come, now, just as you walked in, what would be the most striking thing to do under such circumstances?"

"Why, the most striking thing, Tony, would be to fall down and upset the tea table."

"Oh, I mean in a loving, affectionate sort of way. Come, you understand me, I'm sure, Mr. Dean, and won't refuse a word of advice."

"Well, Tony, if you are in love with the girl, I think the best way is to tell her so in as few words as possible, and then what you next say or do, you know, must depend altogether upon what sort of reply she makes to it. I really cannot say anything else upon the subject."

"Humph!" said Tony.

"But," added Harry Dean, "are you really in love with a nymph with such eyes and ringlets as exceed all description?—for you evidently broke down upon that point, Tony."

"Well—a-hem! I really—am—in a manner of speaking."

"And who is she?"

"Well, I don't know exactly, but I'm to meet her in the bar; and all I wanted to know was, what your opinion might be of the best thing to say. That is all."

"Then, Tony, I will advise you."

"You really will?"

"Indeed, I really will—I have said so, and I will most assuredly keep my word, Tony."

"Then you are just the sort of trump I always thought you was. Well? Well?"

"Then, Tony, you may depend, that in an affair of the heart, it is by far safer to trust to the inspiration of the moment to teach you what to say, than to premeditate any speech; so, if you have to meet ringlets and black eyes in the bar, don't give a thought to what you have got to say until you have to say it, and thus, you may depend, something will turn up from your natural wit much more appropriate than anything previously studied."

"You think so?"

"I know it, Tony. I feel quite assured of it. Moreover, how can any third party have anything like a genuine idea of what you might say? This may be a serious affair, or only one of common gallantry. Which is it, Tony?"

"Upon my life I don't know. If the girl is civil to me I am civil to her. That's all, but no more, I assure you; and how the affair goes on will altogether depend upon what she says herself about it."

CHAPTER XCIX.

WILKINS'S EXAMINATION.

Tony had evidently got the spirit of the old song by heart, which says—

"What care I how fair she be,
If she smiles not upon me?"

For, from what he had said to Harry Dean, it seemed pretty plain that the amount of his affection for the young lady with the eyes and the ringlets was to be as nearly as possible graduated by the amount of favour with which his advances were by her received. This is so obviously sensible a mode of proceeding, and so superior to the absurd practice of the dying-duck order of swains, who love the more the more they are treated with disdain by the object of their fond solicitude, that we unhesitatingly recommend it. When a young lady pouts, let the young gentleman walk off—not very briskly—and we pledge our reputation, that if she does care for him, she will catch him before he turns the first corner; but if she does not, why then let him pursue his way, singing in as merry a tone as an enfranchised blackbird—

"What care I how fair she be,
If she smiles not upon me?"

But we must now leave Tony to get on as well as his mother wit will let him with eyes and ringlets, while we attend to more stern subjects; and now we will step into a cell in Clerkenwell Prison, and take a glance at its occupant. That occupant is Wilkins. Upon his committal to prison until the following morning by the magistrate, the full particulars, as far as they well knew, of who and what he was, went with him; and consequently he found himself quite an object of attention in the prison. Had he been some poor devil taken up for a petty larceny, not a word would have been said to him; but the governor himself comes to the receiving-room to look at a murderer. So much for the nobility of crime. We can fancy some haughty bloated bishop receiving the same kind of polite attentions from a certain Gentleman, expected to be Old, and

"Not mentionable to ears polite,"

in a certain region where the thermometer is usually believed to make a very high temperature indeed. But this is a digression, and quite by the way. We return to Wilkins the murderer.

"You can go into the common ward," said the governor, "or you can have a cell to yourself if you like."

"A cell to myself," said Wilkins, "even at the lowest pit of——. Never mind. A cell to myself I prefer, by all means. I want no company."

He was accordingly accommodated with a dingy habitation, the walls of which were of a dull coloured plaister, the monotony of which had been relieved by different prisoners drawing cartoons thereon, which generally, somehow or another, brought in a lively view of the gallows. There were, too, some lively couplets scratched upon the said walls by prisoners of a poetic turn, such as—

"I John Lucking,
Expect to dance on nothink."

"My name is Timothy Daly,
And the beaks wants to 'xibit me at the Old Bailey;"

and such like specimens of noble rhyme and rhythm, together with a concoction of fugitive pieces upon a variety of discursive subjects, no doubt highly interesting to the turnkeys, who only whitewashed the place once a year. There was a wooden bench close to one of the walls, upon which the lonely prisoner might sit, if it so pleased him; but the moment the door was closed, and the wards of the ponderous lock turned into their socket, Wilkins folded his arms and burst out into a triumphant laugh, exclaiming—

"I have done it! I have had my revenge! Ha! ha! And they think they will make a public spectacle of me, to please the gaping mob, and furnish food for the prying curiosity of newsmongers. No, no. I have had my revenge upon him who would have hunted me to death, and in my own hands I hold the scales of my own existence. Henry Dean, as you call yourself, I have blasted your happiness for ever."

So saying, he cast himself upon the floor of the cell, and covering his arms over his eyes, this remarkable man in a few minutes, seemingly from a mere effort of will, fell into an apparently deep and dreamless slumber. From this sleep he was in about two hours roughly awakened by a turnkey with rations, which were placed upon the bench.

"You can have what you like," said the man, "if you have got anything, you know?"

"Any what?"

"Tippery—blunt."

"Oh, I understand. I want nothing. Leave me."

"Well, you must be precious fond of being alone. Howsomdever, the chaplain will be here soon to talk a little with you, so you will have some company."

"The devil!"

"Lor bless you, he isn't—a what? He's the Rev. Mr. Lovell, and they do say a remarkably stupid—God bless me, what am I saying—pious man indeed."

"Why you are too honest," said Wilkins, "for a turnkey."

At this moment the Rev. gentleman who was a younger son of a highly re-

spectable family, and being found too stupid for anything else, was made an ex-
pounder of the most troublesome subject
in the world made his appearance. He
was one of those sleek light brown-
looking men who walk civilly through
life without saying or doing anything
worth remembering, and with just average
sense sufficient to keep them clear of
downright absurdities. He advanced
with what he, no doubt, intended to be an
imposing air, and slightly inclining his
head to Wilkins, as he said to the turnkey—

"You can come in half an hour,
Brown."

"Yes, sir."

Wilkins looked him calmly in the
face, but said nothing. The look, however, said much—much more than the
reverend gentleman comprehended, for he
began the conversation by saying—

"I hope your unhappy situation will
enable you to turn your attentions to a
subject of paramount importance to all
men."

"Sir?" said Wilkins.

Now, to repeat a sentence is always
awkward, and the reverend gentleman
made rather a mess of his, and at the
conclusion Wilkins shook his head, and
said in a calm collected tone—

"There must be some mistake here,
for I really cannot call to mind that I
have the honour of your acquaintance,
sir, whoever you are."

"My acquaintance? Why I am the
chaplain of this prison."

"Then, sir, I am quite sure it is a
mistake upon your part, for I was
never introduced to any such personage,
and must decline the honour now, since I
believe it is a privilege that is conceded
in society to any gentleman to receive or
not receive whom he pleases."

"But—but—I—it's my duty——"

"To thrust your society on me, sir,
whether I like it or not. How dare
you, after, in the politest manner in the
world, being told by me that I decline
your acquaintance, try to force it on me?
Have you had the education of a gentleman, or have you seen anything of
decent society?"

The chaplain was so confounded at
being met in this way, that he immediately left the cell to solitude and Wilkins, and after that no one came near

him at all till it was time to take him to
the police office. Alas! what abilities
that man had stained by crime, that
deservedly brought him so low in the
scale of society. With the heart of a
villain he had mind enough, one would
have thought, to have told him that
honesty and goodness is honour, and
that a perception of the benevolence and
the greatness of that Deity whose presence shines forth in all his works, was
the right road to happiness. But, no—
Wilkins was a striking illustration of
perverted talents, and consequently he
sunk below the level of the humblest
and most ignorant savage whose conscience was free from his deep and
manifold iniquities. "Triumph!" was all
he said when he was taken from his
cell to be conveyed to the police court;
and, from the look of his face, any one
would have supposed that he was going
to condemn and to glory over some one
else, instead of to hear the recital of his
own criminality, and to be told to prepare himself to answer to his fellow men
for the evil that he had done. The
trial of the examination had collected
many persons together, so that the court
was densely crowded, and when Wilkins
was brought in, there was a pressure
and a struggle of the most inconvenient
character to see him, which the officers,
who were peremptorily ordered to do so
by the magistrates, had the greatest
trouble in suppressing. At length, comparative order being restored, the proceedings commenced, and still the face of
the prisoner bore that strange look of
hideous satisfaction, from which any one
could see that he gloried in the crime he
had committed, and that he was far, very
far from having any dread of the consequences likely to result from it.

"What is your name?" said the
magistrate.

"Joseph Wilkins."

"A—hem! You are probably aware
of the awful crime of which you are
charged—murder, in its most aggravated
shape. I am prepared now to hear what
evidence there is against this man, Joseph
Wilkins; who I see comes before the
bench on remand, charged with wilful
murder. I understand a learned counsel
is present for the crown, who will prosecute in this matter."

"Yes, sir," said a barrister. "I conduct

the case for the prosecution, and shall merely call before you sufficient evidence to justify me in requesting a committal of the prisoner to Newgate for trial. A verdict of wilful murder against him has been returned by the coroner's jury, after a careful examination of evidence; so, probably, your worship will readily commit the prisoner from your custody to that of the authorities of Newgate."

"Very well," said the magistrate. "Call your witnesses."

"Before I do so," added the counsel, "allow me to say, sir, that the prisoner at the bar is aged forty-seven, and is a physician."

"Admitted," said Wilkins. "I know from whom that information was received, and am anxiously looking for that person in court. Now, I allude to one Harry Dean."

"I am here," said Harry Dean, stepping forward, and bowing to the bench. "I am here to watch these proceedings, and to give my testimony upon a subject that I really feel acutely upon."

The face, dress, air, manner, tone, everything of Harry Dean, proclaimed a mind serene and at ease; and Wilkins glanced at him with such wondering eyes, as though he had seen an apparition. He expected, of course, to see Harry Dean in court; but in how different a fashion had his imagination pictured that sight to what it really was when he saw it. Knowing the ardent character of Harry Dean's disposition, and knowing that he loved Kate Destern as few can love, Wilkins thought to behold him prostrated with grief; for still, it will be remembered, nothing had been said to disabuse the villain of the delusive belief that he had taken the life of the beautiful and much loved Kate Destern. But now, to behold Harry Dean looking calm and serious, but with one of the most unruffled brows in the world, was really a thing so staggering to him, as almost to make him doubt the identity of his enemy.

"He must be mad," said Wilkins.

"Who mad?" asked the magistrate.

"No matter—no matter—perhaps I am. Go on."

"In the next place," said the counsel for the prosecution, "I have to state that the prisoner at the bar has, since his apprehension upon the present charge, been recognised by the police as an old offender."

"Very well," said the magistrate. "Is there any one present who can add to the testimony who he is?—if so, it will not be out of place for such information to come in at this place."

An officer of the police came forward and was sworn.

"I well remember the prisoner," he said. "Five years ago a murder was committed at a place called Bishopstoke, and the prisoner was seen by a servant girl actually concerned in it. A man had been murdered, and he, the prisoner, was accurately described by the girl as superintending the interment of the body by moonlight, while a Swede, for the love of whom the wife of the murdered man had, by a word, lured Wilkins to give her a drug that was fatal to her husband, was completely at the secret interment overcome by a sudden conviction of the terrible character of the crime he had mixed himself up with."

"Is this story told to prejudice me," said Wilkins, "or for what?"

"Merely being a fact," said the magistrate, "we take it as a matter of safety, in case, from any unexpected circumstance, you should escape from the indictment that will be preferred against you on account of this last murder."

"How do you know it was me?"

"The girl, whose name was Maria Harrison, swore to your identity," said the officer, "and you left the country immediately. It was said that you had a thousand pounds for the deed. The wife committed suicide one hour after being in custody, and the Swede disappeared no one ever found out where."

Wilkins was silent, and the magistrate then said—

"Prisoner, it is my duty now to tell you, before any evidence is gone into formally, what you are charged with. You are brought before me, I perceive, for the murder of one Martha Lupin."

"No!" cried Wilkins, in a voice that made every one start. Then lowering his voice, he added, "A foolish error—you are reading another case, sir."

"No, no."

"I think," said Harry Dean, "this may be shortly explained. The prisoner at the bar, no doubt, intended to murder a young lady named Destern, but, by this take, he took the life, instead, of a poor old char-woman named Lupin, who, by one of the strangest accidents in the world, occupied upon that night the bed of Miss Destern, and he committing the deed, no doubt, in the dark, did not discover his mistake.

CHAPTER C.

THE SUICIDE.

THERE is no language at the command of human nature that could depict one half of the horrible expressions that chased each other, like a storm upon a lake, over the convulsed features of Wilkins at this crushing statement of Harry Dean's. Hitherto he had been supported solely by a conviction that he had achieved a great revenge, and that although his own death was certain, he had embittered the remainder of the existence of Harry Dean. Like some shipwrecked mariner upon a wide and fathomless waste of waters, he had clung to that one plank of refuge against despair. It was his consolation—his courage—his everything. He had had his revenge against the man whom he had most of all to fear, and he cared little for the awful situation in which he had placed himself. Now, however, by as many words as might be uttered in a breath, all that delusion was dispelled, and there he stood self-sacrificed for—nothing. He convulsively clasped the bar before him, and drawing his breath hard, like one upon the eve of suffocation, he gasped—

"It is not true—it is not true!"

"I rejoice," said Harry Dean, "to be able to confirm it. The young lady, who is my affianced wife, is now at the outer door of this court, waiting to tender her evidence against the heartless murderer of the poor char-woman, who, notwithstanding she appears, from what transpired at the inquest, to have been in a state of intoxication at the time, yet has been most brutally murdered by this man. Her name is sworn by the cook of the house where the deed was committed to be Martha Lupin."

"Foiled! foiled!" gasped Wilkins. "Thus—thus——"

"Heaven protect its own!" said Harry Dean, finishing the sentence for him, "and punish such men as you, Joseph Wilkins; I pity and shudder while I look upon you."

"Horror! horror! horror!" cried Wilkins, and he let his head drop upon the bar in front of him, while a convulsion shook his whole frame. There was a few moments' pause, during which all eyes were directed to that spirit-stricken man. Such mortal agony had not before met the gaze of any then present. In the course of a few minutes he slowly looked up, but the awful change that had come over his face appalled every one who looked upon him. It seemed as though twenty years had been added to that man's age, in those few fleeting moments of mortal agony. He intended to speak, but it was only after several efforts that he could command himself sufficiently to form an articulate word. When he did commence to say what he had to say, so intense was the silence in the court, lest a word he uttered should be lost, that one would have thought all present had been changed to statues.

"At last," he said, turning his gaze upon Harry Dean. "At last, you have conquered me. I have not with my own eyes seen Kate Destern in life this day; but I know she lives, for you could not act the part which now to you is nature. She is yours, and you will be happy, while I bid thus this world, which I hate, and all within its sphere, good night!"

As he spoke these words, he dived his hand into a secret pocket of his coat, and brought out something which he placed to his lips; but on the moment withdrawing it again, he glanced at what he held. It was the neck only of a very small flat bottle. It had contained poison, but probably had got smashed by some accident, of which he (Wilkins) had not been at all aware at the time it took place. A shriek proclaimed the depth of his disappointment, for there cannot be a doubt but that from first to last he intended to commit suicide at the time meant for his triumph; and now, when all was lost, he was quite willing to quit a world in which he had no more hope. The officers were too much accustomed to such escapes of prisoners from the last penalty of the law, not to see at once what Wilkins meant to do; but the disappointment he had experienced was as equally manifest; so that, although they were prepared to make a rush upon him, they abstained from so doing, and looked at the magistrate for directions.

"Handcuffs," said the magistrate. "There is no knowing now what deed of desperation, against his own life and those of others, this wretched man might perpetrate. Secure him."

With that dexterity which officers of the police pride themselves on, a pair of handcuffs were placed upon the wrists of Wilkins, and he was, to all intents and purposes, quite harmless to himself and to others. The neck of the bottle, which, no doubt, had contained some subtle drug,

"A mortal foe to life!"

fell at his feet; and from that moment Wilkins appeared to give himself up to a horrible kind of apathy, which probably would be as deadly, although not so rapid a poison to him, as that which he had hugged himself with the belief that he could take at any time in an extremity of bad fortune; but which, at the last moment, had failed. The evidence which was sufficient to warrant his committal to Newgate upon the charge of wilful murder, was now rapidly gone through, and, still secured and carefully guarded, Wilkins at last seemed to be in a fair way to endure that retribution in this world from his enemies which he had always flattered himself he could at any time escape from, by one passing pang to herald him from life to death. The magistrate had not thought it necessary, in that stage of the proceedings, to trouble Kate Destern at all, although her evidence, no doubt, upon the trial would be considered very essential. In fact, as Wilkins could already be committed under the coroner's warrant, all that took place at the police-office might be considered a matter of form; yet, having him in custody, the magistrate was bound to hear enough to commit him or to discharge him. In another half hour, from the moment that he had made the attack upon his own life, in which he had so signally failed, Wilkins was in a cell in Newgate, and a man sitting up with him, and keeping a wary eye upon his slightest movements; but by some cunning and desperate means, he still made

an effort to deprive himself of that life which was justly forfeited to the laws. Harry Dean made his acknowledgments to the magistrate, and then left the court—as he did so, he met the officer who had given the strong evidence concerning Wilkins's former crime, and he spoke to him—

"Ah, sir, he's a regular bad fellow," said the officer.

"I know it well," said Harry Dean.

"You see, sir, he resided a short distance only from the gentleman who was so cruelly murdered at Bishopstoke, and carried on an intrigue with his wife, and the poor devil of a Swedish captain was regularly hoodwinked in the whole affair, for the woman tried all her arts to attract him, as a kind of blind for her intrigues with Wilkins, and actually cajoled him with aiding in the murder of her husband; but, however, this affair will hang the fellow."

"No doubt," said Harry Dean, "and if ever a man really deserved death from the hands of his fellow creatures, Wilkins is that man; although, perhaps, it would have been better for society if he had succeeded in the attempt upon his life."

"Lord! no, sir," said the officer, "don't say that; why there has not been a hanging for this year and a half—oh, dear me, no. There's nothing like having things done in a regular legal sort of way. Good morning, sir, we shall meet at the trial."

It was a good relief to Kate not to have been called at the examination of Wilkins, and when Harry Dean came back to the hackney-coach in which she was waiting at the door of the police-office, and told her that Wilkins was committed, he found her almost fainting.

"Good Heavens! Kate," he said, "what is the matter?"

"Nothing, nothing, Harry; it was the sight of him."

"Of whom?"

"Wilkins. A moment or two since they brought him hurriedly out, and placed him in a coach, which was driven rapidly away. I caught but one passing glance at his face, and it was horrible—most horrible—why his hair has turned nearly white, Harry."

"I saw the change, Kate. The hour of mental retribution has come at last for Wilkins, and men of his violent passions feel these things most acutely. When I saw his face, after he had hidden it from all but his Maker, for a few short moments, I noticed the awful change that had taken place in it. I felt more of pity than of anger against him."

"Alas! alas! I too can pity him."

"We will not talk of him, Kate; our judgments must condemn frequently what our feelings pity; a worse man than Wilkins, it would be impossible for any state of society to produce, and he has not the common excuse of ignorance, for he is a man full of knowledge and

TONY'S FORMER MODE OF LIFE.

costly acquirements. But we will drop the ungracious theme, Kate, and talk of happier things. I am poor, Kate."

"Poor!"

"Yes. Poor and rich—rich in your affections, which are priceless, but poor in pocket. You have no doubt at times seen or fancied you have seen mysterious indications of wealth and power about me, but all that has passed away."

"Well, Harry?"

"I merely wish to let you know that by marrying me you marry poverty, and perchance entail upon yourself a life of hardships, Kate, ill-suited to you. Our daily bread must be procured by daily toil, and the home I must take you to, will be one so humble that I shall dread your turning your eyes upon its miseries."

"Oh, Harry, Wilkins is not the only person upon whom a great change has taken place."

"You thought me rich, then?"

"I do not allude to that, but to the grievous thing that it is that you should think it necessary to say more to me than that you love me, to be sure that any lot in life with you would be full of that contentment which is joy sanctioned by reflection. Oh, Harry, is it kind or gentle of you—is it at all like you to talk to me in this way? Say no more —say no more."

"I thought it right to tell you, Kate, as I had hoped better things."

"What better?"

"Wealth, and power, and station."

"And you regret that they have passed away

"Like the baseless fabric of a vision." Oh, Harry, I will not even ask you what were your hopes, and what are now your fears. Do you think I will not toil for you—do you think that the demon of idleness has taken possession of me, Harry, and that from morn till night I would shrink from any amount of labour that would contribute to make you more happy? Do not regret the loss of fortune. We will be poor, but not humble— we will be among the lowly, and possibly in the world's eyes, but what a kingdom shall we not possess in the dear consciousness we shall ourselves have of loving and being beloved.

"Harry Dean listened with a charmed delight. He could so have listened for hours to the sweet tones of Kate's voice, as she uttered sentiments that each moment more and more endeared her to him by letting him see more than ever what a treasure he had won when he made that gentle heart, by the force of love's own eloquence, his."

"Say on—say on, dear Kate."

"Have I not said enough, Harry?"

"Yes. Yes, you have said more than enough to convince me that I am unworthy of you, Kate. You are as superior to me as——"

"Nay, now she cried, as she placed her small child-like hand upon his mouth, I will hear no more in such a strain. We will make a bargain each to believe the other to be all perfection, and so, translating every word and every action by a reference to such a standard, we shall never quarrel, but our lives will pass away like a golden dream. We shall escape even a knowledge of any suffering from the "seasons' difference," for in our hearts there will be eternal summer."

"This," said Harry Dean, "is nature's true nobility, Kate; in the muster roll of angels you must be an empress, for the glory of heavenly thoughts and divine sensibility is about you, and—"

"Ah," said Kate, again stopping him, "more flattery—since when, Harry, have you learned to think that I would permit you to make me so many fine speeches? Speak to me simply as your Kate, and that is eloquence enough for me."

"But you know, Kate, I really wish——"

"No, Harry, you must not, as you will set me racking my invention to tell you how brave an Achilles you are— three handsome as the Trojan boy, who won the heart of the Queen of Love herself—and how when you speak——"

"Mercy! mercy!"

"A truce then, Harry, and we will both descend from the clouds and be plain mortals, loving each other in the old Darby and Joan fashion; so no more talk of poverty, or of blighted hopes, or of angels, or of empresses, or of beauty and eyes, and all that sort of thing, Harry. Let us be as sensible as we can, and so here we are at our temporary house; and there is our friend Tony anxiously looking out for us."

"Ah, there is Lucy, likewise."

Kate and Harry Dean related at length, both to Lucy and Tony, the full particulars of what had happened at the police-office, to which they both listened with the most intense interest that could be imagined—Lucy's eyes filled with tears, and Tony, after drawing a long breath, ejaculated—

"Poor devil, it's a pity he didn't take the mixture as before, 'that he was going to pop on' as a sort of extinguisher to his candle-light of life when he bade the world good night."

"I think so too," said Lucy, "for he is so very wicked that nobody can wish him to be alive to kill more people, which no doubt he would do if he could, I do think, Kate, he is quite as bad as the dreadful woman who took the life of Madame Zadzed."

"By the bye," said Harry, "the trial of Swam and a man named Carter for that very murder will take place at the same sessions, now close at hand, during which Wilkins will no doubt be convicted."

CHAPTER CI.

TONY'S COURTSHIP.

WE must not omit to do justice to Tony's courtship. The fact is, that we feel as we hope our readers do by this time, considerable interest in Tony and his affairs; in addition to which, we cannot help likewise feeling some amount of interest in the pretty face and laughing eyes of the damsel with the ringlets, so that we have two motives for peeping into the bar-parlour, just to see how Tony is getting on. Of course, he was true to his appointment—true, do we say!—he was, like all true lovers, more than true—that is to say, he was dodging about in everybody's way a good half hour before he was wanted. But this only showed Tony's wisdom, as it could not be very offensive to eyes and ringlets. The hour, however, as hours commonly do, came at last, and Tony made his appeal at the little bar, upon the inner side of which was the piece of fascination that had won Tony's heart, so busy, doing some indescribable something to a muslin stuff, that she could not hear or see Tony, not she. Oh, hypocrisy—thy name is woman!!

"A—hem!" said Tony, a—hem! "Here I am, miss."

"Eh? Oh, is that you—what did you please to want, sir?"

"I don't want anything now," said Tony. "If the moon was only just peeping through a cloud, how the man in it might, seeing your two eyes, say, 'Ah! pretty stars, you have come out to-night.'"

"Ha, ha, ha! Oh, really, no. What's your name?—I didn't think that your madness took that turn, indeed, I didn't."

"My what?"

"Your madness, to be sure. I heard that you were a poor cracked fellow, and the gentleman up stairs they call Dean, was your keeper; ain't it so, now? Come, answer truly."

A small amount of indignation took possession of Tony, but when he glanced at the laughing eyes of the young girl, he saw the jest, and replied—

"Oh yes, it's all right, and the doctor said the only thing to bring me to my senses again was a kiss of the prettiest girl in all the world, let the next be whom she may."

Tony knew enough of oratory as a science, we must suppose, to suit the action to the word, and the word to the action, for bouncing into the bar at the moment he made this extraordinary statement, he kissed, as fairly as ever ruby lips were kissed, the pretty barmaid, as she really was.

"You impudent wretch!—you good-for-nothing——"

"Don't say that I am good-for-nothing, now."

"What impudence?"

"Why, I've done what the King of England could not do—kissed the prettiest lips that ever the bees mistook for roses, and scampered after in a crowd for honey."

"I'm afraid——"

"Of what?"

"That you are a very bad young man, and say a great many things that you don't mean. Come, you must not sit here, you know; she don't allow anybody inside the bar. Hush! hush! Oh, there's nobody coming—my heart was in my mouth, do you know. Now Mr. What's-your-name?"

"In your mouth!" said Tony, "among all those little bits of mother-of-pearl, you call teeth, I suppose, and that fairy bell-clapper, that all the little loves in the world gave you for a tongue. What's your name?"

"I told you, stupid."

"Mary Ann. Oh! ah, I remember—why, in thinking of you, my mind was so taken up, that it drove your name clean out of my head. But, come now, will you answer me one question, and answer me truly upon your word and honour?"

"That depends upon what it is. I won't make any promises to you, I won't indeed. Hush! hush!—what's that?—do you hear any nobody or anything?"

"No," said Tony, kissing the pretty cheek this time, "I don't indeed. Is that dear little heart of yours among the noises again? Come, don't look so frightened. Do you love any one? That is the question I wanted you to answer."

"Oh dear, yes."

"Yes—you—you—really do—no!—you don't mean—that is to say, you do mean that you don't—do—no—come now, Mary Ann, you have made me miserable."

"Don't I love my mother?" said Mary Ann, with a smile that made Tony again violently essay another kiss; but Mary Ann thought there had been, as she said, "enough of that;" and so she met Tony by a slight puncture with the point of a needle, which cooled his ardour a little, and made him a decided convert to the opinion that 'every rose has its thorns.'"

"Keep your distance," said Mary Ann, "and don't let's have any nonsense. Say your say, fool—what do you want here? Come, be quick; for my aunt will be down in a minute. Besides, I can't tell a moment whether there was some one knocking at the door."

"I love you," said Tony. "Will you have me for a sweetheart?—I shall never have anybody else as long as I live, and if you say no, I promise that I will love you still well enough never to annoy you by coming in your way, or trying to make you in any way unhappy."

Mary Ann was silent, and one of her little feet went pat—pat upon the floor; and then she said in a low tone, "I don't know you, and I am a poor friendless girl, and my aunt is not—very—very kind to me."

Her eyes swam in tears, and, with a gasping sob, she covered her face with her hands, and wept.

"I'm a wretch!" said Tony. "I'm Blue Beard and the Baron Bumbustikus all in one. This is all owing to me, I have made her get the better of herself in this way. Oh, Mary Ann, I'll fly to Crim Tartary, or Winchester, or any other infernal suicidal place, and you shall never hear anything more of me while you live; but, on the contrary, *vice versa* as we say, if you don't mind quite the other sort of thing, and have the smallest notion of how pleasant bread and cheese and kisses are, only say the word, and I am yours, and yours only, for evermore, to the end of the world, and three days past it."

"My—my aunt——"

"Well?"

"She—that is my—my aunt, you know."

"Oh, the damned old cat! Murder! murder! Good gracious; murder!—fire—! what the deuce did you do that for;—eh?"

Somebody had seized Tony by the ears, and given him such a shake, digging some by no means despicable nails into his flesh at the same time, that he thought a couple of loving hand-vices had got hold of him; but when he was released, and turned quickly round, he saw the identical aunt of Mary Ann staring him full in the face, and looking strangely expressive of—"This dose to be repeated." Mary Ann made a rush from the bar, and fairly took to flight up stairs, where it is believed she shut herself in some bed-room, and there remained until the ire of the old lady was somewhat diminished by calmer reflection. Thus Tony had to bear the full brunt of the battle alone.

"And pray, sir," said the landlady, swaying her head from side to side in the manner of irascible females, "may I take the great liberty of asking who you are?"

"Oh, certainly, mum," said Tony, "you may take any proper liberties you like with me."

"You impudent low-lived wretch! Get out of the house, you old——"

"Old?"

"Thomas! Thomas! Thomas!"

"Yes, missus," cried the waiter, rushing to the bar, with a napkin in his hand.

"Count the spoons, Thomas, and see that the pepper castors have got their tops on them, before the person with the plate-stealing look leaves the house."

"I'm not going to leave the house," said Tony; "and as you are looking about, Thomas, just see if you can find your missus's decency in any odd cup or basin, and her temper in another. I don't wonder there's no cat with whiskers and a tail kept in this house, where there's such a regular old mouser behind the bar, in a blond cap and wig, one glass eye, and a cork leg, I shouldn't wonder."

The landlady gave a shriek of passion, and dropped upon a chair in the commencement of an excellent hysterical exhibition.

"Lor!" said the waiter. "What, supposes she *busteses* a blood *wessel?* What's it all about, I wonder? Missus —missus, don't take on so. Come, you know I loves yer."

This was said in a low tone, and the landlady, with a deep sigh, responded—

"Do you really, Thomas, or are you like the rest of the men?"

"I don't think I am like the rest of the men," said Thomas, "but I knows what's what, and I loves you, so don't take on now, missus, and atween you and me and the post, if you will only say you will be Mrs. Candy—you know my name is Thomas Candy—we will make a good thing of the Hotel."

"Hush! Is the villains gone?—Is the thief out of hearing, Thomas?"

"Yes, missus."

"And Mary Ann, Thomas? Is she gone, too—the young love-making ugly sinner?"

"Yes, missus."

"Then, Thomas, I've got a revelation to make to you. Listen, oh, listen."

"A revolution, missus?"

"No, a revelation. Thomas, when old Hermit died, as was Mary Ann's father, he said to me, 'Sister,' says he, 'the hotel, and all I have in the world, is Mary Ann's; my will is in the left-hand small top drawer of the walnut-tree chest, in No. 5. Give it to her, and tell her that I asked you to stay here, and be a mother to her, and that my dying wish was, that she should never forget to be kind to you. I could have died easier if she had come home from boarding school in time for me to see her; but tell her my last words were 'God bless her.'"

"You—you don't mean that, missus?"

"Yes I do. These were the last words he spoke. "Mary Ann came home from school two hours after, and I told her——"

"You told her?"

"Yes, that with his dying breath he

had left all to me, and that I had in return promised to be a mother to her. I—I did not say a word about the will at all, Thomas."

"Capital!"

"Well, since then, now going of two years and more, I have been mistress here—and I have let every one know it, too; but here's a fellow coming courting the girl, and I'm alarmed that the thing may get wind—I am indeed. You understand all that, Thomas?"

"In course I do. But still, you know by law, she could take all, whether the old man left it to her by will or not."

"Yes; but she said to me, 'Aunt,' says she, 'the wish of my father is my law; I throw myself upon your kindness. Take all, and only let me be as happy as I can, and as useful as I can, to you.'"

"Of course you flummaxed the will, missus?"

"Did what with it, Thomas?"

"Burnt it!

"I couldn't; and I'll tell you just why I couldn't, Thomas. I made up my mind to do it one night about a week after the funeral. I kept a good fire in my room, which you know is next to No. 5, being No. 4. It was about half-past twelve, when everybody was in bed, and the house all shut up, that I stepped into No. 5, with the key of the walnut-tree chest of drawers in one hand and a light in the other. The house was as still as a family vault, Thomas."

"Yes, missns. Go on."

"I did go on: I went into the room, and right up to the chest of drawers, without thinking of anything but the will; when, who should I see standing close to the corner drawer, but my brother himself, in his old dressing-gown with the two tassels, just as he looked in life."

"You don't mean that, missus?"

"Yes, Thomas. Yes; I fell down in a sort of fit, and the sun was shining when I came to myself; I got up, and got back to my own room without anybody knowing anything about it, and I lay ill for a week, and got up, looking almost like a ghost myself. It makes me tremble now."

"But the will, missus. The will?"

"Is there still."

"What, there, in the corner drawer

for two years and more. The will that makes Mary Ann mistress of the hotel and all in it ? It's freehold, too, and she won't so much as condescend to look at me, missus ?'

"Yes, Thomas."

"I'll tell you what it is—if you'll say yes to what I asked you before, that will shan't trouble you very long. I'll soon get hold of it. Why, it's like being in a firework manufactory, when you don't know a minute but you may be blown up, for such a thing to be come-at-able by everybody. What do you say, missus ?"

"I am yours, Thomas."

"All's right, then. You make your mind easy about it. Now, listen to me. You know I sleep up stairs, but if you take good care to have a fire in your room to-night, I'll slip down when all is quiet, and soon make the will into ashes. I'm not afraid of ghosts.'

"But it was horrid, Thomas."

"Oh, stuff, you only fancied it. I don't go for to believe in any such nonsense. Ghosts, indeed! Psha! I tell you it was all fancy. Naturally enough you was thinking of the old man, and so when you got into the room, all of a tremble, and the candle flaring about in the cold air, you fancied you saw him, and down you went in a faint."

"Oh, no, no !"

"But I say—oh, yes; and you shall find no ghost will trouble me. I don't mean to say but I might be scared if there was such a thing, but as I know there ain't, why it's quite another affair, so don't you make yourself at all uncomfortable about it, missus, but just trust to me. Shall it be as I have said to-night, eh ? Only say the word, that's all, and it's as good as settled then ?"

"Yes, Thomas, and I can only say it will be a great weight off my mind when it's all settled, for every time I pass the door of No. 5, I am all of a tremble. Let it be to-night, and as for Mary Ann, I really don't know what to do with her, I hate the sight of her about the house."

"Oh, turn her out, and make her go to service, or get her living any way she likes. What matters it to us ? She never had a civil word to say to me, except in the way of business."

"Very well, Thomas, then we quite understand each other, and that's all arranged satisfactorily."

"Is it ?" said Tony to himself, as he walked lightly up the stairs, after listening to every word of the above conversation. "Is it all arranged satisfactorily, really ? Well, I begin to think it will be, but not exactly in your way."

CHAPTER CII.

A NIGHT ADVENTURE.

TONY was a little puzzled, and when he got up stairs he sat down to think. The result of that thought was the wise determination to seek the advice of Harry Dean. A more prudent step than this he could not possibly have taken. When Harry Dean heard him to an end, he said—

"Why, Tony, this is quite an adventure ; what are your own notions upon the subject ?"

"I'm very sorry," said Tony, "that Mary Ann is entitled to so much, and that I happen to know it."

"Indeed, Tony, and what makes you sorry for that ? One would have thought you would have rejoiced."

"Why, look here now," said Tony. "When I speak to her again of loving her, she may think that it's all for what she is worth, and it won't be so, for I loved her when I thought she was only a poor girl, and pictured to myself the pleasure of working for her, and keeping her so nice. That's really too bad—it is—for now there's no saying what she may think."

"I think, Tony," said Harry Dean, "that you take an exaggerated view of this matter. You certainly, as I can testify, fell violently in love before you had the least idea of the financial condition of Mary Ann, and therefore you have nothing to fear. Moreover, it appears to me that, as you will be the means now, in all probability, of restoring to her what is her own, you will materially increase your claim upon her affections."

"You really think so ?"

"In good faith I do. And I look upon Mary Ann as yours from this time forthwith."

"You don't know how you please

me by saying that. I'm quite easy now; but what ought I to do about this affair of the will? It won't do to let Mr. Thomas and the old lady put it into the fire to-night quite so comfortably as they wish, and expect, no doubt, to be able to do. Will it?"

"By no means, Tony. It's rather a delicate affair, take it altogether, and probably Mary Ann would prefer any way of managing the business to making a police affair of it, as her aunt is concerned in it. Do you think yourself a match for Thomas, the waiter?"

"What—I? Why, I'd double him up in about half a minute, so that he'd think himself packed up suddenly for a long journey. Oh, if it was only to come to that, I'd soon cut the matter quite short, that I would."

"Very well then, Tony, the grand thing will be to catch them in the fact of purloining the will, and take it from them yourself, which I think you may do very well, as you will only have Thomas and an old woman to contend with, and both of them will, no doubt, be pretty well terrified at the idea that they might see the ghost of old Hermit. I dare say, if the door of No. 5 is locked, it is some every-day lock that every key may open; and suppose, now, at a little before twelve, you were to manage to get into the room, and there secure yourself."

"I will," said Tony, "it's settled, and if I don't give Mr. Thomas a fight, as well as the old vixen of an aunt, my name is not Tony Thorpe."

"You know," added Harry Dean, "that my bed-room is close at hand, and I will leave my door only just closed, so that, should anything occur to which you require a witness, you have only to call to me, or push my door open, and I shall be with you quickly."

"A thousand thanks," said Tony, "it's as good as settled."

"And you will, I hope, be the happy husband of Mary Anne."

"Oh, yes, I hope I may; what a change for me! Lord bless you, Mr. Dean, if I was only to write my history, you would be astonished, that you would. I ain't old, but I've gone through odd scenes, and lived in all sorts of ways; why once, for a whole winter, I lived with a man and his wife and a dog, and

a blackamoor, in all the wild out-of-the-way places that could be found out. He'd done something or another wrong, I believe, but he was kind to me, and many a time we have all lived for a day upon a rasher of bacon, held on a stick over a wood fire to cook, and I shall never forget it how the dog used to look on, just like a mahomedan."

"Like a what? Tony—a christian you mean."

"Ah, well, its meant the same, only there are mahomedans, but no christians. We had a horse that used to carry our luggage, such as it was, and at night we used to put up a sort of a rude tent, and horse and dog, and blackamoor, and I, and the man and his wife, all got under it together and snored away, for all the world like singing for the million at Exeter Hall, only there was some sense in our proceedings, but there is nothing but humbug in that, as all the world knows, but the noodles who part with their money for such nonsense."

"You are right, Tony, but now I must leave you to the management of your own plans. Mind you don't betray yourself; and I would seriously caution you to say nothing of the will to Mary Ann, for she might say or do something that possibly would give her aunt such a hint as to induce the immediate destruction of the will before night."

"Leave me alone, for that's all right," said Tony, "I mean to be as close as wax, you may depend upon it. This is just what I like—an adventure. Lord bless you, it makes me feel quite another thing to have an affair like this on hand; I would not give a pin's head for things to go on all as smoothly as possible; give me a few difficulties and adventures, and all that sort of thing, and then I'm all right."

"I believe that is really your disposition, Tony, and I only hope you will manage this affair, in which you are personally interested, with your usual tact and discretion."

So saying, Harry Dean left Tony to his own devices, and not a little pleased was the latter with the whole, although, had the aunt or Thomas had the least suspicion of the possibility of Tony knowing so much more than they wished any one to know, his man-her would seriously have alarmed them. There was a very stern look upon his face as he moved about the house, and he trod softly, as though he were intent upon always catching somebody by surprise, and more than once he went to the door of No. 5, and there executed some extraordinary antics, such as throwing himself into attitudes of offence and defence, and in an imaginary manner half strangling a waiter. Then, if he heard any one coming, he would affect to be looking upon the floor for something, or to be catching some fly upon the wall, or whistling some popular air with all the unconcern in the world, and the most deceptive way imaginable. He could fain have had a few moments' conversation with Mary Ann, just to tell her not to mind her aunt a brass farthing, and trust to luck and to him; but the old woman kept such good watch and ward over her niece, that Tony had not the ghost of an opportunity of saying one word, or of even making any telegraphic signs; which was just as well, for no doubt, however extraordinary and graphic they might have been to him, they would, probably, have been quite unintelligible to Mary Ann, and might only have tended greatly to the confusion of her faculties for the remainder of the evening. And oh, how Tony did sigh for that evening to slide into night—and the night to quietly become deep and dark until the hour of twelve, when the proceedings were about to commence that would make the fortune of Mary Ann, and visit with a retributive justice the aunt and the waiter. Long looked for will, however, come at last, if folks will but have a little patience; and eleven o'clock arrived and found Tony broad awake in his own bed-room. It would, however, be an hour yet before the hotel would be tolerably quiet; nevertheless, it was high-time that he, Tony, should see if he had the means of effecting an entrance into the haunted chamber, No. 5. This in all prudence he should have done before, but several times that he had sallied out with such an object, he had heard, or fancied he heard, some one coming, and had retreated into his own room again, fearful of a discovery of the plot, which he would not have had frustrated for the world. Ren-

dered desperate, however, by eleven o'clock striking, he resolved, armed with the key of his own room door, to make the attempt upon No. 5. Shutting his ears to all slight noises, he made his way to the door of the haunted chamber, and hastily and easily unlocked it. To walk in and lock the door on the inside, so that it should have no appearance of being tampered with, was the work of a moment. He put the key in his pocket, and there he was in a strange room, which was as dark as a dungeon, and in which he had the comfortable assurance that a ghost had been seen most clearly. And this ghost story was not like many others, added to, and illustrated by two or three narrators—no, Tony had had it —which is quite a phenomenon in ghost stories—at first hand. He had heard it from the lips of the person who had actually seen it. It was far from being such a common case as—'There was a friend of mine, whose step-mother's aunt had a cook, whose first cousin's second husband knew a very respectable man, who saw, &c., &c., &c.' Oh dear, no; it was nothing of that sort! But Tony had done one courageous thing already. He had done what the nerves of many brave men would not have permitted them to do. He had locked himself in a strange dark room, which he was told was haunted. There was a damp musty smell in the atmosphere of the room—a sort of earthy grave-like flavour, as though everything in it was intent upon resolving itself to its elements as quickly as possible, through the instrumentality of damp. No doubt everything there, if Tony had looked about him, had a mouldy aspect. The spirit of neglect, disease, and desolation, was in the odour of that long-shut-up room, in which Mary Ann's father had breathed his last. Truly it was a room cut out for the occupation of a ghost, and if no ghost was there, we should like to know where else a ghost would be likely to be?

Tony stood profoundly still upon the same spot from which he had been enabled to lock the door, and then he listened with that almost painful intensity which in a short time is tolerably certain to act sufficiently upon the imagination to create the semblance of the sound the ears expect to momentarily drink in. All was still in the room, and Tony drew his breath freely, for he had done what he had done in a sort of flurry, for fear of interruption, but now there was no dread of such an event, as the door was locked safely.

"How very dark !" he said, in that low tone which people speak in when they think they are alone, but are not quite sure about it. "How very dark —a-hem ! Well, who's afraid ?"

An odd noise, most likely occasioned by the still atmosphere of the room being altered in temperature, and disturbed generally by Tony's presence came upon his ears. It was one of

those noises that furniture will make at times from purely atmospheric causes, but it sent a cold chilling feeling to Tony's heart.

"What's that ?" he said, "what's that ? I—I don't want to interfere with you, you know; I only want to do what's right, that's all—What do you say ?"

All was still again.

"Well I never !" said Tony. "I know what I ought to have done. I ought to have come into the room in the daylight first, and found out where every thing is—I—I must feel my way now Perhaps the shutters are shut. They must be too, or it would never be so confoundedly dark as it is here.   I'll try and find my way to the window."

Tony moved slowly along in the direction that he thought the window lay, but, owing to having turned round twice or thrice, his notions of topography, as connected with that room, were rather in a confused state, and he suddenly touched something that he thought at the moment must be the ghost of old Hermit, for it was soft and yielding.

"Murder !" said Tony.

He stretched out both his hands, and felt that he was close to the side of a bed, and that the object which he had touched was the curtain at its foot.

"Why this is the bed," he said, "that the old man died on, I suppose, and everything, no doubt, is in the room just as when he kicked the bucket. I wonder whereabouts the walnut-tree chest of drawers is, that the old aunt spoke about ?"

Since he had found the bed, there was every likelihood that, with a little diligent groping about, he would be able to lift open the chest of drawers in which was deposited the precious document that was of such importance to Mary Ann. He accordingly commenced his researches in a very cautious manner along the room. Of course he managed to run against nearly every article in it, and to feel all sorts of apprehension as he did so. He kept his hands stretched out before him for fear of actually having a tumble, and he suddenly grasped a something that came down upon his head and nearly smothered him. By a violent series of kicks, Tony did succeed in freeing himself from the sudden infliction of such an incumbrance, but he could not for the life of him make out what it was, for he was in by far too great a fright to have all his senses sufficiently active about him to enable him to come to any rational conclusion. He began to wish devoutly that he had not undertaken the adventure, but one thought of the bright eyes and the ringlets of Mary Ann always gave him fresh courage in the pursuit of the adventure.

"Now," said Tony, "if any one had told me I should be so very uncomfortable, I should have told him he didn't know me, or he would not say that. Eh !, eh ?"

He actually fancied he heard a deep groan, and the perspiration broke out upon his brow in large drops. Truly Tony was doing as much to win Mary Ann as any knight adventurer of old ever essayed for the love of lady fair.

"What was that ?" he said. Eh ? Did anybody speak ? Don't mind me. It's only Tony, old chap. I haven't come to do any harm."

He listened intently, and all was still again. He began to feel a little reassured, and to think that some purely accidental noise, as was indeed the case, had deceived him. He wiped the large drops of perspiration from his face, and drew a long breath.

"Oh, Mary Ann ! Oh, Mary Ann," said Tony, "if this affair turns up, as no doubt it will, a trump card for you, you ought to think of me."

Tony now groped about, until he found a chair, upon which he sat with great caution, as though he feared it might by some unexampled act of treachery slip from under him, and let him down.

" I won't stir," he said, "from here now, until somebody comes. That I won't ; and when they do come, if I don't frighten 'em a bit for the fright they have given me, my name ain't Tony, that's all. I never thought, upon my life, sitting all alone in a room where there was a ghost was half such work as it is. Not I."

It was not a very pleasant amusement for Tony to sit there, and look at the darkness, which seemed to him anything but a philosophical nonentity, for there appeared to be all sorts of arch goblins sailing about the black atmosphere, with which he, Tony, was surrounded, and each seemed to be quite intent upon driving him into a state of permanent distraction. It was at this moment, that the clock upon the landing-place of the staircase, and not very far from the door of No. 5, began to execute the chimes, which was a prelude to striking the midnight hour.

CHAPTER CIII.

A GHOST.

"One—two—three—four—five—six seven — eight — nine — ten—eleven—twelve!" counted Tony, and then he drew a long breath as he said, "twelve o'clock! Well, I never before felt what a rummy sort of hour twelve o'clock was. How all-overish I do feel, to be sure. I have often heard about the spectres of the midnight hour, but somehow or another, I never felt about them just as I do now. It ain't at all comfortable. What's that?"

Some faint noise from within or without the house came upon his ears, which was certainly upon that occasion preternaturally acute, and he shook from top to toe.

"I can't stand this much longer," he muttered. "Ah! now I hear 'em shutting up the house as safe as bricks, and they will soon be here. I like the human sound of those bolts, and bars, and shutters. They make me think that I am in the old work-a-day world again, and not altogether given up to ghosts and spirits, and all that set of ugly customers."

The sounds of nightly precaution in the way of house fastenings were now quite unequivocal, and Tony listened to them with real pleasure. At length they ceased, and Tony heard divers footsteps upon the staircases, and doors shut and fastened. The folks were retiring to rest, with the exception of the night porter, who always slept all day, and sat wide awake in the hall all night. Tony felt better, and slowly rose from the chair.

"I think," he said, "I had better try now to feel about the room, and find some hiding place for myself before they come, and then I can pounce upon them quite at unawares, and frighten 'em out of their wits. Oh, I hope that nummy old aunt will come. Don't I long to give her a turn, the old cat, for her treatment of my Mary Ann."

Tony, it will be seen, was already beginning to assume a kind of property in the landlady's fair niece. "My Mary Ann," sounded pretty well for a beginning. By dint, now, of groping about the room for some time, he found what he had no doubt, from the feel of the old-fashiond handles, was the walnut-tree bureau, and he was about to cheer himself up by a remark to that effect, when something soft fell upon his head; and Tony dropped to the ground with a full conviction that the ghost of old Hermit, mistaking altogether in the most horrible way his, Tony's, intentions, was, to use his own phraseology, "down upon him." So sudden was the surprise of this encounter to Tony, that he lay upon the floor for some minutes, before the rather rational supposition occurred to him, that all that had occurred was the falling upon him of some article of dress that had been hanging on the wall close to the bureau, and which, in all human probability, had rotted off its perch. When once he admitted to his mind such an idea as this, its rationality strongly recommended it; and he began a careful manual examination of the soft article with which he was encumbered. The result of this examination was highly satisfactory, for nothing could be more clearer to Tony than that he had now in his possession some sort of coat with very long and ample skirts.

"I have hit it," cried Tony; and then, fearful that he had spoken too loud, he said—"Hush!" Then, in a more cautious tone, he added—"I'd lay any wager that wasn't downright ruination to ose, that this is the old man's dressing gown, and that it was a sight of it hanging against the wall close to the bureau that helped the conscience of that old vinegar-cruet of an aunt of Mary Ann's to conjure up the ghost of the old man."

We think so too, Tony. This idea was a comforting one, and Tony did not feel that his nerves were in half such a state of flutter as they had been. All that was supernatural in the whole affair was, as supernatural things mostly do in the long run, fading gradually into the natural, aided largely by superstition.

"All's right," he said. "Mary Ann, you will have what belongs to you in good time now, or I shall be able to state some remarkably good reason why not."

Scarcely had Tony given utterance to this remark, than through the key-hole of the door there came from the outside a thin pencil of light, and he heard some whispered conversation. Inclining his ear, he caught the following words, faintly uttered in the voice of the waiter—

"Is this the key?"

"Yes," said the aunt. "I know it is by the piece of string round the handle; besides, it's been on a nail in my room ever since that night when I saw——"

"Well—well, we won't talk about that just now."

"You ain't afeard?"

"I afeard! I think not, rather. Only what's — what's — the — the use, you know, of talking about ghosts and such like things at a time like this? Of course no ghosts will interfere with us. A-hem. We don't mean any harm, not we. Every one for himself, and God for us all."

"That's my motty," said the aunt. "Now let's be quick about it. Can't you open the door?"

"Oh, yes. There it is. How dark it does look inside, to be sure. Is it a big four-poster?"

"Yes, to be sure; and the very best bed in the house; and a sin and a shame it has been to let it be shut up here so long. I—I—can see it now."

"Why how odd you look, missus!"

"Do—I?—So—so do you. Your eyes seem taking a start out of your head, and you are all of a shake."

"Ah!" said the waiter with a groan. "It's earning the money; but here goes. Come in."

"What?"

"Come in, I say. Why you don't mean to stand shivering and shaking there, do you, missus? Come in, do now, with me?"

"No, not if I were at my last gasp, I wouldn't and couldn't. I told you I'd seen enough in that room already, and I ain't going to try it again. No, it's no use saying anything, I ain't going."

"Oh, stuff, missus—stuff, I ain't a bit afeard in course, and I only want you to come and see as I ain't."

"I shall be quite satisfied of that, by your going in. Nobody but you, or a clergyman in a suit of armour, could do it."

"You don't mean that, missus?"

While this little dispute was going on, Tony had had time to thoroughly digest a plan of operation. He carefully slipped on the dressing-gown, and stooping down by the corner of the room, close to which was the walnut-tree bureau, he waited with some little anxiety the appearance of the waiter. That personage, with all his fears, was sufficiently urged on by his cupidity to run almost any risk, and when he found that nothing would stir the resolution of the landlady, he took the key of the drawer in which the will was from her hands, and with it projected out before him like a pocket pistol, and a lighted candle in the other hand, he slowly made his way into the haunted chamber. His teeth quite clattered in his head, as he said—

"I—I—I don't—see—anything to be afeard, of—missus. What a fool you—must be."

"Quick! Oh, be quick about it," said the aunt. "I shan't feel no more happy till that will is in the fire in my room."

"Then—the left-hand drawer is it?"

"Yes, yes. The left-hand drawer. Speak now and then, to let me know you are alive."

"Yes, yes. I will—I will."

Slowly the rascal made his way towards the walnut-tree chest of drawers, which the light came faintly glaring upon, shining up the faded lackering of the old handles, and making everything seem to shake about as he held the light in his trembling hands.

"I see it—I see it," he said, in a muttered tone. "I see it. The left-hand drawer."

Now Tony had no idea of in any way interfering in the affair until the will was actually produced, so he kept profoundly quiet in the corner where he had hidden himself; and if he had been much worse concealed than he was, the fright of the waiter was by far too great to have enabled him to observe anything but the walnut-tree chest of drawers, to which he was bound. With trembling agonies, having now got so far without any interruption, either by sight or sound, he commenced unlocking the drawer; but a man in a state of nervous terror is always particularly unhappy with locks, and the waiter fumbled for some moments at the long disused one of the left-hand drawer before he could persuade it to open. At length with a click it unlocked, and he pulled the drawer about half-way out, and held the candle eagerly to it. Tony was too low to see into the drawer, but he heard a rustling of papers, and then the fellow said suddenly, with an air of triumph—

"Here it is! Missus—missus."

"Yes, yes."

"I've got it."

"Bring it here at once. And there's no ghost."

"Ghost! No, come in—come.—There's nothing to frighten a mouse here. Only think of my courage; now, missus, you'll remember how I marched in here as long as you live, won't you now?"

"But where's the will?"

"Here it is, tied up by a piece of tape. The last will and testament of——"

"Drop that!" said Tony, in a sepulchral sort of voice.

For the space of time, perhaps, that it would have taken any one deliberately to count six, both the waiter and his mistress were so struck with horror and amazement, that they remained transfixed, as though suddenly paralysed by these two words that Tony had uttered. Then the spell was broken in both of them at once. The will and the candle fell to the floor, and their sole object was to see which would get out of the room first. Tony added to their terror by rising up and saying—

"I'm coming—I'm coming. Oh you wretches, I'll be on your backs in a moment."

The waiter tried to struggle past his mistress and she tried to struggle past him, so that, of course, they seriously impeded each other, and naturally enough they fell down on the floor, where each supposing that the ghost had hold of them, they lay roaring for mercy, and pummelling each other at a great rate. Tony snatched up the will, and trampling over them both as they lay, he gained Harry Dean's room, the door of which he opened without any ceremony, and bounced in. Harry Dean was up and reading.

"Well Tony," he said. "What success?"

"All's right—all's right. Here's the will!"

"That is the most important thing of all. But what is all that row about, Tony? Hilloa! I hear people calling murder."

"They are them."

"The aunt and her intended, I suppose? Why the whole inn will be alarmed in a moment or two. Did you ever hear such a racket? Give me the will, Tony, I will put that in a place of safety, and then we will sally out of our rooms as though disturbed by the uproar."

"Help! help!" shouted the waiter.

"Murder, fire," screamed the landlady.

The natural consequence of these alarming cries was, that the night porter flew up stairs with a small hand lantern in his hand, and rushing into the room, he fell sprawling over the landlady and the waiter. Doors, however, began to be opened in all directions, and many lights began to flash upon the scene, while, among the rest, came Harry Dean and Tony, looking as innocent as possible of knowing anything of the real cause of the disturbance. The scene that met their eyes was a sufficiently ludicrous one. The night-watchman sat with his nose in his hand, for it had from some stray blow received a severe concussion, and the landlady had a good grasp of the waiter's hair, while he in his hands bore, as a trophy of the battle, her cap and false front, which looked just as though he were some Indian warrior who had succeeded in scalping his enemy. Harry Dean thought he might as well take the initiative in the matter, so, before any one else spoke, he said—

"What is the meaning of this disturbance? Are people to have no rest in this house?"

"Ah, what is the meaning of it?" cried everybody.

"The meaning!" groaned the waiter.

"The meaning!" shrieked the landlady.

"I don't know," said the night-watchman. "All I have got to say, is, that hearing somebody cry murder upstairs, I came, when somebody knocked me down and pummelled away at my nose as if they were gold-beaters, and it was to be made into leaf from lump."

The landlady and the waiter rose and looked with horrified gestures into the room they had just left, and Harry Dean said—

"What do you look so terrified into that room for?"

"Is there a ghost there?" said Tony.

"A ghost!" said everybody, and a very respectful distance was kept from the chamber door.

"Don't ask me anything," said the landlady. "Don't say anything to me. I feel that I shan't be long for this world after to-night, I am as good as a dead woman."

She tottered away to her own room and closed the door.

"Well," said Harry Dean to the waiter, "it is pretty plain that you have been at some villany or another, so we will trouble you to explain the affair."

"No, no.—I'm very ill, very ill indeed.—I—I—can't explain anything.—Oh dear, oh dear, I never was so frightened in all my life. I would'nt go into that room again for fifty-thousand pound done up in a great heap, that I wouldn't."

"What's your objection to that room?" said Tony.

"Nothing—nothing, I don't want to say anything about it. I'm very ill—very ill indeed—that's the plain fact; and—and do let me go, will you? I have only just dropped a paper there."

The waiter was recovering a little, and beginning to ask himself whether he might not, by some manœuvring, yet get possession of the will.

"A paper!" said Tony. "Oh, I'll go in and get it for you."

"Thank you, thank you. It's folded up, and tied with a piece of red tape. You will be sure to see it. You can bring it direct to me, if you please, sir, as it's private in it's nature."

"Very good," said Tony, "I ain't afraid of ghosts—never was. Thank you, this light will do."

Tony walked into the bed-room again, and carefully shut the drawer of the bureau, as well as everything behind it, out of sight with the old dressing-gown, by the assumption of which he had been able to terrify to such an extent the aunt of Mary Ann, and her intended, the unscrupulous waiter.

Returning then rapidly, he said, "I can see nothing."

"Nothing? Why—why it's close down by the chest of drawers; and—and one of the drawers is open."

"Certainly not, sir," said Tony. "Everything is all shut up quite close, I assure you, there is no drawer open."

The waiter gave a shudder, for he was now more than ever convinced that there must be some supernatural agency at work, since the drawer he had opened was closed against all conviction he had of having opened it. With a groan, arising from the horrid thought, that as now he had once awakened the attention of a ghost towards him, he might be tormented for the remainder of his existence, he tottered away to his own bed-room, no doubt, like most rogues when they fail in their roguery, bitterly repenting the share he had taken in the infamous transaction that had been proposed to him by Mary Ann's aunt.

CHAPTER CIV.

WILKINS'S LETTER.

TONY was abundantly satisfied with the result of this adventure, and so was Harry Dean; for, quite independent of his regard for Tony, he was one of those who always felt a degree of honest exultation in the defeat of any offers of villany and the establishment of right.

"Go to bed now, Tony," he said, "and we will talk about this matter in the morning, with the assistance of a lawyer."

"A lawyer!" said Tony.

"Yes. This affair will require one."

Tony shook his head, as he said—

"Well, I'm sorry for that; they are such blundering rogues, you know."

"Not all of them, Tony."

"Oh, dear, yes. You don't know 'em as I do. Lord bless you. If one of 'em was to try to be honest, he'd have to leave the profession, he would. Whatever you do, Mr. Dean, don't you have anything to say to lawyers."

"Well, well, Tony, we will have as little to say to them as possible, for, even if they are not all downright thieves, I believe a more waspish and narrow-minded set of men don't exist in the world—so that I have no great inclination for their society at any time; but in this affair it would be absolutely dangerous to the interests of Mary Ann to proceed without one."

"Very well," said Tony, "have a dozen of 'em. Stop a bit, I've thought of a good idea."

"What is it, Tony?"

"Why, it's as regards a lawyer, Mr. Dean; and it was suggested to me by a nice little story I heard once."

"What was it? Will it take long to tell?"

"Not two minutes. There was a man travelling in Spain, with a considerable sum of money about him, and knowing that a particular road he had to pass was infested by two notorious thieves, he found out where they both could be seen in the town—for the thieves there walk about, and are as well known as the lawyers are with us. So that as we point out a man, and say that's Mr. So-and-so, the notorious lawyer, they point to a fellow in Spain, and say that's Don So-and-so, the notorious brigand."

"Very good, Tony. Go on."

"Well, this man, who did not want to lose his money, called upon each of the brigands separately, and said—'I'm afraid of such a one,' mentioning the other, 'robbing me to-morrow upon the road to Castille, and if you will meet me about a mile on, and escort me, I will pay out of a thousand crowns, I have with me, fifty.' Well, they both agreed to the proposal, making up their minds, at the same time, to have the whole thousand crowns, but they were each quite obvious in their determination that the other should not touch a single coin."

"I see the drift of your story, Tony."

"I dare say you do; howsomdever, just listen to it to an end. The traveller set off, and presently one of the robbers found him, and had scarcely given him a 'good day' when the other came up, and they looked at each other like two strange cats, each saying to himself—'ah, now, if I had not been spoken to by this traveller, he would have been robbed, and perhaps his throat cut by that vagabond.' The traveller pushed on at a good pace, and presently, from

words, the two thieves got to blows, which mightily amused the traveller. One killed the other, but not without being himself so badly wounded that he could not move, upon which the traveller said to him—'Good day; the road is clear now, and I perceive that there is nothing in the world like setting a thief to catch a thief. Hurrah for Castille!'"

Harry Dean laughed at Tony.

"Stay," he said, "I suppose from this you would have me draw the inference, Tony, that it is safer to employ two lawyers than one."

"Oh, much, much, and give each of 'em ten per cent. upon all the charges he can knock out of the other's bill."

"Well, Tony, I don't know but you may be quite right, and the plan is worth trying, but yet I think I do know that *rara avis*—an honest lawyer."

"No."

"Yes, Tony; and, at all events, if I make a mistake so far, I will take good care that Mary Ann shall not suffer from any totally unexpected bill of costs. Good night."

"Good night," said Tony, "and may you have all the pleasant dreams in the world."

"The same to you, Tony."

*　　*　　*　　*

"When the morning came, it shone upon the various parties connected with the over night's proceedings at the hotel in a very different fashion, such difference being the result of the widely varying feelings with which they severally named it. The landlady was in an awful state of perplexity to know what possible and probable explanations to give of the night adventure, and the waiter was in a perfect agony to think that all his expectations of greatness had vanished from before him,

"Like the baseless fabric of a vision." He was too thorough a rogue, however, not to make up his mind to take all the advantage that he could of the affair, and he rose with a determination to make his way into the haunted chamber in broad daylight and secure the will, and if he found such further obstructions and terrors as to effectually stop him from doing so, he thought the possession of his mistress's secret might furnish him with a capital pretext for demanding what he chose of her. Mary Ann was about the only one who rose quite calmly upon the morning so eventful to her. It is true, that she had heard a noise in the night, but as it had wholly ceased, she did not think it at all necessary that she should show herself upon the field of dispute, for some quarrel was what she supposed it to be. As Tony himself particularly remarked, she looked as serenely nice that morning as she looked the day before, and it was quite a satisfaction to see her. During the night Harry Dean had found time to look at the will, which he found to be just as it had been by the aunt described, absolutely in favour of Mary Ann, and entitling her to property over three thousand pounds in value, which he, Harry Dean, determined that she should not be long now kept from the enjoyment of. He thought that it would be better to put the whole affair in proper legal train, before Mary Ann knew anything about it, for otherwise her aunt, by tears and entreaties, might influence her to make some indiscreet promise, which might probably defeat what was right. Harry Dean accordingly sent Tony to a solicitor in Lincoln's Inn with a note, desiring him to come to the hotel as soon as possible. The note had the desired effect, and the solicitor made his appearance, upon which Harry Dean, in the presence of Tony, related to him the whole affair, concluding by saying—

"Will you glance over the will at once, and see if it is in proper legal form?"

"Certainly, sir."

The solicitor looked over the will, which was uncommonly short, carefully, and then said—

"This will is not only in proper legal form, but it is uncommonly well drawn, I know the professional man quite well whose name is here at the foot of the endorsement."

"Then we shall have two lawyers said Tony.

"Two lawyers? What do you mean?"

"Oh, it's only a fancy of his," said Harry Dean, "he likes to have two professional men in a case, that's all. What will be the first step to take?"

"Why there is no trustee named in this will. It is what is called an absolute demise, and the young lady to whom the property is wholly bequeathed must take out letters of administration at once. The aunt can be proceeded against criminally for concealing a will, which the judges always consider a very serious offence, and she and the waiter can likewise be indicted for a conspiracy to commit a felony by destroying a will."

"Very well, all that must be left to Mary Ann, and I think at this juncture of affairs we are bound now to speak to her upon the subject. Just ring the bell, Tony."

Tony did so sharply, and the waiter made his appearance, looking rather cadaverous.

"Did you ring, gentlemen?"

"Yes," said Harry Dean, dexterously concealing the will from his observation. "Yes, give my compliments to the young lady down stairs named Mary Ann, and say I should be obliged to her if she would step up here for a few minutes."

"Compliments!" gasped the waiter —to—Mary Ann!"

"Yes, and my love," said Tony.

"Love—I—I—what do you want with her?"

"Pray, what is that to you?" said Harry Dean, "how do you ask such a question? Leave the room, and do what you have been ordered."

The waiter retired, but in lieu of summoning Mary Ann, he rushed into the bar, where the aunt was raising her spirits with a tumbler of mulled port, and cried—

"There's something up! there's something up! They want Mary Ann upstairs."

"Mary Ann! You don't say so. That child will be the ruin of me yet."

"And of me, too," said the waiter; lifting the large glass of mulled port to his lips, and finishing it off at a draught.

"How dare you, sir," said the landlady with anger in her eyes, "take such a liberty. Do you know who I am sir?"

"Yes, you was my missus afore that critical affair, but now, as I know the secret as would turn you out of house and home, I mean to be your master.

The landlady took a fit of trembling, and while she is recovering from that, we will look at Tony, as he waits inside Harry Dean's sitting-room door for the expected arrival of Mary Ann, upon whose lips he certainly meditated an assault, the exact character of which we must leave to our readers to determine. Now it so happened that Mary Ann was upstairs, so that the waiter, with the best intentions in the world instead of the worst, could not have sent her to the room where Harry Dean and the lawyer were anxiously waiting her appearance,

but by pure accident down she came, and seeing Tony, she gave quite a nice little shriek, as she said—

"Why who would have thought of seeing you here ? How stupid you are to frighten folks so."

"Am I stupid ?"

"Yes, to be sure you are, and what's a good deal worse, you are ugly—precious ugly, too."

"Really ! Well, I'm glad of that, because when we are married, you have quite enough sense o' beauty for any two people, that you have, Mary Ann."

"Go along with you. Married, indeed ! You don't suppose I'd love you, do you? And, besides, I don't intend to marry at all, so you need not say any more about it."

"What, do you want me to go and commit suicide?"

"You may commit what you like, ugly, only don't come near me. eep your distance now, stupid."

"Well, but I really have got something to say—a great secret, but you must let me whisper it in your ear."

"I dare say it's some nonsense or another. Well, be quiet. I only wonder at myself for wasting my time upon you. What is it? You need not come so close to me."

"Oh, but I must, for I wouldn't let anybody else hear it for the whole world."

How simple it was of Mary Ann to let Tony put one arm round her neck, and then, instead of a secret in her ear, Tony—oh, Tony!—imprinted a kiss upon that inviting pair of lips that went pouting about the house with such a "Come kiss me now!" sort of look, that St. Anthony himself could not have resisted the temptation. It was at this interesting moment that Harry Dean, wondering where Tony was, and why Mary Ann did not come, flung the door open to go down stairs to look for him, and exposed the little episode of affection to the admiring eyes of the man of law as well as his own.

"Bravo!" cried Harry Dean.

"Very good, indeed," said the lawyer.

"The deuce!" cried Tony.

Mary Ann uttered a slight scream, and would have fallen down stairs like a startled hind, had not Harry Dean stopped her quickly—it did not require great force—and said—

"We really do wish to speak to you upon most particular business."

"Oh, no—no—I can't stay—I must not—I won't—I can't——"

"Exactly," said Harry Dean, as he led her into the room. "Pray take a seat, and tell this gentleman in what position and situation you are in, in this house, for, as the advertisement says, he can in return inform you of something to your advantage."

Mary Ann looked all the surprise she felt. She had one of those ingenuous faces which are ever like the open page of some honest book, for all to read.

"May I ask your name, miss?" said the lawyer.

"Mary Ann Hermit."

"And the best and prettiest darling of a little angel in the world," said Tony.

The lawyer bowed, and Mary Ann blushed.

"Yes, bless her," added Tony, "there she sits like a rose, making the room look like—like——"

"A greenhouse," suggested Harry Dean.

"No—no. But she is the prettiest and the best. Look at her nice little hand, with the fairy looking dimples by way of knuckles.—Look at her little mouse's head of a foot, just peeping from under her—what do you call 'ems. Look at her——"

"I won't stay here," said Mary Ann, starting up.

"Tony," said Harry Dean, "I am surprised at you, and shall advise this young lady to order you out of the room at once, while we speak to her upon a serious matter of business."

"Go!" said Mary Ann.

"Mercy!" said Tony. "You don't mean that! Oh, dear!—oh, dear! I'll promise to be as mute as a fish."

"Go!"

"I'll look out of window.—I'll look at the wall. Only do let me stay."

"Go!"

With a series of sighs, Tony got up and left the room, when the lawyer said—

"I think, Miss Hermit, you have served him right, and shown great and becoming spirit in the matter. Now what are you supposed to be here, and what is your position in this house? Tell me frankly, as a friend."

"Have I a friend?"

"Indeed you have," said Harry Dean, "if you will but consider me as one. Speak freely."

"My aunt keeps me here from charity, as she frequently tells me, and she never says a kind word to me, while I have had even blows from her; so you may imagine why the tears come into my eyes if any one tells me they will be my friend. You see, sir, my poor dear father left all to her, and thought she would be kind to me; but she is not; and sometimes I do think she wishes I were dead, she looks so strangely and frightfully at me ; and altogether I am a poor unhappy girl, though I strive to shake it off at times."

"A letter, a letter for you, Mr. Dean," cried Tony, rushing into the room at this moment, glad of the excuse. "A letter for you ; and they say that it has come from that fellow Wilkins, in Newgate. Ah, Mary Ann, how are you, you duck ?"

CHAPTER CIV.

THE MYSTERY.

"From Wilkins ?" said Harry Dean. "How are you sure of that ?"

"A man came from Newgate on purpose, and so, when he told me who it was from, I thought the best thing I could do was to bring it you at once. Oh, you cruel little bundle of perfection."

"Do you mean me, stupid ?" said Mary Ann.

"There she goes again," said Tony. "She always applies opprobrious epithets to me, when she knows that my heart has been made over to her complete, like a snug little freehold property, from the first moment that I ever saw her, the duck."

"Don't duck me."

"Well—well," said Harry Dean, as he put Wilkins's letter in his pocket. "You can say what you like to each other at some other time. Now we are upon business. Miss Mary Ann, may Tony stay in the room ?"

"Oh, I don't care. Any piece of lumber may be brought in, for all I care."

"Thank you," said Tony.

"Well, Miss Hermit," said the attorney, "it is my duty, at the request of Mr. Dean here, to inform you of a something which will very much surprise you. But, first of all, will you answer me one question ?"

"Yes, sir."

"Are you your father's only child ?"

"I am, now, sir ; but I was not when he died. I had then an elder brother, who turned out very, very bad ; but he is now no more."

"Very good. That accounts for the only point that puzzled me in the whole transaction, because you see, Mr. Dean, if this young lady had been the only child of the late Mr. Hermit, she would, without a will at all, have inherited what he might happen to be possessed of."

"Are you talking of my father's property, gentlemen ?"

"We are."

"Then I can tell you that, upon his death-bed he gave all to my aunt ; and as his slightest word would be law to me I cannot take any steps to dispossess her."

"But, my good young lady," said the lawyer, "you can speedily and easily be convinced that your father made no such bequest to your aunt upon his death-bed. On the contrary, he left a will which made you the sole inheritor of all that belonged to him, and in the face of that document he could not have made an oral distribution of his property."

"A will, sir ! My father left a will, say you ?"

"Yes. Listen to me, and you shall hear all. Mr. Dean, will you allow me just to turn the key of the door, to secure us from any interruption, for this is rather an important piece of business. I think you (to Tony) had better first state the conversation you overheard last evening between the young lady's aunt and the waiter."

"Very good," said Tony. "Here goes."

He then without the slightest exaggeration—for, in matters of fact, Tony had a conscientiousness to truth—told all that he had overheard, and he told it so well, that he was permitted to go on with the narrative ; and at its conclusion the attorney said—

"And here is the will, drawn up in proper legal form, under the authority of which you can take possession of every species of property that belonged to your father."

Mary Ann burst into tears, and pointing to the will, she said—

"And is that his hand-writing ?"

"No, not the body of the will, but there is his signature."

She pressed a kiss upon the name of her father, and then said—

"Does he not mention my aunt ?"

"He recommends her to your consideration and kindness merely. Those are the precise words. And now, Miss Hermit, will you permit me in this case to act as your attorney ?"

"Yes, sir. Yes."

"And what shall we do with your aunt and the waiter? You can have them both apprehended if you like, for their proceedings lay them open to a criminal charge; but let me warn you, you cannot pick and choose the law's victims. If you give the waiter into custody, you must likewise give your aunt."

"I will forgive them both."

"Reflect, young lady, reflect. Their conduct has been most infamous."

"If this house be really mine, inasmuch as my aunt has, by her proceedings, insulted the memory of my father, she shall not sleep another night beneath its roof; but I will, after that, be to her what my father orders me, kind and considerate."

"Very well, the waiter can be kicked out of the house at once."

"Which I will do with all the pleasure in life," said Tony.

"Now listen to me," said the attorney. "Since no criminal proceedings are to be instituted against the people, it will be a great satisfaction to you, Miss Hermit, to hear from their own lips a confirmation of all we have told you, and then no doubt can ever insinuate itself into your mind."

"Will they confess?"

"Oh, yes, under a threat of consequences they will, no doubt. I will now ring for the waiter. Unlock the door, Mr. Tony, if you please, and just run down and ask the aunt to step up here a moment. We will have them both together if you have no objection, Miss Hermit?"

"None, none," said Mary Ann. "I only wish it was all over; I tremble as much as though I were the guilty party, instead of they who have made me suffer so many unkindnesses."

"Ah, but you only tremble from agitation and the novelty of these events, while they will tremble from real guilt. Do not say anything until I have terrified them a little—that is but a small punishment for their serious misdeeds towards you. You promise me that you will not interfere?"

"If I promise, I promise."

"Did you ring, gentlemen?" said the waiter."

"Did you send for me?" said Miss Hermit the elder, and both she and Thomas showed symptoms of the most extraordinary agitation, for they saw Mary Ann seated, and there was a peculiar look upon the faces of all there present.

The attorney rose and adroitly placed himself between them and the door, as he said, in firm cool accents—

"Now, Mr. Tony, if you will be so good as to open the window and call out as loud as you can for a policeman, we will soon settle this little affair."

"Oh, yes," said Tony. "Don't I wish I had got a stunning good rattle, wouldn't I bring a lot of raw lobsters round the house in a few minutes. All's right—here goes."

"Call a what?" shouted the aunt.

"A po—lice—man!" gasped Thomas. "You—you don't labour under any—sort—of mistake about my character, gentlemen, do you? because I'll just run and fetch a friend, who will speak for me."

"We are not under the slightest mistake," said the attorney; "we have decided upon giving you and that female into custody, for conspiring to destroy a will."

"A—a—will?"

"Yes, and here it is. Now, Mr. Tony."

The waiter dropped with a flop upon his knees, and bawled out—

"Oh! gentlemen. Oh! Miss Mary Ann, have mercy upon me. It was the old woman as tempted me into the affair—it was indeed. Oh, sir, that ever I should come to such a pass as this here. Oh, you old cat, if it hadn't been for you, I should never have thought of such a thing."

The landlady that was, immediately made a rush at Thomas, and executed summary vengeance upon his countenance, which in a moment bore the marks of ten rather long nails.

"I will confess something," she cried, "if you will but promise to get him hanged."

"We can, probably, madam, do you that favour," said Harry Dean, "for there will be, I understand, two charges against you, and only one against him. Have you no shame in your disposition?"

"Mary Ann! Mary Ann!"

"Yes, aunt."

"I am your father's sister."

"And, as such, I forgive you, aunt."

"Then I do not care that for any of you," she exclaimed, snapping her fingers so close to the lawyer's nose, that he jerked himself back in alarm. "Come down stairs, Mary Ann, and we will soon come to a good understanding, I'll be bound. Follow me, child, directly."

"This is assurance itself," said the attorney.

"Are you coming, Mary Ann?"

"Listen to me a moment," said the young girl, in a mild quiet voice; "yesterday, if you had had to ask me twice to do anything, the last order would have been answered by a blow. I have forgiven you for all the past, but I order you now to quit this house within one hour, on pain of being given into custody for your crimes, and prosecuted if you refuse. I will allow you a small weekly sum for your maintenance, and you will, I hope, yet live to repent of your wickedness. You may take your clothing with you, but nothing else."

"Bravo! bravo!" cried the attorney, "that is capital. Come, madam, are you panic-stricken?—can't you move, or say one word to let us know which way you have made up your mind?"

"Oh, my own brother's child!" suddenly exclaimed the hypocrite, "come to my arms."

She made a rush forward to catch Mary Anne in her arms, but Tony so abruptly interposed that she embraced him instead, to which he expressed the utmost repugnance, and got out of her clutches as soon as possible.

"Don't be hugging me," said Tony, "I hate the sight of you."

"Aunt," said Mary Ann, "I am firm. This conduct of yours fills me with disgust, more than your crimes did. I have given you one hour—make good use of it."

"Curse you all!" she said, and walked out of the room. The waiter was following her, when Mary Ann said—

"You will leave the house, Thomas, at once."

"Yes, Miss," he whined.

"And there's something to keep you on," said Tony, as he accelerated Thomas's progress by a kick that sent him rolling down stairs, pretending to be much more hurt than he really was,

with a view of exciting an amount of pity that might save him from further consequences;—Thomas would have sat upon the dining room fire rather than have been introduced to a policeman.

"You have acted bravely," said the solicitor to Mary Ann, "and you will not be troubled, I think, by either your aunt or Thomas; but if the former should be any annoyance to you, stop the supplies peremptorily, and you will soon bring her to her senses."

"Well, Mary Ann," said Tony, "I give you joy of having your own. When I thought you poor and friendless, I—I hoped to be able to show you how well I could and would love you, but now you are quite rich——"

"Well, Tony?"

"Well, Mary Ann, you—you will perhaps marry a very different sort of fellow from poor Tony Thorpe?"

"And you, are you poor?"

"I am destitute, Mary Ann, only I think I have a friend in Mr. Dean here, who would have done sufficient for me to have made you comfortable. There is only one thing, before I go, that I want you to take notice of, and that is, that when I told you in the bar parlour that I loved you, I had no more idea that you were worth a penny piece, than I have now of flying—I mean to say as to money, for as to yourself, you are worth all the mines of gold and diamonds in the world.—So God bless you, I'm off."

"Off, Tony?"

"Yes, I'm off, Miss Hermit."

"And pray, how dare you be off, or talk of being off? Do you think that because you loved me when you thought me destitute, I am not to—to—I will say it—love you when I have what my poor dear father meant me to have. Oh Tony! Tony!"

"Why, what? You really—you—you will have me?"

"Go along, stupid!"

"Ha! ha! ha!—hip! hip! hip! hurrah! three times three—nine times nine, and one cheer more!—hurrah!"

"Are you mad, Tony?"

"No, Mary Ann, but I'm—I'm—I don't know what I am. Only look at her, gentlemen, now, and tell me upon your words and honours, did you ever see her equal?—look at her dear eyes—her cheeks—her lips. Look at her hair, look at her hand, and the dear baby-like dimples——"

"Tony! Tony!" said Mary Ann, " if you say another word I won't have you."

"Well," said Harry Dean, " I don't know when I have so much rejoiced in other people's joy as I have to-day. I can tell you, Miss Hermit, that an honester hearted lad than you have chosen could not be found. Your conduct upon this, really most trying occasion, has proved how worthy you are to possess that property which your father left to you, and I hope that you will always consider me as an intimate friend. This gentleman, you may trust implicitly with the management of your pecuniary affairs, and now you are, in a most incredibly short space of time, provided with an estate, a lawyer, a husband, and a friend.".

"I owe you all many thanks," said Mary Ann. " Heaven reward you for the pains you have taken to do me service."

"May I speak ?" said Tony.

"Well, what is it?"

"Oh yes, duck. That's all for the present. I—I think some snuff must have blown in at the open window, my —my eyes water so—I'll run down stairs and see whether Thomas has gone or not. I'll soon be back. Oh yes, duck! That's all at present."

So saying, Tony, to conceal the tears of satisfaction which would come welling up to his eyes from his heart, trotted out of the room, and down the stairs, like lightning. It was well that he did so, for he got to the bar just in time to prevent Thomas from going off with all the silver spoons and forks. Tony again, by sundry applications of his boot toe, facilitated Thomas's progress off the premises, and that exercise having sufficiently recovered him, he found himself able to see about putting things to rights a little. He called up from the kitchen the cook, and told her to take care of the bar, and was about to leave it himself, when the aunt came down.

"Get out of my way, wretch," she said, and was making her way to the till, when Tony said to the cook—

"Run to the door and fetch a policeman. Miss Mary Ann is mistress here now. Her father's proper will, leaving her all that's in the house, and the house too, has been found."

"Oh, ain't I glad," cried the cook. " I'll get John White, No. 22, as comes arter me and sops in the pan."

"Oh, no—no—for God's sake, no! cried the aunt. I—I—am going. Oh, dear me, I'm going. Where's Thomas?"

"Why," said the cook, " it's to be hoped he's gone home to that poor half-starved wife and family of his."

"Wife and family! Thomas a wife and family! Then I'm an undone female ?

Down dropped the aunt in a fit of hysterics, which did not in the smallest degree excite the sympathy of Tony, who walked up stairs to report progress.

———

CHAPTER CV.

THE ODD VOLUME.

HE found Mary Ann weeping, and upon looking surprised to know the cause, Harry Dean said, with a smile—

"You must not be at all alarmed, Tony, Miss Hermit has only been telling us a little episode in the life of her mother."

"What is it ?" said Tony.

"Just this," said Mary Ann, " that when my father, who was but a country lad at the time, got secretly married to my mother, who was the only companion of her aged grandmother, and they both went before the old lady, to ask for her blessing and forgiveness, she said quietly, as she sat in her old arm chair, and they stood before her—'My good children, your happiness is all in your own hands. If you be good and truthful, and forbearing to each other, you may be much happier than kings and queens.'"

"Right," said Tony, " that old girl was a trump."

"Well," said the attorney, " I must now go, and will take the necessary steps regarding the will. Good day, good day to you all."

"And I," said Harry Dean, " must, I suppose, read this letter that has been sent to me from Newgate by the villain Wilkins ; I expect, it is some appeal for that mercy which it is out of my power to show, since he is in the hands of the law.

So saying, Harry Dean retired to his own oom, after telling Tony to speak to Kate Destern and Lucy, and introduce them to Mary Ann, who, if she pleased, might tell them her history."

When he got to a private room, he carelessly enough opened Wilkins's letter, and approaching the window so as to get as good a light as possible for the perusal of its contents, he read the following rather astounding statement. The letter was headed thus:—

"*Newgate Cells.*

"SIR,—At the first sight of this epistle you may feel some surprise at being addressed by me, but I have a revelation to make, which I thought to have gone from this world without making, had you not, indeed, defeated my wishes in the manner you were a witness to in the police office at Bow Street. I am aware that you have a suspicion that the young lady who names herself Kate Destern is not the daughter of the old woman of that name who nursed her. Such suspicions are well grounded, and since you have set your best affections upon this young person, it will, probably, be no small satisfaction to know really who she is. Kate, then—for Kate is her name—is my daughter. I placed her with Mrs. Destern to nurse when I was by the force of circumstances obliged to fly the country, and I would recommend, if after this you marry her, that your nuptials take place upon the morning of the execution of the bride's father. I know you will doubt this—perhaps you will laugh at it, but if you want proof, come to me in this prison, and I will furnish you with such as you will never utter a word to question. This is from your old enemy,

"JOSIAH WILKINS."

"Infamous slanderer!" cried Harry Dean, as the letter dropped from his grasp. "It is true, that I am well aware, as is Kate herself, that she is not the daughter of old Mrs. Destern, but she is not the child of this infamous man. This is the last fangless bite of the adder—the last contortion of the wounded snake. No, no; you cannot make me believe this, Wilkins. Ah! what is this? a postscript. Let me see."

"P.S.—I demand an interview with my daughter."

"Insolence!"

Harry Dean, without a moment's hesitation, placed the letter in the fire, and watched it burn with all the calmness in the world.

"No, no, Kate," he said, "you shall not have your pure mind troubled with the wild throes of this man, who has yet some revenge against us all before he dies the death that he so richly deserves. But yet, it would give me some pleasure to find out the mystery of the birth of Kate."

There seemed no mode at present of discovering this mystery, so, after some thought, Harry Dean made up his mind to take no manner of notice of Wilkins's communication, and yet it would obtrude itself continually upon his mind, and, like a spectre, haunted him so much that he resolved to call upon the lawyer in Lincoln's Inn, and speak to him about it. In the meantime, Kate and Lucy had seen Mary Ann, and had heard all the particulars of the affair in which Tony was so largely interested. They condoled with her on the past, and congratulated her upon the present and the future, while Tony was here and there, and everywhere, in the hotel, giving himself, at the request of Mary Ann, all the airs of its master, which he was soon to be in reality, for she now made no sort of secret of her predilection for Tony, while he thought, without the shadow of a doubt, that she concentrated in herself all the charms and excellences that could possibly belong to woman.— Happy Tony!

"I shall soon return," said Harry Dean, as he entered the room with his hat in his hand. "I am going to make a call. Tony is in the house, you know, in case your aunt or Thomas should try to take it by storm."

"Just let 'em," said Tony, "that's all! I'd show 'em what was what. A Mary Ann to the rescue!—down with scaling ladders!—stride over the heaps of slain!—hang out our banners on the outer walls!

——'Come death, come racks—
At least we'll die with harness on our backs.'"

"Well, Tony," said Mary Ann, with a mischievous twinkle of the eyes— those eyes which had played such havoc with Tony's heart—" if they do come, you can hide in the pantry, you know."

" Hide !—hide !'

" Yes, to be sure. And the safest thing for you to do, I think. What should I do if you were to get killed with, as you call it, harness on your back! Now, recollect, your place is the pantry in any danger."

" The devil! Pantry me. No—no. I know my place better than that."

While they were thus disputing in so facetious a mood, Harry Dean made his way to the lawyer, to whom he showed Wilkins's letter, and explained how the matter stood.

" The mere assertion of this fellow, that he is father of the young lady, will always be a disagreeable thought to you," said the lawyer, " and therefore I advise you to see him in Newgate, and really put to the test the proofs he pretends to know of the assertions he makes in his letter."

" You really think so ?"

" I seriously advise it."

" Then I will do so. But I am far from being uneasy upon the subject. It is nothing but an invention of the fellow to make me wretched, as he knows that the thought of such a thing would do since that young lady, to whom he claims such close consanguinity, will shortly be my wife."

" At all events, hear and see his proofs if he have any."

" I will go at once. I suppose I shall be admitted ?"

" Oh yes, to a prisoner merely committed. After conviction, it is quite another matter, 1 believe; but if you have the slightest desire that I should do so, I will accompany you."

" You will much oblige me, for I would rather have a witness to my interview with Wilkins. Can you now accompany me ?"

" Certanly, I can. There is nothing that requires professional presence for some hours, so we can walk quietly to Newgate, as the distance is so short."

They walked quickly, and soon the dark, frowning facade of Newgate was aefore them in all its gloom and coldness. They ascended the few well-worn steps leading to the small wicket entrance, and the solicitor, upon giving his card, was at once, with Harry Dean, admitted. Upon signifying their wish for an interview with Wilkins, the turnkey rather hesitated, but Harry Dean put an end to the discussion by saying—

" If you will show me into the governor's apartments, I dare say I shall be able to get an order from him.'

" Very well, sir. This way."

" I will wait here for you, Mr. Dean," said the attorney; " for, as I am not the professional adviser of Wilkins, and have no sort of desire for that honour, I cannot claim the privilege of seeing him."

In the course of about three minutes the turnkey and officers of the prison were rather confused at the arrival of the governor himself with Harry Dean, to whom he was evidently paying the most polite attention, and when they reached the vestibule, the governor said—

" Allow this gentleman and his friend to see Wilkins, and pay them every attention."

At this command all was obsequiousness to Harry Dean, and the attorney was rather astonished to know what magic there was in the presence of plain Mr. Dean to produce such an effect— but he had no time just then for reflection; and if he had, he was too well-bred a man to ask any questions, for they were both ushered into a room, in which there was a table and likewise some chairs. Writing materials were likewise there. In fact, it was the room in which attornies might, upon demand, see such prisoners as they were professionally engaged for, and for whose proper defence private consultations might be necessary. It was a dim and gloomy-looking place though.

" We will bring him to you, gentlemen," said an officer, " if you will sit down for a few moments."

" Thank you," said Harry Dean.

The few moments that now elapsed before the door of this little reception room was again opened, were spent by Harry Dean in looking at its appointments, and he had just made some remark concerning them, when an officer came in and said—

" Twenty minutes, gentlemen, is the usual time allowed for an interview, but the governor desires me to say, with his compliments, that you need not restrict yourselves to that period of time. I shall be within hearing, if you touch that little hand-bell."

"Thank you, that will do."

The door was now flung wide open, and in walked Wilkins. The door was instantly closed again, and the murderer stood in the presence of him whom he had tried to injure more than as though he had taken means to compass his death. Wilkins started, as he exclaimed—

"You are not alone ?"

"No," said Harry Dean, "I will not speak to you without a witness."

"Then I return to my cell, leaving unsaid that which you came to hear."

"That may be as you please," said Harry Dean. "If you decline to say what you asked me here to listen to, in the presence of that gentleman, I am quite content that it should remain unsaid. I care nothing for it, inasmuch as your assertion that you are the father of Miss Destern, I heard with all the contempt it deserves."

"And yet it rankles at your heart?"

"It does not."

"Well, well, I only ask for two minutes of your company alone. I will then tell you upon what proof

I ground my assertion. It is surely worth your whil e to listen to me for a few minutes."

No, not without a witness."

"Are you really so resolved?"

"I am. I thought you had already known sufficient of me, that when I say I will not do a thing, even to my friends, I am commonly firm, and to my enemies I am immoveable as a rock."

"Fool!" said Wilkins. "Fool! May your whole life now be embittered by the conviction that what I have said is true: and may her, whom you take to your bosom as your wedded wife, learn in time to curse the man who hunted her father to the gallows. May your children hate you!"

"Impious man," said Harry Dean. "These idle curses but fix deeper in your own heart the damning circumstances of what your crimes have at length brought you to. I grieve that I came] here at all, to [incite in you so wild a frame of mind in your sad] condition."

"Indeed, do you regret?"

"I do from my heart, bold and bad as you are."

Wilkins had gradually advanced upon Harry Dean as he spoke, but it was done in so suspicious a manner, that both Harry and the solicitor thought he meditated an assault of some kind, and they were right enough, for suddenly, with a yell of rage, Wilkins sprung forward, crying—

"This is what I intended!" and made a blow at Harry Dean's neck with a something he held in his hand. Luckily, being upon his guard, Harry stepped back in time, and with the force of his own disappointed blow Wilkins fell to the ground. The solicitor rang the little bell, and in a moment an officer came in.

"Hilloa!" he said. "Anything the matter, gentlemen?"

"Yes," said the solicitor, "the rascal has made an attack upon this gentleman, and I think he has something in his hand."

"The deuce he has. We commonly look pretty sharp after that sort of thing. I can hardly think it possible how he can have. Now, my man, we will trouble you to get up."

Wilkins sprung to his feet, and would have darted upon Harry Dean again, but the officer caught him round the waist from behind, saying—

"Come—come, don't be a fool now; what is the use of you giving yourself all this trouble?—Jem! Jem!

"What's the row?" said another officer entering the room. "Anybody's eye-tooth come out?"

"Only a skrimmage!"

"Oh, is that it?"

"Yes, pop the darbies on him, and it's ten to one if the governor don't accommodate him with a pair of lead garters—I have got him. Ah you may kick away my rum 'un. It won't have no more effect upon us than as if you was all for to go to knock your stupid head against the wall."

"All's right," said the other officer, "all's right."

Wilkins was duly secured, and when he found himself quite impotent to do further mischief, his rage was so excessive that he bawled again in the intensity of it.

"Wretched man!" said Harry Dean, "and so, for the poor revenge of taking my life, you asked me here?"

"No," said Wilkins, assuming a sudden calmness, "no—no."

"For what, then?"

"I declare solemnly the truth of what I asserted. Kate Destern is my daughter."

"Impossible."

"I say she is. She is, and marry her when you will, the name of Wilkins shall be perpetuated in your memory, and you will feel that you hold to your heart the daughter of a murderer. Ha! Ha! I am pleased at that. To kill you was a foolish and sudden impulse, but to plant such a thorn as this in your heart is much more in my way. There is a book which belonged to old Mrs. Destern. It would prove the truth of what I now so confidently assert. Kate Destern is my daughter, and no earthly power, no juggling can trample out that fact. I know that to you the thought is gall and wormwood, and I glory therefore in it."

———

CHAPTER CVI,

KING'S EVIDENCE.

THIS mention by Wilkins of a book a once brought to the mind of Harry Dean a recollection of all he had from time to time heard of a certain mysterious volume which had been in possession of the late Mrs. Destern, but which had unaccountably disappeared. The reader will probably recollect that Madame Zadzed had obtained possession of this book, little thinking she was so ardently pursuing her own schemes of revenge that she was so soon to fall a victim to the cruelty and cupidity of others. Therefore, upon Wilkins making the statement with which we concluded the last chapter, Harry Dean said to him with some eagerness—

"Where is that book ?"

"Aye, where is that book ?" You may ask the question, but I will not tell."

"Because," added Harry Dean, fixing upon him a stern scrutinizing glance, "because you don't know. It is in vain, Wilkins, that you attempt to impose upon any one who knows you so thoroughly as I do. Your threats go for nothing. Your most solemn sounding assertions pass by me like the wind; I hear them, but I heed them not; and now, disgraced and foiled in your last attempt to injure me, I leave you to the sting of your own conscience."

"Oh, there's no doubt he meant to do for you, sir," said one of the officers. "He had saved up that old nail on purpose, I can tell you."

"No," said Wilkins, "I say no ; it was intended for myself."

"Gammon! We know pretty well what fellows is. You ain't the sort to commit suicide, not you, my old cock—oh dear no. You'll come out and be locked up quite comfortable, so don't make any more words about things in general, my tulip, but come along."

"A plague light upon you."

"A what? A plague?—why that's you. A greater plague can't be. I suppose, gentlemen, you don't want to say anything more to this here piece of goods ?"

"Not I," said Harry Dean.

"Nor I," said the solicitor. "He requested this interview solely with the hope of being able to take this gentleman's life, and being foiled in that, he is, of course, in a most desperate state from disappointment."

Wilkins ground his teeth together with rage, and in a deep hollow voice he said, as he fixed his eyes upon Harry Dean—

"We shall meet again yet."

Harry returned him no answer, but taking the arm of the attorney, he at once left the prison.

"I never met," said the lawyer, "with such a determined villain as that in all my life, and he is really a man of education, is he not ?' '

"He is indeed, and, as a physician, I believe him to be a man of rare skill, but such a melancholy instance of perverted abilities I never saw."

"Nor I. But do you really put no faith whatever in his assertions regarding the parentage of the young lady in whose fortunes you are interested."

"Not the least. That there is a mystery surrounding her birth I fairly admit, for many concurrent circumstances prove so much, but that it is a subject upon which I am very solicitous, I deny ; as she is, I intend to make her my wife, and, as I am no believer in hereditary criminality, were those who can claim kindred with her ten times more wicked than Wilkins is, which I apprehend would be impossible, she would still be the same to me."

"I honour your sentiments, sir, and with such you cannot be otherwise than happy in your approaching union ; but still, as a matter of curiosity, it would be quite as well if the affair were settled one way or another, don't you think so ?"

"Most unquestionably it would, and no one would take more pains than I to bring it to such a settlement, but I do not see yet how I can set about it."

"Is there any one who you think knows ?"

"None but the dead. From all I can gather, and that, after all, is but very vague, the murdered woman named Zadzed knew all about it."

"Ah, indeed. Then it is more than likely that among her papers something may be found that would tend to settle this affair. The house is in the custody of the police, but I dare say leave could be got in a matter of this kind to look over the papers she has left. I have heard that no one has come forward to claim the slightest consanguinity to the woman, and consequently her ill-gotten means will fall into the hands of the state."

"She was, I believe, for many years

the wretched pander to the vices of the late Lord Battaney," said Harry Dean, " and I have a peculiar wish to see if she have left any memoranda connected with the deceased nobleman."

" That man was a disgrace to the peerage."

" He was," said Harry Dean, gravely, " but there are circumstances which make his name peculiarly displeasing to my ears ; I pray you do not mention him again unless there should be an urgent necessity."

" I will not, sir ; but to return to this Madame Zadzed. Did you ever see her, sir ?"

" Oh yes,—did you ?"

" No, but I have heard that she had been in early life one of the most beautiful of women, and that her amours upon the continent were the scandal of more than one large city. That however was, of course, long ago. What a wretched existence must be that of such a woman, after she has outlived all her glaring and meretricious attractions—when the voice of flattery no longer sounds in her ears, and when her vices and her cruel passions show themselves in all their deformity, completely stripped of the gloss of youth and beauty, which for a time had covered their grossness, as a corpse may be covered with rich and stately garments. Oh! what a hell must the heart of such a woman then become !"

" It must, indeed."

Both the lawyer and Harry Dean were now silent for some minutes. Their minds were full of such reflections as an acquaintance with the world's villanies will at times engender. They had walked direct back to the hotel, which might be called Tony's, since by the grace of ringlets and bright eyes he was soon to become sole master of it. At the door the attorney paused and said—

" Mr. Dean, between this and the evening I will endeavour to get an order to look over Madam Zadzed's effects, and if successful, I will call for you at eight o'clock, when my professional business for the day will be over, and we can go upon that expedition together."

" I shall be well pleased to do so," said Harry Dean, " and will take care to be here at the time you mention.'

With this they parted at the door of the hotel, the lawyer to go after his business, and Harry Dean to that house, in which he was now a friend instead of a customer. Nothing had happened worth recording during his absence, and he found Kate, Lucy, Tony, and the " Bride elect "—as Tony would insist upon calling Miss Hermit—all in excellent spirits. Harry forbore to say anything about his interview with Wilkins, and it was soon quite an all-absorbing amusement to him to see how perfectey happy and comfortable Tony was making himself. He was up stairs and down stairs, and in and out of the bar in the most pleasant manner in the world, and having made himself acquainted with the contents of every room in the place but the old man's death-chamber, he at length spoke about that.

" My dear," he said to the bride elect, " what an uncomfortable thing it is that every time one goes up or comes down stairs, one is forced to look askance at the door of your father's room."

" It is not agreeable, Mr. Thorpe."

" What ?—what ?"

There was a mischievous twinkle about the eyes of the bride elect.

" I said ' it was not agreeable, Mr. Thorpe.' "

" And pray what have I done, eyes and ringlets, to be called Mr. Thorpe ? I'm Tony, eyes and ringlets, and you know it. Don't insult me by calling me Mr. any more. It's a shame and a disgrace, that's what it is, eyes and ringlets. I'm Tony, and Tony I mean to be. Come—come, pretty, don't be provoking ?"

" But why should I call you by your christian name merely ? The young and handsome Charles Theodore de Beverley never liked me to mention him but by all his names."

" The what ?"

" He wasn't a *what*. The *whom*, you mean, I suppose ?"

" The devil !"

" Far from it. He was decidedly the handsomest young man I ever saw. His long chesnut curls hung——"

" Confound his curls, and his chesnuts too. Don't tell me about him."

" Yes—but I must tell you what he said."

" I won't hear it."

" But you must. ' Beautiful being !' he said, and all the nice little dimples played round his moustachios, and his eyes danced like stars in a wash-hand basin, while his elegant hands——"

" Do you want to drive me out of my wits ?"

" Wits ? wits ? Why, I never supposed you had any."

" Didn't you. It's a good thing, then, that you have, for you must make up for my deficiencies when we are married."

" When we are what ?"

" Married, and made one, to be sure."

" Married, and made one! Well, I never! What in the name of all that's droll, put that in your head ?".

" What ?" said Tony. making an examination of the top of his head rapidly. " What ?"

" Why, about the marrying ? How can I need any one but my heroic preserver. The day was as fair a one as ever peeped out from the heavens, and the birds sang melodiously upon every twig. The gallant steed upon which I rode pranced and gambolled with frolicsome glee, when suddenly, with a cry of agony, the animal darted forward, and at a furious pace, sought the cataract."

" The what ?"

" The cataract. I thought myself doomed to certain destruction, when I heard another horse's legs coming on like a wild avalanche, and in a moment De Beverley caught the reins of my maddened steed, and lifting up his own horse in one hand and my horse in another, he preserved the life of one who exists but to pour the soft tale of her affections into his ear."

" The deuce he did ! Only let me catch him. Oh, eyes and ringlets ! Is this the way you mean to treat me ? Is this the reward of affection ? Is this the everything and the nothing ?"

" Lor, Tony ! what a goose you must be, to be offended at my telling you what I read in that charming novel I was devouring this morning."

" Novel ? novel ? You don't mean that. Who wrote it ?"

" How should I know ? But hark, somebody rings. Lor, Tony, how could you be such a ninny as to believe there was a De Beverley ! And as for my father's room, let you and 1, when we have a spare hour, go into it and take a thorough look at what is in it, and then it shall be cleared out. There must be no room in this house to cast a gloom upon the young joy that shall make its home within its walls."

" Now that's sensible."

" Is it, Tony ?"

" Yes, and a great deal better than all that affair about Charles Theodore De Beverley, and be hanged to him. I shall never hear that name again with any patience."

" And so, Tony, after all that had passed, you really thought it possible I was so light—so frivolous—and so little to be depended upon, that I intended to play the coquette with you, and deceive you ? But know, Tony, that although men, judging from themselves, have little faith in woman——"

" Stop, eyes and ringlets !" said Tony. " Don't say anything more about it, or else you will drive me out of the house, and perhaps out of the world. You may say what you like about anybody, and I won't take offence at it, I assure you. Only don't look at me in that way."

" Don't you deserve it ?"

" Yes."

Tony made a snatch at a kiss, and got —a cuff! After this, eyes and ringlets ran off, and left the master of the house, that was to be, rather crest-fallen.

" What a little teasing, pleasing, perplexing, vexing, pretty natty creature she is, to be sure," he soliloquised. " Ah! well, bless her heart, and eyes, and ringlets, I do love her."

Tony took up the newspaper, and the first words his eyes fell upon were—

" Death and confession of Eliza Swam, the murderess."

The paragraph went on to say that after turning king's evidence, and making a full and complete confession of the whole particulars of the murder of Madame Zadzed, the wretched woman had gradually sunk into a state of collapse, and, notwithstanding all that medical skill could suggest, had expired in Newgate ; and concluded by an intimation of the ample manner in which she had vindicated any one else from the charge, except the real partner of her guilt, whose trial would come on at the approaching sessions. Judging that this would be interesting to Harry Dean, Tony took it to him at once.

"It is no more, Tony, than might have been expected," said Harry Dean. "They were sure to accuse each other, but it is a mercy that the woman is dead, for, however, in such a case stern justice would have condemned her to death, there is something that looks so awful and so cowardly in a lot of men taking a woman to death, that the mere fact that such things are done is almost enough to stamp a nation with indelible disgrace."

"That's my notion exactly," said Tony. "Men who are warring with each other in the active business of life, may and must make hang laws to protect themselves against each other, but to drag a woman to execution, let her be ever so bad, is horrible."

"And yet young girls have suffered that death before now."

"Yes, and a crowd has looked on. Well," added Tony, drawing a long breath, "I don't know what human nature in some of its varieties is made of, but if I were to be made king of England, as a payment for so doing I could not, and would not, have been a witness to one of those barbarous sacrifices."

In such like conversation as this Harry Dean and Tony passed some time, for although there was a vast difference between them in education, yet Harry Dean always found that Tony got hold of the right end of a subject, and although he might not succeed in always expressing himself in the most elegant language, yet there was a rough honesty in his manner that especially recommended him to Harry Dean. As the day wore on Harry was very solicitous concerning his expedition with the attorney in the evening; he wished he had made an arrangement with that person to let him know earlier if it were to be undertaken but he did not take any steps in the matter. It was therefore to him agreeable when the attorney came, at eight o'clock, and said—

"It is all right, we are to have full liberty of rummaging in Madame Zadzed's house. I have got an order to that end from a magistrate, and if you please we can go at once."

"Directly," said Harry Dean, "I am all impatience."

CHAPTER CVII
THE NIGHT SEARCH.

Tony had during the evening several times solicited eyes and ringlets to name a time for the visit to the chamber of her deceased father, but she had naturally enough shrunk from doing so until Tony pressed the matter very much, and then she consented.

"We will go together," she said, "when the house is shut."

"Humph!" said Tony; "don't you think broad daylight would be better, eyes and ringlets, to go upon such an expedition?"

"If you be afraid, Tony, I can easily go by myself, my poor father loved me while living, and I will not believe now, if such things be possible, that he would terrify me when no more."

"There is something in that," said Tony, "only, from all I have heard of ghosts they are such an eccentric set that I don't depend much upon them, you see. Their principal fun seems to be in frightening people, and perhaps, after all, they think us very stupid to be at all alarmed at them.

"Why, Tony, you speak as though you were a believer in apparitions."

"Pho!" said Tony, "it's all gammon, I know well enough; but the real fact is, I don't care one straw one way or the other. There aint any such things, or the fact would have been well proved long and long ago; but if there even I don't care—won't let them frighten me."

"Then we will take an examination of my poor father's room to-night, Tony; for as you feel no fear, I don't see any reason for delaying it until to-morrow."

"Very good, only I thought you might feel a little nervous, that's all."

"Never mind me."

"Yes, but I will, and do mind you, and mean always to mind you, but that's not the question just now. When the house closes for the night we will meet in the bar, and then make our way up to the room if you keep in the same mind."

"Which assuredly I shall, Tony."

Miss Hermit did keep in the same mind, and as she and Tony met with rather an adventure in the haunted room we will, with the reader's permission follow them upon the expedition. By the time the hall closed for the night, Harry Dean had not come from his visit with the lawyer to Madame Zadzed's, and the consequence was, that Tony looked upon himself as the guardian of Kate and Lucy, as well as of " eyes and ringlets," as he still delighted to call Miss Hermit. Like all person invested with new authority, Tony was wonderfully particular about fastenings, and gave his directions to the night porter with quite an air, for he was resolved to let everybody know that he was master, and determined to show his authority early.

" Now, old fellow," said Tony, " you make yourself comfortable in your arm-chair, and don't be a fool."

" A fool, sir !"

" Yes. That advice sums up everything in a few words," said Tony, " and if you keep on thinking upon it, you will be quite a clever fellow in time, and whatever you do, don't do it again."

These directions, although they might have been highly philosophical, yet they were by no means very remarkably clear, and the porter might well look astonished and confused at such directions, and sink into his large arm-chair with a terrible aspect."

Kate and Lucy sat up in " eyes and ringlet's" bed-room, after fruitlessly offering their company to Tony and the bride elect upon their expedition, but Tony was too valourous to permit so strong a force to go with him'; moreover, there was something pleasant and engaging to him, in the idea of going with no other companion than the fair daughter of the ghost along with him. Perhaps, too, Mary Ann thought something might be found that only she and Tony should see, for she joined him in deprecating any further assistance. The clock in the hall had struck the hour which usually heralded the family to repose ; when Tony, carrying a light and the bride elect, a key, they approached the door of the haunted room. How widely different were their feelings and views to those of the last couple—the aunt and the waiter—who stealthily crept to the apartment on the preceding evening, with a key and a candle. They went upon an errand of iniquity — these upon an errand of

kindness of feeling, for it was with a kind and a reverent soul that the young girl sat at such an hour to look upon what relics of her father might there be found.

' It's a very still night, Tony."

" Very. Don't you hear the rain though, just beginning to make itself heard upon that skylight at the top of the stairs. There it comes, rolling away."

" I do indeed ; to-morrow this room shall be thoroughly cleared out, and no longer shall it be surrounded by gloomy associations. No doubt we shall to-night be able to remove any papers belonging to my father that I would not wish to meet the eyes of strangers, and then I will not again enter the room until its whole aspect is changed."

" We can have it fresh papered and painted," said Tony.

" Yes, so we can."

They began now, these deserving young people, to say we when they spoke of any project in which they were mutually engaged. There was no coquetry now, about the manner of the young girl ; and her eyes were filling with tears as she was thinking of the dead.

With trembling fingers she unlocked the door. It creaked upon its hinges, and then she and Tony entered the room; Mary Ann closed the door behind them, and with much more nerve, considering the hour and the occasion, than could have been expected from her, she approached the walnut-tree chest of drawers, saying as she did so—

" Now, Tony, if there are any papers in my father's hand-writing at all, they are in these drawers, and as there is no other lock-up piece of furniture besides in the room that I can see, we need not trouble ourselves with anything else.— You hold the candle while I search the drawers."

Yes," said Tony. " How very silent everything seems here."

" This house just now is unusually silent, on account of the next one being to let, so that there comes no noise from that side indicative of life or of human feeling."

" That must be it," said Tony.

Mary Ann had by this time opened the drawer from which the will had been taken, and there appeared quite a variety of miscellaneous articles within it, consisting of papers and other things. There was a large packet of letters, and immediately beneath them, when Mary Ann lifted them up, appeared a gold watch with a heavy chain and seals attached thereto.

"That has escaped," said Tony. "Do you know it ?"

"Oh, yes, it was my poor father's. Often and often, when I was a careless laughing child, how he has held this watch to my ear to let me hear and wonder at the mysterious and life-like movements of the machine working. Alas! it has like him, been long silent. Oh, my poor father! my poor father! You should have lived until now, and seen that there were some who loved me."

Tony wiped his eyes and looked amazingly sympathetic.

"Ah, poor fellow," he said. He's gone, sure enough, but we can wind up the watch, can't we? Only we can't wind up the old gentleman, who has gone the way of all flesh."

"No, Tony, we can't," said Mary Ann. "Take the watch, it was reckoned a remarkable one by my father, and cost £50, and not dear."

"Yes, love!"

"What do you mean, Tony ?"

"Why, only that all the affections ought not to be on one side, you know, and as you said 'dear,' what in the world, my darling, could I say but 'love ?' Wasn't it natural, Mary Ann—wasn't it natural ?"

"Don't say it again if it be, Tony. "There is no time for trifling. Take care of the watch, Tony."

"Oh, yes, I'll take care of it for your sake, Mary Ann."

"Now, Tony, tell me what letters those are, for—for the truth is, my eyes are so full of tears, that I cannot look at them."

"Never mind," said Tony. "There's a little ticket upon them, and it says, miscellaneous letters of *no* consequence."

Tony himself had put in the negative.

"Then lay them aside, and look further, Tony."

"Hilloa, what's this ?" said Tony, lifting up a little packet, and reading upon it's outside.—"My dear sister,

pray, when I am gone, hand the enclosed to my darling child."

"And she never gave it to me !" cried Mary Ann, bursting into tears. "Ah, cruel, cruel, aunt ; you might like wealth, but you should have given to the orphan what was left in the hand-writing of her father. Oh, was it not cruel, Tony, to keep from me this, no doubt, dear remembrance of my father ?"

"Yes, love. The seal is open, and inside there is a letter addressed, 'To my dear child, Mary Ann.' Come, now, don't you be crying in that way, or else you'll make so many tears fall on the floor that they will make a slop in the room below. Come, come, Mary Ann, be a man! Don't go on crying in that sort of way, as if you had found a spring in your head, and were determined to show all the world what a fine one it was."

"You have no feeling, Tony."

"If you say that, I shall have to kiss you again, that I shall."

This speech of Tony's betokened a foregone conclusion. We are afraid that he had already tried kissing as a means of relief for the tears. At all events Mary Ann would be obdurate, and told him again that he had no feeling, upon which, what could he do, but kiss her again ?

"Nonsense, Tony," she said, "let us look what else is in the drawer, and then we will take a glance in the others, and leave, for this visit to my father's chamber has been much more painful to my feelings than I at all imagined it would have been. I fear I shall not be able to look further."

"Oh, don't say that ; won't you read your letter ?"

"Not now ; I could not do it—I could not do it. A few written words of affection from him is now to me like a voice from the dead. No, Tony, I will keep it in my bosom, and read it when I am alone."

"Well, Mary Ann, I think you are right in that, as I must say, my dear, you are right in most things, so just put it away, and we will go on with our search. What's this ? "Life Policy £1,000, in favour of my dear child, Mary Ann." Why you are a £1,000 richer than you were half an hour ago. What with this and the inn, and all that's in it, you are worth something handsome, while I——

"Well, Tony."

"While I am a poor fellow——"

"With nothing but one priceless jewel."

"Eh?—what jewel?"

"An honest heart, Tony. Ah! what worlds of wealth would be by those who have it brought into the market of their affections, if they could purchase with it an honest and a loving heart!"

"Come to my arms."

"Go along with you. Look what else there is in the drawer; there seems to be many papers yet, Tony."

"Yes, there is. Oh, this is some great piece of parchment connected with the house. The lawyer that Mr. Dean knows ought to see this. Let me see, here is a lot of receipts, of all kinds and descriptions, too. I don't think there's anything else of any consequence."

"Close the drawer, then."

Tony did so with such suddenness that he created a blast of air that puffed out the solitary light they had with them in a moment. One! struck the old clock upon the stairs, and they both stood for a few moments in profound silence, and in the most impenetrable darkness, listening to the solemn echo that the single sound seemed to summon out of the night air, and which, like some sad and mysterious spirit, appeared to pervade the whole house. It is strange what there can be in those hours of the night, that makes them come with such solemnity upon the ear. It is strange that, in joy or in sorrow, in prosperity or in misfortune, the imagination alike feels the strange mysterious influences of midnight and its adjoining hour.

"Supposition! supposition—! you have, indeed, much to answer for!"

"Mary Ann," said Tony, in a faint whisper.

Yes, Tony," she replied, in the same tone.

"Don't be frightened, I'll get a light. Don't you stir an inch, mind, from where you are, or you may run against something and frighten yourself, you know, Mary Ann."

"What's that?"

"What?"

"I hear a noise upon the drawers, exactly like the ticking of a watch. Don't you hear it, Tony?"

"Why I laid your father's watch down there. Lord bless me! I hear it fast enough! Why, after all this time, and without being wound up by any human hand, the old watch is going."

Tick! tick! tick! tick! went the old watch, with a clear and distinct intonation, laid upon hollow wood work as it was, and in a room so silent as that now was. No doubt the watch had stopped without running entirely down, and the moving from the drawers to the top of the walnut-tree chest, had had the effect of starting it off again, as it would many watches, but still, under the circumstances, the thing had a very startling effect, and certainly, with nine folks out of ten, would have smacked strongly of the supernatural.

"You still hear it?" whispered Mary Ann; "it is not my imagination."

"Not a bit of it," said Tony; "I hear it, but don't you mind about such a thing as that. Only wait while I get a light."

"Down stairs you must go. We ought to have provided ourselves against such an accident as this. I'll go, Tony, I know the way better than you do. You dont mind being left alone here?"

"Not I, I know what that is already; don't you recollect when I waited, I don't know how long, for your aunt and that beauty that she would have made master of the house here, if she could but have managed it?"

"Oh, yes—yes. Don't move, Tony. How very strange that the old watch should begin to go in such a way, when we might least expect such a thing. How very dark it is."

"Never you mind about that. Mind how you go now, dear, and don't run against anything and hurt yourself. There you go. What was that?"

"Only a chair, I think, Tony. All's right. What are you making that odd noise for?"

"Odd noise?—I ain't making any odd noise. It's you that seem to me as if you were scraping something."

"Hush!"

They both listened, and heard distinctly a scraping sound, as if some one was at work with a trowel or some such implement upon one of the walls of the room. It was a very strange sort of noise indeed, and yet it sounded as if it might have been much louder if the party who was making the noise had not been particularly careful to control it. Both Mary Ann and Tony were convinced from what they had said to each other that neither of them were occasioning the odd sounds, and after a few moments' intense listening, she said—

Tony, it comes from the wall next to the empty house. Don't you think it does

"I am sure of it, provided the empty house is to my right hand."

"It is, Tony, if you have not moved."

"And that I have not to my knowledge, Mary Ann. Can you hazard a guess as to what it can mean?"

"It is of no use guessing, Tony. Let us remain as we are without a light, and perhaps we shall soon know for a certainty. Our visit here to-night may, after all, be something of a providential character.

———

CHAPTER CVIII.

A DISCOVERY.

It is now necessary, in order that the reader may thoroughly understand the meaning of the mysterious noise in the chamber, that we should for a very brief space, pay some slight attention to the movement of what may be considered to be rather an insignificant personage. We allude to the waiter, who had been so ignominiously kicked from the hotel by Tony. We own our regret at leaving Mary Ann and Tony in so critical a position, but if they cannot endure each other's company for a short time without our interference, it is a very odd thing indeed, so we will leave them together while we take this necessary glance at the waiter. That personage, as he left the door of the hotel, was rather profuse in his promises as regarded the amount of vengeance which he would take upon Tony, and upon Mary Ann, and upon every one, indeed, who had in any way taken upon themselves to interfere with him in the carrying out of his rascally projects. There never is any one so indignant as your disappointed lofty schemer.

"I will have my revenge yet," muttered the fellow, "if I swing for it."

Now, any gentleman of strong passions and loose morals may have his revenge if he consents to swing for it, only there is required, in addition to the strong passions and the loose morals, a certain amount of courage, where swinging—Anglice, hanging—is to be the result, that your fine, high-minded, revengeful gents, are by no means famous for. We shall see, however, how the waiter got on. He took his way hurriedly into the city, and diving down one of those courts at the back of Lombard-street, where the light of day is a rare guest, he made his way into a wretched-looking den, which had a dilapidated counting-house aspect, and asked a miserable old frowsy-looking man there present if Mr. Zadok was at home.

"No—yes," was the reply. "Have you a card?"

"Yes, and I am No. 37."

The old man peered at him for some few moments in silence, and then opening a kind of ledger, he said—

"What, and who are you to the world?"

"John Such, a waiter in a tavern just now."

"Humph!" said the old man, shutting the book with a clap, as he found the description tally with what was there recorded of No. 37. "You perhaps know his room, young man?"

"I do."

"Go on, then; you'll find him disengaged; and I can tell you, that he thinks very highly of you, by the memorandum that follows your name in the book—ah, very highly indeed, young man. You have nothing to do but to go on and prosper."

There was a strange sinister expression about the old clerk's face as he uttered these words, that John Such did not exactly like, but he made no remark merely nodding his head and passing out of the room and down a narrow passage which terminated by a door conducting into the private room of Mr. Zadok. Before, however, he was half way down the passage the old clerk had struck a bell-wire which let Zadok know that one of the initiated was coming, and then opening the book at John Such's name, he chuckled and coughed his satisfaction at what he saw there recorded.

"Ha! ha! Let me see what he says about John Such—ha! ha! let me see. Oh, here it is. 'John Such, a hot tempered hasty fellow, must be transported shortly, or he will do some mischief, and if kept in England, will never achieve anything great.' Ha! ha!"

The book was closed again sharply. The old man evidently took a peculiar pleasure in flopping the book about, and then he sunk into an old leathern chair, in a seeming doze, but it was the doze of an angry dog who watches while he sleeps. John tapped at Mr. Zadok's door.

"Come in."

He opened it and entered the room, which was about as dingy a hole for any human being to sit in as could be imagined, but then Zadok could scarcely be called a human being. He was, as his name implied, one of the chosen people—one of those who have long since forsaken the God of Abraham for the

God of Mammon; and there he sat, old, deformed, and hideous, like some gaunt monster in a cell waiting for any chance prey that might come within reach of his insatiate fangs. This libel upon manhood peered in the face of the new comer, and then with that facility of recollection which was said to belong 'o George the Third, who had the instinct of a brute if he had not the capacity of a man, he said—

"No. 37, I think."

"Yes, I am 37, and desperate."

"Any more spoons or forks from the hotel?"

"I am kicked out, I tried hard before I left to take all that was at hand, but they were down upon me, and I have been forced to leave without anything but the lids of the cruet-stand bottles, and they ain't worth much."

"Nothing at all," said Zadok, as he swept with his shrivelled hand the articles that the waiter laid upon the sort of counter before him into a large chest without a lid, that was by his side, "nothing at all, What are your views now, 37? Speak out—what do you think of doing? Can we help you in any way?"

"I want revenge."

"Bah!"

"You will not help me to it, I know."

"Certainly not; I am a receiver of stolen and mislaid property, not an Italian bravo. Revenge is an article that won't melt up in our cauldron. It is a luxury, my dear 37, that I never allow myself to indulge in, so let me seriously advise you, as an older and wiser man than yourself, to have nothing to do with it."

"But if I can get my rvenege, and put something in the cauldron at he same time.—How would that look?"

"Much better, I assure you; 37, and if that is the case you are welcome to as much of the article as you can get hold of—Go on."

37 cleared his throat with a hem! and told the Jew all that had taken place at he hotel, not omitting any one particular, and concluded by saying—

"In the drawer where the will was, I saw a gold watch and seals, and I am pretty sure there was other property of value there; however, if you will assist me to rob the house, I shall be revenged, and for aught I know the will may still be in the drawer."

"And so, after you had it in your hand, 37, you were frightened at a ghost '

"I—I was.

"Can such things be!—I tell you what it is, 37, if I had the thinnest silver spoon that ever was made in my thumb and finger, not all the ghosts of immaterial space should get it from me."

"You are a man among a thousand. Can you, and will you help me?"

To rob the house?—yes, if practicable. Call again in an hour, and I shall be able to give you an answer, yes or no. It will be decisive either way. Go along with you now, some one is coming."

John left the room, and a few paces up the passage he met a lad with a carpet-bag in his hand. The lad passed timidly on, and the door closed. John Such lingered a moment or two out of curiosity, and placing his ear against the panel of the door, he heard the lad say—

"I brought it from a railway station. There was an old fat fellow waiting for the train, and I bothered him so to let me carry his bag for a penny, that he gave it to me, so I came right off with it.

"Have you opened it?"

"Lor, no, sir!—I haven't had time."

"A sovereign on the chance; I dare say I shall lose by it."

"Give us the tin."

The waiter continued listening, when suddenly he felt a sensation upon the top of his head as though his very brain was taking fire. The pain was horrible, and darting back with a yell of dismay, he looked up, when he saw the face and arm of Zadok, and in the latter a red-hot poker, with which he made an envious effect upon the head of No. 37—an effect which was still manifest by the agony of a serious burn upon his scalp.

"Dear me, I hope you ain't hurt."

"Hurt. The devil take you, why did set my head on fire?"

"How should I know your thick head was there, my dear friend? What should such a confidential acquaintance as you want behind the door, when you might walk in. I often amuse myself with the hot poker. Do you know it rarefies the air if waved about a little.

"Rarefies the deuce! I shall be distracted now with this burn. Confound anything and everything."

John Such rushed from the Jew's house in no very amiable frame of mind, but as he and his head cooled together, he thought that he would let his indignation against Zadok sleep for a while, and keep still alive his desire of doing something at the hotel. He, therefore, made his appearance punctually at the hour again, and Zadok, without making the remotest allusion to the hot poker business, at once said—

"There is an empty house next door to the hotel; I will find you two companions upon whom you may depend, and at midnight they, with you, will enter the empty house. The wall between the two houses happens only to be cloth and plaister, so that with care an opening can easily be made into the very room you wish to get into. Will that suit you?"

"Capitally."

"Very well, come here at half-past eleven to-night, and you will find those who are to go with you; but don't, when you are in the house, and have secured your booty, be fool enough to linger for any personal contest, for those who are going with you will not aid you in it. Let the robbery be the revenge, or you will be left to your fate; now be off with you, for I have much more important matters to look to."

John Such was very well pleased at the prospect that now presented itself of having some amout of vengeance against Tony and Mary Ann, and he thought that nothing was more probable than that as yet the will remained in its original place of custody, in which case he ran now a very good chance of getting possession of it, and so of inconveniencing Mary Ann. The reader is aware, however, that the will was placed immediately in the safe keeping of the attorney, to whom Harry Dean had entrusted the task of taking the necessary legal steps with regard to it. At half-past eleven o'clock the waiter made his appearance at Zadok's, and was there introduced to two gents of the burglarious or cracksman school; and the beautiful trio set off for the hotel amid a drizzling rain, that made even the police glad to linger beneath a door-way or a balcony for a few minutes at a time, in order to avoid the weather without getting a mouthful of it.

"Is there much plate?" said one.

"Yes," replied John Such, "a good stock of it. I know the premises, of course, well."

"That's everything," said the other.

"Oh, it will be by no means a troublesome job," added John; "and besides, nobody sleeps down stairs where the plate closet is, so that we can pack it up as easy as look at it."

"Very good. One had need now and then light upon a good job in these hard times. The worst of it is that old Zadok grabs such a lot for himself."

"Yes," said the other; "but one advantage of being connected with Zadok is, that a fellow is never driven to commit any stupid petty robbery, and run all the chances of being grabbed from pure distress. He enables us to wait until there are good chances, and he will keep one that he knows he can depend upon to manage a first-rate job when a chance shows itself, six months or more in idleness, rather than let him throw himself away upon some petty affair that is dangerous, and nothing to speak of in the way of profit if successful."

"Right," said the other. "That's how the old man keeps us together, and the establishment going."

Talking thus of their affairs, as if they were engaged in as legitimate a thieving business as a lawyer or a parson, the three housebreakers reached the empty house next door to the hotel, which was to be the object of attack and robbery, at that still hour of the night.

"Where's the policeman?"

"Didn't you see him at the corner?"

"Not I."

"It's all right. He was looking after a drunken gent, who looked as if he ought to have something in his pockets, whether he had or not in reality, and all the cribs upon his beat may be cracked for aught he'll know about it. Come on. The empty crib, of course, is only locked?"

"Yes. But there's one good of making way through an empty house; you are quite sure always that the chain is not up, and none of the bolts are shot. Come on. Why what are you shaking at, stupid?"

"I only feel a little nervous," said the waiter.

"Nervous! What's that?"

"Oh, nothing—nothing. Only you know, gentlemen, I ain't quite so well used to this sort of thing as you are. My experience has not gone quite so far, although I have brought a trifle or so to Mr. Zadok."

"You'll improve. Come on. Don't be lingering here. Now then for the lock."

Click went something at the lock of the door ; and then, as if by magic, the street door opened. In another moment they were all three inside. One of them closed the door again, and shot the top bolt into its place, saying as he did so—

"Mind, if a hurry-skurry takes place, that it's the top bolt."

"All's right. This way. Zadok says that the first-floor is the place to work through. Have you got your tools ?"

"Oh yes, plenty for a lath and plaister job. We shall soon get down enough to slip through—we are none of us very big ; a cracksman should be small and active as a horse-jockey."

They made their way up-stairs without a light, but when they reached the first floor, upon finding that the shutters were all fast closed, and that they fitted tightly, they ventured upon lighting a small taper, which they placed upon the floor, and then looked about them."

"That's the wall," said one. "Now, Mr. What's-your-name, are you quite sure that nobody has taken a fancy to sleep in that next room ?"

"I would stake my life upon it," said John Such. "They believe it to be haunted—at least, some of them do—besides, it has been shut up for years, and who would go and sleep in a bed that a man had died upon a couple of years ago, and that bed never have been touched since ?"

"Well, that's all right, then, no doubt. Let us set to work."

"Hush !"

"What's up now, Bob ?"

"I thought—I thought I heard something move, do you know, in the next room ; let's listen. Clap your ear against the wall."

Both of the highwaymen, for such they were, as well as housebreakers, did so ; but, as good luck would have it, that was at the very moment when, overcome by her feelings at finding the letter addressed to her by her father, Mary Ann

was silent, and Tony was likewise silent from sympathy.

"All's right, Bill."

"Yes ; it was nothing."

The thieves spoke in cautious whispers, from which, upon such expeditions, although they freely believed themselves to be safe from observation, so that their voices did not reach the ears of our friends in the next chamber ; and hence it was not until that mysterious scraping upon the wall, which took place after the candle had been accidentally extinguished, came upon their senses, that Tony and Mary Ann had the least intimation that anything of an unusual character was taking place.

CHAPTER CIX.

CATCHING A TARTAR.

WE are happy to find ourselves once more in the company of Mary Ann and Tony. They were, it will be recollected, in the dark, in that mysterious room, and the watch, which had really gone on far to awaken all the latent superstitious feelings of both of them, went on in that slow and solemn sort of way in which an elderly watch of sound discretion may be supposed to execute its evolutions. Tick ! tick ! It seemed as if the departed spirit of the old man had got into that machine, and was making itself manifest in that way to the feelings of his child. Mary Ann felt through the air until she reached Tony, and then, grasping him by the arm with both hands, she whispered—

"Tell me—Oh, tell me what it is ?"

"Thieves !"

"Thieves ?—but where, Tony—where, and how could thieves set my poor dead father's watch going ?"

"I don't say anything about the watch," replied Tony, "it's the scraping on the wall that I'm listening to, and if that's not occasioned by something in the next house, trying to work a way through, I know nothing."

"But who—who would think of such a thing ?"

"Lots. Be quiet, darling, for a minute, while I go and listen."

"Yes, Tony—yes, I will be uiet ; but somehow I would rather keep ast hold of you."

"Lord love you," said Tony, "I only hope you'll be of the same opinion as long as you live; you keep fast hold of me, and I'll keep fast hold of you, and so, like two precious souls that hold to each other, and look to God, we shall float down the great world's tide to the ocean of eternal life."

"Yes, Tony—yes. Ah, how strange it is that at times you speak quite a different language to what you do at others?"

"Do I?"

"Yes. Who now, that knew you, would have supposed it was you just now spoke? Why are you not always so?"

"I don't know, Mary Ann. The fact is, my mind is something like a storehouse, in which are thrown many things, mean and exalted, fair and foul, in most admired disorder, and as I go rummaging about among them all, I sometimes find a jewel, and sometimes only some shallow thing of paste and pinchbeck. Do you understand me?"

"I think I do. But listen at the wall, Tony."

"All's right. There goes my ear flat against it."

"What do you hear?"

"Somebody scraping away like a good one, and a whispering of voices. Now, Mary Ann, there is something very queer going on here, and I want you to do just what I tell you."

"Yes, Tony, I will. Only say what I have to do, and you will see that I shall do it. Go on, Tony."

"Well, then, creep down stairs, and awaken the night-porter?—he's always asleep. Then open the street door, and be sure you stand at it until a policeman passes."

"Lor, Tony, did you ever know a policeman pass when he was wanted?"

"Well," said Tony, " I must confess I never did. You must send the night-porter, then, to the station for two or three blue devils, you understand, and bring them up here, and all I have got to say is, that the quicker you do it the better; for if they don't come, this may be some desperate plan, for all I know to the contrary, to murder us all in our beds."

"I am gone, Tony."

Mary Ann slipped from the room, and Tony was alone, with all the probability staring him in the face that the thieves might make good an entrance through the lath and plaister wall to the room before Mary Ann should succeed in bringing the police to the house.

"Pleasant this," said Tony.

The housebreakers continued to work away at the wall, and had it not been that they thought it was a great object not to make no noise, or at all events, as little as possible, they would soon enough have found their way into the room. As it was, however, they got on rapidly, and Tony could each moment more and more distinctly hear their rapid approach to the paper upon his side the wall. By attentively listening, Tony ascertained with tolerable exactitude the precise spot upon which they were employed, and by spanning it from the ground, he found that it was not above three feet up the wall; no doubt they thought an aperture about that position would be the most convenient to creep through. A lucky thought came across Tony's mind. He went softly as foot could fall to the walnut-tree cabinet of drawers, and spanned the height of them. They were considerably higher than the spot was from the floor at which the thieves were at work. Moreover, the drawers were not above six feet from that spot, although they leant against the wall at right angles with it. By feeling, Tony found that it ran upon castors.

"I have it," said Tony. "It will puzzle them a little if I can move these drawers with the back of them right against the wall. I'll try it."

Placing his shoulder against the drawers, and exerting a sturdy strength, Tony found that he could quite easily make the walnut-tree cabinet glide along, and so, hitching them on by degrees, he at length firmly placed them against the wall upon which the thieves were at work. Scarcely had he succeeded, when the housebreakers actually perforated the wall, and to their chagrin, found themselves opposed by very hard wood.

"What the devil is this?" Tony heard one of them say. "There's no more plaister, but here is something as hard as a rock."

"The deuce there is!" said the other. "What is it? Let me look. Why it must be the back of some piece of furniture. What is there in the room, you John What's-your-name?"

" Nothing against that wall but a chair or two," said the waiter, " I'll take my oath, for I looked particularly round all the walls when I was in the place. Give it a good push."

Tony was prepared for this, and set his back against the drawers, so that, although the thieves did give it as good a push as the limited space they had to push against enabled them to do, they did not move it a hair's breadth, and they began to be both puzzled and troubled to know what to do.

" It's like a stone," said one.

" What on earth can it be ?" said the other, panting from his exertions to push the obstacle away. " It won't budge an inch. It's confoundedly mysterious."

" Shall—shall—we go ?" stammered the waiter.

" Go ! What for ?"

" Why—why things are getting rather uncomfortable, you know. I—I don't comprehend it."

" Nor we either; but we mean to comprehend it before we have done with it, I can tell you. Tell me, Bill, you are an old hand. What do you really think ?"

" Try again somewhere else."

" Good."

" And set about it quick. It must be a book-case, or something infernally heavy against the wall, that we have had the bad luck to hit upon, that's all. You see we have no power to push it away from here, but we won't give it up quite so easy."

" I should think not. The night is young yet."

Scrape ! scrape ! scrape ! began the process of making their way through another part of the wall, about six or eight feet from the spot where they had met with so serious and unexpected an opposition to their further progress. Tony was mightily pleased at the success of his plan, to gain time until Mary Ann should be able to bring him efficient assistance. Indeed he now expected her every passing moment. But there is more difficulty than any one would imagine in procuring the aid of the authorities in London, and policemen are something like love,

" Follow them and they will flee,
Fly them, and they will follow thee !'

so, although Mary Ann awakened the night porter, and the night porter flew to the station-house, the inspector upon duty happened to be one of those philosophers, of which there are so many who doubt everything they hear. No doubt this vice of the mind had originally been engendered by exaggeration.

" Thieves !" said the inspector, as though he had never heard of such a variety of the human species. " Thieves ! You don't mean that ?"

" Yes I do," said the night porter, rubbing his eyes.

" God bless me.—What makes you so sleepy ?"

" Cos, you see, I gets twelve shillings a-week to keep awake."

" Oh ! that's it. Very well. 223, and you, 230, just go and see what it's all about. I dare say it's nothing, after all."

The two policemen roused themselves for action, and accompanied the porter back again to the hotel ; but he could not induce them to adopt anything like a good pace upon the occasion. Mary Ann was waiting, as the phrase is, with the door in her hand, and the moment she saw the uniforms of the police, she flung it wide, saying—

" Come in.—Come in. Do not make any noise, I pray you. Follow me, and you shall hear what it is. The haunted-room is up stairs. This way.—Hush ! This way. Tread softly, or they may take the alarm and make their escape."

" The haunted room did you say, miss?" asked one of the policemen.

" Yes, but that's nothing. This way —this way."

" Ain't it nothing?" muttered the policeman, " I can only say as I've never been quite right in my inside since one night arter a gent had treated me to such a lot of lobster-salad as never was, and I seed my grandmother's ghost with a lobster's claw in each hand, sharpening 'em one agin the other like a pair of carving knives."

" Don't be a fool," said the other policeman, who prided himself upon his pronunciation of hard words. " You know you was a suffering from what we calls *indigustion*."

"Hush! hush!" said Mary Ann. "This talking is most indiscreet."

The policemen were silent, and followed her until they reached the door of the haunted chamber, when each of them drew out his truncheon, and put on a "Come, come, move on!" sort of look.

"Tony! Tony!" said Mary Ann.

"Here you are."

"Come here. The police have come. What are the thieves doing now, Tony? Come out here and tell us."

Thus abjured and summoned, Tony put in an appearance at the door of the haunted room, and Mary Ann was so

CLANDESTINE TRANSACTION AT MRS. DESTERN'S COTTAGE, HAMPSTEAD.

delighted to see him quite safe and sound, that she could not forbear giving him a sly pinch, which, in the rather excited state of his mind at that time, made him give a jump of alarm, and both the policemen threw themselves into attitudes of defence.

"What was that?" said one.

"Only me," said Tony. "It's a way I've got."

"Don't do it agin, then, young man, but tell us what you have got to say—a-hem! Look me in the face."

"Don't be a fool," said Tony.

"What?"

"Come, come; nonsense! Say what

you like afterwards, but come in now and listen to what I have been listening to for this half-hour nearly. If you manage right you will be sure to catch them. Come along. Tread light."

The policemen, with the most mysterious looks in the world, went into the room. After listening to the workmanship going on against the wall for some few moments, one said—

"It's the old dodge."

"Oh, yes," said the other. "Empty houses do more mischief than enough. Policemen's wives and families should be always put in empty houses to take care of 'em."

"Certainly," said the other. "There ought to be an act of parliament providing such; but what can you expect from the Whigs? That's what I ask, if anybody can answer me."

"Now, be quiet both of you," said Tony. "I am quite convinced from what I have heard that there are three men making their way in here. Now there are three of us, and if we don't take them all, we ought to be made the laughing stock of the parish. It will be easily done if you only hide yourselves up in a dark corner by the bedstead there."

Scrape! scrape! went the housebreakers against the wall, and just as the policemen and Tony had hidden, and Mary Ann had closed the door of the room, and flown to the chamber of Kate and Lucy, in order to tell them what was taking place, a clear orifice was made through the lath and plaister. One of the thieves looked through.

"All's dark," he said.

"And safe, I suppose," said the other.

"Oh, yes; there's not a mouse stirring. Hand me the light."

The little taper was handed to him, and holding it through the opening in the wall as far as his hand would go, he took a good look into the room. It were well that Tony and the two policemen were well hidden, or the thieves would speedily enough have taken the alarm, and left the empty house, probably before the force could have got round to capture them.

"All's clear," said the fellow, "we have nothing to do but to come on."

"What was it stopped us before, Bob?"

"A large chest of drawers that we happened to come just at the back of, as it unfortunately happened, for we have lost twenty minutes by it.'

"It is impossible," said John Such, "the drawers don't stand there. They are against the wall that the window is in, I tell you; I noticed particularly, and cannot be mistaken.''

"Look for yourself then."

The waiter took the little taper, and with a trembling hand, held it into the room; and then, sure enough, he saw that the drawers were the obstruction, and that they occupied the place in the apartment that they had done when he, in conjunction with the aunt of Mary Ann, had made an attempt to steal the will."

"It's very odd."

"What's odd? Get out of the way."

"Why, the drawers have been moved, I'll swear."

"Pho! You were in a muddle for fear of the ghost, when you made your way into the room before; you hardly knew, by your own account, whether you were upon your head or your heels, so it ain't likely you could be very clear about where the drawers stood."

John began to think that, after all, he must have made a mistake, and while the housebreakers were busy wiening the aperture sufficiently to make it available as a mode of entrance into the room, he was holding a strong contest between his fears and his doubts, but at length he succeeded in convincing himself that he really must positively have been mistaken altogether regarding the topography of the haunted apartment.

CHAPTER CX.

THE SEARCH AT MADAME ZADZED'S.

"Is all right?" said one of the housebreakers, placing an emphasis upon the is, as he held the taper light close to the face of John Such, indeed so close as almost to scorch his nose; for this robber was a great physiognomist, and wished to judge by John's face as much, if not more, than by his words.

"I suppose it is," said John, jerking back his head, and hitting a severe blow against the wall behind him—" I suppose it is."

" Oh, you are a nice article to come out with men on a job like this ; I only wonder at old Zadok not knowing you better. Work away, Bob."

" All's right, I'm getting on, but you know the two toughest things in the world are an old woman and a lath, so, as I have got ever so many of the latter to get through, I am forced to take my time about it."

At this moment there came a loud rat ! tat ! at the hotel door. The housebreakers suspended their operations to listen, and John Such, while his teeth chattered, and he shook in every limb, managed just to stammer out—

" Who's that knocking at the door ?"

" Pho !" said Bill, " I shall go on, in course ; people lodge here, and must come late if they don't early, and it ain't very likely they'll come into a room that hasn't been used for years."

He went on with his work, and in the course of five minutes more he had broken away quite enough of the wall for a man who was not encumbered by too much flesh to creep through.

" Now for it," he said ; " come on, John What's-your-name."

" I told you coming along, that my name was Such."

" Ah ! so you did, and a regular nonesuch you'll be, if you show us where we can light upon a box of plate."

" That can I, and that will I. Only you keep between me and all danger, for, somehow, I ain't quite the thing to-night, and I rather think I might run away if I were to meet anything. You quite understand me don't you ?"

" Rather, you're a coward—that's all about it. Get through."

" What !—me first ?"

" To be sure. You know the way, and we don't."

" Well, if I must I—I must. I only wonder who that was knocking at the door. Dear me, there's a man always in the hall of a night to see who comes, and so, ' It's no use knocking at the door.' I—I am all of a perspiration for fear. ' There's somebody in the house with——' Eh ? What was that ? I heard a noise and saw a footstep."

" What do you mean ?"

" There's—some—somebody in the house, I know."

" Confound you," said one of the robbers, as he drew a pistol from his pocket, and placed the barrel against the temple of John Such, " if you give us any more of your nonsense, I'll blow your brains out. Get into the room at once, will you? Are we to be trifled with in this way ?"

" Thus admonished, John Such got through the opening in the wall, and stood in the haunted room—that room which was now haunted by something much more inimical to the interests of the housebreakers, than the ghost of Mary Anne's father would have been. The two thieves quickly followed John, and by the aid of the piece of lighted paper, they just saw dimly about the room. The policemen, however, as well as Tony, were too well hidden to be so easily detected, and the robbers advanced under the full impression that everything was turning out exactly as they would wish it. When they had got sufficiently far from the opening in the wall, that a sudden escape that way would have been impracticable, Tony, who was upon his hands and knees upon the floor, crawled behind John Such, and seizing that gent by the ancle, he cried—

" It's the devil knocking at the door."

Down fell John, for he verily believed his infernal majesty had come for him. With an oath one of the robbers made a rush to the opening in the wall, and he naturally enough fell over Tony and John Such. The other thief immediately blew out the light. A few hearty cuffs were given and received in the dark, and then Tony cried—

" Lights ! lights ! lights !"

The door of the room was flung open, and Harry Dean, with a pistol in one hand and a lighted candle in the other, made his appearance. The scene at this moment was sufficiently picturesque. Tony was upon the ground, holding John Such by the throat with one hand, while with the other he had a firm clutch of the leg of one of the housebreakers, who was making vain attempts to reach the hole in the wall. The other robber was bolt upright against the walnut-tree chest of drawers with a pistol in his hand, while the two policemen stood at bay, one of them holding up his hat before his face, as though that would shield him from the bullet, should it come his way. Harry Dean was not one to hesitate much when he saw his way clearly, and comprehending at a glance the posture of affairs, he fired at the robbers with the pistol, and then followed up the shot by springing forward upon him. The police were emboldened by the presence of such an ally, and they ran in upon the thieves as well; so that although Harry Dean had purposely missed shooting the fellow, he was quickly taken and disarmed. Prudence had forbidden him from firing his pistol, and one of the first things he said after his capture was to Harry Dean—Sir, you will take notice that I might have taken a life, but refrained from doing so. I hope, sir, you'll remember that to my advantage in another place. Harry Dean did not think himself called upon to commit himself in any way by an answer to this, and cried aloud for more lights. In the course of a few moments the night-porter appeared with plenty of lights and two more policemen, who had been sent from the station to know what had become of the others. Handcuffs were speedily put upon the housebreakers, and then Tony, looking at John Such, said—

"Now you see you couldn't let very well alone. You were let go once, but that wouldn't satisfy you, and now the consequence is that you'll take a voyage, John, for the good of your country; but you were quite right about the chest of drawers, if that's any consolation to you, I moved them."

John only groaned.

"Take them away," said Harry Dean to the policeman. "Take them away. The peace of this house has now been sufficiently disturbed. I rejoice that I chanced to come home in time to give some assistance in this affair. I was surprised, Tony, to find the door fast, instead of yielding to the touch, while the night-porter was in the hall, and I rapped rather sharply."

"Oh, yes," said Tony. "John, here, heard you knocking at the door."

John gave another groan.

"Now, my tulips," said one of the policemen. "Come on. This will be a lagging affair, and in old times it would have been a scragging one, so you may quite congratulate yourselves that you live in these enlightened times, and that policemen is gents. Come on."

The housebreakers seemed to take their capture very much as a thing of course, and with a sullen sort of philosophy they followed the two policemen who went before them, while the two others held them in a scientific manner by the cuffs of their coats. John was honoured by being permitted to walk between the two foremost policemen, and so, in grand procession, off they went to the station-house. During the latter part of these proceedings, Mary Ann had made herself visible, and now she spoke, saying—

"I will quiet the apprehension of Miss Destern and her sister, and now I beg that you will all go to bed, and we will talk of this affair in the morning."

"Come with me, Tony," said Harry Dean, "I want to speak to you."

"I'm a coming," said Tony. "Good night, Mary Ann—lord bless you, how pretty you look."

"What's that to you?"

"What's that to me? Come now, that is a good joke. I'll tell you what it is, Mary Ann—I think, after all the fighting and squabbling with no end of housebreakers to-night, I'm entitled to just one. The deuce! Well now, I call that too bad."

Tony had slowly followed Mary Ann, intending to snatch a kiss, but she had retreated until she got just within the bed-room where Kate and Lucy were, and then at the critical moment when Tony was about to make the attempt, she banged the door shut, inflicting upon the most prominent features of Tony's face, rather a severe blow.

"It serves you right, Tony," said Mary Ann. "You should never try to kiss before company."

"Don't mention it any more," said Tony, as he rubbed his nose. "It's a sore subject. Don't mention it."

He followed Harry Dean into his dressing-room, and when the door was closed Harry said—

"Well, Tony, I think I have made some progress in finding out who Kate really is."

"I am rejoiced to hear it."

"I knew you would be. But as the

adventures of this evening have been rather peculiar, if you are not sleepy, I will relate them to you now at once."

"Sleepy?" said Tony, "I never was less sleepy in my life, and I shall be quite rejoiced to hear them. Pray go on, Mr. Dean."

"I will. Stir the fire, Tony."

"Done," said Tony; "there's a nice blaze now, it's a comfort to see such a fire, ain't it?—upon my life, I wouldn't go to bed on any account."

"Well then, Tony, you know that the attorney, having procured an order for us to view the effects of the late Madame Zadzed, I started with him full of hope that something might be elicited of a favourable character, as regarded the parentage of Kate. When I say favourable, of course, I mean such evidence as might prove, beyond the shadow of a doubt, that she was in no way akin to Wilkins."

"I'm convinced of that already."

"We may be convinced ourselves of many things, Tony, that we would yet gladly be in a position to prove to other people, who know nothing of the parties."

"That's true enough. Go on."

"Well, Tony, since the murder, the house of Madame Zadzed has been shut up completely, while in the kitchen, it appears, a policeman and his wife reluctantly live. When we arrived, the wife was at home, and, as her husband was upon duty, she seemed really quite pleased at the idea of some people being in the house, even if it were only for a few hours. We were shown up-stairs into a handsome enough drawing-room, and as the place, from being long neglected, was chill and damp, we got the woman to light us a fire in it, and soon had a cheerful blaze in the grate, which made the place look amazingly different."

"I should think so," said Tony.

"Well, there was in this drawing-room an oaken book-case with a number of drawers under it, and it was there that we first directed our attention; upon opening it, we found many papers, and among the rest was this, which, by its tenor, was evidently in the hand-writing of Madame Zadzed. Read it, Tony, if you please."

Harry Dean handed to Tony a paper, upon which were written the following words:—

"You will go, Swam, again to Hampstead, to the cottage of old Mrs. Destern. It appears from all that I can gather, that, after her decease, a man arrived in the village, sought out the cottage of an old woman, whose daughter was in the cottage of the late Mrs. Destern, minding it. To this old woman he gave two sovereigns, on condition that she got her daughter to look at the back of a cupboard between the paper and the wall for a packet of letters there concealed. How this man got his information, and who he was, Swam, I cannot discover. The old woman, it appears, went into the back garden of Mrs. Destern's cottage, which communicated with her own garden, and called her daughter to a latticed window there, and the result was that she found the packet of papers, and handed them out of the window to her mother, who, heedless of what their real value might be, thought she had disposed of them well for two sovereigns, and the man rode off with them. Now, Swam, I want you to go to Hampstead, and find out, if you can, what those papers looked like, and who the man was. The old woman's name is Finch."

"What do you think of that?" said Harry Dean.

"Why," said Tony, "there can be no doubt but that it was written by Madame Zadzed, to that woman, Swam, who is dead."

"Yes, unfortunately."

"What can you make of it, Mr. Dean?"

"Just nothing, as it stands. But here is another piece of paper, more mysterious than the former. What do you make of this Tony."

Tony took a little scrap of paper that was handed to him by Harry Dean, and read upon it the following truly mysterious words:—

"Int. hel. eg. oft. hec. abin. et."

These few cabalistic looking words were written in bold characters, and the piece of paper upon which they were, had been carefully enclosed in an envelope.

"The deuce!" said Tony; "what language is that?"

"None," said Harry Dean; "but it has its meaning, no doubt."

"It may."

"I am convinced that it has, Tony, and the probability is, that that meaning is very simple, if we could but discover it, and that when we do so, we shall wonder at ourselves for not having done so before."

"The deuce take the woman!" said Tony, "why could she not write plain English while she was about it? Did she expect that her papers, after her throat was cut, would fall into the hands of none but some conjurer, I wonder?"

"It looks like it, Tony."

"What does the lawyer think of it?"

"He don't know what to think. I have left him still at the house, where he says he will make a further search, although I don't think he will find anything to repay him for his trouble. He has taken an exact copy of this mysterious paragraph or sentence, if it may be called either, and puzzles himself about it very much. Some of it is Latin."

"Is it?" said Tony.

"Yes, but the rest is not. Now, Tony, I wished, before you went to bed, to give you these mysterious and puzzling words to think of; so now we will bid each other 'Good night,' and I hope by the morning that your ingenuity may have discovered some solution of the enigma."

"I don't think it likely," said Tony. "However, they will keep me awake all night, I don't doubt, for all that. Good night, Mr. Dean, and a sound repose to you. Confound folks that write in riddles, say I. Good night."

CHAPTER CXI.

THE LAWYER'S ADVENTURE.

As he had mentioned to Tony, Harry Dean had left the lawyer at the house of the late Madame Zedzed, still engaged in rummaging over her papers. That there was some secret worth knowing in the cabalistic words of which he had taken a copy, and the purport of which so much puzzled Harry Dean and Tony, he, the attorney, did not entertain a doubt, and it was most peculiarly provoking to him, that, with all his profes-

sional acumen, he could not find it out. The clock of a neighbouring church, St. Ann's, Soho, had pealed forth the hour of midnight, and there still sat the lawyer, with his head resting upon his hands, and his elbows upon the table, while between them lay the exact copy of the mysterious document. The house was profoundly still, and a feeling of loneliness began to creep over him. He stirred the fire, and the cheerful blaze that it shot up somewhat restored his spirits.

"Confound it!" he said, "I would give something to know what this means."

Over and over again, then, he read the paper, and was just about to give it up in despair, when there came a tap at the room door.

"Come in," he cried.

The door opened, and the policeman's wife made her appearance, saying—

"It's raining cats and dogs, sir."

"Raining what?"

"I mean very hard indeed; and my husband's just come, and he says shall he shut up the house for the night. He by no manner of means wishes to hurry you, sir, only he always locks up at twelve, and if you like to stay, there's a well-aired bed up-stairs."

"Does it rain so very hard?"

"Hark at it, against the windows."

Splash—dash—rattle, and splash again came the rain against the windows of the room. The attorney was a single man, so he had no one awaiting his return home. The fire looked cheerful, and he had paid well for it."

"Just get me," he said, "a pint bottle of ale from the nearest house if you can, and bring it to me with some bread, and I will stay. There's a shilling."

"My husband can get it, I dare say, sir," she said, "although it is past twelve."

"Oh, I forgot that. Let him try."

The woman left the room, and that her husband had been successful in getting the required repast, was very soon sufficiently evidenced by its production on a tray.

"Give the change to your children," said the lawyer, "and I shall not trouble you any further; I shall only sit another hour. Which is the bed-room?"

"The one exactly over head, sir."

"Thank you, good night."

The woman executed a curtsey, and bidding him good night left him to his moderate supper and the puzzling memorandum of Madame Zadzed, from the meaning of which he found himself just as far as when he first set eyes upon it. Again he stirred the fire, and took a drop of ale, and then he said to himself—

"Well, I will to-night give an hour to this affair, which my vocation to-morrow, I know very well, would not permit me to do, and if I can't find it out by then, I shall give it up as a bad job altogether. It may, after all, be like the celebrated riddle—"Why is a pig looking out at an attic window, like a dish of green peas?" to which there is no meaning at all."

This was a provoking idea.

"Well, well," he added, after a little more time spent in looking at it. What a pleasure it would be to me to find it out, if it be anything to find out, and how provoked I shall be if some one else at a glance were ever to find a meaning to it."

This idea inspired him with fresh perseverance, and taking another sip of the bottled ale, which was particularly good, he twisted and turned the paper in all directions, but there it remained as great an enigma as the Sphynx in Egypt, which everybody thinks is a riddle of old King Cleops for all the world to addle its brains over. Thus another hour passed away. One! pealed forth from the church clock, and then giving the table a blow with his fist, that made the now empty ale bottle and the glass jump again, he cried—

"Confound it, I only wish she'd come herself, if it were from the infernal regions, and explain what the devil she means."

Tap!—tap!—tap! came at the door of the room. The lawyer turned pale, the candle immediately exhibited symptoms of guttering all down on one side, while the rain against the window panes suddenly ceased, and a coffin flew out of the fire, creating a very uncomfortable odour by burning the hearth-rug. Tap! —tap!—tap!

"W—w—what's that?" gasped the lawyer.

Tap!—tap!—tap!

"Co—co—come—in—come in——"

The door of the apartment slowly opened with a lazy sort of scream upon its hinges. Horror almost froze up the faculties of the lawyer, as he saw upon the threshold a tall female figure, the neck of which was closely enveloped in numerous bandages, while the face was ghastly pale. This figure carried a light in its left hand, and as it stood upon the threshold of the room, it solemnly beckoned to him with its right to follow her. He felt his hair bristling up on his head, while a cold perspiration dropped from his brow like rain. He made several inarticulate efforts to speak, but could only produce an odd gurgling noise in his throat. Still the figure beckoned him, and then sufficiently recovering from his first fright, he managed to say—

"Who—who—what—are—you?"

The figure was still silent, but pointed significantly to its bandaged throat, and shook its head mournfully.

"Good God!" thought the attorney. "This is, indeed, the apparition of the murdered Madame Zadzed. Oh, that I had nerve sufficient to enable me to go through this dreadful interview."

The figure solemnly beckoned him again. Calling then to his aid all the courage and all the intense curiosity that education had given to him, he clutched the arms of the chair and rose. He could have exclaimed with Hamlet—

"Lead on—I'll follow thee!"

for such was now his purpose, as with a staggering gait he neared the door.

"Where—where would you lead me to?" he just managed to gasp out.

The figure again pointed to its throat, and then indicated the stairs that led to the upper part of the house. Making a desperate rally from his fears, the attorney said—

"I never harmed you in life, nor saw you; why, therefore, should I fear you in death? I tremble with what, I suppose, is a natural fear, but I will follow you. Lead on—I come—I come."

The apparition at once slowly and solemnly began the ascend of the stairs, and holding, with cold and clammy hands, the balustrades, as she ascended the lawyer slowly followed. His eyes were iated; he drew his breath short and thick, and more than once he thought if he had not had that balustrade to hold by, his knees would have sunk under him, and he should have fallen. Never had he experienced such horrible sensations as those which now found a home at his heart. Step by step, up—up these creaking stairs went the apparition, and up went the attorney, feeling each moment as though, if he were to live for a hundred years, he should never forget the sensations of that night. The figure paused upon the landing. The attorney twined his arm round the balustrades, and spoke in a hoarse thick voice—

" No further !—no further !—no—no —no!"

The figure beckoned him on.

" No, no. Speak here. Tell me what has summoned you from another world ! If you have a revelation to make to me, make it here at once, and do not seek to drive me mad by protracting a state of mind that even now is bordering upon insanity. Speak—oh, speak !"

The figure pointed to its throat, and then to the door of a room opening from the landing, close to where it stood, and then it beckoned the lawyer again.

" No !" he cried ; " No—no further! Not a step ;—I cannot—I dare not ! Here I take my stand ! Speak to me here, or vanish from my sight, and leave unsaid that which you have come to say!"

The apparition slowly turned and commenced the descent of the stairs again, and then, as if from some new impulse, it turned again and ascended. It crossed the landing, and pushing open a door, entered a room, upon the threshold of which it turned and once more beckoned him on. Rendered desperate by the horrors of his position, and with all his feelings wound up to the highest pitch of excitement, he abandoned the kind of vantage ground he had by his hold of the balustrade of the stairs, and ascending the remaining few steps, he followed the ghost into the chamber, whither it appeared to be the most particular wish of the spectre to lead him. It was a good sized handsome enough room, with a large gloomy looking bedstead in it, past which the apparition went until it reached a dressing-table, upon which it placed the light it had, until then, carried steadily in one hand.

" Now," thought the lawyer, as he paused, and kept between him and the ghost a large arm-chair that was in the room ; " now I shall hear what dreadful revelation has summoned this woman's erring spirit from beyond the grave. Speak now !" he said ; " speak now !"

The apparition again pointed to its throat, and in a strange voice, said—

" It's enough to throttle a body to speak with such a sore throat ; but I'm the policeman's mother, you know, and as Jane told me you meant to go to bed at once, I thought I'd wait up to bring you a chamber candlestick, and here it is."

" What ?"

" I wishes you a very good night, sir, and all I can say is, if I don't soon get the better of this cold in my throat, it will send me to kingdom come. Good night."

" The devil!"

" Lor! sir, how skeared you look. Oh, my sore throat !—oh—oh—oh ! I wish I'd sent Jane, for all this talking has done my poor throat no good, that it hasn't ; and I, too, that, if I am well, can talk anybody sand blind ! Oh, dear ! —oh, dear ! what a world we live in! There's nothing but ups and downs. Oh, dear ! I suppose it's all for the best. Good night, sir. Dear me, you are an odd-looking man !"

The attorney was so completely staggered at this unexpected *denouement* to the affair, that he sank into the great arm chair in silence, and the old woman with the cold in her throat, who had caused him such exquisite apprehension, coolly walked down stairs, thinking she had been amazingly polite, and never dreaming that she had nearly frightened a professional man out of his wits. For about ten minutes there sat the attorney trying to recover his usual frame of mind, and really prevented from doing so by the anger which he felt upon the occasion of having been made such a perfect fool of. It is astonishing, when the imagination is suddenly freed from the trammels of any strong impression that has been for a time made upon it, how angry the judgment is at having given way to the deception.

" Oh, that I, at my time of life, and with all my experience," said the attorney, " should have been such a fool as to follow with fear and trembling the ghost of an old woman."

Disagreeable as it was to his judgment, and hurtful as it was to his vanity, he had done so; and now he set to work trying to remember every word he had said, so as to learn how far he had committed himself in the affair, and to judge how it would tell if the old woman chose to make a story of it to her son, the policeman, and others. The result of this self-examination was anything but satisfactory.

"Well, well," he said, at length, "it is done and can't be undone, but if I be not ghost-proof after this, I deserve to be frightened every night in the week."

Hurriedly denuding himself of his

apparel, the lawyer stepped into bed now, and was soon in a sound sleep, which for a wonder was so, for one might have expected, as a result of his recent mental agitation, that his repose would be anything but dreamless. In the morning he laughed at what had made him angry the night before, and as he had made an appointment to breakfast with Harry Dean at the hotel, he rose and left the house of Madame Zadzed at an early hour. Before he left, he spoke to the policeman and his wife, but he could not detect that they knew or thought anything of the preceding night's adventure, so that he came to the conclusion, that after all, although she might have thought him rather an eccentric person, the old woman was too stupid to have observed the effect she had produced upon his nerves. This was so far satisfactory, and *en route* to the hotel he made up his mind to tell the story to Harry Dean as a good joke. This was the best course he could pursue, for, although, no doubt, he wished he had stood the test of strong superstitious feeling better than he had done, there are very few men of keen imaginations who, under the circumstances, would have acted differently from what he did. It was a full quarter to nine before he reached the door of the hotel, but he found every one up, and Harry Dean, in fact, delaying breakfast upon his account. The morning's meal, therefore, was sat down to immediately upon his arrival. The parties present at the breakfast consisted of Harry Dean, the lawyer, Tony, Mary Ann Kate Destern, and Lucy. The presence of the ladies, and a certain arch look which was always upon the countenance of Mary Ann, would have had the effect of stopping the attorney from telling his ghost story, even if his tongue had not been withheld by knowing that Harry Dean did not wish Kate to be disturbed about this question of her paternity. The talk ran, therefore, upon the attempted robbery at the hotel, and the attorney listened with great attention to the details.

"You may depend," he said, "that your lives would not have been worth ten minutes' purchase if those men had got fairly into the house, and found no more opposition than they had power to master."

"It is a capital thing," added Harry Dean, "that that waiter has committed himself so far, as he will now be disposed of. I fully expected, from the looks of that man, that sooner or later he would try some plan of revenge."

"And I likewise," said Mary Ann, "but now," with a sly glance at Tony, "we may venture to feel happy."

CHAPTER CXII.

THE SOLUTION OF THE MYSTERY.

TONY was quite enchanted at this little speech of Mary Ann's, particularly as it was accompanied by so pointed a look towards him. The pleasure of his heart danced in his eyes, and he was about to say something that no doubt would have been particularly apropos, when Mary Ann suddenly cooled his ardour, by saying—

"Dear me, Mr. Thorpe must be ill, for he has been looking at me in the most extraordinary manner for the last five minutes."

"Ill," said Tony, "I ain't ill."

"Oh, I thought you were. If you please, Mr. Dean, does he often make such extraordinary faces as those?"

"Oh, yes, very often," said Harry Dean, with a laugh. "But you will have leisure enough to cure him, you know. That will be one comfort to you."

Mary Ann laughed, and Tony muttered something about people blowing hot and cold, which he thought particularly applicable to his intended. Harry Dean turned to the attorney, and said to him—

"Have you made any progress in deciphering the enigmatical memorandum of the late Madame Zadzed?"

"Indeed, no," he replied, "I have puzzled my brains to no purpose, I confess."

"And I too," said Tony.

"Is this anything," said Mary Ann, "in which my guessing power can be of any assistance?"

"Oh, dear, no," said Tony; "it has defied even me, and I flatter myself I am rather a good one at a riddle, but this is a regular teazer, so it's no use your knitting your pretty brows about it, Mary Ann, or screwing up your nice little nose into a state of perplexity. Leave it alone, there's a duck."

A roar of laughter from Harry Dean and the lawyer did not make Mary Ann a bit more pleased with this speech of Tony's, which they all saw was a little bit of revenge for the discomfiture he had met with a few moments before. He gave now a sort of nod at Mary Ann, as much as to say, "Never try on any pun at my expense, for, you see, I am more than a match for you," and this look certainly had the effect of urging Mary Ann to revenge. It was such a triumphant one upon the part of Tony, that Harry Dean said—

"Mary Ann, if you mean to rule as all prudent wives will try to do, you must not give in so soon to Tony's Blue Beard-like tyranny."

"I don't mean."

"Very good!" said Tony, with the air of a man who makes some idle threat; but in a moment his countenance changed, and he said—"Good God! What's that? Murder!"

"What's the matter?"

"I don't know. It's down my back, that's all I know about it. What is it? An animal? Murder!"

Tony jumped up, and executed some such extraordinary capers about the room, that the most serious individual in the world must have laughed at. As for Mary Ann, she was in convulsions of merriment, while Harry Dean and the lawyer looked amazed at the curious efforts Tony made, as if to wriggle out of his clothes. They laughed with Mary Ann, who, they guessed was the author of the mischief, and when Tony got a little more composed, she said to him—

"Now, Tony, don't you ever again hilloa before you are out of the wood. It's an old proverb, and it happens not to be a foolish one."

"Good gracious!" said Tony, wiping the perspiration from his face, "what was it? I didn't hilloa at all. Well, something went down my back that was enough to make the devil himself do so. What was it? If it was a joke, tell me."

"A joke, Tony!"

"Yes. You all seemed to think it was, though I can't see it yet for the life of me."

"Nor won't, Tony. It was not a joke."

"What was it, then, Mary Ann?"

"Why, it was a cup of hot chocolate. And now, Tony, when you want to be particularly grand and triumphant, all I shall say to you will be—'Remember the chocolate!'"

Tony made a wry face as he held out his hand to Mary Ann, and said—

"I give in—I give in. Come, be friends, Mary Ann; I give up com-

pletely, and, as you have got the best of it, don't harbour malice."

"Go along with you, Tony."

A spoon that was of a fiery heat was laid in Tony's palm instead of the fair hand of Mary Ann, and he gave another jump, to the great amusement of Harry Dean and the attorney who laughed most uproariously.

"Come, come," said Harry Dean, "we will avail ourselves of woman's aid. Just look at this little piece of paper, Mary Ann, and tell me what you think of it. Read it out, if you please."

He handed to Mary Ann the mysterious document, and she read it as it appeared, namely :—

"*Int. hel. eg. oft. hec. abin. et.*"

"Yes," said Harry Dean; "now what do you make of that?"

"Ah!" said Tony. "I'll give you a kiss, and a promise of future favours and a sixpence, if you can find out what that means, Mary Ann."

"Will you really; and what will you give, sir?"

"My best thanks," said Harry Dean; "for it is probable it may be to me useful information, and if not, it will relieve me from the anxiety consequent upon the idea that there may be something I much wish to know locked up in that mysterious language."

"It is easy. But what say you, sir?"

"I," said the lawyer, "will thank you with all my heart, and I would admire you more than I do at present, but for one little circumstance, and that is, that it is impossible for me to do so."

"The deuce!" said Tony.

"Then, gentlemen," said Mary Ann, "the merest accidental thought would enable you to read this paper with the greatest facility. I remember finding one something similar once, and that remembrance instantly gave me, as it were, a key to this, for at a glance I tried it."

"And can read it?"

"Yes."

"Then pray have pity upon my impatience," said Harry Dean, "and let me know at once what it contains."

"The words are these. *In the leg of the cabinet.*"

The lawyer and Harry Dean looked

at each other, and Tony, giving himself a punch on the side of the head, cried—

"Well, I never! Was anything ever so stupid. In all my life now I never made such a blunder about anything. Oh, it's as easy as kiss my hand. Oh, I see it. I see it."

"So do we all now," said Harry Dean. "Mary Ann, I am much beholden to you."

"And I," said the attorney.

"Don't think of it," said Mary Ann. "In a little time some of you must have thought of it, and there's no merit at all in the matter. You see at a glance now that the interpretation I have given is the correct one."

"Oh, yes, yes!"

"Come to my arms," said Tony. "I acknowledge that your wit and intelligence, Mary Ann, are so great, that they are only equalled by your beauty, and that, we know, is about what it ought to be to go on towards the manufacture of an angel. In the leg of the cabinet! Dear me! Dear me! Of course it is. But what is in the leg of the cabinet, and what cabinet is it?"

"The cabinet in which it was found," said Harry Dean, "of course."

"Yes," said the lawyer. "This came out of a small drawer at Madam Zadzed's house, and it is in some secret receptacle in the leg of that cabinet, that we shall, I hope, find papers which will have the effect of clearing up the mystery in which you, sir, (to Harry Dean,) feel so deeply interested."

"Ah!" said Kate, "what mystery is that Harry? Have you any anxiety or absorbing interest of which I know nothing?"

"Pardon me, Kate, and allow me to keep yet for awhile this affair a secret. Have you sufficient confidence?"

"Have I confidence?"

"Ah, I see that it is that complexod, but not real doubt, for which I ought to ask forgiveness."

"It is indeed, but it is awarded as soon as asked, and you must pardon me, Harry, for assuming the right to ask you what gives you uneasiness."

"There now," said Tony. "There now, Mary Ann, you see how nice and amiable other folks are. Why don't you take pattern by Miss Destern? You don't see her pour a cup of red-hot chocolate down Mr. Dean's back, do you? I wonder at you."

"Will you pardon me?" said Harry Dean. "For my impatience to know what is hidden in the leg of the cabinet is so great, that I cannot conceal the impulse I have to go at once, and satisfy my curiosity. Will you accompany me, sir?"

"Yes," said the lawyer, "if you will permit me just to write a note to my clerk first, to tell him that I shall not be at chambers for an hour or two; and probably Mr. Thorpe will go with us, as in such a case it is always best to have as many witnesses as possible."

A tap came at the room door, and a female servant of the hotel peeped into the room, and looking at Tony, said—

"Oh, if you please, sir, a policeman has come for you."

"A policeman for me?"

"Yes, sir. He says he must have you at once, and can't wait no longer. Oh, here he is."

A tall gaunt-looking policeman made his appearance, and touching his hat, he said—

"Your servant, ladies and gentlemen. I can't wait. Come on, if you please, Mr. Thorpe. I think that's your name. You are wanted at Bow-street, if you please."

"Why, what have I done?" said Tony.

"Done?"

"Yes. What the deuce do you want with me? It's some mistake. This is another joke. What do you mean?"

"Why, only that if nobody appears agin them three fellows we took out of this house last night, that they'll be discharged. That's all. So if any more of you is evidence, you had better come, but one will be enough to commit 'em, and you, sir, I think saw most of it along with the beautiful young lady."

"Hark you, my friend," said Tony. "I'll come with you, but it don't matter just now whether the young lady is beautiful or not, so just be so good, when you speak of her again, as to say *the* young lady, and drop the *beautiful*."

"No offence, gents," said the policeman.

"None in the least," said Mary Ann.

"Come along," said Tony, pulling the policeman out of the room, for fear Mary Ann should say something in acknowledgment of the compliment that had been paid to her. "Come along—first of all, you say you can't wait a moment, and then you stand grinning here as if you had all the day at your disposal."

Tony marched off to the police office at Bow-street, with the complimentary member of the force, and Harry Dean, with the attorney, proceeded again to the house in which Madame Zadzed had breathed her last, in order to find what mystery the leg of the cabinet contained. The policeman's wife made no objection to their resuming their search in the house, and they at once made their way to the drawing-room in which was the bureau or cabinet in which had been found the mysterious document so happily translated by Mary Ann.

"How shall we set about it?" said the lawyer. "This article of furniture, as you perceive, Mr. Dean, has six legs, and none look at all, from their size, likely to be the receptacle of papers. I'm afraid, after all, that this is either a mere blind, or that there is something more to find out in it yet than we have had the good fortune to discover."

"It may be so."

"It looks very like it, I think, sir."

"The woman to whom this house belonged was such an adept at intrigue, that I should not be surprised at any complexity connected with her affairs. Nevertheless, as the leg of the cabinet is mentioned, I think we should not shrink from an immediate examination. Your strength and mine will suffice to turn upon its side this piece of furniture."

"Oh, yes."

They both set about it, and with as little noise as possible they succeeded in turning over the cabinet, by which process three of its legs were free for examination. It was in vain that they shook them, and at any place where the lathe had made an incision or an ornament, they tried hard for a screw. Not the least symptoms of anything of the kind appeared, and Harry Dean himself began to think that the lawyer's suspicions concerning the affair had more in them than at first he had been inclined to suppose. Still the other three legs had to be examined and until they had passed through the same ordeal as the first one, they could not be said to be foiled in their attempt. With some difficulty they got the cabinet which was very heavy, being made of massive Spanish mahogany, over upon its other side, so that the other three legs were at their disposal. Harry Dean commenced an examination of one of them, and the lawyer of another.

"No," said the lawyer. "Mine won't move."

"Behold!" cried Harry Dean.

The lawyer looked up and saw that he had found a place in the leg of the cabinet at which it unscrewed at about the middle of its length.

"I suspected this leg," said Harry Dean, "for it was, I saw, a trifle shorter than any of the others, so that it just cleared the ground, and escaped having any of the weight of the cabinet upon it; and here, no doubt, is the object of our search."

As he spoke the screw moved, and he got one half of the leg quite off; when a hollow space was visible, and within it was a thick compressed roll of papers. Harry Dean turned pale with excitement, and his hand trembled so, that he could not hold the papers, which the lawyer observing, he said to him—

"Allow me, sir, if you please."

"Yes," said Harry. "You read the endorsement to me, for the letters danced before my eyes, and I could not do so, I pray you read it to me."

The lawyer read in a clear voice an endorsement upon the roll of papers to the following effect—

"Papers and documents connected with Amilie Beaufort, and the birth of K——"

"The mystery will be quite unravelled," said Harry Dean. "It can only mean her who is called Kate Destern."

———

CHAPTER CXIII.

MADAME ZADZED'S PAPERS.

HARRY DEAN's feelings had been so strongly excited that he was compelled to sit down to try to recover himself. He had never before felt so overcome.

"You are faint," said the attorney. "Allow me to ring for a glass of water."

"Oh, no, no, I shall be all right in a moment or two. I am so deeply interested in all that in any way concerns that young lady whom I hope soon to make my wife, that I did at the instant feel a little indisposed. It is going off now."

"I'm glad of it, you looked very ill."

"No doubt. The fact was, I had worked myself up in this matter to too great a pitch of excitement, and then the sudden discovery of these papers, after having, in a manner of speaking, prepared for a complete disappointment, produced a revulsion of feeling that for the moment overcame me. You see I am better now."

"Yes, your colour has returned."

"Oh yes. I am now as usual. But you see, sir, of late, my nerves have been much shaken. I have never, and I don't think I shall while I live, get over the shock of supposing, as I firmly did, that Miss Destern had been murdered by the villain Wilkins. I only wonder it did not kill me."

"Time will do wonders in restoring you."

Harry Dean shook his head, as with a faint smile he said—

"I would not have Wilkins to know how deep a revenge he has really had. But let us look at these papers at once. I only hope, whoever they may prove Kate to be, that I shall find her the child of an honest man—I care not for his gentility of birth; but be she whom she may, she will be the same to me, for she is good enough and pure enough to redeem a world."

"Ah, Mr. Dean, you deserve her."

"That is the greatest compliment you could pay me. But open the papers, I give you full authority to do so. Open them at once, sir."

The attorney untied a piece of green silk that held the papers together, and the first one he took up was a letter addressed "To Miss Amilie Beaufort, Verona." The handwriting looked as though it had been disguised, and the paper was of that thin gauzy texture which is common on the continent.

"Shall I read it, sir?" said the lawyer.

"Yes. But by whom is it signed?"

"It is anonymous."

"That is a disappointment. But read on, sir. Is it a long letter?"

"No. A very few words."

"Go on then with it, I pray you, at once; I can listen to you, although I really think that just at present I should not have courage to read the documents myself. I pray you go on, sir."

The lawyer read as follows:—

"My Amilie—Can I resist, on the eve before that day which is to make you mine, writing to you a few words, to tell you how happy I am. To-morrow sees the fruition of all my dearest hopes; and, by the aid of a priest of that denomination that you have by your mother been taught to prefer, you will be made mine. Ah, my Amilie, I am happy, happy, happy. This is from him who is your own upon the muster roll of angels."

"Is that all?"

"Yes," said the lawyer. "Short and sweet, that is. But, Mr. Dean, let me advise you to wait for a few hours, until you are more yourself, before you dip deeper into a correspondence that may in some of its features much distress you. Shall we make an appointment for this evening?"

"Yes," said Harry Dean. "I feel that it will be better to do so. Will you come to me at eight o'clock, or shall I come to you?"

"I will wait upon you, sir, at the hour you have named, which is a specially convenient one for me. In the meantime, I shall feel better pleased for you to keep these papers than as though they remained with me."

Harry Dean mechanically thrust the packet into a pocket in the breast of his coat; and then having between them restored the cabinet to its usual appearance, and screwed on the leg again, they left the house. In the meantime, Tony was at the police-office in Bow-street. The two housebreakers, whom we may call very clever practitioners, took the whole affair in a perfectly easy way; but the waiter, who made his appearance at a police-office for the first time on so very serious a charge, looked the very picture of physical and moral prostration. He had to be fairly assisted into the court by the police; and when in the dock, he seemed like a man deprived of all power of self-support, and ready to double up at his joints, and fall in a heap to the floor. The charge had been duly entered as a burglary, and the first person examined was Tony, who was asked to detail all he knew of the case. He created no little merriment by the mode in which he told the tale ; but what excited the risibility of the spectators as much as anything was, a hideous groan from John Such, the waiter, at every pause that Tony made in his narration.

"I wish, prisoner," said the magistrate, "that you would not make that hideous noise."

"I can't help it, your worship."

"Oh, nonsense. You can help it very well. Have you any legal adviser in this affair ?—for if you have, I should strongly advise him to advise you not to make yourself so disagreeable. It won't do your situation any good."

"I have no legal adviser," said John Such, "but I want one. I've got money."

"Money," said an attorney who was present, sidling up to the prisoner, and adding in a whisper—"how much ?"

"Five pounds."

"Hand it over. That'll do. Ahem ! Allow me, your worship, to request, as the evidence by no means touches my client, Mr. Such, that he should be discharged at once. He is a highly respectable gentleman, I assure your worship, and is far above committing himself by any such transaction as that in which by some accident he has become a little involved."

"If he is above committing himself," said the magistrate, "I shall not be above committing him."

"Really ?"

"Yes. Really sir. So if your client has anything to say, perhaps he had better defer it until he is at the Old Bailey, for it won't avail him here. Juries sometimes believe things that magistrates won't."

"Of course," said the attorney, "Mr. Such will listen quietly to the evidence, and then give, through me, a triumphant reply to it."

"Very well," said the magistrate, "go on with the evidence."

The two policemen deposed to hiding in the room, and finally to the capture of the thieves ; and the case being so far concluded, the magistrate asked the prisoners individually, what they had to say, and the two housebreakers at once replied—

"Nothing at present."

John Such looked anxiously at his lawyer.

"Really your worship," said the lawyer, "when you come to consider my client, the highly respectable John Such, only went to the house to see what good he could do to the inmates of it, whom he so much respected, the case alters its aspect, and if he be remanded, I am prepared upon another examination to bring forward a gentleman who is now a little way out of town, to prove that he some hours before announced his determination to go and look to the safety of the hotel, as, having seen some suspicious looking men lurking about, he was apprehensive of something."

"Indeed," said the magistrate.

"Yes, your worship. So, a-hem ! John Such being innocent, as is clearly shown by what the witness Thorpe has sworn—"

"Go to the deuce !" cried Tony, " I never swore anything of the sort."

"Come—come," said the attorney, "did you not swear that John Such said ' here they are. Seize the thieves ?'"

"No."

"Be cautious. An indictment for perjury, young man, is a very uncomfortable thing, recollect."

"Perhaps you know that by experience," said Tony.

There was a laugh at this, which disconcerted the lawyer, but he returned to the attack, and said, in a tone of bullying, to Tony—

"Come—come. Books are kept here ; recollect yourself. Did you not say that John Such only joined the housebreakers for the purpose of giving them into custody ? I have no doubt but the two prisoners at the bar will themselves admit as much."

"Gammon !" said one.

"Walker !" said the other.

"It's all nonsense," said Tony— "he's the worst of the three."

"Very good," said the attorney. "For all these reasons, I hope your worship will see the propriety of committing the two men who have given the names of James and Tomkins, and of only remanding my client until this day week, by which time I dare say I can bring forward evidence entirely to exculpate him. He is evidently a highly respectable man. Is it likely that a man with this in his pocket, would set about a common house robbery?"

As he spoke, he produced the five-pound note that John Such had given him, in order to add point to his argument; and as he did so his eyes for the first time fell particularly upon it, and in one moment his countenance changed.

"What's the matter now?" said Tony.

"Oh! you guilty vagabond!" said the attorney, shaking his head at John Such, who resorted again to his groans; "I now perceive, that not only are you guilty, but that you are decidedly the worst of the three. Why you deserve hanging."

"Dear me!" said the magistrate, "what has so suddenly changed your opinion of your client, Mr. Roberts?"

"Why, your worship, this note is—is—oh, you wretch!—is upon The Bank of Elegance, instead of the Bank of England!"

A roar of laughter followed this announcement, in which the magistrate most heartily joined, and when silence was restored, he said—

"Then, Mr. Roberts, you have no objection to the committal of your client?"

"None in the least."

"I apply," said John Such, "for a warrant against that rascal of an attorney. He is well known as a thief and a murderer, and he has changed the note I gave him, which was a genuine one of the Bank of England, for that which he holds in his hand."

"You infamous rascal!"

"Stop!" said the magistrate, "I cannot allow such language here; and since a charge has been made of a serious nature, I am bound to attend to it. Officers, take that person into custody."

"Me?—Me?" asked the lawyer.

"Search him, and see if he has in his possession a genuine five-pound note."

"2040," whispered a voice in John Such's ear; and upon turning he saw no one near him but a very grim-looking policeman. But yet he took the hint, and he said at once—

"Please your worship, the number of my note—it was the only one I had—was 2040. I gave it to that man to defend me; and he, I suppose, finding that I was poor and friendless, thought he would rob me of my money and leave me to my fate."

"Here's a note, your worship," said an officer who had been searching the lawyer's pockets. "Here's a note, your worship."

"Give it to me. Humph! The number of this note, which is a genuine one, is 2040."

"Ha! ha! ha!" said some one in the court.

"Silence! silence! Officer, find that person out, and bring him before me. I will commit him to prison."

A stir was made, but no person was found. The lawyer passed his hand several times across his forehead, as though all his cunning had deserted him, leaving him in such a state of mental confusion, that he was incapable of defending himself. The magistrate shook his head with great gravity; but before he could speak, the attorney recovered himself sufficiently to say—

"I am being made the victim of some suddenly concocted plot. This is horrible. I had a good five-pound note in my pocket as well as the bad one I received from the prisoner at the bar."

"How did the prisoner at the bar know the number of the good note that you had in your pocket?" said the magistrate calmly.

"That to me is inexplicable."

"Well, we are bound to act upon evidence. I shall remand you until this day week, as you are rather fond of remands for that period. Take him away, officer. The other three prisoners stand committed for trial."

"Remand me!" shouted the attorney, "remand me!—an attorney!—oh, good gracious! no.—Please to consider my professional reputation!"

"Your professional reputation is a matter that the least that is said about it is, I think, the best," said the magistrate. "Officer, remove your prisoner."

"Bail, your worship—I apply for bail?"

"I refuse it."

The lawyer was duly handcuffed, and led, not in the most gentle manner in the world, out of the court. Again a voice said—"Ha! ha! ha!" and again an active search was made for the person who said it, but, as before, without avail. As for John Such, he was rather bewildered at the whole transaction ; for, in good truth, richly as the rascal deserved every kind of retribution that could come over him, the attorney was victimised by some one. John Such hoped that, whoever that some one was, they would prove friendly to him,

since by so strange an accident he had become an instrument of their revenge ; for the fact was, and he knew it perfectly well, he had given the attorney the note upon The Bank of Elegance, and he had only done so with the hope that before detecting it the attorney might do him some service. Tony was quite delighted at what had taken place, and he felt very much inclined himself to say ha! ha! ha! as well as the unknown producer of these sounds of revengeful jocularity. As it was, he put on an air of mock-condolence, and as the lawyer passed him he said—

"How do you feel now?"

"Revenge!" growled the attorney.

"Oh, for shame!" said Tony. "Remember, you ugly rascal, that books are kept here, and that your name will occupy a very unenviable place in them for the future. I wish you joy where you are going ; for I really never saw such an ill-looking rogue in all my life. You ought to be shut up, Mr. Roberts, for fear of frightening women and children."

CHAPTER CXIV.

THE MYSTERIOUS DOCUMENTS.

THE document which Harry Dean, in conjunction with his solicitor from Lincoln's inn, had so mysteriously obtained possession of, now filled up, by the many conjectures they awakened, the whole imagination of Harry Dean. And with a feeling which he in vain tried to analyse, and which he could not rally from, he shrunk from an investigation of those papers. It seemed to him as though some hidden monitor had addressed to him—" Be content with what you know, and if these papers really concern her whom you love, what more can they tell you of her than that she is young, and beautiful, and innocent?" But yet was it in human nature to know that there was a secret, which required but to be looked at to be revealed, and yet to look not at it? Has there ever lived in this world one man who, even in the plenitude of a rare philosophy, could have exercised such a controul over his feelings and his passions? We may venture to say, not one. No: prudence may preach to human nature to be content with wealth—to be content with station—to be content with knowledge—but when was it content with either? When did the intellect of man prompt him to say, while there was before him an unexplored landscape—" Thus far will I go, but no farther?" And thus, although his better intellect told him not to look at those papers, so strangely removed from the depository in which Madame Zadzed had placed them, Harry Dean eagerly awaited the hour when he was to look on them in conjunction with the attorney whose assistance he had enlisted. The longest expected, and most distant hour, will come at last; and so, at length, the reader will please to peep into a small private room, in which he will find Harry Dean and the solicitor sitting, with the papers taken from the leg of Madame Zadzed's bureau before them. There is visible agitation upon the face of Harry Dean.

" Take courage, sir," said the lawyer, " it is extremely unlikely that there is anything here that ought to give you real uneasiness."

" It may be so, and yet my heart fails me."

" Shall I take the papers home, and look over them first ?

" Oh, no—no—no."

" Well, I did not propose doing so because I would advise such a course, for your imagination is now so much affected, that if you did not become acquainted with every word that these documents contain, the probability is that your imagination would supply the omission by making you believe there is to be found in them much worse than any reality can be."

" That is my own opinion," said Harry Dean, " and, therefore, I will not shrink from the expression of it. I pray you read them to me, and not, from any fancied regard for my feelings, keep back a paragraph or word that they may contain."

The lawyer bowed his assent, and after looking at the topmost paper of the lot, he said—

" Here is a sort of evidence, which, by being of an explanatory character, it is as well I should read to you."

" I pray you do so."

The lawyer read from the paper as follows :—

" Fancying that I may meet with death at some moment when I may be either not willing or not able to give the requisite information regarding a subject that will, I hope, help me to have revenge upon the only real enemy I have in the world, I have thought proper to commit to writing certain matters in full, that may be implicitly relied upon. The transactions to which the accompanying papers refer are so curious and out of the commom order of things, that were there not living witnesses to some parts of them, it would be impossible for me to hope for credence. I shall, however, give such dates, and such circumstantial evidence, as will set completely at rest all scruples, and convince the most sceptical of the exact truth, undiminished and unexaggerated, of what is to be found in the accompanying narrative. I have thought it better for the sake of brevity and conspicuity, to relate the incidents in the third person, and so speak of myself as an actor in the scenes through which I passed, as I would speak of any one else, only with this difference and advantage as regards myself, namely, that knowing my own thoughts and my own hidden springs of action, while I could only guess at those of others, it is my hope and expectation that before these lines reach any mortal gaze my vengeance will be fully consummated' against Lord Battaney."

"Battaney!" exclaimed Harry Dean.

"Yes, sir, that is the name."

"Go on—go on."

"That is all, with the exception of the signature, which is 'Madame Delcroix, Zadzed.'"

"It is as I expected."

"Indeed. Pray what?"

"Go on, sir, I beg you don't pay particular heed to any disjointed expressions that may fall from me. when we have concluded the examination of these papers, I make no doubt but that I shall see sufficient cause to make you confidentially acquainted with all that is so deeply interesting to me.

"I shall be proud of your confidence, sir."

"In the meantime, pray proceed with the papers. Do they seem to be in regular consecutive order, as they lie before you?"

"They do, sir."

After a few moments' pause, the lawyer commenced, what may be fairly enough entitled

MADAME ZADZED'S NARRATIVE.

The sun of a Neapolitan autumn was gilding the waters of the glorious bay, and glancing upon the fluttering sails of a fleet of galleys and gay craft, when, from the marble steps of a chateau, which was situated so close to the bay as to have its principal approach from its waters, an eight-oared galley with a crimson covering was pushed off. The sail was set, and with a gentle breeze fanning it, the little craft quietly stood out for the open sea. It was the intention of those, who in all the gaiety and exuberance of youth, formed the passengers in that gay galley, to make sail about four or five English miles from the shore, and then return with the setting sun behind them, enjoying the soft cool land breeze that at that hour was always incidental to the latitude. The party consisted of a lady, rather stricken in years, who was the widowed proprietress of the chateau, from the marble steps of which they had embarked—her son, a youth of about, nineteen years of age, and her niece— an orphan recently from Languedoc, and whose name was Maria Delcroix Zadzed. The elderly lady's name was Castro, and the niece was the only child of her sister, who had been left destitute, and had found at Naples an asylum with her widowed aunt, who, living as she had done alone with her son, Felix, felt the want of female society, and was glad to welcome her sister's orphan child to the comforts of an almost princely abode, for her husband had been a merchant of great wealth and repute. He had died five years previous to the evening upon which I commence this narrative, leaving her with the young Felix, then fourteen years of age. All was life, joy, and animation on board that little bark, as it gaily floated over the pure waters of that unrivalled bay, and no thought of danger occurred to the imaginations of any of the party, either to themselves or others. But this feeling of security was not to last long. As the sun set of a fiery redness, some black clouds, rare enough in that latitude, began to strew themselves, and to give notice of one of those squally storms in the Medeterranean which sometimes, to the surprise of all navigating that sea, bring desolation in their track. In the course of ten minutes, the black clouds had increased in size amazingly, and so powerful a wind arose, that for safety sake the sail was compelled to be taken in. From the moment that the unmistakeable appearance of a squall had shown itself, the two men who had charge of the boat, had turned its head towards the shore, but the boiling surge for a time baffled all their endeavours. However, as regarded actual danger to the little vessel, there really was not much, and Signora Castro was cheering the falling spirits of her niece, Maria, when Felix cried—

"Behold yon felucca! She sinks !—she sinks !"

All eyes were immediately turned in the direction to which he pointed, and a felucca was seen with tattered sails labouring heavily in the trough of the sea. We found afterwards that her principal injuries had resulted from a collision with some other vessel of superior weight, for there was nothing in the actual storm which ought to have reduced her to such a condition as she was in. She settled for a moment in the water—gave a convulsive kind of shiver from stem to stern, and down she went. It is as needless as it would be impossible, to attempt to describe the feelings with which the people in the boat of the Signora Castro witnessed this sad catastrophe. The head of the boat was, by the orders of the lady, immediately put about, for the purpose of making an attempt to save any of the crew of the vessel that had gone down, who might be struggling in the waves, but for some few minutes no one was seen. The Signora Castro was upon the point of giving up the search, and proceeding to her own home with as much expedition as possible, when her niece observed a dark object rise at times to the surface of the waves. She pointed it out to the boatman, who by great exertions at length succeeded in recovering it, and then they found it was some one faintly swimming. By great exertion, a young man rudely attired was got into the boat from the sea, and in a state of insensibility he there lay until the servants of the chateau carried him to a chamber. There was nothing peculiarly interesting about the apparel of this stranger, who had been thus rescued from death. On the contrary, there was upon his face an expression of libertinism that was displeasing, but he had youth in his favour, and the romantic circumstances under which he had been thrown upon the care of those who had saved him endeared him to them. During the few days of repose which were necessary for his recovery, he was waited upon by Marie Zadzed with as much care and tenderness as though he had been her brother, and when he was able to walk in the gardens of the chateau, no one could be more profuse in thanks than he was, for the kindness he had met with. He announced himself to be a Lord Battaney, from England.

At this juncture of the narrative, Harry Dean made another exclamation of intense interest, mingled with surprise, and the lawyer paused for a moment or two.

"Go on—go on," said Harry Dean.

He then proceeded without taking any further notice of the interruption.

To comprehend why Marie Zadzed so soon—as she did—gave her heart to the Englishman, her position should be considered. She was an orphan, and utterly destitute, and although she had everything to expect, and certainly nothing to complain of from her aunt, the spirit of independence was strong within her, and when this Lord Battaney whispered the words of love in her ear, his were the first lips from which she had heard the gentle accents. No wonder, then, that she yielded to the influence of new feelings and new passions, and as his professed intentions were of the most honourable character, there seemed to her young heart nothing to apprehend.

" My aristocratic friends in England,' he said, "will not be pleased at my marrying a young portionless French girl ; but after a time those prejudices will vanish, particularly when they understand that you are willing to be married according to the form of the Church of England, and to conform to the Protestant faith."

He had previously talked me into so much submission. In vain did Marie even then, after she had given her consent, implore him to allow the ceremony to be likewise performed in a manner conformable to the Catholic faith. He would not do so.—He swore that it would exasperate his family, and for ever shut the door upon reconciliation.

"No, Marie," he said, " we must be married by an English clergyman who is now in Naples, and who is a friend of mine. Your aunt, even, must not know what has happened for some days. Then her forgiveness will be easily obtained, and after that, I will break the matter to my family."

In an evil hour Marie consented to this secret marriage. She had to meet him by the great entrance of the theatre

San Carlos by the hour of sunset, and she was true to her appointment. In a few minutes he joined her with an air of exultation upon his face, which she mistook for real, honest love.

"Ah, my charmer," he said, "you have indeed bound me to you for ever."

"To your hands I commit my happiness," she said. "God will see how you keep the trust. I have believed all that you have told me, and——"

He interrupted her impetuously, saying—

"Ah, do you doubt me now at this eleventh hour? Is it now that you would cast the stain of suspicion upon me, when my heart is only full of the most sincere affection for you? Oh, Marie! Marie!—is this right—is this kind of you?"

The only reply she could make to this passionate appeal at such a time was to declare that she was his and his only. He clasped her arms closely in his, and hurried her to a house not far from the theatre, the door of which was open.

"I shrink," she said.

"Shrink?" he cried. "Oh, why is hesitation? Only tell me, Marie, that you no longer love me, and I will at once return with you to your aunt's palazzo, where, amid the gloom of its faded rooms, you may congratulate yourself upon having broken the heart of one who loved you as never yet was woman loved."

"Oh, no—no—no!"

"You do not repent—you would not retract?"

"No, no!"

They both hastily crossed the threshold of the house, and in an apartment dimly lighted, and hastily, as it appeared, prepared for the occasion, they found an English clergyman in his canonical costume. This was a sight which raised the drooping sprits of Marie. Willingly she reproached herself for having for one moment shrunk from ratifying the promise she had given to one who had stooped from his high estate to sue for the hand of the poor orphan girl, who could give him nothing but her heart in exchange for wealth and rank.

——

CHAPTER CXV.

THE NARRATIVE CONTINUED.

"Now," he whispered, "are your doubts satisfied?"

"Ah, I should have had none," she replied. "Forgive me! They were high treason to your affections. I will never again doubt your lightest word."

"How charming," he said.

There was a something in the tone in which those two words "how charming!" were uttered, that jarred upon the feelings of Marie. She had certainly never heard such a tone from Lord Battaney before, but was she, at that moment when he was about to make her his wife, to shrink back, and refuse to ratify the contract, because he had some particular note in his voice which she had not before observed, and which, after all, might be quite imaginative upon her part?—no, no, she could not.

"Are the parties ready?" said the clergyman, in a solemn tone.

"Yes," said Lord Battaney, "I am here, and here is the lady."

"Have you duly reflected, my lord?"

"I have, and I hope, reverend sir, that at this juncture you will be content to perform your office, and spare me any further entreaties or remonstrances upon a subject, concerning which you must feel my mind is thoroughly made up."

From this, Marie guessed that the English clergyman had opposed himself to the match, no doubt, from its great inequality.

"I will say no more," remarked the clergyman, mildly, "and will certainly perform my office for you. Upon our last meeting, I begged your lordship to consider the step you were about to take. If you have done so, and still persevere in it, it would ill become me to oppose you."

"I am satisfied," said Lord Battaney, and I am quite sure that in a short time even you will see good cause to congratulate me upon being so fortunate as to win the affections of so accomplished and beautiful a young lady."

All this, as may be well supposed, was most distressing conversation to Marie and she hung down her head until it was over. The clergyman seemed to think it necessary to say something, and in a gentle voice he remarked—

"Pardon me, young lady; if I tell you candidly that I have made an effort to persuade my friend from this marriage, I did so from conscientious motives, fearing that where there was a great inequality of rank, happiness was by no means secure."

Marie merely bowed, and Lord Battaney said, rather impatiently—

"Happiness is never secure, but all we can do in this world is to take the most likely way that presents itself for securing it, and my opinion is, that for me, that way is to unite myself in the holy and indissoluble bands of matrimony with my fair and excellent Marie."

After this the clergyman did not think proper to say more upon the subject, and the ceremony commenced. To be sure Marie, in a low voice said to her husband elect—

"Ought there not to be witnesses?"

"No, darling," he replied, "not to marriages of the nobility."

She was content with this lie, coming as it did from lips that she thought, in the fondness of her heart, could not lie, and the ceremony went on, being conducted by the clergyman in a very feeling and sombre manner indeed. In less than ten minutes Marie fancied herself Lady Battaney. The clergyman closed his book.

"Mine and mine only!" said Battaney, as he kissed the cheek of his bride.

Marie burst into tears.

"Nay, dear one, why do you weep? Are you not happy now? Are we not now one, and what power upon earth can separate us? Why those tears, my Marie? Dearest and best, be of good cheer."

"Do not blame *all* the tears," replied Marie. "Some of them are tears of joy."

Marie felt very, very happy. Now she felt that there was one in the world who clung to her, and to whom she could cling from pure affection, and the tears that she shed upon that occasion were indeed tears of joy.

*   *   *   *   *

Five months elapsed, and all was joy. By various excuses Lord Battaney had made his young wife believe that circumstances were of such moment that he could not take the steps he wished; and

from the lips of those we love any excuses suffice. In her dream of joy Marie was not very special in her criticisms. And yet there were times at which she would press the subject rather closely upon her husband. One soft and gentle evening, in particular, she did so.

"My aunt," she said, "and my cousin Felix, both now rejoice in my union with you. Oh, when will the time come for your friends to know that you have taken to your heart one who loves you so well as I do?"

"Soon—soon."

"But that word 'soon' has been your only reply to me for many a long and weary week."

"Long and weary week? Do you want to quarrel, Marie?"

"Quarrel?"

"Aye, quarrel! that is the word. If you want to quarrel with me, say so at once."

Marie shrunk back, and the once devoted and tender Lord Battaney left the room with such a scowl upon his face as she had never before seen it wear. She sat for more than two hours inactive—indeed the twilight had deepened into night, and she did not move. God only knows what evil passions passed in grim array before her imagination during that period of time. She could not herself detail with anything like the concise order of narrative what she then felt. The summing up of all was to be found at last in the faintly uttered words—

"He loves me not."

From that time her eyes were seldom undimmed by tears, and the light of joy had gone from her—her step lost its bounding elasticity—her cheeks lost their bloom, and in six weeks more she recovered but the shadow only of her former beauty—for she had beauty. The bright and beautiful summer had come again, and had reached its height, when, with a countenance upon which some anxiety was manifest, Lord Battaney approached her with an open letter in his hand.

"I have heard from England," he said.

The face of the sufferer flushed for a moment, but she said nothing.

"Do you hear me?" he added, hastily.

"Yes."

"Well, it will be necessary formly to return immediately. Some family affairs render such a step now absolutely necessary."

"And—and—I——"

"Ah, that is what I wished to tell you about. What do you think of doing, Marie?"

"Doing?"

"Yes. Hang all sentiment and tears, and that sort of nonsense. I don't mean to play you a shabby trick, and never did. You shall have as much as would keep you comfortable, even in England, but in Italy you may live like a little princess, so I don't see that there need be any fuss about it; for my part, I don't like a woman who is always melting into tears, and your aspect, for some time now, has really been enough to give any one the horrors."

"I—I will endeavour to be more cheerful with you."

"With me? Ha! ha!"

"Whom should I be with but with you? If I am not with you, I am out of my place. If you will but sometimes—only sometimes—speak to me as of old, I shall yet be happy; I am not so very unreasonable as to suppose that the first furor of passion is to last for ever, but let it be tempered down to a quiet feeling, and you will find me such again."

"Psha! nonsense! You know my will by this time, that you cannot go with me. I am about to show myself among my equals. I believe my Italian intrigues have made some noise even in London, but I am not going to import any of their practical results."

"Listen now. Can you say this to a wife?"

"A wife? Ha! ha! A wife?"

"Silence, Lord Battaney. Listen to me. Am I not your wife?"

"Certainly not. Don't think to deceive me. Upon my life, you act your part well, and I don't know now but it would be a good thing to take you to London, and introduce you to the stage. Come, come, a scene is what I detest. You know as well as I do that our marriage was a delusion; the clergyman was an old friend of mine—an artist. Don't think to deceive me with an idea that you have been hoodwinked as to the real character of your position for so long."

Marie held her head for a moment or two with both her hands, and then she fell senseless to the ground, with a shriek that appalled even Lord Battaney.

*　　*　　*　　*

"Where am I?" said Marie, in a faint voice, as she awakened and found herself in bed; "where am I? Oh, God, what a frightful dream''

"Hush!" said a voice, " husha You must not speak yet; your medic-attendant forbids any sort of conversation at present."

"But tell me where I am?"

"In your aunt's palazzo, to be sure. Where else should you be? I am a nurse employed to attend you; so now be quiet."

At this moment Felix came to the door of the chamber, and cried out—

"Ah, Marie, you are better, for I hear your voice."

"Come in! come in!"

"No," said the nurse, positively, "no. It must not be. The learned Doctor Stolfe says that it must not be, and so it must not. Well, Master Felix, I wash my hands of it, and won't stay while you stay; and if any harm comes of all this, it will not be my fault. What's a doctor and a nurse for, if they are not to say what is to be, and what is not to be?"

So speaking, the nurse bounced out of the room in a great passion; but Felix tenderly approached the bed-side of his cousin—she seized his hand, and looking with streaming eyes into his face, she spoke to him—

"Felix, by the devout hopes you have in this world and the next,—by all your expectations of eternal bliss, answer truly to me what I shall ask of you."

"I will—I will."

"How long have I been here?"

"A night and a portion of to-day only. Lord Battaney brought you here, saying that you were unwell, and he could not get you so much attention as we could in our affection for you bestow upon you. My mother, instead of a hireling, would have been by your bed-side, but indisposition confines her to her couch."

"Felix! Felix!"

She felt half choked, and yet she had made up her mind to tell him.

"Felix, do you know the cause of this sudden attack of insensibility? Tell me truly, if you do."

"Indeed, cousin Marie, I do not."

"Then Felix, it arose from Lord Battaney informing me that I was not his wife, and that the ceremony, which I, and we all thought made me such, was a mock one. At the instant of that communication I fell to the floor as if struck by the destroying angel. That is the truth, Felix. Tell your mother for me. Tell her all, and then pray, Felix, that I may be soon with the dead."

Felix spoke not one word, but pressing her hand for a moment, he rushed from the chamber and left her in tears. What happened to Felix, Marie was not cognisant of for some time, but as she afterwards became fully cognisant of it, she is able to append it to this memoir. When he left his cousin's bedside, he did not go near his mother, but proceeded direct to the furnished palazzo that had been hired by Lord Battaney. There he found everything in confusion. The hall was filled with trunks and imperials, and there was every indication of a journey of some extent being on the tapis. Forcing his way onwards, Felix asked for Lord Battaney.

"His lordship can't be seen," said a courier.

"Why not?"

The manner of the young man forced a reluctant civility from the courier, who replied with more respect—

"Why, sir, his lordship will leave Naples in two hours, and he is busy making some arrangements for his departure."

"And yet I must see him. Where is he?"

"He is in the room up stairs. Above here, sir."

"Thank you."

"But, sir, I shall be blamed if you proceed to force your way into his presence. Pray, sir, consider."

"Fear nothing, I will take care to explain that you did all in your power to keep me from interrupting his lordship."

Felix ascended the stairs, two, and sometimes three at a stride. He was then not quite twenty years of age, and by no means so powerful or large in frame as most young men of his years, but what nature had denied to him in physical power, she had attempted, if she had not succeeded, to make up to him in courage, and that rare spirit which calculates nothing in the shape of danger when something that it is right to attempt has to be accomplished. A partially open door, immediately at the top of the staircase, disclosed to Felix a room in which he had passed so many pleasant hours in the society of his cousin Marie, beneath whose feet he then little suspected such a mine was about to explode for her destruction. Felix entered the room without a moment's hesitation. Lord Battaney was packing a small writing case with private papers. In spite of an effrontery that rarely fell to the lot of any one man to possess, the face of Lord Battaney flushed crimson at the sight of the young man, and he affected to be so busy packing his papers, that he could not look up. Assuming, however, a carelessness of voice, he said—

"Ah, Felix! A fine day—be seated. I hope nothing that may have happened, or that may still happen, will deprive me of the pleasure of your acquaintance, and of the hope of serving you. If you will come to England, I will undertake to get you some employment that will make a man of you."

"Lord Battaney," said Felix, in a calm deep, clear voice, that rung through the room, "you are a villain."

The note case dropped from Battaney's hands, and he glared at Felix as though with a glance he could kill him.

CHAPTER CXVI.

THE REVENGE OF THE BLIGHTED HEART.

PROBABLY Lord Battaney thought such a glance as he bent upon so mere a youth as Felix, would have the effect of intimidating him, but if such was his impression he was most miserably mistaken, for still regarding him fixedly, Felix repeated—

"You are a villain!"

"And pray, sir," cried Battaney, raising his voice, "who authorised you to be a judge of my actions?"

"God," said Felix, "who gave me the heart to loathe them."

"Begone, sir, I waste not my time upon boys. Begone, or I will call my servants and have you turned from my doors with ignominy."

"You base coward," said Felix, advancing. As he advanced Lord Battaney stepped back, for there was a something about the youth's aspect which bespoke him dangerous, and the forward movement of the one, and retrograde movement of the other, continued until Felix was close to the table at which Lord Battaney had been arranging his papers. He happened to cast his eyes

upon the table, and there he saw a pair of richly mounted pistols.

"Ah!" he said, "if these be loaded I am avenged."

By the cry that came from the lips of the coward Battaney, Felix felt convinced they were charged, and if any further evidence of that fact had been wanting, he would have found it in the manner in which Battaney now crouched before him."

"You do not mean to murder me?" he said.

"It would not be a murder," said Felix, "if I were to shoot you through the head now. It would be the execution only of a great criminal, but it shall not be said that I took even the advantage over you that chance has given me. You shall fight me."

"As you please," replied Battaney, wonderfully recovering himself when he found Felix was not going to shoot him at once. "As you please. If you feel yourself aggrieved, you have but to name the time, place, and weapons, and you will not find me backward in meeting you to give you the satisfaction you require."

"Agreed! The time is now; the place, this room; the weapons, these pistols—no doubt well charged by yourself. Take one."

As he spoke, he threw one of the weapons across the table to Battaney, who, turning of a death-like paleness picked it up.

"I will not fight," he said, "without the usual formalities. If you kill me, people will call it murder, since we were without witnesses."

"Of future consequences I am regardless," said Felix. "Here you shall fight, or here at my hands you shall receive your death without fighting. Take your place, sir, and fire!"

"I might," said Lord Battaney, "take a most unfair advantage of you, but it would be contrary to my character as an English nobleman to do so."

"You have already shown that it is not contrary to the character of an English nobleman to take the most cowardly advantage of one much weaker than I. You are a coward! a villain! and as a natural consequence, a liar!"

"You did not hear me out," said Battaney, his pale lips quivering with passion. "You have not heard me out. I was about to tell you that although my pistol is, that which you hold is not primed."

Felix cast a glance immediately at his pistol. Lord Battaney at once took that opportunity of the young man's eyes being off him, and raising the weapon he held, he shot Felix through the heart. The young man stood while any one might have counted six, during which he made an effort to speak, but his voice failed him, and he fell dead upon the floor. One servant, a valet to Lord Battaney, who afterwards upon his death-bed declared that he had listened to the whole

of the preceding scene, rushed into the room.

"My lord! my lord!" he said, "say he shot himself

"Yes, yes. Do you know?"

"All—all!"

"Depend upon your reward, then, and keep the thing quiet."

When the servants and the courier, who were below, reached the room, which they did a few minutes after they had been alarmed by the discharge of the pistol, they found Felix lying upon the floor dead, and with a *discharged* pistol in his hand. Battaney and his valet had adroitly changed the weapons. That very day Lord Battaney sailed for England.

*   *   *   *   *

It was about two hours after that transaction that Marie was aroused from a light slumber, into which she had fallen, by a scream, and upon looking up, she saw her aunt by her bedside. The appearance of the Signora Castro was terrible in the extreme, as with a loud and vehement voice, she cried—

"Marie! Marie! He is murdered! My Felix—my son—the joy of my heart! He is murdered! and his murderer is Battaney—Battaney, the man who has been the bane of your happiness and of mine!—Battaney, the betrayer! the murderer—the—the—vengeance!"

A gush of blood came from her mouth, and she fell to the floor. A blood-vessel had given way upon the lungs, and the Signora Castro went to rejoin her son in that world where there is no sin and no sorrow. The senses of Marie nearly gave way under this accumulation of disasters, and she lay for a long period hovering between life and death. Physicians were summoned from all parts to minister to her, and at length she was declared convalescent, and told that she inherited her aunt's property. She was alone. It was twelve months after that before she fully recovered her strength, and during that time her appearance had entirely changed from the girl to that of the woman. During that twelve months she cherished but one idea, and that was how to be revenged upon Lord Battaney. Her child—yes, a child was born during the delirium of her illness—her child lived. It was a boy; but Marie could not regard it with any feeling but dislike and horror, for there was upon even its infant face all the worst expressions and features of its brutal and inhuman father. She placed this child with poor people to bring up, and they eventually, at her solicitation and her expense, removed to England with it. Marie even once thought of killing Battaney.

"Why should I kill him?" she said to herself. "Death is the inevitable lot of all, virtuous as well as wicked! By killing him I may only be saving him from the much worse pangs of some disease that otherwise would kill him. What revenge would it be to me to kill him? None—none—none!—I will make him suffer—death is no punishment—a momentary pang, and all is over. I would have him live and suffer. The knife and poison would soon put an end to his career; but no, I must and will have a deeper revenge than that!"

It was about this time that Marie got acquainted with an English physician, named Wilkins, whom she found, after a time, to be a very unscrupulous agent in her affairs. He, by some means, was always able to give her information of Battaney, and finally, it was by him she was informed that he, Lord Battaney, was upon the continent again. After a long and painful struggle with her feelings, Marie resolved to see him, and she repaired to Florence, where she understood he was. She merely sent up to his hotel a message that a lady wished to wait upon him at a certain hour, and at that hour she went. It is unnecessary here to say that pure and innocent as Marie Delcroix Zadzed was when Lord Battaney first became acquainted with her, she was now no longer so. A reflection upon the injuries she had suffered had destroyed all her confidence in Heaven's goodness and fostering care, and consequently she had cast off all religious feelings. Revenge, which was always uppermost in her heart, had changed her from a woman to a fiend, and the Marie who waited upon Lord Battaney at the hotel in Florence was as different a person from the Marie with whom he had contracted the mock marriage at Naples, as one person could possibly be from another. He did not know her when she entered the room, but he was unaltered. There was the same smile—a smile, which now that she saw

it again, she wondered had ever deceived her. He rose and handed her a chair.

"To what happy circumstance," he said, "am I to attribute the honour of this visit, madame?"

"Do you not know me?"

The voice startled him. There was something in it that struck familiarly upon his ears. He looked at her fixedly, and then said—

"Is it possible? are you——"

"Marie!"

He involuntarily rose and plunged his hand in the bust of his apparel, as though to search for a weapon there concealed. She saw the movement, and perfectly well understood the purport of it.

"Do not be alarmed," she said, "there is no danger."

"No—no—danger?" he stammered.

"None in the least. I am four years older since last we met, and twenty years wiser."

"What do you mean, Marie?"

"Mean, my Lord Battaney? Why, that my folly was as much to blame, if not much more so, in what took place between us, as your villany."

"And—and—what brought you here?"

"Only the wish to convince you that your lesson in vice had not been thrown away upon me, and that I was now as bad—aye, as bad as yourself. You have nothing to fear from me. Vice has its attractions, and I have made up my mind, since I cannot enjoy the bliss of being a saint, that I will at least revel in the enjoyments of being a sinner."

He drew a long breath of exquisite relief, and then said—

"Truly, I am rejoiced at this meeting, and I hope you do not give credence to the reports that were raised to my prejudice by some people as regarded Felix."

"What reports?"

"Why—why you must know that there were people who did not scruple to say that I—I—murdered him, and that the story of his having, in his passion, shot himself was only fabricated."

"Oh, certainly!"

"Certainly what?"

"I have no doubt you shot him, and he richly deserved it for interfering in other folk's affairs. What was it to him that I was a dupe, and you were a cowardly betrayer?" Are you the only villain who walks about in ease and safety beneath the blue sky of Italy? I say, my Lord Battaney, it was most absurd of Felix to interfere in the matter."

"You don't know how pleased I am to meet with you."

"The pleasure is mutual."

He placed a bank bill for a hundred pounds in her hands, as he added—

"Marie, you might, if you chose, be so very useful to me."

"Indeed!"

"Yes. I—I almost hesitate to tell you how, but yet I hope you will not feel offended. I can only say that if you choose to do as I wish, you may live in luxury. I suppose you are poor?"

"Yes. Very!"

She did not think proper to say one word to him about having inherited the estate of her aunt.

"Well," he added, "I want such a person as you for the purpose of assisting me in my—my intrigues!—I may as well out with the word at once. I want an unscrupulous female who will do anything for money in the way of betraying others."

"A female pander?"

"Yes, yes."

"It is an office, my lord, that will suit me very well, and I accept it. Henceforward we are in alliance together. I shall expect you to be liberal, and you may depend that no amount of what the world calls villany will ever shock me. I have got rid of all religion—of all morality—and of all feeling."

"You almost, Marie, make me shudder."

"Nonsense; but don't call me Marie."

"What name would you prefer, then?"

"Madame Zadzed call me, and the sooner I am out of Naples, the better; for my story is rather too well known there, and within that principality I should not be able to do you such good service as elsewhere."

"Then go back at once and arrange your affairs in that city, and then come to me here. Ah, Marie, do you not remember our delightful walks by the volcano's ridge, when——"

He took her hand, but she drew it from him with loathing.

"Listen to me," she said. "Our compact ends the moment that you touch me again. I can bear anything in this world but the contamination of your hands. This sounds strange from my lips, but it is true, and probably it is the only strong feeling left me unconnected with sensual gratifications—a loathing of you personally."

Lord Battaney bit his lip until the blood nearly started, and then he said—

"Am I to take your last words as a jest?"

"No, my lord. I treat you with the utmost candour, as throughout this interview, so pleasant upon both sides, you must have found. I have told you that I was ready to accept the degrading situation you offer me. What would you have more? As for my own little antipathies, surely you will permit me to have them if I please."

"Well! well!"

"You agree to the terms?"

"For anything you please. You are a singular woman. But if you do me the service you promise, you will find me everything you can desire in regard to money affairs. Go back to Naples, and arrange for your immediate departure from that city. I will wait for you here, and shall only expect that you will not keep me waiting longer than you can help."

"I will not."

She at once left the hotel, and when she reached her own, where she had put up, she fainted, and did not recover for three hours. The strain upon her nerves during the interview with Battaney had been too much for her, but that was the last occasion upon which she betrayed so much weakness; after that she was cool, calculating, full of life and energy, and as devilish as any fiend from the lower regions.

CHAPTER CXVII.

MADAME ZADZED EXPLAINS HER PLANS

THUS there was a compact—an unholy alliance formed between Lord Battaney and his victim, which was equally satisfactory to both, but from different motives. He, no doubt, thought that she was really what she pretended to be—a person lost to all human feeling and human honesty—a waif and stray upon the surface of society, that might be picked up by any one, and brought into use. Early taught that money was omnipotent, which it is in England, he thought that he, by being liberal to her, could always command her services; and as for her personal antipathy to him, which had been so warmly expressed, he looked upon that as one of the eccentricities of a woman whose vanity, that prevailing characteristic of the sex, had been wounded, and, in fact, he cared little about it. She, on the other hand, considered that, filling the situation she now did, surely some opportunity would offer itself of being revenged upon Lord Battaney, and if the worst success attended her, and she found that there was nothing more satisfactory to be done, she told herself that by the aid of some poisons that she had procured from her friend Wilkins, she could at any time put him to a death of agony. Little did he suspect that he was about to pay a person liberally to keep near him who only would not put him to death, because she hoped to inflict upon him some torture that would exceed even that. How little do men know the precipices upon which they stand when all seems safe and well around and about them. Madame Zadzed proceeded to Naples, and soon settled her affairs. She left her property in charge of a scrivener, who was regularly to account to her for the proceeds, and then she again proceeded to Florence, and formally entered the service of Lord Battaney, who was on a tour through the Italian cities, with the exception of Naples, where he considered he was too well remembered to make it desirable that he should show his face again; and Madame Zadzed did all in her power to strengthen him in the determination, for nothing was further from her mind than to visit that city again. It would be quite foreign to the purpose of these pages to follow Madame Zadzed and Lord Battaney from city to city in Italy, and to detail or comment upon the various villanies committed by the latter with the aid of the former. Let it suffice that the worst case of deceit in which they were both engaged, consisted in the pretended marriage upon the part of Lord Battaney, with a young lady at Florence. Upon the evening before this mock marriage was to take place, Madame Zadzed met Wilkins, the physician, in an obscure street of the city. The recognition was mutual, and they renewed their implicit compact to be of service to each other, to the utmost of their ability so to be. To Wilkins then, since it was necessary she should have a confidant, Madame Zadzed confided her wishes, and as she accommodated him with a sum of money he wanted, he readily promised to assist her, and he kept his word—perhaps the more readily, as he was doing something to be revenged upon Lord Battaney, whom he considered had not been sufficiently liberal to him, on account of some signal service he had done to his lordship. What was the nature of that service he did not tell Madame Zadzed, and she forbore to ask him, for she well knew that to press for a secret is generally to bespeak a lie.

"What I wish," she said, "is that you should help Lord Battaney to a wife."

"A wife?"

"Yes, a real wife, instead of, as he expects and wishes, a mock one."

"Ah, I begin now to understand your wishes, but how can I help you to the accomplishment of them, I should like to know?"

"Easily. I am entrusted with the task of procuring a clergyman, or rather some one who will personate that character, to perform the ceremony of marriage between Lord Battaney and his new victim. Whoever I present he will be content with. Now, if such a thing as a real English clergyman could be found, would it not be trick upon trick to make him really marry his lordship to the person whom he wishes to deceive?"

"As he deceived you?"

"Yes, precisely."

"Depend upon me," said Wilkins, "it shall be done. I will consider it as an instalment of the revenge I owe to his lordship."

"Ah, now I am sure of you."

"What do you mean?"

"Why I mean that now I find your own passions enlisted in the same cause with mine, I am certain that you will do me good service. I will rely upon you to find me a real clergyman, and to bring him to me at six to-morrow evening, at the Palazzo Gurgioni. Leave the rest to me."

Wilkins, when he undertook anything

really, he seldom failed in it, and among the many English visitors to Florence, he easily found a gentleman who was in holy orders, and to him he said, " that if he did not consent to perform the ceremony, it would be done by a Roman priest, and both parties most probably would, in consequence, be lost to the Church of England, as by law established."   This was a conclusive argument with the divine, who was decidedly evangelical in his views, and with all the eagerness of a zealot he kept the appointment, and was duly introduced to Madame Zadzed, who soon found that she had to do with a fine specimen of one of the two species or classes into which clergymen of the Church of England were divided, namely, rogues or weak-headed enthusiasts.   This young clergyman decidedly belonged to the latter class.   He was weak-headed, very devout, and consumptive, as most pious folks are.   It wanted but a small portion of the cant always at the command of Madame Zadzed to enable her to convince this young divine that she was a most exemplary person, and he consented to perform the ceremony, and to say nothing to Lord Battaney, who was represented by Madame Zadzed as being so unholy in his religious belief, that a few words only with a Protestant clergyman might induce him at once to join the Church of Rome, where he would find no lack of complying priests. All this from the tongue of a still pretty woman had a powerful effect upon the mad head-piece of the young divine, and the ceremony was duly performed to a miracle, Lord Battaney being quite delighted with the admirable manner in which—so he told Madame Zadzed — the sham parson had *acted* his part.

"It is capitally done," he said, "one would almost swear that a parson he was to all intents and purposes."

"Yes," replied Madame Zadzed, "he has performed his part to my entire satisfaction, and I am pleased to find that it is to yours."

"It is, most certainly."

Now Madame Zadzed had cautioned the young divine to say nothing to Lord Battaney; but if any means could be invented by which the tongue of a religious zealot could be silenced, we might next very fairly expect to find the perpetual motion.   No sooner did the parson see Lord Battaney upon the point of departure with his young bride, than he stepped up to them and said—

"Now, my lord, I hope you will duly consider that as you have been united to her whom you have raised to your own rank in the Protestant faith, you will see the propriety of remaining in it, and so save your soul alive."

"Eh ?" said Battaney.

"And so save your soul alive !" repeated the parson, as he triumphantly walked away.

"Capital ! capital !   Is it not capital ?" whispered Madame Zadzed.

"Very good !" said Lord Battaney, "but rather over acted.   That is the worst of a fellow who does anything well. He is so confoundedly apt to overdo it."

"Oh, yes, yes ; that is a fault."

"A serious one ; but give him what you please for his trouble, and then charge it to me.   Who is he, by the bye? One may want him again."

"A young man on his travels merely; a professional man, but it is of no consequence ; you won't want *him* again."

Lord Battaney saw that Madame Zadzed was in a state of a little excitement about something, but one of the things upon which he prided himself was in being quite indifferent to what he called the humours and fancies of women ; and, therefore, after staring for a few moments at her exultant-looking countenance, he merely shrugged up his shoulders, and passed on with his young wife, as Madame Zadzed knew, but victim as he thought, leaning upon his arm. About two hours after that Madame Zadzed procured from the young clergyman a full certificate of the marriage, which both she and Wilkins witnessed; for out of pretended zeal for the service of Lord Battaney, and for fear anything should go amiss, as he said, he had been present at the ceremony.   The look of Madame Zadzed's face, it is said, when she placed the document in her bosom, was of such a triumphant character that it astonished even the clergyman, and almost gave him a dreamy sort of notion that there was something more in the matter than he had at first imagined.   As nothing further was said, however, no doubt he soon forgot the transaction. Lord Battaney took up his abode with his young wife in a beautiful suburban villa, about a couple of miles from Florence, and there she enjoyed as much happiness as could fall to the lot of one united to such a man as Battaney. Of course, it was upon her part a most grievous mistake to suppose that she could ever find happiness with such a man. In due course he neglected her, and in due course she wept and complained. Then comes the Marie story once again. He told her she would not suit him if she could not wear a cheerful countenance. To this she responded a little warmly, and then out came the fact that she was only his mistress—so he believed; and so he told her. It did not then chime in with the views of Madame Zadzed to inform the young wife of her real position."

*　　*　　*　　*　　*

　　*　　*　　●　　*

"Is there a hiatus in the manuscript?" said Harry Dean.

"Yes," replied the solicitor, "it seems so. You look unwell, sir."

"I am, I confess, deeply affected by this narrative. As it proceeds it seems as though some curtain which had hitherto hidden from my perception many things in which I felt deeply interested was slowly rolled from before my mental vision. I seem as if I had myself been an actor in the scenes depicted in these papers."

"This Wilkins is, no doubt, the same man now in Newgate."

"The same."

"I thought as much when I came to his name, and this Lord Battaney is the nobleman who is said to have perished in the flames of his villa at Fulham some time ago, I rather suspect."

"He is the same."

"Mr. Dean, you do, indeed, seem deeply affected by what I read in these papers. Perhaps you would much rather that I did not proceed at present. If so, at any other time, when your own inclination and leisure may serve you, I shall be most happy to come and resume."

"No; go on now. That is to say, if you are not fatigued. Pray pardon me for urging you. Doubtless you are fatigued, for you cannot, like me, feel an amount of interest in these disclosures sufficient to overcome bodily depression."

The lawyer would there and then have gone on with Madame Zadzed's documents, but Harry Dean was too considerate to allow him. He ordered some refreshments to be brought to him, and insisted upon his taking an hour's rest.

"If compatible with your convenience and your feelings," said Harry Dean, "I confess I should be obliged by your remaining until we have gone through the papers, for I see there are but very few remaining; but if not, I will finish by myself."

"Do not think of it. I am sufficiently interested to go on. I am rather surprised," added the lawyer, after a pause, "that Madame Zadzed has said so little of her son."

"I expect we shall hear more of him," said Harry Dean. "Such a woman, admitting that her child lived, could not fail to make some use of him, as indeed she made use of everything in the prosecution of her revenge."

"Perhaps, then, we shall hear of him as you say; for if that child had died, it seems that it would have been one of those facts that would not have escaped her in her narration."

"You may depend that child lived."

"Perhaps, Mr. Dean, you have some special reason for believing as much. No doubt the reading of these papers to you affords many a clue to circumstances and events, of which I am in ignorance."

"In good truth they do."

The attorney nodded his head as though he would have said, "I guessed as much all along;" and then made haste to finish some wine that was before him, in order that he might bring the refreshments and the rest to a close, for he could not help fearing that Harry Dean was really in a state of the most nervous impatience for him to begin again.

The wine was finally pushed aside, and the lawyer again opened Madame Zadzed's manuscript at the page where he had left off.

"There is one thing," he said, "which is an important omission."

"What is that?"

"Why, at the commencement of this

manuscript she talks of affording proof of its contents by dates and documents, but as yet we have not found either."

"Probably we shall yet find information upon that head."

"I hope so, for, as it plainly appears that the principal event here recorded, and one upon which some important results evidently hang, is the real marriage of Lord Battaney, at Florence, Madame Zadzed would have done well to endorse the certificate of the ceremony really being performed, and which she says she got from the clergyman within two hours, and witnessed along with the physician Wilkins."

"That is an important document wanting," said Harry Dean, "but pray go on, I cannot think she will be so explicit about these things, and yet leave us in ignorance concerning the whereabouts of a document of such importance."

CHAPTER CXVIII.

THE NARRATIVE CONTINUED.

THE next page of the brief memoir of Madame Zadzed began as follows :—

"Sixteen years—sixteen long weary years, and yet no vengeance!—sixteen years, and yet this man—no—not this man, but this fiend, Battaney, still lives uncrushed. And Marie has been waiting for a great revenge. A thousand opportunities of petty vengeance—a thousand opportunities of striking him dead in the very middle of all his pride, and all his vice, have occurred! and yet she has spared him with the hope that some rare opportunity might yet come, at which she could say to herself,—"This vengeance shall be effectual!" Had she been satisfied with any ordinary measure of revenge, it would have been gratified long before, but her thirst for a something that would plant the iron into his very soul!—a something that would drive him to despair, and perchance from despair to madness!—then her vengeance, perchance, might cease; but, oh, what agonising steps Battaney might be compelled to take before misery worked such havoc in his brain. It was those steps she wanted to behold. It was those agonies she would have gloried in being a witness to : and the more she reflected upon the exquisite gratification they would afford her, the more she looked with a contempt upon any petty vengeance. During the long period that she had been in the service of Lord Battaney, she had accumulated a considerable sum of money, and as Italy had long been distasteful to her, she was not sorry when Lord Battaney one day announced his intention of removing himself and his vices to his own country, England. The preparations for departure were very quickly made, and within ten days of the resolve to leave the continent being made, his lordship's suite, including Madame Zadzed, landed at Plymouth. From thence they proceeded direct to the metropolis, where Madame Zadzed was not long in finding that money, in England, would accomplish much more than it did anywhere else, powerful as it is in all countries. Nowhere, however, did she find the same slavish adulation to wealth, merely for its own sake, as in England, while never had she found such an amount of hypocritical rascality cloaking such an amount of vice. This state of things suited Madame Zadzed's views very well, but upon her arrival in England there were some matters that she felt anxious to inquire into at her very earliest convenience, and the principal of these was as to what kind of personage her son appeared. She had during the whole period of her sojourn upon the continent with Lord Battaney regularly transmitted to England the necessary funds for the support and plain education of this son of her's, and no wonder she felt a little anxious to see what description of being he was. To the slight inquiry of Lord Battaney upon the subject, she had said that her child was dead, which had perfectly satisfied him. The feelings of Madame Zadzed were of a strangely mixed character when she waited for her son to be introduced to her. There were at moments some yearnings of affection towards the unknown one that showed all feeling was not dead within her, while at other times she would wish that there were no such remnants of her intrigue with Lord Battaney in existence in this world. She had had an interview with the people with whom he had been brought up, and she had given them golden reasons for keeping secret the fact that she was his mother, so that when the youth was introduced to her, he had not the smallest notion of the relationship. He was nearly twenty years of age, but looked some years older. By the orders of Madame Zadzed he had been given the name of the people who had brought him up. That name was Mayston, and they had him christened Alfred. He knew himself, therefore, by no other appellation than that of Alfred Mayston. When he was introduced into the room where Madame Zadzed waited for him, she took care to give herself the advantage of turning her

back to the light — a movement that secured her a good view of his features, while it shaded her own. She was a tolerable judge of human nature, and at the first glance at Alfred Mayston, she saw there was not the smallest approach to a gentleman about him; and at the second glance, she made up her mind that he was a blackguard. She knew that most comprehensive English word. Half an hour's conversation with him, let her know that he was ignorant, unprincipled, coarse, and rough in his tastes and habits, and altogether a most repulsive personage. From that time she determined he should never know his consanguinity to her. If he had been different from what he were—if he had shown any feeling—any tenderness or goodness of disposition—any of that fine sensibility which forms so charming a feature in some intellects, she would at once have moved him to finer senses, and given him an opportunity of learning something very different from what his father even was ; but she knew enough of human nature to know that it is quite useless to throw away culture upon a barren soil. She was satisfied it would be as impossible by education or cultivation to convert Alfred Mayston into a gentleman, as it would by similar means to convert a bull-dog into an Italian greyhound, and therefore she was not foolish enough to make the attempt. She had often, in the affairs she had had from time to time to manage for Lord Battaney, felt the want of the assistance of some unscrupulous man, and the idea at once struck her that if her Alfred Mayston was calculated for anything in the world, it was for such a part. However, he might assist in the vengeance she yet hoped to perpetrate upon Battaney, and any blow that might be struck through his, Alfred Mayston's, instrumentality, might be made doubly severe by the after information, that it came from the hands of his own son. She questioned Alfred upon his feelings as regarded such an appointment as bully and jackall to Lord Battaney.

"Are you brave ?" she said.

"Yes, if I find the other party is not so strong as I am."

"Have you had any personal quarrels ?"

"Plenty."

"And what were the results ?"

"I got beaten the first time I fought, so after that, if ever I quarrelled with any one, I laid wait for him in some lonely spot, and came upon him behind at unawares."

"The courage of an assassin!" muttered Madame Zadzed. "Well, Alfred, if you like to be well paid, and do what I may require of you from time to time—that is, implicitly to obey orders, you may do very well. You will be engaged in highly discreditable offices, and therefore it is for yourself to consider whether you will stoop to them or not."

"What do I care, so long as I get money!"

"That will do ; I can perceive you will do."

"Of course I shall, madame, if I am well paid. Folks don't scruple now to call me a scoundrel, and I may as well be one in reality, you know."

"Precisely, you take a very reasonable view of the affair. Here is some money on account, and I shall expect you to make your appearance here every morning for orders as to what you are to do, or to report upon the progress of any affairs which you may have in hand."

This was highly agreeable to Alfred Mayston, and he was thus fairly admitted as the protegee of Madame Zadzed and the pander of Lord Battaney. It was some time after this arrangement that Alfred Mayston informed Madame Zadzed that there was at Hampstead a beautiful young girl of the name of Kate Destern, who, if she could be got there, would be a principal ornament of Battaney's new villa at Fulham. Madame Zadzed herself, accompanied by a woman whom she had recently taken into her service, of the name of Swam, went to Hampstead and saw the girl. A glance satisfied her that Alfred Moyston's report of her was not exaggerated. She at once gave Alfred Mayston a *carte blanche* of action in the matter. Alfred took a lodging in the same cottage with this beautiful young girl, and after a time he informed Madame Zadzed that the principal obstacle to the obtaining possession of the young girl, and giving her up to Lord Battaney, consisted in the watchful protection of a young man named Harry Dean.

"This young man," said Alfred Moyston, "has gained the confidence and affection of the whole family, consisting of Mrs. Destern, Kate, and her young sister Lucy, and he is so continually upon the spot, that I am convinced, without his removal by force or by fraud, nothing can be done. Who and what he is, I know not."

Madame Zadzed immediately ordered Alfred Moyston to spare no pains nor expense in ascertaining who and what this Harry Dean was, for upon knowing that, she did not despair of finding some ready means of destroying him. Alfred, however, was completely baffled, and so full of rage was he at being so, that, after a time, he declared to Madame Zadzed that the affair should be no longer protracted, for he would take an immediate and effectual means of getting rid of Harry Dean. He did so, for he informed Madame Zadzed that he had shot him, although the dead body had, by some mysterious means, disappeared. At all events, he was got rid of—that was the main object, and shortly afterwards Mrs. Destern died, and an attack being made upon the cottage, Kate Destern was fairly carried off by force to Lord Battaney's villa at Fulham. He, Battaney, paid Madame Zadzed two hundred pounds for that abduction, and she gave fifty to Alfred Mayston, with which he thought himself very well paid, not knowing the amount she had received. It was at this juncture that accident gave Madame Zadzed a clue to something which at once promised her all her long delayed revenge. She had reason to suspect that this very Kate Destern was the daughter of the young lady to whom Lord Battaney had, sixteen or seventeen years before, been actually married in Florence. From the moment of this suspicion arising Madame Zadzed scarcely slept or tasted food in her intense anxiety to prove it."

* * * * *

There was a considerable hiatus here in the manuscript. The attorney looked up in the face of Harry Dean, and he saw there so much emotion that he instantly rose and approached him.

"This is really too much for you, sir."

"Just at this moment it is. The revelations in these papers, I must own, are to me of an astounding character."

"Different from what you expected?"

"Quite so—quite so."

"At all events, Mr. Dean, this young lady, Miss Destern, in whom you are so naturally interested, seems to be satisfactorily proved not to be the daughter of Wilkins."

"I never for one moment supposed she were such; but I am indeed surprised to find she is, what these papers state her to be—the legitimate child of Lord Battaney. I would indeed have wished that she had borne some other name than that."

"It is not a very creditable one, Mr. Dean, but still it cannot affect her. She may be, and no doubt is, purity itself, notwithstanding her father died with a character that few men would have chosen to have clinging to their memory even for all his wealth. What a truly dreadful woman this Madame Zadzed must have been."

"Dreadful indeed!"

"I think, in all the course of my experience, I never heard anything approaching to her diabolical and protracted wickedness. One can hardly think it possible that such a being could ever have been pure and innocent as she pretends she had been before her encounter with Battaney. He is the only parallel one can find for her. As for Alfred Mayston, he was evidently a vulgar villain, who in France or Italy would have been a bravo."

"No doubt—no doubt. How frightful it is to think that one man, such as Battaney, utterly destitute of all feeling or honour, should be able, by the accident of wealth, to disseminate the poison of his own vices so widely around him. I shudder to think what may yet be contained in these papers."

"Courage, sir, courage! There is one thing of which you are well assured, and that is, that whatever terrors and temptations Miss Destern was exposed to, she escaped them pure, and thus Madame Zadzed was, after all, foiled in the most diabolical scheme of revenge that ever, I think, entered the brain of a human being."

"Thank God, yes. Yes, she was foiled in that dreadful plan of selling for gold to Lord Battaney her own child. Oh, horror, horror!"

"And that, too, through the instrumentality of his other child, Alfred Mayston."

"Yes, into what an abyss of sin and horror had not that man's vices dragged him. Oh! if there be a hell in human conscience, certainly he must feel its bitterest pangs. The thought of all these horrors brings the cold dew upon my brow, and I tremble to my very heart."

The attorney poured out a glass of wine, which he insisted upon Harry Dean partaking of; and then, instead of as before advising him to let the remainder of Madame Zadzed's frightful narration wait until some other opportunity, he said to him—

"Let me advise you now to hear all. There are but very few pages wanting now to finish this record of crime, which I think is the coolest confession of iniquity I ever read. How the woman could sit down to write such things of herself transcends all belief."

"It does—it does."

"Are you better, sir?"

"Much better; and I am of your opinion, that it is far better I should know all, now that I know so much; so I pray you, sir, if you be not fatigued with what you have already read, that you will proceed with the frightful narration."

"I am too much interested to feel fatigued."

"Then go on at once, sir."

The lawyer refreshed himself with a glass of wine, and then he turned over Madame Zadzed's papers again until he came to where he had left off. After glancing at the contractions for a few moments, he said—

"The style as well as the handwriting of what follows is very different. It seems to have been put down under the strongest impulses of passion, day by day, as events progressed."

CHAPTER CXIX.

THE CONCLUSION OF MADAME ZADZED'S PAPERS.

THE conclusion of the narrative of Madame Zadzed was as follows:—

"She is his own child! He suspects nothing, but loves her with an unholy passion; he swears that no power on earth shall sever her from him. The consummation of my revenge is at length close at hand. A fiend-like joy fills my brain. I can write no more, for I must hasten to Fulham.

  * * * *

"He has had a furious quarrel with Alfred Mayston. Kate resists him, and seems inclined to prefer death to dishonour. Alfred tells me that the young man named Harry Dean, whom he shot, is not dead, and he anticipates trouble upon that score. He swears vengeance against Lord Battaney. Kate Destern

is looking pale and wan, but more beautiful than before.

  * * * *

"Another day. I am feverish and ill. Swam has done me good service, for by the evidence she has brought me, she has moved every shadow of doubt that might remain regarding the birth of Kate Destern. *She is Lord Battaney's legitimate child!*—Ha! ha! ha!—I laughed, and the laugh seemed to be echoed by fiends, deep down in the earth's centre. I laugh again. They again echo me.

  * * * *

"Battaney has killed Alfred Mayston! Killed him!—His own son, too!—Ha! ha! It seems to me as though there was liquid fire in my brain, and yet I rejoice! I do not expect, and I do not wish to outlive all these events, I only hope to see them finished. To be able to tell myself I have been revenged; and then to be able to go and whisper in his ear—*now* I have been revenged! That is all I wish. Yes, Alfred is dead! Already is Battaney the murderer of one of his children, and he will be the worse than murderer of the other. Ha! ha! I am going to Fulham directly."

  * * * *

"*She has escaped!*"

"Go on—go on," cried Harry Dean.

"That is all," said the attorney.

"All?"

"Yes, Madame Zadzed's narrative ends here; but there are other papers—also the certificate of the marriage at Florence is here, and some letters likewise. This case is now, Mr. Dean, perfectly clear."

Harry shuddered.

"Lord Battaney," he said, "was saved by Heaven from the commission of the worst crime that he was incited to by that female fiend, Madame Zadzed. He died a terrible death—I have but to hope that the infinite mercy of God will even include him."

"But tell me candidly, Mr. Dean—do you fully believe what is here recorded? Could there be such a monstrous piece of iniquity as this woman? To sacrifice her own son, and glory in it!"

"Yes, said Harry Dean, solemnly, "I believe it all, and the grounds upon which I do so are, that it is within m own knowledge and power to fully corroborate by far the most important part of the narrative. Wherever I happen to know the real truth, this manuscript is singularly correct, and therefore I am well warranted in believing that which I do not know is equally veracious."

"That is good reasoning, sir."

"It is," said Harry Dean, as he placed his hand upon the manuscript, "it is; and from my inmost heart I believe this to be a genuine confession."

"You are the best judge, sir."

"Under the circumstances it happens that I am, and the only thing that now troubles me is, that I shall have to make a painful communication to Miss Destern."

"Is there a necessity, sir, for making it?"

"Not in itself, but I have gone upon such a principle of candour in all things with her, but one, that I hardly know how I can keep the facts from her knowledge. However, I must take the best opportunity that I can find for enlightening her upon a matter that ought, philosophically speaking, to be of no importance to her, but which the vitiated fashion of society at large renders of moment. On my faith, I would rather have found that she was the daughter of the poorest man in England, provided he was an honest one, than have made the discovery that she owed her birth to such a libel upon human nature as Lord Battaney certainly was."

The lawyer fully acquiesced in this feeling of Harry Dean's, and as there was nothing in the papers that called for his professional services, he rose to go.

"I shall not now," said Harry Dean, "interfere in the remotest degree with Wilkins, except as an enforced witness upon his trial. The law will doubtless for his last crime mete out to him the punishment he has long deserved—for I really call the murder for which he will be executed a minor crime in comparison with many that he has committed."

The lawyer took his leave, and Harry Dean carefully locked up the papers which Madame Zadzed had written, and which no doubt she intended should,

in case of her decease before Lord Battaney, fall into the hands of some one who would, to his confusion, proclaim the facts to the world. The escape of Kate Destern, however—the death of Lord Battaney—the awful manner in which it took place, and her son's murder, were events that it had not occurred to the imagination of Madame Zadzed to suspect might happen, and hence the documents had been left unfinished, and had fallen, at last, into the very hands which, of all others, she probably least expected would have ever held them. Such are the inscrutable decrees of a mysterious destiny, which jumbles together people and circumstances in a manner to defy all critical calculation founded upon the experience of the past. After much consideration, Harry Dean resolved upon taking a peculiar course with regard to the disclosures in Madame Zadzed's papers. He the next day sought Kate Destern, and said to her—

"Kate, I am in possession of the secret of your birth."

"Oh, Harry!"

"Hush! I, in my judgment, do not think you ought to know just yet that secret: will you have sufficient faith in me to adopt that view, and not to ask me. If you do ask me, I will tell you at once."

"Tell me when you think proper, Harry, and not before. If I had not faith in your judgment I should not——"

"Go on, Kate—go on."

"Love you as I do, nor should I be so candid as to tell you as much."

He looked at her for some few moments in silence, and then, as he held her hand between his own, he said—

"I do not know how it is, or by what miracle I have deserved so much happiness as to be loved by you, Kate, but thanking Heaven for that amount of good fortune, I can only endeavour to deserve it."

"It is more than deserved, Harry."

"No, no; do not tell me that. But now, Kate, can you for a few days forgive me for being very much absent from you?"

"Yes, Harry, while I regret it."

"You shall not have to regret it long, for——What noise is that?"

A miserable howling noise from the next apartment at this moment came upon their ears. They listened intently, and they heard a voice cry out—

"Yes, yes, it's all over now. It's all over!"

"What can be the meaning of that?" said Harry Dean ; "and who is it talking about something being all over?"

"I cannot guess."

The door of the room at this moment opened, and Tony made his appearance, looking uncommonly flurried and vexed.

"I beg your pardon, Mr. Dean, and you, Miss Kate," he said, "for bouncing in in such a way, but the fact is, the old 'un is taking us all by storm."

"The who?"

"The old 'un. The—the, confound her, the old woman—Mary Ann's aunt. Do come, Mr. Dean, and help me to shovel her out of the window."

"Help you to what?"

"To get rid of her in any way. Oh, bother her ! she has nearly smothered me, and now she's a trying it on in the suffocating line on Mary Ann, and I can't get her away at all single-handed."

With this Tony flew out of the room again, and Harry Dean with Kate followed him, for they were both not a little astonished at his report that Mary Ann's highly criminal aunt had had the unbounded impudence to show herself again in the house, after what had occurred in it regarding her. The scene which presented itself to the eyes of Harry Dean and Kate when they entered the room was truly ludicrous. Mary Ann was there, at least so they conjectured, for they could see nothing whatever of her head and shoulders. The fact was, that the aunt had arrived, enveloped in an immense shawl, which completely, as she violently embraced Mary Ann, covered her up, and that was the process of semi-suffocation which poor Tony had suffered from only a few moments previously.

"It's all over ! It's all over !" cried the aunt.

"Is it though," said Tony, as he seized Mary Ann by the waist and violently wrenched her away from the aunt. "It would be all over soon, you old dragon, if nobody was here."

"Oh, dear yes," continued the old woman with a strong nasal twang, which no doubt she meant should in-

timate the strength and depth of her forgiving disposition. "It's all over now."

With this she pounced upon Tony again, before he was aware of what she intended, and held him in such an embrace, that although he kicked vigorously, it really required no common exertion to rescue himself. He did do so, owing to his not being very scrupulous.

"Confound you !" he cried. "What do you mean? Murder ! Do you want to take our lives, you old cormorant?"

"Ah ! dear me," said the old woman, who was evidently, from her constrained manner, acting a part, "we ought not after all, to forget in this world to whom we are related. Forget and forgive is my motto, and so we will all live quite happy together now, and say nothing of the past. Let oblivion roll over us. Come to my arms, Mary Ann—my brother's own child——"

"Hold off," cried Tony.

"Come to my arms, and remember that I am your own aunt. Did you, could you think that I would desert you? No! We will never recur to the past, but we will all live happily together—and remember, I approve highly of your choice."

Then finding she could not catch Mary Ann, she made another demonstration against poor Tony, but he eluded her. She was, however, evidently not to be discomfited by a trifle, and forcing a whole shower of tears, she added—

"I hope we are all christians?"

"It's a great pity," said Tony, "one of us isn't a policeman."

"A what?"

"A policeman ; but as it is, I dare say, if Mr. Dean will keep Mary Ann from being actually smothered, I shall be able to get one in a minute."

"Oh, dear—oh dear!" said the aunt. "How facetious he is too. What things he says, to be sure. He is the image of a young man at Wisbeach, who won the hearts of all the females. Come to my arms."

"You be hanged," said Tony.

"Oh, my Mary Ann, we will forget the past. It's all over ! It's all over ! What's the use of reaping up old stories that only make relations quarrel. Remember, I'm your poor dear father's own sister."

"Aunt," said Mary Ann.

"Oh, yes. Is's all over and done with now. I'm sure when families are disunited and quarrel among themselves, what hope can there be of anything like concord and good feeling among strangers?"

"Will you hear me, aunt?"

"Yes, my dear, but don't fall back upon old grievances whatever you do, and as for you, Mr. What's-your-name, I'm quite sure I shall take to you as if you were my own son, that I shall."

"Aunt," said Mary Ann, in the most persevering manner in the world, "I look upon this as an audacious attempt to force your most unwelcome society upon myself and my friends. You shall not want, but once and for all, I tell you plainly and distinctly, you shall not reside beneath a roof of mine."

"Good," said Tony. "This dose to be repeated if the patient is fractious. What do you say to that, old female? Come, bundle."

The aunt looked at one and then at the other of them for a minute or two in silence, and then down she fell upon the floor in a real or pretended swoon, which it was, at that moment, no one there could take upon themselves to say, whatever their suspicion might be.

CHAPTER CXX.

TONY'S DANGER.

THE aunt was playing a deeper game than any of those upon whom she had so very strangely and so very unconsciously thrust her society, imagined. What may be the ultimate result of her pretended compunction for the conduct which had so deservedly brought upon her the bad opinion of all those whose good feelings she ought sedulously to have taken pains to cultivate, we shall soon see. Tony shook his head, as he said—

"I don't like this affair, and it would be no use of me to pretend that I did. Mary Ann, my dear, I only wish you could convince me in some way that this old—a-hem!—lady was not your aunt."

"I wish I could convince myself of so much," said Mary Ann.

After some little time spent in consultation, Tony said that the aunt should have shelter in the house until she was better, but that the moment such a state of things was manifest, she should quit again. The designing woman was accordingly taken up stairs to the bed room she had been so long in the habit of occupying when she considered herself to be—fairly, in fact, but most unfairly as regarded the truth of the circumstances that gave her that title mistress of the house, and there they left her. This little episode did not greatly disturb the happiness of the party at the hotel, and yet they could all of them perceive that there was a shade of melancholy upon the countenance of Harry Dean. The reader will be able, although those who looked upon him with such interest and affection at that hotel were not, to understand easily why he felt full of sad thoughts. The recital that he had listened to from the papers of Madame Zadzed had had a great effect upon his spirits. Harry Dean was far, very far indeed, above the vulgar prejudice of supposing that anything in the shape of a stigma should attach to the child for the criminality of the parent; but yet, in his honest heart, how devotedly he wished that she (the object of his dearest affections) had been the daughter of any one but Lord Battaney. There was another view, likewise, to take of the affair, and that was, that as the legitimate daughter of Lord Battaney, Kate was rich and noble. Considerable estates must of necessity be her's, if she put in her claims to them, and that very villa at Fulham, within the unhallowed precincts of which she had suffered so much mental torture, was her own. How strange are human mutations! The victim that was attempted to be made, had become now the sole arbitress of the fate of many who had lent themselves to the unholy task of achieving her destruction. The debate that was taking place in the mind of Harry Dean was how, and in what way, he should make Kate acquainted with the remarkable change that had taken place in her position and prospects, as regarded worldly wealth and station. Of one thing, however, he felt quite clear, and that was, that it would not be justifiable upon his part to delay making a communication that was of so personal a character to Kate; and, accordingly, he took an opportunity during that day of saying to her with ill-concealed emotion—

"Kate, will you listen to me for half an hour?"

"For half an hour, Harry?"

Kate smiled as she uttered these words, and the obvious signification of them was, that it would indeed require many half hours of his company before she should be tired of listening to him. He took her hand and pressed it to his lips, as he added—

"At once then, my Kate, at once, I have really something important to say to you."

He rose, and she followed him to a room that was close at hand, and where it was not likely they would meet with any interruption; and when they were seated, he commenced by saying—

"I am well aware, Kate, that you know there is a mystery surrounding your birth."

"Oh, yes—yes."

"That mystery is solved."

Kate shook like an aspen leaf.

"Nay, be not alarmed, Kate. Look at me."

She did look at him, and upon his countenance there was such an expression of unutterable love and kindness, that she could not resist the impulse to throw herself in his arms, and bursting into tears, she cried, sobbingly—

"Oh, tell me all—tell me all, Harry, now, for I can well perceive that you love me still."

"Love you?"

"Yes, Harry. Let me be who or what I may, if you love me—still I am your own happy girl; but tell me all, for an unknown dread is at my heart, and it seems to me as though what you were about to say was a something that would place a barrier between us."

"It is not."

"Oh, what an existir elief."

"No, dear one, what I have to say is nothing that will prevent me in the broad, open face of day calling you my own, and I hope that the time that must elapse before I do so may be now easily counted by hours."

"Go on—go on. Tell me all."

Harry paused for a moment, for he hardly knew where to begin in the narrative, but seeing the look of anxious expectation that was upon the face of Kate, he could not keep her longer in suspense, and at once commenced his story with the account of the motives that had induced Madame Zadzed to enter into the service of Lord Battaney —a service that had resulted in so many important particulars. From that point in the strange and eventful history of Madame Zadzed, he had no difficulty in proceeding right on until he came to what more particularly concerned Kate. He then told her all, and concluded by saying—

"You will thus perceive that you are entitled to append the title of lady to your name, and in all probability you will be rich, for it is very unlikely that Lord Battaney died with a will."

For the last five minutes of his discourse, Kate had uttered not one word, and now she suddenly slid from her chair, and but for the protecting arm of Harry Dean, would have fallen heavily to the floor. The various agitating feelings that had been called into existence by what she heard, had been too much for her, and she who, amid dangers that would have affected many, preserved her senses and her courage, now lapsed into a swoon at the dreadful thought of what a precipice Lord Battaney had stood upon when, by his vile acts, she, his own child, was forced to become an inmate of that house at Fulham, from the dangers of which she had only so narrowly escaped.

"Alas!" said Harry Dean, "I thought this much."

He was not alarmed particularly at the swooning of Kate, for he knew well it proceeded from mental emotion, and not from any heavy ailment. He kissed once the pale lips, and then, gently laying her upon a couch that was in the room, he immediately left to get the assistance of Lucy and Mary Ann. It is needless to say that they hurried to the room and took every care of Kate. Poor Lucy, as she wept bitterly, said—

"Oh, how cruel of you Harry, to frighten Kate so."

"My dear Lucy," he replied, it was absolutely necessary that I should tell her something, which has very much agitated her nerves, but she will soon be better. I was not justified in keeping it secret."

Lucy thought she had said something unkind to him, so she pressed his hand in silence, and he returned the pressure, saying, as he did so—

"If Kate should ask you for me, I will come to her in a moment. She may have some questions to ask of me, which I am bound to answer."

"Yes, yes, Harry."

He left the room, and took his way to the little apartment below, which was called the bar parlour. In that room there was a screen, which shielded any draught from the repeatedly-opened outer door, and as Harry Dean then was in no mood but one which induced him to commune with his own thoughts, he got quite behind the screen, and sat down in comparative darkness. There was no one in the bar now, for the fact was, Mary Ann had been there, and upon his summons had hastily left it for the purpose of attending upon Kate, and Tony had slipped out for a few moments.

Harry Dean, however, had not been long behind the screen where he had so innocently hidden, when he heard a soft footstep approaching the room along a passage that was covered with floor-cloth, and which approached it from the upper part of the house. Attracted much more by the stealthy manner in which the person was approaching than by anything else, Harry Dean, by slightly shifting his position, peeped out from behind the screen, and to his great surprise he saw that it was the aunt, who had been left up stairs, apparently so very unwell. She peeped into the bar-parlour, and then seeing that it was apparently empty, she entered in the same slow and cautious manner which had characterised her movements from the first moment that Harry Dean had observed her. Upon a small shelf two decanters were always kept, one of which was full of port wine and the other of sherry; and Harry Dean saw her deliberately pour some dark liquid, from a little bottle she produced, into the port wine, after which she retreated as silently as she had come, and was soon out of sight and hearing of Harry Dean.

"What on earth can be the meaning of this?" said Harry Dean.

He at once emerged from his place of concealment, and looked at the wine, but he could perceive no difference to the eye, and he was not quite so imprudent as to taste any of it, in order to ascertain if there was a strange taste to it. At all events, he made up his mind that no one should run the risk of being poisoned by partaking of any of the drugged liquor. He accordingly at once placed it in a cupboard, which he locked, and just as he had concluded that operation Tony came in.

"Well, Tony," said Harry Dean, "I have something to tell you of your aunt that is to be."

Tony made a wry face.

"That is an unwelcome subject?"

"Very!" said Tony. "Bother her, I don't bear malice, and if she had done anything to me, you see, Mr. Dean, I should have been the last person in all the world to say a word about it, but it's Mary Ann that she for so long made a galley slave of, and that I feel here."

Tony touched his chest as he spoke.

"I don't blame you," said Harry Dean, "but it strikes me forcibly that your aunt is very anxious to make us all feel here."

Harry Dean indicated his stomach as he uttered these words.

"The deuce," said Tony, "what do you mean?"

Harry Dean then told him exactly what he had seen regarding the aunt's trafficking with the port wine, and Tony looked at him with an amount of amazement that made his countenance look truly hideous. With open mouth and eyes he glanced at Harry Dean, and then he said—

"Why, goodness gracious, she wants to be the death of Mary Ann."

"No doubt of it, and of everybody else beside."

"Oh, the old——. Oh, dear! What shall we do, Mr. Dean? Why, she's a regular Guy Faux, that she is. Lor! what a paragraph for the Sunday papers. A whole family, including a Mary Ann, poisoned by an old woman. It's enough to make one's blood chill, and all one's flesh to go with a creep. Mr. Dean, what shall we all do? Ah! I have it, I have it. Now for it."

Tony at once procured a decanter of similar pattern to the one which had the drugged wine, and in that he decantered a bottle of port, and placed it on the shelf again.

"What do you mean to do?"

"Why, look you here, Mr. Dean, I'll tell you what I will do. I will quietly wait till the old girl puts in an appearance below here, and then if she don't have a taste of her own handy work, it shan't be my fault. Give me the key of the cupboard."

Tony poured out from the drugged decanter just one glass of wine, and hid it behind some bottles on a shelf, and he had only just completed this manoeuvre when Mary Ann came down stairs, and said—

"She is quite well again, Mr. Dean."

"She!" cried Tony. "Who do you mean? What's been amiss?"

"Nothing particular," said Harry Dean. "Only Kate was rather affected at something I had to tell her, that's all. Ah! some one comes."

To the amazement of Mary Ann, the aunt suddenly made her appearance in the room, saying as she approached Tony and her niece—

"Oh, my dear children, can you forgive me all the past? Better thoughts and better feelings have come over me now, and I will love you, and do my duty by you."

"We don't doubt," said Tony, "but you would do anything and anybody, but we can do for ourselves. I can tell you, we ain't quite such babes in the wood as you think us."

"Aunt," added Mary Ann, "I have again the disagreeable task to perform of telling you that I will not and cannot stay in the same house with you."

The aunt squeezed out some tears.

"No," added Mary Ann, "I will not forget that you are my father's sister, and you shall, in consequence, never want; but I cannot have you under the same roof with me, so get out of my sight at once."

"No," added Tony, "we don't want any old females here, kicking up rumpusses, and setting young married folks by the ears, not we."

"Well, my children," said the aunt, "for I shall always call you such, since such is your positive wish, I will go; but do not let us part in anger."

"Well," said Tony, "I don't know that we've any need to do that."

"No, I'm sure we may part very good friends yet, and I shall have the pleasure of speaking to whoever I may be living with, in future, of my dear brother's child and her affectionate husband."

"Yes," said Tony, "you may talk all you like about Mary Ann's affectionate husband, for you may be assured he will be an uncommonly kind one."

Tony was about to turn away towards Mary Ann, when the old aunt said—

"Wait a minute, we will take one friendly glass of wine together, and then I will no longer trouble you with my society."

"I don't object to that," said Tony.

"Very well, then. Fill our glasses out of the port decanter, my dear Mary Ann, and let us, for once in a way, feel that we are Christians, and forgiving and forgetting."

"Allow me," said Tony.

Mary Ann, who was completely in the dark respecting what was going on, was quite surprised at Tony's ready acquiescence in this matter, and she looked on in no small amazement as he took some glasses, and went to the decanter of port upon the shelf to fill them.

"I'll take sherry," said the aunt.

"Oh," said Tony, "I'm sorry you won't drink with us. There was not any left in the port decanter after pouring out all our glasses, so I was just going to tap a fresh bottle for you. Here goes."

"A fresh bottle?"

"Yes. There you are."

Tony had picked up, from among a row of bottles of port wine that was upon a shelf near the floor, a fresh bottle, and with his back towards the aunt, he pretended to pour her glass out of it, but in reality he brought her the drugged glass he had so dexterously hidden before she came down stairs.

"There," he said, as he handed it to her; "you will find yours the best, I dare say, and the freshest."

He then placed a glass before Harry Dean, another before Mary Ann, and a third before himself. The old woman glanced up to the shelf, and saw the decanter was empty, for Tony had poured all that remained, after filling three glasses, into a pint mug that was upon the shelf, and so she thoroughly believed that all was what she considered right, namely, that she had the only fresh glass of wine, while the other three came from the drugged decanter. Had she no compunctions? We shall see.

"Now, my dears," she said, "may you be as happy as loving hearts can make you."

"Amen!" said Tony, and he drank down his wine.

The others did the same. The aunt tossed her's off with an air, and then she said—

"Ha! ha!"

"Did you cough, mum?" said Tony.

"Yes, I did, stupid; and I shall cough more soon. How do you all feel? He! he! he!"

"Why, as regards myself," said Tony, "I'm uncommonly comfortable. How are you?"

"Perfectly well; but I don't think you will be long so. You will find that I am not exactly the sort of person to be

ill-treated with impunity. I—I—eh?
—oh dear !—How—how—dark, and odd
—I can't keep my eyes—open—easy—
what—murder! I—I—have drunk some
of it myself ! Oh, you—you—wretches
—you wretches ! I'm a dead wo——"

Down went the aunt in a state of total
insensibility to the floor to the great surprise of Mary Ann, who was not at all in
the secret.

"Run, Tony," said Harry Dean.
"Run for a doctor. By-the-bye, you
may as well stay here and tell Mary
Ann all about it, while I—"

"Well, good folks," said some one
looking in at the door at that moment,
"how are you all?"

"Dr. Bell," cried Harry Dean, "you
are indeed welcome. Just look at this
old lady, and tell us, if you can, what
poison she has taken, for that she has
got something of that character in her
stomach we happen to know."

The physician paid all the attention
that was requisite to the aunt, and he
was very soon able to announce that she
had taken some narcotic poison, although
he doubted much if it were in a dose
sufficient to produce any serious consequences.

"And that," said Tony, "was kindly
intended for us."

"No doubt of it."

"Well, Mary Ann, she is your aunt,
so you shall decide what ought to be
done in such a case as this. Only say
the word, my dear, and I'm quite sure
we will all attend to your wishes in this
matter."

Mary Ann could not speak for the
tears that would keep coursing each
other down her cheeks, and then Harry
Dean taking her hand, said kindly—

"Cheer up, Mary Ann, we all understand your feelings. You know that
your aunt is deserving of punishment
for this atrocious attempt, such as the
law would inflict upon her, but at the
same time you cannot forget that she is
your father's sister."

"Oh, yes. That is it—that is it."

"Then leave all to me."

Harry Dean consulted with Tony
and Dr. Bell, and the result was that
they procured a coach, into which they
placed the unscrupulous woman, and
took her from the house. When the
aunt did awaken from her lengthened
sleep she found herself in one of the
Metropolitan Hospitals, and was not a
little amazed and discomfited at the utter
failure of her scheme.

CHAPTER CXXI.

THE DEATH OF WILKINS.

KATE DESTERN soon recovered from
the sudden shock which the communication of Harry Dean regarding who
and what she was, had given to her.
She wept much, but her natural good
sense soon enabled her to recover her
cheerfulness. Harry Dean spoke to her
upon the subject of her new condition
in life.

"Kate," he said, "I continue to call
you by that old name, but do you know
that your real one is Lady Kate
Wortley?"

Kate looked in Harry Dean's face as
she repeated the name of "Wortley—
Wortley."

"Yes," he added, "Battaney was
merely a title, and not the family name;
it was the one under which all the
villany was practised that that bad man
was guilty of from time to time ; it was
the one that his minions knew him by.
He was fearful, with all his various
propensities, of tarnishing the name of
his ancestors, which had passed through
many generations without a stain on its
honour. It would not have been safe
for him, reckless as he was, to have
openly violated the strict honour of his
family, for there was a sufficient number
left to have dealt a severe retribution on
the delinquent. And now, Kate, only
look at me and ask yourself if it is right
and proper that you, of high birth and
with a title, should ally yourself to one so
humble? Only consider, Kate, what the
world will say—what your new high-born
aristocratic relations will say."

"The world, Harry, and new relations?—what of the world? what have
we to do with the world's opinion when
our hearts have been united so long ?
Have we not exchanged our vows of love
and fidelity to each other, and endeavoured to live on in the mutual love
that fate has kindled in our breasts, and
that we have so long nourished with a
jealous care?"

"Yes, Kate, yes. You may, you know, now look for a union with one of the noblest families of England. Your newly recovered title, in addition to the wealth that is sure to follow it, will make you a fit match for the proudest of the land. Soon as you are introduced to the fashionable world, there will be no lack of suitors for the hand of the lovely and rich Lady Wortley."

She approached him, and led him nearer to the light. She seemed to be too much astonished to speak for some moments, but continued to gaze steadfastly in his face, as though she would trace every ligament of his features. After she had satisfied her scrutiny, she said—

"Let me look at you well, to be sure that you are my Harry. The voice seems like that of Harry's—the features seem the same, but the words are not those of my ever affectionate Harry Dean. No, no, they cannot be his; they are foreign, they are entire strangers to his heart."

"Do you doubt it, Kate? Could you believe that I, who live in a humble station, would ever be a bar to your attaining rank, wealth, and honour? I, who am without a name, could not presume to be a hindrance to your reaching that position in life your worth deserves."

"I may well do so, when I hear from your lips words which do not belong to you; and so, Harry, I am to turn away from you, who have loved and protected me so long, for fear of what the world and some folks, who by accident are able to call themselves new relations, may say? Oh, Harry—Harry, is this like you? When was it that you turned traitor to true affection, and spoke such high treason to the majesty of honest Love?"

"A very pretty sentiment, Kate, and well expressed. You will permit me at some other time to put you in mind of it."

"At any time, and at all times; and now, since you will have it, Harry, that I am in so wonderful a position that it might be supposed to warp my better judgment, and to have an effect upon my long cherished affections, it behoves me to speak so, Harry—I, Lady Kate Wortley, offer myself to you, Harry Dean."

Harry caught her in his arms, as he cried—

"Ever—ever the same, my own, own Kate. Ah! we shall indeed be happy."

At this moment the lawyer from Lincoln's Inn was announced, and Harry, with Kate's acquiescence, ordered him to be shown into the room in which they were. After the usual salutations, he said to Harry—

"I presume this lady knows all now?"

"Yes, all."

"Then I may say that I have made every enquiry into the condition of Lord Battaney's property, and find that he died absolutely pennyless, and that every bit of landed property he possessed is mortgaged up to its full market price and above."

"Then I inherit nothing," said Kate.

"Absolutely nothing."

She looked at Harry Dean with a smile as she said—

"Why, Harry, how apprehensive you were that I was about to bring you some great fortune. We shall be poor together now."

The lawyer looked rather puzzled, but Harry changed the conversation, by saying—

"If I mistake not, sir, the trial o Wilkins comes on to-morrow."

"It does; and there seems to be no doubt entertained of his guilt," said the lawyer.

"None. The infatuated man has been carrying on a guilty career for some time. He is of a worse description of notorious characters than any that have been brought before the public for some time."

"Yes; his connection with that unfortunate nobleman was to be lamented. We cannot, of course, say which of the two were most to blame. They were both very vicious characters. The one was brought to an untimely death in the midst of his wickedness, and the other is likely to expiate his offences on the scaffold. His conviction is certain. To-morrow is Friday.

"Ah! yes, and on Monday he will expiate his crimes upon the scaffold."

"There cannot be a doubt of it"

Kate shuddered, for she knew that

she had to attend this trial, and that there was no such thing as 'escaping the ordeal. Harry Dean, too, was a witness, and Dr. Bell; therefore almost all our friends, in whose fortunes we have been interested, will assemble at the Old Bailey. Wilkins had made two determined attempts at suicide, subsequent to the visit that had been paid him in Newgate, by Harry Dean and the solicitor, but by the vigilance of the officers, they had both proved failures. On the morning of trial he was sullen and morose, and no one could extort a word from him. It seemed as though he was in deep thought about something, and there was very little doubt but that the wretched man was busy thinking of some mode of evading the sentence of the law if he should be found guilty. That he should be so, he could not himself scarcely entertain the remotest doubt. An immense assemblage of people came far and near to witness the trial, and by an early hour in the morning the doors of the court were quite beset. The rush to get in when the doors were opened was something truly tremendous, and a full half hour elapsed before anything like order could be obtained. It would be but a work of repetition for us to go through the trial, for the reader is already aware of the evidence that was to be adduced against Wilkins—evidence so clear and so conclusive, that even the stupidity of a jury must be triumphed over. Suffice it to say, that by half-past four o'clock in the day a verdict of guilty was pronounced against the wretched man. He made no remark, until the judge, in his customary manner, asked him if he had anything to say, why sentence of death should not be pronounced against him, and then he said—

"It is a solemn farce to ask me this; but I have one request to make."

"Name it."

"I am willing to make a full confession, but in order to do so perfectly, I must have access to a small writing-desk that was at my lodgings, and which is now in the hands of the police."

"It is not within my province," said the judge, "to make any order in that matter; all I have to do now is to perform the most painful part of my official duties, and that is to sentence you according to law."

The sentence was passed upon him in due form, and he was conveyed back to gaol. With great calmness and apparent resignation, he again pressed his request concerning the little writing-desk that had been taken by the police, and as it was in the governor's apartments in Newgate, that personage looked carefully into it to see if there was in it anything that could enable him to commit suicide. He found nothing but papers and a bottle of ink, so he began to think that all was well, but he had the prudence to send for one of the sheriffs, to consult about it. The sheriff looked as wise as possible, and declared his inability to detect any danger; so they called in an experienced officer, and told him the case.

"Why, gemmen," he said, "all I says is empt out the ink and pour some fresh into this bottle, and then we is quite sure as there's nothing else any harm can come of."

This was a precaution that looked quite like an unnecessary one, and seemed to both the sheriff and the governor as overdoing the matter; but still they did as the officer suggested, and the little ink bottle of Wilkins's desk was duly emptied of its contents, and then filled again from the governor's resources in that line. After this, the desk was taken to him in the condemned cell. They saw that a flush of satisfaction came over his face as he saw it, and with an eagerness that quite made his hands tremble, he looked for the ink. Now, two men were watching him, and they were not a little surprised to see him suddenly raise the ink bottle to his lips and drink off the greater part of its contents.

"Ha! ha! ha!" he cried, "I am poisoned now, and not all the art in the world can prolong my life another minute."

The two men, who knew nothing of the manner in which the ink had been changed, gave an immediate alarm, and the governor came to the cell. Wilkins was sitting upon the edge of the truckle-bed that comprised its only furniture, and looking very pale.

"What's the matter?" said the governor.

"He says, sir, he has poisoned himself by drinking some ink."

"Oh, nonsense, nonsense. I changed it."

With a cry of anger, Wilkins would have sprung upon the governor, but his fetters prevented him, and he only fell to the ground half fainting from vexation and chagrin. Between that time and the morning of his execution he lay in a kind of stupor. All hope of evading the sentence of the law had entirely passed away from him; and when, at about three minutes before eight o'clock, he made his appearance upon the scaffold, before a concourse of persons, amounting to about five thousand at least, he seemed already more dead than alive. In taking his last look at this world, the most horrible agony of mind seemed to come over him, and looking at the fatal cord, he said—

"Quick! quick!"

Those were the last words he spoke.—In another minute he was in eternity! And thus finished a man who, if his acquirements and his talents had been properly directed, might have been a distinguished member of society. How many men have carved for themselves a place in the muster roll of a nation's worthies with far less real pretension than Wilkins!

* * * * *

On the following Monday, Carter, the vile accomplice of Swam, in the murder of Madame Zadzed, was dragged shrieking to the scaffold. While we are disposing of the criminal portion of our *dramatis personæ*, we may mention that John Such, notwithstanding all his cleverness, was transported, while the attorney Roberts escaped from the peccadillo in which we left him, and still practises as a thieves' lawyer in London.

CHAPTER CXXII.

THE CONCLUSION.

A WEEK has passed away, and the shuddering horror with which Kate had listened to the public details of the death of Wilkins had passed away. A bright and beautiful morning was shining out of the heavens, as though some special angelic jubilee was taking place, and the inhabitants of the earth were, so far as sunshine and such a blue sky as our northern clime seldom sees, permitted to share in it. The birds were singing from every hedge, and the pleasant rustle of the tall trees came upon the ear with grateful music as a small party of five persons only entered the church porch of the picturesque ecclesiastical edifice of Hampstead. These five persons were Harry Dean, Kate, Tony, Mary Ann, and Dr. Bell. It was the wish of Kate to be married at Hampstead Church, for in the little grave yard adjoining it lay her who had played the part of a mother to both Kate and Lucy—namely, Mrs. Destern; and it seemed to Kate, as she said, a blessed thing to take the most important step in life that she could take beneath the roof of that edifice where she had been first taught to lift up her infant voice in prayer to the Ruler of all things. As for Tony, so that he was married to his Mary Ann, he cared not where the ceremony took place, and so, from all this, the reader will naturally conclude that we have, upon this occasion, introduced him to a wedding party. This was indeed the fact, for upon that eventful morning Kate was to become the wife of Harry Dean, and Mary Ann had consented to become Mrs. Thorpe. Dr. Bell was to play the part of father to both the brides, and so, with as little parade as possible, the important step was to be taken that could not be drawn back. But who is this that comes bounding from the church door, all smiles and dimples, and at once kisses Kate, and then kisses Mary Ann, and seems fully disposed, upon the very smallest amount of encouragement, to kiss everybody? It is Lucy. Yes, little Lucy, who would not be away from the wedding if you would give her the weight of the whole party in gold, not she. "Ding dong! ding dong!" go the chimes of the church. It is half-past twelve. Just in time are they all, and now an old paralytic woman makes a score of curtsies to them all, and gets half-a-crown from Dr. Bell at once, seeing which, the beadle throws himself immediately into a perspiration of zeal in the service of the bridal party, and makes such a banging of unnecessary pew doors that it is quite awful to hear him, and what cushions he places, too, by the rails of the communion table, and what a a flourish of a great yellow silk handkerchief, as big as any ordinary banner, he gives, as he hopes everything will be found comfortable. Then in the vestry, he tells them all, there is such a cheerful fire!—so in they go, but they have hardly got there when it is time to rush out again and be married—a nervous sort of operation to go through at the best, but such things will happen. But the strangest thing was, that neither Kate nor Mary Ann looked in the least alarmed about it, and there was decidedly no occasion for volatile salts, or any of the one thousand and one means and appliances for enabling young ladies to go through what they have been dying to accomplish. The clergyman comes in, looking as grand and solemn as possible, and then Tony says to Mary Ann, "Now for it!" and the beadle says, "Hush! if you please, sir," and looks as bland as possible. What a domestic man that beadle must be. The service begins and goes on all right, with the exception that the parson wants to marry Kate to Tony and Mary Ann to Harry, but that is quickly put to rights, and in exactly seven minutes and a half the knot is tied, which is the most difficult to loosen of any that the imagination of man ever invented. Two little gold circlets and a few words have done the business, but Tony and Harry are quite resigned, and Dr. Bell, before anybody could possibly be aware of what he was about, saluted Kate, and then he saluted Mary Ann, and he did it with such unction that the parson gave an odd sort of look and wiped his lips with the sleeve of his gown, as though he would have said—

"How I should like that, now, if I dared."

The very beadle looked envious. Then Harry Dean kissed Mary Ann, and called her Mrs. Thorpe, which made everybody laugh. How easily folks laugh when they are pleased at any rate. After this, they all went into the vestry and signed the register and paid what was to pay. The beadle coughed dreadfully, and was under everybody's feet in some odd sort of way, so that Dr. Bell was obliged to give him five shillings to get him to be commonly quiet. Then the clerk wanted something, and the pew-opener, and the sexton, and the bell-ringer, and some half dozen supernume-

raries connected with the church besides, so that Dr. Bell, who took upon himself the office of almoner, had enough to do. However, all this was got through at last, and a one-horse chariot, in which they had come to Hampstead, was gained, and into it they all got. Tony had insisted upon a general return to the hotel to dinner, so off they went, and in about half an hour they all crossed the threshold of the hotel again, looking as happy as possible. Tony was quite a great man and played the host to perfection, and, to tell the honest truth, the drive to Hampstead and back again had given the whole party quite an appetite, and never did dinner pass off with greater *eclat* than that one. Numerous toasts were drunk, and then coffee followed, and at last the twilight came soon to deepen into night.

"You will dine with me," said Harry Dean, "all of you, this day week—I shall esteem it a favour."

"But where?" said Tony.

"Why, at present I own that my address is a secret. Lucy will remain here with you for a week, at the end of which time you will hear from Kate and I."

"But you will tell me, Kate," said Lucy, "where you are going?"

"I don't know, Lucy."

"Not know?" said Mary Ann, with astonishment.

"Not know?" said Tony.

"No," added Kate, "I do not know. Harry will take me to his house, and where that is so that he is there, I care not. It will be my home."

"Bravo!" cried Dr. Bell. "That's right—put your faith in Harry Dean, Kate, and you'll never be deceived."

Harry now rose, and Kate got on her bonnet and shawl to accompany him. They took a kind and affectionate farewell of their dear friends, and so sallied out into the streets. A light misty rain was rapidly falling. Kate clung close to Harry Dean.

"And have you no apprehensions, Kate," he said, "for the future?"

"I am yours, Harry."

Oh, what a world of eloquence—true, pure, eloquence of the heart, was in those few words, "I am yours, Harry."—To be his silenced all apprehensions, and comprehended the sum of her felicity.

These words came upon his ears like the sweetest melody.   After a pause of some few moments, he again spoke—

"What if you find me poorer, Kate, than even I have hinted to you I was. Alas! the home I am now going to take you to, will owe its principal grace to your presence."

"To love.—To love, it will owe all its grace."

How the rain fell now.   The light shower deepened into a cold regular penetrating rain, and as Harry Dean and his young bride traversed street after street, they suffered more and more from the pelting of the pitiless storm.

He conducted her through various streets at the west-end of the town, long, broad, streets with handsome houses in them, and at last he turned a corner abruptly, and paused at a doorway which was in total darkness.

"Is it here?" said Kate.

"Yes, dearest.   The humble have to wait upon themselves."

He took a latch-key from his pocket and opened the door.   All was profoundly dark within, and then he closed the door again, and taking her by the hand, he said—

"Follow me, Kate. Follow me, dear, and fear nothing. We may be happy, although poor."

"We will be happy, Harry."

Up some staircase he led her. It consisted of many steps, and then he pushed open another door, but still all was darkness. He led her by the hand until by feeling about he found a seat on which he placed her, and then kneeling by her side, he spoke—

"My Kate, it is a poor return for all your devotion to me, to bring you to a home in which gaunt poverty, and at times absolute famine reigns, and you so nobly and so generously, when you thought you had rank and wealth, dashed aside all obstacles to make yourself mine."

"I did do so."

"And do you not regret?"

"No, Harry."

"What if your high and proud relations should find you out and say, why have you allied yourself to this poor and untitled man?"

"I should say I heeded not his poverty, and that as to titles, he was one of nature's own nobility by right of his honest, noble heart."

"And then they would scoff at you."

"I would smile at them, and pity them."

"They would neglect you, never coming near your——"

"I would cling the closer to you, Harry."

There was a silence of some few minutes' duration, and then she heard distinctly that he was sobbing bitterly.

"Harry, Harry, whence this passion of tears?"

"Because I am unworthy of you, Kate."

"Unworthy?"

"Yes, I have deceived you, deceived you very much; and yet, I am very, very happy. Will you forgive me, Kate, now, if I tell you candidly in what I have deceived you?"

"Deceive me in anything but your love, Harry, and I will laugh away the imputation."

"Give me your hand, Kate. Now the other. Thus let me hold one to my heart and the other to my lips—my darling—my best, truest, proudest, noblest girl."

He struck his foot twice upon the floor. Kate started.

"Hush," he said, "you are with me. Do not be alarmed, dear one, I am an enchanter, and will transform you to a countess."

At that moment the darkness, as though obedient to him, began to disperse. A faint twilight shone into the room, and each moment increased. Kate looked about her in amazement as by the rapidly increasing light she saw she was in an apartment of spacious proportions and the most superb description. The ceiling was one blaze of fretted gold, and everywhere that the eyes fell they encountered something rich and rare.

"Oh, Harry, Harry! Is this a dream?"

"No," he said, "listen. I am the Earl of Crowsborne, and nephew to the late Lord Battaney. We are cousins, Kate. I am wealthy far beyond the ordinary wealth of nobles, and you are my countess."

It was now Kate's turn to burst into tears.

"And you have stooped," she sobbed "you have stooped, Harry, to wed one who——"

"Hush! let us have, to use your own words, no 'high treason against the majesty of Love.' Look around you, Kate—all is your own, the happiness of Lucy Destern shall be my care; as for ourselves——"

"Harry, Harry!"

She fell upon his breast, and sobbed—

"Dry those tears, dear one, and tell me you forgive your Harry, his first, last, and only deceit."

"Forgive! oh, my lord."

"Kate—Kate, call me Harry, if you love me."

"My Harry."

"Ah, that has about it the golden sound of our early love, Kate—the future is before us in all its beauty. It will be our own faults if we allow it to be dimmed by shadows of the past."

*   *   *   *   *   *

But little now remains to be told. Harry Dean was indeed the Earl of Crowsborne by the death of his father, who had unquestionably been poisoned